THE TIGER WAITS

BY ANTON MYRER

THE TIGER WAITS

ONCE AN EAGLE

THE INTRUDER

THE VIOLENT SHORE

THE BIG WAR

EVIL UNDER THE SUN

A Novel by ANTON MYRER

THE

TIGER

WAITS

W · W · NORTON & COMPANY · INC ·

NEW YORK

FIRST EDITION

Library of Congress Cataloging in Publication Data

Myrer, Anton.
 The tiger waits.
 I. Title.
PZ4.M998Ti [PS3563.Y74] 813'.5'4 72–10355
ISBN 0–393–08672–0

1 2 3 4 5 6 7 8 9 0

To
Ainslie and Barbara Burke

When vice prevails and impious men bear sway,
The post of honor is a private station.

—JOSEPH ADDISON

THE TIGER WAITS

ONE

JACOBI AWOKE, all at once and fully, to the soft, sea-green hull of the great plane's lounge, a flurry of voices he knew. The stewardess, a handsome girl with straw-colored hair, was gazing down at him; a faintly troubled smile. Bad dream. There had been a vast hall with marble pillars and blue brocade draperies, and one of the Chinese envoys—it wasn't Ch'en Pu-tsao or anyone he knew—was shouting accusations, his broad, flat face like hammered brass. Paul had wanted a memo, some memo he couldn't find anywhere—then there'd been a distending panic drowned forever in the measureless collision of all suns, all planets: a universe of glare . . .

He swallowed, rubbed his nose. Outside the window were clouds carved of solid silver. Life poured over him discordant and sweet. He was bombarded by color and sound: Reinhold Vosz's chattering metallic laughter, sunlight on his hands. From a nearby chair Big Bill Donlund, a sheaf of papers furled in his lap, was grinning at him.

"What's the matter, Sid? They have you cornered?"

Embarrassed, he smiled back feebly. "Just about." He was sweating and his throat was dry. Bad dream, all it was. But so *vivid*. The sunlight swayed gently on his hands. Why a dream like that? After they'd broken through—at least for a time, which was all you could hope for. And they were flying home . . .

"Would you, Doctor Jacobi?" The stewardess had just put in his hands an oblong black booklet adorned with gold Spencerian script that read: *Thoughts First and Last*. "Hey, I'm sorry I woke you up like that."

"Not at all," he answered, a shade too brusquely. "You did me a favor." Ever since he'd come to work for the Department people had called him Doctor and it always irked him, stirring each time that gray ghost of his mother's thwarted hope. She had been obsessed with the idea of his being a surgeon—a career he'd known at the age of nine he was wildly unfitted for. Natalie was always taunting him over his aversion to blood. Even now the thought of bending over still, white skin with a scalpel could give him a faint thrill of fear. No, what he *was* was a professor of Far Eastern history—and a damned good one, too, if the truth were known. But no one in Washington was ever in danger of being called Professor.

"The thing is we're only half an hour out," the girl was saying, "and I knew if I didn't catch you now there won't be time later. With the reporters and everything." Her Venetian-red nail tapped the book's cover once. "Would you write something in it for me?"

"—Why, it's an autograph album," he said in surprise. "And a commonplace book, all in one."

"You just put down whatever comes into your mind *first*. Some saying. And then your name." She laughed shyly, her wide violet eyes made larger by the eye shadow. The inclusion of WAVE petty officers as part of the crew on official flights had been one of the President's more welcome innovations. "It's awfully square, I know. It's just a kind of a hobby."

"And think of the value it'll have," Bill Donlund broke in on them. "In years to come. Signatures of all the captains and the kings. You've thought of *that* now, haven't you?"

The girl bridled, a hand at her throat. "Oh, Mr. Vice President—that's not true at all!"

"Not just the least bit?"

"Well, of course everyone likes mementoes of important people."

Donlund threw back his head and laughed. And watching him Jacobi saw the Vice President's weather-beaten face harden in the shrewd appraisal of a suspicion confirmed.

"Bill, you're one of the soundest men I know, but you're an awful cynic."

"Of course I am. Somebody's got to balance you unstable romantic types."

The stewardess was still standing by Jacobi's chair. He flipped through the pastel rainbow pages, scanning the signatures. David Brinkley, Mike Nichols, Hubert Humphrey, Herman Kahn, Georges Pompidou, Elliott Gould. A certain portion of uncertain paper.

"Look, you don't want mine," he protested. "I'm just a spear carrier."

"Oh, no . . ." Her pretty little oval face was genuinely shocked. "You're famous!"

Everything was, after all, point of view. Here he sat, dead-dog-tired and jumpy after nine days and nights of cross-purposes, proposals and rejections and background papers and memoranda, feeling just about as beleaguered as a civil servant could feel—but from this stewardess' point of vantage he was one of the movers and shakers. He could snap his bony fingers and the whole treacherous Burma Triangle Question would vanish in a puff of pretty pink smoke. He was invested with glamour. It was a word he hated more than any other.

"Shame on you, Doctor!" the girl was teasing him. "You're blocking, don't tell me you aren't. It's got to be impulse or it's no good."

Impulse. With a soft smile he got out his pen and wrote on a blank yellow page, without pausing: *The whole earth is a sepulcher for famous men*. Who had said that? One of the Greeks, the good sardonic Greeks.

Below it he set down *Sidney Jacobi, Special Assistant to the Secretary of State*. The whole earth.

"I'm always dying to see what people write," the stewardess said. "I don't understand half of them! Anyway, it'll be fun to look back on when I'm old and gray."

"Oh, but you're not thinking about that, are you?" Donlund asked her. "A lovely, wide-awake girl like you? I can't believe it."

Her eyes narrowed prettily. "Ooh—they told me to watch out for you . . ."

Jacobi watched her flirting with the Vice President. Young, twenty-two or -three, with fine, firm thighs the taut blue skirt revealed palpably; but her gaze beneath the mascara and eyepencil was cool. She was like so many of the youngsters now: that wary appraisal of a world they had so little confidence in. Rubbing his eyes he recalled the nightmare, and his terror. It's because I have no children, he thought with a sharp finality he knew to be absurd. No sons. If I had sons I wouldn't have dreams like that.

The girl had moved away in response to a bell. Jacobi idly flipped back through the little book's pages. Their party had contributed while he'd slept. Bill Donlund's large, loose hand had scrawled, *Wise men learn more from fools than fools from the wise.* Tough, implacable old Cato, who had ended every single senate speech for three years with the terrible admonition that had finally destroyed a great city . . .

Mildly startled, he glanced at Donlund, but the V.P. was reading again, now and then listening to Vosz and the others. He looked out of place in the dun-colored gabardine suit, wrinkled and baggy now after fourteen hours in the air. He ought to have been wearing a checked wool shirt and whipcord trousers, a big felt hat sweated white at the band—that was how Jacobi always thought of him: stalking through the damp gloom of the Northwest woods, blazing trees with a double-bitted ax, or crossing a bobbing corduroy of logs with catlike ease, a peavey balanced in his huge hands; moving in the world of men—and yet somehow solitary and aloof, beyond the common needs.

Conscious of a tremor of jealousy, Jacobi scowled. Donlund was so hard, so indestructible: coupled with his astonishing intelligence and quickness of perception, it made him formidable. For all the stories that had been told of him—the drinking and gambling forays to Vegas, the liaisons with the daughters of publishers or the wives of hard-worked counselors-at-law—he had been a senator who did his homework. He'd been brought up in China, the son of missionary parents, before the fall of the Nationalists, which probably accounted for the benign cynicism; but it didn't begin to explain his astonishing grasp of Asian matters. Jacobi, relatively new to government service, had been amazed.

And the sheer raw energy of the man! It was Donlund who had come forward two days before, when the entire conference had been on the verge of foundering, with the startling proposal for the international rescue and reclamation mission to the devastated areas. It was Donlund, in a masterful four-hour mixture of entreaty and threat—what his old congressional colleagues still referred to as "the velvet hammerlock"—who had overcome the frantic opposition of General Bodawyin, the Burmese leader, and broken the jam. They would have failed—for all Paul Blackburn's brilliant efforts they would still have failed—if it hadn't been for Donlund. How nice it would be to own that easy, deliberate assurance, that remarkable flexibility.

But fancy his knowing Cato . . .

He turned the pages backward. Andy Stinchfield, Assistant Secretary for Far East and Pacific, quite sick with gastroenteritis in one of the berths up forward, had wished the girl luck and let it go at that. Dick Coddington of UPI had scrawled, *Women's Libbers are never any fun in bed!!!* Jacobi grunted, wondering what Natalie would have to say to that. He turned to Paul Blackburn's quick, forward-moving hand. *The instruments of darkness tell us truths; win us with honest trifles, to betray us in deepest consequence.*

Banquo. He closed the book on his thumb. Soon to be struck down in a ditch. Betrayed by an old comrade-in-arms, a most ambitious thane. He thought all at once of a day on Vineyard Sound, nearly becalmed, slipping along through water smooth as oil and Paul, one bare brown arm looped indolently over the tiller, murmuring, "Do you ever wonder about retribution, Sid? The real kind, I mean. The long kind. Take the tragic hero—all that business about the fatal flaw. Isn't that because he knows in his very guts he's broken some higher law and so he *wants* to be brought down?" Jacobi had fought the idea, and they'd drifted into a desultory argument about determinism while the ocher cliffs of Makoniky Head shimmered in the haze. "If my father hadn't given in to my mother I'd have been raised a Catholic," Paul had said after another silence. "Is that why I want to change things? The old crazy Calvinist guilt thing?" And then, with that quick, breath-catching smile: "Maybe I'll regress one of these days. There's always hope . . ."

Jacobi had been astonished when Blackburn had been named Secretary—everyone at Cambridge had been astonished. He'd been even more amazed when Paul had asked him to come down to Washington with him as Special Assistant for Far East. Amazed—and a bit scared. For several weeks it had all seemed like some eerie pop-art joke that had tossed them into those sedate, carpeted rooms on State's seventh floor; that Paul Blackburn had become, incredibly, the latest in that august procession of bewigged, imposing gentlemen who watched them so impassively from the heavy gilt frames on the gallery and reception room walls. My God— *Monroe* had had this job, and Adams and Clay and Webster . . . A part of Jacobi still felt like an interloper. Paul, however, had accepted it calmly enough: it was almost as though he'd intended to wind up there. No one could have charged him with studying to be Secretary of State since the age of five, as Eisenhower had once remarked of Dulles; but it was there all the same—an easy, purposeful assertion.

"Gentlemen, you've heard it said that the Department has become a shadow cabinet, a laughingstock in government," he'd told his bureau chiefs and immediate staff that first clear, cold January morning. "That morale in the Department is at its lowest ebb in a long and illustrious history. There is a good deal of truth in these charges. Well, the President has assured me I am to be his First Secretary. And I intend to be just that: *First* Secretary. State is going to play first violin in this orchestra—as long as I'm sitting behind this desk. The foreign policy of this Administration is not going to be run by a bunch of computer wizards deep in the White House basement, hiding behind executive privilege." He paused; there was a glint in his eye no one could fail to catch. "As for me, I'll be *glad* to be responsible to Congress. It was, after all, the way the machinery was intended to work; and it's worked remarkably well, all things considered, for a good many years. We don't need the furtive worn-out ghosts of Europe to guide us. There are virtues in Mr. Jefferson's system undreamt of in Dr. Kissinger's philosophy. In a word, ladies and gentlemen, State is back at the helm of foreign policy. And State will take the conn."

Exciting words—brave words. His audience, inured to caution and disappointment, had been predictably skeptical. Yet on the whole Paul had made good on them. He'd held his own between the White House Basement and the CIA, he'd effected a thoroughgoing reorganization of the Department none of his predecessors had dared to try, he'd even gained the grudging respect of Congress. Most important of all, he'd given the Department back its self-esteem.

And it hadn't all been toil and solemnity. Neither the memories of Rusk's mandarin circumspection nor Rogers' rather forced candor had impressed him: he'd gone his own way, invested the Secretaryship with a wit and easy informality that never succumbed to vulgarity. State dinners were the liveliest and most congenial in years.

"People are far more likely to agree with each other after laughter than after squints and scowls," he'd said one evening that first spring. "There will be no hairy-chest, hard-nose talk while I'm Secretary—or at least let *me* not hear it! The watchwords will be negotiation, accommodation, the soft answer; and the hotshots can call us just as unsound or subversive as they please. The President has put me here to resolve tensions, not exacerbate them." He seemed more forceful and decisive, harder at the edges than he'd been back at Cambridge. It was true: the office makes the man, the man makes the office. He'd grown. They all had, one way and another. You grew, or you went under.

But even so, he would never have believed that Paul possessed the personal authority, the daring, the sheer persuasive *durability* that could dominate the nine days' conference, determine its direction, allay suspicions—and cap it all by actually inducing the People's Republic of China to cede a piece of its sovereign territory. Incredible! When the Secretary had first broached the scheme Jacobi had thought he'd gone mad—and very nearly ventured to say so. And yet there had been a certain hard, fresh logic to the plan, once you'd thought about it. There was to be a UN-administered plebiscite in the Burmese and Chinese areas concerned; and out of it—drawn from parts of Yunnan, the Triangle and the Shan States—would arise the bouncing new independent state of Dhotal. A master stroke, brought off in the face of all the odds. Who would have believed it possible a bare month ago, with the entire country shattered by two years of the most savage guerrilla warfare and half a dozen dangerous Sino-Burmese border clashes?

Near him Donlund frowned, wrote something rapidly on the margin of a report. Jacobi watched him idly. Of course there was always a price; and the price of Chinese concession had been the Greater Asian Treaty Organization's acceptance of Prince Naungapaya as head of the provisional state. He was an overemotional, spoiled young man who played the valve trombone, gambled incessantly, and worst of all was the long-time protégé of the Chinese, which had already aroused charges in the conservative press of craven truckling to the warlords of Peking. The art of the possible, as the man said. And certain assurances had had to be given to Bodawyin, whose terror of China was matched only by his grinding hatred of Prince Naungapaya. The international relief mission, headed by the American engineering wizard Drachenfels, embraced a huge land reclamation and flood control project for the entire Upper Salween. They had already been dispatched to that unhappy country, and there would be a lot of growling in certain quarters about a return to the spendthrift days of UNRRA and the Marshall Plan.

"But we'll weather that squall when it hits," Paul had told them with quiet elation the night before. "The main thing is, we've stopped the killing and burning. And we have a very good chance of solving the whole hassle once and for all. The saber-rattlers can howl all they want: chalk one up to the inglorious arts of peace."

Jacobi snapped open the little book again, encountered Reinhold Vosz's tense, spiculate script: *Man is something that shall be surpassed; what have you done to surpass him?* Nietzsche, Jacobi groaned half aloud, oh-my-God—Nietzsche, wouldn't you know; and as if in corroboration the Presidential Adviser's rapid, chattering laugh burst in on his thoughts, answered by a raucous chorus from the others.

"No, but Doctor," Dick Coddington protested mildly, "it's a different matter now, he's a signatory to an international—"

"Catastrophic!" Diminutive, squat, with his cropped, bristling head and the octagonal purple-tinted shades he swore were prescribed for an amblyopic condition (he never seemed to be without them, even at night), Vosz looked like an emissary from the dark side of the moon: less stable, more potent than earthlings. "Do you think for one minute the *Chinks* feel bound by it? Look at them! Centuries of superstition and self-abasement. Consider their language, frozen in its eerie pictographs, its weird ambivalences of meaning, nonmeaning—"

"Reiny," Donlund broke in with amusement, "what the hell do you really know about China?"

"Enough! Don't talk to me about your cultured Oriental! Ignorance still calls the turn. Look at him in his communal hall, chanting mesmerically from Chairman Mao's little red book, exactly as his fathers bobbed up and down before the ceremonial wine vessel. Or do you prefer the cultivated African? Among the Shilluks of the Upper Sudan it is the duty— the *duty*, mind you!—of the king's wives to report to the tribe the slightest decrease in his virility. They do. Whereupon he lays his fuzzy old rastus head in the lap of a virgin—and pa-*chooonggg!* Both are forthwith buried alive. Dry your eyes!"

"Reiny," Tom Wales, Director of International Organization Affairs, murmured. "If you ask me, you're still all worked up over the Hughbryce flap."

"And who wouldn't be? Answer me that! Fifteen years of priceless labor wiped out in one hour." Deftly he transferred a hard black rubber grip fitted with a coil spring from one fist to the other, squeezing it compulsively; but his eyes remained absolutely indecipherable behind the purple lenses. "Vicious traitor! And to think I trusted him as though he were my own son."

"Now, Reiny," Donlund said, "you know that's not true. You haven't trusted anybody since you were four years old."

"I wish it were. I do! I am too credulous. Yes, go on, laugh your tonsils loose. It's true. It's my sheltered upbringing. Did you know I was privately tutored until I was twelve? The scars are irreparable. But to think that deceitful little scum should actually seek to make me a global laughing stock!"

And about time, Jacobi almost said aloud. The Presidential Adviser never failed to enrage him. Reinhold Vosz had been considered the brightest of the postwar crop of scholars out of the University of Chicago. He'd made his reputation at Rand with a series of unnerving projections of how human beings would live (underground and undersea exclusively) in the wake of global atomic war—a boon to the proponents of massive retaliation. Later he'd switched to euphoric scenarios on space exploration, a theme that had its passionate adherents during the Nixon years. He had founded the prestigious Hughbryce Institute, a handsome stone-and-glass pile hidden away deep in the Sierra, where (for an equally mountainous fee) government geophysicists and high brass, businessmen and educators were treated to dazzling dioramas of choice in current political and economic problems.

Then, not three weeks ago, a young Hughbryce employee named Lachlan Smith had begun releasing to the press fistfuls of papers the Institute had prepared for various branches of government—schemes for purchasing sheikdoms in Muscat, jamming Soviet radar in the Arctic, inducing seismic convulsions in the Andes, guerrilla actions in Burundi and Khotiane. They were a sensation. Smith, in hiding, hinted at still more devastating disclosures to follow—at which point he was captured by the FBI and revealed as a member of a militant group called Sirius, based in Cambridge and New York City. Jacobi hadn't known whether to be pleased at Vosz's discomfiture or depressed at the further lesion of public confidence in the mysterious workings of government.

"He was everything I am not," the Presidential Adviser was pounding along now in his hoarse, high-pitched voice. "Dispassionate, analytical, self-contained. No family, no friends, no allegiances except to the Institute. A good and loyal servant. He assured me. And all the time he was nothing but a grubby campus radical. Another Maoist apostle, seeking headlines."

"You've hunted up a few headlines in your day, haven't you, Reiny?" Donlund baited him.

"Of course, of course! But in the name of the government. It is a question of loyalty."

"Well, he's being loyal to his side, isn't he?"

Vosz bared his worn, ridged teeth in an extravagant grimace. "There is no loyalty in such scum. None. Only selfishness and destruction." He nodded rapidly, wrenching his neck around in its high starched collar. "He'll pay for it, too. He'll rot away his days in the deepest dungeon this country can produce. I promise you." His face swung sharply left and riveted on Jacobi. "The President values loyalty above everything else— *as* you know. Dry your eyes!"

"Oh hell, Reiny, it'll all blow over in weeks," Donlund murmured soothingly. "Look at Ellsberg. These self-appointed Robin Hoods nail down the headlines for a spell, and then they fade away. No sweat."

"I'm not thinking of myself, Bill."

"No? Since when's that?"

"Laugh if you like." Solemnly he proclaimed: "It is the greatest danger we all face: *each such act weakens the image of authority.*"

Tom Wales began: "But if authority is as rickety as all that . . ."

"No! There is nothing which cannot be subverted, transformed into its very opposite. Fancy the first aborigine—let's call him Pog-Wog—who realizes in a flash of terrifying insight that woman is *not* the primary agent of procreation, but man. Pa-*chooonggg!* Fifty thousand years of matriarchy

wiped out at a blow." He raised a short, blunt hand in warning. "But!—
what happened to our anthropoid genius? Did he go mad with the discovery? Or was he torn limb from quivering limb and eaten with relish by
the fair sex? Don't tell *me* ideas aren't dangerous . . ."

"God damn it, Reiny," Donlund said with dry mirth, "some of the
crap you come up with would unnerve the devil himself."

"An informed public. What a preposterous concept! When you analyze
it. Informed how, toward what end? One man, one vote. Will you prove
to me a professor of political science is no wiser nor more valuable to the
Republic than some idiot refuse collector who thinks *plenipotentiary* means
oversexed? Dry your eyes!"

"It just so happens," Jacobi heard himself saying hotly—God, the man
was irredeemably insufferable!—"it just so happens that as a citizen he
has a certain right to information his—"

"Ballyraggle and claptrap! He has no rights at all—he has never made
them his, he has never *wanted* to take power in his hands. He deserves
nothing!" Vosz glared around him ferociously, shifted the black rubber
grip again. "Are you prepared to tell this kingly commoner of yours everything that happened at New Delhi this past ten days? That Ch'en Pu-tsao,
trapped in the iron politics of Tamerlane, probably has no intention whatever of honoring this agreement because it violates the alliance with Pakistan? that buttery old Musashi has a secret understanding with Taiwan to
come to Burma's aid in the event of 'future difficulties' with Dhotal; that
we have given Bodawyin confidential assurances of aid in return for *his* tacit
promises that *we* may continue to operate air bases at Myitkyina and
Lashio? that the Soviets have participated in this quixotic mission of mercy
only because they hope to drive a wedge between Washington and Peking,
Washington and Rangoon? Truth!" he shouted, "the truth is disastrous—
a concoction your sans-culotte lout can't handle and never could. If I were
Haydn Bonestell I wouldn't give them *anything* but bromides . . ."

*"There is no trouble existing which I fear, or would wish unknown to
the whole world."*

The voice was recognizable instantly: all the heads in the room turned
with that barely perceptible tick of deference. The laughter fell away. Paul
Blackburn was leaning against the compartment doorway in that characteristic manner—the first two fingers of each hand hooked in a trouser
pocket, wrists cocked, his arms hanging loosely. He was staring hard at
Vosz, his deep hazel eyes very intent; and watching him Jacobi was conscious of that quick, pleasurable surge, part elation, part relief, he never
failed to own in the Secretary's presence: the certainty that now, held in
uncommonly good hands, one could relax.

In the attentive silence Blackburn nodded, as though the words had
settled something very thorny and grave. Then all at once he shifted position and smiled, and that astonishing transformation took place. It was

really a rather homely face in repose, when you studied it—the eyes were spaced a touch too far apart, the nose short and rather blunt, the jaw heavy, the mouth overlarge. And then he would smile that quick, full smile and on the instant become another, younger, singularly handsome man. Jacobi had first seen it at a faculty tea years ago at Cambridge, one of those vague, interminable affairs the women always dominated through small talk and overenthusiastic greetings. Harriet Crittenden had looked at him suddenly and said in her finishing-school voice: "Who is that *charming* man?" and turning he had caught sight of a plain, undistinguished face among others.

"Oh, don't you know him?" he'd said. "That's Blackburn—he's in our section. He's just come to us from Foreign Service."

"Goodness—why'd he ever leave it? He'll never stick it out in this wasteland. After tigers and houris and all that stuff."

"But what I don't understand," Jacobi had begun, "is why you called him charming—" and at that instant Paul had caught sight of him and smiled a greeting over the other heads, and Harriet, leaning close, had said:

"See? You see?"

"Yes," he'd answered. "I see."

There was charm in that smile, but there was nothing fatuous in it, nothing facile or calculated. It was an offering—of life, of immensely human warmth. It was a smile that said, Many things matter to me—but right now, you most of all; and there will somehow always be time for us to exchange fears and dreams, to laugh at certain things and even—who knows? —to forgive each other our trespasses in this imperfect world; don't you agree?

He'd been a clean, fresh wind in the history section: he had avoided both the forbidding hand of the old guard and that sophomoric, glozing camaraderie affected by some of the younger and more ambitious Harvard instructors. A healthy irreverence did not presuppose the surrender of all historical values. Wisdom was based on learning—and learning in turn meant discipline, whether it involved memorizing the French conditional mode or the terms of the Treaty of Westphalia. He had managed, astonishingly, to convince his classes that to eschew the lessons of history was not only foolish—it was an insult to one's intellectual forebears: it meant one didn't value the mistakes and achievements of men as good as or better than oneself.

He had met the violence and disruption of the Occupation and the Bust with his characteristic balance of force and charm. They had burst into his class one morning, snake-dancing down the aisles, calling him a government spy, a merchant of death, chanting obscenities and defiance. Quick as light he had singled one of them out:

"Miss Thomas! Miss Thomas! Will you speak for your group? will you tell me what your beef is?"

The girl was pretty, with snarled black hair and wide, staring eyes. "Don't think you're going to fake *me,* Mr. Fink—just because I made the mistake of signing up for one of your fucking classes!"

Blackburn's face showed delighted surprise. "My—were they wilder than I knew?" Amid the ensuing laughter he made his offer. "All right. I will debate with three of you—any three you choose—twenty minutes apiece, on the utter irrelevance of history today. That's your theme song, isn't it? Twenty minutes now—we've just time enough—and forty next class. Okay?" He waved again for quiet. "I have only one condition: that each speaker limit his use of the four-letter fricative to three times per speech. For dramatic emphasis. More than that will only cause us all to lose respect for the act itself."

The class broke into applause. He debated with the spokesmen on that and successive days and moderated the ensuing discussions from the floor with wit and a disarming frankness. "Sure, all arbitrary value systems are suspect, probably. We're *all* alienated from something or other. And there's plenty that's rotten in the old system. But *shut it down* is good as a program only as long as you're willing to dare to put something in its place. Are you? *Shut it down.* All right, come on, carry it through to its logical conclusion: no university, no Establishment, no nation, no natural resources —no inhabitants. No, that's a dilettante's game, and deep in your hearts you know it's so . . ."

He was the sensation of a fearful, vindictive time. When most of the faculty had withdrawn in disgust, he'd gone out to the kids with a quiet, singular passion and reached a lot of them. Now, in and out of the Department, people had the same reaction: They saw that smile, the earnest hazel eyes, the alert, attentive inclination of his head and they said to one another: "By God, do you know, the Secretary *listens* to you! He really cares . . ." That was the thing about Paul—wherever he went he distended the possibilities.

"Or would wish unknown to the whole world," Blackburn repeated now, slowly. "How does that reach you as an idea, Reiny?"

"Rhetoric," the Presidential Adviser retorted scornfully. "Rot and rhetoric. The incurable idiot who said that had absolutely no experience in running a nation of psychopaths."

"The incurable idiot who said that was Thomas Jefferson," the Secretary observed. Jacobi led the burst of laughter that followed. "Does that give you pause?"

Vosz indulged in his satanic grimace. "Yes—but not for long."

"I suppose not."

"What rational individual would be caught dead airing high-level negotiations before that carnival of louts and satyrs down there?" Thrusting out one powerful short arm, he jerked a thumb between his feet. "The mandarins were right all along. Read my scenario thirty-eight-dash-nineteen on the death of secrecy. Look at Metternich's Europe—look at Westphalia, Versailles, Munich . . ."

"The fallacy there is that such decisions are not isolated events," Blackburn answered evenly. "They have sequels; and consequences are what we must care about—or we're no better than the cheapest shill in that carnival of yours."

"Oh, you effing liberals!" Vosz exclaimed. "Now you're going to howl about world opinion, I suppose. In a climate of terror there is only one force operant—power. Why won't you face it? Everything else is sentimental narcosis. Louis Sixteenth sends word to the Swiss Guard not to shoot down the rabble—and an entire political order is wiped away. Informed citizenry! What lunacy. All *he* wants, the pitiful, thrasonic baboon, is to see power exercised; holding his grubby world fast against the terrors of the void. Power counts and power alone—it's nothing more or less than the brutal extension of the ego. Dry your eyes!"

Blackburn watched him a moment with an expression of perfect composure. "Reiny, what I admire most about you—I mean above and beyond everything else—is your discovery, singlehanded and unafraid, of the laws of human behavior. It's something I can cling to in the small hours." When the hilarity died down again, he pointed a finger at Vosz and said: "You *have* to tell him."

"Who?"

"Your thrasonic baboon. You have to tell him."

"Why?"

"Because it is the only way you can repay him."

"Repay him!" Vosz shouted. "For *what,* in the name of Beelzeboob?"

"For his sense of responsibility."

"Responsibility—!"

"Yes. Oh, yes. You're resting on it, Reiny. Such as it is—and it's pretty good on balance."

"The hell I am!"

"Yes, you are. Tell me, have you ever thought of changing places with your garbage collector? Tomorrow morning, say?"

"Collecting *garbage—?*" The whites of Vosz's eyes were visible for the first time behind the violet lenses. "Every garbage collector in the world could fall over dead from apoplexy and my life wouldn't be affected at all . . ."

"Ah, but it would, Reiny. It would. Even if you continue to dwell high in the mountains of truth," he added, and Jacobi, hearing the phrase, realized the Secretary had caught the Nietzsche quotation in the girl's book. "You're snatching at the same straw we all are: an essential faith in the conscientious care of the guy who checks out the jet engine, bleeds the brakes, adjusts the pressure valve on the furnace . . ."

The plane, turning slowly now, sinking through the sculptured clouds, gave a little jolting lurch; and Blackburn, steadying himself in the doorway, grinned. "You see? In case we needed any reminders. That fellow up there"—he pointed toward the pilot's cabin—"may have just had a disastrous fight with his wife; he may even be coming down with a terrible case of Delhi belly, like Andy . . . but we've placed our poor old fragile bodies in his hands just the same. We've got our money on him, win or lose."

A smile was playing around the corners of the Secretary's mouth, but his voice had that edge in it that could make people grave with attention. "The actions of responsible men in society *are* judgeable, they *are* supportable. Blackburn's Law Three-A. Though I haven't written a scenario on it yet." Passing his hand through his bristling black hair, he grinned. "The spirit is—now and then—willing; and the flesh is—usually—weak. That's why the completely responsible man is so rare. He's the only bulwark against your terror-laden void, Reiny. The only one . . ."

He paused, looked a touch ruefully at the carpeted beige floor of the cabin as though in mild disapproval of having run on this way; glanced up again. "But all kidding aside, Reiny: couldn't you have called him a *conceited* baboon instead?"

The cabin broke into quick laughter. Blackburn had already turned and gone forward. The ship shuddered briefly in dense clouds—and then, still banking, they were out of it, slipping down over the puzzle mosaic of houses and pools, the sand-and-tar lace of traffic circles. Jacobi, moving toward the exit with the others, thought: God, how wonderful it must be to be able to do that. Set down that crazy son of a bitch Vosz and his scenarios, weld a roomful of people into a sense of purpose, with a sentence—and then walk off cool as cool: how wonderful it must be . . .

The door swung back. Following the Secretary and one of the security men he stepped out into the June morning, felt the rush of sweet, familiar air, glorious after the rank, damp heat of New Delhi. Below, at the foot of the steps the press was waiting—the crush of cameras and microphones that were a part of the life they led, that never failed to shake his scholar's reticence. Paul was already speaking.

"As you know, I don't believe in bromides. This is not the coming of a new heaven and a new earth. But we *have* accomplished a great deal, a very great deal at New Delhi. The People's Republic of China has generously withdrawn its objections to an eventual referendum in the area under dispute. We have secured guarantees from all GATO members, including India and Japan. And recognition of the provisional state of Dhotal will be first on the agenda when the United Nations reconvenes in the fall."

"What about the question of increased military aid to General Bodawyın, Mr. Secretary?" Landis, the *Chicago Tribune* man, his eyes narrow behind his spectacles. "Have you had any second thoughts about that?"

Blackburn smiled. "Walter, I've answered that question over the past several weeks in San Francisco, New Delhi and Melbourne. I'm grieved that an answer is still sought here in Washington—where as you know we have the answers to everything. However, I deeply respect the fine sense of tradition that impels you to ask it."

There was laughter, followed by some questions of a more or less personal nature; and then Coningham of *Time* called: "Mr. Secretary, do you anticipate a backlash here at home in terms of your acquiescence over Prince Naungapaya?"

"I'm not exactly flattered by your choice of words, Ted. I don't see it as acquiescence. Prince Naungapaya is clearly the most popular leader of the insurgent peoples in the area. I'm confident that the American people realize that his leadership reflects the will of the people in the provisional state of Dhotal."

"Mr. Secretary,"—it was Landis again—"Senator Brickley in a speech to the Denver Chamber of Commerce yesterday called you 'the author of a new chapter of appeasement in American history' and 'a permanently subversive influence on United States foreign policy.' Would you care to comment on that?"

"Why, yes. I'd have to say that inspires me—I've never felt I had a complete enough control over foreign policy to be *permanently* subversive. Let's say that I'm fond of drafting my chapters of appeasement in an occasionally subversive *form.*"

He broke off on a chorus of amusement and left the field to Vosz. The Presidential Adviser was always great copy, though after the Kissinger flap over Pakistan what he said could only be attributed to "a highly placed government official." The reporters were already scribbling away.

Hurrying to catch up with the Secretary, Jacobi said: "Why?"

Blackburn shrugged. "I've had my say. Let him rant. Did you think I should have had him taken off in a mummy case?"

"Hell, no. You should have pushed him out the emergency exit over French Frigate Shoals."

The Secretary laughed. "Don't worry about Reiny. He's a trial but he's all right."

"He's a menace," Jacobi burst out.

"Well, in some ways, yes. In others, no." They began moving through the crowd toward the main exits. Blackburn threw his assistant a quick, enigmatic glance. "Reiny keeps me on my toes. There's that certain competition for the President's ear. Reiny's just mad because we brought it off. He'll get over it."

"But if he's going to keep sniping—"

"Don't worry about it. The President listens to me first. That's what counts ultimately."

Jacobi made no reply. What Paul didn't see—or didn't want to see—was that the danger existed as long as Vosz, or anyone at all, was Presidential Adviser for National Security Affairs. Paul might be Secretary, all right, with the President's airy assurances of a free hand, the pre-eminence of State, the burial of the Little State–Big State hatchet and all the rest of it; but the fact remained that Reiny was *there,* like Everest. With his own retinue of specialists and communications apparatus, just as Bundy and Kissinger had been. And Vosz, as far as Jacobi could see, was more aggressive and power-hungry than any of his predecessors.

"Let's remember," Paul was saying, "the President thinks Reiny has a brilliant mind, and he puts a lot of confidence in his judgment. And therefore whatever we may think we must get along with him. And we will. Won't we, Sid?"

"Yours to command, Mr. Secretary," Jacobi answered gravely. Pausing, the two men looked at each other with that surge of affection only time and respect and a dozen crises surmounted together can forge. Then Blackburn grinned and clapped him once on the shoulder.

"What's the matter, Sid? Still worried about the Student Prince?" It was their nickname for Naungapaya.

Jacobi shook his head. "No—Bodawyin, actually. I don't trust him."

"You know something? I don't trust either of them." Blackburn gave that quick, loosening shrug of his neck and shoulders—a throwback to his swimming days. "What you've got to remember is that *neither* party wanted a solution—each gun wanted to shoot down the other one on a central, nonnegotiable issue. But they've got to hold to it now—they've signed up, they're on board. Ch'en and I are in full agreement. The treaty's behind us. If they—"

"Mr. Secretary . . ."

They turned together. Joseph Carter, Andy Stinchfield's Deputy, came up to them tall and slender; a Sudanese warrior in a slate dacron suit. His hair rose from his head in a magnificent, bushy aureole. "Congratulations, sir!"

"Thank you, Joe." They all shook hands. "Come to carry your bureau chief home on his shield?"

"How *is* Andy?"

"Pretty sick. We're going to want you at the oars for a while. Any new ripples while we were gone?"

"There's a message from Mrs. Blackburn, asking you to come up to the Paling as soon as possible."

"Really? Did she say what it was?"

"No, sir. Only that it was urgent."

"I see. Curious." A shadow of concern crossed the Secretary's face, vanished again. He said: "And how is Under Secretary Stout?"

"Fine. He's over on the Hill right now. He said"—Carter's lips curved —"to tender his not inconsiderable felicitations."

All three of them laughed. This was a reference to Miles Stout's fondness for the double negative—in certain circles of the Department the Under Secretary was known as "the Neg," though no one knew who had invented the term.

Jacobi said solemnly: "It's not that he doesn't mean to be disingenuous about *not* disagreeing with our policy: he doesn't."

"I think—" Carter's eyes glittered, but his face remained as gravely self-possessed as a sergeant major's on parade "—he wishes now he'd been in on the action."

"Does he?" the Secretary said. "He wouldn't have given a wooden nickel for our chances two weeks ago."

Jacobi remembered the afternoon the Under Secretary had begun to raise elaborate objections to Blackburn's appointment of Carter.

"You feel he's unqualified?" Paul had asked.

"Oh, no—it's not that." Stout had pressed back on a cuticle with his thumb. "It's just that it's never been done before. With someone of his— background. In Far East, especially. It would tend to set a precedent."

"Would it?" Blackburn's expression was merely inquiring, but his voice held that narrow steel edge that warned the wary to tread with infinite care. Stout, however, armed in the insular rigidities of thirty years, proceeded mildly.

"Of course I'm not unmindful of the value of the appointment."

"You're not."

"No, of course not. It's a fine gesture. And one must not fail to move with the times, I suppose . . ." But then the menaces of this new world jostled the self-possessed ghosts of Groton and Princeton and Newburyport—he raised a pale hand to his face and cried: "But it's his appearance! That kinky Hottentot hair—it's flying all over his head!"

Blackburn had watched the Under Secretary for a quiet moment. "Well," he said firmly, "he *has* a head under all that hair—which is a good deal more than can be said for certain sartorial splendors in this Department. And that is what I care about, Miles. I know it's heresy . . ."

"I guess I'll fly on up to the Paling, then," the Secretary was saying now. "The President won't want to see me till tomorrow or the next day, anyway. He's all tied up with the new urban reform bill."

"You've got Villarta tomorrow afternoon," Jacobi reminded him, "and after that the Germans."

"I'll be back tomorrow morning early. Will you work up those notes on the Indian suggestion?"

Reinhold Vosz hurried past them, short arms gesticulating, followed by an avid, gleeful mob of reporters.

"—There isn't time enough in the universe to solve all the things we've got to solve," Jacobi heard himself say gloomily.

"What? Of course there is. After our victory? You're just tired. A weary statesman means a pessimistic statesman. Ask Charles Maurice de Talleyrand-Périgord. Or Jeanne Antoinette Poisson Le Normant d'Etioles, Marquise de Pompadour. For the woman's angle." He winked, and Jacobi could see the old curious excitement working in him. "Cheer up, Sid. Things are never so black they can't get blacker. 'Dost thou not know, my son, with how little wisdom the world is governed?' Bet you don't know who said that, Joe."

"Sully?" Carter inquired.

"Wrong. No more chances. Who knows what's in store for us? And a bleeding good thing it is, too—as my son and heir would put it." And his face broke into that radiant, entrancing smile, shadowed now with exhaustion, sadness, a rare fortitude. "It's perfectly simple, Sid. All we have to do is plot a brilliant course between the distasteful and the catastrophic. I don't know about *you* public servants, but this public servant is going for a good, long swim."

Turning, he moved away through the airport crowd with that quick, forward-leaning stride, anticipatory, Vineyard bound.

"Who did say that, Sid?"

"Oxenstern," Jacobi answered absently. With the Secretary's departure he was conscious of a stealthy sense of depression, of gathering threatful events. The high point, he wondered; was it the high point? There always was one. Bemused, weary, he watched Blackburn until he lost sight of him in the surge of heaving shoulders, bobbing heads.

TWO

"—You know something?" Leland Blackburn leaped to his feet—a colt's swift, awkward grace—and confronted them all, looking defiant and handsome. "I find myself out of sync with this whole convention. Basically."

"Bravo," Judge Seaver said with frosty amusement. He was slumped under the newspapers of half a dozen cities; his bony, tapering fingers played over the cramped columns. "That's telling 'em off, boy."

"Father, are you reading the *Times* or are you a part of this conversation?" Eleanor Blackburn asked him.

"Both," he barked. "Guess I can manage two things at once."

"No you can't, you never could."

The Judge shoved his tortoise-shell half-glasses to the top of his head in a fierce, reflex gesture, and squinted at his daughter. "Eleanor, that's one of your cardinal faults: forcing people counter to their basic natures."

She smiled and became all at once the gauche, vulnerable, rather charming young girl Blackburn had first laid eyes on thirty years ago. "You used to say I *had* no cardinal faults, Father."

"Rank self-indulgence on my part. Land takes after Uncle Ben—running close-hauled off a lee shore. The Darcey blood, you can't change that."

"Wrong," Leland retorted in a furious tone, and flung himself deep in the couch again, all elbows and knees and long, bony legs. "Who I take after is myself."

Blackburn laughed. "The last Adam." He slipped off his tie—he'd come straight from the airport—and said: "What's the source of all the hard-favored rage, may I ask?"

"My own business," the boy said with heat. "My own. P-V-T. This is not—repeat, *not*—a global crisis."

"I wish that were true, sweet," his mother answered with her customary coolness. "The trouble is, everything is *somebody* else's business."

"What a bloody comforting thought."

"Especially when you're a minor and there are serious repercussions." She said to Blackburn, "I'm sorry to involve you in this right now, Paul. But it's just come out, and we've been having a bit of back-and-forth about it."

"Mostly forth," Leland said.

"Yes." She straightened, arching her neck, and pressed her fine slim hands hard against her thigh—a prefatory gesture Blackburn had learned to read over the years. He suppressed a smile. Eleanor always functioned like this: the assemblage of principals, the calm, faintly portentous manner, the generalizing preambles. Her ritual. She had begun exactly this way on that long-ago day (it was right here at the Paling but on the sea wall above the beach) when she had told him her father had agreed to their marriage. Of course it had been a foregone certainty long before that; he'd talked with the Judge for nearly an hour that morning; but still there had been that curious little need in Eleanor to make an elaborate mystery out of it. Only then she had been shyer, and a bit tremulous—almost vulnerable in her hesitancy. Thresholds . . .

She said: "The fact is, Leland has been seeing a woman."

"How original of him!" Blackburn exclaimed, and the Judge gave his high-pitched gleeful bark.

"Yes, I imagined it would amuse you. It's only that this particular relationship isn't quite so innocent as all that."

"Suffering Jesus," Leland groaned from the couch.

"I mean he's been having a prolonged affair with her. Up in Cambridge."

Blackburn shot his wife a glance. "Things have changed quite a bit since we were in school, Nell."

"Oh yes—I'm more or less aware of that." She smiled again, a different smile. "She's a secretary in Howard Hannig's office. She's a much older woman." She put great stress on the comparative and Blackburn thought of an evening in Damascus and Michele Franquinet, her thin alabaster face serene in the candlelight, gently holding forth on not only the propriety but the absolute necessity of some older woman's serving as affectionate instructor in every young man's *dépucillage,* to the general amusement of the table—and then, laughing with the others, he had caught the expression on Nell's face. What had it been? disapproval, embarrassment, anger? All of those, and something else . . .

"Is that a crime punishable by death?" he asked now.

"I suppose not." She was determined, he saw, to match his easy style with her own. "She's a good fifteen years older—"

"As a matter of fact, the gap is exactly twelve years and three months," Leland interrupted.

"Twelve, fifteen—what difference does it make? It's an altogether unhealthy relationship."

"Unhealthy—!" The boy threw up his hands. "Maman, your terminology unhinges me, it really does. Yeah, sure, we take showers together—that what you mean?"

The Judge barked with delight, slapping the pile of newspapers. "That's it. Fight 'em, boy . . ."

"Leland," his mother said in a patient tone, "If you could—"

"We even sit up late—in bed, of course—watching TV and eating coconut custard pie. With the same *fork!*" he jeered. "How's that for a gasper, Maman?"

"I *can* think of more edifying things to do."

"Hey, I'll bet you can!" The boy leaped to his feet again. "I'll tell you what's unhealthy. If you're aching to know. What's *unhealthy* is the Right Honorable Arthur McCain, calling off the dogs on that NRT anti-trust suit in return for a prepaid military coup in Colombia. What's un-healthy is your buddy Quantrell picking up a cool thirty-seven thou a year —in addition to his steady academic baksheesh, of course—for checking out atomic warheads with Larch-Zimco. I mean, what a neat rip-off—and it's legal! Not to mention little old Hughbryce, hotting up far-out scenes for everybody else, America the Imperial. There's sickness, all right. I mean, *if* you want to roll away the stone—"

He broke off, facing his mother's rejoinder with an expression of in-supportable outrage. Smiling in spite of himself Blackburn studied the aquiline features and scornful, dark brown eyes. His son, nearly grown. Taller than I am, Blackburn thought with a twinge of mingled pride and regret; a good three inches taller, at nineteen. What collision of inscrutable genes had made him so astonishingly good-looking? His hair, black and silky, lay low on his forehead and he raked it back impatiently. That high partisan extravagance Blackburn remembered in his own father, wedded to Eleanor's uncompromising New England conscience: an inflammable com-bination. Where would it take him? Where it took all of us: into trouble— and even out of it again, God willing . . .

Feeling pleasantly tired, no longer listening, he gazed out at the great English mulberry that had been washed ashore a balled sapling from the wreck of the *Jason,* over a century before. He was still bound in the sense of subdued triumph from New Delhi, a mood heightened by the short drive from the airport: the grass high and green from the late May rains, sur-mounted by the heads of Queen Anne's lace like feathery white coral float-ing in still water, and flowing low along the stone walls the blued canopy of wild grape that had given the Island its name; then the turn north and west into the pine woods, a tremulous dappled light, the rutted wood road winding haphazard, with the foliage thinning in rare promise—all at once cutting away to the tortured calligraphy of beach plum and bayberry hug-ging the shore below the hard salt blue of the Sound, like breaking surface from a dream of a deep sea dive . . . and there beyond the ancient bar-berry hedge lay the grand old house with its railed widow's walk and fine Greek portico, flanked by its congeries of outbuildings: austere, secluded, graceful, proud—everything a house should be. Walking up the broad gray path made from the vertebrae of whales, his lungs filled with the wine-and-iodine smell of the sea, he felt as he always had that high, exultant catch at his heart. It was always a homecoming. No other place had ever equalled it or ever would—not the gloomy structure of his childhood years in San Francisco or the magnificent Bullfinch façade he'd bought in Cambridge after they'd made him a department head. This was home.

The main house had been built by the Judge's Great-Great-grand-father Gamaliel, a tall man with the narrow-set eyes and wrathful demeanor of a hell-fire preacher, though he was a seafarer. Enraged by a plan to fill in the marshlands north of the town he had stood up in Edgartown village meeting and denounced a scheme that would willfully destroy herring runs and the essential rhythm of the tides. If in their folly and unpardonable greed they did this thing, he would never set foot in their wretched township again. The marshes *were* filled, and he was as good as his word: he'd gone up-island, about as far away from Edgartown as he could without getting his feet wet, to a low promontory called Turk's Head, halfway between Menemsha and Lambert's Cove overlooking Vineyard Sound, and had built there on the site of an old fort abandoned after the Indian wars. He'd replaced the crumbling stockade with barberry and hawthorne hedges but it was still the Paling: huddled low to the land, swept by the northwest gales, staring defiantly out to sea, away from the pleasures and capitulations of Edgartown. Beyond the Pale, local wags often referred to it; Gamaliel Seaver had not invited entry.

Gamaliel's descendants had been less austere—though every bit as eccentric. Pilots, ship captains, whalers, they brought back booty from a thousand fearful coasts and enviable isles. Joshua, a bachelor and misogynist, had quarreled with his brothers and built the Fiji House, a salt-box Cape Codder where he lived after a back injury had put him ashore for good, in a jungle of tapa cloth mats and ceremonial masks and painted shields. Mercifully in the rear of the compound his nephew Asa had put up the Pagoda, an impossible Oriental structure which could only be entered on the second floor by means of a nobbly arched bridge. It was crammed with silk hangings and lacquered tables and massive grinning dragons, and the odor of camphor and incense still lingered after more than a century.

It was Asa who had brought home "the Spanish woman"—a Chilean marquesa whose separation from her former husband had never been clearly defined, and who, it was said, required a three-masted bark to transport her possessions. She patronized her neighbors, fought with the tradespeople, and chose to walk the beach in the worst autumn gales, holding a shingle to her face and screaming curses in Spanish at the frantic, wheeling gulls. One fine evening she had disappeared—her dinner unfinished, her robe flung over a chair in her bedroom; it was rumored she had gone off with the first mate of a French packet that had put into Holmes Hole for repairs. But no one ever knew.

There they were—there were portraits of them in the parlor, the dining room, the downstairs hall; young Paul Blackburn had once studied each of them with slow, avid care. It was something he'd never known —a family with so much self-assurance, such a wealth of history. There had been a forebear named Zachariah who, as third officer of a brig, had singlehanded put down a mutiny off Rarotonga at the tender age of twenty-two; another, a bearded whaling captain named Oliver, had led a three-vessel hunt for a notoriously destructive sperm whale named Sunda Jack, and after a wild two-day chase, amid a welter of smashed boats and broken men, had succeeded in personally killing that terror of the Java Sea; most impressive of all, there had been an ancestor—named, appropriately enough, Fortitude—who, captured by pirates off Grand Cayman, had coolly sat on a hatch cover and haggled with the entire band of cutthroats over the price for his ransom—and after four hours or so had beaten them down to what he considered a more reasonable figure . . .

The Judge's father Jeremy had been the first of the Seavers to go off-island: an import-export business which had led to the Massachusetts Legislature and later to New York. He had added the tennis court and built the new boathouse, and his schooner *Ariadne* had been the glory of the Vineyard fleet, twice victor of the Round-the-Island race. He had remodeled and renovated—but the compound was still called the Paling. With its sloping lawns and fine expanse of beach, its fair-weather moorings and the two low breakwaters bounding the property like lean granite arms, it was open to the sea, not to the land behind it. A world unto itself: stalwart, self-sufficient. From the first moment Paul Blackburn had laid eyes on it, coming down from Exeter with Lee—the other Leland, Nell's brother—that long-ago Thanksgiving morning, moving through the chaste, wainscoted rooms, watching the locust logs blazing in the huge fireplace, hearing the congenial rhythms of talk and laughter he had thought with sharp, furtive sureness: *Here* is where I want to be, here is the home I've always dreamed of, *here, this house.* It was as though some unforeseen and extravagant gift had been thrust into his two hands. The Judge dressed in a worn old herringbone tweed jacket had come toward him, his hand extended; he'd taken it, murmuring his thanks for the invitation, had turned back—and seen with dismay that Lee had vanished . . .

He said now: "What is the lady's name, may I ask?"

"I believe it's Hoyt," Eleanor answered. Her eyes, hard with that peculiarly piercing quality the palest blue pupils often have, rested on his for a moment.

"Well, that sounds like a good Irish name," he rejoined in a pleasant, even tone. "Or maybe it's English, I'm not sure."

"—Her name is Jillian Hoyt," Leland broke in tightly, "and she *is* part Irish, and you know something *totally* unhealthy? I'm in love with her."

"Everybody's in love at nineteen," Judge Seaver said. "Didn't you know that, Land? I was, myself. Bar girl at McBride's Rathskeller. Flaming red hair and the fairest skin you ever laid eyes on. Head over heels in love with her—I *was*. She later married Tierney, fellow that got mixed up in the Jamaica Overpass scandal."

The boy watched his grandfather a moment—all at once broke into a sardonic, mischievous grin. "Maybe you should have married her, Grampus."

The Judge's eyes narrowed; he raised both gnarled hands and let them drop. "Maybe I should have, at that."

"That's ridiculous," Eleanor said. "It would have been the biggest mistake of your life and you know it. Why do you say such things?"

"Anyway," Land broke in on her, "I don't know about *everybody*. I only know about myself."

"The particular relates to the general, Leland."

He shook his head vehemently. "Oh no, it doesn't—that's where *you're* out to lunch. The particular relates to the particular."

"Ipso facto," Blackburn said. All at once he remembered plucking Land, at the age of five, out of a melee of shrieking, clawing Japanese boys in Kobe. Land had not been able to understand them, nor they him, and in his frustration and dismay he had struck out right and left. Later, sitting on the edge of his son's bed, bandaging his nose and forehead, Blackburn had tried to reason with him: those little boys hadn't answered him because they didn't know English. They'd never had the chance to learn, just as he hadn't yet learned Japanese. Didn't he see?

Blinking against the burn of the iodine, Land had shaken his head stubbornly. "They wanted to kill me."

"What? No—why on earth should they want to do that?"

"Because my eyes are different. And my nose. I could tell."

"Land, that's silly. Everybody looks different from everyone else— that's no reason for wanting to *kill* someone. You wait: you'll learn to speak their language and you'll all be friends."

The boy had set his jaw. "I'll learn their language but it won't make any difference. My eyes will still be rounder."

"—completely and happily in love with each other," this tall, rebellious, handsome version of his son was saying now, "—I can't seem to get this across. *Happily,* you know? And that's all there is to it."

"No, I'm afraid that *isn't* all there is to it." It was sadly symptomatic of Nell that when she smiled she often didn't mean it; when she frowned she always did.

Land gave a quick, disdainful laugh, his hair looped low over his forehead. "You're right, Nellie—that isn't all. I know none of you can grasp the concept, but she's a wonderful person, a *real* person—not like the phony, temporizing types who hang out around the ancestral hearth."

"I've no idea what sort of person she is."

"Oh—you certainly wouldn't approve of her! She likes old movies, and she doesn't get around to hoeing out the flat for weeks at a time. But I've got riotous news for you. She wouldn't approve of you, either."

"Is she married?" Blackburn asked him suddenly.

"No, she's not married—and it wouldn't make a particle of difference if she was."

"Of course it would, it would make a great deal of difference."

"Not to me!"

"Take it easy now, take it easy," Blackburn told him. "Sit down, will you, Land? You make me nervous, thrashing around. You don't want to make me nervous at a time like this, do you?"

But the boy did not smile; slumped in the couch again he scowled at nothing and picked at a scab on the back of his hand. The wind, southwest and freshening, sent arabesques of shadow and light swaying on the lawn. Beyond the wall the sea looked royal and dense and limitless, irresistible. What I *want* right now is to go swimming, Blackburn thought irritably; I don't want to be sitting in here wrangling about some woman named Hoyt . . .

To his wife he said mildly: "I can see I've come late to this problem —if problem it is. You've obviously thought about it at length. What do you feel should be done?"

Arching her back she pressed down on her thigh again. "I should think the answer to that is obvious, Paul. I think you ought to go up to Cambridge and have a good heart-to-heart talk with her. Something to the effect that it's a highly unprofitable relationship and should end quickly and gracefully."

"Transpierced Jesus," Leland groaned.

Blackburn looked sharply at his wife, looked away again. Never pretty—the broad, angular jaw and high-ridged Seaver nose had precluded that, as well as a curious shadowed concavity in her cheeks and brows— she had improved with age. There were men who considered her "a handsome woman"; Blackburn had heard them. What they meant, more often than not, was that astonishing assurance she wore like a diadem. Eleanor Seaver Blackburn had never doubted who she was or what she wanted. She was, she knew it, clumsy physically, she lacked true charm and beauty; but her arrogance of family contained that—she could afford unorthodox, even eccentric ways. Unsure of his own background, Blackburn had admired this: it didn't matter to her that her flat leather sandals didn't favor her long, narrow feet or that her print skirt was too arty for her tall, angular figure, that the cloth band she wore in her hair was more suitable to a teenager—the sublime Yankee aplomb always saw her through.

She was still watching him levelly—a gaze both compliant and imperious. She should have been her grandmother—the wife of a hard, taciturn sea captain, waiting with inflexible patience for him to return from some exotic voyage, from having met and slept with some equally exotic woman; dressed in a high-necked dark gingham gown with a single cameo brooch at the throat, and over it a bombazine cloak even if the weather were warm, traversing the railed widow's walk with the same firm, measured stride that her man paced his quarterdeck, waiting for him to bring back to her the jade combs and amber prayer beads—the surrogates of his passion and his guilt—that she never wore . . . Why did he always think of Nell as dressed in period costume? Yet he always had—in some odd way it had been part of her early attraction for him. She would never wear the jewelry he'd bought her, either—the delicate gold bracelet from Trebizond, the garnet pendant, the Twelfth Dynasty scarab: they were all in boxes in the right-hand drawer of her dresser. Waiting. She was always waiting . . .

He dropped his eyes again. Tired, his nerves stretched taut from the weeks of travel and interminable argument, he found himself resenting this penchant for swift and implacable judgment she displayed so proudly —almost innocently. How the devil could she be so sure this was the right thing to do? In all probability the girl was amusing herself with Land and would tire of him; or Land's ego was preened by an older woman's attentions, and he would tire of her. And that would be that. Furthermore it was humiliating to the boy—all this analysis and censure, as though he were seven years old and guilty of chronic bed-wetting. But that was Nell. Nell's Way, they'd used to say in Isfahan, in Khotiane; they were still saying it, for all he knew, in Cambridge and Cleveland Park. She'd always felt vehemently—it was one of the things about her he loved— but that abrupt appraisal of people and causes had altered subtly over the years. She still went straight at life with that cool, level sea captain's stare —but more and more she saw it in abstractions, in curiously remote ways. All crises (like this one: did she honestly see it as a *crisis?*) were to be met and solved as policy problems, not as differences between confused, emotional human beings. How could she be so sure! As though the hot red Punjab earth, the churning bazaars and timeless bleak hills had given him new and fearful eyes he found himself thinking: She will go too far some day, with this arrogance of hers . . .

"Aren't we making a little too much of this?" he asked. "I must confess I don't really see the need for such drastic action. Land's virtually a man grown"—the archaic ring of the phrase surprised him; what was it, the Judge's presence?—"he presumably knows what he's doing."   ˙

"Boy, *there's* magnanimity," Leland exclaimed, and cast his eyes at the ceiling. "Orchids from the Prof-O."

Blackburn thought, Imagine looking that handsome and maligned and confident about it all—at nineteen. Let alone enjoying a bang-up, five-alarm affair with a thirty-one-year-old secretary right under Fudgy Hannig's bulbous nose. Amused at his own fleeting envy he said: "Aside from giving Miss Hoyt certain cautionary advice I'm sure she has no need of, I can see very little point in an eyeball-to-eyeball confrontation."

Eleanor's lips set firmly, she looked away at the pale blue shell of sky above the Sound. "I see," she said quietly.

No you don't see, he thought, you really don't, but there's no point in going into all *that,* now. There were times when this Yankee implacability of Nell's could seem as outrageous, as horrifyingly remote as the culinary habits of an anteater. Watching Land out of the corner of his eye he was filled with a sudden, almost overpowering sadness. My son: don't accede to loss, to mortality. You will be forced to, of course—but don't. Defy the foul fiend. My son—

But the boy was glaring at his loafers and picking at the scab again.

Eleanor said: "And then there's the political side."

"Oh, my God!" Land burst out. "I suppose you're going to tell me *that's* relevant!"

"What political side?" Blackburn asked.

Eleanor picked up a few sheets of paper from the end table near her and handed them to him. "Here's a speech Miss Hoyt gave last week on Cambridge Common. I think you might find it interesting—especially right now."

"You're just dragging that in—look, are we immoral or are we subversive? Make up your Torquemada minds, will you?"

His mother smiled at him. "Leland, we're not ogres, you know. We're going to be some day, but we're not now."

"Well, just clue me in on when the mutation's going to take place."

The speech was effective enough, as such harangues went: idiomatic and hot, a naked appeal to the emotions. It accused the government of inaugurating a reign of terror in refusing bail to Lachlan Smith, promised that Sirius would secure his release, and wound up with a savage attack on Reinhold Vosz, calling on all students and political action groups to join forces against "this ultra-fascist apologist for imperialism, clearly the most dangerous man in America since the bloody days of McNamara and Bundy."

Sirius. He folded the sheets thoughtfully on his thumb. Eleanor was watching him again—that calm, measuring glance edged with reproach, through which the narrowest point of vindication glittered: only he would have caught it. Well, nobody could say Nell Blackburn expended her ammunition rashly. He felt a kind of weary admiration. What a terrific diplomat she'd have made! Foreign minister for some lesser Balkan principality, say, squeezing the last ounce of advantage out of each situation with a finely calculated sense of leverage; saving her most telling blow for the precise moment. It was a talent you either had or you didn't. Up to a point it could be learned—as Miles Stout, in his provident, pom-

pous way had learned it, or old Leggett. But on the highest level it was a
matter of feel, inherent and unfailing instinct. A gift of the gods. What a
waste . . .

"Forensic talents, I see," he said aloud. "Sirius. She's a member?"

"More than that," Land answered. "She's Smitty's exec. She draws
up the plans."

"Your son is a member, too," Eleanor said.

Blackburn stared at the boy. "You've joined them? You belong?"

"Shake you up, Prof-O?" Land was grinning, but it was an expression
Blackburn had never seen before; not quite. His eyes were black as jet.
"Dues all paid up, membership card sealed in blood. Savage midnight
rites, you know."

His mother said: "Miss Hoyt's influence, I daresay."

"I think for myself," Leland retorted hotly.

"I'm sure you do, dear. But how nice to be able to share radical
sentiments along with the coconut custard pie."

"Sirius," Blackburn murmured; to cover his dismay added, "Well, it's
a rotten pun, I can tell you that much."

"Yeah, well, we're just as committed as hell. Don't underestimate us."

Eleanor said, "Of course the considerable embarrassment this could
cause your father hasn't mattered to you at all."

"Leave me out of this," the Secretary interposed sharply. "He goes
his way, I go mine. There's never been any thought control in this family
and we're not going to start now."

"Then in that case you won't of course have any objection to this."
And leaning forward again she offered him a copy of the Harvard *Crimson,*
opened to the editorial page.

"Well, well—the dear old Crime." He smiled at the familiar typeface
fondly. "Takes you back."

"Exhibit B," Land muttered. "What would we ever do without the
evidence?"

*Presidential Adviser Reinhold Vosz's recent decision to speak at
Emerson Hall on the 14th is not a courtesy call. Coming hard upon the
persecution of Lachlan Smith it constitutes a mortal insult to every member of the University who values free inquiry and civil liberties. The appearance on campus of this hysterical refugee from a faded Alfred
Hitchcock rerun should be an occasion for hilarity: a stand-up comic's
routine, with belly laughs for all. But make no mistake about him, dear
reader: he is deadly serious, and he is cloaked in enormous power.*

*Those undergraduates who see his participation in the New Delhi
Conference as a cause for hope are deluding themselves cruelly. The facts
are that this "treaty" is intended to obscure the REAL purpose of the
meeting, which was to establish a puppet state obedient to U.S. influence
on the border of the People's Republic of China. While the Naungapaya*

Deal lulls us into a sense of false security, the Angelic Doctor (with the endorsement of a supine Secretary of State) is free to give full scope to his psychotic theories of espionage and aggression—as evidenced in the grim revelations of the Hughbryce Papers.

One point is clear: for all its rhetoric of response and responsibility, the Administration has chosen the path of repression. Lachlan Smith is being held without bail because, freed, he would reveal still more damaging scenarios in deceit and destruction. His release is an obligation in the name of truth.

For the militant liberal everywhere the options (as the Angelic Doctor would say) have narrowed significantly: (1) he faces an Establishment deaf to individual rights; (2) he can no longer look to popular support for his actions; (3) he must pick his targets with great care—and wait for the moment.

"Ah, if youth only knew, if age were only able," Blackburn murmured. He sighed. "The level of editorial acumen seems to have fallen off a good deal since my palmy days—I suppose every old grad likes to say that."

"It's an editorial Leland wrote last week."

Blackburn put down the paper and looked at his son. "Do you really believe this? About the conference?"

"Believe it—of course I believe it!" The boy bounded to his feet again, his hand extended. "Do you think I'd have said it if I didn't? I *know* it's so."

"Know it. What do you mean, you know it?"

"Oh my God—semantics! I'm *aware* of these things. As facts."

"What are your sources?"

"For Pete's sake—they're everywhere! There's J. D. Marks, there's Frénisson in *Le Moule* . . ."

Blackburn frowned. "What would you say if I were to tell you there's no substance to those stories?"

"I'd say you had your reasons for telling me that."

"As a supine Secretary of State, you mean."

"Sure—what else?"

"What if I were to give you my personal word of honor that I have no *reasons* for telling you that: that there is really and truly no substance to the theory that the United States is seeking to establish a puppet regime in the Burma Triangle. What would be your response?"

"Then . . ." Land put his head down; when he looked up again his face wore an expression so hostile Blackburn was startled. "Then I'd have to conclude either that you haven't the faintest idea what's going on —or that you're lying to me."

"Leland!" his mother exclaimed, and the Judge muttered something inaudible; Blackburn waved them both silent.

"If that's what he thinks, I want to hear it . . . Tell me: if someone told you he had it on good authority that the President had hired a group of men to shoot down the plane I was coming back on from New Delhi in order to provoke the Administration into war with China, would you credit the story?"

"Of course I would. Why shouldn't I? Weirder things than that have happened."

"Have they? Are you sure?"

"Sure, I'm sure. The CIA rigged those phony plane shots in the Bay of Pigs operation to con Stevenson with, didn't they? You yourself told me Rusk held out on Hanoi's peace proposals in Vietnam. I remember how sore you were about it at the time. Or the Tonkin Gulf swindle."

"But that's hardly comparable to—"

"How about these Hughbryce Papers—are you going to tell me they're not real? That Smitty invented them?"

"They're schemes, fancies. Vosz's pipe dreams. They would never have been put in operation."

Leland gave a quick, explosive laugh. "Who's to know that?"

"*I'm* to know that," Blackburn answered with some warmth. "I make these decisions, Land. I'm in charge of foreign policy, not Reinhold Vosz."

"Yeah, I know—they're *all* pipe dreams until some Establishment freak gets the urge to run 'em up the old flagpole, see how they'll wave . . ."

"Where do you get some of your ideas—from the Venus probe? I hate like hell to disappoint you, but we really aren't all that irresponsible."

"All right. Tell me: do you think Smitty ought to be busted for wanting to hang up this dirty wash where all can see? Do you?"

Blackburn shook his head. "No. I think it's a mistake, it's too severe."

"Then why don't you do something about it?"

"Because it doesn't fall under my jurisdiction, that's why."

"Yeah, that's what I figured. Cop-out time in old Foggy Bottom . . . Man, what do you think the *next* memos were about—the ones Smitty never got to release?" He nodded grimly. "Well: it'll come out. It'll all come out, anyway, no matter how the Squeezer decides to play it.—Hell, the Nazis rigged those murders to get their citizenry cranked up for the Polish invasion in Thirty-Nine, didn't they? Why not have you zapped if it would set things up the way they want it?"

"Land—believe me, you can dismiss an idea like that out of hand."

"Not me!" the boy cried all at once. "That's the trouble with you— you close your mind . . ." He broke off, but his eyes gleamed restlessly in the cool, even light of the room. More quietly he said: "There's nothing that could happen anywhere in the world—nothing!—that can be dismissed out of hand."

". . . But Land,"—and Blackburn could hear the note of dismay, of hesitant entreaty in his voice—"you have to trust something, somebody, there are things you *have* to take on faith."

"Sorry. It won't wash. You've lied to us too long."

There was a silence. Blackburn gazed out at the fine, innocent expanse of water, thinking of old Leggett at the Korean Repatriation Commission negotiations. "That's how the game is played, Paul. There are ground rules and they've been around a long time; and the Chinese are every bit as cognizant of them as we are." Fingering his wedge-shaped chin delicately with pale, tapering fingers. "It was the same thing with the Japanese in Washington in Twenty-Two. They're unregenerate little barbarians, they always were—but they've abided by the rules most of the time. Certain formalities are not exceeded, you know? It's all part of the framework within which everybody must work. They'll come around. You'll see." And they had come around, after a fashion. Now Leggett was dead of a stroke these three years, and his posthumous memoirs were being held up by the young revisionists as prime examples of diplomatic deceit and Cold War double-dealing . . .

You've lied to us too long.

It was strange: he, Paul Whitcombe Blackburn, had "come to power," as the phrase went, had found himself toiling with some success—and much failure—to hold together a discordant world, to deal with things-as-they-were; even, it must be confessed, buoyed by the hope of leaving a few lesser memorials after he'd departed. It was power he wielded, undeniably —but it was not the magisterial moving of levers he had once imagined: it was a good deal more like riding out a gale in a small boat, driving along at the mercy of a thousand willful elements that forced their own designs on every action. It was strange, so really very strange, when you turned it around: he saw himself as a fairly intelligent, reasonably conscientious spokesman for his government, a cog in a fiendishly elaborate chain of command—cajoling, entreating, threatening, patching here and splicing there, bargaining for time, fearful of the overhasty establishment of a dangerous policy somebody else would have to live with; praying for the sea to grow smooth again . . . Yet to his son he was *they*—a member of a band of criminally irresponsible despots who were blithely brushing this earth off the table's edge of sanity. How nice it must be to see life with that stark, monolithic simplicity again! How comforting . . .

But to be unable to dismiss anything at all—any hypocrisy, manipulation, perfidy, any act of wickedness; to feel that nothing was beyond the bounds of human responsibility, human restraint—*nothing at all on earth:* to feel that, at nineteen—

"—wasting your breath," the Judge was saying now to Eleanor. His glasses, riding high on his head, caught the light like translucent medals.

"Don't inhibit him. Youth has to challenge authority. That's how it was meant to be."

Leland flung back his rich black hair, watching his grandfather with that quizzical, speculative expression. "That's a pretty far-out sentiment —especially for a joker whose initials are SDS."

The old man laughed secretively. "Just figured that out, did you? Also stands for Some Do Survive. Spite of everything."

Land grinned in spite of himself. "Yeah, it also stands for—you know, it also stands for—"

"I know, I know," the Judge wagged his head. "I've tracked that one down too, Land. Little game I used to play on the bench when testimony was unduly boring . . . You know, Land," he offered in a different tone, "I was a radical once."

"You were?"

"Yep. Marched in protest of the Sacco-Vanzetti conviction in front of Dedham Court House. Demonstrated for Tom Meaney."

"Tom Meaney? Who's that?"

"Mooney, you mean Tom Mooney, Father," his daughter said with a trace of impatience.

"Can't see me in a protest march, can you, Land?" the Judge pursued, oblivious. "I was there. Way it should be. Every kid worth his salt has to go through the stage."

Land stiffened. "Well, that's where you're wrong. It's not a stage with me."

"You'll find the way things are run isn't so bad after all. Particularly when you consider the alternatives."

"That was your way, Grampus."

"It's everybody's way. Except for a few hopeless misfits."

The boy's eyes glittered. "Only the number of hopeless misfits keeps growing—there's more of us all the time. What'll you do when we're the majority? Who'll be the hopeless misfits then?"

"Now you hold on, boy," the Judge said irritably, "You're young yet—"

"I'm old enough to know when everything around me has gone rotten!"

"You'll realize the system's got to keep going, that nothing's more important than continuity, a firm hand at the helm—"

"Oh no! You can use that shoddy argument to salve *your* conscience with! I'm not buying it . . ."

The old man got to his feet with sudden wrenching alacrity, spilling newspapers in disordered piles. Red angry welts had appeared at the sides of his neck and high in his cheeks. "You'll see," he muttered hoarsely, wagging his head. "You'll learn." He thumped crossly away through the house.

Eleanor said, "Was that absolutely necessary, Leland?"

"Look, *he* latched onto a seat on the fifty-yard line—I didn't ask him."

"You know how he is now, when he's upset."

Sitting there watching the feathered branches of the locusts swaying in the wind Blackburn thought again of the other Leland, the boy's uncle, long dead, with a sense of deep sadness. The same headlong iconoclasm, the scornful defiance—but Blackburn had been fascinated by it then. Why was that? Why were these qualities attractive in the friend, disquieting in the son?

"It's two different worlds," Land was saying now. "You *believe* in all that stuff—you don't see the fundamental dishonesty in it. All you're doing is sliding us into World War Three-A."

"Not if I can help it, I'm not," he answered sharply.

"But you can't, you can't—that's just it! You were brought up trusting in all that balance-of-power, secret-diplomacy bullshit and we can't! Not any more."

Blackburn hooked his fingers together, pressed until the knuckles cracked. It was too bad. They'd done many things together, he and Land: they'd been caught in a storm off Gay Head, they'd stood silent in the grim, gray pass at Thermopylae and roared with the crowd at the great Dominguín, they'd swum together in the Inland Sea near Kyoto with the Shinto shrines high above them like lordly bleached arbors to heaven . . . He'd lost touch. Had he restored the Department's self-respect at his boy's expense? They were so angry, these kids. So full of mistrust.

"Land," he said aloud, "half your trouble is you get yourself so worked up about everything you don't realize when somebody is on your side."

"Oh, no!" The boy shook his head violently. "That old bromide. No way . . ."

He grinned. "Because I've just turned thirty, you mean?"

"A million reasons." Leland stared at his parents mutely, biting his lower lip—all at once burst out: "I'm in love with her. Can't you grab hold of that? *Real* love. Not the kind of poor sick shadow thing you've got . . ."

Aware that his wife was still as stone, keeping his gaze consciously averted from hers, Blackburn thought: Why is youth so *cruel?* Do they have to utter *every* blasted notion that comes into their heads, no matter whom it hurts, or why? Yes, and were you any better at his age? any gentler? Didn't you lose your temper one gusty afternoon, stalk off in boundless rage—

Quietly he said: "You might one day find out that things are a touch more complicated than they seem to you right now."

"Oh, they're complicated, all right. Some things. And other things are good and simple. This happens to be one of those."

"I see."

From the shop behind the Fiji House there came the high, distant whine of a power tool. The Judge back at his bench, repairing something. Blackburn could see the narrowed eyes, the thin mouth compressed, intent. Silas Darcey Seaver, closing out an eventful life—a thwarted life. One would have to call it that. His father-in-law had changed mightily. With bitterness and deferred ambition had come a resort to mocking raillery, and the sudden, increasing lapses of memory. There were only flashes of the man he had been a quarter of a century ago, when he had already accomplished so much—the Turkish relief mission and the Court of International Justice and the Fore River Shipyard arbitration—and so much more still seemed open to him; when the long verandah beyond the French doors had been filled with houseguests and the rush of wit and argument. Spare, wiry, in his mid-fifties then (he had married late, he liked to inform delighted listeners, in order to rid himself of the romantic illusions that are certain to blight any union between man and woman), with a lofty shock of prematurely white hair and the bold, high-ridged Seaver nose—he was called the Benevolent Hawk by both friends and foes, a sobriquet he secretly loved—he would carry the half-dozen conversations with ease, dealing out commendation and rebuke with an impartial hand, to the chagrin or merriment of the participants.

In those days it had been his wit that struck one first—the pungent, epigrammatic bite of the Yankee mind at its best; and hard on that a sere, unswerving probity which would have no truck with the pliant venalities of a lax age. "Poor old Ninninger," he would say mournfully, "he made only one mistake—but it was irreparable: he forgot to expunge the tedium from his reports." Once when Professor Brooke ventured to chide him over his unpopularity with certain segments of the press over a recent decision, he snorted, "The law is not a popularity contest, Perry. I have no intention of changing opinions the way certain women on Caribbean cruises change costumes." His opinion on enemy aliens had been hailed as a landmark; he was almost certain to chair one of the war crimes tribunals when the Axis was brought to its knees. Flung back in the creaky old rattan armchair, the southerly ruffling his proud white crest, his frosty gray eyes twinkling, he'd seemed to young Paul Blackburn to embody everything the man of affairs, the well-born public servant should be. Everything his own father had not been . . .

But then things had somehow gone wrong. Everyone had predicted —and he had expected—that he would fill the next vacancy on the Supreme Court; yet that ultimate laurel had never crowned a distinguished career. He was a rock-ribbed Republican, tart, outspoken, and Truman had never liked him; he'd incurred Brownell's displeasure during the soporific Eisenhower years; the racy New Frontier had passed him over, and Nixon's people had found him too caustic and unbending. Brilliant, yes—but a crank, a troublemaker. The vacancies had been filled by blander spirits, tighter natures. Not fame but bitterness was the last infirmity of noble mind, Blackburn thought somberly. Alien itself, it yet embraced so many sympathetic passions—blighted hope, a choking sense of injustice, sick betrayal. The Judge, choleric, mordant, was held securely in its ivory jaws: every newspaper article, every television commentary ripped the old wound open again, heightened the angry glint in his goshawk's eye.

Down in the shop the machine whine stopped abruptly, was replaced by a quick hollow pounding: iron on wood. Well, they'd all changed. What was so remarkable about that? We shed old dreams, obsessions like a snake its hyaline scales—and like the snake we emerged no wiser, only —changed.

But, oh kind and merciful God, if only we could hold the leaping green sap of youth through all the bights and snarls of years—

"There *are* things," Eleanor was saying to Land with badly frayed patience, "believe me, there are certain things you can't possibly understand at your age. Mock them all you want—there are standards one must hold to."

"Standards."

"Yes. If you can't see that—"

"I'll tell you what I *can* see, I can see I'm being told exactly how to live my own life."

"If you don't know how to live it wisely."

Land laughed harshly, recoiling. "No, that's right, I *don't* know how to live it wisely—I just want to live it honestly! Isn't that heavy, though? Isn't that out of sight? Honesty—something there hasn't been one hell of a choking lot of around here, you know?" He swung back to his father, extended five quivering fingers. "In case you're in any doubt, I resent this—I resent the drift of this whole, lousy dialogue. I'm seeing Jillie when I want and as I want—"

"Land, if you'd only—"

"—and another thing. While we're covering all the bases. Maybe Lachlan Smith isn't in your jurisdiction, but by Jesus, he's in *ours*. You can tell the Squeezer he better cancel that Emerson Hall speech if he knows what's good for him. He's going to eat shit for busting Smitty, and you'd better believe it! Any number can play. And he's right at the top of the list!" He flung out of the room, his feet drove lightly on the stairs, three at a time, thud, thud, thud; and a door slammed.

"Leland!" Eleanor called sharply.

"Let him go, Nell," Blackburn murmured. "Can't you see it's no good hammering at him like that?"

She turned and faced him. Anger had marked her face and neck with small dark blotches. She reminded Blackburn of her mother, whom he'd known only as an invalid, and he thought, We're old, we're getting old—pushed the observation crossly out of reach.

"Of course," she said in a low, almost threatful tone. "It's easier for you this way. Do you know he's taken an incomplete for the term?"

"No . . ." he answered in dismay. He'd been familiar enough with the practice when he'd been teaching, but the thought of his own son's throwing away half a year's study shook him. It was serious, then.

"Well, he has. Indulge him. Let this ruthless street radical destroy him. Do you think she can't?" She made an abrupt, distressful gesture with one hand. "Why do you turn away from people so? withhold your concern—and leave others with the consequences? It's so *wrong, Paul!*"

"Nell, that's not true. I just don't think that interfering in his life like this—I'm not sure this is the way to handle it."

"You felt exactly the same way about Margaret, remember?"

He stared down at the lovely faded blues and reds of the great Bokhara carpet, tracing the dense, anguillous dance of birds and animals in the single great tree, thinking unhappily of his daughter, remembering the airport at Nice and her face white and wild, slick with rain. "They can do anything they want to me and so can you—I don't care! You *have* to care!—but I don't, not any more I don't . . ." Inconsolable, raging, one quick step away from doing herself irreparable harm. Harry had left her, she was sick, they were still crowding her because of that stupid pot raid, didn't they ever let up on you, ever? She wanted to go and live in New Zealand, a new life somewhere in New Zealand, what was wrong with that? —with starting over, hadn't he ever felt that way? Standing there in the raw, salt mistral holding her tightly, he hadn't known what to say beyond banal reassurances. He'd failed her somehow, let her down, he could see it in her eyes, feel it in her wildly trembling body: but how? what had he done wrong?

"Peg was always a stormy petrel," he said quietly.

"People aren't always *anything*. They *become* something because of the way they were brought up, the values instilled in them. When milk goes sour there's a reason." Eleanor arched her back again, craned her neck in that proud, implacable way he suddenly realized he disliked intensely—he'd never realized before how much he disliked it. "You're too permissive, Paul. You always were, you know that. You indulged her as a child and later, too—it was easier that way. You had your work, your career and all . . ." Her eyes fell, but not before he'd caught the sudden, sharp flicker of resentment at his high success: the anger warring with the pride. Your career. She was ambitious for him, she'd always been—but it wasn't unalloyed, there was this begrudging quality too, the edge that denied; and it angered him. They'd worked too hard, made too many sacrifices for that.

"Yes," he said, "I had my work. Like anyone else."

"It was the same thing with the marriage," she went on, "you were for that, too. And the result was foregone."

He bit his lip. "I refused to forbid her marrying Harry, if that's what you're driving at."

"It was more than that, much more. Don't you see? It was a question of not seeing where certain involvements *lead*."

He started to answer and stopped himself, cursing that penchant in Nell for relentless pursuit of her point which led so frequently to quarrels. If there was anything he didn't want today it was a row. He wanted to bask in the sense of something accomplished in the face of distrust; rest on his oars and drift in a backwater. My God, if he could only sleep and swim and lie around for three full days . . .

"This Smitty," he muttered. "How did Land get to know him so well?"

"I've no idea."

Down in the shop the whine of the drill began again, insistent and hard. What a pit of contrary emotions this family was! Like all families probably, if the truth were known (which of course it never was). Yet how often he'd felt like a wary, dutiful servitor, trying to go calmly about his duties in the harsh progression of judgment and withdrawal: the New England conscience at work and play . . . He got to his feet and went over to the window, conscious all at once of a huge and nameless disappointment. That sense of quiet, contained triumph, of dropping anchor with a broom at the mast, had vanished. Had his illustrious predecessors returned from averting the threat of war in Venezuela, in the Aroostook, in Samoa to face a rupture of domestic relations? And how had impetuous Olney, blithe John Hay, masterful Jefferson, crusty old Cord Hull handled those crises? How well had his idol, imperturbable Daniel Webster, come up to the mark back home?

The breeze had dropped again. Cats' paws ran great burred fingers beyond Fantic Point. Across the Sound, Naushon looked remote, immeasurable. Maybe she was right—maybe Land would up and marry the woman and take off for Valparaiso—he was perfectly capable of it. This political activity—how deep did it go? What madcap plan was in the fire for Reiny? *Could* it be dangerous for the Administration? With a smile he thought of Joe Carter during the Cambodian flap two years ago: "Everything's tied in with everything else, isn't it? You can't ever isolate anything and settle *that* . . ." But hell's bells, he wasn't Vosz's keeper: Reiny had asked for this, it was his hunt. If Reiny couldn't handle the hooting and hollering of a—

"You did the same thing with Lee."

He whirled around, distraught and very angry. "—I thought we had an understanding about that subject!"

"I can't help it. It's true. You *are* responsible, you know."

"It's not fair to bring that up—it's cruel and unfair . . . ." He broke off, saw to his surprise that her eyes had filled. She was shaking her head slowly from side to side as if more distressed at this unseemly revelation of weakness than his catastrophic permissiveness.

"Paul, I've never asked a thing like this of you. Now I am." She was chewing at her lip to keep it from trembling. "Please go up there and see her. Because of—my brother, please do this for our son."

"Nell—" he began.

"Please. This once, Paul."

She looked gaunt and unlovely and defeated—it was an expression he'd rarely seen on her face. He wanted to go over to her and put his arms around her; but still smarting from her accusation and all it evoked he hung there, his fingers hooked in his trouser pockets. Nothing's ever buried, he thought heavily; we never really put anything behind us.

". . . It's so hard," she said after a moment. "I can't bear to have things be all for nothing. A waste, and for nothing!"

"It's not," he murmured. "It's not as bad as you think."

"No—this is worse. I just feel it's going to end badly—I can *feel* it. It frightens me . . ." Her face, stamped now with bewilderment and dread, reminded him of an evening in Khotiane, when Land had come in to them, complaining of pains in his head and neck, and they'd feared it was polio. Gazing at this woman who was his wife, the hypnotic pale blue eyes, the thick, carefully tended hair, now more white than fair, he caught a fleeting evocation of past days together like some lost thread of music he hadn't heard in years, haunting and sad. Well: they'd had their troubles, God knew. Their marriage hadn't been half what it could have been, should have been—but did it really matter now whose fault it was? The years had made it irrelevant. What mattered was that she had stood by him firmly; wasn't that true? There had been the days of privation at those early posts, and then the narrow gray world of the university, and now the tumultuous dislocations and social burdens of the Department—and she had met all of it, resolute and resourceful; pleasing superiors, persuading associates, even bringing him consolation and counsel in the late hours. Anyone would have to say it was so. She had never made difficult demands, like so many women. He owed her a great deal, a good great deal.

And he had never been able to fill the hollows in that face . . .

"Will you go?" She was watching him with an almost timorous eagerness that made him think of a moment around a campfire, long ago. "For me, Paul? This once—for me? Just go and see the woman, have a talk with her?"

Slowly he nodded, held in the old, worn affection; yet knowing too, watching the shadow of that distant, terrible afternoon in her gaze, the shadow that lay between them like a bar of rusted iron, that the most sequestered part of him could never forgive her.

"Yes, of course, dear," he said. "I'll go see her."

THREE

THE HIGHWAY rolled out ahead of him, long and beige and even, flanked by shoulders of dune or dense scrub pine. Off to the southwest the sky was murky with thunderclouds, but Blackburn was running away from them, running north. Refreshed by the hard half-mile swim out to the Mace Rock buoy and back, pleasantly relaxed, he hummed a tune he couldn't place and watched the speedometer needle sway to 60, to 65, and hold there. It was fun driving up to Cambridge, alone in a car for the first time in months, blessing that order of the President's that had done away with security guards for cabinet officers except for special functions or overseas missions; roaring along in Eleanor's old Mercedes, away from the OAS meeting and Villarta and the report to the President: playing truant to it all.

The swim had decided him. In spite of the assurance Eleanor had wrung from him he still hadn't been at all certain he would go and see the girl. It meant several hours at a time when he was extremely tired, and burdened with a terrific backlog of work; and there was the matter of invading Land's world. But gliding along in the easy, effortless four-beat crawl that at one stage of his life had been as natural to him as walking, his hands reaching out and down in a rhythmic litany of greeting and gathering, the sea racing green froth past his eye, he found himself thinking persistently of Land, the furious plea gathered in the boy's intense black gaze. "That's the trouble with you—you close off everything . . ."

Was that true? In point of fact he'd prided himself—though with caution—on the fact that he understood this generation better than most. Their new silence, their resignation were more dangerous than the violence they had replaced. He'd hoped the worst headlands had been passed with the ending of the Vietnam agony and the President's racial and urban reforms; but he'd been wrong. The old values were still suspect. They must all go—the stately protocol, the ponderous machinery of feeler and referral by which nation-states, like strange dogs, got on with one another.

And yet—how could the young deny it?—life ran on symbols. Eleanor was too censorious, with her talk of decency and propriety—and yet what she said was true enough; were we to blithely cast away these invisible bonds that held us on course, defined our powers and limitations, kept freedom from spilling into license, impatience into violence?

". . . Standards." But it was his mother's voice he heard, not his wife's: inculcative and low (she had never raised it, even in the old, bitter arguments with his father; it had been Rick Blackburn who had lost his temper, stormed and shouted), conveying in its very absence of emotion a certainty beyond question. "They are the pillars on which society rests, Paul. This is why you'll see the English foreign service officer sit down to dinner with a white tablecloth and all the proper accouterments, even though he's stationed deep in some jungle a thousand miles from civilization. To relax these standards is to forfeit the hard-won heritage of the entire human experience. Do you see, dear? It's one of those things that is true, no matter how trite it may sound."

Her face had been lined even then, thirty years ago—a delicate tracery that seemed to make her somehow wiser, more poised and compassionate than other mothers. Her eyes, though, were cool and blue and a bit forbidding; it always made him a trifle nervous when that unblinking, calmly assertive gaze would come to rest on him, and that edge of unquestioned prescription would darken perceptibly its mild force. She had always been so *sure*. Again like Nell . . . Now she lived alone on Pinckney Street, an apartment in one of the favored houses overlooking Louisburg Square, ordered her groceries from Brigham and read the *Times* every noon with a steady zeal, cutting out any clippings that bore reference to her son's activities in Vienna or Istanbul. It was a fitting climax to her life. She had been born a Whitcombe; her father, though reared in Boston, had ended his days as minister of a church in one of the sleepy, unpretentious little towns that ring Framingham.

"You are of good stock, Paul," she would say (this was in the house behind Nob Hill, a gloomy, decrepit old ark he knew even then she hated), and her voice held a tremor of bitterness—as though that good stock would be hard put to offset other, less salutary strains. "Your grandfather was asked to preach at Trinity, and *his* father was a distinguished surgeon at Peter Bent Brigham; and your *great*-great-grandfather was for a time United States minister to Lisbon. You are of *very good* family. Never forget that."

Richard Vincent Blackburn had been everything his wife was not: handsome, mercurial and expansive. San Francisco was his native city and he loved it with a genuine, boyish passion—the rumble and thump of the Embarcadero, the brash white pride of the Civic Center, the flat sunlight and the cool surge of summer fog. His boast was that he had never owned a raincoat—though he'd often got wet. "Where else could you find a city this beautiful?" he would demand of any sympathetic listener. "It's the Paradise of the Western World!" And his mobile Irish mouth would curve into a mischievous grin, his eyes sparkling. As salesman for a succession of local firms—coffee, sports cars, spices, he never held one job for very long—he knew everyone, went everywhere, ran into friends in a rush of high exuberance. Rollicking Rick, his friends called him (to his wife's disgust), a great guy, a real live wire, and Paul had been delighted one afternoon after a ball game at Candlestick Park when a pretty blond woman had rushed up to his father and embraced him excitedly. "Laura, baby!" his father had cried; he'd lifted the lady off her feet and winked at Paul. "Right out of the blue . . ." Afterward they had gone to a bar with painted mirrors and deep red plush walls and his father and the blond lady had ordered drinks and talked about a driving trip up to Tahoe. And much later, going home, his father had said, "Let's not tell Mother about meeting Laura, okay?" and punched him gently on the shoulder, and that had seemed all right, too: part of the marvelous, lofty, free-moving sphere of men.

Rick Blackburn could do anything, it seemed—it was his contention that a man, a real, honest-to-God, full-blooded man should be able to master any number of skills: ride a motorcycle, repair a car, sail a boat, shoot a rifle—and at the same time dress impeccably, keep abreast of world events, and be gallant with the ladies. He taught Paul to do most of these things, and took him places. His engaging smile, his quick, full laughter rang through a world of action and conviviality—elaborate fishing trips and theater parties, and now and then men's clubs where the rooms were burdened with massive dark woodwork and the rattle and click of dominoes and the clean, harsh smell of liquor—an odor the boy came after a while to associate with threatful surprise, misgivings, downright fear: times when his father would be helped from cabs by old friends, or when he would lie sick in bed upstairs with the house consigned to silence—or worse, when he would be gone for weeks on end, no one seemed to know where, and Adelaide Blackburn's face would turn unapproachable and stern.

. . . There were two worlds, it seemed: the world of what might be called *true events*—what was happening to you, what you actually thought and felt in the privacy of your mind; and the other world—the one that watched you from outside, measured you, decided whether you would do and why. This was the world that coolly observed you at school and church; it was always waiting right outside the front door, and its judgment was final, immutable, without appeal. Yet *that* wasn't quite true, either, because this second world also divided in two. "The world runs on appearances," he had been told by his father, who was a flamboyant dresser and tipped waiters and doormen far too much, according to his mother. "Your success in this world will stand or fall on how many friends you can call yours when the chips are down. Remember that, son." Charm, ebullience, generosity and manly competence marked you as a regular guy, a good egg.

Adelaide Blackburn despised these virtues (if virtues they were; she more than implied they were nothing of the kind) with righteous candor. There were of course people who needed and derived a certain solace—a sense of vanity was what it was, really—from such an attitude. But the world, the *real* world, the world that counted ultimately, honored frugality, constancy, service. *These* made up the mainspring of social order, and they were far more important than the outward trappings of ostentation and hail-fellow-well-met. These led nowhere. A proper appearance, certainly— good breeding, exemplary manners; but that did not embrace the easy familiarity of the street.

"Your father came from a different tradition, Paul. A different tradition entirely."

—But I'm half my *father!* he wanted to say. Isn't that so? Half from your tradition and half from his . . . But he said nothing. There was that quality in his mother's voice that did not encourage dissent.

How entirely different was borne in on him gradually. Rick Blackburn was Irish and, though not overly demonstrative about his religion, a Roman Catholic. He had acquiesced early in their marriage to Adelaide's insistence that any children be reared in her faith, but there was a part of him that resented the arrangement. He was proud and hot-tempered, especially when he'd been drinking, which was increasingly often; and there were times when, goaded by Adelaide's biting disparagement of his lack of discipline or his origins, he would lash out at her violently. Then the dark old house would quake with sudden storms and stony silences, and the boy would tread warily, his head cocked for the prevailing wind . . .

And then, without warning, came the afternoon that even after thirty-five years could still make his belly tighten and his heart beat thickly, remembering. He'd heard their voices from his room upstairs; he hadn't known his father was home and he'd leaped up and hurried along the hall to the stairs, full of joyful anticipation—then stopped short. It was a quarrel, unmistakably, and he hung there, caught between fear of discovery and the need to overhear.

"—monstrous," his mother was saying, her voice unsteady with rage and mortification. "Do you imagine I was ignorant of it? Of course I know you pride yourself on your marvelous savoir faire."

"Addy, I tell you you're making entirely too much out of a simple—"

"Don't lie to me!—and your friends who cover for anything you do."

"It was a lark, for God's sake, a *lark!* She's not—"

"Couldn't you have had the restraint, the simple basic *decency* to hold yourself aloof from such filth? For the boy's sake, if not for mine?—I know your marriage vows mean nothing to you and never have . . ."

"Addy, that's not fair! I know I'm—"

"But no, that was too much to ask, wasn't it?" His mother's voice had fallen into that low, threatful tone that made the flesh move beneath his scalp. "Not enough that you've saddled me with this dreary, moth-eaten hulk of a place, without proper help or funds to run it—no, you never gave that a thought, did you? Because you're selfish—"

"That's not—"

"—no, you had to humiliate me—you're a moral vagrant after all, without background or—"

"Addy, I'm warning you!—"

"—but of course it gave you pleasure, didn't it?—the rutting of a vulgar Irish hooligan without a grain of—"

He heard it then—a sharp, flat slap and a gasp. Only in the silence that followed did he take in the significance of those sounds. Rooted to the stairs, his heart quaking, he heard his father's voice, very different now; low and suppliant, muffled.

"Addy. Forgive me. Please forgive me . . ."

"No." Another silence and a susurrus of movement, swift and desperate. "Let me—go!"

"Addy, please—"

"I can never forgive you for that."

"Addy . . ."

"I would appreciate it if you would leave. Right now. The last, decent thing you can do is leave. Do you understand that? *Can* you?"

"Jesus God, Addy . . ."

"There is no need for profanity. I merely said—"

"—You're impossible, do you know that? Impossible!"

"If you would be so good as to leave this house—"

"All right. By God, yes. I'll leave. I'll leave. If that's the way you want it, by Jesus that's the way it'll be!—"

And his father burst into the hall, his handsome face flushed, his mouth working; the silver streak was bright against the fine black sweep of his hair. The boy shrank behind the railing but Rick Blackburn never saw him; without a glance he hurried toward the light. The front door crashed shut. Then there was silence, broken only by his mother's rosewood clock in the alcove next to the coat closet, and the clank of a tire iron from the garage across the street. Sunlight lay long and pale on the worn blue rug, mottled with flecks of red and orange from the panes of colored glass above the door.

He ran down the stairs then, almost falling, his heart crushing his lungs, and raced into the living room, to find his mother standing by the fireplace, her eyes closed, still as death. There was a long red oval mark on her cheek.

"Mother . . ."

He stopped again, in consternation. What he'd expected—embraces, tears, a sudden rush of complicity and comfort in the face of this awful breaking of his world—did not take place. Adelaide Blackburn turned and gazed at him stonily for a long moment, as though he were an intruder, some strange little boy who had blundered into her home. As if he were not Paul Blackburn at all. He had never known such fear.

"Mother—"

Crying he ran against her, thrust his face against her belly, clutching at the rough wool of her skirt, half-strangling in his great need.

"I'm sorry, Paul." Her voice was calm but her body was trembling around him. "Oh, so sorry—you had to hear that."

"Mother . . . Where is Dad going?"

"I don't know." She reached out and held him, then—a harsh, quick pressure. "Paul: you must be good. Now. Do what Mother says."

"But isn't—" He had to say it; obscurely he knew he shouldn't, but in his anguish he had to. "Won't he be coming back? Ever?"

"No. He won't." And she drew back and looked down into his eyes, holding him with that mild, incontrovertible gaze. "You must help Mother now. In every way you can. You must promise."

He did. The years—very different years—crept by. His mother divided the old house into what she called "apartments"—they were little better than rooms with kitchens behind folding doors—and later went to work as a filing clerk in a law office downtown. There were no more ball games at Candlestick Park, no more camping expeditions up to Tuolumne Meadows or spur-of-the-moment driving trips down to Monterey. He never saw his father again. He uncrated vegetables for the A & P afternoons; later he lied about his age—he was barely fourteen—and got a job ushering at the movie palace down on Despedida Street. He flung himself into his homework in every free moment he had. Education was the way out of this tunnel—the only way out: his mother hadn't needed to impress the fact on him. He stood first in his class continually; and for his final two years of high school, with what he knew were virtually the last of her savings, Adelaide Blackburn sent him east to one of the two prestigious preparatory schools founded by her father's lifelong idol, Wendell Phillips.

Exeter had been a shock of another kind. His mother's enthusiastic assurances had done nothing to prepare him for this harsh world of caste, the patterns of disdain and ostracism that bound this bleak corner of New Hampshire where winter came so early and spring so late. It was the two worlds all over again—but cruelly simplified: the world of the favored, the world of the outcasts. There were the boys he liked instinctively—the imaginative, the rebels; and then there were the boys who were important, the ones "of good family" his mother had intimated he should cultivate. It was disconcerting. For instance, there were Jimmy Donoghue and Frank Hrdlicka, who were from Worcester and Providence respectively and who went around together, and Walt Fein, who was from New York City and went around all by himself; there were no Negro boys at all. The rest fell into subtly graded phases of precedence, dominated by Bullock and Lothram and Beard, the reigning aristocracy. They decided who was acceptable and who was not.

For the first months he kept his own counsel; he got unobtrusively good grades, played on the club teams; and watched. This was the world that was important, his mother had admonished him on his departure; these were the boys who in later years were destined to lead, to run the country when their turn came. They were being "groomed for leadership" —he was always to remember her phrase. "This is your chance, Paul. Your only chance to make your way. Do you know what I'm saying?" His hand callused from A & P fruit crates, his lungs filled with the stale, greasy air of the theater lobby, he knew beyond any doubt. He must succeed here: there would be no second chance.

What complicated it all was the war. The war was everywhere around them. It dominated these years, raging its minatory way across Europe and Asia and the Pacific, thundering at them from radios and the headlines of the Boston papers, inflaming their hopes, their fears, and made painfully proximate by the masters, who drove them through calisthenics and obstacle courses behind the stadium through the long chill afternoons. They understood. They would go, they would all of them go if the war lasted long enough; and it seemed certain it would last forever. They were being toughened for sacrifice and with a wry indifference they accepted it: they were ready.

Except for Leland Seaver. He went his own way. Slender, sardonic, mercurial, Lee would mutter that they could butcher every last poor son of a bitch in the Western Hemisphere but he was not going. He was going to beat the physical. "You know that trick of shoving sugar under your fingernails and then peeing on them when you give them a specimen? Too much albumen in your urine. Why not?" And if that didn't work there were other ways. The whole country could turn itself into one sweet orgy of tribal messianism if it chose—half graveyard, half lunatic asylum; he was going to sit it out.

"The only sensible creatures on this stupid globe are birds—do you realize that, Blackburn? You think I'm kidding, don't you? You watch them sometimes. When they get disgusted with a certain area they flap their wings and leave it behind." With that stubborn intractability for which his seafaring forebears were famed, he absolutely refused to buy a third of a war bond each month; he would neither collect metal pots nor give blood. He mocked the obstacle-course ardor of his classmates, chose pacifist themes for his English papers, and at odd moments would harangue his listeners with a mixture of derisive sarcasm and calm reason that fascinated Blackburn. Couldn't they see the score? that it was the same old, sick game of national expansion, power politics run riot? "What lawful business do we have in New Guinea—or the Philippines, for that matter? Really—*analyze* it. Or Persia, or Oran. Well, don't just sit there breathing through your mouth—read Bertrand Russell, read Shaw, read Stuart Chase, for Christ sake. Can't you see you're just a bunch of slot-machine tokens being played to someone's grand global scheme?—my God, before you've even had the chance to go to bed with a girl! What chumps . . ."

"You know, you're getting to sound pretty obnoxious, Seaver," Bullock told him one afternoon in the locker room. Bullock was oversize and hard, with a round flat face and humorless little brown eyes; his older brother was a lieutenant with Patton's Third Army. "I don't know how aware of it you are, but that's treason you're talking."

"Treason! Oh, my weary anus . . . what do you know about treason, Bullock?"

"I know it when I hear it."

"Let me clue you in, chum. Treason happens to be an overt act to overthrow the government to which a subject owes allegiance." Kicking his locker door shut with one knee he pulled a sweat-caked jersey over his head. "That's what treason is, chum."

Bullock faced him, scowling. "And that's just what you're doing— making a mockery of the war effort."

"Because I refuse to be turned into a gun-toting robot like all the rest of you chowderheads?"

"As far as I'm concerned you can shut up, Seaver," Bullock said.

"Oh, no!" Leland laughed once. "I'll talk as long and as loud as I feel like."

"Is that right."

"You don't have to listen to me—more's the pity—but I'll be damned if I'm going to shut up because you've got the notion it's unpatriotic or something stupid like that."

"Well, we'll just have to shut you up, then."

Lothram and Beard had come up behind him during the last exchange. It was quiet now between the lockers.

"Why shouldn't he say what he thinks?" Blackburn asked suddenly.

"You keep out of this, Frisco," Bullock told him. "This hasn't got anything to do with you."

But it did. He couldn't say why exactly, but it did. It was impolitic, it ran full in the face of his mother's urgent injunctions—yet there was no doubt in his mind: there was something extremely important about this moment. Naked and beefy in his shorts Bullock was glaring at them; the faces behind him were stiff with hostility. They were so full of righteous candor, those faces—so healthy in their certainties! Their bodies were sturdy with all the best food and medical care and organized athletics this world could offer. Prizing open all those crates afternoons had given him a certain strength, too—but it was not the same kind; not remotely. And there was more to it than that: he knew, with a long-pent surge of anger. *Frisco.* He was the raw Californian, the outsider: he would always be. They would always find him wanting; just as they had this slender, sardonic boy who, New England Seaver or not, was being branded an outcast as well. Standing astride the wooden bench, his gorge rising, he cast his lot and set himself.

"Go ahead," Leland was saying hotly, "try it, then—see if it makes you feel brave and clean and reverent! Look at you—all the lovely instincts of the wolf pack in heat—"

The next minutes were fierce. Lee was borne back against the lockers in a tumultuous crash of sweaty bodies. Blackburn had already moved to intercept the rush. He found himself fighting with a fury he didn't know he possessed. He caught Bullock once, full in the face, and heard him howl with pain—then was half-swamped in a welter of feet and hands and overturned benches. His head slammed against metal; he felt a sudden sharp pain at the base of his neck and his left arm went numb and tingling. But his father, a good amateur boxer, had taught him well; he regained his feet, giving and taking punishment, and had actually reached Leland, pinned now against the floor and groaning with rage, when authority in the person of Mr. McAndrew, a physics instructor and club football coach, intervened. In the sullen, panting silence that followed, the terse ritual of inquiry and denial, Blackburn made up his mind.

"Sir, it was Bullock's doing. He said Seaver had no right to say anything against the war effort. He told Seaver they would silence him by force."

The faces around him were savage. He had broken the cardinal commandment of Exeter, of all prep schools everywhere in the Anglophiliac world, probably: he was snitching to authority. Even Mr. McAndrew's lean Scotch-Canadian face was dour with disapproval. An outcast and a snitcher. But the others had broken the code, too—in silencing another boy, in ganging up on him: that was a graver sin in the scale, wasn't it? —if scales were needed. He thought again of his mother, the threat to his future. But it felt right, what he had done; he would stand or fall on it. Next day there was a hearing in the headmaster's chambers, an inquisition heavy with recitations and silences. But Blackburn stuck to his story. At the end of it Bullock was reprimanded (though not placed on probation: Exeter was proud of its sacrifices in the war) and the affair forgotten, or at least placed in abeyance.

For Blackburn the two souvenirs of the incident were a scar at the back of his head which he was pleased to find required five stitches, and the friendship of Leland Seaver, who invited him home for Thanksgiving, then for spring vacation, and again for the short June recess between wartime semesters. And at sixteen, eager and full of wonder, Paul Blackburn had fallen passionately and irrevocably in love: not with a girl or an idea, but with a way of life. Life as the Seavers lived it on Martha's Vineyard. He loved the secluded coves edged with long scarves of blue water shimmering; the old Water Street houses over in Edgartown with their chaste classic porticoes and fan windows; the rush of surf at South Beach—

more intimate, more ardent than the remote Pacific swells. But most of all he loved the Paling. All the hunger of his childhood years was filled at last in the ancient clapboard house with its low, open-beam ceilings, its mellow hutches and deal tables and scarred sea chests smelling of lemon-verbena wax; the diamond of whale ivory embedded in the cap of the newel post in the front hall; the still, sun-drenched garden with its croquet court and the old bronze sundial with the inscription *Dignum laude virum Musa vetat mori; Coelo Musa beat,* struck in letters so bold you knew it was true—the muse *would* enthrone the praiseworthy man in the heavens . . .

Afternoons there would be swimming parties, and after that impromptu regattas on the Sound, the boats beating wildly along, close-hauled, everyone leaning far out over the windward gunnels, shouting threats and hilarious nonsense; and still later there might be clambakes or corn roasts on the beach below the bluff while the sun sank away to the west, a gibbous red ball, and the sky deepened in strokes of rose and magenta; above the fire's low embers the singers' eyes would flash like pairs of precious stones.

But the mornings captivated him most of all—the leisured breakfasts on the long verandah shadowed with wisteria and wild rose, where venerable professors of international law held forth to young clerks, theoretical physicists argued with historians, literary critics took issue with musicians over the click of coffee cups and the gentle wash of the Sound beyond the lawns. A world invested with so much zest, so much self-assurance! There was nothing like it anywhere, he knew. Camilla Seaver, spritely and frail, with pretty, down-drooping eyelids, would pour him coffee from a swan-necked silver pot, and listening to the talk and laughter Blackburn would press the worn linen napkin to his lips, stir his cup with a coin silver spoon engraved with its coiled, exfoliate *S* and realize with an almost guilty shock of delight that there was nowhere on earth he would rather be than here on the porch of this magnificent Vineyard house; on the shore of another, less barbarous ocean . . .

Lee on the other hand hated the place. He referred to it as the Mossyleum, avoided the social breakfasts and dinner parties whenever possible, and spent all the time he could roaming the moors and marshlands behind the compound. Birds were his passion—nothing else could stir him so deeply. He knew them all; the different species, where they nested, where they fed; he even had names for certain favorites. He led Blackburn on some elaborate stalking sessions through dense thickets of blackberry and swamp alder in pursuit of warblers and vireos, and a few days later took him to what he called "the foretop," a low blind on a little mound constructed between two scrub pines and made of intricately woven twigs and rush, with a slit in its face affording a view of the great dead oak at the head of Tashawena Inlet.

"You built this?" Blackburn asked in surprise, passing his hand over the elaborate wattling.

"Yes. Keep your voice down, now. Do you want to wreck everything?" Lee was already peering through his telescope, a handsome antique piece with nautical scenes and symbols inscribed on its brass tubing, and inlaid mother-of-pearl at its base. It had been in the family for generations. They were lying on their bellies in the warm marsh grass; below them the Inlet was a fine deep blue, brushed with cat's-paws.

"—Yep," the Vineyard boy's voice was quick with suppressed excitement, "here she is, here she is . . ."

There was a high, piercing whistle and looking up Blackburn saw the big bird come soaring in, crested, slate-white, majestic, a thin black mask through its eye, the tinker mackerel an iridescent sickle in its talons; its great wings fanned then, braking hard, it sank toward the ragged, lopsided nest in one of the upper crotches of the oak—all at once lifted away, to settle on a nearby branch; and again there came the high, shrill call.

"Here. Look now. Watch the nest." Lee was pushing the glass into his hands. "No—rest it on my shoulder. Like this." And now Blackburn saw over the jackstraw rim of twigs a bony head, a gaping falcate beak; then another. The parent called once more, hopped to a slightly nearer branch. The young hawk struggled on to the edge of the nest, off-balance, its wings trailing and flapping awkwardly, its gold eyes hard with hunger. The adult called still again, bent over and tore at the mackerel's guts. The young bird lurched forward—backpedalled in panic, wobbled wildly—all at once spilled forward into air in a frantic parody of flight, came up against a lower bough and clung there, peeping thinly; shook itself, riveted its gaze on the mackerel and again leaped, beating the air fiercely now—reached the upper perch and plunged its beak into the slick silver body of the fish; raised its bristling head and looked out over the Inlet with a new and different gaze.

"Caught it!" Lee was whispering, "We caught the day!—the exact day!" His thin, taut features were suffused with pure joy. "There's the real thing, Paul—right there . . . He'll fly now," he murmured, and Blackburn saw he was writing swiftly and neatly in a small loose-leaf notebook. "They both will, now. *Pandion haliaetus*. The noblest of all the hawks. He has no enemies—do you know that? No enemies. Except two-legged sons of bitches with guns. Did you ever see anything so tremendous, so poetic? No kidding." Smiling happily he pointed to the great tree. "That, right there, is more important than anything else happening in the world today."

"Well, I don't know about that . . ."

"Well *I* do. Who's going to prove to me that Napoleon is any more necessary than John James Audubon? Now come on, tell me straight: did you ever see anything as marvelous as that with your own eyes? Did you?"

"No," Blackburn said, stirred by the memory of those great wings, "I don't think I ever did."

"You bet you didn't.—You're the only person I've ever brought here." Lee's eyes held a quick, shy appeal Blackburn had never seen before. "Except for Nell. I knew you wouldn't—you know, wreck it all. Give it away . . . You won't, will you, Paul? tell anybody? I mean it."

Lying on the thick mat of hog vine with the odor of salt and barberry and marsh grass dense around him, Blackburn felt a slow, warm flooding of his heart. A friend, the friend he'd never had, the brother he'd longed for through those lonely years in San Francisco. "I won't tell another living soul," he murmured. "I promise."

"Thanks, Paul. I knew you wouldn't." He pulled a chocolate bar out of his shirt pocket, broke it in two and gave half to Blackburn; passed his thin fingers lovingly over the barkentines and great fish etched on the spyglass barrel. "I've watched them for nine years—it took me all one summer to build this blind." He pointed again at the huge, misshapen nest. "There's a day coming—I'm not kidding—when that scruffy little bird up there is going to be more important to the fate of the world than every last Buck Rogers rocket they decide to send to Mars . . ."

But then there were more somber moments, darker moods. What came as a complete shock to Blackburn was the realization that Lee hated his father. He could not hide his dismay. He dropped the halyard—they were making some alterations on a star-class boat the Judge had given Lee—and stared at his friend. "But—he's a great man . . ."

"Oh come off it, Paul. I know it's nice to be a courteous houseguest and all that rubbish. But you don't have to perjure your indomitable soul."

"I mean it—he *is*. He's everything a father could be."

"More! Way more . . ." Lee's face broke into the wry, sardonic grin. "And just in case you might forget it, he's got the most wonderful ways of reminding you!"

"That's too harsh, Lee."

"He's not a *father*—he's an institution."

"Look—" Blackburn gripped his hands together, frowning "—you take too much for granted. You don't realize all you have . . ."

"Oh yes! I realize it—don't think for one blue second I don't!" He gave the Californian a swift, scornful glance. "Look at this three-ring circus: it ought to be a sanctuary, an eyrie—and he's turned it into a perpetual lawn pary."

"The Paling? Why, it's magnificent—he's done wonders with it."

"Don't be ridiculous. He's made it a showcase for the grand panjandrums. The whole thing makes me want to barf. Come on, let's go for a swim."

Only away from the compound—"Beyond the Pale," as he would say to Blackburn with a wry grin—his shirt hanging open, his hair ruffled by the wind, in pursuit of his elusive sea birds, was he at peace. Simply living at the Paling seemed to exacerbate his destructive rebelliousness. He referred to his father as the O. T.—which he told Blackburn stood for Old Tyrant, Odious Toad, Ominous Terror or anything else that might fit— and in his presence would often turn sullen and resentful. He proved to be a reckless sailor, and an absolute menace behind the wheel of a car. When one of his defiant spells was upon him he would drive his younger sister Eleanor to tears, accusing her of disgusting subservience to the Judge, or drink anything alcoholic he could get his hands on. One evening after the Judge had admonished him mildly over minor injury to one of the dinghies, the boys had driven over to Edgartown to the movies. Slumped down in the back row Lee decided to drink most of a quart bottle of rum (it was all he'd been able to buy, what with rationing), tried to pick up a waitress going home from the Capstan restaurant, lost his wallet and the keys to the car, loudly declared his intention of stealing the badge of Hobie Colbron, the chief of police, and passed out in the municipal parking lot behind the Yacht Club.

Blackburn found a piece of wire and bypassed the ignition and starter circuits by connecting it from the hot battery post to the ignition coil, shorted the connector between the terminals with a screwdriver and started the engine—a trick his father, who was often losing his own keys, had taught him. He rolled Lee into the back seat (where he promptly became copiously sick), drove him home and put him to bed, then went out to the garage and cleaned up the car as well as he could.

The next morning the Judge called him into the study and asked him who had been sick in the Packard. Blackburn hesitated less than a second.

"I was, sir. I had a couple of Planter's Punches on top of a lobster roll. And I guess it didn't agree with me."

Silas Seaver looked at him very intently. "I wouldn't have believed it of you, Paul."

"I'm extremely sorry, sir. I'll go right out and work on it again."

"Don't worry about that—Henry can take care of it. I'm only surprised, that's all."

"I'm sorry, sir," Paul repeated lamely. It was a sad moment—he suddenly realized with a pang how much the Judge's approval meant to him. But loyalty was more important, wasn't it? He owed Lee so much, so very much. He would be loyal, no matter what. Yet the sense of impending loss made him say it: "I wouldn't have had it happen for the world, sir . . ."

"No—I don't imagine you would." The Judge had given him his keenest glance and walked away moodily. He never alluded to the episode again. Yet Paul often had the sense the Judge was studying him, assaying him against some background, some purpose. It excited him even while he worried about it.

"You seem to have a head on your shoulders, Paul," he'd said one evening when there had been a family discussion of the projected United Nations Security Council. "You may think that's the natural condition of the human species. Believe me, nothing could be farther from the truth."

"Of course not," Lee had interposed with false innocence, "there's always the two-faced magistrates—who look both ways: ahead to righteousness and backward to politics."

"All right, Leland," his mother said gently. "That's uncalled for."

"*Nothing* is called for. Everything in the universe is volunteered."

The Judge was gazing at his son with some asperity. "Some people would be well advised to devote time to their studies instead of observing the deglutitory habits of the white-crowned night heron."

"The only proper study for mankind is man, eh?"

"There *are* more profitable fields than bird-watching."

"Of course there are! Why, there's the black market in gas and butter, there's all those luscious war contracts with that nice fat profit margin—boy, it beats the FPA all hollow . . . And Cousin Elliott, you haven't met Cousin Elliott, have you, Blackburn—he's interrogating German prisoners these days. The way he does it—it's ingenious! First he makes them kneel on the edge of a very sharp—"

"Elliott," his father said, "is doing his duty. Like a lot of other people, he is *trying* to deal with the world as it is."

"Right!" Lee's eyes flashed like newly hammered blades. "That's exactly what's wrong with him. How about trying to deal with things as they ought to be? Just for the radical novelty of it . . ."

The argument had gone from bad to worse, and ended with the Judge stalking away tremulous with suppressed rage, muttering about bird-watching as a sign of decadence and social withdrawal, and Lee gazing at his father's back with hot defiance. The Judge was often prey to such outbursts—it was said he'd marred a brilliant start through a largely unnecessary personal feud with Attorney General Palmer—and Camilla would rebuke him mildly; whereupon he would subside in morose, largely incoherent mutterings. Blackburn, listening to the quarrels—father against son, brother against sister—felt troubled: in so wonderful a family there ought to be no estrangements.

A year later, the summer the boys had graduated from Exeter, Seaver called Blackburn into his study and offered to pay his way through Harvard on condition that he room with Leland.

"Actually, there'd be a little more to it than that." The Judge's fine hawk's eyes studied him carefully. "You'd be acting in the capacity of a sort of companion. In and out of school, so to speak. You'd go over to Boston together evenings, spend your vacations together, travel to Europe, things like that; and you'd keep an eye on him. A steadying influence. Do you follow me?"

"Yes, sir. I do." Although he'd already been accepted on full scholarship Blackburn felt his heart leap—he knew instantly what it would mean: a good house, more time for study and sports, chances to travel, the ease of living well . . . but most of all, best of all, it was proof of the Judge's great trust in him, his faith in what he could be—there was nothing that could compare with that.

"—so intransigent," the Judge was saying, "—so wild! There are times when he doesn't seem to care *what* he says or does. God alone knows what made him like this. The Darcey blood, I suppose—they always lived gale force . . . There are two kinds of people, Paul. Those who reach out to the world, and those who recoil from it. Which is only another way of saying: Those who want to hold things together and those who want to tear them apart." His eyes came to rest on Blackburn again; the harsh, drawn features relaxed—his face broke all at once into a radiant smile the boy had never seen before. "You're like me, Paul—the way I was at your age. You want to measure up. Take things in your two hands and move them forward. Not many have it. Oh, they'll pretend they do, but they don't—you can tell at a glance: they're grubbers, most of them, working events for their own ends, making deals. This is something else. It's compounded of conscience, a sense of duty—a lot of things. You can find it in the greatest statesman, or in the lowliest civil servant buried deep in the archives down at Foggy Bottom. You have it. We're a—I guess you could call us a sort of secret fraternity of responsibility. And Paul, it's the only thing that holds the ship on course. The only thing . . ."

The Judge looked away, his mouth working. There was a silence, broken only by shouts and a hoot of boisterous laughter from the tennis court.

"Thank you, sir," Blackburn said after a moment, lamely. "I can't ever tell you how much this means . . ." To his surprise his eyes had filled with tears and he blinked rapidly, swallowing. It was the happiest moment of his life. "I'd like to say—if I could have a father again, I'd want him to be like you."

"Yes," the Judge answered; he nodded, rose to his feet and reaching out gripped the Californian by the shoulders, hard. "I've thought something like that, myself . . . Take care of him, Paul," he said with sudden soft intensity. "He's so impulsive—I'm fearful of what he might do to himself, sometimes. Stay close to him, Paul."

"Yes sir, I will," he said. "I promise."

He kept his promise—he would not have dreamed of refusing (his mother was delighted with the Seaver connection, but it would not have mattered if she hadn't been)—and with that word opened the gate to some of the most exciting years of his life. The war, finally and unbelievably, was over, the University was alive with the return of its best faculty and its veterans. Everything fell into place for him. He reached Group II academic level in his freshman year and never fell below it; he was a varsity swimmer and co-captained the team in his senior year, became a *Crimson* editor and member of Signet Society, and emerged as Third Marshal of his class.

Summers the Judge sent them abroad—an education no university could hope to impart. Blackburn read the little bronze plaques to the dead Resistance fighters around the Hôtel de Ville, plodded through the sea of gray rubble around St. Paul's, sat on a fallen column on the Palatine Hill and felt about his head the heavy, slow hum of the past. Everything he saw he remembered. He watched the ministers sedately mount the stone steps of the Quai d'Orsay, to be admitted by an usher in a black frock coat and white bow tie; he watched the destitute scavenging through the garbage buckets behind the grand hotels on Via Veneto, and ran for his life with a crowd of students scattered by black-helmeted police in Brussels. Peace: there was peace now—a peace of conquest and exhaustion; but how durable would it be if this exhausted world returned to all the old alliances, the outworn enmities?

He thought a lot about this. His honors thesis was a study in comparisons and contrasts between the Potsdam Conference and the Congress of Vienna; and Langer, who was never given to rash praise, told him it was almost good enough to publish as it stood. In his heart—even then—he knew better: it lacked the authority of rude experience to deepen its perceptions. He would try to publish it—but later, after he'd tempered theory with some labor in the field. He wouldn't need to follow the direction of the first solitary crow in flight on leaving Cambridge, like William King two centuries before. He wanted to go into Foreign Service. There was so much he wanted to do . . .

But the core of his life remained that jumble of silver-shingled houses below Turk's Head on the Vineyard. Camilla died in the boys' sophomore year, and the loss of her levity and moderation sharpened the antagonisms among the survivors, despite the presence of her spinster sister, Charlotte, who had come down from Camden expressly in the hope of softening them. The Judge gave way to more frequent explosions of wrath, Leland responded with redoubled defiance; Eleanor tried to make peace between them, but she lacked her mother's serenity and sense of humor. She was an awkward, diffident girl; her blunt candor embroiled her in the quarrels more often than not. Blackburn saw her now and then—she was at Dana Hall—took her to an occasional dance or football game; but his attitude was that of an older brother—bantering, mildly affectionate. He did not take her seriously.

He took Leland seriously, though: he had to. Instead of growing steadier with the comparative ease of undergraduate life in one of the nation's most relaxed colleges, Lee seemed increasingly obsessed with the need to scourge himself and everyone else with a wild hatred of authority. It was a hard-drinking, fractious place, the Harvard of the immediate postwar years, and Lee drank and quarreled more than anyone else. He was in an unending series of jams. He brought a girl up to their rooms one night and insisted he was going to set up light housekeeping with her; Blackburn got her out by the simple but desperate expedient of luring the janitor away from their entry with a well-timed phone call. He extricated his ward from an ominous wrangle with an ex-paratrooper outside the Oxford Grille; he lent him his notes, sat in for him occasionally during those years of compulsory lecture hall attendance, put him to bed when he was drunk, got him up for classes and exams, sent out his laundry and even bought him shirts and socks.

He didn't mind this—it was part of the pact he'd made with the Judge and he carried it out ably and well. Besides, he knew Silas Seaver grieved over his son's often dangerous vagaries. When Lee was hungover and contrite Blackburn could reach him with various pleas and threats, and now and then he would try to reform. But then he would meet with his father, and the ever more violent cycle of drinking and self-destructive action would rush on him again. He spent whole days bird-watching at the Arnold Arboretum or in the Lynn Marshes, he flunked exams out of perversity, got a Radcliffe girl pregnant and then refused to see her at all—one rainy night, very drunk, he even stepped out of their windows on the fourth floor and made an entire circuit of the building on the fourteen-inch ledge, to reappear laughing savagely, while Blackburn, powerless and sick with fright, gaped at him.

"Afraid, weren't you?" Lee demanded, his handsome thin face distorted, slick with sweat. "Sure—scared witless the old goose was going to smash up all those golden eggs. Weren't you?—you stupid, prudent soul . . . Think you're taking care of me, don't you? Yeah. *I* know how you're taking care of me."

All of which had only been prelude to that afternoon on Stonewall Beach, with the fire snapping, and the angry voices, and the surf . . . Terrible. Terrible. And yet no one could say he hadn't done all he could—after he'd come back, anyway. Wasn't that true? What more could he have done? What could anyone have done in the face of so prideful, desperate—

—Police car. Swelling in his mirror, bearing down on him. Thrust back to the present Blackburn glanced at the speedometer. He was going well over 80. Horrified he braked—realized his tail lights would only give him away further, and grinned nervously. The cruiser was nearly abreast of him now, its conical turret flashing a pale garnet in the still, flat light; and now the siren burst close against him, a mounting growl. He saw the set face, the quick, peremptory hand, slowed sharply and rolled on to the shoulder. Why in heaven's name had he been batting along like that?

The patrol car pulled in ahead and now backed toward him. With that insolent deliberateness common to all state troopers the man got out and began walking toward him. Feeling vexed with himself Blackburn took out his driver's license and opening the glove compartment began hunting for the registration, rummaging through a crushed wad of outdated road maps, repair bills, facial tissues, congealed strips of trading stamps, peppermint rolls, a plastic flashlight. It was curious—for someone as organized and neat as Eleanor, to leave all this junk—

"License and registration."

That and nothing more. The trooper was looking in at him. A heavy face, not unhandsome if fleshy; stern now with the prospect of an unpleasant duty to perform. Or was it a pleasant duty? The eyes, impenetrable behind wrap-around sunglasses, gave no sign. How they dehumanize a person, Blackburn thought, remembering Vosz on the plane; all public servants should be forbidden to wear them.

The policeman was still staring at him in silence. A face that could go either way—to leniency, to brutality, depending on the circumstances. Which could be said for any one of us.

"Here's my license," Blackburn said, handing it over. "I'm sorry, I can't seem to find the car registration, my wife's obviously hidden it in some inaccessible place here."

"That's all right. Take your time." The trooper took the license, straightened—bent forward again into view. "Mr. Secretary?" he said quickly. "Secretary Blackburn?"

"Yes."

"I'm sorry, sir. I didn't recognize you. Without the official car . . ." With one deft motion he removed his glasses, revealing rather ineffectual pale blue eyes, paler now with concern. "You *were* driving pretty fast."

"I know I was. I—"

"Is there an emergency?"

Blackburn laughed. "No—I can't claim that."

"Can I give you an escort anywhere?"

"Oh no, it won't be necessary." Leaning out of the window he smiled and said: "To tell you the truth, I'm launched on a cross between a secret mission and a sentimental journey: I'm going up to Cambridge to see a young woman my son's apparently very serious about."

"Oh—sure . . ." The trooper handed him back his license. "Sorry I stopped you."

"Not at all. You were quite right—I had my mind on other things and I simply forgot. I had no idea I was going that fast."

"Trouble is, a tire blows at that speed—I've seen some bad ones this spring, I want to tell you. Lying all over the road, smashed up . . . We don't want to lose *you,* you know."

"I'll watch it, I promise."

"Okay, then." The trooper paused, shifted his cap brim. "My wife saw you on TV just this morning. At the airport. Boy, I'll bet it was hot over there in India."

"Couldn't be any hotter."

"I'll bet you're glad to be back!"

"Indeed I am."

"Well, take it easy . . ." The trooper paused again, then turned with an airy wave of his hand. It was something Blackburn had noticed often since he'd been made Secretary—this almost wistful need people had to be near him, stay near him, as if they derived a kind of emotional nourishment from the contact. The Indians even had a word for it— *darshan:* that beneficial glow that came from being in the presence of the great. The flame could be consuming, however. And in his own case one would have to say it was pretty diffused.

Pulling past the police car he nodded again—felt in spite of himself the old, furtive, adolescent twitch of elation (got out of it this time!), smiled wryly. Power. Power had given him privilege, had rendered him immune to many of the mishaps that afflicted the run of men. Not all of them though, by any means. Land would have been furious—he could hear him now: "You see? You count on it, you *know* you're safe simply because you're a member of the power élite. You abuse it the way the honorable heads of state always do . . ."

Power. He had sought it, true enough. What purpose (save sentimental romantics) was served by denying it? It was mainly what had drawn him back to the Paling after Korea. He'd seen very little action—he'd been assigned to artillery—but he'd seen a lot of other things. Sobered and shaken by the shuffling columns of refugees, the bloodshed and incessant shelling; profoundly dislocated by its sheer remoteness from the American experience as he thought he understood it, he had hurried back to familiarity, authority, tradition—and yes, to be near the only center of power and stability he had ever known.

The Paling, too, was changed. Everything had changed after that afternoon at Stonewall Beach. Terrible. Terrible . . . The violence had gone out of the household, but also much of its vitality. The Judge fell into fits of morose introspection laced with flashes of caustic rage. The ebb and flow of houseguests had stopped; the boats were put up, the tennis courts were flawed with weeds. The old house seemed to crouch behind its stone and shrub barriers as though defying the world to seek contact with it as it had in the days of mad, misanthropic Gamaliel Seaver . . .

Eleanor had changed, too. She surprised him. In place of the awkward girl he had left, a self-possessed young woman now drank martinis very dry and wore her cropped hair in a feathery fair clip around her head.

"Well," he'd said, watching her. "And what have you been doing with your time?"

She shrugged. "One thing and another. Preparing myself, I guess."

"Preparing for what?"

"Oh—for the Fabulous Fifties. For life. Isn't that what we're all doing?" She was smiling at him but her blue eyes were very large and earnest.

She *did* surprise him, mightily. She knew a lot more about political matters than he'd ever suspected. The old dogmatic certitude—abrupt, almost rude—had been tempered to an engaging candor. She deplored the choice of Dulles to negotiate the peace treaty with Japan, she felt Acheson was neglecting Asia in his obsession with Europe, she was excited about the candidacy of Adlai Stevenson.

"And what does your dad think of that?" he asked.

"Oh, he makes fun of me about it. He'll go to his grave hating the Democrats. Except you—he's never held it against you."

She wanted to go to work for UNRRA, or perhaps land a job as secretary in some overseas embassy—she wanted to see more of the world than New England.

"There *is* a world out there beyond Gay Head, isn't there?"

"Oh, yes," he said. They smiled at each other for a moment.

"This is silly," she broke off. "I want to listen to you—I want to know what *you're* thinking." Her eyes held a sudden direct entreaty, the concave planes of her face seemed to deepen. "It's been a terribly long time. I mean when you add the months all up, end to end . . ."

She had been waiting. Blackburn sat there holding his drink, gazing at the beautiful scale model of the *Ariadne* on the mantel. She'd been waiting. A girl with a head on her shoulders, with balance and purpose, a girl who had prepared herself for what life might offer; and beyond that—he saw this with a sudden soft shock, almost fearful—in spite of his absence, in spite of what had happened between them, she was still head over heels in love with him . . .

FOUR

RUNNING ALONG THE Southeast Expressway the traffic thickened around him; and that curious sensation returned—of floating over this crabbed, compressed, provincial town that had been so difficult to traverse only twenty years before. Blackburn stared at the grimy baroque façades, the somber tower of the old Customs House and thought: Our lives are all mapped out by some celestial magistrate before we are ever born; we go where we are thrust—our lofty claims to self-will, to forging our own destinies are so much twaddle . . .

Why else had he done it—married Nell? What had impelled him? Nothing answered this better than the simplistic *It was in the cards*. There had been the Judge, bereft now of his only son, looking to him with fierce entreaty; the fine old Vineyard home with its world of authority and grace; and Eleanor, handling the jib sheets for him, answering his call, "Ready about!" with her own eager, *"Ready . . ."*—her blue glance following him with an almost fearful ardor. In the cards. He got his MA, took his exams for the Foreign Service a month later, passed them impressively. Two weeks after that they were married, a simple ceremony held in the garden at the Paling behind the sundial with its sanguine Roman motto, and no one had been more pleased about it all than Silas Darcey Seaver; Blackburn had never forgotten the look of high satisfaction on the old man's face during the reception. The weather had been perfect.

Isfahan had been half a world and several centuries away: a land of gaunt blued mountains, and then this improbable oasis in a wilderness of red dust. Everywhere around him Blackburn could feel the somber beat of history—the shades of Alexander and Tamerlane and the good Shah Abbas moved against the gaily colored walls that enclosed graceful balconies, cool fountains and still, exotic gardens. As Administrative Officer his duties were to see that the code clerk was up on his cables, that American tourists or businessmen got assistance whenever they wanted it; that the vehicles at the consulate were kept in good running condition, the hedges trimmed and the plumbing in good order. Not exactly what he'd had in mind during Langer's seminar, but it gave him plenty of time for reading up on Persian history, and even for occasional trips to nearby ruins or up into the mountains.

The Paling had gone with them too, in a way: there was the big mahogany box of heavy flat silver with its elaborate *S* monogram, there were cases of linen and crystal, even certain of the Oriental rugs.

"We're going to the land of great carpets," he'd protested. "Do we need to take all this?"

Eleanor had stared at him in mild astonishment. "Of course we do— there's no sense buying things we don't need. We can put our money to better uses than that . . ."

She'd handled most of the packing herself—she always did. She was always superbly organized. She kept typewritten lists, in duplicate, of all their goods in transit; the boxes and crates were cleverly identified by crayoned symbols. She mastered Persian with amazing speed and took to frequenting the bazaars—she was always coming home with things: little inlaid mother-of-pearl caskets, an ivory chess set, leaded crystal decanters, candlesticks exquisitely worked in silver—purchases, she told him, she'd made at a good price; the merchants expected you to drive a sharp bargain with them, they were actually disappointed in you if you didn't.

"My itinerant Yankee," he'd said, and taken her in his arms, "—shades of Great-Great-Uncle Asa!" And she'd laughed; but still she brought the small treasures home and displayed them on mantels, on shelves and sideboards.

She'd learned to give impeccable dinner parties. She had the best cooks and servant girls among the junior officers, and her service was the envy of the wives. Only—there was that odd little element of constraint: she ran an evening like a field problem, an exercise in hospitality. Finally he'd broached the matter, gently; they had a long talk about it.

"But I want it to be *right,*" she said with some distress, "—don't you see?"

"It was, it was . . ." he smiled at her fondly. *Only nobody had a good time,* he wanted to say; *don't you see? You dry up the juices of conviviality with all the protocol—and self-enclosure.* "Sometimes it's more important if people—well, feel at their ease . . ."

He hadn't realized she was so unsure—her airy candor had misled him. Gradually he found ways to build her confidence, get her to relax. He in any event was immensely well liked, and her intelligence and deference pleased their superiors; his Performance Evaluation Reports were filled with superlatives. At Damascus, his second post, they'd done still better—of course, as he'd pointed out to Nell, she had more substantial resources than the wives of most minor secretaries. But even so, they'd worked well together—he running his department, she hers, and in the evenings achieving that nice balance of wit, gossip and serious discussion that can give a dinner form if not consequence. Maybe they'd even got too good at it. "That deadly Blackburn team," one of the staff had called them once. And it was true—now and then, glancing down the table, watching

Nell drawing out the Counselor of Embassy, he would have the sense
that he scarcely recognized her. Was this true of him, too? was he becoming someone else, someone alien?

He had been in Khotiane just four months, as acting first consul at
Plei Hoa, when the CIA man Kirby had flown up from Cau Luong to
brief him on the contingency plan for United States intervention in support of the French. The plan called for six divisions, reinforced; an amphibious landing with extensive air support and naval units. Taipei had
given unequivocal assurances of assistance in force.

Blackburn had been shocked into vehemence. "But—that's war," he'd
finally protested. "That's armed invasion of a guaranteed neutral . . ."

Kirby was a big man with a pale, freckled face and sparse gray hair;
he'd worked with the OSS in Burma during the war, and then with the
Dutch in Indonesia in '47. "The French are in trouble up here, Blackburn.
It seems to me you ought to be aware of that by now."

"I *am* aware of it."

"What you going to do—let the God damn Reds starve 'em out?"

"That's De Montherlot's problem, not ours . . . Vuoi Khol's people
will throw in with the Hai Minh in a matter of hours."

The CIA man's eyes narrowed. "What do you know about Vuoi
Khol?"

"A lot—a hell of a lot. I talked with him for three hours, just last
week. And with Hoanh-Trac, too. Look, they've got it anyway. The French
position is untenable. Don't take my word for it, ask any competent
observer—"

"That isn't the way Washington sees it."

"Do you think these people have been fighting and dying for eight
years for the privilege of swapping the French for the Americans? Whose
brainchild *is* this, anyway? Do they *want* Peking in here with both feet?
There's no better way to do it, I can tell you that."

Kirby was watching him with an expression of bilious distaste. "How
did you think little girls got to be moom-pitcher stars? You've got a lot
to learn, Blackburn."

"Is that right."

"Don't be naive. This is what's in the works, and this is probably—
very probably—what is going to be put into action." Kirby heaved himself
to his feet with a ponderous sigh. "My advice to you—I can tell you right
now you better take it—is: Forget about Mr. Vuoi Khol and get things
set up for this eventuality. See you around."

It was a hard decision to make. Very hard. He tried to reach Dorrance, his Chief of Mission down in Cau Luong, without success; started
two reports and tore them up. His sense of loyalty struggled fitfully with
his frustration at not knowing exactly what was planned, and a genuine
anger at the stateside fire-eaters who would dream up a hare-brained, disas-

trous operation like this and expect it to solve all Khotianese—good God, all *Asian*—problems at a stroke. It was wrong, all wrong. After another attempt to contact Dorrance he sent off a night action cable and followed it up with a carefully documented report to both the Far East desk and Cau Luong, giving the reasons for his opposition to the plan, and listing the probable Khotianese and Chinese reaction.

He had grievously misread the mind of John Foster Dulles, who he knew would see the report, given the nature of the crisis. He had banked on the Secretary's New England probity; he had failed to perceive the religious fervor with which Dulles met the specter of world communism, his capacity for self-righteous wrath. The reverberations were swift and they were intense. Dorrance, a Princeton man with bulging brown eyes and a waxed mustache, summoned him down to Cau Luong in great perturbation. What the devil did he think he was doing? What was he taking upon himself?

"But I sent you a copy of the report, sir."

"I can't read everything, Blackburn—you must know that. I have a good many pressures on me."

"I understand that, sir. But—"

"The Secretary himself is *very* angry with you—I have no hesitation in telling you that. So is Far East desk. And so, I hasten to add, am I." Dorrance plucked at his cuffs crossly. "I had no idea you were at odds with government policy in this area."

"I don't believe I am, sir. It was my understanding that we are in the process of *formulating* policy, particularly in the light of Vuoi Khol and the neutralist elements."

"Acting consuls in Asian backwaters do not formulate policy, Blackburn—do I need to tell you that? Besides, there's no such thing as a neutralist element out here. Those who are not for us are against us. You know the Secretary's position on that. In a world in conflict one seeks *allies* . . ."

"Yes sir, but my understanding was that this military operation was a projected plan, not something already committed."

"Hang it all, man, you're not *that* naive! You know which way the wind is blowing . . . Can't you see this was a high-level decision—that it does not concern you and what your *understandings* are?" The Chief of Mission went into a violent coughing fit, his face apoplectic and tight. "Now how in the name of God are we going to extricate ourselves?"

There proved to be no need for that. The amphibious assault never took place—some high personages had decided against it, Blackburn never knew why—but he was not to be forgiven, nonetheless. When he was passed over on the next promotion list he understood. A policy of accommodation with Asian Third Force adherents was not only inadvisable, it was anathema. Containment, intrigue and intervention were the order of the day.

That was all the story. The measured answer was out of fashion, and apparently it would be for some time to come.

At the Mystic River Bridge he swung left, dipped down from the Expressway, his tires snarling on the ramp; and the gentle curve of the Charles River began. Far ahead of him he could see the towers of Harvard slide into view like a fine old print. Off to the southwest over the Fens thunderheads were massing, slate and silver.

The moments in one's life. It had been another hard decision—in some ways the hardest of all. He'd had his heart set on a diplomatic career; the life excited him, it was something for which he knew he was singularly well fitted. But if a man's career was to be destroyed simply because he told the truth as he saw it, because his recommendations ran counter to Washington's iron preconceptions . . . Eleanor for once was uncertain as to what he ought to do; the Judge was emphatically opposed to his resigning. "Let it blow over, Paul. Foster Dulles won't last forever. Even Presbyterians die eventually. Wait for a shift in the wind."

In the end he resigned. He wrote an article on United States policy in Southeast Asia that none of the foreign policy magazines would take, but which provoked a lot of talk in certain quarters. Old Langer asked him back to Harvard to teach; and to his surprise he loved it. His courses became immensely popular—legendary, Sid Jacobi liked to say. He was appointed to the prestigious Council on Foreign Relations, caught the attention of Schlesinger and Hilsman and Galbraith, and came to share in the brief vigor and elation of the Camelot years. He served on the commission for the Thai-Burmese border dispute, and after that Chet Bowles made him Assistant Secretary for Far Eastern Affairs.

Then came Vietnam. From the very start he was profoundly opposed to American involvement. It was wrong, all wrong—he had listened to Vincent and Service and Davies and the others, the men who had been rewarded for their honesty and the accuracy of their predictions by summary dismissal, or by an indifference so chill that they took their talents elsewhere; and his own memories of Khotiane were still vivid enough. It was a blind alley, a delusion based on false premises, outworn fears. He watched with dismay the relentless pressure for escalation building all around them: they weren't really going to commit this folly, were they?

After the massive troop commitment of March, 1965 he decided to leave the Department in protest again. By all odds it should have been the end of his public career—that was evident enough. Eleanor fought him tooth and nail this time, and they had one of their few really serious quarrels. But he left, returned to Cambridge and worked slowly and carefully on his book, which called for a system of interlocking regional councils as the most effective means of breaking down international tensions and boldly attacked the old policy of containment of a monolithic world communism as unimaginative and rigid. Mainland China, not Japan or

Taiwan, was the pivotal power in Asia, the awakening giant without whose friendly participation no stable world order was possible. And the sooner we realized that we had put our money on the wrong horse, and recognized Peking, the better for everyone concerned.

He smiled wryly, remembering. It was everything he believed, it was well written—but for all that he'd been lucky. So much in this world depends on timing—who had occasion to know that melancholy truth better than he? The book made its appearance at a time when public mistrust of the Cambodian invasion and other oily artifices of the Nixon Administration was at its height. *A World Revived* became the center of intensely partisan heat, attacked and defended in the colleges, even in Congress—and gained powerful adherents among the revisionists. Harriman and Clifford in particular had praised its bold new doctrine. A year later the dramatic defeat of the purblind American stratagem over China in the United Nations and Washington's belated overtures to Peking had combined to give the book a prophetic power. He *had* been vindicated, in a sense . . .

Larz Anderson Bridge, looking antiquated and proud. He turned right and crossed the Charles, idly watching a man in a singles shell pumping his way downstream, skimming on the slick dun water. It was curious, when you thought about it. He'd done things out of expediency now and then, with an eye to repercussions—to avoid controversy, to attract notice or support. Who in public life hadn't? There was never anything to be gained that he could see by hiding one's light meekly under a bushel. Yet that book, which he'd written without thought of favor or advancement—that sober little *J'accuse* he'd forged out of an aroused conviction that American foreign policy (not to mention State itself) desperately needed mending—had done more for his career than all the posts and commissions, the Cambridge gatherings or Washington receptions or sailing parties out of Hyannis. Was there a lesson there for him? Doubtless—the world was full of them.

When the new Administration had come into power, reform and response were the watchwords. The President-elect had called him out of class to talk to him—had invited him down to Washington and apparently decided on him on the basis of a twenty-minute interview. The President was like that—impulsive, aggressive, as quick to make up his mind as when he'd been running the mightiest automotive corporation in America; but even so, Blackburn had been far more astonished than the disgruntled senior men at State or even his detractors in the press, when the President revealed his intentions. The most Blackburn himself had dared hope for was an Assistant Secretaryship. He'd have thought the President would have wanted someone with more experience in the hit-trip-and-tumble of the international arena, and in his amazement ventured to say so.

"What's the matter, Paul?" The President-elect's eyes were snapping behind the rimless glasses; his sandy hair, as always, was immaculately combed. "Don't you think you can handle it?"

"Yes, sir. As a matter of fact I do."

"Good. That's what I wanted to hear."

"I was only—surprised."

"No, you're what I want, Paul. I've liked your ideas about bringing poor old State back into the government again. That's where it belongs. My predecessor just about wrecked it for good. They say Jack Kennedy wanted to be his own Secretary of State, and I guess he was. Well, all *I* want to be is my own Secretary of Commerce, Labor, Interior and HEW. *And* Attorney General." He grinned and bobbed his head. He had a funny little habit of hitching up his trousers and leaning forward, his shoulders hunched, as though he were about to charge the problem before him and bowl it over, take it out of contention. "I'm going to get things rolling again, right here at home—housing, race relations, the kids, inflation. I want to restore confidence in the meaning, the *structure* of the government." Reaching out he had tapped Blackburn on the wrist once. "All that out there—" he tossed his head toward the window, east toward Europe, Africa, Asia "—I'm going to leave to you. I haven't got the slightest desire to play the Great Statesman, and the people that elected me don't expect or want me to. State is your baby. I'll back you up if, as and when. But my own thrust is right here. At home. We've had all the Vietnams and Cambodias we need. Do you follow me?"

"Yes sir, indeed I do."

"Just run it flawlessly, that's all. *Molliter et molle manu.* You know?" The President was fond of salting his conversation with Latin and Greek phrases, which gave an unlooked-for dimension to his talk: he had never been a classics scholar. His long experience in business had never given time for that, and while he subscribed to some of the economic tenets of the Charles River School his real teacher had been the factories of Detroit and Cleveland and Gary. "A soft answer turneth away wrath," he said in a musing tone. "My grandfather used to say that like nobody on earth—I can still hear him.—I want foreign affairs out of my hair, Paul," he said with a certain definable sharpness. "Ever since Forty-One we've splathered ourselves all over the globe—airlifts and police actions and undeclared wars and incursions and everything else you can think of. Well, the time for that is over. What's important now is Operation Bootstrap, right by the fireside. We're going to seek accommodation, relaxing of tensions—wherever our friends and foes will allow it, anyway. No more Asiatic adventures, no more muscle-flexing in Berlin or name-calling in Chile. No more *gloire* with a capital *G*. I want four years of peace, Paul. That's why I wanted you—I know you'll push for that harder than anyone else."

Blackburn had smiled. "That's a tall order, Mr. President."

"Sure it is. The only orders worth filling are tall ones. But there's this: you're loyal and you inspire loyalty. People will listen to you and then go out there and knock themselves out for you. I've heard them. That's good. A man can't do everything by himself any more—he can't do half of it." With a characteristically brusque movement he picked up the transparent model of an internal combustion engine—one of the innumerable flood of gifts and mementoes a chief executive receives; his desk held several of them: a bright yellow bulldozer, a World War II Sherman tank in olive drab—and turned it slowly, critically in his pudgy fingers. "There are going to be a lot of noses out of joint over at State, and over on the Hill, too. You're going to hear a lot of flak about how I picked you for cosmetic purposes, or as a fall guy, or to please the eggheads in New York. Some of them are going to be after you with both hands—Goldwater and Buckley and Thurmond, the Hard Line. You're going to have to take the heat for a while. But don't worry about confirmation. They'll work you over a bit, but hell, that's part of the game, they've got to make some noise. We've got the votes and they know it."

He was right: the confirmation struggle was short. Blackburn's opponents fumed and glowered and insinuated, calling him an academic theoretician, a cloistered esthete. But he could give the lie to that. He had served on thorny international commissions and run a desk at State; but more important than that he'd walked among the legions of beggars in Calcutta, he'd watched Korean faces gray with despair, he'd seen French paratroopers, crazed with the specter of defeat, looting and raping in Plei Hoa. And he had been a poor boy in rich men's schools—and that had been the most searching tutelage of all.

They said he was too young, his detractors; that he was overly ambitious; that the charm, the personal magnetism and tensile grace for which he was famed were no more than a façade behind which he had driven his way to power. Well, it was true—he *was* young; and he *was* ambitious. Was that such a crime? Who was not, in some sphere? Possibly he was even overly ambitious—a rather broad human failing, truth to tell . . .

But deceitful—no. It was during the second day of the committee hearings that he realized how much—how really terribly much—he wanted the post. It meant an opportunity that ran beyond the formulation and implementation of policy, crucial as that was. It was simply—he saw it all at once in the crowded room, the clatter of voices and cameras—that he was as much his father's son as his mother's. A native Californian, son and heir of the late, unlamented Rollicking Rick Blackburn (dead in a six-car Bayshore pile-up eight years ago), he could never see the world entirely through the eyes of the Eastern Establishment—what Bill Donlund liked to refer to in his sly, sardonic way as "the Sainted ABC: the Atlantic Brahmin Coronet." Blackburn had remonstrated with him once, telling the ex-lumberjack he was beating a dead horse, that world was gone. Donlund had given him his slow, amused wink and said: "They're still there, Paul. Don't fool yourself about that. They're just biding their time, that's all. Us West Coasters know what the score is. We've got to stick together, or they'll swamp us again."

Blackburn had laughed and nodded, but the Oregonian was wrong: the golden years—the illustrious foreign policy years of the Welleses and Achesons and Harrimans and Lovetts, when the voices went forth and the earth trembled—were dead. At their best they had been nothing short of brilliant, but there had always been that shadow of complacency, of mild but unmistakable disdain for the marginless fields of the Republic rolling west of the Hudson. He had felt it in Miles Stout's snappish retort to Marvin Kalb, who had expressed a perfectly well-grounded apprehension over a certain aspect of policy in USIS: *"That* question must have originated in the advertising section!" or the Judge's remark after the disastrous Chicago Convention in '68: "They don't *know* what they want. They have to be shown the way, Paul." It was the voice he remembered most clearly of all from the locker room at Exeter: "You keep out of this, Frisco. This doesn't concern you."

But it *did* concern him: he was damned if he was going to keep out of it. Standing astride the two worlds he'd seen it as a personal obligation to balance them, fuse them—to refurbish the fading Coronet, pour in fresh blood from those despised hinterlands and restore it to its tradition of vigor and disinterested service. Miles Stout was a Brahmin of Brahmins, Mike Hudela had come out of the Pennsylvania coalfields, Joe Carter was the son of a Chicago South Side janitor, Andy Stinchfield looked as if he could still do a full Arkansas field day if he had to, Hugh Pearmain down in Buenos Aires was a Philadelphia Main Liner. This was what he'd been after—a balance, a coming-together, an end to disdain and resentment. The climate, after the divisive rifts of the Nixon-Agnew years, was propitious.

"Go over there and shake the place up, Paul," the President had told him after he'd been confirmed. "Jesus Christ, they're living in the eighteenth century, half of 'em think they're Richelieu or somebody. The rest gave up when Nixon started playing the privy-counselor game with Kissinger, and Rogers caved in. Shake it up and get it rolling." And then the boyish grin, the famous dry snort. "Just give me a clean slate on all major issues. I won't ask a drop more than that from you."

Well, he hadn't done that, God knew; but in two and a half years he'd been able to accomplish a good deal. Both Israel and the Arab world had adhered to the Beirut Pact after the futile Sinai battle, and the Canal had been reopened. The infamous Indochina war had at last been brought to a true end, GATO had been realized. He'd made the new formal diplomatic relations with Mainland China meaningful for the first time, and assuaged Japanese fears with a fresh trade agreement even the Republicans hadn't been able to find too much fault with; and now the terrible China-

Burma conflict was ended and a new state about to be born. Not a bad record for an academic theorist, a poor kid from Frisco with lots of ambition . . .

The Yard, looking relaxed and inviting behind the old brick dormitories, the iron gates. He swung right and rolled down the underpass below the gloomy bulk of Memorial Hall, thinking of wars and their dead, of President Lowell and Henry James, turned left and then left again, working his way back from the University, past the pizza restaurants and fruit stores, checking the street numbers.

The house depressed him. It was one of those dreary two-story, gray-and-brown clapboard affairs wedged between two others nearly identical, cut up now into what avaricious landlords liked to call studio apartments. His watch said 5:42. Just about right: she would be home from work, would have changed, perhaps have had a drink. Overhead the sky was still clear but the air was moist and oppressive. He parked a few doors down the street and climbed the worn, scaling porch. A little boy playing with a bright orange metal grader squinted up at him and said: "Hi."

"Hi there," he answered. The old pine flooring sagged under his weight. Yes, there was her door at the far end—a faded peace symbol in blue and under that, more recent, a dog-shaped star-cluster and lightning bolt that he assumed was the insigne of the Sirius faction. And the name: HOYT, a harsh scrawl of letters. He raised his hand—on an impulse he could not define used the Blackburn family knock: one rap, a brief pause, then three taps in quick succession. Steps crossed the room, a swift, sure rhythm; the door was flung open.

"I don't know why you—"

The girl—she was younger than he'd expected but it was she, all right: he knew—broke off in sudden consternation. Blackburn was conscious of a thin, expressive face and eyes that flashed like mirrors tilted, full of lights.

"—Oh," she said, and recoiled. Then all at once her eyes narrowed, and Blackburn knew she had recognized him. "That is a perfectly foul trick," she said distinctly. Her voice was pleasant, a warm contralto. "I suppose it's something you picked up from your CIA friends."

"Force of habit," he answered. He had an impulse to laugh, he didn't know why—by all rights he ought to feel guilty, at a disadvantage: it *had* been a mean trick. And yet the very opposite was true. "I'm really sorry— I didn't think."

"They *said* you were all voyeurs, you power-seekers. In Psych Twelve. And I thought that was too simplistic." Abruptly she turned her back on him and moved off; he followed her inside and closed the door after him quietly. The room—it seemed to function as a kind of living room, dressing room and study—was in a state of great disorder. Sweaters were flung over the backs of chairs, magazines lay in rough stacks on the floor, torn newspaper clippings and overflowing ashtrays littered the surfaces. Blackburn had the impression that a wind had swept through the place, churned everything up in one wild burst, then let it all settle again. On the wall facing him was a poster of three guerrillas—Blackburn presumed they were guerrillas, they wore patrol caps and oversize bandoleers—moving against a skyline; and next to it a placard that had obviously been used in some street demonstration, of a stylized grenade with a tag on the ring that said *CIA,* and for a legend the phrase he himself had coined with such elation: *An Age for Dialogue.*

"Talk about acting in character . . ." The girl had retreated to the center of the room, near a large round oak table awash with notes and papers. What struck Blackburn was her quick, supple grace—even angry she moved with a deep awareness of her body: it was animate with life. She had high cheekbones that gave a faintly Oriental cast to her face; her chestnut hair fell away from it in an easy sweep to her shoulders. She was dressed plainly, in pongee slacks and a sleeveless orange silk jersey, a thin gold chain at her throat; yet there was a kind of elegance in the way she stood there, her weight on one leg as if poised for flight—or perhaps for attack, you couldn't be quite sure—one hand to her chin: the fine, flowing line of a Brancusi figure. Well, Blackburn thought, the boy has taste, at least. I must compliment him on it. Some time.

"Did you think I was going to barricade myself in here," she demanded, "and shoot it out like Che Guevara?"

"I'm quite alone," he murmured.

"I suppose I ought to be grateful for that." She had regained her poise but she was still very angry, and now in reaction he was annoyed with himself. Why the devil *had* he knocked that way? This was no run-of-the-mill sexual diversion on Land's part, he could see that clearly; there was a lot more involved here.

"You people are never alone. Even when you are." Her lower lip protruded stubbornly. "You know, I'm disappointed in you. Really. I thought you had more—more finesse than this."

"Oh, that's a press invention," he answered. "You expect too much from your public servants."

She laughed once—two low notes half an octave apart. "Not enough, I think. Not nearly enough." Then her face set again. "You know—you're just what I thought you'd be."

"Good." He smiled. "I've confirmed your worst suspicions. Now all that remains is for you to confirm mine, and then we can hate each other to destruction."

"—Oh, stuff it!" she burst out all at once. "Save that for your diplomatic types. Do you think I'm so stupid I don't know why you're here?"

"Even today's parents have to go through the motions. After all, Land *is* only a minor, Miss Hoyt."

"He's more mature than you are right now, if you want to know. Which you don't." She moved off toward a disheveled bookcase—whirled around again with a swift contortion of her body, that lovely, flowing Brancusi thing. Her face kept catching sudden planes and facets of light. "Does this thrill you?" she demanded. "I mean, do you get some sneaky orgasm out of it or something? Be honest—go ahead. Do you?"

He watched her impassively. "To tell you the truth, I'm not very *macho* as a type."

"Oh, but you *are!* Women think you are—I've heard them. The charming, the magnetic, the irresistible Professor Blackburn. Secretary now, of course. That helps. Nothing like JFK, you understand; but it's there. For those who respond to that sort of thing." She had a way of frowning and looking up from under her brows that was attractive. Did she know it? Probably. Blackburn crossed his arms and settled his weight on the balls of his feet. The raillery, the flash of assault were not really native to her; there was something else behind it—some deeper, darker goad, and it piqued him.

"Jesus, I'm sick of paying for the sexual emptiness of people like you," she exclaimed. "Or doesn't that apply, Mr. Secretary? Perhaps I've wronged you cruelly. Have I? Tell me."

Why, she can be really quite nasty, he thought in slow surprise. "You don't aim for the legs, do you?" he murmured aloud.

"I say what I want, if that's what you mean."

"Yes, I can see that."

"That's all we've got left, you see. *You* wield all the power."

"That's a debatable point."

"Don't mock me!" she cried. "That's disgusting . . ." She plucked a crushed package of Trues out of the confusion on the table. "Yes, I say what I want," she went on. "Do what I want, too."

"Doesn't that ever trouble you?"

"Why should it? I've earned the right." She swept back her fine chestnut hair with a peremptory toss of her head. "Oh, yes. Don't make any mistake about *that*. Ways you'll never know." There was a mutter of thunder—the storm rolling up from Providence, or maybe it was only a jet plane over Logan—and she threw a quick, furious glance toward the solitary window, though there was nothing to be seen outside but the shank of a poplar and the grimy clapboarding of the house next door. "I know—I'm supposed to offer you tea or a drink or some such garbage . . ."

"It's sometimes a civilized thing to do."

"Yes—well, I'm not civilized, you see."

"Yes, I do see that."

"I've *had* all that. I've been civilized by experts! *Right out of my skull.*" The thunder—it was unmistakably that, Blackburn could feel it in the air now—broke with a low, rolling crash and the girl raised her voice above it. "You think you're going to *handle* me, don't you? The way you handle Ch'en Pu-tsao and the others. Don't you?"

"No . . . no, I don't." He cleared his throat, feeling depressed and tricked. "To tell you the truth, Miss Hoyt, I'm afraid of you."

"Bullshit," she said in implacable tones. "Lying bullshit." She laughed again, once, watching him. "All right: why are you afraid of me?"

"Because you're so *sure.*"

She drew on her cigarette furiously, waving the smoke away from her face. "Tell me: do you feel I'm being counterproductive?" she taunted him. "That my life style stands in the way of your global dream? Well, it does—it damned well does, and you'd better get used to the idea, you imperial types. Your day is just about over . . ."

"I wouldn't take Reinhold Vosz too seriously if I were you," he said. "His bark is worse than his bite."

Her head went back as if he'd put his hands on her; her eyes—an intense green—dilated with angry amazement. "So that's it!" she cried. "Oh, that's too good, oh that's really priceless. The Squeezer! A member of the sacred, bloody team . . . Jesus God, you're all alike—computers in place of honest-to-God flesh and blood. Every time. The options for today, the odds against tomorrow."

"Vosz fires for effect, Miss Hoyt. He likes to be thought of as out-rageous, unpredictable." He could not repress a smile. "You've known people like that, haven't you?"

"Not people who put away a man like Lachlan Smith—no." She stared at him narrowly. "If you believe that, you're really naive—a soggy ro-mantic fool."

"Aren't you?"

"Certainly not. If there's anything I'm not it's romantic."

"I see. So often the really romantic people never believe they are."

"*Analysis,*" she spat. "On top of everything else. Yes, you're both after the same thing. That's why you take him with you on your errands of peace-and-harmony, unquote. He can run interference for you, he masks what you *really* want, doesn't he? The clean, well-lighted police state. Well, let me tell you something—"

She launched a furious diatribe against American foreign policy, its aggressiveness and duplicity: negotiations without faith, the unholy trium-virate of government, business and the academy feeding on war and the underdeveloped nations, a world safe for American capital; while the storm, high overhead now, bumped and rumbled sullenly and the frayed monk's cloth curtain at the window ebbed and sucked against the screen. Blackburn shoved his hands deep in his pockets and stared glumly at the poster of the grenade. Why were they all so *doctrinaire,* these embattled young radicals? They claimed they were liberated—racially, politically, sexually—innovative and free . . . why in God's name did they mouth ideological slogans worn ragged forty years ago? There she stood (she certainly could stay on her feet long enough, doubtless it was all the marching and demonstrating), her eyes shining as if with tropical fever, ranting away . . . So certain!—she was so *certain,* this slender, volatile whip of a girl. And he, facing her (on very tired feet), was one of the most powerful men on this earth—it was said; and he was besieged by a perfect torrent of doubts and fears.

"Do you know something?" he inserted quietly into a pause. "Do you know, you remind me of no one quite so much as Reinhold Vosz."

She gasped in rage. "That's—that's cheap and vicious and insulting! And I'll tell you something else: come Wednesday morning you're going to rue the day you ever threw in with him—"

"I haven't *thrown in* with him. He was appointed by the President, just as I was."

"—supported his plans for turning the Third World into a test tube for his little imperialist infrastructure. By God, he'll wish he'd never decided to stand up on that podium. I know—you think we're ineffectual, a lot of faceless shadows. You think when the Days of Rage ended we came all apart, freaked-out in splinter groups, you think we can't organize and carry out resistance any more—well, you're wrong! Time is on our side, and so is history . . ."

He glanced at his watch. There was a tight crash of thunder and the room dipped into gloom. He'd left the windows of the car open. Nothing further would be accomplished by staying on here, shifting his weight from one foot to the other, listening (and partly listening) to this harangue. The protest over Vosz posed no threat—Sirius hadn't any plan beyond chanted abuse. And the affair with Land would not last, either; she was lovely, yes, and volatile—there was something attractive in her very vehemence, but it wouldn't hold the boy. There was nothing more to keep him here.

"I'm afraid we're getting nowhere rapidly, Miss Hoyt," he broke in on her in his most authoritative tone. "I know you will see it as an egocentric fancy, but I do have a few other claims on my time."

"You haven't been listening anyway, I realize that."

"My dear girl—"

"Don't you *dare* call me your dear girl!"

"I've heard these arguments half a hundred times—"

"Yes, and forgotten them just as quickly." There was a high, abrupt clap, the room shimmered in the lightning flash, and rain came in a fine, hissing roar. They both had started. "Because we don't count, do we?"

"Good afternoon, Miss Hoyt."

"—All right for you to go *your* merry way, isn't it? Smash up everyone, everyone's lives . . ." Her voice had risen with the thunder and rain —it held a note of vengeful deprecation that set his teeth on edge. "Yes—

Vosz is pure apeshit, right out of a horror film, but you're worse, do you know that?—*worse,* because you kill out of indifference. Out of superiority. Yes—kill!" she pursued, watching his face with fearful intensity. "Hear the truth just once, before you go back to the Pentagon—"

"Miss Hoyt, I've—"

"—that's what's behind all the pretty speeches and the conference tables and TV. Death!" She threw one arm out, pointing full at his breast —a senseless, overdramatic gesture. He moved toward the door. "Oh, you're a perfect success at it—perfect! Looking the other way. Yes. Well, keep looking! Worried about your son? Well, we're even, Mr. Secretary— you murdered the boy *I* loved!"

He turned. "I? *Murdered* him?"

"Yes. In Vietnam . . ."

Astonishment and a peculiar kind of fear held him rigid. "Why, I wasn't even in office during the Vietnam war—I was only a minor functionary. As a matter of fact I resigned when—"

"It doesn't matter." Doggedly she shook her head at him; and all at once her eyes filled. Outside the rain was spanging on some hollow metal surface. "The end of everything. Right there."

"But can't you see—"

"There's only power, anyway." She made no effort to get a handkerchief, or even to wipe the tears away with her hands. "That's all there is. I know. The ones that have it and the ones that don't . . . Poor Dave," she said, and shook her head again, slowly, as though to clear it; he could hardly hear her now. "Sitting there in the airlines terminal twisting that silly overseas cap like a washcloth. He believed you—all the fine grand truths, and off he went. Burned to death. That's what he got for believing you. Served him right, didn't it?" She hadn't moved, but for Blackburn this sudden stillness in her, poised against the uproar of wind and rain outside, was more compelling than all her wild extravagance before. "Maybe you do always win. Always break us, one way or another.—Go away now," she murmured, her voice thick with grief. "Please go."

"Miss Hoyt, I'm—"

"Go *away*—!"

He stopped, his hand on the knob. She was so wrong—so brutally and pathetically wrong about this . . . and yet she wasn't. For the third time that day and against his will he thought of an afternoon dark with clouds and high wind, and the surf booming: angry weather, angry words. Staring at the Hoyt girl's grief-dulled, accusatory eyes he knew she was right, too— in some labyrinthine way neither of them could ever divine.

"Maybe you're right," he said. "Maybe we all murder once."

Abruptly he closed the door.

"I think I ought to tell you a story," he said gently. "A story about me,—that I've never told anybody." He paused. "I'd like to tell it to you, if I may. Will you let me?"

Her mouth was working; she looked shocked, utterly beaten, defenseless. Not at all the dogmatic zealot of a moment before. A different girl. Still watching him she nodded soberly, and rubbed at her cheek with the back of her hand—a child's furtive gesture.

FIVE

"DO YOU SEE THAT CLOUD?" Leland Seaver demanded. He pointed to a particularly ominous thunderhead off to the southeast. "It's the end of the world. When that cloud hits the beach we're all going to die. In convulsions."

This provoked moans of protest from the group, and Beth Welliver said, "Oh Lee, you're so morbid sometimes."

"That's not morbidity, that's insight. Don't you want *insight,* for heaven's sake?" He swayed above them, his thin, pale face flushed from the fire and several Tom Collinses. "What's the matter with you? Don't you wonder what it'd be like if we were all six inches tall, or our brains were transparent? or if you—" he pointed accusingly at several of the girls huddled around the fire "—were male and we were female?"

"Then I could rub *your* face in the sand," Libby Mewden cried.

"Right! Better yet, you could go to Korea instead of me . . ."

"Yes, and I'd *go,* too!" She was a tiny little thing with her hair in a ponytail and the face of a Victorian street urchin. She rode a unicycle around the Island, and for years had kept a pet boa constrictor of immense proportions—an arrangement that had ended only when the snake had crept into one of the furnace flues to sleep and got cooked when the heat came on suddenly one evening. Islanders still talked about the smell. The Mewdens were considered eccentric even by Vineyard standards, which was what had attracted Leland to Libby in the first place.

"Yeah, you're just balmy enough and stupid enough," he agreed. Drinking he eyed his sister narrowly. "What's the matter with *you?*"

Hooded and swaddled in two ratty beach blankets and an oversize sweater, Eleanor said: "I'm *cold* . . ."

"Pure imagination," he told her cruelly. "Go home. Or have a drink."

She shook her head but Blackburn, sitting on the sand beside her, couldn't tell whether it was refusal or a convulsive shiver. "I'm always colder than anyone else at the beach," she said to him. "Even on good days. I don't know why. Mother used to say it was because my circulation is slow. She said I took after Aunt Carrie—"

"Well, just make sure that's *all* you take after her," Lee retorted. "Vicious old biddy-bat. Terrorized the town of Sherborn for forty years. Castrated Uncle Anger with a pair of stainless steel scissors—"

"Lee, stop it!" Beth shouted.

"Figuratively, *figuratively*—which was a lot worse! Can't you face up to the truth?"

"It's too cold for the truth."

"Sybarite!"

"Sadist!"

"Chicken!"

It *was* cold—astonishingly cold for mid-June. The wind, hammering out of the east, was savage; it tore at voices, caps, the flames from the fire. No day for a picnic, but it was to be the last one for a time—perhaps for a very long time. Leland had insisted on it, and so they were camped, nine of them, on Stonewall Beach, where the waves bowled in all the way from Safi and Dakar. Everything had gone wrong. The water was too cold, the surf running too high for swimming, the wind had wrecked the touch-football game. Intermittent bursts of rain damped the fire and soaked the blankets. The chowder had spoiled somehow or other, and Lee had tripped over one of the insulated buckets and sprayed sand on most of the hamburgers and buns. All of which he'd taken a perverse pleasure in, pouring out drinks with riotous abandon, firing at bits of flotsam with an old .22 rifle, and giving Blackburn and Russ Conklin unwanted advice on how to rebuild the fire. By midafternoon everyone was peevish, chilled, at loose ends; and yet somehow constrained to stay on, as though to leave now would destroy the conviviality and promise of the past four years. The portable radio, an imitation leather and brushed aluminum set that ran on two large dry-cell batteries, stuttered and howled as the mood and the airwaves took it, and the fire hissed and snapped and roared back.

"Won't you go?" Hugh Stanhope asked Leland. "If they call you up?"

"Of course he'll go," Russ answered.

"You shut up, Sea-Conch," Leland said. "They'll have to tie me down and shoot me full of Old Glory serum before I'll go."

"But—what'll you do? Go to jail?"

Lee laughed harshly. "I'm going to go to Mexico and lead an invasion. Sailing from Vera Cruz with a Washington heading. I'm going to burn the White House—*with* Dolley Madison inside—and declare a socialist republic dedicated to gin, poetry and bird-worship."

"Sailing!" Russ crowed. "You'll never make it—you're the world's worst sailor from here to Hatteras."

"Don't give me that."

"How about the Regatta last July? A reach genoa in that wind—if it hadn't been for Blackburn you'd have got us all drowned."

"Just because I don't sail like a frightened old auntie . . ."

"Is he serious?" Beth Welliver asked Paul. "About not going?"

Leland heard her and laughed his harsh, defiant laugh. "Of course I'm serious! Let Blackburn go and get himself blown out of a gun—he took ROTC. Foresight, ya know. He and Conklin.—You chumps," he taunted them. "Don't you see it's all for your benefit? You ought to be grateful."

"What the hell do you mean by that?" Russ demanded crossly.

"Just what I said. It's all arranged. So that each generation—each college generation, I mean—has a war for its ownest own. You don't want to be *without* one, do you? Ask Blackburn, he's up on all that balance-of-power candelabra. They sit around the old conference table, all the honorable heads of state, passing the jug, and all of a sudden one of them smites himself full on the forehead and says, 'My God—it's 1949: we've had *four years of peace!* Do you jimokes realize that? The kids'll never stand it.' So then old Acheson tweaks his mustache and gets off a hot wire to Prince Whang-Dong to crank up an invasion, and we're off and running again. There's really nothing to it."

"You mean you don't think it's a simple case of armed aggression?" Stanhope, who was a physics major, asked him soberly.

"Oh, you poor wrinkled prune. *Of course* it's armed aggression! Armed aggression against *me.* Defense of the free world—what do I care, if they turn me into rancid dog food in the process?"

"Lee, for heaven's sake—"

"Do you think I give an oily rag about the march of democracy among my little brown brothers? I want to live to a ripe old age, that's what *I* want." He spread his long arms. "I want to see pandion-baby come soaring in over Tashawena like a beautiful Aztec god, watching over me with his golden eyes . . ."

"Lee," Blackburn told him, "you're the original Vineyard existentialist."

"If we didn't look after ourselves, who would? It's something you can't comprehend and never will. Hell, we should have seceded back in 1812 or whenever it was—then we'd have been rid of the whole mucking machinery."

"Your father thinks the UN action—"

"—Don't tell me what my father thinks!" Leland said with quick savagery, "I'm sick to puking with what my father thinks. I know *you* think he's God in a sultana roll—but that's your problem, not mine . . ."

"Lee, that's a rotten thing to say," his sister protested.

"Truth too much for you, doll? Feel safer with your head in the sand?"

Eleanor started to say something else. Blackburn caught her eye and shook his head tersely. All afternoon Lee had been churning along like this, lashing out at first one old friend and then another. Blackburn had never seen him so contentious and wild, so choked with that ungovernable need to hurt anybody within reach.

Not that there wasn't cause enough. Only the week before the dean's office had notified Leland that he'd failed to graduate—a laconic report on his finals exams that had shaken even his airy indifference.

". . . Gee, I thought I'd made it all right." He'd looked diminished, strangely young. "Except for that one gov exam, I thought I was okay, Paul—I really did."

Blackburn was furious. In one of the courses they shared he'd tutored him for days—midway through the exam itself he'd looked up in horror to discover that Lee, exhausted from nights of frantic cramming, had actually fallen asleep; he'd waked him with a savage kick in the ankle that had brought the proctors hurrying to their side of the hall. All the notes and digests, all the years of advice and exhortation, even threat—and now this.

"Jesus, how could you *do* it?" he cried with sudden unexpected vehemence.

Lee gazed at him for a few moments, wordless and miserable. Then his mouth drew down in the old reckless disdain. "Oh, take it easy, Blackburn. What the hell does it mean, anyway?"

"It means everything—it's the door to anything you want to do . . ."

"Speak for yourself, chum. Piece of lousy parchment you can't even wipe your ass with, it'd give you hemorrhoids. What I'm going to do is follow the cerulean warbler down to Panama. Did you know it's increased its summer range? Or maybe hole up in a fire-watcher's tower and do some writing—that's what I should have been doing the past four years, anyway."

"The hell with that!" Blackburn shouted at him; he felt utterly out of patience, thwarted and betrayed. "Don't you see what this *means?* Your father will never forgive me."

Lee sprang to his feet. "Screw my father! You let *me* worry about my father, okay? Hell, you ought to be pleased—think how much better it makes you look! He can get all excited over *your* triumphs—he'd prefer that, anyway."

"Oh, knock it off, Lee." Fearful of his friend's resentment he'd often tried to deprecate the Judge's occasional comparisons; yet it was almost exactly what had slipped through his mind, and this made him even angrier.

"Isn't it?" Lee was saying with sly malice. "Isn't it, old protector, old alter ego? Well, now you can forget it. The millstone's cut adrift—now you can go on to grander things. Carve out a career for yourself . . ."

They'd driven down to the Paling that evening in sullen silence, thinking their own thoughts. The ferry trip from Woods Hole, usually a festive interlude, was the scene of a further argument when Lee dented a fender on one of the stanchions. Next day Lee had been summoned to the Judge's study—a long stormy scene. Blackburn, pulling weeds in the tennis court behind the house, could hear the clash of voices. Lee had emerged white-faced and trembling and shut himself up in his room for the rest of the afternoon. Worried and contrite, Paul had gone by once and knocked softly on his door; there was no answer.

Dinner that evening, despite the presence of the former Attorney General and his wife and a bright young sociologist from Yale, had been rather constrained. It was only at dessert that the Judge, thawed by several glasses of Vosne-Romanée, had offered the toast to Blackburn.

"In case you didn't know it, Daphne, Paul has just been awarded a Rhodes. Unfortunately it'll have to be held in abeyance until he's done his military service. But I have the feeling it'll be waiting for him when he returns." Smiling he turned to the Attorney General. "We're going to be hearing from this young man, you can take my word for it. Of course he's an unregenerate Democrat like you, Jeffrey; but as we seem to be condemned to the rule of that party forever, it should only help him on his way."

The Attorney General smiled his vulpine, courtly smile. "Sometimes it helps and sometimes it doesn't. What field have you chosen, Paul?"

"Foreign Service, sir."

"Ah, that terrible oral! Think you'll pass it?"

"He'll pass it," the Judge answered for him. "He'll pass it with flying colors. I've never known a boy with so many capabilities. It's uncanny, Jeffrey! Things you never knew about. He can receive and send in Morse, he can prune a grape arbor, he can splice rope—he can even start a car without the ignition key." He looked at Blackburn, his eyes twinkling. "He's the best middle-distance swimmer the University's had since that Hutter fellow . . ."

"—And that talent he has for always saying the right thing," Lee broke in. "Don't forget that! Imagine if he'd just said he wanted to organize migrant labor. Or publish a pornographic magazine—"

"Lee!" Eleanor cried, "can't you ever be quiet?"

But the Judge, with the exception of one baleful glance, had chosen to ignore his son. "We're going to miss you, Paul," he said after a short pause. "All of us. And on this occasion—I want you to have this." Rising he picked up a long, narrow package wrapped lumpily in tissue paper and handed it to Blackburn. "It's a Yankee gift, Paul: something you can use, as my grandfather used to say."

"Not very gracefully packaged, I'm afraid," Aunt Charlotte said.

The room had fallen silent; there was that little stir of attentiveness such moments always bring. Blackburn untied the string and opened the paper. It was the Voigtlander telescope, the heirloom. The inlaid mother-of-pearl pieces glowed like deep water in the candlelight. Engraved neatly on the old brass, centered on the arched back of a leaping dolphin, was the legend: *Property of Joshua M. Seaver. 1787.*

"—Oh, I can't," he stammered. He could not look at Lee. "I can't accept this . . ."

"Of course you can," the Judge said. "Nobody in this family deserves it more than you do, Paul."

—But it's Lee's! he almost burst out; his favorite—he's used it for years, watching the . . . He looked down, full of consternation. He should not take it, he didn't have the right, really—a family treasure like this. *Words are easy, like the wind; faithful friends are hard to find.* He wanted to be a faithful friend, a good and faithful friend. Didn't he? He ought to hand the glass back to the Judge with thanks, with profuse thanks.

But the Judge himself had put it in his hands. The Judge was looking at him now—that fierce, importunate affection of four years before had flooded his narrow hawk's eyes.

"I can't begin to thank you," he heard himself say aloud. "I'm very —moved by this . . ." His voice was trembling, he felt himself strangely near tears. What was the matter with him? "There's nothing in my whole life that has meant more to me than being here—with all of you. A kind of small part of this family, now and then." He felt his hand tighten on the telescope. "I only hope I can be worthy of this. And of you all."

And then, gazing around the table to the low murmur of approbation, he had finally encountered Lee's eyes—and saw they were filled with an anguished outrage that turned him to stone . . .

"I'm going to write you." Eleanor was watching him now from under her blanket—that diffident, level, demanding gaze.

He winked at her. "Me—a scurrilous West Coaster?"

"Oh, you're not, really—you're like all of us here."

"You mean I'd actually be accepted, a bona fide, dyed-in-the-wool Vineyarder?"

She laughed then and shook her head. "You'd be an Off-Islander if you lived to be a thousand."

"That's what I thought. No, East is East. Blackburn's Law. You can't change something like that."

Propped on his elbows he watched the sea, still building mightily, the crests of its breakers tearing off to leeward, and measured it against the Pacific. No matter what they said, California was a land of conclusions: the Vineyard one of beginnings. Even the phrase "the Islands"—uttered as though there were no others anywhere, only these two sabuline triangles flung out into the Atlantic like a pair of great kites set adrift and whirling— embraced a sense of departure, of romantic and far-flung voyage. Men had reached the Pacific weary from traversing the Great Plains, the harsh wall of the Rockies, the wide salt agony of Carson Sink, the Sierra—eager at last to settle down, write finis to the Homeric trek. But here on this flat land girdled by water a man's eyes leaped outward to all points of the compass: north to Boston, south to Washington, east to Paris, London, Vienna. That was where he wanted to look. Oceans laced the world together. The sea had never seemed a barrier to him, as mountains or desert did. The sea could be grim, even frightening, as it was now; but it was relenting, too; it bore you up, it could blow you across its vast belly to alabaster palaces like dreams of paradise—

"*I* can." Nell was leaning toward him, her hands locked around her knees, as if to isolate them from the others. "I can," she repeated with soft stubbornness. "You'll always be an Islander to me. You'll always be everything to me."

With a start he realized she was in love with him—implacably, irrevocably. Was that true? He looked away, watching Lee quarreling with Russ Conklin. She'd had a crush on him for years, he'd known that—a schoolgirl crush, mawkish and rather touching, and he'd met it with the indulgent condescension of an older brother. But this was different. He found himself looking at her again—a quick, harsh scrutiny: the shadowed, gaunt features, oldly young, pinched now with cold; the high-ridged nose and small, gravely determined mouth. In her blunt, gauche, committed way she was in love with him, it was as plain as the pole star . . . Bemused, a touch apprehensive, holding the slow intensity of her glance he dwelt for the shadow of an instant on montages of a life together, the fine old creaking ship of a house tucked away on Turk's Head, children and friends, the whole Island world of pre-eminence and tradition—then thrust it away with annoyance. What the hell kind of way to think was this? She was a Seaver, a member of the family he loved beyond all reason, and that was it. She was a kid, just turned seventeen. A homely, likable kid, a kid sister determined to propose to him . . .

"I'm going to miss you." Her eyes had never once left his face. She was going to say something more. To avert it he said, a touch callously:

"You'll have forgotten all about me in three weeks."

Doggedly she shook her head. "Not me. I never will. I wish we—"

"And how about me? You know you can't trust anybody from west of the Hudson River."

"I know I can trust—*oh!*"

The beach ball—a huge, lurid, blue-and-yellow rubber one—hit her full on the side of the head. She rocked over, bobbed up again, her hand to the side of her face. Leland was laughing at them maliciously.

"Lee," she cried, "that hurt!"

"Of course it did! That's the object of it . . . We're going to play a new game," he announced, hefting the ball in one hand, peering at it as if it were the globe itself. "It's called Caprice. No—Fate. Yes, the wingéd shaft. Or shafted wing, as the case may be." Without warning he flung the ball full force at Russ, who ducked; the ball caromed off his shoulder and knocked the hamburger out of Libby Mewden's hand.

"Aw, Lee—look at that! And I just spent the last ten minutes trying to get the sand off it."

"That's one of the hazards. The innocent must perish with the guilty."

"But what the hell are the rules?" Conklin demanded.

"Rules? There *aren't* any rules—that's why it's called Fate, you blue-behinded ape." Leland had retrieved the ball again and was waving it high over his head. "It simply comes out of nowhere, no warning—and pow!" He slammed it down at Eleanor again, pointblank.

"Damn it, Lee!" She was glaring at him, her lip trembling.

The ball had bounced clear of the fire and was rolling off down the beach, blown hard by the rising wind. Blackburn leaped to his feet. Leland, watching him, spun away, and Blackburn raced him for it. But he was no runner, never had been: Lee, who could have run sprints if he'd ever wanted to train for them, reached the ball first, snatched it up and whirled around, laughing defiantly.

"—Can't pull off everything, can you?" he panted. "No—not every bloody thing . . ."

"That wasn't very funny, Lee," Blackburn said.

"No? I thought it was hilarious."

"Why don't you lay off?"

Leland gave a harsh, malignant grin. "Who, Frisco? Lay off *who?*"

"Nell—everybody . . ."

"Nell? She's tough—she's a *Seaver,* for creep's sake! She'd better learn how it is."

"Why don't you take it easy?"

Leland turned away. "Why don't *you?* School's out, Jackson. You know? You can relax, now."

"She's just a kid, Lee . . ."

The Vineyarder whirled back again. "Do tell. That doesn't bother *you,* though, does it?"

Blackburn frowned. "What does that mean?"

"You think I don't know why you've hung around all this time?" His chest was heaving and his eyes were dark with rage. "Steady old, reliable old Paul. The prodigal's pal. Why don't you shove off out of here?"

"Look, if you—"

"Christ knows I'm no paragon—but I'd have been all right if it hadn't been for you: doing the martyred good Samaritan caper, in three-D—the answer to a tyrant's prayer. Do you think I'm paralyzed that I can't see what you're after?"

"Lee—"

"—the O. T.'s power-and-influence in high places, all the fat connections—"

"—That's not true," Blackburn stammered.

Leland broke into coughing, raging laughter. "Oh no, Jesus no! Not you—not Probity Paul, the All-American Dreamboat . . ." His face stiffened. "Well, now I've got a word of advice for *you,* sport. You keep your filthy fucking hands off my sister, you understand?"

"What?—I never touched your sister . . ."

"No? No? But you want to, though, don't you? Sure, you've got *that* all taped, just like everything else. You've conned all the rest of them, but not me, pal—I've been on to you, all the way . . ."

Blackburn said coldly: "You've had too much to drink."

"Oh, no. Just enough! Just enough to tell you every lousy, rotten thing you are—!"

The blow was quick and hard on his face. He ducked the next wild swing; more to check the desire to hit the Islander than anything else he caught him around the waist and threw him to the sand. Rubbing his cheek he said thickly: "Don't do that again."

Leland scrambled to his feet. "I'm warning you, Blackburn. Fair warning. You keep away from Nell. You don't I'll kill you! That's a promise."

"Leland, I swear to God—"

"Oh, why don't you just move your ass out of here? Go find someone else for a change. You've used us long enough . . ."

Blackburn stared at his friend mutely for a few seconds, then turned away; he could not trust himself to speak.

"That's right—take off!" Leland's voice pursued him, torn by the wind, the roll and crash of surf. "Find someone else to fatten on, you phony son of a bitch—!"

He walked quickly away down the beach. The sea broke on his left hand, flung long, eddying fans of foam at his feet. His face, his fingers were numb. Bound in the protective responses of five years he turned. Leland had rejoined the group, now a dense little knot around the fire, indistinguishable. The hell with him. He walked on eastward, into the wind. If that was how the spoiled bastard wanted it, that was how it would be. The bloody, bleeding hell with him—let him smash up the car on the Chilmark Road, drink himself into a perfect stupor and get picked up and jugged by Chief Colbron. The utter and final hell with him. He was sick to death of playing nursemaid, tutor and valet to a drunken, rebellious, destructive idiot who didn't care who he hurt or why—

He heard high raucous shrieks, looked up; terns were moving above his head, fighting the gale. He was in their nesting area. He threw himself down on an old timber, white with salt and wind-blast, and sat there in a turmoil of anger and mortification, hands between his knees, gazing blindly at the baleful parade of breakers, towering jade walls. Blown sand stung his face. How long had Lee thought this? Was that what they felt about him? It wasn't true. By God, it wasn't the least bit true—he loved the Judge, loved and respected him like his own father; he wanted nothing on this earth so much as to serve this assured, replete family, earn its approval, its affection . . . no one could say he had come to them under false pretenses, used them—*no one* could!

The terns still hung above him, sideslipping and diving crazily, shouting their reedy, accusatory cries. Far out, a squat black object—a barrel maybe, or a balk of timber—rose and sank in the tumbling, foaming crests of surf. It was blowing as hard as he'd ever seen it. What should he do now? Pack his bags, leave the clothes that the Judge's money had bought in the closet in his bedroom, the small one next to Leland's and down the hall from Nell's, the one he'd used since that first vacation from Exeter? Make some excuse or other—a letter from his mother, illness—and say his fare-wells? Something like that. He couldn't stay on now. Not after this. No matter what the Judge might say. If there was even the *chance* they thought he was using them . . .

Rain began to fall, spitting on the white sand. He gripped his hands together and ducked his head, shivering. Well: it could look that way to anyone. Seen from one point of view. But if you genuinely loved a person, a family, a way of life, how could that be time-serving or opportunistic? To emulate was to praise, wasn't it?

Sore at heart he looked back toward the fire; but he had rounded a little point of land. There was nothing but a tumbling crash of surf, the strident terns, the quick, chill rain.

". . . Good people. I'm so pleased, Paul. So very pleased." His mother had met the Seavers, she had come east at great expense for his graduation from Exeter, she was coming again for commencement the following week. "The friendship of a great man can change one's life." She had nodded firmly. "I'm so pleased for you. They are the people who count."

This had troubled him—he'd turned with an awkward smile. "But all people count, don't they? Shouldn't they?"

Her eyes rose steadily to his. "Of course, dear. In that sense. But there are those who lead, who guide the common run of mankind." Her eyes were shining densely. "He sees it in you, you know."

"Sees what?"

"That quality." She smiled her secret, certain smile. "He recognizes it—Judge Seaver: he knows you're going to be one of the people who get things done."

He was shivering. He didn't know how long he'd been sitting on the bleached, splintered wood. It was what the Judge had said too, of course: that select little fraternity of duty, the people at the helm. Yet maybe too much adulation was a danger—maybe in the process you forfeited some of the self-reliance that made a man most exceptional of all. It was hard to say. Anyhow, it was over. He could not stay now, he'd have to go his own way. Into the army, and then the Rhodes and Foreign Service, if the war—

"—auuuuul . . ."

A figure was moving toward him, hanging in the indeterminate pale margin of the squall. Now running, he could see. A girl—it was Nell. Running wildly, calling to him. She seemed to make no progress in the terrific gray expanse of sand.

"*Paul . . . !*"

He eyed her approach with glum resentment. Yes, and now come hotfooting it after him. Oh, it was perfect! Another piece of absurdity, another petty crisis, and of course they were sorry, they were *always* sorry afterward, and he was expected to leap into the breach and pick up the pieces, mend, placate, set it all right again. The same, my lord, and thy poor servant ever. Well, he was sick of it, he was sick to death of putting it all right again. Faithful old Horatio wasn't going to leap into the breach this time. They could—

The girl swelled nearer suddenly, shrinking distance, her feet lifting and falling, her hair wild in the rain; her eyes were white with fear.

"Paul, come! Lee—he went in. The ball! . . ."

He got to his feet. She reached him, fell against him, trembling violently, gasping words. If he hadn't held her she would have fallen.

"In what?" he demanded. "In the surf, you mean? He actually—"

"Went after the ball—swam—after the ball. He's gone!" Her eyes rolled up at him without focus; he could feel the panic in her voice. "Oh-my-God *hurry,* Paul! Go back—!"

"Swimming in *that*—?" The God damned stupid fool! He glared down the beach, the wind-whipped charging sea, looked again at Nell, who had collapsed on the log, holding her side.

"You can't—stand there . . . like that!" Her eyes were hollow with accusation. "You can't—oh! Paul, he's in *trouble!* You're the only one—"

He started back up the beach then, walking angrily, kicking at the sand. The only one. Oh of course, Jesus, yes. Nell called something after him—a piercing, indistinct cry. He was trotting now, in mounting slow dread. Rounding the promontory he could make out figures, a dark little knot at the edge of the surf. Suddenly he was running hard, close along the sea's edge, where the sand was packed firmer. Rain stung his eyes. In the water nothing was distinct. They had seen him now, were waving frantically to him. Drawing nearer he caught a glimpse of a head beyond the first breaker line, in a swirling raw foam churning—gone all at once to reappear again, arms clutching and clawing in a frenzy. A towhead. Conklin. But Russ was no swimmer—

No one else was visible. Jesus. He pulled off his sweatshirt and kicked out of his slacks, looking for Russ again, measuring the seas. Someone was running toward him calling, but he paid no attention. He had only been in surf this rough once before—a gale off Monomoy, on a bet, and he'd been glad to get out of it after a few minutes, battered and weary; but then he'd had Jonesy and Bob Shawn, two good distance men, right there with him . . .

The water was shockingly cold. He gasped, wading hard, driving his thighs against the pull, hurrying toward the first breaker sweeping down in high-furling, implacable might—plunged under at the last second and felt the tremendous surge wrench him backward. He surfaced in a sliding white trough, pulling hard, dove again and thrust his way forward underwater, frog-kicking, again surfaced. He could see nothing in a wilderness of undertow and spoondrift. Waves were still bursting ahead of him in the shallows, bearing down like doom—one caught him unfairly, twisting, and sent him tumbling and writhing back through its driven gray-green mass. He went lower, fighting down fear, gasping for air each time he surfaced. He already felt tired. Glancing back once he saw that wind and current were driving him west from the fire, down toward Gay Head. This was bad, bad as it could be. Breaking water deep in another sliding trough he saw—or thought he saw—a leg or an arm. Gone again. Timing the next breaker he dove shallow and swam frantically through a tangled mat of torn seaweed and came on Conklin—an anguished face, dead white and straining. He knew that look—he'd worked as a lifeguard one summer at Nakesset Hollow. Grabbing the other man under the armpits he shouted, "Go back! Back in!—too much for you! . . ."

"—Can't . . ." Conklin's eyes fluttered open, closed again. "Can't— make it . . ."

Big one, breaking early. God, they were savage. He pulled Conklin down with him, felt the formidable tug of tons of water move them. When they rose again he called: "You see him? Lee?"

Russ shook his head numbly, his eyes closed; he had a stranglehold on Blackburn's neck. "Not after—I went in . . ."

"Which way was he headed?"

"Don't know . . ."

"Go back in, now! You can't stay in this!—" Blackburn waved frantically toward the little knot of figures in the shallows, left Conklin and pulled his way out through the tumbling, heaving seas, burdened with dread. He swam and struggled, he extended himself more than he ever had in the furious meets against Princeton and Yale, until his arms were so heavy he could barely lift them and his feet dangled like meaningless appendages strapped to his trunk. He dove again and again in the gray-green, swaying murk, straining to see—all at once found himself praying, a dull, fear-riven litany: *Oh God, please let me find him. Oh, have mercy. Let me find him. Oh please, God.* And still he dove, until his heart gripped in fiery bands and his stomach churned and blood was streaming from his nose—until in his sick exhaustion he could no longer even pray . . .

Finally, looking toward shore, he saw the battleship-gray jeep and several figures in black rubber suits; and gave up. The sea had beaten him, and now it swept him helpless toward shore with the ease of eternity until a final breaker, mightier and more pitiless than all the rest, took him up and flung him through a ponderous, strangling universe of darkness and violence, spun and crushed and battered him and spewed him into the terrible impact of another, and still another. Sobbing for air he struggled, a parody of swimming, until hands seized him and lifted him free to the sand, where he fell on all fours and retched and retched until his belly heaved in empty shuddering spasms. Later he lay wrapped in a blanket, smoke from the fire stinging his eyes; lay stunned and beaten, oblivious of all faces, all voices—even the wild, reproachful eyes of Eleanor Seaver—and cried as he had never cried before in all his life.

"And that's what happened to me." Blackburn drew a deep, slow breath and passed a hand through his hair. He felt all at once immensely tired and confused. Why had he insisted on telling this anguished tale? Outside the rain fell with a soft reluctance. The girl, sitting on the ratty old apricot couch facing him, nodded without smiling.

"So now the sea means death to you, as well. Death and—" she paused.

"Yes. And dereliction. I don't know why I told you all that."

"I'm glad you did."

"I just felt I had to. I've never told a soul. Isn't that strange?"

She shrugged. "That's how it always is: you guard something like that with your life—and then you throw it away in front of a total stranger. Maybe that's the best way, too.—Did they find his body?"

Blackburn shook his head. "Not the frogmen. Fishing boat picked it up two days later."

There was a pause. The girl was still staring at him with that astonishingly direct, stark gaze; without hostility. "I'm sorry," she said all at once. "It's hard to fail, isn't it?"

"—It's terrible," he heard himself answer. *"Terrible . . ."*

"I think you could use a drink." She rose in that electric way and then paused. As if entirely herself for the first time that afternoon she seemed embarrassed, ill at ease. "I guess I don't know what you offer a Secretary of State."

Slowly he smiled. "Even imperialist establishmentarians can use a whisky. Or gin. Whatever you have. Yes, I would like one."

She went over to the sink and poured whisky into two fat tumblers and brought them back to him and said: "Here goes nothing."

"Cheers," he answered.

"Is that why you married her—to prove him wrong?" Before he could even begin to answer she added, "Hey, I'm sorry. I shouldn't have said that. Land's made a few remarks here and there. It's none of my business—I know that. It's just that you're such a *personage.* An—emanation or something. You don't understand how it can be. It's like sitting in the same God damned room with Talleyrand."

"*Mentir et démentir*—the soul of diplomacy. I'll try to level with you a little better than Talleyrand."

"No, I mean you don't realize what you *mean* to people. Really. It's impossible to talk to you the way one can to just anybody—there's the big GATO Conference, and the Great Debate you had with al-Zobeir at Beirut and all that kind of thing. It's hard not to be afraid of you." She struck her front teeth with her thumbnail, musing. "It makes a person want to smack you in the face just to turn you into a human being—to *make* you be equal. Do you see what I mean?"

"Yes. I think so."

She looked at him a moment—that grave, steady glance; shook her head suddenly and said: "Well. You're not to blame. People are more important than ideas."

He found he was smiling. "Do my ears deceive me?"

"I know. After all the stuff I shouted at you. But it's what *people* think, not the thoughts . . . That's all mixed up, isn't it? True, though. Everyone's got his own private hair shirt, itching and scratching away, driving him crazy whenever he can't get his mind off it. Even the mighty like you. That's what my grandmother used to say, when some wealthy people would go by in a big car and furs and jewels and all that junk, and one of us would ooh-and-ah about it. 'Humph! Never know what's gnawing *their* vitals!' " Wryly she smiled. "And then after a while *we* had the cars and furs and jewelry, just like the good old American dream—and sure enough, things were gnawing our vitals, all right . . ."

She had been reared in Connecticut, first in a drab suburb of Bridgeport, then in fashionable Fairfield County, as the family fortunes improved. Her father was a stockbroker, and their lives reflected the feast-or-famine oscillations of the market speculator. "One Christmas he gave my mother a book—something about a British gentleman's travels in the Orient but that wasn't the point of it, he never read anything. But it had five hundred pages exactly—and inserted between each page was a ten dollar bill." She smiled her quick, wry smile. "Kind of a cute surprise, you see? Right out of Norman Rockwell. Only *next* month of course he had to come to her and ask for it all *back*. Pleasant little scene. We had quite a few of them. Kept you limber—if you were the good, elastic type. Mother wasn't." Her mother had been a Montana farm girl, and these incessant switches in resources and status terrified and finally unhinged her. She had to be institutionalized with increasing frequency during Jillie's adolescence. "Then *I* was head of the household—till off I went to dear old *Smith*." She bit off the last word tartly. "Lousy stinking country club—it ought to be burned to the ground. They divided their time with beautiful impartiality between bridge-playing, man-baiting, and man-hating. But I got through. I did what they wanted."

And then one evening in the summer after graduation she returned from visiting friends in New Hampshire to find her father alone in the kitchen, red-eyed, with a full glass of neat whisky trembling in his hands.

"Daddy—what's the matter?"

"You wouldn't understand. You wouldn't believe it if you did . . . To think—that they could do this to me. Oh! To *think*—" He was a heavy man with a weak, fleshy, handsome face and hair streaked on the sides with silver, and he was very drunk and weeping with shock and rage. "And I trusted them! God help me—I *trusted* the bastards . . ."

Shaken, confused—she had never seen her father like this—she understood very little at first. It had something to do with an attempt he and some associates had made to drive down the stock of an aerospace firm in order to take it over; and then some conglomerate had induced his friends to sell out to them without his knowledge, and now he was wiped out. "To think," he muttered. "Out of nowhere . . . Squashed like a fly against a wall—!"

She felt a dark cold fear deep in her belly. ". . . What about Mother?" she whispered.

His eyes wavered toward her, wavered away. "Well. I—you see, I had her put in Crowayton."

"Crowayton! But that's—that's a *state* asylum, that's a horrible place. Dad, you didn't do that—!"

His mouth went slack. "What could I do? She's past helping, you know that . . . I'm broke!" he cried. "I'm broke, Jillie, I'm through! I haven't got a dime to my name." He drank. "Anyway, you're all right," he muttered after a short silence. "You're graduated, you're all right."

"—So long as I find myself a nice, rich young boy," she burst out, "in a nice, rich brokerage house! Like you—is that it? Like you!"

His eyes were full of fear, pleading. "Honey, don't say that."

"So I can join the PTA and take my turn on the old car pool and watch *him* double-cross his best friend—in line of business, of course—"

"Honey, don't look at me like that . . ."

"You're everything that's wrong with this filthy world—you are!"

"Ah, don't say that, Jillie—you don't know . . . It's because I never had enough capital," he moaned, and he squeezed the nearly empty glass between his hands as though he might somehow force the necessary funds from its mouth. "If only I'd had enough *capital*—*!*"

She had left the house that night and stayed with friends. "I got into social work in New Haven for a while. And then I signed up for Bolivia. Oruro. Peace Corps volunteer. No more Lake poets, no more Lope de Vega. I wanted to get my hands into reality. I got it, with a big *R*." Her full, pretty mouth hardened. "I thought I'd seen a little in the way of poverty. Jesus. I hadn't scratched the top layer. They'd come out of the mines, the Aymaras, staggering, too exhausted to talk. Salamanca Tin Corporation, a subsidiary of Barstow Mining and Manufacturing. As you might imagine. Old men at thirty, wasting away with tin pest, the women hollow with cold and childbearing. And the kids—rickets and trachoma and hunger hunger hunger. It was all there, and they had it. And nobody cared about them, nobody even tried. Their little bellies were swollen and I was trying to teach them to *read*. Quaint. There was one little boy whose eyes were so bad—"

She broke off, shook her head violently. "I'm a weepy bitch today. It must be the weather. Anyway, what started me on my sinful path was when the baby died with this family I knew, and the man stayed away from the mines that day for the burial. And the cholo foreman beat him for it. 'My baby died,' Joaquin kept saying, and the foreman kept beating him. And then Joaquin apologized to the bastard. I couldn't believe it. I said: 'But why!—*why* did you apologize?' And he looked at me, so sadly, so hopelessly. 'Well,' he said, 'I had no right to be absent.' 'You did!' I told him, I was almost out of my mind by then, '—you have more right than anyone!' 'No,' he said, and he shook his head over and over. 'I have no right.' I couldn't get over it. I thought, If a man—a human being—is ashamed because he leaves that black hole of hell for one day to bury his baby—

"Hopeless, hopeless. It was like trying to shovel a dry path across Cape Cod Bay. And down in La Paz the rich slobs with their villas and Ferraris and Pucci gowns and Gucci loafers. After just so much of this you saw you had only two choices: do a brain-scramble on yourself and slink back to the old system, or join the people who were fighting for land reform, nationalization of the mines."

That was where she had met Lachlan Smith, who was in Bolivia with a technical assistance group. Through him she met survivors of the suppressed PIR and helped carry out a raid on the big Barstow warehouse in Oruro. "God, we were such amateurs. We did everything wrong—and it worked. We got food and blankets and money, and we got away clean. And we gave the stuff to people with our own hands. I was terrified right through the whole thing, but I did it." Her jaw set. "And I'd do it again, tomorrow."

On her return to the States she joined the New Left. She showed a real talent for organizing demonstrations, and her work in Bolivia had earned her authority with the Movement's leaders. She moved up rapidly in the councils. She took part in the bitter factional struggles for control of SDS and the march on the Pentagon, where she was beaten and jailed; and finally found herself in one of the Weatherman collectives during the Violent Summer of '69. "I'd lost Dave the year before, I hated everything and everybody, I didn't know *what* I thought by then. That was the trouble with the Movement by that time—it was too much. Everyone was living out his own home-movies of Czarist nihilists or Maoist sons-of-the-soil, or some freaky sad thing."

Blackburn murmured: "It seems so unlike you. Weatherman."

"Isn't it?" She gave her quick, wry grin. "Well, you're right. I couldn't hack it. I was one of those who got purged. Too weak, they said. It was really crazy finally, the whole scene. Kids like Terry and Bill and Diana, good people essentially but they'd gone over the rim after Chicago. Any rational thought was hateful, they didn't even *try* to argue principles any more. The Blacks and the grease and the little old ladies in Keokuk were all going to follow them because they'd turned outlaw, because they'd cut every tie. What they refused to see was that there wasn't a single black auto worker or white machinist who would blink one eye if they all held hands and dived into a lake of fire in Lincoln Park.

"You can't imagine what it was like in the collectives then. No one could who wasn't there. Karate practice at three AM, all-day fasts to save bail money for busted members, briefings on police interrogation, explosives. Shades drawn at all times, windows wired, doors barred with timbers. Everyone hungry and snapping at everyone else. Regis Debray couldn't have dreamed it up if he'd tried . . ."

But the trashing sessions were the worst of all. Group Criticism to self-criticism to transformation. Sitting crosslegged on the stained mattresses under the bulb's mean yellow glare, a litany of accusation and denial; on and on and on.

"—of course you don't see any *need* for it, for the simple reason that you're still hung up on your smart-ass bourgeois Smith–station wagon–Bonwit Teller values . . ."

"That's not true, I hate all that, I've hated it for years—"

"—all part of the same disgusting individualistic shit, Hoyt. You think you're past it but you're not. Well, that's got to be flushed right out of your skull!" Terry, his face hollow and white and wild, his fist high over his head. "You're a tool of the revolution now, you haven't *got* any outs. Dig? Your thoughts aren't your own, your life isn't your own, you're in up to the guts!"

A brief silence. The light from the bulb stung her eyes, her belly hurt. They were waiting for her to say something. Criticism becomes self-criticism becomes transformation. Maybe. But into what? Into just *what?*

"I fail to see," she said doggedly, "why revolutionary motivation has to subject every last private thought and feeling to group analysis. Why it has to mean screwing every stud in the whole crew . . ."

"Because it's the only way you're going to get over your obstructionist obsessions," Karen said sharply, her narrow mouth working. "We smashed monogamy in Cleveland, it's out, you know that. But you still think you're too good for us."

"No, I don't think I'm—"

"Of course you do, you're still hung up on your sacred little middle-class pussy! What are you saving it for—that poor slob that got himself knocked off in Vietnam?"

"You bitch," she said. "You dirty rotten no-good bitch."

"Got to you, didn't it?" This from Terry, gleefuily. "Because it's still there, you see? How do you think you can stick a pig with a knife if you can't stop *feeling?* How do you think you can bomb a restaurant, women and babies, Hoyt, can you do it? *Can* you?"

"—No," she said dully, "no, I can't."

"Now I'll tell you what *that* is—that's just plain bourgeois and defeatist. And defeatism equals individualism and individualism equals counterrevolutionary obstructionism!"

"There's no logic to that, no logical basis for—"

"Oh shit! An *intellectual.* Logic, we're not into logic, we're into action and action alone!"

"Oh great, just like the Nazis!" She was crying now, it was impossible to keep from crying after just so many hours of this. "How to take the D out of SDS—"

"You're a cheap bitch, that's what *you* are. And always will be. You refuse to submit to the discipline." Tom's voice now, low, flat, inexorable. "I vote she be purged from this collective."

The faces ringing her were all alike, eyes suffused with the same terrible, exultant glare. Fearfully she gazed back at them. Were these dirty, wolf-eyed creatures the same eager kids she'd marched with at Lincoln Park? Was she herself? That honest defiance—had it all been ripped away? They want it, she thought all at once and shockingly, it's what they've come to. They will kill now, they're ready.

"I felt as if I'd been hypnotized for months and somebody had just slapped my face. Wide awake. All it meant was death. And they wanted it —theirs and everyone else's. They weren't going to *accomplish* one fucking thing for the whole human race . . . I went out that door and heard the bar thump down behind me and I was still crying but I never looked back once. And you know what? It was a blue-clear summer morning. Christ, I hadn't even known what *year* it was."

She took a deep breath and shook back her hair. "I came straight on to Cambridge and enrolled in some courses, got a job as a secretary. And here I am. So to speak. Life story."

There was a little pause. Blackburn sipped moodily at his drink. "And yet you're Lachlan Smith's assistant in Sirius."

Her glance was quick and penetrating. "Oh, I believe what I believe, all right. Don't make any mistake about that. But those heavy days are gone. When Weatherman burned the SDS files on West Madison on New Year's Eve and went underground they slammed the cover. Rage-in-the-Streets had turned everybody off, and in their guts they knew it. The Smith-Hoyt Formula has been vindicated. Keep your cool and hold your fire, man. We're moving more intelligently now."

"I hope so," Blackburn answered. He paused. "What happened to him?"

"Who?"

"Your father."

Her chin came up. "I haven't the faintest idea. I haven't laid eyes on him for six years. I'm told he's a salesman for a wallboard firm."

"You're not through punishing him, then."

"Maybe not." She bit at a hangnail, severely. "Yes, I guess that's it. I'll tell you one thing: I try not to lie to myself about things. I had enough of that at home. Enough and to spare. I know you think I'm a bitch, and maybe you're right—but at least I'm going to be an honest bitch. Not the current American model. Look, I refuse—I absolutely refuse to deceive myself about the hypocrisy and cruelty going on in this great big laughing academy."

It was curious: sitting deep in the faded armchair he had the impression that her features had softened, relaxed in gentler planes—or maybe it was only the early evening light sifting in through the window. The rain had stopped; somewhere in the pinched alleyway there was a slow, musical dripping. Our lives are molded by happenstance, he thought somberly, by caprice, by unlooked-for catastrophe and extenuating circumstance—and we present our sad little briefs to one another, plead our own cases. How desperately we need to do it! None of us is consummate culprit, none unparagoned judge: how many times do I have to learn that? . . .

The girl was talking about Cambridge now, about her job in Fudgy Hannig's office, about her love of Yeats, about the Anderson boy who'd been killed in the big Tet Offensive back in '68; and he listened to her attentively; watching the way her face kept catching bits and facets of light as it moved, the mirror dance of her eyes, the fine mobility of her mouth, the way her open hand would cut the air in sudden emphasis. All the hard, vengeful hostility was gone. Essentially she was a reflective, gentle creature—this made her vulnerable and so she resorted to cruelty, anticipating cruelty and rejection by others. Thresholds. Bemused, aroused in some strange way he did not understand, he saw her plain, immaculate, fragile, stripped of invective or dogma, the Medusa glare. And was moved . . .

A bell tolled thunderously. Memorial Hall tower—he would have recognized it anywhere in the world. They were still within reach of the University. He got to his feet and set down his glass.

"I'm afraid I must go," he said. He felt curiously awkward, and this puzzled him. "I want to apologize. I had no business coming here. Dropping in on you like this." Her face expressed a vast surprise, which pleased him. "Your life is your own, yours and Land's—God knows I don't even need to say it. I came for—ancillary reasons."

She was smiling. "Ancillary?"

"Unworthy, yes. I won't intrude on you again." He ran his eyes along a shelf of books: Thucydides, Colette, Stendhal, Camus, Bakunin—and at the far end a photo clipped from some magazine and tacked to the wood, of a woman, an Oriental woman swimming, laughing into the sunlight. No, that wasn't quite it. He bent forward to see better—realized with a sharp small shock his eyes had deceived him. The woman was indeed in the water, swimming—or fording—a deep stream, but one arm clutched desperately at some kind of liana lifeline, the other supported a feeble old woman, a baby was clinging like a leech to her neck; her mouth was parted and her eyes were shining, but with a distracted terror so vast she did not know which way to move—backward to death and spoliation, forward to—

He thought suddenly of Michael Williams the night before Agincourt, and the King; murmured: *"That's more than we know."* All at once he wanted to be off by himself, holed up somewhere in a cabin on the edge of a far expanse of still water, rereading Thucydides and Camus. He said: "That's the trouble with government service, public life—you get a distorted idea of your ability to solve problems that aren't properly your own. That are sometimes best let alone to solve themselves . . ." She was still staring at him—a frank and troubled gaze, utterly ingenuous, as though he had mesmerized her in some nefarious way. He said: "May we be friends? you and I?"

"—Of course." She leaped up with that flowing quicksilver alacrity and extended her hand. He took it—and now it was unmistakable: a surge of current, swift, consensual, excitant. Her features underwent a quick little tremor; they released each other's grasp in haste.

"I saw you once," she was saying, moving ahead of him toward the door. "I was going down the hall and you were coming out of Professor Marsh's office. It was just before you went to Washington. He made some remark about somebody high up in the government, I've forgotten who, and you laughed and said, 'I know—he'll always be controlled by the most disagreeable person around him. Perhaps I can qualify.' Do you remember that?" Blackburn shook his head. "And I glared at you and thought, Yes, by God, you certainly could!" For the first time that afternoon she smiled fully—a radiant opening of her features that made him think of suddenly revealed sunlight in the midst of a squall on the Sound. She forgave as readily as she attacked, this girl. "But you're not disagreeable at all."

"Oh, I can be downright obnoxious—you should see me in action."

"I have!" She laughed now, and shook her head. "But you're not *basically* disagreeable, is what I mean. You seem too—I don't know: too gentle to be Secretary of State."

"Too gentle?"

"No, I don't mean that either." She put her hand to her throat. "I don't know what I mean . . . It's as if you're beyond all that fakery and backstabbing. Better than all that."

"We're none of us any better than what we do," he said.

Her sea-green eyes were very wide. "Do you believe that?"

"Absolutely. I'd stake my life on it." He smiled slowly, held again in that groundswell of affinity. "Blackburn's Law. Nine-C. And I'd better be getting back to doing it, too. Goodbye."

"Goodbye," she said.

Outside the air was cool, clearing northwest in a dusk as dense as smoke. When he got in behind the wheel he was surprised to find that his heart was beating as if he'd swum a mile.

SIX

"It's a bit puzzling, I'll admit," Sheldon Tremayne said. Setting the single piece of paper on his desk he snapped it with thumb and middle finger. It spun on the point made by the four-way fold, spun round and round on the polished wood. *Faites vos jeux,* Blackburn thought, watching it; *faites vos jeux, 'sieurs-et-dames.* When he looked up again Tremayne was frowning at him. "I don't know what to tell you, Paul," the CIA Director went on. "I doubt if we have much more on it than you do. Of course Naungapaya's people have been recruiting for some time. You knew that."

"Even Europeans and Americans, Shelly?"

"Why not? Conquest needs its technicians, like anything else."

"Shades of Katanga, eh?"

"Competrin's had its professionals out there for some time. And there's the usual assortment of comic-opera types—cashiered military, stranded engineers, drifters. It's a kind of end-of-the-line place, you know."

"I know."

Tremayne leaned back in his chair, hands behind his head. "Where there ain't no Ten Commandments, and a man can raise a thirst . . . Chid Jackson bailed out over there in World War Two. C-Forty-Seven. Engine quit and he hit the silk. Said he wandered around in there for days without seeing a soul, creeping up and down the mountain sides, frozen half to death. Finally some people found him. Lisus. Women wear great wide turbans and have silver bangles hanging all over them. Chid said the women wanted to go to bed with him and the men wanted to put him in a pot and eat him. No Ten Commandments, all right."

The two men smiled. Sitting hunched forward, elbows on his knees, Blackburn found himself watching the CIA man with the old familiar twinge of envy, half-amused at himself. Sheldon Tremayne was easily the handsomest man he'd ever known—there were the prettily sculptured features of the matinee idol of the Twenties, but harder, more virile. Someone at Universal had actually given him a screen test on graduation from Amherst, and for a short time he'd contemplated a film career; but oddly it had never gone to his head. Nubile girls gaped at him in idiotic admiration, even self-possessed embassy secretaries fluttered or forgot their lines—Blackburn had seen them—yet Shelly remained for all that a good family man who took his kids to see the Redskins at Kennedy Stadium and passed canapés deferentially for his wife, a moderately handsome German woman he'd met during a tour of duty in Bonn.

In one of those curious coincidences that link people's lives, he and Blackburn had both been freshmen Foreign Service Officers at Isfahan—though for Shelly the post had already been a cover. One of the youngest of the "Knights Templar," that urbane, dedicated and—it was often thought—overzealous group who ran the intelligence establishment in the adventurous days of the Fifties and Sixties, Tremayne had carried out his missions skillfully—the drops, the secret rendezvous and guileful ruses; then he had adapted just as smoothly to the shift from flamboyant derring-do to the lower profile of objective information-gathering and cautious appraisal effected by Helms. If he missed the good old days of cabal and coven he never showed it. He and Blackburn had served together later on the Burma-Thai border dispute commission; and the Secretary had found him controlled, resourceful, open to suggestion.

Reporters had become fond of coupling them in articles—their charm, their poise, their curiously entwined careers: the Looks and Brains of the Administration, Tyrone Power and Adlai Stevenson come to government, two national security managers who could collaborate brilliantly on some thorny problem, furnish a generous amount of the wit a few hours later at a Washington party, and wind up the evening over a chessboard with a scotch and water. In fact it was largely a press invention. Blackburn liked Shelly well enough, he respected his competence, but something in him deplored the Director's long years in the hooded caverns of the CIA, and he knew Tremayne had disapproved of his own two resignations from State as sophomoric indulgences inconsistent with government service. Their wives disliked each other intensely.

"But to accuse a good-will mission like this one of fomenting insurrection," Blackburn muttered aloud. "He isn't out-and-out crazy by any chance, is he? I never heard of such a flimsy pretext for power-grabbing in all my life."

"I told you that one would bear watching,"

"It doesn't make any sense. Why should the Russians get involved in something like this? Ragozhin wouldn't be that stupid. Or sly, either."

"That I'm not so sure of."

"But Shelly—a hare-brained scheme like this . . ."

"If it's true."

"If it's true, sure."

Tremayne studied his fingertips. "My own feeling, for what it's worth, is: it's all a little adventure Naungapaya's got infatuated with."

"Where does he think that's going to get him? International arbitration—the UN airing—is his only hope and he knows it. He wouldn't last six weeks against Bodawyin, even in that country. And the Chinese—! Besides, I made it abundantly clear to him just five days ago that we weren't going to tolerate any war dances." Impatiently he ran his fingers through his hair. "If he blows this sky-high, after all the work we put in on it, I'll personally wring his scrawny playboy neck for him."

"You might have done that long ago, as far as we're concerned," Tremayne said with a trace of reproach. "Now he's a head of state."

"He's *not* a head of state. Not yet, he isn't—it's a provisional government until UN ratification, and he knows it."

"People's appetite for vanity is boundless, Paul. They surround themselves with a little army of schemers and yes men and everything begins to look like a diabolically clever piece of statecraft . . . Consider Hassan Dagh: sitting there in that collapsing fleabag of a palace telling me he would accept nothing but full and immediate Anglo-American withdrawal —the poor sod didn't have three hundred men he could rely on, and he'd worked himself up into believing he was the new Genghis Khan."

Fuming, half-listening, Blackburn let his gaze wander around the room. There were no windows. Illumination came from cleverly concealed honeycomb clusters in the ceiling and walls: a light without shadows, depthless and oddly disconcerting. From somewhere behind him—or above him —came the purling, favonian hum of an air conditioner; there was no other sound. No dirt, no sunlight, no dust or birdsong could penetrate these sleek beige walls. Over here there was none of the ponderous, cranky chaos of State—that damned old Byzantine bat's nest, Sid Jacobi had once called it in a fit of frustration—and yet Blackburn liked it better that way; the confusion and additions and renovations reminded people they were human beings, fallible, hopeful, concerned. Out here at Langley everything was quick and silent and efficient, couched deep in woodland and supported by that legendary, covert expense budget. Invulnerable to inquiry . . .

Inaudibly Blackburn sighed. The fact was we loved secrecy, inside maneuver, skullduggery—our perennial American fascination with whodunits and espionage thrillers spawned and abetted it: if a matter was secret it *must* be important, crucial—far beyond what we average citizens could ever hope to encompass. "They" knew things we didn't (obviously— else why would they have this $46,000,000 hideaway in the Potomac woods?), "their" decisions were therefore both momentous and exotic, wise beyond our troubled ken. The only difficulty was, *"they"*—suitably boiled down—meant dapper Shelly Tremayne who, as the romantic lead in the Scheherazade Players' benefit performance of *The Masquerader,* had wrecked the production by dropping two crucial lines in the second act; who had been one of the most vociferous champions of the Bay of Pigs operation, and ten years after that had pressed for the ill-starred Laotian "incursion" . . .

"You're sure you're not making too much of this, Paul?"

Blackburn raised his head. The CIA Director's right eyebrow was cocked at him. "An episode like this—my God, they're a dime a dozen. Look at that Uruguayan flap."

He nodded without smiling. "Maybe," he said. "Maybe I am. It's easy to do in this business."

Joe Carter had brought the report in to his office at ten that morning, right after he'd finished talking with Archie Grace at the United Nations.

"This may be just a tempest in a China teapot, Mr. Secretary. But you said you wanted to see anything out of Dhotal."

The provisional state of Dhotal was thrown into more confusion yesterday when the forces of Prince Naungapaya, in a dramatic and perplexing move, seized all members of the International Rescue and Reclamation Mission and have been holding them incommunicado. In a statement issued this morning from Pao Shan, Naungapaya angrily denounced the mission as "This sinister scheme by the imperialist superpowers to spread dissension in a people's democracy standing on the threshold of a unique destiny," and promised "swift and pitiless punishment." The reference was presumably to the United States and Soviet teams, principal participants in the mission organized as part of the New Delhi Pact to bring relief to the areas devastated by three years of bitter struggle on the China-Burma border.

A particularly virulent strain of cholera has broken out in the vicinity of Lushui and Meng-p'eng, further devastating those areas most ravaged by the Sino-Burmese conflict. Meng-p'eng is the site of the new flood control project for the Upper Salween, where the mission under the overall leadership of Dr. Kurt Drachenfels had already begun preliminary work before its seizure.

When queried about Prince Naungapaya's action, Chinese authorities refused to comment officially, although one highly placed official expressed grave concern. Rioting has reportedly broken out in Pao Shan itself—

He looked up. Carter's eyes were dark with worry. "It's a Reuters dispatch, Mr. Secretary."

"Who's their man out there—Daetwyler, isn't it?"

"Yes, sir. He's always been reliable enough."

"Nothing from our people?"

"Not as yet."

Blackburn bent the sheet of paper back and forth in his hands, aware of a quick surge of exasperation. The Burman guv us Irrawaddy chills. Why was it everything of unknown origin had to be the product of someone's malevolence? But to *seize the mission*—

"Has Sid seen this?" he asked.

"No, sir. He's at the meeting."

"What meeting?"

"Under Secretary Stout's staff meeting, sir."

"Oh, Jesus. Is he still holding those?"

Blackburn groaned. Walla-walla time in old Foggy Bottom. When he'd first come into the Department under Rusk, that inscrutable, ceremony-rapt soul had held a staff meeting from 9:15 till 10:00. Then, liberated from that, they had all attended the Under Secretary's staff meeting on operations from 10:00 until 10:45—whereupon the assistant secretaries were to inform *their* staffs of what had gone on at the previous two convocations. After that, it was the turn of the deputy assistant secretaries. For all Blackburn knew, the ritual reached on down to the janitors. By then of course it was time for lunch. "Day half gone and nothing done yet," the Judge had used to say with wintry Yankee humor; which was about the size of it.

As far as Blackburn was concerned staff meetings served only two valid functions—to impart essential information quickly and easily, and to give subordinates a sense of participation in large events; beyond that they usually fell foul of either excessive caution or dissension, and they devoured time and energy like seven-year locusts. As Secretary he'd cut his own staff meetings to one a week, and let it be known he frowned on the practice generally—an observation that horrified Stout and Spofford and most of the Old Guard, who promptly spread rumors that the new chief was bent on destroying State in one fell blow. For a while his disapproval had stopped the daily ritual, and things got done; but then, like some creeping fungus, they'd started up again. The trouble was that Miles loved to hold them. Whether there was anything of importance to be covered or not, they gave him the sense of ordering each day neatly, a sense of moving in the minuet paces of hallowed procedure. State Forever, stately . . .

"I don't seem to be able to get that point over, do I?" he said aloud. "Call him out, will you, Joe?"

"Who—Secretary Stout?"

"God, no—it'd ruin his entire week. Just get Sid." And as the Acting Assistant Secretary swung away, "And Joe: unobtrusively—casually. I don't want to start wild-eyed rumors flying around."

Alone he read the dispatch again, fighting his anger. Sinister scheme to spread dissension. Of course Daetwyler hadn't been up there himself, that was obvious—the piece was datelined Chungking. The man might simply have been low on copy and seized on some rumors. Or it could be a hoax, some lurid invention of Naungapaya's to stir things up again. He let his hand fall to the desk with a thump. If that sloe-eyed, saxophone-tooting playboy had taken it into his head to play the swashbuckling bravo after he'd given them all a solemn promise to submit the entire matter to arbitration; if he actually thought he was going to jeopardize the labor of months, the finest uphill victory they'd achieved in three harassed years—

In the corner of his office next to the walnut Chippendale secretary from the Paling the huge illuminated globe seemed to float in space, offering its illusion of unity. He'd always loved globes—that prevalence of blue . . .

So many seas: he had seen most of them: the Indian glittering like an anvil under the sun's hammer, the Aegean a hard salt lapis against its white-walled upslanting villages; the feathery, milk-and-hyacinth iridescence of the Mediterranean, the Caribbean streaked with brilliant amber and indigo bands under the purple headlands . . . All that wide blue canopy flowing serenely around the divided continents, the discordant, multicolored nations, binding them all together. Sea. Nell saw water as the end of land, the way her Great-Grandmother Tirzah did, waiting implacably for treasure to be brought her over its threatful expanse; for him it had always been a beginning, fount and origin, the elemental source of life. As a boy he'd loved nothing so much as to read about the voyages of Hakluyt and da Gama and Frobisher and Cook, his mind dancing with mighty deeds on far horizons . . .

He got to his feet and walked over and pushed at the globe with his fingers; it rotated slowly, silently, came to rest again. Under his eyes Southeast Asia hung voluminously in the cobalt-and-azure swirls of the Pacific, lopsided scrotal sack and absurdly wasted member; lure and graveyard of the American expansionist dream. He had turned to the Atlantic as the mood-filled bridge between his country and the European legator; but it had been the Pacific that had pursued him, sought him out again and again. At times it seemed to him that half his troubles had stemmed from that tormented corner of Asia. There had been Khotiane, and later the Vietnam agony; on the Burma-Thailand boundary dispute commission he'd caught malaria and lain sweating and shivering in a room at the embassy in Rangoon, visited by all the lurching hobgoblins of fancy while the sun, an immense, red-hot ingot, slid into the jungle and night fell like a thrown cloak . . .

When Jacobi came in he handed him the dispatch without comment.

"—Why, the pimp!" Sid exploded. "The dirty little sneak. After all his rutting royal word about doing nothing to rock the boat—"

"If it's true."

"If it's true, sure . . ." Sobered by Blackburn's impassive manner the Special Assistant chafed his ear furiously. "Swift and pitiless punishment—for what? What's he after?"

"Something diabolical."

"Hostages, then." Jacobi nodded, his lips compressed. "Leverage toward some kind of concession."

"I've thought that, too," Blackburn said slowly. "The Indians have got a team there, the Japanese, the Thais—"

"But what's he stand to gain? It sounds crazy, completely crazy from any logical point of view. And the *Chinese*—that's all they'll need . . ."

Peering out toward Arlington, the Lee Mansion, Jacobi screwed his eyes into slits, looking rather Chinese himself. "Only thing is—"

There was a brisk knock and Katherine Ross, Blackburn's secretary, stepped inside the room, eased the door closed behind her and said: "Mr. Secretary, you have that appointment with Ambassador U Mein Thaw."

"Oh, no!" Blackburn protested. "Not today—I'm not up to it." He grinned. "Do I have to see him, Kitty?"

"You'll be sorry if you don't." She was a thin, wiry woman with a long pointed nose and pale, almost waxlike skin. "He's in the Monroe Room now with Assistant Secretary Carter."

"All right. Better face it." He turned again to Sid. "The only thing is—?"

"It—it has the ring of authenticity . . ."

"I agree. Let's do some checking. Can you? Are you free?"

"Yes, sir."

"Who's up at Pao Shan? Umphlett, isn't it?"

"That's who. Our problem boy himself."

"Let's get off a flash to him, see what he knows. Then contact Tom Van Kleeck in Peking and Stew Davis down in Rangoon. Somebody must know something, even if it *is* the Department."

"There's always a chance."

"I mean, if he's actually going to try and play T. E. Lawrence it'd be peachy to know a little something about it. When you get a chance, tell Joe's people I want all messages to China and Burma desks to come to me direct from now on. Okay?"

Jacobi got up. "Right, Chief."

"And keep checking with the wire room, will you? There's got to be a Chinese reaction somewhere along the line . . ."

Ambassador U Mein Thaw was a round little man with incredibly smooth, drum-tight skin and large liquid oval eyes. He had been educated at Oxford and his pride in his proficiency in the English language was exceeded only by an overweening obsession with archaic turns of phrase. Conversations with him were like a weird time-machine audience with some Jacobean functionary. After one such session Blackburn had referred to him as the Lexicorn—and the sobriquet had raced through the Department's higher echelons. Whether it had ever reached the ears of the Burmese Ambassador Blackburn had no idea; there were times when he fervently hoped so. For now, he knew the Ambassador would be apprehensive over the New Delhi Treaty and especially the Naungapaya agreement. He nodded to Carter and greeted the Ambassador with forced cordiality.

U Mein Thaw made a bouncy little bow. "I trust you will not find it amiss were I to jubilate over your fortuitous recursion to your native littoral, Mr. Secretary." Blackburn agreed that it was indeed good to be

back home. "Might the occasion have been vouchsafed you for a perusal
of the splendiferously bedizened Black Pagoda at Kanarak?"

"Uh—no, I'm immensely sorry, Mr. Ambassador. I wanted to, of
course, but there simply wasn't time. As you can imagine."

The Burman's eyes began to shine still more wetly. "A veritable
morisco of erotomanic pererration!"

Blackburn nodded gravely, thinking of Owen Spandrell, former Officer in Charge at Calcutta, who had studied every erotic façade in all India
with fanatical zeal, and who, it was said, had approached every situation
in thirty years with a closed mind and an open fly. He kept his eyes resolutely deflected from Carter.

Ambassador U Mein Thaw caught himself up all at once with a
quick little quiver and coughed behind his hand. "Ah, I fear that must
suffice for such *plaisanteries*. You are aware that my government has been
deeply distressed by the direction of the negotiations at New Delhi."

"I'm sorry to hear that, Mr. Ambassador."

The Lexicorn sighed, and scratched delicately a smooth olive cheek.
"The infelicities of the diplomatic existence . . ." He thereupon unfurled
a highly baroque disquisition on the Burmese government's extreme apprehension over Prince Naungapaya's premature assumption of power in
Dhotal, expressed fears of a revival of Chinese expansionism and the increased dangers of a new border war in the Triangle; and closed with the
inevitable plea for $15,000,000,000 in foreign credits and matériel. Black-
burn and Carter tried to sound reassuring yet noncommittal. The talk
again turned to lighter vein; and at long last U Mein Thaw rose to take
his departure.

"This has been a source of coruscating delectation, as always, Mr.
Secretary."

"Yes. It's been—thoroughly enjoyable." Moving toward the door
with the Burmese Blackburn felt himself twitching with impatience. He
had an almost ungovernable impulse to thump the little man between the
shoulder blades, tell some raw and ribald story and roar with laughter.
God keep me from ever taking myself seriously, he thought with a little
shiver: the day I do I'm done for . . .

But at the door the Lexicorn turned again. "I partake of the sentiment that you have not encountered any unforeseen impeditions, Mr. Secretary. The Asian world finds itself in a condition that is—what shall I
say?—dementate?"

"Dementate is the word, Mr. Ambassador."

"Burma is so vulnerable. We crouch between the eagle and the
dragon, so to speak . . . I flatter myself that you will seek to apprise my
government of any minacious eventualities." The Burman's large liquid
eyes showed no change whatever; his full red lips curved upward in the

most gracious of smiles. He knows, then, Blackburn thought with increased irritation. He's got wind of it already; of course.

"You can be assured my government will honor our commitments to any member of the Greater Asian Treaty Organization, Mr. Ambassador," he answered.

"Even under circumstances which might prove to be most—teratical?"

Jesus Christ. Teratical. The Burman's eyes now held an unmistakable glint of amusement. He forced himself to smile once more. "This world is full of monsters, Mr. Ambassador—and wonders, too. Let's hope we can slay the former and dance to the latter."

U Mein Thaw laughed and bowed. "An inspiriting thought! I will cling to it, Mr. Secretary." He bounced away over the thick beige carpeting.

After the Lexicorn, Blackburn met with Mondabele of the new Pan-African Federation, and after that had luncheon with Kleist and Hagendorn, who were pressing hard for a new trade agreement with Bonn. He was back in his office going over his briefing book and scanning the flood of cables when Jacobi came in.

"It's for real, chief. Something is, anyway. Here's Van's flash."

FM AMEMBASSY PEKING
TO SECSTATE WASHDC
CLAS PEKING 97Ø5
    ENTIRE INTERNATIONAL MISSION IN CUSTODY DHOTALESE PROVISIONAL GOVERNMENT. BEST AVAILABLE SOURCES INDICATE NAUNGAPAYA IN COMMAND OF SUBSTANTIAL MILITARY FORCE DEPLOYING SOUTH TOWARD LASHIO OVER OLD BURMA ROAD. FOREIGN MINISTRY OFFICE WOULD NEITHER CONFIRM NOR DENY WIDESPREAD REPORTS CHINESE FORCES MOVING TO SEAL OFF YUNNAN-BURMA BORDER AS "PRECAUTIONARY MEASURE" IN EVENT DHOTALESE-BURMESE HOSTILITIES. REQUEST INSTRUCTIONS SOONEST. VAN KLEECK, PEKING.

"Best available sources." Blackburn was conscious of a slow, fanning ripple of dismay, then a dart of anger. "What does he mean, *substantial*—five hundred or fifty thousand? Ministry office—why doesn't he dig out Ch'en Pu-tsao himself? What's he waiting for, a bloody engraved invitation? I've told you, Van's too reticent at times like this. Doesn't he see he's got to act *now*, before everybody starts hauling out his saber and playing hero? I don't like this, I don't like the way this is going at all . . . What have we got from Umphlett?"

"Nothing, sir."

"*Nothing!* Didn't you get off a flash to him?"

Jacobi nodded. "There's been no reply out of Pao Shan at all. There's something fishy there. Flnch told me a routine cable started coming in last night, requesting supplies for Drachenfels' people—earth-movers, dozers, demolitions, stuff like that. And then it just broke off. Of course they've got to encode by hand out there. Could be nothing more than some routine foul-up."

"Hell, yes—let's make sure it's just routine, just the normal state of affairs . . ."

The joys of command. Something happened out at the far corners of the world, in Nootka Sound or Pakanbaru, and you struggled to find out what its components were, in order to chart a deft and responsible course. Your representative in the general area knew more than you did—but not enough, not nearly enough; and your man on the precise spot (assuming of course there *was* a man on the spot) knew still more—perhaps knew the very elements that could unlock the riddle. If you could contact him, that was: if he was where he could relay some of that indispensable knowledge, and if he possessed that rare-as-rubies ability to winnow the important from the trivial. And here at the nerve center—Jesus! the *nerve center* —you sat, and waited, and fumed, wild for tangibles you could hold in your two hands, the blessed marlinspikes that alone could pry open the knot. There were times when you felt, like tart John Adams, that the best solution was to recall *every* overseas minister and be done with it. For the second time that morning he thought of Jillian Hoyt and her fierce, monolithic view of him as the omniscient wielder of power, and smiled grimly.

"Well, let's let it simmer. We've got to have more scoop than this. That God damned, epicene Lexicorn knows more than we do. Get off another flash to Pao Shan, will you, Sid? And give Van the needle, tell him to contact Umphlett by goat cart if he has to. He must be up there somewhere . . ."

"I hope so, chief." Jacobi paused, his thin bony hands on the edge of the desk. "There may be a problem there."

"Umphlett's all right," Blackburn replied, a shade tartly. "He just needs to gain a little confidence, that's all."

"Yes, I know—that's what you're always saying."

The two men looked at each other, thinking their arguments. Clarence Umphlett was an introspective young man with staring, nearsighted eyes and a prominent Adam's apple that pulsed rhythmically when he was excited. He was intelligent, hard-working, fluent in both Burmese and Mandarin—a great rarity—and his field reports were brilliant. The trouble was that he had an unfortunate way of putting things—he was always being misconstrued. Up at Hankow, two years before, Van Kleeck had come upon him unshaven, his clothing rumpled, asleep at his desk, and had asked him rather testily what was wrong. Umphlett, raising haggard eyes, replied that he'd just lost his wife. Abashed and mortified—why hadn't someone informed him about this?—his chief, ordinarily an un-demonstrative Dutchman, gave such comfort as he could, sent him home for a good rest, and made arrangements for emergency leave—only to find out several hours later that a handsome Portuguese copra trader, not the Grim Reaper, had taken Nancy Umphlett to his bosom. Earlier there had been the seaman from a Soviet freighter who had sought asylum at the embassy; Umphlett had described him as Polish; the Russians had maintained he was Russian and demanded his return. It turned out the sailor was from Vilna—from "Old," prewar Poland. By the time Van Kleeck had learned the seaman was indeed a Soviet citizen the affair had become very strained indeed.

The nautical associations in both episodes, coupled with a forlorn attachment to the daughter of a member of the Brazilian trade commission, had been too much for the wits in East Asian and Pacific. Poor Umphlett became known (surreptitiously) as "Cockswain"—Meskill, economic officer at Canton, who had given him the nickname, even insisted on the archaic spelling to drive the point home a bit further. Blackburn nevertheless liked Umphlett and defended him. What the boy needed was increased responsibility, he'd decided—a post where he could make full use of his talents, free of Van's forbidding exactitude. He'd had him transferred to Pao Shan to a chorus of dark predictions. Now it looked as though some of them might be coming true.

"The only thing," Jacobi was saying now, "is whether you'll be able to put any credence in what he says, if he does give us anything."

"Don't worry about him, Sid. He'll be all right. Remember Bob Rossow up at Teheran, in Forty-Six? cabling all that dynamite on the Russian invasion out of a clear blue sky, and everybody back here thought he had blown his stack?"

"Sure, sure—the problem here will be to *get* information first."

"Fear not, Doctor!" He knew the term irritated Sid—which was why he always used it at such moments. "Just get a report out of him—that's *your* detail. Mine is to send as many unqualified people as possible to the wrong place at the wrong time . . ."

Later that afternoon there was the National Security Council meeting on forthcoming NATO commitments. An unhappy business. Defense always wanted more hardware—through their implacably marshaled arguments ran the old, wearisome fallacy that arms in ever greater number made for peace. Not a milligram of the anguished wash of history would ever shake their Roman conviction: *If you would have peace, prepare for war.* Fred Semmes was reasonably inventive and ferociously efficient, but like most businessmen he was beguiled by the short-term expedient: move the product today, tomorrow will take care of itself. But tomorrow *didn't* take care of itself any more than today did—the vexing attitudes of tomorrow grew inexorably out of the summary decisions of this very afternoon. A product of the Great Bull Market and the dogmatic certainties of the Johnson Administration, Semmes could never seriously entertain the idea of arms as a mainspring for paranoia and reprisal; surely fighter wings placed here, or RCTs with tactical nuclear capabilities placed there, would *solve something* in a final, irrefutable way. The argument swung back and forth, bending between Semmes' and Vosz's insistence on beefing up the Spanish and German bases and occasional warnings by Blackburn and Donlund of the inevitable Soviet reaction. In the end the meeting broke up without anything having been decided.

As they left the conference room Blackburn nodded to his own Director of Intelligence and Research, Michael Hudela. "Cheer up, Mike. We'll come to a decision one of these days—and then you'll have the fun of uncovering why it was the wrong one all along."

Hudela grinned ruefully. "Jim Osborne isn't going to like this very much, I can tell you that. He says Perenyi has been hinting strongly at a Soviet alliance."

"I wouldn't worry too much about that, Michael," Miles Stout murmured. "It's believed he's losing favor with the Soviet faction."

Blackburn suppressed a smile. There it was again: that vaguely impersonal passive tense—the inculpable passive, Sid called it. Stout used it incessantly. Someone was widely mentioned as a possible appointee for such and such a post, something else was held to be a source of potential conflict. It was so convenient: it gave weight without responsibility, it was the perfect mode for the Washington atmosphere of gossip and evasion.

"*Who* believes it, Miles?" he asked.

Stout blinked at him imperturbably. "Well, that is to say it's a feeling generally held out there."

"I see." *Out there.* What was it the British said? The chaps in the Foreign Office think that all the chaps in the field are crazy, and the chaps in the field *know* everyone in the Foreign Office is crazy. He started to make a rejoinder—caught sight of Vosz and Donlund talking alone at the end of the corridor and thought, Seize the moment. "Go ahead," he told the other two, "I'll be over later." Vosz was bent forward in a state of high excitement, his legs spread, his short powerful arms working; the Vice President was listening with patient amusement. His glance encountered Blackburn; without any change of expression the big man winked once. As the Secretary came up Vosz broke off, his teeth locked in the perennial glare.

"Well well well—the master mariner! And how was the glorious land of vines?" Vosz himself had bought a house on the Vineyard only the year before, an ostentatious pile out on West Chop. "Did you go for a sail in that antique scow of yours?"

"Didn't have time. I wanted to. Domestic problems." He paused. "I did get up to Cambridge, though. Feeling's running pretty high over the Smith case, Reiny."

"Ah yes—the champions of the downtrodden. Dry your eyes!"

"It might not be a bad idea to cancel your speech up there. After all, you have to make that address at the Council, later on."

Vosz broke into delighted laughter. "Paul—such solicitude! A few wild-eyed campus radicals?"

"It's more general than that."

"He's got a point, Reiny," Donlund said. "Postpone your appearance, maybe. Pressures of office or something. Or don't you feel we've got enough problems as it is?"

Vosz's mouth popped open. "Perhaps so. It might be wiser." He studied the Secretary mischievously. "You look worried, Paul—has State actually decided to recommend the purchase of the *entire* Louisiana Territory?"

"No—we're pushing for war with both Napoleon *and* Alexander. As a means of uniting the nation."

"Delightful! Perhaps the Student Prince will accomplish that all by himself."

Blackburn stopped smiling. Without preliminary he produced the report from Van Kleeck. "You both know about this, then."

Vosz scanned it at a glance and nodded. "Yes-yes-yes. Charming little game they're playing."

"Who's playing, Reiny?"

"When the lion's skin runs short it must be eked out with the fox's. Pa-*chooonggg!* How to turn a diplomatic defeat into a game of blindman's buff. The Greeks used to poke around in a sheep's smoking intestines. Your Russky consults a crystal ball—*and* the gospel according to Karl Marx—and says: 'What would I like most to have happen in the dear world today?' And there you are."

"What the hell have the Russians got to do with it?"

"You're so touchingly naive over at C Street; it's your most appealing trait. Drachenfels cabled us the Russians approached him even before the Mission took off from Calcutta."

"What about?"

"They offered him half a million cash if he would detach their team. Send them on up to Meng-po-lo, give them a free hand there."

"But for God's sake, why?"

"Oh, to keep the iron cauldron bubbling. As ever."

"But why approach *him?*"

"Presumably because Drachenfels was once a Russian subject. The Bolshevik mind is quite logical—in an inscrutable sort of way."

"And how did he handle it?"

"He told them to go fly one of those lovely Burmese kites . . . Why such amazement, Paul? You find it outlandish? You cannot believe it of old *Ursus slavicus?*"

It sounded outlandish, all right. To seek to suborn a prominent American engineer, the head of the entire International Mission . . . Still, it was possible, all things were possible. And why hadn't Drachenfels reported this to him? It was State's primary responsibility. Suppressing his resentment Blackburn said: "Do you buy this, Bill?"

Donlund creased the piece of paper along its folds thoughtfully, peering at it. "It'd serve their purposes."

"Kind of Machiavellian, isn't it?"

"It's got a lot of extras. Removes pressure from their own border troubles with the Chinese, busts up our New Delhi Pact—at best it kicks off a spanking new war between Dhotal and Burma. It seems pretty good to me, more I think about it. This all that's come in?"

"So far, yes. If only the Chinese weren't clamping down this way . . ."

"Yeah, looks as if they're off on one of their crazy paranoid spells."

Blackburn said crossly: *"Now* of course Bodawyin will start screaming for US hardware—invoking everything since the Atlantic Charter."

"You're not going to oppose it?" Vosz demanded.

"I don't know what I'm going to do. I want more information before I decide on anything. I want confirmation on that Drachenfels story. Let me know if anything more comes into that blockhouse command post of yours, will you, Reiny?"

"Of course, of course." The Special Assistant waggled a stubby forefinger at him. "You'll be making a serious mistake if you withhold support from Bodawyin. He's fighting our battle out there."

"If it's true."

"Oh, it's true! It's true, all right . . ."

Blackburn nodded and moved away thinking, I've got to see Shelly. Just as soon as I can.

Now, an hour later, sitting in Tremayne's office listening to the liquid hum of the air conditioners, he sighed and passed a hand through his hair. "It's just that I have such a funny feeling about this one. It—touches on the wrong nerve . . ." But this cloistral, antiseptic room was no help: here, bound in durance to computer consoles and over-the-horizon radio scanners and electronic surveillance satellites no human scheme, however monstrous or cataclysmic, seemed impossible. Man, the runaway ape of bewildering moods and terrifying ambitions, loomed large in these hermetic walls. Like Land, like Jillian Hoyt, you caught yourself thinking about "them": in the fevered, amoral dance of the printed circuits of "their" minds, what were "they" concocting?

"Shelly," he said suddenly, "this isn't the kind of question I like asking, but I've got to ask it. Are your people involved in this, in any way?"

The CIA Director picked up his pipe and put it in his mouth. After a moment he smiled, but there was no real warmth in his eyes. "I should have thought you'd obviated the need for that question," he said after a moment.

Blackburn was silent. It was the answer, the tone he might have expected. When he'd come in as Secretary he'd made it an indispensable condition that State was to be absolute master in its own house: chiefs of mission abroad were to be exactly that, *chiefs of mission*—all intelligence activities of whatever nature were to be cleared with them in full. Resentment in the Department had run high after Guatemala and Laos and Iran—the *Vaqueros*, the *Sea Supplies*, the *El Diablos*, the *Hatchets* that had led to such angry distrust of the American diplomatic presence abroad; matters hadn't been improved much either with the controversial reorganization of the intelligence community under Helms and Kissinger in '71. Tremayne had fought him tooth and nail, but in the end the President had acceded to Blackburn's demand. State was to have final approval of all intelligence activities, no matter how "black." And there it had rested, though the CIA and the service intelligence people still bitterly resented it.

"You know the Agency is required to inform you," Tremayne was saying quietly.

"I know, Shelly. I appreciate that. Only I know things aren't always that simple. You still have people operating out of Nam Lieu, don't you? And there's the *Conestoga* thing in Medinilla . . ."

Tremayne lifted a hand and looked at his fingernails. "I don't think we need to wander down memory lane. We do what we're directed to do. What's deemed necessary at the time. Just the way you do."

"Of course. It's just that—well, sometimes certain actions have a habit of gaining their own momentum, taking on a life of their own."

"Indeed they do. *On fait ce qu'on peut,* as the lady said. Don't forget, Paul, we get stuck with the unhappy consequences, too."

Blackburn said slowly: "You have reservations about the New Delhi Treaty? Go on, say what you think—I want to hear it."

The Director swung forward in his chair. "All right, I'll tell you what I think. I think you moved too precipitously, Paul. You got the bit in your teeth and you tried to wrap it all up—one big happy package. Naungapaya means nothing but trouble: you know his word is worthless, he'll never honor any international commitment. And a joint mission like this—it invites manipulation. It's just the kind of situation the Russians have been looking for—conflicting interests, espionage, the possibilities for a puppet regime. Not to mention the Chinese . . ."

"It was Bill's idea," Blackburn said with some surprise.

Tremayne shrugged. "Well, whoever's. It's a bad situation. If the Chinese in their wisdom have decided to seal off the area, maybe we have a certain obligation to try and find out what's going on in there. Surely you can understand that."

"Maybe. Let's hope it won't come to that." He locked his fingers, pressing till the knuckles cracked. "Shelly, I want your word that if there's a move to take any covert action in the area you'll let me know."

"You have it."

"Thanks. I'm sorry to have to force this. But I had to know, in this case. It's too important for—well, for credibility gaps and suchlike. I know you'll understand that."

"Of course, Paul. Chances are I'd have come to you if the shoe were on the other foot."

There was a silence. Tremayne was smiling at him—a faintly sad, faintly rueful smile. The Secretary got to his feet, chagrined that he had caused Shelly to adopt a smaller opinion of him than he'd had thirty minutes before. Doubt induces suspicion, which breeds hostility: Blackburn's Law Five-B. It was too bad; they'd made a lot of voyages together.

SEVEN

THE AIR IN THE STUDY was heavy and warm; light from the single desk lamp drained away to its far corners, a fine brass dust. Blackburn sat deep in the cracked leather chair beside his desk, rolling a pencil up and down his nose and staring at nothing in particular. The whole house was still. During the summer months Eleanor stayed at the Vineyard with most of the staff, coming down to Washington only for important functions, and so he was alone here except for the cook and his chauffeur Stollens, who also served unofficially as a kind of valet.

Eleven-fifteen. He kept rolling the pencil over his nose. It was the time of day he loved most—when with the day's clamor and dislocations behind him he could draft key letters and speeches, write in his journal, or simply slump here in his shirtsleeves, turning some problem over and over in his mind. There was the same almost furtive pleasure he'd known as a graduate student, in his book-weltered cubicle deep in the stacks at Widener, bound in inaccessibility, in silence: a miner oblivious of the deafening crush far above his head, picking at the stubborn rock, picking at the truth, the dense, obdurate essence of things.

The dimensions had shifted significantly, however . . .

There had been another disquieting cable from Van Kleeck around six (God knew what time it was out there, he'd never been able to keep track of time zones); Sid and Joe had both come in with it. Naungapaya in an even more inflammatory speech had accused Drachenfels of leading a band of foreign mercenaries dedicated to bringing Dhotal under the Burmese yoke, and was fulminating away about a "monstrous plague sown in our very entrails by these deceitful assassins of imperialism"—presumably a wild-eyed reference to the cholera epidemic, which did seem to be spreading with astonishing rapidity. He had made no reply to Van's protest. Peking had finally spoken, calling on their arrant protégé to release the International Mission and meet with Ch'en Pu-tsao and other Chinese leaders at Kunming. The Student Prince had noisily refused, and immediately proclaimed the formation of an Army of National Liberation consecrated to the ousting of all foreign influence in Asia. He had then embarked on some sort of haphazard campaign through the Kaolikung Shan, recruiting as he went, finally crossing the Burmese border at Wanting.

This had been more than enough to set off General Bodawyin, who had called up his reserves and fired a frantic appeal to the President, begging for "clouds of planes, rivers of armor"—a phrase that had sent Sid Jacobi into sour derision. There was still no contact with the Pao Shan consulate—there were ominous though unconfirmed rumors that Naungapaya's people had occupied it and set it on fire. Van even cited an equally unconfirmed eyewitness report that Umphlett had not been with the consulate staff at the time of the incident, but had been seen "moving in concert with Dhotalese units."

"What does *that* mean—are they implying he's *enlisted?*" Blackburn hadn't been able to keep the consternation out of his voice. "That he's actually joined up with this Vagabond King—?"

"Looks that way, sir," Joe Carter had said somberly.

"I don't believe it. This whole business has as many wild rumors as a dog has fleas. Umphlett may be impulsive but he's not insane . . ."

Their eyes had met his lugubriously and dropped away. Blackburn had drafted a protest note to Naungapaya himself, ordered Van Kleeck in no uncertain terms to hump himself down to Yunnan and find out precisely what was going on, and cabled Stew Davis in Rangoon to use every persuasion short of truth serum to keep Bodawyin from driving off the cliff; and there they'd had to leave it, at least until they had something more to go on than threats and fairy tales.

A gust of wind riffled the papers on his desk, sent two sheets skirling to the floor; he bent over and picked them up. The Alaskan salmon fishing fleet had sent a furious protest over the ramming of one of its vessels by a big Soviet trawler twenty miles southwest of Cape Fairweather; the American captain, foundering and in helpless rage, had fired on the Soviet ship with a 30-caliber Winchester, wounding two seamen—or so the Russians charged. It was the third such incident in five weeks. Blackburn had finally induced them, after months of labyrinthine bargaining, to join the North Pacific Fisheries Convention, and they had damned well better adhere to the new treaty. He would send Timofyevna a stiff note in the morning.

Hugh Pearmain reported from São Paulo that Campilhas' people, armed with Czech weapons, were definitely infiltrating the Mato Grosso region from Bolivia, and that the new insurrection posed a serious threat to President Da Pardas. Former comrades-in-arms of the Hoyt girl's, maybe, spreading the old, inflammatory—but oh so just—doctrine: *Land to those who till it!*

Embassy Moscow noted an air of unmistakable cordiality displayed by Ragozhin at the current visit of the Japanese Foreign Minister Musashi and equated this with the Russian Premier's recent speech threatening swift reprisal against any power, great or small, which would seek to upset the stability of the Asian mainland. Was this a sour reference to New

Delhi? or was Ragozhin alluding to Naungapaya's antics? Any rumbler can bray, as Land would put it. Great or small.

He had that speech Friday evening on the peaceful uses of the sea floor. It would serve as a good warm-up for his address to the UN in September. "That exercise in utter futility," Acheson had called the General Assembly's opening debates. But for all his brilliance Acheson came out of another era—the day of chalk lines drawn with cold severity on a dozen fronts. We knew better now—at least we'd learned differently. The worst diplomats were missionaries, fanatics, and lawyers, as old Harold Nicolson said. In the brash flood-tide years after Hitler we had subverted some governments and muscled others, invaded and garrisoned and intrigued. We had deceived to a fare-thee-well—not only others but our own citizens. In Vietnam we had burned a helpless people for eight terrible years. We didn't have the recipe any more than Communists or heliolators or flower children did. Look out for your true believer in any guise—at some crucial moment he will abandon thought and reach for his gun. And be gunned down in turn.

And yet—it was true, irrationally and absurdly true: something inside him believed that the sea could solve everything; if we yielded to it, let its healing, revitalizing force wash over us in a foamy saline baptism . . .

Smiling at himself he dropped the papers with the others on his desk and crossed to the opposite wall, where a blown-up photograph had caught him sweating, half-naked, struggling frantically to set a spinnaker, his eyes slitted against the sun. The Judge's last big race—second place in the Edgartown Regatta. The sea: all his troubles seemed to begin and end with it. Joys, too. You could tell so much about a man, sailing with him: if he was overly prudent, rash, indecisive, if he was a fraud or a mainstay it would be revealed to you in an hour or so, pounding through the blue water. Reinhold Vosz was a perfect case in point. Along with that turreted Gothic pile the actress Delia Manyon had built overlooking West Chop, he'd purchased the *Tanager* Uncle Dan Harden had once won the Round-the-Island race with, and had it redesigned and rechristened. To watch Reiny try to sail that rakish, volatile greyhound of a boat could put your heart in your mouth: all his fury came boiling out, his grinding need to prove he was as mettlesome as any old salt on the Sound. The little-man syndrome, but it was more than that, too: he seemed to want to outrage some fancied audience of peers. If he'd had his way, this Burma hassle would already have turned into a duel of wills, with Americans and Chinese playing chicken in a forest of deployed missiles and troop concentrations—

Abruptly he went back to his desk, got out a map of northern Burma and began to study the area along the Upper Salween. Maps always gave him a sense of proximity—an illusion he knew was false but nevertheless indulged. The Seventh Floor *was* so far away from tangibles . . . Here was Meng-p'eng, where the dam was to be built, and which was not to be confused with Meng-po-lo, farther upriver, where Drachenfels had told Vosz the Russian team had wanted to be detached and given "a free hand"—whatever that meant; and farther on Pao Shan, on the old Burma Road, where Naungapaya either had or hadn't seized and destroyed the consulate, and where Umphlett either had or hadn't joined this Cook's Tour or Children's Crusade or whatever it was. Naungapaya's movements seemed to be describing an arc around the area invested with this surprising cholera outbreak. A dilettante with dreams of "destiny." Blackburn could see him right now, all togged out in a military tunic and a peaked cap and crossed bandoleers—a merry desperado, half Carranza, half François Villon, "arousing the people." He was the most dangerous of all demagogues—the impulsive romantic: he never paused long enough to recognize that the passions he excited to support him restricted the very freedom of choice he needed, and left him only extreme solutions. He had painted himself right into a corner—and in some of the cruelest, most inaccessible terrain in the world. A wilderness of gorges, dense forest, lonely mountain hamlets. He would always be a tool for those who could exercise greater craft and force of will.

The question of course was: *whose* tool . . .

Blackburn leaned back and with his two hands rotated his head and neck on his shoulders—an unthinking swimmer's habit, part therapeutic, part talismanic. Was he making too much of this, as Shelly had intimated? He was still tired from New Delhi, dog tired. That was the trouble with this job—you never could get sufficiently rested from one crisis, one particular effort, to be able to meet the next one with the requisite clarity and force. The history of international relations is nothing more than a melancholy record of the hasty decisions of weary—and therefore irritable —men. Blackburn's Law Six-D. There was so much—so eternally, infernally much—that could go wrong.

Thumbs hooked in his trouser pockets he wandered over to one of the windows. Most of the lights were out, even in the bedrooms. Sensible people. Two doors down, across the street, a woman in a paris blue housecoat tossed a magazine on a table and swayed out of his scan of vision. The breeze was damp and warm on his throat. A tempest in a China teapot, Joe Carter had called it. Maybe that was all it was. Yet there was something deeply disquieting about the episode—it was filled with such absurd and contradictory components. Who—even an addlepated, jazz-loving, girl-chasing playboy like Naungapaya—would be insane enough to launch an insurrection aimed at both Burma and China—*China!*—and lock up the representatives of all the GATO powers? If he *had* assaulted the Pao Shan consulate they'd have to take strong measures: that kind of thing would have to be met head on. Of course the Chinese were justified in sealing off their borders if they chose—it was, after all, still Chinese territory until UN ratification; only then how could you get *at* anything? Could Umphlett actually have elected to join this band of idiots and dime-store heroes—Umphlett who, whatever his other failings, was simply incapable of deserting his post, particularly at a time like this—? And why above all should the whole business have erupted right after he'd given both Naunga and the Shan chiefs firm assurances of his government's good offices before the next session of the General Assembly? They had barely waited until he'd stepped off the plane from New Delhi . . .

Things were not what they seemed—very often; but sometimes—he'd heard Acheson say it one tense night—they were *just* that. Wrestling with the problem, worrying it, letting the unrelated pieces sift to the bottom of his mind, he became aware of voices downstairs: a woman's and then Stollens', in swiftly rising altercation. Irritably he went to the head of the stairs to hear the woman saying, "But it's important, don't you see I *must* see him—" and then Stollens, sharp and forbidding:

"I'm sorry, Madam, *no one* is permitted to see the Secretary at this hour . . ."

"But he will *see* me, I know he will!"

"—can't force your way in here like this and expect to—"

"What is it, George?" Blackburn called sharply.

Stollens moved back from the vestibule into view; his face, upturned, was flat and angry. He began: "There's this—person just barged in, one of these liberated types, with some story—" and at the same time the woman moved forward saying, "Secretary Blackburn? I've got to see you —it's important!" and he saw it was Jillian Hoyt. He put his hand on the pommel of the newel post, invaded by a curious swift lightness of the heart.

"It's all right, George," he called. "She may come up."

"Just as you say, sir."

Stollens stepped aside, dourly dismissing any responsibility for this unpardonable intrusion; and Blackburn watched the girl rise toward him, bemused. He should be irritated, for a host of reasons, and he was not— he clearly was not. Her hair was still in that charmingly tousled disorder; she was dressed much the way she had been the other afternoon, but in a skirt now and with a blouse of the same rippling orange material, though with long sleeves. A large worn green suede shoulder bag rode high on her left hip. She wore no make-up, but Blackburn was conscious of the faint scent of sandalwood as she drew near him.

"Hello, there," he murmured.

"Hello."

"What brings you down to this cruel citadel of the imperialist infrastructure?"

"Well, I—I had to tell you about something. Something very important." Moving past him into the study at his indication she didn't seem to know where to dispose herself or how—she started to sit on the oversize couch he occasionally used for napping, checked the impulse, wavered again, and finally with that easy fluid motion perched on one arm of the big leather chair by the desk where he'd been sitting. "Then on the way down I had the feeling you'd probably heard it by now, anyway. I don't know." Scratching lightly at the side of her cheek she smiled—a quick, eager, half-fearful smile that stirred him strangely. "Anyway," she said with an almost merry defiance, "the President says we ought to seek out dialogues with our national leaders. So here I am!"

"Dial away," he said. "But first let me get you a drink. May I?"

"Yes—thanks very much." She still seemed oddly constrained and this, too, pleased him. As he put ice in their glasses she began to look at the walls with their maps and blown-up snapshots of what he liked to refer to, wryly, as Grand Occasions: the signed photos from President Kennedy, Harriman, Piers-Monckton, Couve de Murville. Washington had always been a portrait-swapping town.

"Is that Rusk with you—near that funny-looking mosque there?"

"Yes, it is."

"Cozy, devious little mano." Her mouth hardened. "That purring silky-southern voice. Phony-genteel, wasn't he? Now be honest."

He grinned at her. "At risk of unpardonable disloyalty to my former boss, I'd have to say I found him circumspect, indecisive and tradition-ridden."

"I should think so. How could you even work with him?"

"To tell you the truth, up until the Vietnam horror, he was such a relief after Dulles I was humbly grateful." He handed her a drink. "After all, Rusk had a much harder job."

"Harder?"

"Sure—he tried to personify the Foreign Policy Establishment for the past half-century; Dulles only tried to represent God, which is a lot easier."

Her laughter was deeper, more resonant than he'd remembered it. When she threw back her head quick planes of light struck her cheeks and brows; her hair swung in a loose chestnut skein. "You don't let things get to you, do you?" she said. "I mean crises and power struggles and that kind of thing. You can see it all objectively. As a kind of a game . . ."

"Not at all. I blow off regularly twice a week, whether circumstances warrant it or not. A good, low flash point is a great help—it warns certain power-snatching types to switch to some more tractable soul down the hall."

"I wish I could be like that. Able to control my emotions—"

"Don't."

The word had more force than he'd intended: her eyes flashed up at him again, bright with surprise, fell away. Abruptly she rose and sat on the couch with her small, shapely knees close together, her body bent over her drink. Without preamble, watching him gravely she said:

"There is a very big plot going on right now. In Dhotal. The CIA has a scheme to have Prince Naungapaya assassinated by an ex-Nazi general. So as to force a war with China. Do you know about it?"

". . . Not entirely."

He saw that she was completely serious. Mildly astonished that she knew anything at all about what they were referring to in the White House basement as the Naunga Switch—nothing much had been released to the press after official Department reaction to that first Reuters dispatch—and amused by this incredible hash of fact and fancy he swung the liquor around in his glass thoughtfully. "Who's the ex-Nazi general?"

"Drachenfels. You must know that."

"I see. Tell me: do you honestly think a branch of our government would undertake something like this?"

"Of course they would. Why not—what's so far-fetched about it? They've had people put out of the way in Guatemala, they killed Diem in Saigon—not that he didn't deserve it of course, the little monster. Look what they did in Laos . . ."

She was staring at him—a frank surprise edged with disappointment; it made her look very young, very appealing. She *was* young, too—she was nearer by far to Leland's generation than to his; and the thought gave him a pang. He remembered Land storming around the living room at the Paling the other afternoon, flinging his arms about. What a gulf it was! And yet she *was* over thirty. No kid. She fell almost exactly between their generations, his and Land's. She was certainly old enough not to accept so blandly the idea that Shelly's people would cold-bloodedly arrange for the assassination of a head of state, even a provisional one—

Gently he said: "I'd have to ask you the same question I'd ask any member of my own staff: What are your sources?"

Her temper flared. "I'm not an informer, I can tell you that! It's simply something I thought you ought to know. Assuming of course you don't."

He smiled and bobbed his head. "I'm very grateful to you—I really am. Only, why such solicitude for my welfare? I'd have thought you'd want to see me felled by an unforeseen crisis."

"Don't make fun of me. I know you probably know about the whole filthy business—you've probably dreamed it all up yourself, as far as that goes."

"No, it's news to me. Believe me, it's news to me. Aren't you violating the first precept of the good revolutionary? Embarrass the existing center of power?"

"I suppose so." She rubbed the base of her nose with her forefinger as though to avert a sneeze—a child's gesture, ingenuous and charming. "Smitty once told me I don't have the temperament for it. That I'm incapable of the ultimate commitment. That you may never *need* to make it but you ought to be capable of it. That's why I work on plans, mostly. I suppose he's right. I never believed in violence—not even at Chicago. I've always hated it, avoided it whenever I could." Abruptly she said: "Vosz has canceled the Emerson Hall appearance. We just got the word. Why did he do it, do you know?"

Blackburn said carefully, "I imagine he was prevailed upon to see the wisdom of the move."

"Did you have a hand in it?"

"I spoke to him, yes. I told him I didn't think it was stunningly appropriate in view of the climate of opinion up there."

"Now why—!" Indignation gave her face a curious, quite pleasant heightening of color. "Well, it doesn't matter—we'll still get to him, you know. Wherever he is."

"I thought you were against Action-in-the-Streets."

"I am—we are. But certain kinds of confrontation can be effective enough." He could see her forcing back her resentment. "Tell me: why should Smitty's case be considered more 'criminal' than Ellsberg's?"

He set down his glass and ran a hand through his hair. "The line of argument seems to be that the Pentagon Papers were historical documents, a transcript of past events. Whereas these Hughbryce Papers deal with *projected* policy, plans that could still be put into effect under various contingencies. And therefore they come under the Official Secrets Act."

"Oh, crud! That's too ridiculous even to answer . . ."

"I won't pretend I like it. Or understand it, either. But I'm no legal beagle. In my opinion Reiny's enraged because it's Hughbryce, and so he's acting with unwarranted severity—and using rather dubious technicalities."

She leaned forward. "But couldn't you—I mean since you feel it's all wrong—couldn't you talk to them? Persuade Vosz to release Smitty? At least let him out on bail?"

"Dear girl, I'm not the Attorney General. I have no authority in the matter, it's completely out of my jurisdiction. You must see that . . . I'm charged with the execution of foreign policy—"

"But they're all mixed up with each other! The Papers are all about Muscat and Chile and Burma, all the things *we're* planning to do there. How can you say it hasn't anything to do with you?"

He sighed. "You're right, in a certain sense. In a certain sense *everything* is intertwined with everything else. But we harassed civil servants have to stake out areas of responsibility or we'd all end up climbing the walls. Believe me, I regret the whole business. But there's truly nothing I can do about it."

"I see." She crossed her legs and folded her arms tightly. "I know," she declared in another tone. "I've heard it all before. You liberals deplore this, you're sorry as hell about that. The truth is you haven't the balls to tear the whole building down and start over."

He got up and moved across the room to his desk and leaned against its bulk. "But look," he said suddenly. "Suppose you were sitting there. Right there. You're Secretary of State, you've just been given the job."

"Fat chance—!"

"But as a hypothetical question. There you are. You're told: This exists, and this, and this. Resolve them as best you can. With what you've got."

"That's just it—I wouldn't, anyway."

"Why's that?"

In the alien, bureaucratic voice he'd heard in Somerville, as though reciting a hard-learned lesson, she proclaimed: "The duty of the radical intellectual is implacable hostility to power, repudiation of power."

"Why?"

"Because power corrupts, that's why . . ." Her voice had risen a note. "Or are you by any chance unaware of that?"

He locked his fingers and peered at them—he suddenly wanted very much to reach her on this. "You've got to decide," he told her. "It's a cruel choice maybe, but you've got to choose. Either you accept the responsibility of power, and take the chance of being corrupted by it; or you repudiate power—and run the risk of irrelevance."

"Is Thoreau irrelevant? or Rousseau, or Diogenes?"

"Yes—in the sense of immediate pressures, social needs. Look: suppose you had a sort of Aaron's rod—I don't mean to tempt you unduly. But suppose you had one and your friend Smitty was wrong, you *were* angry enough to raise it—and the head of every political and social organization in the country dropped dead, right where he was standing."

"Happy day," she murmured with a mischievous grin.

"That's right. All of us—the whole blind, malicious power élite, with all our staffs and assistants. Wiped out. What would you do?" Her body moved restlessly and he raised a peremptory hand. "No—think hard, now. That's the clean slate you want, isn't it? Perfectly clean. There is nobody anywhere in America to give a single order. No one. What are you going to do? You're walking briskly down Pennsylvania Avenue to the Capitol. You enter the White House and climb the stairs, stepping over all the corpses, to the President's study. There you are—and now what will you do? Will you proclaim an agrarian republic? a federation of free thinkers, an anarchist soviet, a thousand love communes? You've got to do *some-*

thing, you know: the clock is ticking very fast—there's a food shortage, garbage is piling up everywhere, there's the danger of epidemics. People are looting the stores, terrified citizens are nailing planks across their front doors and shooting at shadows. Yes, and the heads of other governments are looking on in apprehension, thinking of trade agreements, treaty commitments. There are even several heads of state who are uncommonly eager to dismember and absorb this geographical entity you've just inherited—they've already started to put certain contingency plans into effect. What are you going to do about *them?*"

She shook her head slowly, as though just awakened. "That's too far from reality," she said. "It—just couldn't happen."

"Yes, it could. That is just what will happen. Eventually we will die and you—your generation—will be there. In the offices."

"But not like that. It's a fantasy," she burst out in the old, impetuous way, "you're living one yourself, you see? You don't really believe what you say you do—you like to pretend you believe in all this community-of-peoples, hands-across-the-sea jazz, but actually you *know* it's all jungle, dog-eat-dog. The big fish and the minnows . . ."

"I don't see either position as absolute. I see possibilities in restraint, in communication, I see tendencies toward ruthless Realpolitik." He ran his hand through his hair. "My God—the world is a welter of an awful lot of things, a million colliding fragments of hope and malice and cynicism and good will. And the purposeful man tries to do what he can with them: he hopes and struggles—he even arranges international conferences, God help him. He fears disaster, Christ yes, but even so he believes he can effect—"

"You have to believe that!" she cried softly. "You haven't any choice! That's the trouble—you feel your life has *meaning.* Yes! You think your career is going to bring something, something historical, to the political course of the country. Everything pushed you that way—Boston, Martha's Vineyard, Exeter, Harvard—that's what the Brahmin is trained for, that's what he always believes . . ."

Blackburn watched the girl a moment in silence. Her face, cut by the lamp's broad path, was animate with light and shadow, flaring nostril and dilated eye; a spendthrift impassioned bounty, essentially Irish, that made him think of other days long gone, and moved him strangely.

"—I'm not a Brahmin," he heard himself saying aloud. "I know they call me one now and then, but they're wrong. I'm an eager-beaver California Irishman from a broken home. Who wants to put things back together again. If he can."

Her emerald eyes seemed to darken as she listened. He became all at once aware of the late hour, the still, impervious bulk of the room beyond the glow of the lamp, and that unmistakable hum of current between them. Why had he told her that? Yet it seemed so natural, so utterly and

unanalyzably *right*. He was sliding toward something, he didn't know what
exactly but he was—like a boy in the mill race at Tashawena Inlet bobbing, spinning, borne swiftly out to sea; and the thought filled him with a
quick, exuberant joy.

"I've been fighting a certain kind of man all my life," he added
slowly. "I've wanted to do one thing, bring about one kind of peace, truce,
reconciliation—something or other. And I suppose I'll go right on doing
it. You're quite right: you don't change what you are."

Her gaze met his as though he were the last person she might see on
earth. "I'm sorry I said some of the things I said the other day," she
offered; her voice had fallen so low he could barely hear her. "I was—well,
being defensive. I was awfully angry at you."

"I know. You were right to be."

"Well . . ."

"I said some things I shouldn't have said, either."

"No, you didn't."

"Well: I *thought* them . . ."

Their laughter rang together, broke off.

"You *can't* be any good as Secretary of State," she declared.

"Why's that?"

"You're too—you're too honest."

"Only now and then."

"I wanted to say—" she began. Her eyes were very large and green
and grave. "I wanted to tell you—I'll break off the thing with Land. If
you want me to."

He was more surprised than he'd been all evening. "But that's *your*
decision—yours and Land's . . . I haven't any right to intrude. I told
you—"

"I know."

"It's not my province."

"Isn't it?" A moment longer she gazed at him, as if something most
momentous lay in the room's somber stillness, as if it were an instant
utterly outside of time. A car passed slowly below, hunting for some address, and the night wind, hot and intimate, whistled against the screens.
A long moment, while he stood in front of a temple near Cau Luong and
watched a stone goddess, bare-breasted, bare-bellied, dancing with stately
undulant largesse, smiling dreamily down at him . . .

Jillie Hoyt caught herself up and leaped to her feet.

"I've got to be going," she said almost tersely. "I didn't mean to
barge in on you like this. Really. It was—just impulse. I *do* respect people's time, privacy, stuff like that. I know I don't act as if I do, but I do."
She moved off toward the doorway. "I hope this hasn't made any problems for you—a bomb-throwing radical like me here in your sanctum
sanctorum, I mean. Anyway, I wouldn't think—"

"Don't go."

He had said it without thought—he'd had to say it, had to rise and move in her direction like a man under hypnosis, a man in great and desperate need. Here right behind him were the NATO treaty renewal and the Micronesian Republic dispute, and de Mortier's angry note over Somaliland, and the Alaskan fisheries wrangle and this nagging, tortuous Burma Triangle incident; all the tangled patterns of confusion and ignorance and design, and the lonely, arduous struggle to unravel them—yes, and beyond that, too, the tangled patterns of the Paling, exigent and sere, the gray odyssey of an arid, loveless marriage . . . and here before him stood this girl, quick with that astonishing force, that impassioned pulsing vividness—who now had whirled around at his words. Her face was frozen in wonder; her eyes shone.

"Stay," he said. "I need you . . . to stay." He had reached her. His hands, alive with the clamor and denial of twenty-five years, touched her shoulders—and that earlier vibratory throb caught at them. Perfectly erect, almost defiant in her stance, she was trembling violently. He started to speak, checked himself and shook his head slowly and drew her to him. She gave a short, gasping cry and her arms slid around his waist and clutched at him like a person drowning. Her throat was smooth and full; it quivered against his lips.

"—Ah," she said after a moment. "Oh God! They're right, you know. About you."

"Are they?"

"Oh my God, yes. All of them. I mean it! But I'm the most right of all . . ."

He found himself bemused: half dizzy with shock at what, after a quarter century of essentially constant behavior, he was doing; bound in astonishment, disbelief, a fevered exultancy. This—this right here—was life he was holding in his two arms, in the person of this lovely, headlong, vivid girl he scarcely knew—and knew so utterly. Her breath came hotly against his jaw, she was murmuring something, her voice tremulous and a bit hoarse with urgency. She certainly said what she felt, this girl; and yet that too was right, partook of the simple astonishing complicity of the moment. It was true—he wanted her immensely, omnivorously, with a fierce singleness of recognition that shook him even as it swept him with delight. A sheer, undeflected longing such as he had never known before. Her lips drew him, caught at him, lulled and quickened him at once, her body arched to meet his with a soft, lithe force only dreamed of now and then, and rarely.

"I want you, Jillie," he said. "I want you now."

There was no recoil, no query or circumspection—he realized he'd expected none. For answer she gave her lips to him again; her quick, suppliant tongue.

"Then let's," she breathed. "My God, *let's* . . ." and she scratched the back of his neck tantalizingly with a fingernail. In spite of himself he laughed.

"What a world," Jillie Hoyt murmured, and bit her lip. "What a kooky, lopsided, unpredictable little old world." She was kneeling astride Blackburn like a proud and faintly weary horsewoman, or a classic statu- ette; her breasts swung like dull silver pendants in the darkness. The sound of cars, of late footfalls, had ceased. Around them the Capital lay shrouded, contained, waiting for day. Their fingers clasped, they thrust each other's arms back and forth in indolent, unthinking rhythms.

"And I hated you so!" she went on. "I really did. I used to have fantasies—" She broke off, marveling.

"What kind of fantasies?"

"Never mind all that. Can't tell you now." She stirred restlessly, and a small, strong wave of sensation mounted in his loins. "Some day when I'm in an exposé mood."

"I want you again," he said. "Isn't that perfectly ridiculous?"

"No, it's not—it's right as rain."

"Yes, it is."

"And high time, too, I'd say. *High time* . . ."

Smiling he brought her to him again, amazed beyond amazement. Their love-making had been a fiery-sweet dance, a true, tumultuous voyage of bestowal he could not possibly have foreseen. Under his eager lips Jillie burst from crest to crest of delight, flying off and then returning like some wild seabird; together they soared to still loftier pinnacles of sensation, tumbled through dream sea surges to a panting calm—only to be caught up all over again in this lazily swinging golden net of desire. Her nipples swelled to taut coral cones, the sea lane of her drew him with its drenched sweet mollescence, her mounting cries—finally, exultantly, "Stars—stars—*stars!*"—stirred him with the boldest ardor. He was bathed in a triumph he had never remotely imagined.

"I knew it!" she breathed in broken, panting phrases. "Oh, I—knew it . . ." And still later, leaning over him, brushing his lips and nose and chin with her own, she murmured: "You are younger than your son."

Caught in a tumult of conflicting emotions he couldn't analyze, he was silent.

"What's the matter? It's true! You're embarrassed by my saying that," she declared in affectionate accusation, "you *are*. You sweet, *sweet* idiot—why not admit what's true? Kiss me here, put your sweet lips here, *here*," she went on, a light fevered importunity. "Oh, you can do any- thing! You can make a woman cry, laugh, shriek like a demon deep in hell—there's nothing you can't do! Do you know it?—you enter me like a god . . ."

And caressing tenderly her breasts, her mount, her firm slender thighs, feeling her fine electric body writhe and tremble and moan beneath him, he knew it was true. He could, all at once and magically, make love like a god. He was somehow another kind of being—free, freed in a bound, at the brisk tap of a trident, from the great gray weight of his marriage, its barren constraints and calculated elusions; delivered too from that moment he could never erase, that night in the dilapidated, ponderous old villa in Isfahan, the third week of his marriage, when he had made love to the silent, recumbent form that was Eleanor his wife (it was always still, the fearful immobility of a small animal, as though she were awaiting some stealthy, inescapable harm, injury, defilement: but waiting)—lying in the high, canopied bed where grand viziers had slept, sirdars, imams, military eunuchs for all he knew; caressing the lean, angular body, the small, hard, oddly narrow breasts, murmuring tones of endearment he knew ran dangerously close to reassurance, almost propitiation (for what? in the name of *what?*); finally entering as gently as he could—a grainy, arescent narrows that troubled him (they'd had no sexual relations before their marriage: she'd promised Father, she'd said, she'd promised him years ago and they must honor that; and Blackburn—sensing an undefined, essential fear as well as the pledge itself, had acquiesced), moving in a slow, faintly arduous pattern, wondering uneasily why this love-making was so different from the two experiences he'd had before, convulsive and hurried as they'd been; why Nell, by daylight so forthright and articulate, should be at night so furtive, so remote and still; wondering if perhaps it had been his dereliction in failing to rouse her adequately, thinking of the long, sun-dappled verandah at the Paling, thinking of the Inlet and the osprey's nest, and Lee . . . all at once feeling himself pause, rigid, intent, incredulous, conscious of a marked, unmistakable rhythm in her breathing.

She was asleep.

He could not believe it, could not accept the fact. Hanging in astonishment, wordless, he could feel his ardor shrivel in its grainy keep. It was impossible! Not now, not at a time like this . . . Her still, lean form never stirred: yes, she had fallen asleep. Outrage, mortification, a slow, cold guilt assailed him—finally a kind of wild panic that froze the breath in his lungs. Stealthily he eased his body away from hers. Waking then, distantly distressed, she murmured confused childlike words of apology and he comforted her, staring sightless at the gloomy brocade canopy above their heads. He didn't know what to do. He tried to make light of it, but he could not: it had happened, and nothing could be the same, he knew it was so; hot with bewilderment and shame, and a still more poignant fear (was he unable to bring a woman to full pitch? he knew better—he *felt* he knew better—but was it possible?), he realized nothing between them could ever be quite the same again.

Not that he hadn't tried, of course. They'd both tried, as everyone must try. Yet that had been all it was—a sliding away rather than a con-joining: she fell asleep again, many more times, and the act of love shriveled like a plant in darkness. Sore at heart, uncertain, he gave way. There was so much to fill their days—the long hours of work, the late hours of entertaining. Nell grew in assurance and tact, for which he was grateful. Only in sleep did she reveal her anxiety—a tense, breath-caught *"Where are you going—?"* that could, at two-thirty in the morning and drugged with sleep as he was, scare him half out of his wits. "I'm going to the toilet to piss in it," he'd told her once with a savagery he knew was completely unjustified. "Where did you think I was going—Samarkand?" She'd made no answer: under the white coverlet her body lay like the sculptured figure on a sepulcher.

After that there had been only the frantic moment in Damascus with Michele Franquinet—an affair (if one could call it that) which had raised more questions than it answered. Michele, hating André, hating the diplo-matic life, had wanted to be a mischief, the architect of petty vengeances; Blackburn, bred to graver things, could not follow her. One made one's bed, one continued to lie in it—to coin a phrase; one remained loyal, constant, held the ship on course, no matter what the weather or the wind, sought consolation in the rigors of the assignment, the needs of parenthood. Life was never all a man might hope for . . .

And now this wild, mercurial girl had restored him in a flurry of passionate abandon—had demanded of him nothing he could not meet in the most glorious abundance. Eleanor, timorous, withdrawn, unyielding, had always taken; this girl gave and gave again, in a tidal surge of naked bestowal; and it was (he saw it now) what he himself had always sought to do—the spendthrift largesse his own blood clamored for.

"Do you love me?" he asked now, softly. "Do you love me, Jillie?"

"God, I don't know," she groaned. "I doubt it."

"What—!" For an instant he felt a genuine shock, then he laughed. "You're positively wicked."

"No—I haven't the faintest idea. I suspect it's a three-alarm infatua-tion. Don't you? The sexual thing—I was right about that, it's there all right, you're never wrong about that. And a certain glamorous aura that hovers around your darling head. Your glorious, majestic, Jovian head . . ."

She wasn't teasing him, then: she actually believed this. Amused, he was yet conscious of a dart of unfocused jealousy, almost exasperation. He thought of Land's uncommonly handsome face, so unlike his own; the lithe tall form, the crewman's shoulders. Nineteen . . .

"You're angry!" she exclaimed in delight. "You're actually out of sorts. You dear, delightful idiot."

"Don't be silly—I'm in Elysium, with a fair wind at my back. Only you might have put a more affectionate face on it."

"*Face,*" she retorted, and indulged in one of her swift, violent grimaces. "All your big, dangerous words. You use so many of them—do you know that? And they mean nothing but bad news. To us groundlings." Arching her back she gave a deep, pleasurable moan. "Don't you see? *This* is everything—*this minute now.* The two of us, swinging in our big beautiful golden net . . . Oh, how can you power-élite types *keep* from turning into hell-roaring existentialists?"

"Talent. And concentration." Fascinating as he found these outbursts of Jillie's, his emotions could not vault through such grand arcs of romance and practical candor. "And then you see, there's always tomorrow morning."

"What have you got tomorrow morning?"

"I've got to keep some American and Russian salmon fishermen from blowing each other out of the water, for one thing. And I've got to try to get de Mortier to cool down over the Somaliland squabble. And I've got to write a speech on the peaceful uses of the sea floor—"

"Lovely!" she crowed. "The sea floor! You don't have to give a speech about it, you just *did* it . . ."

"Yes. We did, didn't we?"

"For all you know we could all be dead tomorrow. Probably will be."

"You kids." He sighed. "You accept that so easily."

"Of course we do. It's *true,* for God's sake: why waffle about it? All that junk about immortality, posterity, rosy-fingered-dawn—that's a moldy Victorian kick." She stared out at the warm night, her face looking small and tough; part naiad, part street urchin. "Life isn't such a prize package, you know—take it in bulk. Even if most people don't advertise the fact. It's not so hard to want to smash all the mirrors in the hall now and then . . ." Her body moved abruptly beside him. "I tried it myself. Cut my wrists once. With a Gem blade. Single edge."

"—*Oh, no,*" he protested. In a purely involuntary movement he took her hand in his. The thought that this sweet, dear flesh could be skeleton and mold was unendurable to him.

"Don't worry—I'm over it. You get over everything. I guess. It was funny," she mused. "It hurt so! As dear old Dorothy Parker once said. I didn't think it would, somehow. All I thought about was dying—not the side effects, if you know what I mean. The good doctor over at Holyoke Center was plenty angry at me."

"It was the boy?" he asked in a low voice. "Dave?"

"That and a lot of other stuff. Things get to be too much at times. Why not ring it down?"

"But—you've so much to offer . . ."

"To who? General Motors? The DAR? Suffering humanity? Don't kid yourself—nobody would have missed me for five fornicating minutes. That's what you don't clue. You think everybody *matters* . . . Then I came close to jumping once. The freight elevator at the end of the hall, at the University office. Dotty Lorber caught me. A real tough baby—do you know her? Works for Dean Marriott—really gone through the wringer: breast removed, acute alcoholism, some son of a bitch who deserted her with two kids to feed, years before that. The works. She rolled one big, frosty eye at me and said: 'Yep, it's a long way down, all rightie,'—and kept on walking down the hall. Never even broke stride. That did it, though. So I went back to the office like a good little professor's helper and typed up a perfectly snazzy letter from Fudgy Hannig to some CIA sachem acknowledging how immensely helpful the Committee on Foreign Policy had been in reorienting US influence in the Middle East. You get the syndrome."

Holding her in his arms he said somberly: "I've never understood it. Suicide. I've never really comprehended how a person could do it."

"Hallelujah! You've actually said out loud something you're thinking —I'm getting to like you more and more." She tossed back her hair with that quick, proud movement of her head. "The thing is that people—a whole lot of people—are hanging on to life by the barest thread, half the time. It's like those big-game fish on TV—they leap out of the water and thrash about, and it seems impossible that tiny line could be holding them. But it is. Most of the time, anyway. And then there's that comfort in another person—the habits of domesticity, the animal warmth. That helps. And you find yourself longing for that with all your might, even though you know it's phony as hell."

"And yet you've never married."

She shook her head violently. "Thanks a lot. I saw enough of that at home. Look at the sainted American wife!" she cried, and thumped a hand on the pillow. "She's a programmed freak. Half con man, half whore. TV and the car pool and being a nice, deadly little career back-up man for hubby. There isn't one girl in a thousand who is being herself, who can really take *care* of herself, make her way in the world with any real dignity . . ."

"You must be a Women's Libber, then."

"Sure, I'm all for them, I joined up once. But sometimes their methods bore me. They could take all the marbles in political action if they weren't so busy blowing their minds over clitoral orgasm or denying the fact that some of the Sisterhood are just basically better in bed than others. Sure, men can be slobs—don't think I don't know that—but I've found them as generous as women, if not more so. And after all, why shouldn't the man be on top? It's still the best position, all around." With an almost fierce little movement she placed her hands underneath her breasts, thrust them forth in sweet and reckless oblation. "I want to be just what I am now—I want to be a living, breathing, love-making woman. That's the hardest thing to be. The American housewife—all she's done is

turn herself into a well-paid whore. Not even an honest one. All right—
that's what they are, most of them . . ."

Laughing softly Blackburn nodded. She could be so scathing—yet it
was a defiance born of honesty and bewilderment. She was genuinely confused yet she refused to lie to herself, and this moved him inordinately.
Intransigence—the perilous, solitary kind—had always held for him a
peculiar distinction; even as a boy those isolate, defiant spirits had existed
as a kind of venerable fraternity. It was so hard, so very *hard* to press
after the often unwelcome truth in this world.

Lying there with her on the hard narrow couch in his study, listening
to her fine, easy contralto, absently tracing the line of her hip and thigh
with one hand, an untutored sculptor, he realized that the chemistry of
the moment had changed: he had already moved from the first flush of
triumph, of a prowess discovered and exulted in, to the more somber reflection of a sense of loss, of time irrevocably past and gone. *You've
actually said what you're thinking!* Her exclamation echoed and re-echoed
through his mind's corridors, staggering the rigors of two dozen years in
the flash of an eye. The public image he had striven so arduously to
create—that had, in large measure, slipped over him unbidden—had
walled him off from the intense, uncompromising young Foreign Service
Officer who had sent that angry report to John Foster Dulles. It was true:
he was not the same man. He hadn't meant to become webbed in temporizing, self-serving patterns but that was nevertheless how he'd wound up,
this warm June evening—and Jillie's fierce probity had thrown it into high
relief.

What was he to do? Tenderly he stroked her head, listening to her
bittersweet tales of despair and resolution and thinking his own thoughts,
carrying the two worlds simultaneously in his mind as he'd taught himself
to do; the habit of years. What he had just done marked a divide in his
life, a gigantic turning point that could alter everything he thought and
did. What he had done, for his kind of man, was—unthinkable. Or nearly.
Yet he had done it, and found a sinewed joy that left him transformed,
green with life . . .

He ran a free hand through his hair, listening to the ship's clock
striking in the hallway downstairs, the plangent double strokes. Eight bells.
And all's well. He needed to love, to be loved—simply, unreservedly: that
was the heart of it. After all the circumspections and evasions of a quarter
century, of permitting the slow avalanche of considerations of career, ideas
and policies to determine his responses, he needed the heedless plunge of
pure emotion, lips to breast, hand to loins, the dense union of heart and
body, the sweet vainglory of giving without stint or reckoning. Of loving.
Eleanor, for all her austerity and sense of sacrifice, had tried to own him,
control him, help him move in the channel of a particular professional
image. Now, here, on the eve of this last third of his life, he was seized

with the urgent need to slough off the scales of this sense of waste; to explore in opulent depth the tremendous possibilities in this girl, to recover some of the old, pure, discordant dreams of youth he'd known before time and discretion had ironed him out, turned him into a creature he no longer entirely—

She had leaped to her feet with astonishing suddenness; in the dull blued light from the windows he could see her groping about for her clothes.

"Where are you going?" he asked.

"Away. Like Shenandoah. It's after four."

"I know." He swung his feet to the floor, watching her. "Jillie."

"I've got to put on a light—I can't find anything."

"Jillie—"

"Yes *sir*, Mr. Sec!"

"Don't be *too* facetious . . ." Who had said that to him only recently? Someone or other. "I want to see you. Again soon."

"All right."

He was brushed with panic. A roll in the hay? Was that all this meant to her—a capricious bang, nothing more? But he knew in his belly it was more than that. It had to be . . .

"Circumspect," she was saying crisply, stepping into her pants. "We *must* be circumspect—the fate of nations hangs in the balance. Christ, it probably does. Is there a secret underground passageway I can use? that all your adoring lovers use?"

"No such luck, I'm afraid." He watched her from the couch, reluctant to move, to shatter this moment, render it unrecoverable. How fragile life was: how achingly fragile! Here was this girl, who had come within an ace of jumping into that elevator shaft in Cambridge because her lover had been—

"I'll drive you home," he said. "Where are you staying?"

"No, you won't—I won't hear of it."

"Yes. It's better that way."

"All right . . . if you think so." Yanking at her hair with a comb she swung on one foot—all at once ran to him and gripped his face in her hands, pressing it hard against her belly. "Oh, you've corrupted me already," she groaned. "All my noble principles. Anyway, I hope you're grateful."

He felt his eyes widen in consternation. "That's hardly the word . . ."

"Oh, I didn't mean *that!*" Fully clothed—she had dressed with a speed that was amazing—she moved away again. "I meant for that inside scoop on the CIA ploy. I hope to hell you're grateful—it wasn't the easiest thing in the world to divulge. What are you going to do about it? Of course it's none of my business."

He rubbed his face slowly. "Why, call an emergency meeting of Ex-

Comm, have Shelly Tremayne put to death by firing squad, and commence full-scale invasion of the Chinese mainland with unrestricted use of nuclear weapons. What did you think?"

She laughed, then stared at him uncertainly. "That's the trouble with you biggies—we never know whether you're kidding or not. Not entirely." Bending deftly she snatched up her bag. "Ah, everything's gone bonkers. La Pompadour and what's-her-name, the other one—they used to shuffle history around like card games."

"You have, too," he said. "You just have."

She made a face at him. "Don't put me on, old Sec. You'll be happily stirring up war with Upper Slivonia tomorrow. Without a care in the world." She put her hands on her hips. "You think *you've* got a reputation to uphold—what about me? What do you think my revolutionary friends would say? No," she mused in another tone, "I've always made the wrong moves. Don't tell me, I know it. When I was five years old I got the cookie-batter bowl to lick. And since then it's all been downhill."

He crossed to her in three strides and embraced her. "You're wonderful, Jillie," he murmured. "I've got to see you soon. Really soon." She was silent; to hide his agitation he smiled. "For the first time since I was a kid I wish things—were different . . ."

"Just power-crossed lovers, that's us." Then the rueful-wry little girl's expression vanished and her face looked wan and sad and uncommonly beautiful, as though seen deep under water. "Yeah," she said. "Isn't it fun to think that?"

EIGHT

"THIS WAS FOLLOWED BY the note of the nineteenth from Peking, stating that it would regard any Burmese incursion of Dhotalese territory as an act of war, and that it considered it primarily a Chinese responsibility to avert any possibility of conflict within the provisional state of Dhotal." Joseph Carter paused; his eyes, moving around the dull mirror of the long table's surface, encountered boredom, exasperation, mild amusement. "How this will affect Prince Naungapaya is not yet clear," he went on imperturbably. He was secretly pleased with the way his voice rang in the conference room—its deep, booming tones. He'd never spoken before the Coordinating Action Committee of the National Security Council (facetiously dubbed Co-Ax Co-Ax by its critics); he wouldn't be speaking now if Andy Stinchfield wasn't over in Walter Reed, felled by that horrendous case of gastroenteritis with complications. Here he was, however, holding forth royally.

"In any event Naungapaya has refused to surrender either the American or Russian teams to the Chinese authorities. In reply to Ambassador Van Kleeck's protest he has stated that he was seriously misinformed as to the Reclamation Mission's goals from the very first."

"What does he mean—*misinformed?*" Reinhold Vosz demanded. "How can he be misinformed about a GATO agreement to which he was himself a signatory?"

"We have no confirmation on that point, Doctor," Carter answered; he subtly increased the booming quality of his voice. "He merely repeated his earlier charges that the American and Soviet teams—he named Drachenfels from ours and Neshevsky from theirs—had been sent in for the express purpose of subverting the government of Dhotal to make it ripe for Burmese conquest."

"Hah! Trying to keep in solid with the Chicoms," Vosz barked. "As if *they* gave a broken pair of chopsticks . . ."

"I assume you're referring to the People's Republic of China, Reiny," Secretary Blackburn said from the head of the table.

Vosz wagged his head. "Official appellation purely."

"Yes—I blush for it. What do you suppose they call *us?* Yankimps? Amcaps? Let's explore what conditions Naungapaya would insist upon before releasing the Mission."

"Conditions—!" Vosz exploded. "The ungrateful little basilisk—we agree to give him a whiff of power and right away he starts lopping off heads . . . You don't mean to tell me you people are falling for all this tartuffery, do you?"

"Keep your shirt on, Reiny," Blackburn answered mildly. "We may be unregenerate doves over here, but we're not gulls."

"The whole gambit's a fraud. The Chinks were afraid the plebiscite wouldn't go their way, so they put the screws on him to take over."

"Wouldn't have to put them on very tight," Vice President Donlund said with a grunt. "From what I've seen of Laughing Boy, he'd sign anything they handed him." His amused, faintly contemptuous gaze rested on Carter for an instant, moved on. "Of course he wants to discredit the whole caper, now he's jumped the gun. And our boy Drachenfels is stuck with the lease."

"Who *is* this Drachenfels?" Secretary of Defense Semmes asked. "Why are they unloading on him like this?"

Carter said: "He's ostensibly a genius in hydraulic engineering."

"Ostensibly!" Vosz bounced tensely in his seat, jammed a hand down in his coat pocket. "That sounds like a Department answer. Don't you *know?*"

The voice of power. Carter regarded the Presidential Adviser for a brief moment—the coarse, leathery skin laced with its millions of finely cut lines, the bared yellow teeth, the dim flash of eyes behind the violet lenses: a copper engraving plate etched by a madman. Well, it came in all shapes, all sizes. For the flicker of an instant he felt a desire as piercing as hunger to grip that thick muscular throat in his two hands—an impulse replaced as quick as thought by the old indulgent, contumacious mirth. ". . . Mister *Dip*lomat." Matt Warfill's high, hoarse voice, lazily taunting. "What you think they going let you be—Jesus H. Napoleon or somebody?" Now Matt was dead, shot to bloody rags by the police in what Cronkite or Chancellor or somebody had christened the Battle of Wabash Avenue; and here he was, Cozy Joe Carter, the Voice of Southeast Asia (pro tem., be it admitted), all tangled up in this kooky China-Burma guessing game and the old Squeezer, of all people, playing the Man. And across the table the Neg looking fastidious and nervous in his custom suit straight from J. Hoare of London, scared flatulent the house nigger might tell Vosz to go shit in his chapeau. Which he just might, one of these days. But not today.

Still riding on the amused defiance, thrusting just a shade of it into his voice he said: "No, I *don't* know, sir. In all truth I'm not sure who does. There seems to be a fair measure of controversy surrounding Drachenfels' background. His appointment was urged—"

"Why not let's hear Shelly on that?" the Vice President intervened. "If that meets with your approval, Paul."

The Secretary nodded without expression. "What can you give us, Shelly?"

The CIA Director drew a single sheet of paper out of the breast pocket of his jacket and unfolded it. Tremayne was famous for these sheets of onionskin, single-spaced typed memoranda that never exceeded one page. "Brevity is the fruit of clarity," he was fond of saying. Long-winded analyses got short shrift out at Langley.

"He's forty-three. He was born in Friedland, now Pravdinsk, in East Prussia. His parents were killed in World War Two, and he was brought up by an uncle, a stonemason. He showed unusual mechanical aptitudes as a child and was graduated with high honors from the prestigious Voskolskaya Institute. He worked on some of the more important hydroelectric projects beyond the Urals."

Tremayne paused and glanced briefly at Carter. His eyes—a rich, deep hazel—had an almost magnetic force in their density. "He first concerns us as part of the Soviet team that built the Aswan Dam in Fifty-Six. While there he defected to our embassy, was granted asylum, and received American citizenship in due course. The name Drachenfels is an alias, of course. His real name was Otto Diefenbach. His remarkable competence was quickly recognized in our own engineering community. Since then he's taken part in a number of reclamation missions abroad, most recently the Magdalena River project in Colombia and the Brahmaputra Basin reclamation in Bangladesh. He was the logical choice to head up our Dhotal mission."

There was a short pause. Blackburn said: "What's he like as a person, Shelly?"

Tremayne looked up. "As a person? He's quite interesting. There's the typical engineer's outlook, of course—matter-of-fact, pragmatic. And then there's the Russian extravagance, the extremes of emotion. He's a vegetarian and a mystic, a person of considerable charisma. An engineer who's worked with him for years says he's utterly fearless."

"Utterly fearless." The Secretary's features had taken on that alert, inquiring edge, and the shadow of a smile.

"That's what my friend said. He said Drachenfels seems to have a faculty for inspiring complete loyalty in his subordinates."

"Happy man," Blackburn murmured. Peering down the table he said: "And now what do you have on him, Mike?"

Hudela opened a plain tan cardboard folder and studied it for a moment. He was balding and run to fat—one of those men whose mildness and girth are completely deceptive. Carter knew because he'd played some exhausting games of squash with State's Director of Intelligence and Research over the past months.

"Our file is substantially in agreement," he said quietly. "There are a few discrepancies, however. He was jailed in Bogotá in Sixty-Seven for getting into a fight with a Colombian government official over a woman. It caused quite a stir. Our people down there were instructed to extricate him quickly and quietly and they did; but it took some doing." He looked at Tremayne over his lenses. "You knew about that."

The CIA chief nodded. "It was a relatively minor thing. There was an OAS meeting coming up, and the consensus was to try to settle it with a minimum of flap."

"And then there was another episode in Gauhati," Hudela pursued softly. "A lot like Bogotá. Only this time he put the guy in the hospital."

"Extremes of emotion seems a mild way to put it," Semmes broke in, and Donlund laughed.

"Haven't you ever got in a fight over a woman, Fred?"

"Hell, no . . ." Semmes stared at him. "Have you?" But the Vice President only gave his amused, sardonic grin.

"That's all very well," Ernest Hazbrouck, Chairman of the Joint Chiefs, said cautiously. "But if he's going to keep getting in fist fights all over the world, creating international incidents . . ."

"I don't know whether he's a vegetarian or not," Hudela went on, "and I haven't got anything on his 'charisma. But people *I've* talked to tell me he's got enough personal vanity to satisfy Napoleon—he feels nobody ever pays enough respect to his talents."

"All right, gentlemen," Tremayne said with a trace of irritation, "he's a problem of sorts—he always has been, he's contentious, he's in and out of trouble. But he's a genius, they'll all tell you that. What are you going to do? He's absolutely invaluable in his field."

"But he *is* reliable, Shelly?" Blackburn asked him. "We can put credence in what he says? Provided we can reach him?"

The CIA man flashed his quick, matinee-idol's smile. "I guess it depends on which paper you read."

"I want to read them all," the Secretary answered flatly.

Tremayne pressed his hands flat on the desk. "All I can tell you is I'm satisfied about him. I think he's creditable enough, within the scope of his activities. He's no fly-by-night defector, I can tell you that—if he says the Russians were in touch with him over some loony scheme, you can bet on it."

"We're all betting on it," Blackburn answered; and watching his chief's face, intent, unsmiling, the broad mobile mouth all at once very firm and even, Carter thought: By God, this flap has got under his skin, all right.

The Secretary asked General Hazbrouck for a summary of the military situation in Burma then, and Carter sat back again and let his mind wander, watching the principals: Blackburn at the head of the table, his weight thrust to the side of his chair, his expression troubled now, curiously preoccupied; Vosz squeezing away on that black rubber grip in a frenzy of resentment (these meetings had been chaired by the Presidential Adviser in other years), twisting his head around in the high French collar; Semmes, with his good, humorless banker's features, his wary little eyes; Donlund, massive, immobile, his broad harsh face perfectly imperturbable and composed; Tremayne, handsome and urbane, taking a few notes with a slender gold pen. And Sid Jacobi, slumped across the table from him between Curran from Defense and one of Vosz's assistants named Wentzel. Actors in a play for which no one had written the second or third acts.

God it was fascinating! They were the center of power, these bored, irascible, assertive men—but the center of power was not what Carter had thought it would be, those years back on Wabash Avenue or at Michigan: a vast and superbly functioning machine moving toward a series of defined goals. Thou too, sail on, oh Ship of State! Baloney. It was more—it was a good deal more like a sackful of alley cats drifting across a mill pond . . . "Mister motherhumping diplomat." Matt Warfill's voice again, and the thick, smoky sunlight of the fire escape, a spider dance of people below, the Cubs game on Chink's transistor a dull sea-roar of sound. "Going to play Whitey's game for him, uh? Going to be one of those sweet-talking Rastus flunkies hustling papers around, driving them places, wiping their smooth white asses? Going to be a happy house nigger, Cozy-man?"

Teetering on the dirty black iron he'd grinned. "Nope. I'm going to make Secretary of State and then I'm going to drop the long bomb on all the honky powers, the world over."

Chink cried, "Who you skit-skooting, man—no black has ever got anywhere in the State Department, ever!"

"Bunche," Veezee said.

"Sad sack Uncle Tom," Matt declared softly, his big glistening arms riding his knees. "Going to tunnel from within, Coze? One them Trojan Greeks? That the petoot?"

"Why not?" he said, half defiant.

"Shiiiit, man—they won't even let you file the *used* toilet paper . . ."

He'd laughed with them, squinting at the flat gray sky, the shutter-storm of pigeons. Old Cozy, running off at the mouth. Yet he had been harder than any of those old friends and brothers: he had been harder, if only because he had schooled himself to crush his outsize passions into a ball and thrust them beneath the ebony stone of his composure whenever he chose. His Tecumseh mood, Blackburn had called it once, and he'd laughed in spite of himself; the Secretary didn't miss a hell of a lot.

But he'd made it serve him. A thousand nights up at Ann Arbor he had reviewed this personal foreign policy, armed it, perfected it. He was not going to wind up washing cars, or in jail, or a battered corpse. He would use this society as it had used the bodies and souls of his fore-bears, he would even the score a little—and his weapons would be not guns but covert calculation, the coolest manipulation of the very centers that had insured these centuries of white Brahmin control. He would curb all tendencies in himself toward hostility, defiance, open rebellion, no matter how great the provocation or how justified his anger. It would cap his education—it would be his true tutelage under the formal façade of the Foreign Service.

He'd been lucky in drawing Bangkok for his first tour. The ruinous American misadventure in Vietnam hadn't yet begun; the French were out to stay and that was that. The country pleased him, its ornate temples and black, bound jungle masses, the purple hills. His chief was a quiet, cultured type who liked chamber music groups and was about as enlightened as most Ivy League types got. Third Secretary Carter was deferential, circumspect, conscientious. What the doctor ordered. São Paulo proved even better. Back in Washington between tours he'd married Frances and brought her down there with him. The Brazilians loved him and he them. He roamed with the crowds on Avenida del Sol, played tennis in the long, breezy afternoons, and got good reports. All life was a trade, and he was learning his, keeping his nose clean, moving up. The American Way.

Then came Umbara. He'd been immediately pleased at the assignment—Consul General at Nouvelle Liège, second city of the new black republic. A time of turbulence, even occasional violence, sure—but a crucible meant heat, and light, too. It might even be a kind of homecoming. He was greeted warmly at the airport by Prime Minister Gambala, a tall, hawk-faced man with powerful hands, and hurried to a military review, a fertility rite, and a boisterous banquet at the palace, where he feasted on suckling pig and a native drink that looked exactly like mint jelly and burned like a bank of acetylene torches. Black men embraced him, danced for him, brought him gifts. He went to bed in a blur of Afro-American bonhomie, celebratory fireworks, and the decision to have Fran fly up from Stanleyville with the baby the following week.

The next afternoon he was dragged from his car by a squad of Umbaran infantrymen, manhandled into one of the abandoned Standard Oil offices and left there. The door was locked from the outside; the view of the street included two soldiers who pointed their rifles at him playfully; he moved away from the windows. When he called the Ministry of Internal Security he was greeted by a roar of laughter and the line went dead. Around five o'clock a sinister figure in a forest green uniform with a choke collar and carpet slippers came in and handed him what was clearly an expulsion order.

"But this is impossible—this means I am non grata . . ."

"It has been established that you are in reality a colonel of paratroopers and that you are seeking to overthrow the Central Government of Umbara."

"Established? What do you mean *established?* There has been a mistake. I am a United States consul, I am accredited . . ."

"That is your assertion. But we know differently."

"How do you know differently—what evidence do you have? This is ridiculous. Look, I demand to see Prime Minister Gambala."

"Prime Minister Gambala is no longer in power. He is no longer in Umbara. In fact, he no longer exists." The man had a curious yellow complexion and short black teeth. "You will leave at dawn tomorrow. Traitor!" he hissed, and left the room.

There was fighting outside. Certain bursts of gunfire were answered by others, and once he thought he heard the dull thump of artillery. But the attitude of the troops seemed to be one of intense festivity: they squealed around corners in jeeploads, spilling half the occupants; they sang various slogans, they drank mountainously from bottles or gourds or gasoline cans and fired joyful shots into the tropic night. But Carter's own guards never left. Virtually untutored in Swahili he couldn't make any contact with them.

Around ten o'clock Acting Foreign Minister Bandikuvu entered and introduced himself. He looked like a black Bacchus, fastidious and merry.

"This is merely a courtesy visit," he announced in rapid, excellent French. "Not official, you understand. I am delighted to inform you that I have the necessary documents. Exit visa and other papers required." He sat down at the vanished oil official's desk and massaged his small fat hands as though he were washing them in grease solvent. "Well, Mr. Carter: and how have you enjoyed your stay in Umbara?"

Carter stared at him. The Acting Foreign Minister's expression remained perfectly genial. There was a shout some distance away, gunshots and a prolonged falsetto howling.

"Needless to say, Your Excellency, I have not found it very enjoyable. One hardly relishes being held like a common criminal—neither informed of the source of such astonishing charges nor permitted to communicate with one's superiors. And then served an expulsion order—"

"Ah, no-no-no-no. It is not a question of expulsion, not a question of that at all." The Foreign Minister opened his little fat hands. "There is merely this suggestion that your *current* presence here is inauspicious, at-this-moment-in-time. Later, when circumstances improve . . ." There was a terrific crash outside, as though a refrigerator had been dropped from some rooftop, and then a chorus of wild laughter, echoed by a burst of automatic rifle fire a few blocks away. "There is no formal expulsion order, however, my dear Mr. Carter—you have my heartfelt assurances on this matter. Our supremely cordial relations with the United States will continue unchanged, absolutely unchanged."

"I see. I am delighted to hear that. In that connection possibly His Excellency might care to examine this." Carter handed Bandikuvu the order, sat back and folded his arms. Bandikuvu read it through and looked up again, smiling merrily.

"I see. Yes." He spread his hands on the desk and pushed them back and forth on the oily wood: they left a dull damp trail. "There are of course certain quarters in which this could be construed as an expulsion order. That is to say there *is* that interpretation. But you have my personal guarantee, as Acting Foreign Minister of the Republic of Umbara, that you are under no surveillance whatsoever. None whatsoever."

There was a violent commotion on the stairs outside the room: something dropped, something falling, and then glass in a quick treble shower. The door was flung open and crashed against the wall. A figure lurched into the room: a giant in a powder-blue blouse and tropical shorts. A submachine gun was cradled in one arm, and a slender black whip dangled from his other hand, slithering on the floor. A rope made of a dozen strands of red-and-gold braid was wound around his neck and shoulders, and there was the single lion's-head pip of an Umbaran colonel on one shoulder board. Behind him were two soldiers carrying rifles. Swaying, grinning hugely he turned, and Carter saw then the oversize scarlet sergeant's chevrons, like dress chevrons of half a century ago. With a deft flick of his wrist he sent the whip's end writhing softly on the floor: Carter and the Foreign Minister both stared at it. The big man laughed silently, his eyes half closed—all at once raised the submachine gun until its short blue snout pointed directly at Bandikuvu's belly.

The Foreign Minister crossly waved a small pink hand, speaking in Swahili. The sergeant—or colonel—shook his head ponderously, then gestured toward the door with the gun; a quick, peremptory movement. Bandikuvu sprang to his feet with an alacrity surprising in a man so fat. He was showing his credentials, a forest of papers, Carter's exit visa, talking all the while. The giant looked at the visa, turned it upside down and peered at it again, scowling thunderously—scaled it away across the room; leaflike it descended to the floor. The Acting Foreign Minister was speaking more rapidly now; sweat stood out in slick chains on his cheeks and neck, staining his fine silk shirt. Carter heard his own name mentioned repeatedly, caught a few words here and there. Bandikuvu was telling them to go, they could go now, they had carried out their duties admirably, they were *free to go*. The sergeant-colonel stared back at him balefully—all at once cracked the whip full force on the desk. Carter and the Foreign Minister both jumped. The giant laughed raucously, snapped his fingers. One of the soldiers behind him produced a squat, dark bottle and the sergeant took a prolonged drink, his throat cords rippling like a python's skin while they all watched him.

Bandikuvu launched on a new tirade of expostulation, his hands moving like pale fans in the hot night; his face was ashen now, his lips puffed and compressed in his urgency. Slowly the sergeant's great head came back, slowly he swung the gun's evil blued snout to the center of Carter's body and held it there. It was a strange weapon, all slick cylinders and outlandish knobs, Russian possibly, or Czech; Carter looked feverishly for the safety—saw with a flash of fright the giant's finger crooked hard on the trigger. Bandikuvu's voice raced along, thin and importunate, saying God knew what. He was going to be shot. Shot as an American, as the agent of a white imperialist power by his big black brother, full of emerging national consciousness and booze. That was exactly what was going to happen if he didn't do something. Now. At once. Frantic, he found his gaze riveted on the mammoth chain of gold braid, a child's dream of a fourragère, looped around the man's neck and shoulders.

"Be silent!" he said to Bandikuvu.

With infinite care, forcing himself to stare back into the wild, blood-shot eyes, he rose to his feet. The gun's muzzle followed him up. The giant growled once, threateningly.

"You wish to see my credentials?" Carter asked in French. "My official papers? But of course." With all the discipline he possessed he forced himself to smile, and extracted his wallet; and then in the smattering of Swahili he'd picked up before leaving Washington: "Excuse me, revered Colonel. I did not understand." With the most ponderous deliberation, while the giant scowled and muttered and Bandikuvu gazed at him as if he'd just descended from Saturn, he searched importantly in his wallet and plucked out the honorary airlines card they'd given him when he'd crossed the international date line years ago—a lavish gold card spangled with red seals and escutcheons and the embossed portrait of one of the legendary pioneers in American aviation. In his grandest Tecumseh mood Carter handed it over.

"I am ambassador—American," he went on in Swahili. "Minister give me honor. Honor American ambassador. You see?"

The sergeant took the card and looked at it—his features broke into pure delight. He nodded. Happily he showed the card to the soldiers, then to Bandikuvu, who peered at it in amazement edged with terror. The gun's muzzle swung away to the floor, the sergeant visited on Carter a torrent of conversation, glancing admiringly at the card—finally extended it with great reluctance to the American.

"No," Carter said, demurring, managing his best smile. "You. I give you. For—American friendship."

The giant laughed in sheer pleasure. Still holding the airlines card he brought his whip hand up in mighty, quivering British salute, broke it away. There was a final exchange that Carter couldn't follow, and then the warriors departed in a tumult of shouts and laughter, crashing their way down the stairs.

Acting Foreign Minister Bandikuvu sat down quickly and shook his head in fastidious displeasure; he seemed to be dissolving in his own perspiration—it was as if the bones had been suddenly withdrawn from his bouncy, corpulent little frame.

"It is a matter for genuine sorrow, my dear sir, that certain servants of our infant republic possess not the slightest comprehension of the nuances of protocol . . ."

General Hazbrouck was still talking; as was to be expected. He was a tall, slender Alabaman with the grave, earnest face of a society dentist. The military situation, suitably boiled down, seemed to be that they had virtually no idea of the strength of Naungapaya's forces or where they were headed, but that it was probably a good idea to assume something or other; and that the Burmese government could probably repel an invasion if that eventuality arose—especially with vigorous close-in US air support, interdiction of the Burma Road and other principal routes and trails. As the Chinese were already moving to isolate Naungapaya's Liberation Army and block the progress of its advance units toward Lashio, none of this seemed too pressingly vital. Still, you never knew. When Chinese armies moved—

Across the table Sid Jacobi was following Hazbrouck's dissertation with an air of intense distaste which made him resemble that hatchet-faced Hollywood actor who always played claims adjusters or loan agents; meeting Carter's gaze he rolled his eyes to the ceiling and then closed them. Why *had* Blackburn called this meeting right now? From everything Carter himself could see, too much was vague and unresolved, the reports still hadn't added up to a coherent pattern. But probably the Chief had his reasons.

Meanwhile he himself had work to do—he was half crazy to get back to grappling with part of the avalanche. The Lexicorn was pressing him for American military aid; a mob had tried for the second time that week to sack the embassy in Rangoon; Ace Clark, the head of CARE, was screaming about a desperate shortage of rice in the Mogaung region—it seemed impossible especially after all their efforts to introduce IR-8, the new miracle rice seed, that there could be *a shortage of rice in Burma,* but there was one; there was Premier Shiraga's impending visit, and the mounting uproar over Peking's enthusiastic welcome of the United Black Congress leaders Jethro and Cummins, who had evaded U. S. customs officials disguised as members of a folk-rock band, and now seemed to be embarked on a triumphal tour of the Orient.

And over and above everything was Van Kleeck's latest cable on Naungapaya's seizure of the Pao Shan consulate which had come in not three hours ago and filled them with more confusion and dismay. Only Blackburn had been singularly unmoved. "Gentlemen, gentlemen," he had said in the voice that could silence any squabble, "in itself it's nothing, the incident is nothing. It's how we react to it that's important. There's no reason to assume this was planned, or that Peking ordered or even sanctions it. We've made our share of mistakes, wouldn't you say? Let's allow them a gaffe or two. Things will be clearer in a little while . . ."

He found himself watching the Secretary now, admiring that curious balance of vigilance and ease. It had been Blackburn who had reached him, sponged away some of the raging disgust he'd felt growing in him for the better part of a decade. After Umbara, after the obsessive butchery of Vietnam and the cunnythumb deceits of the Nixon years, Blackburn had been like a gulp of pure oxygen. He had walked into the auditorium that first afternoon and faced them all simply, directly, his thumbs hooked in his trouser pockets in that easy, characteristic gesture.

"Some of you know me. Many of you do not—a condition I'll do my best to rectify as quickly as possible. We need to know each other. The ship is already underway." That alert, inquiring glance had encountered each and every one of them, it seemed—the administrative and Institute people, the geographical bureaus, even the code clerks and secretaries who were present; it rested longest on the gravely hostile faces of the older career men—some of whom had openly resented his appointment—with the faintest glint of amusement.

"The Department has had its rajahs, its buddhas, its corporation lawyers—even its glamour boys. I shall try to avoid all of these clichés—and doubtless tumble into one of my own. In any event I'll try my best not to disgrace you." There was a low, amused murmur in the hall. "There is one thing I'm *not* going to be: I'm not going to be a shadow. I am going to be Secretary of State. And if negotiations are carried on with Peking or Moscow or the Pan-African Federation, *I* will carry on these negotiations, and no one else."

There was a short pause, and again he passed his glance over them all. "You are people of marked excellence in your respective fields—you wouldn't be here if you were not. And I am going to give you unqualified support in the expression of that excellence. In return I shall ask one thing of you above all else: that you have courage, and the imagination and irreverence it commands. I am not interested in those who wait to see which way the wind might be blowing, and cite protocol, or who qualify any subject right out of existence in the name of discretion. I shall seek out the person who holds strong convictions, and who knows *why* he holds those convictions—and who is willing to take on the President himself if he feels he is right about them. And I will be standing right beside him when and if he does.

"If you have any grievances, ideas on policy, crises you can't resolve I shall try to hear them, all of them, this side of exhaustion. I shall try not to demand of you more than you can bear—though the Department has always done just that, in one way or another. And I suppose it always will. The plaque downstairs has recorded its names, and deservedly so—but there are many, many other Joel Barlows and Victor Stanwoods and

Maddin Summerses who have held the fort, moved with wisdom and fortitude in desperate situations—even though there was no one to sing of them in sacred verse."

He had paused then and opened his hands—making them a single group in that one impulsive, hortatory gesture. "Hard things have been said of you these past years—you have heard them. That State is a shadow bureau, that it is moribund, that it has forfeited its right to pre-eminence in government. Well, whatever truth there may have been in such talk is now at an end. The foreign policy of the United States of America has never been a secondary role in this Department, and it is not going to be now. Let there be no further thoughts of circumspection or survival. It still continues to be true that sacrifice and anonymity are the lot of the public servant—that pride in a quiet competence is the real stuff of heroism. That will never change. But in this swiftly moving world of ours the most trivial incident, the most solitary decision may well have long and fateful consequences. That is why every single one of you is important, why every one of you is needed. We are going forward from here, together."

"I think he means it," Fran had told Carter later, her eyes shining. "All those things he said. I think he's wonderful."

"You broads all fall for him. He's got some sneaky sort of appeal."

"Oh, stop it! He's really different from Rogers, Rusk, the rest of them."

"Sure. His name is Blackburn, and he was—"

"No. In a funny, deep way. For God's sake, he made you a DAS . . ."

"Why not? It's good politics to have a few lovin' pickaninnies sprinkled around in the geographical bureaus."

"Don't be ridiculous—it'll only mean trouble for him and you know it. What a cynic you are, Coze."

"That's right. Us leopards don't change our spots. Especially the dark ones."

"Well, you ought to try it sometime. Same old spots get boring, you know?"

She was smiling, but her eyes held that edge of challenge, of calm appraisal he respected. "You're right," he said. "He sounds good—I know. I only wonder—if push came to shove whether he'd put his body on the line."

"He would." She nodded somberly. "I bet he will. You'll see."

He wasn't sure—he still wasn't sure. At first he'd distrusted the Californian's darting wit, the easy, poised urbanity; it was only with the passage of months, of harried afternoons and sleepless nights, as he watched his chief threading his way through the shoals of cross-purpose and obstinacy and conflicting will that he'd seen the fine steel underneath —and the gelid, Chicago South Side cynicism that had been his mainstay,

the prop of his peculiar brand of defiance, had begun to melt around the
edges. Early in the negotiations over the creation of the Federated Republic
of Micronesia he remembered finding Blackburn still at his desk, though
it was nearly two in the morning, engaged in arduous research on the
inhabitants of Ponape and Truk.

"Why do that, sir?" he'd asked in astonishment. "You've got Marv
Richards and Phil Geissen for that kind of spade work. And me. I hope
you don't mind my saying this, but you can't know an awful lot about the
Caroline Islanders and their problems."

The Secretary had given him a somber, weary smile. "That's why,
Joe," he'd answered. "That's just why."

"Don't be too unforgiving, will you, Joe?" Blackburn had said to him
another night, late; Carter had been quarreling earlier with Miles Stout
over the latter's opposition to Japan's inclusion in the GATO treaty. "We've
all of us got grievances of one kind or another, we're all feeling our way.
It's a horribly imperfect system, but it's all we've got to work with. Unless
you want to blow it all up and start over again. You don't want to blow it
all up, do you, Joe?"

There was a shade of gravity in the Secretary's face that made Carter
hesitate. "No," he answered slowly, "no, I don't want to blow it all up.
I got over that idea long ago. But I'd certainly like to see some changes
made."

Tilting back dangerously in his big chair, Blackburn had locked his
hands behind his head. " 'I came into this world, not chiefly to make this
a good place to live in, but to live in it, be it good or bad.' Know who
said that? A revolutionary—maybe the best one this country ever had."
He sighed, and passed his hand several times through his hair. "No, the
older and tireder and more discouraged I get, the more eminently sensible
Mr. Thoreau sounds . . . I used to think I'd like to make the world over
in three strokes of a pen. Pa-*chooongg!* as Reiny puts it so eloquently.
Now I'm not so sure that what *I* was so sure of is exactly the true prescription for the other three billion sons of perdition." Abruptly he
slammed himself forward in his seat. "But by God, some things are
clearly, demonstrably right or wrong," he declared with a grin. "And those
things we *can* do something about. And we're going to . . ."

Carter straightened in his chair. Jacobi had just passed him a note
across the conference table, scowling. Very slowly Carter unfolded it. It
said: *Drachenfels is not (as we thought) the illegitimate offspring of Erich
von Stroheim and the Blue Angel, but ACTUALLY Maria Ouspenskaya
in drag.*

Frowning just as intensely Carter wrote below it: *Watch that. Some
of my best friends are* straight *Aryans,* and handed it back. Wentzel was
watching them with ill-concealed, avid annoyance, his eyes squeezed to
slits behind his glasses. State secrets. The Afro-Jewish power bloc at State,

tunneling from within. Ernie Hazbrouck, still perorating about the current field efficiency of the Burmese army, glanced at him, moderately startled. Carter nodded back, to show his vehement support of those sentiments. Sid passed him the note again. Crowded down at the bottom, almost indecipherable now, it read: *Oh, I'm FOND enough of them—the only thing is they all* look *alike. You know.*

Carter folded the paper and nodded rapidly at Jacobi, as if in intense confirmation. It seemed to have worked, however: Hazbrouck broke off and leaned back, shoulders squared, chin out. Hut hoo ree fom, I hear the beat of a China drum. A staff man after Korea, he'd been with SHAEF in Germany, thus neatly bypassing that Vietnamese slit trench that had blighted so many careers, military and otherwise. Like all good high brass, though, he'd never lost his instinctual distrust of State.

"And so where does that leave us, if at all?" Vosz was saying, flexing his shoulders in a rapid, nervous rhythm. "Full of condolences, all best wishes. Toodleoo, so long, goodbye. I would say we are presented with five options. We can offer Bodawyin full military aid short of American manpower, we can—"

"I'm not interested in options as yet, Reiny," Blackburn broke in on him. "I'd like to put a few things together first."

"And meanwhile Rome burns, along with London and Washington. It seems to me we've put together all we need to. In any case I have to be back at the White House in ten minutes—no more no less." He flung himself savagely around in his seat. "The *essence* of the matter is that Competrin's position becomes more serious every day. Not to mention the Michelin people and Tonkalloy. It's a farce! The fire begins to burn the stick, the stick begins to beat the dog . . . or do we calmly sit here and let them sink without trace, mmmmh?"

Blackburn smiled. "Why, Reiny—I didn't know you were so solicitous about the needs of our overseas capital. Has your broker switched you over to Competrin this week?"

"Merely weighing another of the options, my dear Paul. The President thinks of them. And so therefore should we. Don't you agree? Meanwhile our rufulous little friends make hay. What's this flap from Rangoon—the embassy trouble there?"

Carter said quietly: "The latest cable from Ambassador Davis informs us that it is under control. It was a sporadic demonstration, mainly students and unemployed teak workers. They dispersed in two hours. There was no discernible leadership, and no damage aside from a few broken windows."

"What about the Dragon Lady?" Semmes asked. This was a reference to Naungapaya's wife, the Princess Yawlat, a querulous thin woman with a growth on her neck who was credited with having held the Prince neutral for years.

"They say she's up at Likiang," Mike Hudela answered. "In seclusion."

"She's of no consequence." It was the first time Donlund had spoken in some while. "It's that dancer, the one he's been shacking with. The Eurasian baby with the dreamy eyes."

"Anaïsa," Tremayne offered.

"That's the one. That's when Laughing Boy started to go wrong. I want to tell you, *affaires d'état* and *affaires de glande* don't mix. You want to play Attila you've got to tend to business. Some of the Shan chiefs have been in a fit ever since."

Tremayne said, "Our sources say she's still in the pay of the Chicoms —oops, sorry, Paul: slip of the tongue." He grinned, but the Secretary, staring at him somberly, unseeing, suddenly got to his feet and walked over to the window and looked out, his back to the group. "I'm told her grandfather was one of the heroes of the Long March," the CIA chief went on, "and she's been trying to talk Naunga into an escapade like this one as a prelude to Chinese annexation. But hell, you can hear anything you want to if you listen long enough."

"Curious," Vosz said after a short pause. "An equation with more unknowns than givens. Why should there be so many unknowns?"

"It's a singularly inaccessible corner of the world," the Neg offered. "And with the imposition of this *cordon sanitaire* by the Chinese . . ."

"I know, I know all about their sanitary procedures." The Presidential Adviser shot the little black grip from right hand to left, went on squeezing it convulsively. "Well, let's deal with what we *do* know. What about this deplorable situation in Pao Shan, Mr. Carter? Do we gracefully acquiesce, let this red riff-raff invade our territory, lock up our people and laugh in our faces, for all the world to marvel at? What, if anything, is being done?"

"Negotiations for the release of the consulate staff have been momentarily interrupted," Carter answered slowly. He stole a glance at Blackburn, seeking his attention, but the Secretary was still gazing out of the window. "Pending the Chinese efforts to induce Naungapaya to turn them over to their jurisdiction, along with the Drachenfels mission itself."

"Yes yes yes—I know. But our ambassador—he's been in touch with them, hasn't he?"

"Yes, he has."

"And what does he say, if I am not being too presumptuous?"

Vosz's face was smooth and expressionless, but his lips quivered oddly. If you could only see the little bastard's eyes! Carter drew a deep breath, glanced for intercession at Stout: the Under Secretary's gaze flickered with alarm. He said, "Ellery Hopkins, our Deputy Principal Officer there, was seriously injured during the occupation. Consequently we—"

"Well, your consul there, your man in charge—what is his report?"

Well, it was too bad. It was probably inevitable, given the circumstances, but this was going to end badly; he could feel it. He answered casually, "There's been nothing definitive, beyond the facts that Naungapaya's forces burst into the consulate, rounded up our personnel and confiscated the files. It's our feeling that until the Chinese have—"

"Mr. Carter," Vosz broke in on him with icy tones, "I have never suffered fools gladly, as you may know—and I suffer deceivers even less. I am not elated when information is being withheld from me." He reared back in his seat; the whites of his eyes were dimly visible now. "I am not *interested* in your feelings, or your artful dodges—now suppose you give us the report from your consul at Pao Shan—and let's be quick about it!"

Control. Control, and an iron dissimulation: his weapons. Beating down rage he drew another slow breath. Blackburn was still standing with his back to the conference table, staring into space. Stout was signaling him, half frantic. Well, here goes nothing.

"I'm afraid I can't do that, Doctor," he said evenly.

"And why not?"

"Consul Umphlett, our Officer in Charge there, was not available."

There was a low murmur of surprise around the table. Vosz cried: "What do you mean—not available?"

"He has disappeared."

The room was very quiet. The Presidential Assistant glared at him savagely—all at once burst into his racketing, metallic laugh. "Ah, that's marvelous! That—is—consummate . . . And so what will you do now? send a delegation to Pao Shan?—four nautch girls, a star quarterback from the Dallas Cowboys and a Unitarian minister? Defected to the Reds, has he?—now *there's* a thought to dwell on: sensational!" And with sudden harsh ferocity: "Is that how you run your bureau? *Answer me!*"

But he was ready now: the rage was gone, the hollow consternation and his disgust at having to evade this odious, malignant little man. He gave Vosz his full, easy grin, knowing that would enrage him beyond anything else, far more than his flare pockets and Afro haircut, his smooth black skin.

"Check, man," he offered in lazy, drawling tones, "I encourage French leave on the part of *all* chiefs of mission—most especially in time of flaming in-ter-*na*-tional crisis. It's just like nocturnal shakedowns in the army. Keeps everybody on his toes, dig?"

"—Enough!" Vosz shouted; waggling his head he coughed a rattling chain of phlegm high in his throat. "We have a crisis here, a dangerous crisis in the making—do you think we are gathered here to listen to your aboriginal blackamoor wit?"

"No—yours, Reiny!"

Blackburn had whirled from the window. His voice, flat and strident, overrode the sudden tumult of voices in the room. "We *always* want to hear you at your waggish best." He leaned forward over the table, riding on his powerful shoulders. "That is an entirely offensive remark you have just made to a distinguished member of my department. Offensive and insulting. I demand that you withdraw it this very instant."

Vosz flung himself back in his seat. "I!—withdraw!"

"Exactly."

Carter began, "Sir, I don't need—"

"Never mind, Joe," the Secretary interrupted him sharply; his eyes were still fastened on Vosz. "Reiny, I demand that you apologize to Secretary Carter."

The two men measured each other for several seconds. It was utterly silent in the room. A troubled group portrait: Blackburn, his face bloodless and very hard, his lips compressed, bent forward over the table; Vosz reared back, quivering, wrenching and wrenching his neck against the tight high collar; the others caught in attitudes of irritation, chagrin, blank dismay. A long moment in which Carter's rage ebbed, and a swelling alarm seeped into its place. Then all at once Donlund's rough baritone said mildly, "All right, Reiny, come on now, you've had your little drama, tell him you didn't mean it," and at nearly the same instant Vosz's teeth bared in his satanic grin and he crowed:

"Of course of course of course! A joke, I was making a joke purely. Did you think I was serious? Dry your eyes—I always say things I don't mean, mean things I don't say. Don't you know that by now? *Of course* I apologize for any misconstructions, any innuendoes . . ."

"Good," Blackburn said softly. "I'm immensely glad to hear that.— And now I think we've gone as far as we can for the time," he said to the long table. "I'm grateful to all of you gentlemen for giving time for this, it's been most helpful . . . Don't let me hold you any longer from your pressing schedule, *Doctor,*" he said to Vosz with heavy emphasis on the title, and smiled his radiant smile.

"Not at all. Believe me, I'll look forward to a subsequent meeting, Mr. Secretary." Gathering up his papers, calling to his aides, the Presidential Adviser hurried from the meeting.

As the room emptied Carter went up to the Secretary, who was talking to Jacobi. "It—wasn't necessary to do that, sir," he murmured. "But thanks, anyway."

"Don't be silly, Joe. It was utterly necessary. Like most court jesters, Reiny goes too far."

"Typical nigger reaction," Sid said; he was wearing his most pinched claims-adjuster expression. "They're just too uppity—we never should have let them off the plantation."

"Or out of the ghettos," Carter retorted. "The shtetel, isn't it?"

"How'd you come to be such close friends with the Angelic Doctor, Joey? How do you get along, living together and all that?"

"Oh, we get along just fine. As long as he doesn't use the bathroom, I mean."

Blackburn laughed shortly; he was writing something in the little blue notebook he always carried. "Remember, boys: in the world of diplomacy it's better to be feared than loved. Uncle Niccolò said so."

"But it's even better to be despised," Carter heard himself say suddenly.

The Secretary threw him a light, sharp glance. "Really? Why?"

"Because it gives you more maneuverability—you see things you wouldn't see any other way. It hands you the element of surprise. Ask Sid —he knows what I mean. How'd you think the Jewish bankers got to be running the country?"

Blackburn frowned through his grin. "It would seem the initiative rests with Reiny, right now."

"I'm sorry about that Umphlett business, sir," Carter said.

"Don't worry about it. It would have come out sooner or later."

"I should have handled it more adroitly, I know."

"What could you have done? He put it to you directly."

"I know. That's the one thing that bothers me."

"What's that, Joe?"

"I keep wondering what there is in this whole Burma Triangle hassle that warrants such—such excessive heat."

"Yes." The Secretary gave him that alert, piercing gaze, nodded rapidly. "Well, these are heat-laden days. Let's hope we don't all get cooked to a turn." He picked up his briefcase. "Sid, come on back with me, will you? There are a couple of things I want to talk over with you."

"Right, Chief."

"And Joe—you'll bring me anything from Van as soon as you have it."

"Yes, sir."

"We've got to have more to go on—it can't *all* be that mysterious. And it isn't. It damned well isn't."

Following them quickly along the stately, well-carpeted corridor, past the mildly disapproving portraits of Blackburn's predecessors, Carter found himself staring at the Secretary's broad back. It was so strange—a lapse like that. Standing at the window, back there; as though he hadn't heard any of them. As though he were a thousand miles away. It wasn't like the chief at all.

NINE

"*Italy,*" Félice Narandji read from the slip of paper in her clear, curiously accented voice. "*Italy: Army Venice invades Trieste.*"

"No!" Blackburn exclaimed. "There's a mistake somewhere."

Reinhold Vosz gave a sharp crow of delight, and Félice said: "Please, Mr. Secretary. Your protocol is slipping. I'm reading Italy's field orders as written." She smiled her slow, serene smile. She was Sino-Indian, the daughter of New Delhi's Finance Minister and the latest in that glittering parade of Big Bill Donlund's lady companions—and she was by far the most beautiful of them all.

"*Fleet Adriatic moves on Albania. Army Greece supports Fleet Adriatic.*" Leaning forward she gently pushed the small green blocks across the cardboard national boundaries.

"Oh, dear," Natalie Jacobi murmured. Vosz crowed again, and clapped his hands.

Blackburn gazed at his son in consternation. "But—you gave me your word!" he protested. "A defensive alliance. You gave me unconditional guarantees—"

The room broke into laughter.

"That's diplomacy." Land looked wolfish and gleeful, holding an unlighted cigarette between his teeth. "You just never know how the old flag will wag, now do you?"

"I'm playing this game under protest." Blackburn grinned at the others. "I appeal to the United Nations."

"No United Nations," Donlund answered. "No UN, no League, no World Court, no nothing. This is Europe as she used to be, Paul. When men were men, and devil hook the low man."

"But this isn't *diplomacy!* This is nothing more than international anarchy, naked military aggression . . ."

"You see?" Vosz appealed to Eleanor Blackburn. "Reliance on these flimsy international tribunals has sapped his fiber."

The Vice President shook his head. "No, he was trapped by history. That Aehrenthal ploy. And look where *he* ended up, poor bastard."

"Now, Bill," Félice said. "Don't act superior."

"But I am." His white counters were all over the board, his and Vosz's. "Can I help it if I am?"

Félice raised her hand and said, "Quiet, everybody," and now Blackburn could hear the bellbuoy off Turk's Head, desolate yet comforting in the warm night air. "Dispositions: Support for Austrian Army Serbia is cut. Italy occupies Trieste. Austrian Army Bulgaria dislodged, Austrian Army Serbia annihilated." She removed the little red cube. "Russia occupies Bulgaria."

"Disaster," Sid Jacobi muttered, scowling gloomily at the map of 1905 Europe. "Irre-*triev*-able disaster."

"Isn't that what always happens?" Eleanor asked. "Austria collapses, and drags down Germany?"

"Yes, relax and enjoy it," Vosz chortled. "Since it's inevitable."

"Reiny," Natalie said, "that's positively obscene . . ."

"Perfidious is the only word for it," Blackburn said to Land. "What did they do? Did they promise you Trieste and the Tyrol? Just try and get them—you won't have any more luck than Orlando did. And what about him?" He nodded toward Dunlund, who was sitting perfectly inert now, bourbon in hand, watching the ships' riding lights moving on the Sound. He was wearing a beautiful clear yellow sport shirt of raw silk and he looked impervious and massive, a north woods Buddha. "What makes you think you can trust *him?*"

"I can't," Land answered with the same mischievous grin. "Any more than anybody else. That's the game. You're hung up on the wrong value system."

For the past three hours they had been playing Diplomacy. Natalie and Sid were houseguests at the Paling for the weekend, Donlund and Félice were staying overnight with Vosz at West Chop, and Eleanor had invited them all over for dinner. Félice had introduced the game to Vosz, who'd brought it along with them, extolling its relevance to world politics.

Blackburn had objected. "Reiny, that's preposterous—a parlor game! At best it's a caricature."

"No, that is what's astonishing. The parallels, the scenarios are uncanny. You'll see."

One thing had led to another and they'd begun to play. Félice appointed herself Gamesmaster. It *was* uncanny—there was an almost overpowering tendency to fall into the old alignments: Triple Alliance, Dual Entente, the incessant wooing of Great Britain by everyone, the clashes in Belgium, in North Africa and the Balkans. The heart of the game was in the pattern of "diplomatic" tête-à-têtes held in the far corners of the living room and out on the verandah; whispered huddles gathered all around Silas Seaver who, chin wedged in one bony shoulder, slept on under his quilt of newspapers in a wing chair, now and then breaking into a sudden barking snore. The Judge had ridiculed them all—grown people wasting their time in such childish tomfoolery!—and had promptly gone to sleep.

Blackburn found himself inclined to agree with the old man. It was hectic somehow, disturbing—fun and yet not fun: you found yourself continually rejecting the old, failed policies, and then falling into others just as bad. Your very professional knowledge got in your way. Why hadn't they made up a mythical Europe, a squabbling congeries of Ruritanias and Erewhons? Yet of course that was half the appeal: you *were* Delcassé, Bülow, Salisbury, guiding your nation through those early years of the century when time had been so long and events so measured, and even the war clouds gathered with a kind of baroque majesty. You would succeed where they had failed . . .

"—A clutch of power-hungry little boys playing chicken." Blackburn smiled. It was almost impossible to resist Jillie's saucy analogy, watching Vosz chortling with high glee, annexing the Low Countries, or Donlund moving with sure stealth against Prussia and Constantinople. A game and yet not a game. What he noticed first was his own instinctive desire to avoid conflict—he found himself writing *Army Galicia Stands, Army Budapest Supports Army Galicia,* and in the secret diplomacy sessions arguing for defensive alliances, arbitration, détentes—anything to keep the drums from beating. Hung up on the wrong value system, Land had said. *Was* he trapped in history? But hell, that was not only inevitable, it was wisdom: you learned from Bethmann Blank Checks and forty-eight-hour ultimatums, or you sank back into the old disastrous patterns. Yet, smiling ruefully at the chaos on the board, the ruins of his policies, he decided that was certainly not the way to play *this* game . . .

"Looks like abdication time in old Vienna," Land was saying, biting savagely on his cigarette.

"Don't gloat!" Félice chided him. "It's bad form, Land."

"Form, who cares about form? I want revenge."

"And it's also dangerous!" She threw her most dazzling smile at him. The night wind blew full in her face, which glowed in the soft light of the lamps. It was as if the finest elements of the two Oriental races had been distilled and fused by a master of all sculptors: an almost frightening delicacy of feature, huge glowing eyes, the flawless *castaña* skin. She was attracted to the boy: a quick, sensual interest, formed, dallied with. Blackburn saw it, but it didn't stir him with parental solicitude as it once might have. He found himself watching Félice with a simple, disinterested pleasure, as he would a brilliantly rendered porcelain. All the heat of his passion—fancy and appetite conjoined—drew to one fierce diamond-point of wanting in a dilapidated cabin on Tashawena Inlet, half a mile away.

"The diehards play on until only one Great Power is left," Félice was saying to Eleanor. They'd decided to terminate the game; it was getting late, and she and Donlund had to fly back to the Capital the next morning. For a few seconds she ran her eyes over the map of Europe; a diminutive exquisite goddess, assaying destinies. Kuan Yin. "Reiny controls more supply centers than Bill. But Bill has better strategic possibilities."

"No, let's quit," Vosz said. "After all, the climax has been reached—we've finished off Blackburn. Say no more!" Bouncing forward he poured some brandy into his glass.

Blackburn rubbed his eyes. "Well, back to the old Seventh Floor, Sid, where everything's simpler."

"A Jew should never draw Imperial Germany." Jacobi nodded at them all lugubriously. "The internal conflicts are terrible."

"What about me?" Natalie demanded. "With the Turks—! No, you both better go back to Cambridge if that's the best you can do."

"Oh, they weren't concentrating," Eleanor told her. "Paul certainly wasn't. I can always tell."

"Can you?" Félice asked her with interest.

"Heavens, yes. When he pinches his eyebrow like that and stares across the room you can be sure his mind is a thousand miles away. Wasn't it, Paul?"

It was as though a curious silence had fallen, as though time had been checked: everyone frozen in the instant, watching him tautly, waiting. There were the principals, family and friends, and behind them Albert fussing almost noiselessly by the dry sink, mixing a drink for someone, and behind him the fine, austere plastered walls .edged with their beaded blue wainscoting and adorned with prints and masks and weapons; and beyond that the depthless wall of night sky and sea, rendered still darker by the rhythmic flare of Vere's Point Light across the Sound. All of it still with expectancy, waiting for this moment. What he said now, whatever words he uttered would alter all their lives.

"Not at all," he answered lightly. "I was right here—on the Island." His eyes met Sid's—a flicker of sadness and alarm so intense Blackburn felt it must explode in their faces, destroy them all. Then everything, obediently, moved again. He raised his glass and sipped at the melted ice with deliberate care, thinking of Jillie, her breasts cool against his cheeks and throat, the dense boom of surf and a gull, high aloft, right against the sun, wheeling.

"Beautiful," Donlund was saying. His eyes narrowed, the big man was gazing at the long silk scroll on the wall across the room: a tiger, leaping out of deep shadow with one paw raised, while cranes rose in panic from the edge of the marsh, scattering water in a soft rain of light. Beyond them the hills seemed to hang in space, uncaring, remote. "Really exquisite. Northern Sung. Li An-chung, is it?"

"Right you are," Jacobi answered. "His name seals. Though he usually preferred birds to animals."

"What the symbol is to the peony, the peony is to the Unknowable." Donlund smiled at Eleanor, who said:

"Old Asa brought it back on his last voyage. He was an inveterate collector."

"Rip-off artist," Land said darkly. "Translator's note."

"Oh yes, the China trade," Félice murmured, and gave Eleanor her lovely, serene smile. "What would you have done without us? Without our silks and porcelains, our Chou jades?"

"—And the tea," Silas Seaver boomed all at once, making them start. His bony hawk's head glared at her around the high back of the chair, blinking himself awake. "Don't forget the tea. Kept us alive nights so's we could scheme up more ways of bilking the little yellow devils."

Donlund laughed. "I never thought of it in exactly that way, Judge."

"Well, you want to."

"What else did we do, Judge Seaver?" Félice asked him. "How else did we corrupt the West?"

"Your women." His hands caused a convulsion in the blanket of newspapers. "Crews went ashore, Foochow, Whampoa, Tsingtao, and sampled the topgallant delights of Oriental love-making, aphrodisia, erotic inventions—" He broke off with a dry bark of a cough. "And then they came home to a cold house holding a cold bed holding a cold woman." He slapped the chair arm abruptly. "Source of two centuries of domestic fury. Do you see this floor?" He pointed at the two-foot-wide pine boards, scarred and glinting like old horn. "Great Uncle Oliver hadn't been back *one day* from a three year's whaling voyage when he painted a black line right down the middle of this room. Dining room and kitchen, upstairs, too. Divided the house neatly in half. 'Alvina,' he said, 'you're not to cross this line for any reason at all. I'll answer for my side.' And that's what they did. For thirty-seven years."

"I mean, you can see I come of real sturdy stock," Land said to Félice.

"What puzzles me is that it didn't take," she pursued. "If it was such fun, all that erotic foreplay—"

"Didn't *want* fun!" The Judge half flung the heap of papers on the floor beside him. "That's the whole point. The Yankee woman *wanted* cold beds and long silences. That made it all worth it, don't you see?"

"To punish him—yes, I see that," Félice answered. "But she kept the trinkets all the same, didn't she? The jades and porcelains."

"Oh, we're all collectors, you'll find," Eleanor broke in on them. She was smiling, but her chin had come up, and her eyes held that level, implacable sea captain's gaze. "Men and women. East and West too, I daresay. Some collect tangible objects—Bill and I are like that. We like to hold things in our two hands. Other people like to collect—other things. Sacred moments. Minds and souls."

"How very true." Félice made her the barest suggestion of a bow.

Blackburn sighed, listening to the Vice President who was talking about China now, about Chou Dynasty bronzes. Donlund had beautiful pieces in his elegant bachelor apartment out in Rock Creek Park, ceremonial vases and jade tigers and dragons and T'ang horses in delicate overglaze enamels. His father had collected them. Nell always loved to go there—she would pass her hands over the things with a strange, loving restraint that always troubled him. They *were* alike, she and Bill. He supposed they had to collect whatever they liked—a singularly American obsession, was it? Yet they showed a kind of veneration for those objects that was touching. Donlund was probably the kind of man Nell should have married: certain, acquisitive, guarding the amenities. A kind of ritual. She was attracted to Bill, he'd always known it; why shouldn't she enter his life—if not as lover then as curator, companion? Was that so absurd a thought? Or was it wishful thinking . . .

He stretched his legs and rotated his shoulders slowly, no longer listening to the conversation. The brief swim on his arrival hadn't relaxed him. He found himself in a state of vast dissatisfaction with things as they were, a kind of benevolent exasperation—all he wanted to see before his recently bedazzled eyes were new constellations of change, partnerships forming, dissolving, reforming in unpredictable ways: Vosz and Félice, dressed in evening clothes, gambling at the Sands in Las Vegas; Sid, in camouflaged Army fatigues, leading an insurrectionary patrol in the Mato Grosso; Nell and Donlund lecturing to vast, attentive audiences at the World Museum of Oriental Art; and he himself—

"And then the houseboy would say, 'Mu-shih, I sold it for thirty yuan.' " Donlund sipped at his highball. "And my father would say: 'Sold it! I never told you to sell it. Why did you sell it?' And Feng Ma-fei would look reproachful. 'But Mu-shih, it was *worth* thirty yuan.' 'All right, all right,' my father would say, 'where is the money?' 'Oh, I gave the money to Mr. Hornbeck.' 'But Mr. Hornbeck is not there, he is at Chung-tu. You couldn't have given him the money.' 'Ah no, Mu-shih, I gave it to his houseboy down there.' 'Down where?' 'Down at Kua-ling-pa.' 'But there is no houseboy at Kua-ling-pa—there is no *house,* there is no anything else of Mr. Hornbeck's at Kua-ling-pa. You know that.' 'Oh, yes, Hsien shêng, I did give it to him.' "

"Oh my God," Natalie exclaimed in the general laughter. "Are you making this up?"

"Not remotely. So then my father would assume a faintly amused manner. It fooled nobody, least of all Feng. 'Now Feng, *what did you do with the money?'* And Feng, with tremendous forbearance, a sage instructing some laggard pupil: 'Mu-shih, I gave it to the other man.' 'What other man?' 'The messenger. From Mr. Hornbeck.' 'Mr. Hornbeck? Mr. Hornbeck *has* no messenger!' 'No, Mu-shih, he was going to Mr. Hornbeck.' "

"Stop it, stop it," Natalie gasped. "But what *did* happen to the money?"

"Nothing." Donlund cupped his hands. "Feng had never sold the teapot. He hadn't done anything with it at all. My father found it on the chest in the hall next morning."

"But that's impossible! That he would invent all that—"

"Part of him believed it, you see."

"But then how did anything ever get *done?*"

Donlund shrugged. "Some things did, some did not. It's the action and the symbol again. For the Chinese intention, imagination, conjecture assume a different dimension from the occidental's hard-and-fast ground rules. If an idea strikes him as gracious or clever he often translates the thought into the deed. He's 'done' it, you see. He goes on to something else."

"But *why?*"

Félice nodded with remote pleasure. "Because that is how we are!"

"Have you ever met Hsien-huan?" Eleanor asked Natalie, who shook her head. "He's Bill's major domo—butler, social secretary, privy counselor. He's absolutely formidable. He's like the last of the Ming emperors."

"How old *is* he, Bill?" Vosz demanded.

"God alone knows. He admitted to being seventy-two once, about three or four years ago, but that's ridiculous—he'd been on my father's household staff a long time when I first remember him. And he looked exactly the way he does now. He was still wearing the queue when I was a kid."

"Hsien and Bill are exactly alike," Félice said. "They both long for the return of the Manchus."

Vosz gave his clattering laugh. "Bill, you aren't suggesting China ought to return to the days of the warlords?"

"Oh, I'm delighted they've got their collectives now, the new rice strains and tractors, the bicycles, their share of world markets. Creature comforts, sure. God knows, I've worked hard enough to help them get them. That damned trade commission, all the rest of it . . . Only *that*—" he pointed abruptly to the Sung painting "—where is that, now? Or anything remotely resembling it? What will there be in all that rabbit warren to nurture their souls? Or ours?"

The mournful *cling-dang* of the bellbuoy came over the water on the rising wind, and Donlund raised his head intently, listening. "Can't ever hear one of those without thinking of San Francisco Bay.—There's a problem of diminishing returns. Look at us: as civilized man, I mean." The hooded, sardonic shadow was back in his face again, and the rejected fatigue. "Of all those tens of centuries of palace intrigues and wars of conquest and famines—of all that endless wash of human proposing and divine disposing, only the bronze and silk testaments are left for us to marvel at. And a few ruins." He shrugged again; his voice, deep and even, seemed to fill the long room. "Look at us here: it's tempting to beguile ourselves with the notion that we ride the whirlwind and direct the storm, as the man says. Power—it's flattering enough. But how paltry that is—measured, say, against the Analects, or Angkor Wat."

"I can't buy that." Land, sitting erect and rather tense, the lamplight falling full on his left side, throwing half his face in shadow. *"People matter!* A single man standing in a rice paddy, singing . . ."

He broke off, agitated, and Blackburn recalled the moment; an evening in Khotiane, the farmer's voice astonishingly clear and birdlike in the swiftly rushing dusk. His limpet hat was tilted back on his head, his arms were raised; around him the paddy had been like a stippled green-bronze disc. Beyond the hills they had heard the rippling pop of automatic rifle fire: a handful of French marines clinging to the underside of a continent. Strange that Land would have remembered . . .

"That man is more important than all the Sui sculpture and Ming vases in the universe. He *is* . . ."

"Do you know, I'm not so sure of that," Donlund said.

"Would you make the trade?" Land asked him. "You—your life—for the greatest work of art in the history of the world. Would you do it?"

"What a bizarre idea!" Félice exclaimed.

"No, it's a perfectly legitimate question," Donlund answered. "Or is it a challenge?" He paused, while the others watched him. "I think . . . I think I'd be inclined to make the exchange."

"Bill, you don't mean it," Blackburn said.

"Of course the price would have to be high!" The Vice President laughed, running his knuckles along the edge of his jaw. "Right up there with Michelangelo's David. Or the great Lung-mên Bodhisattva."

"And how about the farmer in the rice paddy?" Land asked softly. "Would *he* be worth the David?" He looked away then, but Blackburn saw in the boy's eyes the flash of something outraged and unappeased. "Well, it will come," he muttered thickly, and drained his glass. "It will come."

"What will come?" Donlund queried.

"The end of all this . . . make-believe."

"What a violent boy!" Félice cried softly, watching him. "What insistence! Don't you know the world is unchanging? That human destiny is the progress of a colony of ants across a thousand miles of sand? Look at me: I am descended from two races, and both had reached the highest pinnacles of civilization when America was a gloomy forest, where naked men shivered in tents . . ."

"Maybe that's why it's got to come from here."

"Why is that?"

"Because we haven't bogged down in fatalism. In indifference. At least the idea of equality, a *real* equality . . ."

Land lowered his voice; but his eyes, flushed with that fevered exasperation, wavered unsteadily. He picked up his empty glass, set it down again. Why, the boy's tight, Blackburn thought with a little shock of amusement, he's smashed. He felt a fierce, covert pride. Hot, vulnerable, intransigent, this was nonetheless his son. Land would do things he himself never had. He was sure of it. And more power to him. Twice he had been on the point of intervening in the argument, now he was glad he hadn't. Land had the Darcey blood, as the Judge was fond of saying: he would always question, dissent. Bound in his mother's fearful caution Blackburn had accepted things too readily. Of course Land would suffer more: life was a two-edged blade—

In the plaza behind the royal palace in Cau Luong the officer had sung out his commands, and the turbaned guards in their yellow pantaloons and scarlet vests lunged and recovered, their great curved swords swept up and down and up again, swirling tongues of light under the feathery canopy of the pepper trees. Land, sitting on Blackburn's shoulders to see better, had said: "Why do they all do what he says?"

"Because he is their *warisang,*" he'd answered. "Because of the gold sunburst he wears on his turban. See it? And the purple sash around his waist. Those are the symbols of his authority."

"Do they have to obey *everything* he tells them to do?"

"Yes—he is their *warisang.* Their captain."

Land had been silent a moment, squinting, watching the slow ceremonial dance of the guards, the flashing swords. Then: "But what if he took them off? His turban and the sash. What about when he is taking a bath? Would they have to obey him then?"

He'd laughed, startled and pleased even then at the hard acuteness of the question. At five years of age. "Well, yes, they would have to obey him. But if he were taking a bath he probably wouldn't ask them. It's in uniform when he must be obeyed."

Not too satisfactory an answer, truth to tell. It was curious, sitting here now, watching Land flushed and impassioned and Eleanor stiff with disapproval, feeling the south wind moist on his forehead and thinking of Jillie only half a mile away, sitting under a kerosene lamp, reading. Was that what she was doing? What *was* she doing, right now, this instant? The need to be with her now, rush to her, catch her up in his arms and cry out his love, his joy, the wild exultant immanence of his rebirth, was like a fist in his kidneys. "Sometimes—where the emotions are involved, we do things we wish we hadn't, later on . . ." When had he said that to Land? A rainy afternoon down in the boathouse, a year or so ago . . . but over what? in the name of what?

"—for the simple reason that it's sacred," his son and heir was telling the company now with undue intensity. He was high all right, which was strange—Land had always held his liquor well. Like most of his generation he had contempt for people who drank too much and badly. "I mean, all your philosophy and art is so much crappola if there's nobody around to feel it."

"My point," Donlund answered.

"No, no—you've got it upside down. People have got to live in—in truth and dignity, *first*. That's where it's at. Then if art comes, okay."

"I hope you're right. The only trouble is that every time one of these high-minded revolutionary societies of yours comes to power, it never seems to get around to any art or philosophy worth the name. Could there be a coincidence? Knock the Renaissance tyrant if you want to, but he commissioned some of the great monuments to human sensibility—yes, and he paid for them, too."

Land's lip curled. "Out of vanity. Cheap self-glorification."

"Sure. What motives do you think usually drive men? And what difference does it make, essentially? For centuries other men have been lifted out of the prison of their mortality because of the tyrant's vanity. Doesn't that justify it?"

"No way. If the premise is fouled up, the conclusion has got to be."

"An absolutist!" Vosz broke into his high-pitched laugh. "I never knew a revolutionary who wasn't."

"Or an earnest young boy," Félice amended.

"No—you're the absolutists!" Land came to his feet all at once, one hand extended. "You think you've got power, you *are* power, you hold it in your hands, you're secure—"

"In *politics?*" Donlund interposed, and the others broke into laughter.

"Yes you do!—you think nothing can reach you, you can pick up the phone and say ten words and everything's going to change for a million poor sons of bitches in Gavutu. But is that true? Is it? If I, a kid, a perfect nobody, standing here *boring* you with all this apeshit—hell yes, I know I'm boring you, of course you're bored, the only thing that *grabs* you is power, don't you think I see that? Of course, standing here shooting off my face, if I armed and threw this grenade—like *this*—!"

With an abrupt violent gesture he plucked the hard round object out of his pocket, ducked down and sent it rolling and bumping heavily over the broad dun boards into the center of the room. A dark, furry sphere, indistinct, rumbling its way along. Someone gasped, one of the women cried out. Blackburn had only time to think, *My God, he means it then, he's that wild*—and then Donlund was on his feet with darting catlike agility, had pounced on it and plucked it up before it had traveled eight feet. He tossed it in the air with a laugh, caught it again. No one else had moved.

"Taped!" he said easily, peering at it. "What did we used to call them? Nickel rockets?"

Everyone was talking at once now. Blackburn was standing, staring at Donlund, at Land, at Sid. He had no sensation of having got out of his chair. Land was grinning savagely at the Vice President, his eyes alight.

"Yeah! *Then* who has the power? Okay?"

"Land," Blackburn said sharply, "that wasn't particularly funny."

"It wasn't intended to be!"

Donlund was still hefting the friction-taped baseball in his huge, rough hand. "But you see—it *wasn't* a grenade."

"But if it *had* been?"

"But it wasn't. That's the point. The world doesn't run on hypotheses, Land—it runs on deeds. That's why we were safe ultimately, you see. The issue was never raised.—Power," he said quickly, in a different tone. "That's what you want, isn't it? Like everybody else? Isn't that what you want? . . . You have to act, then. Not pose game theories, like this." With a brusque, disdainful gesture he indicated the Diplomacy map board with its gaily painted little counters.

Land stared back at him, his face working—then he turned abruptly: "Doctor Vosz, please drop the charges against Lachlan Smith. Please let him go."

"What?" The Presidential Adviser, who had been talking to Jacobi, twisted around in his chair. "My dear young man—"

"No—I mean it. Please. This one thing. A final request."

"Leland," Eleanor said, "you're presuming upon—"

"Please let Smitty go. If you don't it'll start something nobody will be able to stop."

"Leland!" his mother said in the flat, cutting tones that always prefaced her strongest rebukes. "That was completely uncalled for . . ."

"Was it? Was it? Everybody my age in America is calling for it!"

"You have no right to ask such a question and you know it!"

"Why not? If a man can rot his life away in jail for the 'crime' of waking the country up to—"

"Leland, *that is enough.*" Eleanor walked up to him briskly. "Now we had an understanding about this evening and you've chosen not to honor it. You have my permission to leave the room whenever you wish."

"Gladly, Maman." Blackburn saw that the troubled, importunate look was gone; Land's eyes were glittering with the old defiance. "Gladly." He turned and walked out of the room.

There was a curious little silence. Everyone, standing now, seemed not to know what to do with himself. Félice broke it. "A lovely boy," she said to Blackburn with her dreamy, secretive smile. "Difficult—but lovely."

"I'm sorry for this episode," Eleanor murmured easily. "If episode it was. Please sit down. Bill, have another drink. Leland's idea of a joke sometimes leaves a good deal to be desired."

"Oh, he wasn't joking." Vosz indulged in a series of harsh grimaces. "He was serious, perfectly serious. They all are. They are *unhinged* on this question of Lachlan Smith, they seem to feel the need to build him up into some sort of culture hero. More populist romantic hogwash."

"I told you playing the avenging angel would have its repercussions," Donlund told him quietly.

"You think I've taken this position for my personal gratification? An act of treason of this magnitude?"

Blackburn began: "Oh Reiny, *treason*—"

"Yes! A mortal threat. Not to me, you understand: that is of no consequence, that is nothing. But to that authority of which I am merely the symbol." He spread his short, thick hands before him; he'd drunk a good deal of brandy himself. "Power is force channeled downward, disseminated: force, acknowledged and obeyed. If I show weakness here, I block the flow of that current—and my value as a servant of the President is ended."

"You're wrong, Reiny," Blackburn said gently. "You are guilty of a great confusion. Power is an instrument of government, but it is not government. Any more than lust and a need to possess define love."

"Why, Paul," Félice exclaimed, "what an arresting comparison!"

"Ballyraggle!" Vosz went on as though she hadn't spoken at all. "Power is government, government is power. Anything else is an illusion. When the mob seeks power it is insurrection. When the citizen seeks it, it is treason."

"Then you're no better than the wildest revolutionary," Blackburn answered, "if you crush him. You bind yourself to him, by your use of force. And you'll find cruelty buys peace at the very highest price."

"A point we might bear in mind," Donlund said. Stifling a yawn he stretched his powerful shoulders. "It's getting late, Reiny. Drive us home. I've got that early flight . . . You're too quick to take offense. Everybody's got enemies, if he's worth his salt. You're not running a popularity contest on TV, you're a hustler for Administration policy. Look at Paul, here—the hawks have been screaming for his scalp for three open seasons. Jesus Christ, even Fred *Semmes* has got enemies. You give the whole thing too much importance when you put the screws on this way." He leaned forward, tossing the taped baseball rhythmically.

The Presidential Adviser glanced at Donlund and shrugged. "Perhaps you're right. Perhaps you're right, at that." Biting on his lip he peered up at the dark chestnut beams overhead.

"If I were you I'd begin gently to call off the bloodhounds."

"Can't." Everyone glanced at the Judge, who was awake again. Blackburn had forgotten all about him. Now, glasses riding high on his head, he yawned mightily and massaged his face with one hand. "What you Administration flunkies can never understand: you initiate a legal process, and certain things follow. They follow!" He studied them all a moment—shrewd mirth edged with malice. "Then the panic is on, and you start scrambling for the hatches, all of you . . ."

Félice broke the awkward silence again. "He must be a curious man, this Smith. To have aroused such passions in the young people." Her eyes came to rest on Blackburn. "Your son seems so—*involved* . . ."

On the wall the tiger crouched forever in impotent rage, the cranes perpetually rose in a storm of wings. Pursuer and pursued, against the uncaring mountains. Looking at the painting Blackburn was brushed by the most stealthy, far-reaching dread.

"Yes," he said, "he's involved."

TEN

BEYOND FANTIC POINT the land fell away in a dense green mat edged with ocher at the beaches, pale against the sea's hard, electric blue. Waves leaped tumbling at the yawl's stern, surging and falling off in mesmeric persistence, and then hurrying on east to Monomoy and Stone Horse Shoals. The sun, lightly veiled in the southwest haze, was warm. Jacobi, sitting forward in the *Arcturus'* cockpit, glanced up with a not very professional eye at the strained, trembling swell of the jib, his responsibility, and then across a hundred yards of running sea to the vermilion-hulled sloop tearing along a few points off their beam, spray in a fine rainbow sheen at its bows. Silas Seaver, an ancient, stained, floppy-brimmed hat pulled low over his eyes, grunted and said in his gravelly thin voice:

"Thinks he can sail that fire engine all by himself, does he?"

"That's it," Blackburn answered. Naked except for a pair of faded khaki shorts he eased the wheel over a few points, eased it back, his eyes slitted against the sun. "Reinhold Vosz against the seven seas."

"How long's he been sailing?"

"Not long at all. He got Henry Hildreth to teach him some of the finer points. Henry socked him good for the privilege—twenty-five dollars an hour and expenses."

The Judge emitted a fierce cackling bark. "What is he, made of money?"

"No. Oh, he's got enough, I suppose. It's what he happens to want right now, that's all. Reiny's going to master blue-water sailing, just the way he took over Rand and Hughbryce and the White House basement."

"Well, he's got a lot to learn. Going to be sailing her underwater he doesn't watch out." The old man studied the other boat and its solitary figure in a yellow jacket hunched over the wheel, his seamed face pinched in disapproval. "These power-grabbers—they always come to grief sooner or later. Look at Bob McNamara, look at that fellow Kissinger. Look at Bobby Kennedy, playing both ends against the middle. He's riding for a fall, you mark my words."

Jacobi and Blackburn exchanged a glance. The single most disconcerting thing about the Judge were these astonishing memory lapses. All at once, in the middle of a perfectly lucid observation he would speak of contacting someone long dead, or decide on some course of action that would resolve a crisis ten years past. Both Paul and Eleanor treated it as of no consequence, nothing more or less than one of the hazards of age, but such moments upset Jacobi profoundly. His historian's respect for the fixed orbit of events was offended. Hearing the old man utter such remarks, sprung so in place and time, Jacobi had a sense of measureless chasms opening at his feet, an unchronicled void where mindless creatures prowled and anything was possible. Without the ordered world of memory—

"Bobby was all right," Paul was saying now, mildly, in the rising wind. "He learned a lot, those last days. About life and people and responsibility, the rest of the country out there . . . Arthur told me once you could actually see the change."

The Judge was silent, peering morosely at the horizon. It was impossible to tell whether he'd caught the gentle correction or not. "One hand for yourself and one for the ship," he muttered. "That's what Grandad used to say . . . He's like the rest of 'em. Your exalted boss, same thing. Never been up against it."

"I wouldn't say that," Blackburn answered, and Jacobi said:

"I thought he was great on the Union Square Massacre, the way he handled that."

"That's different—he didn't have much choice there. It was either release the pressure or start up the old Nixon-Agnew repressive cycle again." The hooded hawk's eyes fastened on him. "This other thing's different. Had his own way too long. The President looks *out* at other people to see what they think, how they're going to react. He doesn't go ahead and do what *he* thinks, and to hell with the consequences." Jacobi nodded, more from habit than out of any essential agreement. "The Gnome, there—" the Judge pointed toward Vosz's tense, crouched form in the other cockpit "—same thing." To Paul he said: "They understand each other. If it comes to a showdown between you and the Gnome, your boss'll choose him. Not you."

"Why, Dad—that's such a summary judgment," Paul chided him lightly. "I rather flattered myself that I had some influence with the President."

The Judge either did not see or ignored the quiet smile his son-in-law gave Jacobi. "They're all alike now. Frozen in conformity. *I've* seen them," the old man nodded vengefully. "Any honest soul who gives a tinker's damn for their opinion, in or out of office, deserves what he gets."

Jacobi, busying himself with the jib sheets, made no reply, nor did Blackburn. On this subject Silas Seaver was not to be trusted too far. Thwarted ambition had pinched his nostrils and compressed his already attenuated lips. He still held his legend—the cantankerous Yankee magistrate, incorruptible—in an osprey's grip; but that was all. Shrunk to this little measure—the Paling, his shop, the Sound—he turned chess pieces on his lathe and fulminated against the temporizing, lily-livered souls now sitting on the high court, running the Justice Department. Still, the legend was something in this arrant world where nearly every man had his price, his fatal enticement; how many men could leave forty-five years of public life with a record as spotless and austere? Why couldn't the old man rest on that achievement; why did he need to rage so against the infirmities of lesser men?

"Tacking," the Judge said crisply.

Jacobi looked across the sliding hills of waves to the rival boat. For a moment he could see no change; then the vermilion hull seemed to shrink, to foreshorten mysteriously, and jib and mainsail started their taut fluttering.

"Ready about," Paul called from the helm, and Jacobi answered automatically, "Ready . . ."

"Hard alee!"

There was that brief, curious, premonitory skidding motion, the steep dip and spank of the bow, and then the racketing whine of the mizzen sheet tearing through the blocks as with a sudden sharp pull the boat drove under way again, heeling over hard.

"He does carry on," Blackburn said.

"Genoa rigged too far aft. She's fishtailing." The Judge shook his head irritably. "Crossed all of thirty seconds early. I don't know why you didn't call him on it."

"Don't *worry* about it, Dad," Paul retorted, a touch sharply. It was the third occasion on which Seaver had referred to the fact that Vosz had passed the Number Three marker—the starting line—ahead of the time they'd agreed on. "Let him have his fun. What old salt Reiny didn't know last night was, with a wind like this we'd have had to get in the main, anyway." He laughed once, his head back, looking tousled and boyish, and winked at Jacobi. After their return from New Delhi the Secretary had seemed changed—at once more irascible and relaxed, as though both international controversy and some private struggle were unfolding simultaneously. Administrative trivia and ceremony vexed him, but the larger problems, the overbearing pressures of the Burma crisis, didn't appear to throw him at all. He seemed outside it, in some curious way; a bored traveler killing time between trains.

Then a week later, driving home together from the Department, Blackburn had turned to him and said: "Sid, I've got something to ask of you. Would you do me a great favor?"

"Of course, Chief."

"It's not a professional matter—I wouldn't ask it of you except that there's no one I can trust . . ." The Secretary's face was working oddly in the blue, reflected light. "Natalie's going to be staying on up at Rockport for a while longer, isn't she?"

"I'm afraid so. It's too hard to run back and forth between there and the Vineyard. At least until her father's back on his feet. She'll be down for Nell's weekend on the twenty-third, though."

"The camp on Tashawena—could you let me have it for a few weeks, in that case? I'd pay you for the use of it, of course."

"Why sure. It's not very palatial digs for visiting firemen."

He was mystified and a bit irritated—he was wondering what extraordinary scheme of Eleanor's could have taxed even the Paling's capacious accommodations when Paul said, "Sid—there's this girl. Sid, I'm terribly, terribly in love with her. I have to see her . . ."

Listening intently he could feel his face change: a mixture of astonishment, shock, elation that fused swiftly into frank alarm. It seemed fantastic, it seemed inconceivable that Paul Whitcombe Blackburn, his old friend and academic colleague and now—my God!—Secretary of State of the United States, this same man who had actually charmed Premier Ragozhin, who had blunted the wrath of Ch'en Pu-tsao and with unique determination, moderation and grace had converted the wrangle of the Kuala Lumpur Conference into the Greater Asian Treaty Organization; that this same Paul Blackburn could be sitting here telling him these things on Pennsylvania Avenue in the hot, gusty night—

He thought tensely, numbly, The risk, *the risk,* and to his dismay was invaded by the image of a man slipping from some high place, teetering absurdly, beyond his reach, bound in a terrible and soundless fall.

"You mean—there on the Vineyard?" he asked softly. "Right there— that near the Paling?"

"Yes. I've worked it out. It's the only way at certain times we can see each other for now without drawing attention."

"But—the *danger* . . ."

"There doesn't need to be any. Don't you see, I can walk over there from the Paling, through the woods—I won't have to drive, be seen by anyone . . ." The Secretary's face, moving against the garnet and emerald lights, held a high excitement flawed now with desperation. "You will do it for me, won't you, Sid? And cook up an excuse to keep Natalie away? There's no one else I can trust. I've got to see her, Sid. I've got to be with her—that's all there is to it."

"Of course, Paul. Anything I can." He fought to keep the alarm, the heavy, dislocating shock out of his eyes. For months now he'd been the attendant lord, the responsive subaltern following his chief's competence, looking to him for guidance; now—he realized it with a flash of pure dread —he would have to help him, fend for him. Maybe he would even have to lead . . .

On the flight up to Boston next day they had worked out the details, a little like schoolboys, a little like archconspirators. Fortunately they didn't have to worry about a security detail. Over the years after the Kennedy assassinations and the Wallace shooting, security precautions for cabinet officers and other high officials had been carried to absurd lengths. It was one of the first things the President had decided to curtail. Round-the-clock security guards for virtually everybody, as well as the President and Vice President, gave the average citizen the sense that he was the subject of an armed state, ruled by leaders secluded behind a bristling palace guard; they were expensive and they were unnecessary, except for overseas conferences or election campaigns. "Three or four determined people with automatic weapons can knock off anybody they want to, no matter how many bodies you've got around you. And it *might* happen, sure—but this Administration is going to be relaxed and it's going to be accessible. Maybe the nuts won't be so likely to try it if they don't get full TV and security coverage." Most of the cabinet had agreed with him.

The cottage lay on a curving neck of land between the Inlet and Vineyard Sound, open to both but screened nicely from any casual gaze by stands of scrub pines and beach plum. The woods beyond it abutted on the Paling, and by leaving his work cottage, a converted ice house that stood in the far southeast corner of the Compound, he could reach the camp in under ten minutes by walking rapidly along a little-used wood road. There were only two other camps in the immediate vicinity, and the Secretary was known to take long solitary walks; they could see each other without arousing suspicion. It was impossible for him to get up to Somerville very often, and Washington—that supremely provincial of all national capitals —was simply too dangerous.

That same evening Jacobi had gone to see the girl. He'd disliked her intensely. He tried not to but he couldn't help it. He'd been horrified when he realized who she was: Paul *couldn't* have done this. A firebrand, one of the leaders of Sirius! If Vosz ever got wind of it . . . God in heaven. Her manner with him had been brusque, almost sullen; she clearly saw his presence as an intrusion and resented it, which angered him. Do you think *I* like having to do this? he wanted to tell her. All this—this subterfuge and chicanery? Can't you see what you're asking him to risk—what makes you think you're worth it? What makes you think *anybody's* worth it? He held his tongue, however, with effort. People did strange things, dangerous things, disastrous things in this disordered world. His sole obligation was to his chief—and this was what Paul wanted, there was no doubt whatever about that . . .

On life's vast ocean diversely we sail, Reason the card, but passion is the gale. How true. Dear old Pope, who'd never had to steer the great vessels through these corsair seas of world rivalry. Still, he'd had his own adversities. Watching the vermilion-hulled sloop falling slowly astern, cringing every now and then from the spray which had begun to whip over the weather bow in the still-rising wind, Jacobi wiped his face with one hand and cursed Reinhold Vosz with all his heart. He wished he were back on shore and he and Paul were playing a hard, no-quarter set of tennis. He was no sailor and never would be.

The idea for the race had originated the previous evening. Vosz, flushed with victory in the Diplomacy game and a good deal of Paul's Courvoisier, had begun to hold forth about the sloop he'd recently bought from Dan Harden and rechristened the *Zara*—"For *Zarathustra,* naturally!" The Judge had offered a few patronizing remarks on the Presidential Assistant's seamanship, and before they were through Vosz had challenged them to a race to the Tashawena Buoy and back—on the condition that Paul did not raise his mainsail. To Jacobi's surprise—he knew enough about sailing to realize this would give Vosz a decided advantage against the yawl, especially in light airs—Paul took him up on it. And here they were, out in wilder weather than Jacobi had ever seen, tearing along, and leaving a very angry Vosz behind. Served the arrogant son of a bitch right. But when they could be back at the Paling, with that good clay under their—

They dipped hard, again, hit with shocking force, and a wall of spray soaked him. He gasped, though the water was not really cold. Paul laughed and called, "Don't let it throw you, Sid!"

He grinned back. "It certainly is blowing . . ."

"Blowing?" the Judge said. "No, it's not blowing." Craning his corded neck he peered up at his son-in-law. "How about that run from Block Island, Paul? In Fifty-Six? *Then* it was blowing . . ." Another wave drenched them to the bone but the old man sat like a flint figurine, water streaming from his hat brim, his eyes bright. "Spinning log wrecked, just about had the dinghy in the cockpit with us every few seas. Lost her finally. Painter parted." He shook his head. "Pretty little thing. Lapstrake cedar."

"You couldn't recover it?" Jacobi asked.

"In that sea?" The old man glared at him. "You'd have risked excessive strain on your sails if you brought her up at all. Damned good chance of ramming her before you could ever have secured her, anyway. Harry McNaughton was so sick I had to lash him down to one of the cockpit benches to keep him from rolling overboard. Looked exactly like a corpse —face green, fingers green. Went over and felt him once to see if he was still alive. He was." The Judge's deep-set eyes were boring into Jacobi's with malicious mirth. "Sure! Jib tore away like a girl's slip, engine quit— distributor head soaked through. Everything in the cabin afloat and swimming. Paul had the helm. Seven and a half hours. Know what that means? No, I *guess* you don't. Gorry, what a sleighride that was . . ."

"And Dad hit the Number Four buoy right on the nose," Paul broke in on him. "You couldn't see your hand before your face by that time—

we just about ran her down, swamped in the seas. I couldn't believe it."

"You mean you could actually plot a course in a storm like that?" Jacobi asked in amazement.

"Christ Almighty!" the old man retaliated. "Did you think there'd be a pillar of fire?"

"All right, Dad," Paul said mildly. "Yeah, he was down there, clinging to the chart table like the ghost of Nathaniel Bowditch. Allowing for sideslip, subtracting for tide, all the rest of it. He yelled at me, 'Forty-three! Your course is forty-three!' I said: 'You're sure?' and he hollered back, 'Do you think I made it up?' "

The Judge said: "Finally we cleared West Chop and we were in smooth water. Just like that. And Harry got up and went forward to take his position at the bowsprit. Not a word—like someone risen from the dead. And we ran in past the breakwater, down anchor, down sails, we didn't have the strength to harbor-stow a blasted thing. We just sat there and looked at each other."

"It sounds—pretty scary," Jacobi said cautiously.

"*I'll* tell you," Paul answered. "Only thing that kept me going at one point was Dad. His face was like rock—not a trace of fear on it. Incredible! I remember I thought: Hell, it can't be as bad as I think it is. I'd better pull myself together."

The Judge slapped a bony knee. "*Fact* of the matter was, it was looking at Paul that held me together that day . . ."

Blackburn stared at him. "You never told me that."

The old man nodded—a mirthless Yankee grin. "Didn't want to spoil you. I was saving that for future gales."

"You old deceiver!"

The two men laughed at each other, shaking water from their caps and faces, and Jacobi watched behind them the low, blurred shoulder of land, far off now. Four miles, maybe five. Could he swim it if he had to? That strange attitude he now and then encountered in other men, a kind of wild hilarity in the very outrageous desperateness of some situation, always made him a little nervous. He had never been in a desperate situation, gazing death full in the eye; his life had moved quietly from New York City to Georgia (where he'd done his military service) to Japan (where he'd been on an exchange professorship) to Cambridge. Even about sailing he had mixed feelings: he liked it, the open, rolling motion—but he was never entirely free of a visceral dread. Paul had given him the helm on occasion and he'd proved competent enough; but at such times he was— he recognized it—in a minor storm of nervous tension. A boat this big, this beautiful, with all its fine woods and countless unique appurtenances—what in God's name did it cost? Twenty thousand? Fifty? In spite of himself, in spite of the fair sky and lazy sea his mind would reel with visions of masts snapping like tinder, rigging and canvas raining down like doom—or worst of all, a solitary arm raised feebly in a churning waste of water—

"No, what you ought to do," the Judge was saying without preamble, "is tear it wide open. Give Bodawyin's people the hardware they need and let them go in and clean out this bunch of hell-for-glory idiots." Blackburn, watching the other boat, now a good hundred yards astern, said nothing, and his father-in-law stared up at him mutely for a moment. "You want my opinion you let things drift too much, Paul. That's always been the trouble with State. It was true with Frank Kellogg and it was true with Cord Hull and it's the same way now. You're all accustomed to sitting on things, letting them slide. Figure if you wait long enough it'll all go away . . . You ought to go in with both feet."

"Yes, that's what he wants, all right," Blackburn answered.

"Who?"

"Your Irrepressible Gnome." Paul nodded aft toward the red sloop.

"He does? Well, he's right, then. Hate to agree with him, but he is. They're all watching you. Manikarto, Shiraga, Thanarat. The Gandhi woman, too. You don't take firm action they're going to start that paper-tiger business all over again. You ought to send in a MAAG team at least."

"And bring China in?" the Secretary asked with sudden quiet intensity. "That's precisely what I want to avoid. Peking has shown surprising for-bearance, take it on balance."

"Forbearance—you call setting up war crimes tribunals for the whole Mission—"

"They haven't done it yet, they've only said they're going to. There's a difference." Blackburn stared hard at the Tashawena Buoy, a scant hundred yards ahead, rolling and sinking crazily, the sound of its bell fading down the wind, mournful and thin. "There are some parts to this puzzle that still just don't sound right. I want to let it unravel a bit more."

The old man grunted. "Let it unravel much farther you'll find you won't have any more rope left to work with."

Paul made no reply. They jibed smartly around the buoy, then—red-rusty, plunging, streaked with gull lime—and began to run before the wind. Jacobi too was silent. Even so, there was some truth in the Judge's warning. The past several days had been rocky—events seemed to be gain-ing a fearful momentum of their own. The Chinese had caught up with Naungapaya at Chefang; he'd agreed to hand over to them both the rescue missions and the Pao Shan consulate staff, but categorically refused to with-draw his forces from the region, where the cholera epidemic—a new and deadly variant—was spreading with awesome rapidity. Bodawyin, con-fronted with Chinese divisions astride both the Lashio and Myitkyina roads, had become nearly hysterical, declaring a national emergency and invoking the aid of every ally, past and present, real and imagined, all the way back to the Portuguese treaty of 1519. El Hopkins was in critical condition from the blow on the head he'd received during the consulate hassle. Van Kleeck's overtures to Naungapaya had been greeted with a torrent of abuse. Umphlett was still nowhere to be found—a highly suspect report had the Cockswain hiking through the mountains beyond Mangshih.

Blackburn had met it all with his characteristic vigor and discretion. He'd approached Ch'en Pu-tsao directly on the release of the Americans, expressed his deep concern over the cholera outbreak and offered the services of the Mission's medical personnel as well as special epidemiological units from America; in a stiff cable to Rangoon he'd deplored Bodawyin's warlike posture and warned him expressly against any border incidents which might flare into open warfare; he'd pushed Van Kleeck to locate Umphlett at all cost; and in an artfully worded statement requested French Premier de Mortier's good offices in arbitrating the dispute pending a UN hearing. Ch'en had replied graciously enough, calling the occupation and sacking of the Pao Shan consulate "most regrettable," promising the prompt release of the staff, and welcoming American medical aid. De Mortier had agreed to chair an arbitration commission, Bodawyin had agreed—reluctantly—to abide by its decisions. Paul could be snappish on small issues, but when the big crunches came he was utterly calm, imperturbable. He was like a very good chess player: he took his time with the dangerous moves.

Then day before yesterday had come the dismaying news from the Chinese press agency Hsin-hua that Drachenfels and the rest of the American Mission were to be turned over to a people's tribunal and tried for crimes of aggression, and angrily denouncing Bodawyin as the agent of a nefarious American scheme to destroy the independence of Dhotal. To all Department queries Peking remained ominously silent. This had provoked a hurried Executive Committee session at the White House. The President was not in attendance but Vosz, supported by Fred Semmes and Ernie Hazbrouck, pressed hard for all-out military aid to Bodawyin and formal withdrawal of the support given to Naungapaya at New Delhi. Paul had disagreed vehemently, and the meeting had broken up in some acrimony. The press was becoming increasingly impatient—Reston in the *New York Times* had complained of this two days before, in his dour, senior-statesman way, hinting at the possibility of an "unofficial policy" at State to abandon the Bodawyin regime. Meanwhile the true state of affairs in Dhotal—the Chinese official position, the whereabouts of that crazy bastard Umphlett and now the fate of all the Americans in the Mission—still lay shrouded in a fog as dense as the mountain mists of that wilderness of blue rock and crashing torrents. And they waited.

"Regular Jack-a-dandy, ain't he?" the Judge was saying. Jacobi looked around, saw with amazement the old man was squinting at some photographs of Drachenfels that had been in the sheaf of background material on the Reclamation Mission Mike Hudela had given the Secretary. "Shave that beaver and barroom-quartet mustache off him, and I could tell you just where I've seen him before."

"For Christ sake, Dad!—what are you doing with those out *here?*" Paul complained. He threw Jacobi an exasperated glance and shook his head. When the Judge had retired to the Fiji House he'd offered the use of his old study to Paul; but recently the old man had fallen into the practice of rummaging through his former desk, fuming and fussing, as though collecting bits and pieces of himself.

"They're just going to blow away on you out here—you'll get them all soaked . . ."

"Wanted to look at him some more, that's why," the Judge retorted defiantly, though he made the ineffectual gesture of wiping them against the front of his shirt. "You ever know me to lose anything overboard?"

"That's not the point—that's a Limited Distribution file."

"Won't do 'em any harm. Running before the wind now, anyway . . . Looks like an undertaker who ran off and joined a carnival. Doesn't he?"

Jacobi grinned in spite of himself. The image was apt. Drachenfels, leaning forward in some harsh tropic light, barrel-chested and massive—a wrestler's torso—had a gaunt, almost skull-like face, with a thin beak of a nose which was bent curiously to one side of his face. The head had nothing to do with the body—it was like some eerie practical joke of nature. He stared hard at the camera's lens, mute and challenging. The Judge grunted, put a thumb over the broad mustachios, shuffled to another shot of the subject, in coveralls now and with a rucksack slung over one shoulder, a map in his hand. In profile his face looked more sensitive and natural; the disfigurement of his nose was not so noticeable.

"Yessirree, I've seen this bucko before," the Judge repeated. "Right here, too."

Blackburn and Jacobi exchanged another glance. Paul asked, with an edge of sarcasm: "You mean, here on the Vineyard?"

"No, no, *no,*" the old man said irritably, "here in the States. Washington, New York City . . . Those German submariners who came ashore near Boca Raton in Forty-Two. Had ticket stubs to a Miami movie house in their pockets, too. Did you know that? They were wearing their uniforms under civilian clothes, so we decided not to execute them. Could have, of course."

"Seems unlikely, don't you think?" Paul asked him mildly. "Since he would have been nine years old at the time."

"Eyes are too close together," the Judge declared as though his son-in-law hadn't spoken. Looking up he caught Jacobi grinning.

"What does that signify, sir?" the Far East Assistant asked, to cover himself.

"Why, it means simply that the man's too obsessed with his own wants and reactions to be able to measure anything larger."

"That's very interesting. Is the obverse true as well? Wide-set eyes—"

"No: doesn't follow at all . . . I know: you Freudians think it's all in the mind, the cranial convolutions or some damn thing. Well it's not— it's in the physical characteristics, the shape of a man's skull, the condition of his liver and lights. One of these days they're going to wake up to the fact that our bellies determine our ambitions, love life, everything . . . He's gaining." The Judge tossed his head to indicate the *Zara*. Vosz was rapidly approaching the buoy. Sailing before the wind, as they now were, the tacking vessel gave the impression of moving at much greater speed. "He'll have more canvas going wing-and-wing, Paul. Less hull to pull. He'll overhaul us, most likely."

"I don't think so."

"You wait and see." In place of the gleeful pugnacity he'd displayed that morning the old man now semed morose and peevish. "No kind of a day for a race, anyway."

"Want to call it?"

"No, I don't want to call it! I never called off a race in my life, and I'm not going to start now."

It was blowing still harder. The horizon had dissolved in a silver broth and the waves piled full on each other, tumbling in disordered eddying hills, the spume whipped from their crests. Jacobi, wet and shivering and trying not to show it, flexed his arms and shoulders, listening to Paul and the Judge discussing the set of the mizzen; they were perfectly at ease. Now, with the pitching, sliding motion of the following sea he began to feel squeamish, and gripped his hands in apprehension. The Judge would be merciless toward anyone who sought the lee rail.

"Got her sheeted down pretty smart," the Judge said hoarsely. "He better look out, now . . ."

Hating Vosz with all his might Jacobi started groping in his slacks for the pack of Beeman's Pepsin chewing gum he kept for such emergencies. He was not going to be sick, he was not. It was just a case of breathing deeply, focusing your eyes on objects with—

There was a flat crack like a pistol shot; the Judge gave a muffled exclamation. Gazing aft dully Jacobi saw no boat at all. It had vanished.

"Gone over!" the Judge cried.

Near the slant red cage of the bellbuoy there was a quick fluttering of canvas, and then the saurian swell of the hull, an electric blue below the waterline; Paul called, "Ready about . . . Hard *alee!*" The rail lay down, and they ran back in long, slugging lunges, half-blinded with spray.

"Regular old salt, is he?" The Judge gave vent to his wild cackling laughter. "Sail her singlehanded! The God—damned—fool . . ."

The *Zara* lay on her side, sliding heavily in the waves that broke over her rail in long, creamy chains. They came up fast, much faster than

Jacobi would have believed—all at once they were there, hanging off to leeward, luffing, and Paul shouted: "Where is he? I don't see him . . ."

The mast lay nearly level, like a long black lance at rest. Around it lay a swirling confusion of canvas, lines, cushions. There was no sign of Vosz.

"Can swim, can't he?" the Judge was shouting at him. "Damn blasted fool does know how to *swim*—?"

Blackburn called, "I see him! Take the wheel . . ."

"Look, now—" the old man cried, but Paul was already above them, poised on the weather rail, knees flexed, hands held at his waist—then he was gone in a long, arching dive, reappeared almost instantly, cutting through the water in a quick, powerful rhythm. He was at the mast, he paused—then his head bobbed under the rippling gray tide of canvas. Jacobi stared hard. He had no force, no volition; he had left his body, he was nothing but a tormented eye straining to take in this tableau of sodden sails and fouled lines and débris that seconds before had been a sleek, sturdy sloop. Just like that, he thought dumbly, gazing; no warning at all. Paul was in there, *Paul* was under all that mess—

"Go forward!"

The command snapped him back to his body. The old man was spinning the wheel hard and glaring at him under the crazy, tattered hat brim. "Let her go!" he roared, indicating the jib sheets. "Boat hook—in the bow! *Look lively!"*

He nodded and ran forward, bound in an almost pleasurable release of muscular movement, caught up the gaff and crouched there, his arm hooked around the stay. What should he do now? He glanced aft but the Judge, holding the ship into the wind, was expressionless. The boat reared and plunged drunkenly, the sails rippled and snapped like gunfire. Paul, he thought, in a spasm of pure fear. He would have to go after him, go and find him somehow, there was no other way. He let go the boat hook and raised himself to his feet on the heaving, shuddering bow.

"No! Stay with the boat!" the Judge shouted at him. "Stay there! He knows what he's doing . . ."

He gazed back at the seamed hawk's face, speechless . This had turned all terrible. If they didn't do something—

There was a commotion at the edge of the mainsail, a slow flurry of movement. Paul's head popped out under the boom, then Vosz, his slick skull lolling loosely. He'd lost the wrap-around dark glasses; his eyes were closed. Jacobi heard himself cry something, he had no idea what. He felt a rush of physical relief as sharp as voiding. The capsized vessel kept sliding toward them in clumsy, dreamy lunges while they rose and sank, waiting. Paul was making his way through the tangle of lines and stays, holding Vosz around the chest. Jacobi extended the gaff. Blackburn cried hoarsely, "No! I'm—all right. Ladder!"

Jacobi darted away, threw over the ship's ladder in a paroxysm of need, crouched there and reached down, straining—caught Vosz under the arms as Paul worked him alongside. Jacobi heaved once, again. He would never have believed Vosz was so heavy. The Presidential Assistant's eyes rolled open, rolled closed again, he coughed weakly; his body hung in the water like an impossible cumbrous sack. Jacobi cursed. All at once he hated Vosz more than anyone or anything he'd ever known. He trembled with savagery—he had a powerful impulse to shove that ugly, cropped skull under, smash it with the gaff . . .

"—Bastard," he gasped. He gave a tremendous heave and got Vosz over the rail and dragged him roughly into the cockpit bench.

"Roll him over," the Judge ordered. "On his belly."

Jacobi complied. Vosz, his free arm dragging on the floor of the cockpit, began a rhythmic choked retching, belching up sea water and bile that hung from his mouth in stringy looping skeins.

"Shove his head overboard," the Judge said crisply. "No sense getting it all over the cockpit."

Blackburn hoisted himself on board and sat down with a grunt. "Got himself fouled—in the gear," he panted. "Got one arm—around my neck—before I knew where I was at. Christ, he's strong." Blood was running in several matted streams from a long open cut over one eye.

Jacobi exclaimed: "You're hurt!"

The Secretary felt his forehead, winced. "Yeah. Bumped it against something. Hatch cover, I guess . . . Hey, what a crazy deal." He laughed, watching Vosz pull himself feebly to a sitting position; his head was hanging, his belly still heaved uncontrollably.

"Here you go." Judge Seaver handed him a beautifully wrought glass-and-pewter flask. "This'll draw the miasmas."

Vosz took a drink—fell into a furious fit of coughing and vomited it all over the side. The Judge snatched the flask back. "Perfect waste of good liquor," he said tartly.

"Sorry, sir," Vosz answered in a feeble voice. "Very sorry—to do that."

Jacobi stared at him; it was the first time he'd ever heard Doctor Reinhold Vosz apologize to anyone on this earth.

"Come on," Paul was saying. "Let's get that baby secured before she rams us and we go down with all hands."

They started the engine, got the *Zara* on a long towline, gaffed floating objects out of the sea, everything they could find, and started back in half a gale, hauling the great dead weight of the sloop which looked fat and ungainly now, a piece of fouled slick flotsam. Vosz sat silent, huddled in waterproofs and a blanket. All the headlong bravura had fled him. His hands kept clasping and unclasping vaguely.

"It was so sudden!" he muttered. "Fantastic . . ."

"Yes, it'll go like that," the Judge agreed. The fierce, tight glint had come into his eyes again. "Sea look pretty big to you, did it?"

"Only those who brave its dangers, Comprehend its mysteree," Blackburn chanted from the helm.

"Fine thing!" Jacobi heard himself burst out all at once. "The two men responsible for American foreign policy get themselves drowned in a stupid, ridiculous sailing accident! No, I can't see the humor of it, Chief—"

"Now, Sid," Paul said, placatingly. "Now, Sid . . ."

"No, I mean it," he went on. He couldn't seem to stop himself. Reaction to any crisis invariably turned him snappish and sour, but now he was trembling, almost tearful, caught in a mounting rage. "Look, I'm willing to risk my neck as—as readily as the next man, but it's got to be for a *reason*—yes! Suppose both of you had got drowned just now. Suppose it had happened. Fine bloody thing!"

"—And leave you holding the sack?" Blackburn called. "All those troubles!" Running his fingers over the spokes he laughed boisterously. "Can't you see the Neg now, calling staff meetings at nine-forty, ten-twenty, eleven-ten? Trying to decide whether to include Willy Wentzel? where he ought to sit, all that poop?" The rescue seemed to have blown clear his somber, abstracted mood of the night before. With the bloody compress stuck low over his eye and his hair wild with salt he looked like a kid after some hell-raising prank. "Days of protocol and peril . . . Reason, Sid?—we had a reason. We had a race to see who was the best imperialist-power-élite sailor on the Vineyard."

"—I'll never forget what you did, Paul," Vosz said with sudden hollow entreaty. "Never. No matter what happens—"

"Don't worry about it." Blackburn winked at Jacobi mischievously. "What the hell—you'd do the same thing for me, Reiny. Wouldn't you?" He laughed again, his head back, and the Presidential Assistant's lips turned up in a brief, soured parody of a smile, then drew down again.

"Of course, of course," he said. He kept staring at the low ridge of land off to the southwest—the object of some terrible pilgrimage: a new land of milk and honey. Bereft of the purple-tinted goggles his naked eyes blinked in slow fearful amazement. Like the car crash on the Turnpike with Natalie that time, Jacobi thought. Nothing looks the same, nothing's quite there for granted; for days. A dream that's real. He can't get over it. But there's something else, too . . .

Paul, exuberant and droll, was off on a shipwreck anecdote from the last century, a grisly tale involving men, their hands and faces encased in ice, dropping from the yards like stunned bees, and a ship's officer kneeling on the quarterdeck in vociferous prayer; but Vosz was not listening.

"No—I owe it to you," he said with an effort. "After this . . ."

The Secretary looked down in surprise. "Owe me? You don't owe me a thing."

"Going to owe Josh Clough's shipyard plenty," the Judge said, and Paul laughed and called:

"That's the truth. You'd better throw your checkbook away."

"No, this is different." His eyes were fastened on Blackburn's as though he might not see him again for years. "Something I should tell you."

"It'll keep. Save your strength. Did you ever hear the story about Maw Lummet, the Queen of the Chatham mooncussers? You know what they used to do? There'd be an onshore gale, and they'd get a kid with a lantern on a long pole and make him run up and down—"

"No, you don't understand . . ." A moment longer Vosz struggled with himself, his lips tremulous and blue. Jacobi watched him attentively: the hesitant, importunate tone, the pallid eyes were disturbing—as unlike Reinhold Vosz as Reinhold Vosz would ever be. Alert, a bit apprehensive Jacobi waited, sensing something in the air. Of course it could be the girl. But Vosz wouldn't bring her up with the Judge there—even Reiny wouldn't be that heedless . . .

"Sure I do," Blackburn was saying easily from the wheel. "You've just had an adventure, and it's sprung all the apertures. Those iron posterns we keep closed most of the time. Good thing, too. Mike Hudela was telling me once about the Punjabi riots—they were hitting him, kicking him, a boy of fifteen stabbed him twice. He said he felt as though he were acting in a movie the whole time, watching himself fending them off, keeping his feet, backing away, until the car pulled up and they hauled him in. Perfectly fine, in control of himself—until ten minutes later when he came all apart, began to blubber like a baby. Said he kept seeing that kid's face, and the knife—"

"Deuermann!" the Judge barked suddenly. Squinting up the slender bare shaft of the mainmast he nodded implacably. "I'd know him anywhere."

"Who's that, Dad?" Blackburn said.

"Your undertaker, there. What did you call him—Dunkenfuss?" He pulled a wet, limp photograph out of a pocket of his jacket and glared at it. ". . . But he was innocent!" His mouth went on working vacantly; he looked all at once like a harassed, frightened old man. "The case was *closed* . . . What are they raking up all those dead ashes for?"

"What dead ashes are those?" Paul asked him.

Jacobi began: "You mean you knew this man from some case—" He broke off when Paul shook his head warningly: the Judge's recurrent confusion over time and events again.

"They're pretty sure of his identity, Dad," Blackburn offered mildly. "There's a good-sized dossier on him."

"Riff-raff," the old man went on as though he hadn't heard him. "Do anything for a price. *I* could have told them that but they knew it, anyway. Sent him to Marazkirt later on to set up the missile sites."

"Who, Drachenfels? Dad, he's a hydraulic engineer—he builds *dams* . . ."

"It's the eyes," the Judge said, musing. "They can hide everything, change everything but the eyes." He shot Jacobi a fierce, suspicious glance and jammed the photos into his pocket again.

"Turkish missile sites," Blackburn mused. "You know anything about it, Reiny?"

The Presidential Adviser shook his head. His entire demeanor had changed during Judge Seaver's outburst: his eyes had tightened, his head bobbed in the old fiery way. "Nothing whatever. In fact I very much doubt if the gentleman in question was ever in Turkey."

"Well he *was,*" the old man retorted. He jerked a bony thumb over his shoulder. "If your man Dunkenpuss wasn't setting up sites in Turkey I'll make good on all the repairs for your fire engine, there . . ."

"Hey, hold on," Blackburn interrupted him.

"—and if he was," the Judge continued implacably, "you'll owe *me* a set of sails. Do you accept?"

"Of course, of course I accept—my profuse thanks, Judge Seaver." For the first time that afternoon Vosz emitted his clattering, metallic laugh; he had got hold of himself again. "On Mundareva, in the Admiralty Islands, the man who loses a wager—an important one, a vital one—must surrender all prerequisites of power and leave the tribe. On pain of death."

"Wouldn't be many eminent souls left in Washington at that rate," the Judge observed gloomily.

"No, there wouldn't!" Paul laughed loudly, his head thrown back, full in the sun; the irrepressibly merry mood was still on him. "We're born gamblers, every last mother's son of us—we're ready to risk the work of a lifetime on one throw of a four-year term, and we're delighted at the chance.—I'm going to go see Ch'en Pu-tsao," he said in a different tone.

"What?" Vosz cried, "—go hat-in-hand to that conniving rogue?"

"Yep. Tomorrow. Or have him come to me. One or the other."

"And get to the bottom of things? Confront the ultimate wisdom? Dry your eyes—there are too many impediments, too many dark designs."

"Exactly. Which is why coming together face-to-face might solve a few of them." He passed a hand through his waving crest of hair. "Yep: it's the way to untie this particular Gordian knot."

"You are such a romantic, Paul. This is no Gordian knot—it's a rather simple plan to destroy our position in Asia, no more, no less. You're willing to risk your whole career on a move like that?"

"Ever hear of a man named Joe Oliver?" Blackburn asked him. "It's an interesting story. Right up your alley, Reiny—esoteric anthropological data. Joe Oliver was a black jazz trumpeter in turn-of-the-century New Orleans. He and Mutt Carey were considered the best two horns in town, and neither one could stand being called one-of-the-two-best. You know how it is. So they decided on a duel of cornet solos in Clongowes Square one night, to settle the issue once and for all. It was a battle of giants, but in the end the crowd gave Carey the biggest ovation and declared him the winner. And Joe Oliver threw away his cornet and vowed he'd never play again."

"Idiot," Vosz declared. "To put his fate in the hands of the mob."

"Don't we all?"

"Sentimental fool—all he needed to do was go to some city where they'd never heard of this Mutt Carey."

"You miss the point, Reiny," Blackburn said with that quick, electric intensity of manner. "The point is that *he'd* heard of Mutt Carey—even if he went to the end of the earth."

Jacobi could contain himself no longer. "What were you going to say, Reiny?" he demanded. "A few minutes ago—that was so vital. What were you going to tell Paul?"

The Presidential Assistant's face broke apart in the old ferocious grimace. "It will keep, it will keep. For a later time, a more propitious occasion than this." Humming, he began flexing his powerful hands rhythmically. "You are such a romantic, my dear Paul," he said, smiling. "Dangerously so, I fear."

Blackburn laughed openly. "For going into the water to save your megalomanic old hide, you mean?"

"He might have done better," the Judge muttered.

Vosz nodded, though his slitted eyes were unreadable. "Even for that. A romantic should never aspire to guide a nation."

It became quiet in the cockpit. The Judge coughed up a huge ball of phlegm and spat it fiercely over the side. From behind the wheel Blackburn watched the Presidential Assistant, his blunt broad face nicely balanced between indignation and amusement.

"Maybe you're right," he said after a pause. "Maybe you're right at that."

ELEVEN

THE WATER WAS still as still—a fine, broad, quicksilver plate. Standing immersed to her neck, her feet just touching bottom, Jillie Hoyt watched Paul swim toward her down the sun's path with that serene, lazy crawl, his round arms lifting and dropping, lifting and dropping; all washed in gold, in sliding, darting flakes of gold . . .

"Like magic," she murmured. "It's all like magic." Underwater, foreshortened, her naked body looked childlike and pale; her breasts lifted mysteriously when she turned. Behind her the cottage—the camp, Paul called it—looked like a lovely skeleton ship that had been stranded and then reclaimed by forest. Whoever had built it had sited it cleverly enough on the narrow curving bridge of land between Tashawena Inlet and the Sound: screened by scrub pine and beach plum and chokecherry it nevertheless lay open to both sweeps of water, laved in their soft airs, bombarded by sunlight. At the far end of the Inlet a skiff moved, its two occupants looming primitive and stark, and a solitary heron flapped ponderously over a green sea of eel grass, hunting. This moment, she thought, simple and complete: the cottage at my back, the Inlet green with morning, and Paul swimming toward me . . . He was there, all at once and magically, swept sliding by in a playful little storm of water and pulled up, snorting like a walrus.

"All out of shape," he panted, grinning. *"All* out of shape."

"Oh, but you're not—you're glorious . . ."

"That's because you don't know swimming. I vowed when I took this job I'd get in a mile a day, no matter what. But there's never any time, somehow. Hell, Bill Rogers never missed his golf game—come rain, come shine he'd be out there swinging a club. McNamara always got in his squash. I ought to break out more."

"I don't see how you breathe," she said. "I can't ever see your mouth."

"Snatch-breath. You breathe in a little air pocket your head makes. I'll show you."

With a subtle, powerful movement of his body he drew close to her; he looked so young with his hair plastered close to his skull. His hands came under her arms and cupped her breasts gently, his naked belly came hard against hers. His skin was warm and sleek, the way she imagined a seal's; around her the water turned suddenly cool.

"That's not teaching me how to breathe," she murmured.

"Oh yes, it is. Yes it is.—See how wonderful water is?" he said, and kissed her. "I'll teach you to swim like a frisky lady dolphin. I will! And we'll swim away together to some undiscovered coral isle and make wild love."

"It's really your element," she told him. "Not earth and air."

He nodded at her happily; his eyes were shining like a boy's. "Don't you see?—no matter how tired you are, how helpless, you can't ever fall."

"I never thought of it that way. To me it always meant danger. I was terrified of the water."

He dipped his head backward, rose to her again. "So was I."

"You were—!"

"Yep. Scared to death. But I got over it when I was seven. And I swam a mile unassisted when I was nine."

"How'd you get over it?"

"My father. Tied a towel around my middle with a rope around that, and held me afloat till I got the hang of it. He used to say a man ought never to be afraid of anything in nature. In itself, I mean."

"I would have liked your father."

"He'd have liked you, too. You were his kind of girl."

She smiled. "What does that mean?"

"Oh, you know: a sexy, crazy, lascivious, hell-around—"

She leaped at him and he plunged up and backward, arching, vanished underwater. She gazed all around her, half-amused, half-vexed, fighting a deepening alarm as the moments passed. Something pinched her toes: she squealed, reached down but again he eluded her, slipped ghostly off—burst upward in a silver fountain of water ten feet away, a dazzling sea god, and sank back again.

"Don't do that!" she called, laughing.

". . . An offering." He glided up to her, held out his hand. In its center lay a slender dog whelk, the palest rose along its channel. "To wear in the fateful hollow of thine ear." He placed it there gently; his hand moved along her chin, her throat, caressed with lazy delicacy her breast.

"You and your peaceful uses of the sea floor," she murmured. She was trembling now, her vitals melting in these golden scales of sunlight all around them. "You turn me into water, too—into all glorious, flowing things. Do you know that?"

He nodded. "My green-and-gold girl. All green and gold in the world's first morning." And now the exuberant, boyish look was gone, his fine steady glance was dark with wanting. That good hard yearning needing face . . . She wanted to bring him golden apples, silver pomegranates in her skirt, ebony-and-ivory caskets filled with fantastic shells; she wanted only to follow him to Valparaiso, to Lhasa, to Ponape and bring him all good things in boisterous abundance.

"You *stir* me so! I feel like the first woman on earth, and you the first man."

"Yes."

"I feel as if God had made me from your dear rib. I do! . . . Will you take me?" she asked softly. "Will you take me with you down to all the pearls and cowrie shells and coral? Down to your sea floor?"

"Sweet my love," he said. His arms, so hard, so gentle, held her suspended. "Come . . ."

"Look at them! Look!"

They came on down the Sound, their spinnakers set, storming along in silent majesty as if the sea were sky, in a tumult of turquoise and vermilion and palest azure, and the afternoon sun fell full on the bellying silk in a high voluptuous sheen; a pride of sail.

"Why, they're glorious!" she cried. "They're like a dream of sailing— they're like exotic birds . . ."

"Aren't they?" Paul was peering intently at the regatta through the telescope he'd brought over with him from the Paling that afternoon, but she could feel the excitement in his voice. "That's the *Cormorant,* that black-hulled yawl. Ben Manter's boat. Oooh, he's a tricky one."

And still they came, swaying in stately elegance—a royal blazonry of bends and crosses and sunbursts and chevrons; the sky was alight with their color.

"That's delightful—why don't they use those sails all the time?"

"Can't, love. That's only when you're sailing wing-and-wing."

"Wing-and-wing—oh, that's lovely! That's like us. They make me think of Byzantium. Pirate ships out of the Levant, laden with spices and frankincense. And Portuguese moidores. Don't you love that word?"

"Yes, and doubloons."

"Not as exotic . . . Oh, it's fallen!"

One of the nylon spinnakers—French blue with a deep saffron ball— began to collapse on itself in slow, rhythmic pulsations, like a wounded bird.

"Stolen his wind."

"But they're *behind* them—"

"Yes, love. So's the wind. That's strategy. Here, look through the glass: you'll see what's happening. No—rest it on my shoulder, like this."

Shot near in the great lens she saw figures reaching, straining, grappling with what looked like a long flat pole; but the frantic human activity dimmed the magic. "Whose boat is that?" she asked.

"I don't know—he's flying a New York Yacht Club burgee. *Come* on," he called with sudden boyish excitement, "—now's your chance, Benbo. Take him!"

She said: "You'd like to be out there, wouldn't you, Paul?"

"Don't be silly." He stopped then and looked at her, his cheeks a full, high copper from the sun, his hair wild from swimming. "Look, I want to be exactly where I am—right here with you. I've sailed in a regatta."

"Do you? honestly?" Part of her still found it fantastic that Paul Blackburn would rather be with her than anywhere else in the world.

"You know I do. You have to know it."

His eyes had dropped to the telescope. She handed it back to him and said slowly: "That's the glass. Isn't it? The one your wife's brother used for bird-watching." He nodded silently. "I'd have thought—" she began, and then broke off. Why did she always speak out before she'd thought about it? What a ruinous habit . . .

He was smiling—a sad, terse smile she hadn't seen before. "Oh, no," he said, and shook his head. "That's too easy. No, I accepted it, you see. I couldn't bear not to. So—now I'm sort of stuck with it. If you know what I mean." He looked away again, toward the regatta, his lips compressed.

"My darling!" She laughed out loud; she felt all at once a tremendous certainty about this moment at the edge of their little beach, gazing out at the gorgeous extravagance of sail. There was nothing she could not do, no triumph she could not achieve—she could even laugh him out of certain harsh rigidities as alien to him as igloos. "You're not stuck with anything! My poor darling—you try so hard to be a Puritan, and it just won't go: you'd look so silly in one of those stovepipe hats with a big, brass buckle, anyway."

He was grinning again. "I don't know. I always thought they were pretty imposing."

"You would. I never yet met a Harvard man with decent taste in clothes—if it's shaggy and baggy and a size too big you think you're well-dressed. Jesus, what snobs!" Still watching him she said in a different tone: "You could have gone sailing today, you know. It would have been all right with me."

He lowered the glass and took her by the shoulders. "You idiot. I want to be with you—can't you understand that? With you. Right here." His eyes were dark with animation. "I'm all alive—don't you see?—for the first time in my life, really *alive*. Everything looks fresh and new, just struck into being. Jillie, I'm what I always *wanted* to be. Don't you see that?"

"Yes. I see that."

"I'm like what I dreamed I could be as a kid—those lion dreams. Only I'm living it now . . . Look at them!" he cried, pointing at the hurrying, festive armada flung out across the Sound. "Did you ever see anything so magnificent in all your life?" He threw his head back, his eyes half-closed, and said: *"Soon far from the rose and the lily and fret of the*

*flames would we be, Were we only white birds, my beloved, buoyed out on
the foam of the sea! . . ."*

"Yeats," she said. "I love you for knowing Yeats."

"What do you take me for—a Hottentot? a heathen Chinee?" Laughing wildly he caught her hand. "Come on, come on—you crazy wonderful
white bird, you!"

Holding his hand she ran with him toward the water.

She danced all at once into view from the bedroom—bewigged in a
brand new floor mop, an old piece of Paisley silk wound tight around her
body, rested one lovely bare arm against the door jamb and struck a wildly
provocative pose, staring at him from under her brows. He burst out
laughing.

"This incog enough?" she said.

"You idiot. You dear, divine idiot. Come here this instant."

"Inamorata of High Government Official Entertains Graciously in
Rustic Vineyard Eyrie. 'A few quiet at-homes,' quobbles Somerville militant
siren. 'Our wants are simple. Relatively.' " She moved on to the porch
filled with imperious hauteur. "I'll have to become a Georgetown hostess, a
swinger. Isn't that what they all do? Or Watergate, that's the ultrajazzy
parage down there too, isn't it? Maybe I could become a Dark Force in
Amurkan Foreign Policy. You'd do all the sneaky things I told you to,
wouldn't you?"

"Yours to command, Madame."

"Like what's her name—you know, that woman who stopped the
war between the Turks and the Greeks. Didn't she?"

He smiled. "It was a bit more complicated than that, I'm afraid.
Venizelos had his own—"

"No history!" She came up to him swiftly and sat on his lap. She
looked bizarre and Egyptian under the mop, strangely attractive. "Do you
suppose we could go to the movies at Vineyard Haven if we wore dark
glasses like the Squeezer, and slumped down in the back row? No, I won't
tempt you," she said before he could answer, "I was only fancifying or
something. I'll wear a tiara and an emerald stomacher and be terribly digni-
fied and aloof."

"Jillie, you're wonderful. There's never been anyone like you since
the Pyramids."

"I like *that!* There's never *ever* been anyone like me."

"No. There never has." He kissed her, loving the way her eyelids
drooped in an almost sorrowful, yearning way as her face swam closer; her
lower lip was like a ripe little fig. She was impulsive, almost wanton in her
joy—and yet there was that terribly vulnerable, fragile quality about her,
like a yearling doe at the edge of a clearing . . .

"Your lips have changed," he murmured. "They're fuller, somehow."

"You've changed, too. You actually walk differently, do you know that?"

"Do I?"

"Yes. There's—an ease. A sense of accomplishment, assurance, I don't know. There was always a kind of desperation in the way you walked before . . . I love to watch you walk, Paul."

"I love to feel you kiss." Her eyes were the very deepest emerald. The southerly blew gustily through the house, rattling the old muslin curtains like sails luffing.

"Tell me more about myself," she said.

"La Rochefoucauld says the reason lovers never tire of being together is because they are always talking of themselves."

"Clever old La Rochefoucauld."

"I love you, Jillie. I love you more than any man has ever loved any woman since 784."

"Why 784?"

"I don't know." He had to keep telling her he loved her, as if saying it enough times would determine some great question in human affairs. "Jillie, I want you tremendously."

"I knew I shouldn't have sat on your lap."

"That great swinging golden net."

"Darling, I just put the lobsters in . . ."

"Were we only white birds, my beloved, buoyed out on the foam—"

"—Poor lobsters!"

He sat on the little deck behind the house repairing a broken rung in the back of a chair with glue and some small C-clamps he'd found in the pump house, and watched the light falling, a dove-and-magenta radiance.

"You know how to do so many things," she said. "My father was impossible—he couldn't change a light bulb without giving himself a shock. A man ought to know how to cope . . . You look so *contented* when you're repairing something."

He smiled slowly. It was true: that need to reclaim, restore—why? Because he'd come over the years to feel that something had been irretrievably lost; was that it?

"Tell me more about your father," he said. He wanted to know everything about her—her childhood fears and womanly triumphs, how she'd spent her vacations, what school subjects she'd detested, her preference in desserts. It was a hunger he couldn't begin to satisfy. In the space of two weeks she had come to stand for everything in life that was feminine. When he pictured the queens of history or the heroines of novels they moved, thought, laughed, loved like Jillie. The idea of having gone on through life and never known such happiness could make him stiff with dread.

"I don't want to talk about him now," she said. "I want to talk about sweet and glorious things.—Look, there's that big bird again. It's not an eagle, is it?"

He raised his head, watched the fish hawk's long descent downwind, the catch and balance, and again the deep eddying glide. "No. That's one of Lee's ospreys. Could be descended from one of the broods we used to watch in that dead oak down at the end of the Inlet, there. The nest is gone, though. Almost all of them are gone. They're practically extinct, you know."

Sitting there relaxed, profoundly at peace with himself and the world, he felt he understood Leland Seaver for the first time: that healing simplicity of solitude, the pervasive solace of moving animal-like on the earth, open to it, bound in its glorious privacies and revelations. *Elementals,* he thought suddenly, I'm back to elementals: free again, holding the moment like quicksilver in the palm of my hand—the way I felt when Lee and I followed the birds . . .

He set the repaired chair aside and wiped his hands on his handkerchief. Far down the Inlet the two Clough boys were working on their houseboat—a crazy, wonderful patchwork structure of plywood and old balks of timber. A mammoth baluster rose up in the prow—Blackburn assumed it was the prow, there was no other way of telling—like a wild phallic totem, there was a black-and-orange striped awning above one of the window holes, and a ship's ladder led up to a kind of top deck where a heavy oak chair stood all by itself. The whole edifice canted drunkenly forward, turning now and then as the boys, naked except for blue jeans sawed off at the thigh, clambered over it, adding more superstructure. The tap of their hammers came festive and trivial across the water.

"I check up on their progress each morning," Jillie was saying. "They've worked so hard! Their summer's project, I suppose. Will they take it sailing when they're finished?"

"It's not what you'd call a sailing rig. No, they'll be lucky if it just plain floats."

"But all that wood . . ."

"Some of the lumber is waterlogged, most likely. It's the mistake all kids make—you see a grand old plank lying up in the witch grass and you add that on, and then another, and another. And before you know it the whole contraption just settles in the shallows and stays there."

"Oh, you're such a pessimist! I think it's wonderful."

"So do I. But it won't float—and you couldn't steer it if it did. Hell, the fun's in building it, the mariner dream . . ."

He fell silent, watching the dusk steal in over the Inlet like smoke, the lights coming on here and there at the points of land. Jillie was reminiscing about a tree house she and two other children had built in a neighbor's backyard in Bridgeport and he watched her, tracing the delicate Oriental cast to her cheeks, the full white sweep of her throat. He wanted to sit there forever, a little apart from all the world, even Jillie, and hold this glowing, soaring sensation inside him, examining it from all possible angles, like some mad diamond cutter who has acquired quite by accident the most flawless stone ever mined, and whose rapture is so overmastering he cannot even bear to trace it for cutting . . .

She had stopped—she was watching him, her green eyes very steady and grave. "What are you thinking, darling?"

"I was thinking if I could sit here in this funny old camp with you the rest of my life I'd never ask for anything else."

"And eat off willow ware?" she murmured.

"And eat off willow ware. And wear sawed-off blue jeans, like the kids. And eat clams and blueberries. And bring you a particularly beautiful little shell each morning."

She rose so swiftly he thought she was about to run from the porch—whirled around with that quick, rippling motion and said: "I love you, Paul Blackburn. I love you utterly, I love you hopelessly and fiercely and forever. Do you know how I know?" He had risen, had moved toward her unaware; he shook his head. "Because no matter how I feel about anything, the moment I'm with you I'm instantly all right in the deepest possible sense—I feel as if Grace had descended. I'm only complete with you." She put one hand up to his face as though she were blind. "Your good, strong Irish jaw, and your sturdy nose, and that hurt line I love on the side of your mouth, right there; and most of all your burning dark eyes that turn me to molten gold, set my very veins to singing . . ."

Her voice was low—deep in her throat, her breast, where a woman's voice ought to be; it vibrated with a hidden music that made him tremble.

"Love in the open hand, as the poet said. Isn't it? I fought it so— I didn't want to love you. I didn't. Love makes one timid as well as reckless, doesn't it? I said I'd never love again—it's too painful. How can anyone recover more than once? Now here I am caught by a love I trust. For I do trust you, Paul—completely and absolutely. Quel irony . . ."

He held her, as tenderly as man ever held woman, he knew, and gazed at the Inlet. The only truths lay in contraries, in conundrums: to yield was to triumph, to lose was to find, to give without stint was to gain without measure. It was so simple. The slave was freer than the tyrant, the vagabond richer than the merchant, the lover mightier than the man of war. Blackburn's Law—

"Such a rare and valiant girl," he murmured. He thought of that evening in his study at Cleveland Park when he had gone up to her, thrust along as though by one of Homer's gods, and taken her in his arms; now *she* felt it, was swinging with him in their golden net high over Vineyard Sound, one of the jewels in Big Bill Donlund's Atlantic Brahmin Coronet. Neither of us will ever feel anything again, he thought—nothing like this: how could we? how could anyone?

"Life is simply too short to deny it," she said. "That's all." The wind blew freshly against their faces, and the thread of a new moon forced its way through the sinking dusk beyond the great dead oak. "You make us a five-pointed star, a perfect circle—all dancing moonlight."

"It's true," he said, half laughing,—"by golly, sometimes I think we're like one of those jazzy Greek legends . . ."

"No," she answered quietly. She touched what she called the "hurt line" at the corner of his mouth. "No, we're our own legend, you and I."

"—half-strangled by that time, with the grip Reiny'd had on me, my eyes full of blood and salt water—and there was old Sid, crouched at the rail with a boathook, jabbing it at me. A real Buster Keaton. And you know, for the tiniest part of a second I had the idea he was trying to stab me with it—that he was going to bash me one over the noggin and send me down to the deep six. Yes! Isn't it weird? The things that'll go through your mind at times . . ."

The roof was low and dark, a rough pine sheathing that still bore the ancient fingermarks of the carpenters. The rain drove against it in a dense scouring thunder. Jillie Hoyt thought, It always gets around to raining when we're together, or nearly always, there must be something profoundly symbolic in that. Across the warped trestle table Paul, wearing a frayed old maroon sweater, was tilted back in his chair, arms behind his head, telling her about the rescue; and she listened calmly, watching his face. He was understating the whole affair, she knew: turning it light. He was wearing a huge neat compress that covered his left eyebrow, they'd had to take nine stitches in the cut at the Island Hospital. Men always disparaged such moments, burlesqued them. Why? Feeling the different pitch of his voice more than listening to the words spoken, she realized he'd been badly frightened, that he was now immensely jubilant; and it irritated her obscurely.

"So this time you didn't fail," she said.

His face went slack in surprise, his lower lip thrust forward. "That's right," he answered evenly. "I didn't."

"It was what you wanted to do, then."

"What?" His eyes shot over to hers uncertainly. "Wanted? I had to do it. You don't just sit there and let somebody *drown*."

"No, of course not." She smiled her wry, mirthless smile. "You wait until some pompous idiot has got himself in a mess and then you jump in and get drowned along with him."

"Oh, come on, Jill. It was just a dunk in the drink. It was a lark, for

Pete sake."

The air of boyish exuberance made her furious all at once. "Jesus, I just don't understand you sometimes," she said with heat. "I mean it. You're always talking about a sense of balance, winnowing the essential from the extraneous, all that crap—and then when a hideous, sick creep like Vosz gets tangled up in his own stupid rigging . . . Sometimes you make me want to puke."

"Jill—"

"Risk your ass for that—that freak! Smitty's told me about him. Plenty. Sell out his own mother if the price was right, monogrammed fucking underwear, he can't even go up in a plane without shaking like an old woman—he's a monster. He doesn't *deserve* to survive!"

"Honey, honey, honey . . ." With that lithe alacrity she loved he rose and came around the table to her, raised her to him gently. "You're all tensed up."

"Yes, and so would you be, hanging around in this stupid wooden cage!"

"Honey."

"No."

"Honey girl . . ."

"Oh, God. Oh, my God." His arms were around her; the slow, urgent pressure of his body that stirred her to trembling, made her frantic.

"I want you so, Jillie," he was saying, his lips moving against the shell of her ear. "I'm alive with you—here. Anywhere. Only with you. It's true."

She groaned, and nodded. They had drifted to the disheveled bed in an easy trance. Her body, her senses moved independent of her thoughts, revelling in their high latitude. She could no more not desire this man than she could step through the barrier of time, or live at the bottom of Tashawena Channel, four fathoms down . . .

"You're mine."

It was true. Nothing else was, but this was. His eyes were almost pure onyx at this moment. Reaching deep under her buttocks he brought her mount to him as to a feast. He was tender, he was tireless, he was both subtle and bold—she felt her body sway in distending flares of sensation, heard herself cry aloud in rapture, in heightened need. His flesh was always so warm—as though his blood ran nearer to the surface than other people's. She held his strength in soft ferocity, kissed it, caressed it; sought the instant of his entry—that glorious golden arrow!—a scalding blissful impletion, exulting, *I knew it, I knew it would be like this from the first moment in Somerville, at the door;* caught up now in wave on wave of spattered rainbow hues, birds aloft and dolphins plunging, until she cried she knew not what in ringing, riotous incantation, some sweetly anguished sister far away across the Sound—gliding at last in roller-coaster swoops to present sight and sense as if awakened from the happiest of childhood dreams.

"Stars—oh, stars! . . ."

"Sweet my love."

The deepest of all blue voyages. Yet, holding his slim, round head in her arms she returned to the cold, gray light, the rain, the cramped dark hut that had betrayed her; that didn't seem any longer like a stranded pirate ship at all. In spite of herself she sighed heavily.

"What is it, Jill?"

"Nothing."

"No—tell me."

". . . It's this place," she muttered, yawning. "When it rains here you feel like Noah and the ark."

"I know."

"Oh, it's not the camp . . ." It's *things,* she wanted to say; things ganging up. She'd caught a cold during the week, and yesterday morning walking in the woods they had come upon the child of a local plumber who had recognized Paul immediately. They had passed it off casually enough, but there was no way of knowing whether or not the boy would mention Jillie's presence to his mother. And now this rotten, interminably confining rain . . .

"Can I get you anything, darling?" he was saying. "A drink, or a cup of coffee?"

"No. I'm okay."

She suppressed a sigh, and blew her nose. On the ugly commode beside the bed the clock said 2:19. It had a high, metallic tick that kept her awake nights, but she hadn't brought any clock of her own. He would leave her in an hour. All her glowering resentment swept back full force. A hideaway could become a trap, then—it was all in the point of view. Paul stormed in on her, full of excitement and high ardor, and stormed away again; and she sat here becalmed, waiting for him to fill her sails. Well, that wasn't quite fair, he came whenever he could, worried or not, wearied or not, she knew; it wasn't any picnic for him, either . . .

But—there was no getting around it—he had the two worlds. What wore her down was the unchallengeable fact that Paul was *right over there,* beyond that low, bristling canopy of pine and oak and locust, wining and dining associates at Eleanor's perfectly appointed table; sailing, playing tennis, seeing old friends in Chilmark or Edgartown—basking in the perquisites of power, of status. The sanctity of legitimacy. His wife would count on that: they all did. Impaled Jesus—nothing on this drear bedraggled earth was more cleanly contemptible than the American wife's self-preening—if not hysterical—reliance on the relentless amenities of home and fireside. Which made it all the more galling when she found herself flipping the pages of *Harper's,* listening fitfully to the halting, adenoidal voices over the Yarmouth and Hyannis stations on her battered transistor radio, wondering with a stab of pure anxiety what he was doing at that moment, what he was saying; what would have induced that quick, generous, transfiguring smile.

She was beginning to feel frightened, beleaguered, desperate—she had never felt like this before in her life. She had always moved fearlessly, defiantly, beggar the consequences: this pattern of trysts and deferential circumspection enraged her. One evening early, to exorcise the demon— she told herself that but it was more, much more than that—she had walked brazenly along the wood road to the Paling and seen through the dense privet figures moving on the verandah, huge against the lights inside the house. Crouched close to the pungent little leaves, hating herself, she had listened to the wind-bell sound of ice cubes in a glass pitcher; a voice (it was Sidney Jacobi's, she recognized the New York City intonations) said something indistinguishable, and then Eleanor Blackburn—she knew it was his wife in the very pit of her belly—answered: "Of course. It's just that they aren't going *about* it in the right way, that's all . . ."

You could walk in there right now, she told herself in amused fury; just walk in and introduce yourself—to an anvil chorus of shock, anger, fear, dismay, hatred: and nothing on that clean, well-lighted verandah will ever be the same again. You are the incalculable element, the unassimilable solution. Yes. She felt a constriction across her breast, a sudden dryness in the roof of her mouth—symptoms she knew well. It took all her force of will to wrench her body away from the hedge and hurry back down the road. She *wanted* to be with him, eating lobster at the Spirit Spout Inn or the Albatross, listening to him spin one of his high fancies, or watching some silly film at Vineyard Haven, murmuring hilarious running commentary to each other in the back row . . . She wanted him, and he her, *she* deserved to be sitting on that verandah, not that gaunt, stiff, horse of a woman who'd let his manhood, the rich green sap of his need wither for twenty-five hideous years. The bitch, the frigid, sanctimonious bitch—! She hated herself for wanting to be on that porch, and for her tight, furtive fear; but there it was—a spinning black lodestone at the heart of all devices, all desires. This was what love was, too . . .

"How conscious *are* we of our beliefs, our allegiances?" Paul was staring up at the stained pine sheathing, hands behind his head. "That's the question I can never resolve. Look at Miles Stout, still actually trying to persuade the world that Formosa was China, that Chiang Kai-shek was the parfit gentil knyght of Oriental democracy. Does he really believe these things? if you tied him to the stake would he still cling to them through fire? Or are they convenient cleats on which to hook his calculated sense of how things *ought* to go? What puzzles we all are!" He chuckled softly over the rain, which had softened. "No, a fair face will wither, a full eye will wax hollow, as good, impetuous Harry Plantagenet said; but our obsessions we pack with us to the grave."

"No," she said. "Not to the grave. They stay on and on—and corrupt the next generation."

"Do you think so? Not always, I'd say. Take—"

"Yes: always!" She was surprised at the heat in her voice but she couldn't check it, she didn't even want to. "They're hanging up everywhere like the golden fleece—only they're perfectly approachable, and people take them down and put them on, like expensive clothes. And they *know* they're wrong, siren songs every last one, but they keep on wearing them because it's more convenient, the old boat doesn't get rocked that way."

"How cynical of you, darling heart."

"Well, I've got my cynical contact lenses on."

"What about you?" he said with a trace of amusement. "Do you include yourself in this gold lamé fashion show?"

"That's right—and you too, right along with the rest of us. Don't think you're exempt, Charlie Brown. Just because you're on top of the dung heap."

"Jill, Jill . . ."

"In fact you're worse than the rest of us—you're intelligent, you know better, and *still* you've decided to play the filthy game."

"It seems to me we had a conversation like this once before."

"That's right, we did. And I was right then, too . . . Don't laugh at me!" His tone, a touch avuncular, reproving, angered her. "You made your choices, just the way all of us do. Maybe you were all right back at the beginning, but you got scared—that flap in Khotiane when you stepped out of line and they lowered the boom on you . . ."

He started, his head snapped around awkwardly. "Who told you about that?"

"Land."

"Land? Land told you?" He raised himself on one elbow. "When did he tell you that?"

Sullenly she shrugged. "Three, four days ago. What difference does it make?"

"You saw him—you've been seeing him?"

"Yes, of course. Why shouldn't I? Is there a law against it?"

He sat up, chafing his shoulder with his thumbnail. "I see." When he glanced at her again his eyes had tightened strangely; he looked like an older, colder brother of Paul Blackburn. "I thought—I'd have thought you wouldn't have been seeing him now."

She felt an immense exasperation—she was overborne, hedged about by his presence, his position, the sheer force of his intellect. "Why does that throw you?" she demanded. "It's you I want to be with, you know that."

"Then why don't you keep it that way!" He leaned toward her sud-

denly, very close, his nostrils flared, and she saw he was angrier than he'd ever been. For a moment she expected him to hit her, and the thought gave her a curious little spasm of pleasure.

"Oh, don't be so bloody Victorian," she began, "you put entirely too much—"

"It hasn't a damned thing to do with being Victorian. It's a matter of human decency . . ."

"Decency—!" she cried. "Don't be ridiculous!"

"Look, I forbid you—I absolutely forbid you to see him."

"Don't talk to me that way! I'm not one of your frightened flunkies."

"You told me you'd break off with him, you told me down in Washington you'd—"

"Yes, and *you* said it was none of your business, you told me we had to be circumspect and all that bullshit—which way do you want it? Do you *want* the whole thing torn wide open? Do you?"

He was silent a moment; his eyes looked feverish and hunted. "You mean—you've been with him. Really *with* him . . . ?"

"He came by one night, and then last week—"

"Does he—look, Jillie: do you mean to say . . . does he bring you what I do?" His mouth was twitching; she had a sudden sense of what the question must have cost him. "No difference at all—?"

"Of course not, oh my God, of course not—do you think you even have to ask me that?"

"Then *why—!*" He made a quick violent gesture and swung away. "If what we have does mean something . . ."

"It's not that simple. I can't just break off, like that. It would blow it in a flash. Paul, he's in *love* with me!"

"Yes and so am I!—God help me . . ."

He was nodding at her rapidly, his mouth firm, his face blunt and strangely homely; all at once tears started in his eyes. He gripped her arm hard. "Look, Jillie. An extraordinary thing has happened to me. Yes, really. I don't know how you feel—I mean, I know you look at things in a different way . . . Jillie, I'm in love with you. I mean really and completely. It's just like nothing I've ever felt before—like nothing I even *imagined* I could feel. When I'm with you I feel—like the Emperor of all the French." He locked his hands. "I can hardly think of anything else any more, I have to *fight* to get my mind on work, I can't bear to be anywhere you're not—it's true. I wouldn't have thought it possible but it is, it's happened. I don't care where it leads, where it takes us. Do you see? Do you understand what I'm saying?"

She nodded; with his thick disheveled hair and frantic eyes he looked like a wild forest bird. She felt a thrust of pure fear.

"What's the matter?"

"Nothing. I don't know . . . I'm afraid—when I hear you say it, like that, I'm afraid."

"I know. That makes two of us."

There was a pause. It was still raining, but off to the northwest the sky was lighter. From somewhere she could hear a hollow muttering, like thunder, but more rhythmic, more like a funeral drum.

"It always means trouble when you love too much," she said. "Ends badly. I know."

"I don't believe that. I can't . . ."

She smiled sadly. "You're the romantic."

"Well, we'll just have to—" He broke off, rocking back and forth absently, his arms clamped around his knees. "—All the time wasted!" he cried softly. "All those God—damned—years . . . Do you understand? I *have* to be with you."

"Yes."

"I know you don't love me—not that way."

"I do love you, I told you I love you," she said, conscious even as she uttered the word of a certain impassible difference.

He sprang to his feet—it was as if he had been bound—and moved off across the room, picked up a worn wooden fid and hefted it. The measured booming came again. "I'm sorry I spoke harshly," he murmured. "I'm in a ridiculous state. The whole world goes black when we quarrel—would you believe it?—like a hood coming down over everything. Jillie, don't—turn too ferocious, will you? Something happens to everybody, sooner or later. No one is all he was a lifetime before . . . I have simply got to be with you," he repeated doggedly. *"In your presence."*

He broke off again, shaking his head. He looked trapped, too; fearful, years older. He was one of the three—or four, or five—most powerful men in the world, and he was afraid of her and of himself. She had made him afraid. It was so utterly unreal. Love unmans us, she thought savagely, thinking of her mother. Her mother had been driven mad by love, she herself had been thrust to the edge of an elevator shaft. Never give all the heart.

"I thought everything was service," he was saying now, gripping the fid in his two hands, peering at it densely. "Service and self-denial—it was how I was brought up. I never questioned it. The Great Republic, indivisible, grander and more essential than any one man's needs. The silent satisfactions—work, duty, loyalty, hewing to the line. The nocturnal helmsman, buffeted but resolute." He smiled without joy. "I was driving past the Archives Building the other day. Some kid had written on the stone, nice soft blue chalk: *What is history to me?* He could have said destiny, or foreign policy, or the whole body politic . . . By God, I know just how he feels. *I do.*" He tossed the blunt wooden cylinder in the air, snatched at it as it came down and missed. It clattered raucously across the thin pine floor. "The hell with all that—I want to *live* now, I want to spend myself, pour it all out in a rush. I want to sail away to Halmahera or the Seychelles, some lazy lovely Hottentot place and walk along the beach with you, picking up shells, lie with you under the palms making wild, incredible, demon love, day on golden day . . . One man's life *is* worth more than the whole buggering clanking machine—it *is*."

She leaned toward him and cried: "Don't say that!"

"Why not? Why shouldn't I say it?"

"Because you can't afford to—Paul, you're the fucking Secretary of State! . . ."

He laughed once. "How infernally true. The show must go on. All three rings. Nick Ostrowsky the physicist was telling me one night about the neutrino. 'All my life I'd been taught: There can be no energy without mass. Cardinal law, inviolate. And now some son of a bitch has discovered something *without* mass but *with* energy. Do you realize what that means, Paul? I've got to start all over again.' That's how I feel. As though they taught me all the wrong ground rules, and I'll commit a personal foul every time I make a move."

"You can't think like that," she cried "—you'll just be a sitting duck. They want to get you out of the way, as it is."

"Who's that?"

"Vosz and his crowd. Others, too. You know them. They're scheming now about how to shoot you down."

He shook his head ruefully. "It's curious—I always find the idea that powerful forces are plotting for my overthrow distinctly comforting, absurd as it is. I wonder why."

She made a gesture of impatience. "What is that damn *booming?*"

"I don't know. Naval gunnery. Or maybe the National Guard outfits up at Edwards." He gazed out at the silver slant of the rain, the tortured Oriental blackness of the pines; he looked defeated and gray, his fine broad shoulders drooping. I've caused this, she thought, I've done this to him. He was all right, his life clear and well-charted until he knocked on the door that afternoon in Somerville: the family knock . . . But what could have prevented it, any of it, once that happened?

Abruptly he said: "Let's go swimming."

"Now?"

"Why not? The tide's in."

"But it's raining—"

"The water's always warmer when it's raining. Come on."

"All right."

Naked she followed his hard nakedness down the narrow path to the rim of beach, the rain falling in a million smarting, delicious needles on her breasts and shoulders. The water lapped against her calves, her thighs, closed over her in a sleek green broth, warmer than the rain. She rose gasping, watched Paul drawing away in that even, lazy crawl, smoothly, his hands reaching forward in a sinking litany of offering, his feet beating a fine low rhythm. "That's what he loves to do," she murmured aloud; we should only do things that give us joy. Why not? Eagerly she struck out after him and gave up, all at once breathless and tired—on an impulse doubled over and thrust her way down. The seaweed tendrils rose in soft ribbons and fans, hanging gently in the green-and-amber silence.

"You will die early in life," Marco Retzlaff had told her late one night at Jumbo's pad, under the eerie orange-paper-covered bulbs. "You will die early, and by violence." His eyes had blazed at her, unfocused and mad, pupil and iris fused in large milky magenta rings. Staring into them she had thought of water like this, iridescent purple fronds like death's banners, pendulous and still. "By drowning, Marco?" she'd asked, smiling. "Will I die by drowning?" "No—no water . . ." His eyes, pot-distended, fixed, bored into hers, his breath was like new-mown hay. "No, I see—I see bars of light, long, slanting bars of light and men scream-ing . . ." Bayonets, she had thought, and laughed; I will die on a forest of steel. "Be serious," Marco had told her and turned away crossly. "I speak the truth, the greater heuristic truth of the spheres." Occult powers. He'd been right about Yukio Mishima, he'd predicted the George Wallace shooting, he said Amelia Earhart was alive and married to a second unit man in Santa Monica—

She broke surface again in a tumult of gasping and splashing, saw Paul lying near her, face down, motionless, rocking gently.

"Stop," she called, and tapped his arm. "Paul! Don't do that!"

He raised his head. "What's wrong?"

"You look—I don't like it when you do that. It makes me think of—"

She saw it, then—just above Paul's shoulder: a shaggy dark figure at the edge of the trees, on the rise across from the house; blunted, mis-shapen by the furred edges of the pine branches. Her fancy, sprung by the dive and the memory, claimed it as a bear, a boar. Then, as though it had sensed her scrutiny, animal-like, it moved off in perfect silence—a man now, unmistakably, a stocky figure in a raincoat and a narrow-brimmed hat, slipping away into the woods and rain.

"*Well*," she said "—who's that?"

Paul turned, gazing. The man had vanished.

"He's gone. A man in a hat. He was standing right up there." She pointed. "He looked—he looked like a hunter."

"He had a gun?"

"No. Just the way he was standing." She was shivering now; there was something in the very casualness of the man's turning away, the deliberate stillness of his movements, that was disturbing.

"Will Gleason, probably," Paul said. "He works for various people. He's always wandering around these parts."

"Not with that kind of a hat," she said. "It was one of those lightweight snap-brims." Like what a salesman wore. Or a—detective. "Could it be some security person?"

"No. I'd know about it if it were something like that."

In a few moments they swam back to shore and hurried up to the cabin where they toweled each other briskly.

"Sid thinks that's the whole answer," Paul told her. "Sid says if everyone could swim as well as I can it would relieve the greatest source of human aggression. He's marvelous for the ego." He caught her eye and winked. "Don't worry about it," he commanded. "It was just some city-slicker voyeur who wanted to feast his eyes on your soft young body."

"Paul, he was standing in the *rain*—*!*"

"Then he was a pluvial voyeur. There's an answer for everything. He thought we were the outpost of a nudist colony and he wants to join, but he's too inhibited. Make me a green Tom Collins."

She smiled at him, but the mood was gone again. There was no Vineyard, no placid inlet, no sweet rush of water against her flesh—there were only news commentators and conferences, the hazardous demands on his life and energies, and beyond that the stunning differences in attitude their ages forced upon them; and over all of that a nameless leaden apprehension bound in the leaden skies, the rain. What was I *meant* to do? she wondered sullenly. It wasn't just Paul. If Land found out it wouldn't be just the three of them, or the professional threat to Paul. If Land found out he'd tear Sirius apart, he'd tell the others. And what would they do? Try to exploit such a high-level infiltration of the Establishment? Purge her? Probably. It would torpedo Sirius; and that would be the end of Smitty.

She shivered, scrubbing at her scalp with the towel. What the Christ was her life? Sirius versus Paul. Past and future, red and black, Movement and Establishment. The polarized woman. She had just worked out for Sirius an ingenious plan to broadcast a forced confrontation with Reinhold Vosz over Smitty on the very doorstep of the Council on Foreign Relations in New York City—and she was the lover of the Secretary of State of the United States. Where the bloody hell did she think she was *going?* Last exit before toll. You tried to think about allegiances, about purpose—

"Who wouldn't want to gaze at you?" he was murmuring to her. "You're so beautiful, Jillie. So full of life . . ."

He had dropped the towel, his hands were moving over her breasts, she could feel her body leap in the instantaneous liquefying surge she knew whenever he touched her—sometimes whenever he so much as came close to her, so dense, so vibrant was the emotional field that held them. That first evening here they had made love on the little strip of sand, and afterward lain there watching the terns wheeling and diving over the darkening channel, and at the water's edge across the cove a raccoon hunting for shellfish like a bizarre, fussy little old professor; it had been right below where the man in the snap-brim hat had stood and turned away, as if he'd been watching them for a long time—

"What are you thinking?"

His eyes burned into hers. He's unhappy, she thought sadly, unhappy in his happiness, happy in his unhappiness. He's thinking about it too, he can't help it either—that hurrying awful moment when the summer's over and the cold weather comes, the cabin must be closed; when his wife goes down to Washington. The way time has us in its claws.

"I was thinking how nothing lasts," she answered simply.

"But it does—certain things do."

She shook her head implacably. "Nothing does. We kid ourselves about it, but nothing does."

". . . I can't accept that."

"All right. You don't have to. But it's true just the same."

"Don't see Land. Any more. Please." His face was stern—the way he looked when he was laying down policy lines in some crisis, probably—but his eyes were shadowed with entreaty. "It's important to me. I—please, Jillie. Because I ask it of you, because I love you."

"All right," she said. It was the other world, his generation. They put such store in form, the conventional window-dressing of a thing. He loved her; she was his; therefore she should not be intimate with any other man, no matter what the circumstances. Why couldn't he see it was what the heart commanded, not what the flesh echoed? But he couldn't see that—here he was, agitated beyond measure. It would force another issue, it would maybe even lead to Land's finding out about them—and God alone knew where that would take them all. But if that was what he wanted . . .

"All right," she repeated. "If it's what you want."

"Yes, of *course* it's what I want." He was angry all at once. "Look, a person can't divide his affections, apportion them the way you deal cards—nobody can . . . Can you?"

Smiling gently she shook her head. "I don't know. That's not the point," she said, "the point is something else." She felt much older than Paul suddenly, more balanced and sage. "It's not a question of dividing one's affections, at least not to me."

"But don't you see, if you—"

"It's all right—" she fought the rising tide of irritation "—I'll break it off completely. I promise."

He set down his glass and threw her a quick, rueful glance. "I guess I seem like an awful square to you sometimes. A real, foursquare, dyed-in-the-wool Victorian prude . . . You called me that once, remember?

Something like that."

"No. It's two worlds. Two ways of walking through time."

Hands low on his narrow, naked hips, wrists cocked, he turned and looked at her; she felt troubled all at once, heavy with resentment. What did he *want* of her? What was it he incessantly demanded that she could never for the life of her fulfill? She longed desperately for a cigarette, but he had begged her to quit and to please him she'd done so—an abstention she bitterly regretted.

"Well," he said quietly. "I can't change the way I am. Not now."

"Neither can I."

He seized her, then—an embrace so quick and desperate she gasped. "But don't you see?" he cried softly, "I don't want you to change—that's the whole point of it . . ."

A moment longer they clung to each other while the rain drummed on the dark roof and the distant thunder of guns marked off its column of time. His throat was full and salt against her lips.

"I've got to go, darling," he said finally.

"I know."

Seated she watched him dressing, a sight that always pleased her: he drew on his slacks and pulled his sport shirt over his head with the lithe, impatient movements of a boy—eager to ready himself for something else. After he'd been swimming his hair always stood up from his scalp in a loose, faintly bristling crest, and this too made him look younger, more vulnerable. He was talking about when they'd see each other again, that he would be in Cambridge on Thursday if Timofyevna would only reply to his second note on the Alaskan trawler incident and that God damned hopeless entangled Burmese snarl would begin to unravel itself; if events would only let him alone.

"—the hell with Thursday," she heard herself saying. "The hell with tomorrow and all the tomorrows after that. The only thing that matters is now, this moment, *this* one . . . don't you see that?"

"Won't work, kid." He was lacing his shoes smartly. "Any happy savage can shuck it all. Necessity, responsibility, time—they're right there, waiting for you. That's what tomorrow means."

"And—thank—you, Walter Q. Lippmann."

"Yeah. Profound, isn't it?"

A short while ago they had spoken for each other, offered up each other's arguments; now they were back in character again. She drew the hairy Finnish sweater down over her naked body: warm and abrasive, it chafed her back and breasts pleasantly after the steel chill of the sea, the rain.

"If you really loved me, you'd stay," she declared. "Isn't that the line? Especially while it's raining."

He scowled, caught himself up and drew a long breath. "I never feel I've been with you—it's just as though we've had no time together at all. That's really paranoid, isn't it?"

That tense, cornered look was back in his eyes again. If he leaves this room nothing will ever be the same between us again, the implacable visitant inside her pronounced; just wait and see. It checked everything she was going to say—about her incarceration in this cockeyed cabin and the burdensome proximity to the Paling, and all the tumult of frustrations that sundered her. She went up to him and put her hands at the back of his head, still damp and warm.

"Please smile," she said. "I'm just like all the rest of them—I want to see you smile."

It was a lovely smile, as they all said. It looked into life. It looked gently and deeply into the long parade of human folly; it offered exoneration, sympathy, wonder—and continued undismayed; it was—it was a smile that put its ultimate faith in human beings. It was the smile of a very good man. And only she knew how lordly and vulnerable a smile it was . . .

He had kissed her once, again; he was gone. He never took protracted leave-takings, he hated them ("You either stay and give yourself to the person or situation, or you go on to something else"), he said he couldn't stand people who jittered around as if they had to go to the can, mouthing nonsensical chits and scraps. She watched him move off through the pines, so lithe and purposeful. When he walked his body leaned forward ever so slightly, as if he were poised on some kind of mark, ready to plunge into a race.

He had disappeared. Fog was sifting up the Inlet underneath the rain. There was no depth to anything. She turned, measured the little boxlike room flickering in the lamplight, the wildly rumpled bed, the dirtied blue willow-ware plates from lunch, the empty glasses. On the worn wood of the threshold was a large wet print his foot had made. Her lover, the world's foremost statesman, had been here; he had recounted a tale of minor heroism, they had quarreled briefly, made deft and incomparable love, gone swimming nude (and been observed by either a neighboring plumber or an international spy), quarreled again over her possibly questionable relations with his son; he had left to entertain a renowned professor of international law in the company of his legal wife. What did it signify? beyond the fact that they were as confused as any other wanderers on the earth? Staring at the naked footprint she had a sharp, sure premonition of trouble, like the time years ago driving back to Westport when she'd seen the dead dog at the edge of the road, the knotted guts, the frozen rictal snarl. It was going to end badly, this explosive, glorious, tormented love of theirs. She could not have said why, but she was sure of it. It had nothing to do with the wages of sin, tragic flaws or celestial retribution; it involved—she recognized it instantly—the massing of forces so awesome the gods themselves would blanch and give way . . .

Slowly, tentatively she placed her foot inside the damp print—then to her great surprise she burst into tears, a shuddered tumult of sobbing she hadn't known since Dave had been killed in Vietnam. Above her head the rain kept driving densely on the warped shingles.

TWELVE

13Jul: Must get it all down if I can: flat & unvarnished, without vanity or anger. Or self-exoneration, that deadliest of siren songs. *Just as it happened.* A night for truth. If I can find it—if there is time. Vérité sans peur. No. Fear is there, & worse than fear . . .

Day opened bouffe like all good drama. Wally in early to give me rundown on Burroughs' cosmic blooper. What he actually *said* was: "The Grand Old Coach up there with the big computer would scrap His master game plan at still another attempt to subvert this union," etc., etc. Probably would have passed unnoticed amid all the toasts & oratory if that old troublemaker Safidat hadn't given it a big play in the Press. & Hassan Dagh, ever alert to any chance to keep Middle East cauldron frothing, took it from there: "The God of Mohammed is indescribable. The American official's statement, uttered in the spiritual heart of all Islam, rings with the iconoclastic arrogance of the godless West." Whereupon Burroughs masterfully compounded gaffe by retorting that Allah was by no means the only member of the Pan-Arab Federation who was indescribable. Ergo, Burroughs is now non grata (clearly a blessing), & Hassan Dagh has demanded formal apology (which Burroughs has, incredibly, refused to give) & is howling from every mosque & minaret that B's presence constitutes an intolerable affront to all adherents of THE TRUE FAITH.

So now here we are with desert faithful honing their trusty yataghans to a fine edge, aching to bathe them in the blood of the infidel. Jesus Christ. I mean, inch'Allah. All we need. Fired off one cable to Burroughs instructing him to apologize in full and ordering his *immediate* recall, and another to Wig telling our envoy extraordinary and plenipotentiary to carve *Allah is indescribable, ineffable, unutterable, and Mohammed is his prophet* 300 times on nearest palm, & to assert his UNQUESTIONED authority as chief of mission or face transfer on a slow boat to Bangtang-tikoodoo. These USIS hotdogs give me an abiding pain. They blow into a country without the slightest understanding of cultural or historical forces involved & begin to "implement policy" as if they were Chinese Gordon. The freewheeling hotshot Marco Polo days are over, & that had best be understood at all levels. We've troubles enough without all Islam bursting into holy flame.

Haney came by in a blue sweat over Timofyevna's counterproposal on Alaskan fisheries hassle—wanted to know what to do if The Boys (primarily Frankel and Brodor) press him on question of indemnities. What it boils down to is he's afraid of the UNFORESEEN QUERY—filled with nightmares of dragging State down to ruin with 1 inadvertent phrase. Hell, if he's nervous over *this,* what'll he do when the old chocolate marshmallow really hits the fan? Fear I guessed wrong about him. Doesn't seem to understand it is precisely in saying nothing (& saying it sententiously & well) that his value as PR spokesman lies—an affable screen until decisions *can* be hammered out & facts disseminated. There are 2 kinds of people (still another 2-kinds-of-people): those who can stride forward with assurance & carry others with them, & those who cannot. Haney apparently cannot: he exudes distress like a cornered toad . . .

(*Jillie's* 2 kinds of people are the Aroused & the Complacent, Sid's are the Reflective & the Impulsive, Joe's the Dupes & the Manipulators. & Reiny's 2 kinds? who are they? Zarathustra Vosz & the Rest-of-Humanity, probably.)

Worked through lunch on favorable response to Brandt's NATO requests (thou shalt not muzzle the ox when he treadeth out the corn), ameliorating reply to Timofyevna (a soft answer turneth away wrath), appraisal of maze of options on Brazilian coup (a lion is in the streets).

Review of Dhotal mess not encouraging. Student Prince definitely in Chinese "protective custody," flying to Peking for conferences with Fa-Hsieng. Bodawyin, hysterical over our reluctance to send him a whole trunkful of tanks-&-planes, special delivery, has turned to Russians & Indians for his hardware, Stew Davis hysterical over THAT. Inscrutable Cockswain still apparently roaming boondocks. All manner of rumors coming out of Rangoon—epidemic in Dhotal wildly out of hand, entire population in panic, choking roads, complete breakdown of local administration. Chinese apparently unable to cope—& still they refuse our help & everyone else's, for that matter. Only change seems to be Russian position: they are no longer pressing Chinese for release of their team. Why?

Sitting around mulling all this over when Mike came in with day's first thunderbolt. "You were right, Mr. Secretary. I've just finished running a check on our new candidate. The results are pretty astonishing—I thought you'd better know about it right off."

"What new candidate?" I said.

"This fellow Deuermann."

"Deuermann? Who's that?" I said.

He blinked at me over his lenses, glanced sidewise at Jacobi. "Why—I thought you knew. Sid asked me to get on it . . ."

"What the hell's going on?" I demanded. "Who's this Deuermann?"

Sid's face all scrunched up in apology, looking nervous & cross. "The name the Judge used, Chief. Remember? Those photos. The afternoon Vosz almost got drowned."

"Oh," I said.

"It was a hunch. No-stone-unturned department."

"I see." I stared at him, remembering now. But I'd dismissed it: the Judge & that trouble of his with names, people—

"It's very interesting," Hudela said in that sober, judicial way of his. "He's from the Ukraine—one of those colonies of German extraction. His father was a Nazi, executed as a traitor in '44. He himself was trained as a hydrographic engineer, but it was a cover—he was a missile man. Worked on sites along the Chinese frontier." Scratching at the edge of his bald spot with one finger. "All this came out after I checked with Embassy Cairo. He defected to us during the Aswan Dam construction. Embassy Cairo requested instructions from the Department, got clearance, and flew him on here . . ."

"Wait a minute," I said. "As Deuermann?"

"That's right."

I put my hands on the desk top. "Two?" I said. "Two defections from Aswan? *Two* engineers?"

He gave me that shy, almost painful smile. "Worse than that. Three months later he was indicted in Washington in connection with the murder of a Soviet agent. Acquitted, too. Make you think of anything?"

"Jesus Christ," I said.

"And then he vanishes. No more Deuermann. Just like that." He expelled a long breath. "So—then I went back through Diefenbach-Drachenfels, as well I might. And there's no authentication." We were just staring at him now. "That's right—no Friedland boyhood, the way Shelly said. No stonemason uncle, no Voskolskaya Institute, no nothing. Nothing leads back. Blank wall."

Long unhappy pause. Finally I voiced it (one of the doubtful privileges of rank): "A Soviet agent, then. Is that it?"

Mike nodded unhappily. "Looks that way. Of course in some ways he hasn't been acting like one."

"And just how *does* a pedigreed Soviet agent act?" Sid inquired. Trouble always turns him sardonic.

"Well, chances are he'd have established a deeper cover with us. And the Russian end would have checked out. *Something* would have checked out."

"Have you seen Tremayne?" I asked.

He shook his head. "Came straight to you. But if they'd had any of this over there . . ." Clapping his hands together, palm over fist, his warm brown eyes troubled. "The pieces don't fit—we're not playing with a full deck."

Another silence, each of us thinking his own (unpleasant) thoughts. Trouble with this job is you get so suspicious. In spite of yourself. After you get just so tired, harassed, inundated with schemes, counterschemes and options you're ready to entertain ANY speculation, no matter how outlandish. As all looks yellow to the jaundic'd eye.

Sid said: "Why not contact the Soviet embassy, that fellow Buzarov? Their position's just changed over the release of their team. Is there a connection?"

Mike smiling the pained smile again. "Why should they give us anything?"

"Well, if we forced it. Threatened exposure—he'd be useless to them then . . ."

"There isn't time anyway," I told them.

Stout came in then, followed by Spofford & Geissen. All of us watching clock now, a bunch of kids at 5 AM before a final exam, hoping prof will get scarlet fever, university will be struck by typhoon. To my surprise Miles went after me.

"In my opinion, Mr. Secretary, the Ch'en interview should be canceled as gracefully as possible. It's not inconceivable [up the Neg!] that Drachenfels is a plant by the Chinese to discredit our position in Asia."

"What the hell are the Chinese trying him for, then?" This from Sid.

"They haven't tried him—they've only said they're going to. Even that wouldn't be beyond them. They've done far more ruthless things than that." Staring at me then, his full cheeks pink with disapproval; a baby in need of burping. "Mr. Secretary, I think this interview constitutes a grave indiscretion." A direct statement! Behold the desperate places our emotions take us.

"Then it is my indiscretion," I said.

At 3, Ch'en Pu-tsao.

His demeanor very changed from New Delhi: only the flintlike, obdurate side—no trace of the humor & warmth, the almost delicate wit. Impossible not to like him, all the same. Strong, plain face, fine dark liquid eyes. Curious balance of durable artisan & speculative scholar. (True of me as well?) Plain dark military tunic worn shiny at elbows & collar, no decorations. Soldier of the Indomitable Republic. Well, we all have our vanities—some blatant, some obscure. His gaze fastened on the bandage over my eye, shot away, came back again. I smiled & said I regretted so warlike an appearance at such a moment; he replied that perhaps it was more fitting, given the circumstances. No attempt at humor. A short debate with himself & then said he hoped I hadn't been the victim of the anti-government rioting currently prevalent in my country. Sid's voice very dry as he translated this. I crushed the temptation to retort that *our* Young Guards weren't nearly as accurate marksmen as they were in other lands; summoned my most genial smile & said No, merely a sailing mishap. He nodded gravely, as though he had expected just such a cock-and-bull story.

Obvious there were going to be no more introductory pleasantries. I opened by saying I was pleased he had responded with such alacrity to my invitation; that the gravity of the Dhotalese crisis warranted our best efforts. He replied that it had placed no additional demands on him—that in any event he was on his way to the Security Council meeting, so this was only a short detour. "Two birds with one stone, Mr. Secretary. An American saying."

I refused to take offense at this: told him I welcomed the spirit of amity & conciliation that had brought him here, & said I looked forward with deep interest, now that our two countries had achieved *full* diplomatic recognition, to the day when they would realize the most open and cordial relations. He seemed surprised at this—glanced sharply at his translator, then at Sid—it was clear he felt someone had misconstrued something. There was that shutter-click of an unforeseen possibility recognized & entertained—then firmly rejected. When he looked at me again his expression was noncommittal and hard.

He moved in quickly, then: wanted to know what responsibility my government was prepared to assume in this flagrant violation of the New Delhi Treaty by the Drachenfels invasion.

"You mean the Drachenfels *Mission,* do you not?"

"I mean the Drachenfels *invasion,* Mr. Secretary."

I said there was abundant evidence that Prince Naungapaya had broken the treaty guarantees in a totally unwarranted assumption of power.

"Prince Naungapaya was provoked, Mr. Secretary. Provoked beyond all restraint by the course of events at Lushui and Meng-p'eng."

"But it is my understanding that the members of the American Rescue and Reclamation Mission are in *Chinese* custody at present."

"They are."

"And your government has announced its intention of trying them on charges of espionage."

"No, Mr. Secretary. For crimes against humanity."

Now it was my turn to stare at Sid. "Crimes against humanity—? On what do you base such charges?"

A quick, skeptical, forbidding smile. "It must come to you as no surprise that your man Drachenfels is an agent of the CIA."

"And on what do you base *that* charge?"

"He has confessed to it."

"I see." Two can play that skeptical game. How does Land put it? Any mummer can pray.

"And there is other evidence. A great deal of evidence. Now that the facts have been fully revealed, I believe it is time for a most frank discussion of *all* the issues."

And he sat watching me mutely, content to remain there till doomsday. Didn't know quite what to make of it. Had the sense he was probing

for something—some mirror flash of revelations beyond the structure of
the debate. After matching his silence with one of my own I replied that
I appreciated his government's poise & sense of mesure in the face of the
conflicting issues raised by this incident. It was a time for every nation to
display the utmost calm. For instance, I hardly needed to point out that
the United States had shown much restraint when his government had not
only granted asylum to the fugitives Jethro & Cummins but feted them as
though they were national heroes—an act that could easily have been
construed as a most unfriendly one.

His eyes narrowed at this, his face became harder. "That is quite irrelevant to the point at issue."

"In my opinion, Mr. Minister, it is not. I was under the impression
that we are discussing the question of the responsibilities inherent in
sovereign states. In the case of Jethro and Cummins, your government has
repeatedly honored two American citizens who have been convicted of the
criminal act of theft of my government's property . . ."

"I think you will admit that there is a marked difference between
greeting two alleged fugitives openly, and cold-bloodedly hiring the dregs
of revisionist imperialism to mount an attack on a foreign power. Mister
Secretary, it must come to you as no surprise that the People's Republic of
China is not edified by this latest variant of the Open Door policy."

There is a calefactive quality to these exchanges—once the tempera-
ture reaches a certain height it's better to break off, or duck into some
other avenue of approach. (If you've got one, that is. There was none that
I could see.) Sleepless tact, unmovable calmness, patience that no folly,
no provocation, no blunders can make. Peerless Ben Franklin. Couldn't
rid myself of the atmosphere of some 19th-Century affaire d'honneur:
that Sid or his opposite number would ceremoniously produce the old
rosewood case with the horse pistols nestling in their faded red plush.

I took a deep breath and folded my hands. "Mister Minister, the
world has moved a long, long way from the deplorable days of the Legations, and I beg you to believe that the United States has moved with it.
My government seeks earnestly to respect the sanctity of international law,
and it hopes just as earnestly that all other nations will be so inclined. In
view of the purpose of the Rescue and Reclamation Mission, on behalf of
the President of the United States, I would urge your government most
strongly to reconsider its avowed intention to try Drachenfels and his
associates, and to release them to American authority."

"And I, Mister Secretary, have been instructed to demand a formal
apology on the part of the United States for perpetrating a series of actions
my government has come to regard as intolerable."

That word again. *Pu k'o jung jen ti.* Got that, all right. Ch'en's face
very hard, black eyes snapping. Moment of complete silence. Old Joshua
Seaver's grandfather clock in the far corner stalking the final, reverberant

seconds to the end of the world. A formal apology! . . . The hatred in his eyes alarming. I thought, Have we really come to this? Are we truly adversaries, helpless spokesmen for two implacably opposed systems, bent on each other's destruction? Could we—this man and I—actually rush to grapple, hack and pierce each other in this stately room? No, we are too civilized for that. We would merely create the flash-point instant where millions would do it for us.

("You can't help it, you can't move any other way. The minute you say *The nation-state is an extension of me, I draw my power from its dictates, I will what is for the common good*—once you say that, you've surrendered all personal freedom. You're obligated to serve the state till you die, no matter where it takes you. After that the only source for individual liberty lies in open revolt." Jillie, tossing her lovely little head back, the light flashing on the clean bold planes of her face. Is that true? It is so easy to be angry, to strike, to destroy; so everlastingly, mountainously hard to forgive, conciliate, assuage.)

Could we be friends, this Shensi farmer's son and I? Could we sit together on the high blue-and-ocher cliff at Gay Head and read each other poetry, drink wine from the same slender bottle, run on the level sand stride for stride, shouting into the damp salt wind? Felt inundated with a sorrow so profound, so implacable the tears started in my eyes. Sid watching me tensely, chewing on that crazy God damned pacifier of a marking pen. Ch'en's face closed now, implacable, shadowed with distrust—and something more, too, something worse: repugnance, was it—even contempt?

No: we could not be friends, apparently. Not now or ever. Well: close it out briskly. I said as strongly and truly as I knew how:

"Mister Minister, it is a matter of real regret to me that our conversation has taken so unfortunate a turn. I hope we may enjoy another —and more fruitful—exchange soon. Be assured that I will convey your government's position to the President. Meanwhile I can only reiterate what I have said earlier—that you have my most solemn guarantee that there has been no covert United States participation in the Drachenfels Mission to Dhotal. And now I am bound to say I think we have said all that can be said at this point."

He did not move. His eyes bored into mine as though they would burn through the last recesses of my brain—then he smiled: a small, very formal smile.

"Mister Secretary: what would be your reaction if I were to present to the Security Council of the United Nations concrete proof that your agent Drachenfels has been carrying out a most inhuman experiment? An experiment involving the calculated dissemination of a deadly nerve gas which has *already* destroyed two hundred thousand inhabitants of the Kaolikung Shan?"

Could not keep the astonishment out of my face. Sid stumbled, stumbled again on the phrasing, was watching me fearfully. I said something, can't remember what. Then I said: *"Two hundred thousand people?"*

"Of my countrymen, Mister Secretary. Men, women and children. Who are, it seems, neither living nor dead. But caught in a kind of terrible paralysis, a sleep from which they can never be awakened."

Impossible. Clearly impossible from any point of vantage, any . . . But then why were my hands moist, why had my heart begun to pound so thickly? All I saw was Jillie sprawled in a rice paddy, the fierce green sickle-shoots thrusting past her head, her body arched in convulsions, gasping, blood at her lips . . . I closed my eyes. When I opened them the Foreign Minister's face was altered. That shutter-click beneath the stern, imperturbable features. Curiosity, doubt, surprise? Couldn't tell.

A long, terrible moment. Pulled myself together. Of course it could be a stratagem—a most appalling stratagem. "Mr. Minister, is it my understanding this is not a rhetorical question?"

"That is correct. It is not."

"You—it is your government's contention that the United States has manufactured this gas in full violation of the biological warfare treaty, and turned it over to Dr. Drachenfels for seeding?"

"We have incontrovertible proof that your Central Intelligence Agency furnished this gas."

"I'm afraid you have been misinformed on this point. I have been in constant contact with the Agency's Director from the very first. I have his full assurances that the CIA is not and has not been involved in any way."

"The Secretary is not, then, averse to the forthcoming Security Council meeting on this issue?"

"On the contrary, I welcome it."

Silent again, watching me most gravely. Wanted to believe me, but couldn't; I could tell. Very opposite of me: I *can* believe him (oh Jesus yes) but I don't want to. What is it U Mein Thaw says? The infelicities of the diplomatic existence.

He rose then. Cordial handshakes all around. Assurances we would be in touch on the matter. A last full piercing glance, and they left.

Alone in the room, thinking everything and nothing. Sid looking at me hollowly, chewing on his pacifier. Too scared to be furious. "Is he serious, Chief? Can he be?"

"I don't know," I said.

And I don't. Yet that cold clawlike fear that he is. But in that case is it only the leading edge of a new hard line? some scheme to discredit New Delhi, tear GATO apart—a monster gambit hatched by some bold mind at the moment of seizure of the Mission (why waste those Americans)? Is it some weird cholera variant to be turned to political advantage (why waste all those corpses)?

Or is it possible

Crafty, feline old Shiraga comes tomorrow in full pomp & circumstance, armed with threats over the import quotas; Campilhas will invade São Paulo Province if he possibly can, Ecuador will reject my plan for internationalization of the sea floor beyond the 12-mile limit, Sheik Zaid bin al-Mubarrak will nationalize *all* oil properties without compensation, Burroughs (as a final gesture of good will & understanding) will climb to the top of the highest minaret in Damascus & express the thought that Allah is not only describable but has been reincarnated as Billy Graham.

And I want to be with Jillie. Only that. Huddled with her on that ratty old sofa under the window, *post coitum tranquillus*—no, *voluptuosus triumphans,* her buttocks hot & moist against my groin, her breast nestling in my hand like a sleeping dove. Our voices husky with contentment, murmuring of sandpipers & stratagems. Oh, Mark Antony was right, & so was mighty, credulous Othello: *Perdition catch my soul but I do love thee! and when I love thee not*

"We are all essentially comic figures." André that evening at Petra. Chin sunk on his chest, very drunk, very lucid, eyes red-veined & desperate in the sinking flavous light. "All our self-importance, our engines of obligation. If we were invested with a spark of reality—one *throb* of immanent truth!—we would fling it aside, all this disgusting baggage of avarice and power. Oh yes—and throw ourselves, naked, beneath the nearest incense-bearing tree . . ." Nell watching him with inexpressible hatred, Marjorie's face tense with passion, Denis smiling his well-bred, distant smile, Michele's eyes on mine, asking me something I did not then know. No. Not then.

. . . If we had changed partners that night, yielded to that beat of impulse—if Nell had gone off with Denis, André with Marjorie, I with Michele. Would we have found something, burst into some new constellations of union & release, been altered grandly . . . ? Yes, we would have been altered, I believe it. One moment. At the still point of the turning world. And now behold us: André killed in that crash on National Sept near Montélimar, Marjorie in & out of Davos, Michele remarried to a celebrated composer, Denis growing gray in the Finance Ministry; and Nell & I

"After such knowledge, what forgiveness?" What indeed. *"Think now* [beat] *History has many cunning passages, contrived corridors And issues, deceives with whispering ambitions, Guides us by vanities."* Wise, weary, bitter old Gerontion, waiting for rain. *"Think* [beat] *Neither fear nor courage saves us. Unnatural vices Are fathered by our heroism. Virtues Are forced upon us by our impudent crimes . . ."* Yes. Great God, yes. And yet to fold your hands & turn aside is no answer either. One must

continue to pull one's oar—perhaps because the sight of that one straining back can hold other men to the beat. Blackburn's Law, 17 A. This is why (is it?) Hector is archetypal hero of western civilization: knows Troy is doomed but fights on all the same, brilliantly, resourcefully, even after he knows gods have clearly deserted him. Essence of nobility.

Is that true? Should read more. Would there were TIME (The Public Servant's Perennial Lament). Bill said the other night at Barbara Howar's there is no place for individual heroism in American life because our sense of personal responsibility (the old small-town familiarity & reliance) has been destroyed. He's right of course, but it runs deeper than that. Can the average American really, *viscerally* comprehend the nature of heroism any more? The man enduring public calumny because of a moral stand, the man who goes down to defeat because he will not stoop to base methods to win, the man driven to disaster through excessive sensitivity, adherence to principle?

We no longer value the quality of this defeat—our overweening pragmatism won't permit it. Name of the game is winning. Don't be a loser, Charlie. Nice guys finish last. We despise the loser *because* he is a loser—we want to have nothing to do with the underlying circumstances, the conditions of that defeat. Which is the REAL name of the game. Hamlet, Oedipus, Hector, Prince Andrei, Dr. Stockmann. Losers. (Tell me what hero of fiction you most admire and I will tell you what manner of man you are.) Behind me robust Daniel Webster, the excellent Foster portrait: heavy jowls, generous mouth, the penetrating, lively glance. Old Dan'l, who loved a glass of Jamaica rum & could swing a scythe with the best of them, who twice averted war with Britain & could charm the very birds from the trees—& who destroyed his chance for the presidency in one bitter, glorious hour . . . Yes, what of Webster, Clay, Reed, Wilson, Stevenson? Losers all—& our most illustrious roll.

On we go. All of us—garbage collector and presidential adviser. Bound in our runaway chariots, straining to see through the jittering visor-slit. Do we find ourselves suddenly on bleak mountainsides because we failed to listen to a still voice in the farthest recesses of our hearts? Struggle, duty, self-denial—the iron-handed Moloch to whom I offered up hope & passion & all wild, green things; until the hunger overbore the durance. I am no different from other men (whatever the Chicago TRIBUNE may say). And so now, here, which is the nobler course? To throw it over & set an outrigger for a Danaan shore, white birds, my beloved, borne out on the foam of the sea? or press on through the drummer's beat, deep in the galley's guts?

200,000

No. No statistics. *Two hundred thousand human beings.* People. Like Jillie, like Land. Who are neither living nor dead. *"The tiger springs in the new year. Us he devours."* Jesus yes. Ch'en's homely face terrible in its grief-scored inquiry. At this late hour, staring at the shimmer of lights on the river, the withdrawn stately dignity of Arlington on its gentle hill— shame, & a frantic incredulity: impossible, we have treaties, guarantees, men will honor them. There are—Jesus, aren't there?—things men would not do. Yet something in me beyond dreaming, beyond dread fears it is true, it has happened, it is neither a matter of ruse or invention. That pit-of-the-belly conviction that never lies.

And if it is true, what then? What must I do? What can I do?

If only there were more *time*

THIRTEEN

THE EBONY DOOR swung open with the soundless weight of all rich fittings, and the surf-surge of voices rushed to meet him. There was the long, handsome room giving on the floodlit lawn and pool, where women's gowns—lemon, peach, viridian—glowed against the somber black-and-white of the men; and Blackburn recognized that barely perceptible catch of apprehension, walking into the long oval ballroom of the old Copley Plaza as a freshman, long ago; instantly recognized, instantly dispelled. Shadows.

"Good evening, Mr. Secretary," the butler murmured.

"Good evening, Noland."

Maggie Hendryx had caught sight of him; her eyes dilated in greeting. With just a shade of hesitation she finished what she was saying, broke away from the group and came toward him with her bold, full stride.

"Paul! *Enfin,* sweetie . . ."

"I *am* sorry," he said. "I am. There's been any number of crises. All of them minor, of course."

"I always feel I've earned my merit badge when I can get you out." Her glance darted to his forehead. "Your wound, your *wound!*" she cried. "They're saying Reiny Vosz clouted you with a belaying pin in a policy hassle over l'Affaire Drachenfels. Is that true?"

"Pure invention." Assuming his most serious expression he bent close to her ear. "That's our cover. What *really* happened was the Foreign Relations Committee felt I wasn't showing sufficient initiative—they recommended a complete frontal lobotomy. Now I can face anything."

"Even Comrade Ch'en?"

"Even Comrade Ch'en," he answered, watching Maggie intently, liking her wide-set, good-humored gaze, the flamboyant silk print slack suit and gold lamé harem slippers which, along with her extravagantly long blond hair, comprised her personal trademark. She never missed a thing. That moment of hesitation she displayed in coming to greet him was probably significant—a year ago, a month ago he would have been concerned about it; now, armed with different weapons, he didn't care. That was dangerous, of course—indifference to the nuances of status in the Capital was fraught with peril; but still he didn't care, and it amused him.

"This is the kind of night I love," she was saying. "We've already had two possible assignations, a trial-by-fire and three bons mots—not one of which you can top. Not even you!"

He laughed. Maggie Hendryx's parties were the liveliest in Washington, and the most prestigious. Recently divorced from the head of one of the nation's mightiest conglomerates and daughter of the President's principal supporter, she had deployed her position, her beauty and her flair for encounter shrewdly. Merely to be invited to one of her evenings conferred its own precise categories of status. In reaction to the dreary, humorless insecurity of the Nixon years, the Capital's leading hostesses now sought brilliance and controversy again—an echo of the lost, mourned Camelot years. Parlor games were played with ferocity, dancing was ardent, cameo reputations were made in a small tumult of innuendo and rejoinder. It was at Maggie's that the game of Sobriquet—a complex fusion of the best elements of charades, Botticelli and Twenty Questions—had been invented and refined, where the columnist Mark Pettingill had called Donlund the Administration's deus ex machismo, where Blackburn himself had once observed that if there were no Taiwan it would nonetheless have to be circumvented. It was in these cool white sensuous rooms—an Egyptian monk's idea of a brothel, some wag had dubbed them—that scepters were wielded, lances broken, understandings reached: all the transactions and confrontations that underlay the rituals of power.

"You were wonderful with Shiraga," Maggie Hendryx said. "The perfect blend of protocol and informality. Except for one thing."

"What was that?"

Her eyes narrowed prettily. "I had the feeling—is it silly?—you had your mind on something nonpolitical the whole time."

It was often the best course to say exactly what you thought. "It was as apparent as all that? I'll have to watch myself, then."

"Yes. You will." Her perfect teeth rested on her lower lip. "You've changed, Paul. Do you know that?"

"Into something rich and strange, I hope."

"It's actually occurred to me—" She broke off; Julian Bond and Arthur Schlesinger came up to them; after a few words Blackburn excused himself. He drifted over to the bar and began talking in a desultory way with Max Strauss, who was heading the President's new Committee on Urban Reform, and ran his eyes over the room. Everyone was here—which was to say everyone considered to be of the first rank who was also witty or forceful or controversial. There was Harold Hughes, handsome and weary, his arms folded, listening to a still more handsome, still more weary Eric Sevareid; there was Leonard Bernstein, the newly appointed National Director of the Performing Arts, euphoric and tense, his silver mane impeccably disarranged, his lips parted in the old compulsive, ingratiating need to convince; there was Barry Brickley, looking like the insurance man who has just topped the rest of the sales force for that month, and F. Lee Bailey, who had successfully defended the Fresno Four; there was

dour Ken Galbraith, exchanging pleasantries with a calculatedly languid
Gloria Steinem, the President's Special Assistant for Women's Affairs (it
was the only title that could have lured her into the Administration, it was
said she'd turned down half a dozen others); there was Clarissa Cavanagh,
known as the Duchess, who in her column had designated Nixon—while
he was still President—"the shyster's Miniver Cheevy," and then had
topped that by calling Agnew "the Administration's perfect middle line-
backer—capacious, rapacious and mendacious"; there was Dick Cavett,
the current head of USIS, and Mac Bundy, back in government (though
over in Defense this time, thank God) and still defending his role in the
Vietnam disaster with all the monomaniacal fervor of an Ahab; and
Maury Hennessy, the economics wizard whose alcoholism was beginning
to be no longer disguisable, and Anna Fu Gault, who had sweetly told
Blackburn one evening she was going to destroy him if it was the last thing
she ever did; and of course there was Reinhold Vosz, surrounded by the
noisiest group of all, arguing hotly with someone Blackburn couldn't see.

It went on and on, this elaborate and very serious game, the points
were scored and the alliances formed, but he could no longer look on it as
he had short weeks ago. He had never embraced the feral excitement he
saw in those faces, the smug avidity of their fevered moment in the hot
glare of power. That hard, gray legacy of his mother's, of the Paling, had
always instinctively distrusted it. The goal of public life was service, authority cum obligation—which meant self-denial: life was simply too short
for the jongleur's round of parties and ego-baths that the Capital doted
on . . . Yet now, like the returning invalid for whom family, home,
friends are all at once starkly altered, he had still stranger eyes. He found
himself longing for Jillie to be here, right beside him in this room, wishing
with all his heart that he could call out at the end of some absurd, bravura
flourish of trumpets: *Ladies and gentlemen, courtiers, clowns and rogues,
power-seekers all—this is my beloved! Make of it what you will* . . .

"Well, if it isn't the Great Appeaser!"

He turned casually. Vera Grace Farr, hand on her hip, all her teeth
bared in that weird, hysterical smile. She owned seven papers, wrote a
biweekly column syndicated in seventy-two more, and was a passionate
advocate of America's mission as crusader, policeman and groundskeeper
for a wayward, ungrateful world. "What brings you out from behind the
woodwork?"

"Hello, Vee-Gee," he said.

"I'd have thought you'd be boning up on the files for Eighteen Eighty-
Four . . . or would it be the long, long thoughts of Chairman Mao?"

"Oh, I've read all *those*," Blackburn answered lightly. He had incurred her undying wrath the year before, at a dinner party at Kay Graham's. He and Clarke Tolliver had been threading some of the intricacies
of the French Sudanese crisis, a discussion pierced by interruptions and

asides from Vee-Gee, who finally informed them with happy complacency: "You know, I just don't follow you. I just don't follow you at all!"

It had been a hard week, burdened with the Donaldson appointment and the Peruvian negotiations; it was late, his stomach hurt him, and he had turned to her and said: "The *reason* you don't follow us is because you haven't been listening to a solitary thing Clarke and I have said for the past twenty-five minutes."

"Paul only wants to turn the clock back, that's all," Fred Semmes was saying to her now, with a wink at Blackburn. "Back to the days when knighthood was in flower."

"Knighthood!" Vee-Gee cried. "I guess.—They say you're leaving Washington soon, Mister B," she pursued in her sweetest voice. "Is that true?"

"Only if you'll come away with me, darling."

She laughed with the others, louder than the others—that shivery, high-key glissando laugh that the television audiences loved—but her eyes glittered. "Won't it be marvelous?—to trot on back to fair-Harvard-thy-sons-to-thy-jubilee-throng with the solid satisfaction that you haven't left a single ripple on the whole vast, lovely pond?"

He smiled his most charming smile. "I'm sure I'll always be remembered as the butt of your percipient wit, Vee-Gee."

For some reason this pleased her inordinately. Laughing again she pointed a long, silver-nailed finger at his throat, gave that quick nervous happy waggling of her head—another TV trademark—and murmuring, "Many a truth is spoken in jest, sweetie," whirled away to greet Bill Donlund and John Tunney. The Vice President gave Blackburn his slow, mournful smile, and the patterns realigned again.

"Hey now, that's a jive-ass tempest," Arnold Shamlur crowed. It was he who had been arguing with Vosz. "Now *that* grabs you right in the gonads. You know what I love about this sinkhole, Reiny?" he demanded between his teeth. "Its inventiveness. This whole mother-humping town is just *crawling* with originality . . ."

"Are we having a discussion or not?" Vosz demanded.

"*Of course* we are," Shamlur answered. "Why can't I keep two balls in the air at the same time? All you muff-diving power-brokers do . . ." He winked at Blackburn—a sly, malignant wink, emptied his glass in a rush and wiped his mouth with the back of a big, hairy hand. Arnold Shamlur was Secretary for Cultural Affairs, the spanking new cabinet post the President had created as part of what he was fond of calling the urban renascence campaign. In a certain sense Shamlur had been the logical choice. Thirty years before, at the age of twenty-two, he had written a play about political refugees in hiding in Marseilles—a tense, bitter drama that had caught, with astonishing insight and compassion, the rootless agony of mid-century man. In a matter of weeks Shamlur found himself the darling of the critics as well as a box-office smash—a double success that led him into international symposia, political committees, screenwriting assignments in exotic locations. The success however was followed by two disasters—brilliant theater, some said, steady advances over *The Minotaur* —but the complacent, timorous audiences of the Eisenhower years had recoiled from their harsh iconoclasm; and his fourth play found no backers at all.

Shamlur had been unable to comprehend it. He suffered a nervous breakdown, his marriage blew up, one of his two children fell from their apartment balcony, he very nearly killed himself in a drunken auto crash outside Easthampton. But he proved durable, and resourceful. Taking several pages from the career manual of an illustrious predecessor he began to jab a thumb in the public eye—a rotogravure of personal revelations, love affairs, impulsive gestures. He married in swift succession a notorious call girl, a Danish crown princess, a black militant dancer; he wrote open letters to public figures, he got in fist fights with various celebrities, he snatched at outrageous acting roles (he was said to be the first actor to have urinated, defecated and ejaculated on the Broadway stage, all in one scene) and finally achieved a television interview show "Mix and Mayhem," where uninhibited affront and retaliation (not to mention interminable FCC troubles) were the order of the day. His current plays, though vastly inferior to his earlier work, were heralded as the culmination of Now Theater, he was looked upon as a likely candidate for the Nobel Prize the next time America's turn came round, and he was beyond all odds the most foul-mouthed person Blackburn had ever encountered. In the new Administration, rebounding from Nixonian sanctimoniousness and enamored of what it was pleased to call The New Candor, Shamlur found himself everywhere in demand, in spite of the atmosphere of insult and violence which clung to him like gas. He had made sure of notoriety, the altar at which America worshipped, if not the Nobel.

"You're wasting your time, Reiny," he was saying now. He was a tall man, with a pale, cadaverous face, a walrus mustache and narrow, Oriental eyes that blinked incessantly. "What you refuse to see is that it's all over— the whole big-power, push-'em-around ball game. You haven't read the cables. The pussy-pounding kids don't want to kill slopeys or greasers any more—they want to kill *you*. They want to drag an ice saw down your spine and string your jewelry up all over the White House fence."

"Ooh, that's so graphic," Vee-Gee Farr exclaimed. She had maneuvered her way back into their group again. "Arnie, as a playwright and all that, shouldn't you sort of leave some of it to our imagination?"

"Your *what?* This town hasn't had a fresh thought since the militia decided to shag ass in 1812 . . ."

"That's socking 'em, baby," a girl in a purple silk pants suit and carrot red hair cried. "Come on join Mandy in a little drinkie-boo."

"No—I'm at exactly the right stage. Mean but not morbid." He stared at Blackburn out of his sunken Asiatic revolutionary's eyes. "It's a *very* fine line to walk. Or haven't you ever walked it, Mister Fella Sec?"

"If you possessed *any* vestiges of historical expertise," Vosz was pounding along, "you'd realize that for all the sentimental talk about the international labor congresses before World War One, when the whistle blew every last factory hand—"

"That old bromide." Despite his refusal Shamlur had taken the drink from the girl and downed most of it. He was sweating at the roots of his wiry gray hair, though the room was cool. "Why don't you watch the oscilloscopes? There aren't going to *be* any more wars—only civil mass-acres. Why incinerate a faceless digit when you can watch the terrified mug of a relative or friend? Every kid under twenty-five is aching to splash you ideological totem poles all over the Ellipse."

"Hadn't you better include yourself, Arnie?" Vosz inquired silkily.

"Not me, baby. I'm working from inside. I'm the Trojan humping Horse in the Administration." The look of narrow, malignant cunning was back again. "I'm their great white hope—the kids'. I'm going to be the first hip-anarcho-nihilist president of the old gash-crawling US and A. And the first thing I'm going to do, Squeezer, is sink *you.*"

"Can we monitor the orgasm you'll get with each depth charge, Arnie?"

Blackburn turned at the familiar voice. It was Sheldon Tremayne, looking perfectly tanned and fit, every hair in place. A bandbox matinee idol at a cockfight. He winked at the Secretary.

"Well, if it isn't the poot-pronging spy chief," Shamlur said. "The Indigo Pimpernel and his Seven Pimps. How they hanging, daddy?"

"Lightly, Arnie. Very lightly."

"I wouldn't be surprised."

"I get *my* kicks torturing little brown men in underground rooms—you know that."

"Don't think I don't believe you."

"—How arresting!" Vosz exclaimed. "We all feel the need to come to Arnie to see ourselves. Among the Yoruba—"

"Bugger the Yoruba. You ever wonder what the Yoruba think of *you?*"

In the laughter Tremayne caught Blackburn's eye and gave an imperceptible nod toward the lawn. They moved away together.

"Trouble with Arnie is, he's lost his motivation," Tremayne murmured. "All those years of pot and whip-wielding women and street confrontations and now he's respectable, whether he wants to admit it or not. *He's* the Establishment."

"With a difference."

"You think so? I don't know about that. Take him and Reiny—

at each other hammer-and-tongs all the time. Yet they're essentially alike —they both want the same things."

They moved out through the glass panels on to the floodlit, terraced area around the pool. The grass, beautifully cut, looked not like grass at all but some immaculate felt. People stood in small groups chatting, and a game of Sobriquet was already in progress, provoking shouts and laughter. The odor of mimosa was heavy on the still air.

"That's the refreshing thing about Maggie's parties," Tremayne went on. "If there are any points of friction in the Administration, here's where they're sure to boil out. If you could have tapes of all these . . ." He indicated the knots of conversation.

"Why, I thought you did, Shelly."

The CIA man laughed easily. "Our designs are modest. Times have changed. We've got troubles enough in foreign lands—forfend us from domestic excursions.—We've been checking out our mutual friend," he continued after a short pause, with no change of intonation. "I was talking with Mike about him this afternoon. You been in touch with him since then?"

"No—I've had Shiraga most of the day. What did you come up with?"

"There's a hole there, all right. There's no Diefenbach—or at least not *this* Diefenbach, that's for sure."

"It *is* the same man, then."

"Pretty definitely."

"And he is an American citizen?"

"Yes—there's no doubt about that."

"Christ. A Russian agent . . ."

Tremayne shrugged. "Could be a good deal more complicated than that."

"There's a happy thought. What do you mean?"

"He could be a double agent." Seeing the expression on Blackburn's face he nodded casually. "It's quite possible. He could be working for the Germans, too. Or the Chinese, for that matter. Nobody has a monopoly on this kind of man: he owns no real allegiances. You may think you've bought him but you haven't—you've only rented him till someone comes along and ups the ante."

Blackburn let his breath out through his teeth. "Lovely. Lovely. How in hell did he get so well entrenched with us? Everybody's been singing his praises for years—the masterful technician Drachenfels, the wizard Drachenfels. When you say he's been cleared—"

"You've got to remember he came in back in the late Fifties, when things were different."

"I'll say they were."

"Coordination between various branches was pretty vague at times."

"That's one way of putting it."

"He may have used still other covers. Like that fellow Lotz in Cairo. You remember—he set up the gentleman horse-breeder, SS-colonel background to snow the Egyptians with. Then when they caught him he dropped back to his second line—that sure, he worked for the Israelis all right, but only because they'd blackmailed him into it, by threatening to reveal his Nazi past to Bonn. And the Egyptians bought it. Actually of course he was an Israeli spy all along."

"But all these years—your people must have had *some* indications . . ."

Shelly's lips curved faintly. "He fooled us, Paul," he said simply. "All I can say is we were satisfied about him. He's been very clever. The best of us make mistakes."

"So I see. How much does he know?"

"About us? Not too much, I'd say. Hasn't had the opportunity— he's been abroad most of the time on technical stuff . . . That's why the Chinese are holding him, though. They've probably sweated a certain amount out of him; before they're through they may extract more. Or maybe they won't. It's hard to say, with this kind of man."

The Director's voice was perfectly calm: he might have been talking about his family or the chances of a baseball team. Blackburn glanced around the garden irritably, popping his knuckles. Espionage always made him profoundly unhappy. He could never grasp the mental set of the spy— or his inquisitor either, for that matter. Spying accomplished its objectives now and then but invariably at the cost of confidences misused, the scales of greed and terror artfully played upon. Was it worth it—all this dark machinery of masquerades and double-crosses and torture? He thought again of Ch'en's stubborn, outraged face across his desk, Sid's fearful glances, the *martellato* ticking of the grandfather clock in the far corner of the room.

"And so where does this leave us?" he heard himself say tersely. "I don't like the way this is going, any of it. This mission—and that includes Drachenfels or Deuermann or whoever the hell he calls himself—is State's responsibility. I'm willing and able to take my share of heat when I've incurred it. But I'm not going to take this rap very gladly, Shelly, I can tell you that. This nerve gas business—Ch'en wouldn't make a charge like that without some substantiation . . ."

Tremayne frowned. "You're not really buying that, are you?" The Secretary made no reply. "Look at the possibilities for him: a foreign agent in charge of the American team and the overall mission . . . If it *is* some wild Russian scheme—which it could very well be—he'll have the pretext for a new anti-Moscow offensive. If it's a phony he'll still have focused world attention on Naungapaya and dear little embattled Dhotal. Either way he's ahead. Myself, I rather think Peking has decided to go for broke on this one."

"Did you see Frenlsson's piece in *Le Monde?* He says he's talked to eyewitnesses, that it's really something pretty terrible."

"Oh, come on—you're not going to credit that."

"I'm not sure."

"Hell, he's a Red, Paul . . ."

"No, he's not a Red! Jesus Christ—a foreign correspondent refuses to adopt the official US line and half of you mark him down for a bomb-tossing Bolshevik . . ." He checked himself; his voice had risen. Tremayne was watching him with a kind of circumspect curiosity. He shook his shoulders loose and dropped his head. This wasn't what Shelly had called him outside for, anyway: it was something else. "I'm sorry, pal," he said with an effort. "This has been a trying week for me. As Mike says, we're not playing with a full deck."

"I'll buy that."

"For all I know Comrade Ch'en plans to sell the entire scenario to Warner Brothers and stash the proceeds in a Swiss bank account. But somehow I just don't think so."

They had reached the far end of the pool, a corner bounded by one wall of the garage and some basket-weave fencing edged cleverly by shrubs. Tremayne stopped and began carefully to stuff his pipe. "I guess it's one of the hazards of the profession," he said after a moment. "You see the cards turn up the same way so often that after a while you begin to expect they always will . . ." He snorted softly, drew on the pipe with deep, even rhythms. "Damned awkward all the same. The President's extremely irritated about it, coming at a time like this."

"I know," Blackburn said. "I saw him yesterday."

"It's got the kids all cranked up again. Another rash of plots. Torgerson says several groups are planning to demonstrate in front of the Council on Foreign Relations in New York next week. You know—Reiny's speech up there. It's been decided to move up his hour of arrival, switch things around a bit."

"I thought you were delighted to be out of domestic excursions."

"I am. Oh, I am!" Tremayne was smiling, but that shade of wary speculation had returned. "Jim called me about it because it does concern us, in a way. It was a tip. Not what you'd call hard evidence, really. But it has its overtones. It seems they may even be planning to prevent his speaking." He glanced up suddenly over the pipe's bowl. "You heard anything about it?"

It was Blackburn's turn to stare now. "Why, no—why should I?"

Tremayne frowned, chafed at the edge of the turf with his toe. "I don't quite know how to put this."

"It would be the first time, Shelly."

"Would it? Maybe so . . . I thought perhaps because of Leland.

He's a member of the principal action group they think is involved in the scheme."

Blackburn felt himself become quite still. "Land," he murmured. "You're quite sure of that?"

"Afraid so. Yes. It was the Hoyt girl's influence, of course—though he knows his own mind, I daresay. My kids certainly do."

Tremayne paused again, watching a girl clacking her heels on the smooth concrete coping of the pool, her arms raised. Handsome men have so much more assurance than plain men, Blackburn thought with mounting agitation; the rest of us have to do it on our raddled wits. He remembered Shelly once at an embassy party in Isfahan, telling the ambassador's wife about his school vacations as an Arthur Murray instructor and the parade of women who waylaid him after studio hours, the subterfuges he used to evade them. The ambassador's wife, a squat, overbearing matron with quivering upper arms and the mouth of George Washington, had been charmed . . .

"—terribly vital problem," Tremayne was saying casually. "The security angle. Take that mess in Djebel Qatar—none of it would have happened if Sykes hadn't got himself mixed up with a charming young man who just happened to be a member of a Sudanese irredentist group . . ."

Blackburn folded his arms. "What is it you want to tell me, Shelly?"

Tremayne took his pipe out of his mouth and peered into the bowl, which was no longer smoking. "Jim came to me about it yesterday. It's extremely awkward, I know. He was aware of Miss Hoyt's activities, of course—they've put together quite a dossier on her over the past four or five years. He told me he was convinced you'd decided to sever the connection between her and Land. He certainly supported your move, he was hoping you'd be completely successful. It wasn't till a bit later that he became aware it was—something more than that . . ."

On the far side of the pool they were still playing Sobriquet, hunched forward in wrought-iron chairs around Maggie Hendryx. "The Emperor's favor meant nothing to me," she cried, shaking back her glorious blond hair, "no matter what any of you may think! It was simply that after all those years at court I had to be with the one man I'd *never* ceased to love! . . ."

"Why are you telling me this?" Blackburn asked. With the knowledge that Torgerson's people knew about him and Jillie—that for all he knew half a dozen government agencies were holding emergency sessions on his case—he felt a thick, heavy pressure of indignation, of intolerable confinement in too small a place. He wanted to leap into the air and thrash his arms, plunge into this ridiculous, amoeboid pool—in which you couldn't even swim laps decently—and spray water over everyone, roar defiance at them all. "If Jim Torgerson has something to say, why doesn't he come to me himself? Why do you need to play the duenna?"

Tremayne was watching him impassively, urbanely. "He's troubled about the situation, Paul. That's all. And he knew you and I were old friends."

"And so he got you to make the approach shot. Lovely. Set his gum-shoes on my tail, put me under surveillance like any cheap little syndicate hoodlum—"

"We're all under surveillance in one form or another."

"You know what I mean. Who put him up to this?"

"*I* don't know—nobody, probably."

"Fat chance. What does he want—some kind of New Year's resolution? A certificate of good conduct?"

"Paul, you're the Secretary of State of the United States of America, you're carrying half the—"

"Are you saying that I'm some kind of poor security risk?"

"Paul, she's a member of a militant anarchist *cell* . . ."

"Oh, for God's sake! She's a member of an insignificant protest group —which would have no importance whatever if it weren't for Reiny's ridiculous overreaction to the Lachlan Smith case."

"That's not the way Jim has it. Jim says—"

"The hell with what Jim says! I know what I know."

There was a shriek of laughter from across the pool, and then applause. Someone called, "Wonderful, wonderful!" and then, "All right— you're next, Arthur . . ."

Slowly, sternly, Blackburn forced himself to smile. "Aren't you all getting a little hysterical over this? I'm a fairly good judge—I can assure you there is nothing to worry about from the security angle."

"I wish we could see it that way. Jim's feeling is that it's—not tenable."

"Not tenable."

Tremayne said with sudden low intensity: "Look—I'm not any happier about this than you are. We're not kids out of college any more, horsing around—you see what's involved here. Remember Profumo."

"Thanks."

"You know what I mean. If this got out . . . You can't afford it, Paul. The Administration can't afford it. It's simply too dangerous a connection."

Blackburn set down his empty glass on the cool hard apron of the pool. Arthur Schlesinger, in the center of the Sobriquet players, his eyes snapping behind his glasses, was saying, "I thought he was honest—a faithful and trusted subordinate for the campaigns ahead. I never *dreamed* he would stoop to tactics so vile, so intricate. I'm a simple man, essentially . . ." Someone said, "Oh-my-God," and there was a quick burst of laughter.

Blackburn straightened slowly, hooked his fingers in his trouser pockets. "I'm sorry, Shelly," he said in a low, quiet voice. "I can't give her up, if that's what they told you to get me to do. I'm not going to."

Tremayne was gazing at him as if he'd just shot someone down in cold blood. "—I don't get it."

"No."

"—that's absurd . . . to throw over your life, your whole career, risk the national interest for a girl, a crazy street radical with no more—"

"That's enough!" he said sharply. "That's enough, Shelly. Don't say more than you mean to.—I'm not going to give her up. I'm in love with her. That's all there is to it."

The CIA man blinked, the slender folds above his eyes seemed to tighten strangely, then release. Saying these words here, aloud, gave Blackburn a brief, warm throb of delight such as he'd only felt in Jillie's presence. Shelly was troubled by this declaration, troubled and angered, Shelly thought less of him—which was too bad in a way. But Shelly just didn't know. Shelly's world was structured for people who'd never been spun completely around blindfolded, who'd never come to themselves in some alien, hollow space, beheld the flaking husks of loss and recognized the desperate need to touch, to hold, to lay claim upon the man one could somehow, resurgently, *be* . . . Or did he? Had Shelly perhaps glimpsed that image, and stiffly turned away? Had he known he could never claim it for himself?

"I'm sorry, Shelly," he said again, more softly. "But that's really how it is. You tell Jim if he's got anything more on his mind to come to me with it. And, incidentally, the Republic is not going to suffer for it. You have my word on that."

The two men regarded each other a moment in complete silence. Then the CIA Director nodded, a smart tick of his head, and knocked out the pipe bowl against his palm. "Okay, Paul," he said without inflection. "That's it, then."

Back in the living room after a few casual exchanges they parted; Blackburn went to find Maggie to pay his respects. She was at the bar now, part of an avid, hilarious group clustered about Arnold Shamlur; Blackburn tried to reach her twice through the press, gave it up and stood there, bumped and elbowed by other bodies. He was seething with rage, he was alarmed, he was defiant and panicky and vengeful—he didn't know what he felt. He stood listening dully to Shamlur, waiting for an opening.

The Secretary for Cultural Affairs was even drunker than before. Vosz had departed—probably in disgust—and Shamlur had the audience all to himself. He had reached the stage where nothing on this earth fazed him—"Arnie's fit," his devotees called it—he could vault from the most baleful morbidity to the airiest speculation.

"I love this funky town," he was telling them. "It's so gorgeously irresponsible."

"—*irresponsible!*"

"Shee-it, yo. It's the only place in the Big BM where you can fall down completely on your doogie-ramming job and survive. Wall Street, engineering, pimping, surgery, bookmaking—you name it. In any other field you make some crucial mistake, some disastrous error in judgment and you're through, you've bought it, go get yourself embalmed. But not in little old DC. Jee-sus, dig 'em all, the blood-drinking Vietnam hotshots that were so sure we were going to beat those brown-skinned slopeys into foursquare, fluid-drive, computerized democracy. Bullet Bob, Mac the Knife, the Cheshire Buddha—look at them all. Did *any* of them get stuffed down the Big Crapper while the band played the Dead March from Saul? Hell, no—they're still parading around with all the charisma they can carry."

"Arnie baby," the carrot-haired girl said, "don't you think we ought to be taking off?"

"Climb off my kidneys, will you, twatter-box? . . . Regard the platoons of incompetents who have run this town," he went on, his Asiatic eyes glinting below the pastel lights above the bar. "The big bad Dulles boys, Bundy, Mitchell. Remember Henry the K—the tilting little crisis-manager actually *said:* 'Power is the great aphrodisiac.' You want to know something?—I'm going to rewrite *Faust.*"

"As a musical, darling?" Maggie Hendryx broke in.

"No—as a dong-gobbling morality play. Marlowe got it all wrong, you know? So did Goethe and Mann and the rest of them. The devil doesn't come through with all those big-time kingdoms and conquests— hell no, he gives Faust the most ruinous advice time and time again, cons him into some of the most disastrous moves a man could ever make. *There's* your nooky-shagging legend . . ."

"But then why doesn't Faust drop him?" Hi Carruthers demanded. "If he gives him nothing but bum steers—"

"Because he can't, lame brain. That's just the point. Faust *has* to stick with him—he's accepted Mephisto's lousy judgment, he's identified his administration with it. He's glued to him out of expiation. He's *got* to go on with him for seven years, and then seven more, and seven more . . ."

"Arnie, that's marvelous!" Maggie exclaimed.

"It's iguana turd. But it's right on the money. This glorified brothel of a town operates on error and complicity. Take Blackburn, here—he's about to make the most disastrous mistake of his life, and he can't do one poot-sticking thing about it." He paused; his cunning, mad little blue eyes slid around to the Secretary of State. "Isn't that right, Blackie-boy?"

Blackburn produced a grin. "I always bow to the cultural analysis."

The laughter was quick and nervous. Shamlur shrugged his heavy, sloping shoulders. His gaze fastened on the bandage over the Secretary's eye and a curious look flowed into his face. "Hail to the hero," he said. "How'd you get it—fall head first down the bobo?"

"Something like that." He glanced again at Maggie Hendryx but Carruthers had just engaged her attention.

"It figures," Shamlur said, staring hard at the Secretary. "Why don't you do it? just one time? Kick over the whole snatch-gobbling fruit stand —bust up GATO and put the boots to this disgusting Frankenstein . . ."

"Consider it done, Arnie," Blackburn answered. Turning away he began "Maggie, it's been fun, as always; but I've got—"

One of Shamlur's big hands came down on his shoulder.

"No no no, not like that, Frisco-baby—let's have us a little discussion. You know? Let's see you pull out of Burma, repudiate that bum-buggering Bodawyin. Why not, Blackie? Hell, all it would take is fifteen minutes' courage. You've got *that,* haven't you?"

"—Ooh," someone said.

They were all watching now in a gathering silence, their eyes glittering. This was the stuff of scandal, the climax of the show they had come to see. Worn down from the week's remorseless pressures, the fencing match with Tremayne, Blackburn heard himself say testily: "I don't think my courage needs to be called into question. And I very much doubt if this is the time for a discussion-in-depth of the Drachenfels Affair."

Shamlur's head came up, his shoulders drew down. He set his glass on the bar. "I see," he said. "I get it.—I've shown too high a regard for you."

"Life is disillusioning," Blackburn answered, and again turned toward Maggie when Shamlur pulled him around with a quick, violent gesture. The Secretary for Cultural Affairs had come off his bar stool.

"How'd you like to step outside, Blackburn? We'll take it from there."

A girl gave a high, sharp exclamation, and there was a silence so full a man's voice could be heard from the far end of the pool.

"Arnie, what are you—" Maggie Hendryx began, but Shamlur silenced her with an abrupt thrust of one of his broad, hard hands.

"Come on—I'll give you a *real* chance to be a hero."

Watching the swarthy, sweating, big-pored face, the demonic little eyes Blackburn felt burdened with disgust. "Mister Shamlur," he said, holding his voice perfectly level, "I was one of the earliest admirers of *Depart in Darkness,* and it saddens me to see you behave like this. You and I have far better things to do than bloody each other's faces."

He swung away abruptly and moved off toward the door. He heard Shamlur say, "I've heard a lot—" and then his voice was drowned in the quick release of talk. Young Adlai Stevenson and John Chancellor were listening to a story Barbara Howar was telling them. They nodded pleasantly to Blackburn and he nodded back.

"Paul . . ." It was Maggie Hendryx hurrying after him. "Don't mind Arnie, will you . . ."

"Of course not. He's clearly the life of the party."

"It's not—it's just his way. He says things he doesn't mean."

Blackburn found himself smiling the slow, sad smile of a man who has ceased to believe in the amenities but who must nevertheless abide by them. "Of course, Maggie," he said lightly. "We all have our private vultures. I really must go."

"You *have* changed," she said suddenly. Her glance was level and piercing, not unkind. "You really have."

"Have I?"

"Uh-huh. As though you've come to a decision. A big one."

"No such luck. Maybe I've taken on some of Shamlur's coefficient of disdain."

"Maybe." At the door, pausing, for an instant there in the foyer she looked forlorn, her face beneath the green Tiffany-glass light a touch haggard. She too lived eighteen-hour days, ran her own relentless treadmill. "Don't do anything rash," she said. "You're not going to do anything rash, are you?"

"Me? I'm no Lochinvar."

"—*Lochinvar?*" she exclaimed softly, and her lovely gray eyes gleamed.

"Hotspur. I meant Hotspur, or the Chevalier Bayard. I don't know who I meant." He smiled, amused himself at the slip. "Anyway, I'm not the heroic type, believe me. I'm just a guy who's trying to get a few things done with the least amount of blood-and-thunder."

"I know." Wistfully, warily she looked at him—he suddenly had the feeling that for all her misgivings, the cares of status and royal favor, she was attracted to him as a man. "You be careful, sweetie."

"Indeed I will."

He walked out into the warm, heavy night, chewing on the unsavory incident, raging at Shamlur, angry with himself, wishing he'd done something else (though what he did not know), hating the way the Washington women ran things, hating the backbiting, the gossip, the duels of wit and machismo. What had Rusk called it? An evil town. Yes: that was what it was, all right: an evil town. For once he could agree with his predecessor.

Beyond the roofs, the high-arching shadows of the trees the sky looked tropical, washed with a million enormous, incandescent stars that burned their way through time. Fingers hooked in his trouser pockets he stood motionless, waiting for Stollens to come up with the limousine, and watched them gratefully. All that mattered—absolutely and utterly all that mattered in this immense and drifting galaxy—was that they looked down on Jillie, too; that he would see her in two days.

FOURTEEN

——————————————— the front door was closed. Not that there was anything so special about that, only sometimes when it was this hot she left it ajar so a little air could move through the pad. Sam Spade, Junior, on casual stakeout. From where I was sitting at the end of the counter I could see most of the front porch and the side window, the one in the bedroom. It was open; the shade, drawn against the heat, was tilted queerly. Did that signify anything? Yes: that it was tilted queerly.

Tony Parella came up to me with the coke and said: "You want something else, Blackie-boy?" "Yes," I said, "a Danish, thanks." He reached under the greasy plastic dome, pinched a tired disc of pastry between thumb and forefinger and slid it on to a plate. In front of me again he sucked with satisfaction on a match stem; a taut, clucking sound. Then the phony, agent provocateur's smile. "Well, Blackie-boy. Haven't seen you around much lately."

"I've been working over in Lynn," I said. "That right? Where at?" "Spencer-Snavely." "Firearms?" Narrowed eyes, the coal glint of suspicion. "That's right," I said, "rat-a-tat-tat." The tough grin again—but a touch uncertain now. "No sailing this summer? Boy, I'd like to be out there right now. Fishing for sea bass . . ." Thick red hands on his aproned hips, black hairs stiff as wire against the skin; gazing across the street at the porch, the door, the tilted shade. Then: "What's your old man think of it?" "Think of what?" "Your working at Spencer?" "Why, he's got a subversive warrant out, of course. Shoot on sight." Parella snorted. "Jeez, I wouldn't doubt it." He turned to the two yo-yos pretending to drink coffee down the counter. "Hey, Angie: you hear about this Lagram Smith? Boy, have they ever lowered the boom on *that* hot-rock. Life! They give him life." Turning back to me, flashing his night-club-doorman's grin. "You hear about it?" "Yes," I said, "I heard about it."

Shaking his head, the troubled Somerville philosopher. "I don't know. Some people in this world, they got no sense of loyalty, you know?" "None at all," I said. "What they ain't going to do to *that* cookie. They'll make him wish he'd never lifted those files." "Yeah, well," I said, "it isn't over yet." "What you mean, Blackie?" All their heads raised, perfectly still: Black Bart And His Gang at the Last Chance Saloon. I took a long, easy slug of coke. "I mean, there's always an appeal to the higher courts."

Laughter, on cue. "Oh, sure—they can *appeal*. Only it won't make no difference. They're going to nail that son of a bitch to the wall."

Only thing he'd said I could agree with. Yes, it's going to be a long war. "Hey, you know him, don't you, Blackie-boy? This Lagram Smith." Bright, feigned innocence: old Sherlock Parella closing in. "Sure," I said, "I know him." "How'd you happen to know him?" I finished the Danish and wiped my mouth while they watched me like statues. "Croquet. He taught me everything I know."

No applause. Tony P watching me flatly, not amused. "Jeez, you're a bunch of jokers, you are. You really think that's funny." "What the hell," I decided to say. "We're all harmless enough." "That's not the way I hear it." His eyes shot across the street, back to me again. "Been a long, hot summer already."

He grinned again—a different grin, a joke too precious to conceal, moved away down the counter to his pals. Fascist hard-hat son of a bitch. The enemy. No, only unawakened, Jumbo Erikson said. Blah-loney. They'll never wake up to anything except flag-waving parades in long-ago uniforms, now undersize, and raids on the Linden Street pads, working over the previated dee-verts. Life's simple pleasures. Shouldn't have come in here, I knew better. Unforeseen hazards of sleuthing.

The shade was still tilted. Remarkably. In the street some kids were playing with a wiffle ball and a bright yellow plastic bat. The pitcher went into a windmill wind-up, arms flailing, all that effort, and out came the white ball wobbling and wavering, the batter half broke his back swinging. The air conditioning made me shiver all at once. The sweat was drying on my neck and I wiped at it with a handkerchief. Well, what did I expect— half the Department camped on the stoop smoking grass? The whole thing was ridiculous. That's the trouble with sexually fouled-up types like Nell, they think everyone else is rutting round the clock, a riot of steamy, sliding bodies and crazy moans. All of it behind their honorable backs. The wages of frigidity is phan-tas-ma-GO-ria.

The look on her face when I came in. Standing in the anteroom off the front hall, her body twisted curiously, as though she'd just hidden something behind the curtains. "Well—Mom," I said, "—greetings! Didn't know you were coming up to old Cambridge town." "No, I wasn't, I—just came today." How true. A swift glance, distraught, apprehensive. I said: "Why? What's the matter?" "Nothing. Nothing's the matter. I thought I'd better look in on Grandma Adelaide, she hasn't been feeling well." Not the reason at all. Her back as she turned away had that peculiar stiffness. Watch out for falling rock. Hadn't been up from the Vineyard once all summer: why today? Stood there listening to her prattling along about Grandma and a sale at Jordan Marsh, not hearing her really, still full of the news about Smitty, the session at Jumbo's pad, the long hassle over tactics. *Options*, the Prof-O would call them. Followed her into the living room, a dove evening at three PM with the draperies drawn, conscious of that good old sinking hollow feeling. But of course she couldn't know—how on earth could she know?

She stood there as though we'd just bought the house and she didn't like it but didn't know why. Then she turned and looked at me. I made a nice, clean return of service, not a flinch. She'd always had a God damned fine-mesh espionage net that would make the CI and A look like a pack of Cub Scouts at a weenie roast. "There's not a whole lot of food in the joint," I said, real casuallike. "I've been eating out most of the time. Want me to go out and get some stuff?" "No, that won't be necessary." She sat down on the edge of the couch, almost dropped on to it, her hand to the side of her head. I said: "You all right, Mom?" She pressed down on her thigh with her hands, looked up brightly. "How's the job going?" "Oh—same old stuff. Slipping automatic weapons to the Panthers, pouring sand in the lathes. You know how it is."

Her expression didn't change. Neither amused nor angry. A look I couldn't read—all at once remembered from the time in Khotiane when they thought I had encephalitis. Frightened and trying not to show it. Just like me, like everyone else. Any fumbler can stray. But *Nell* . . . Then she looked down again, at her hands, seemed to be really studying them. Why, she's *old,* I thought, she's grown old, just this summer, she's an ugly old woman—and I felt a twinge of distaste, really intense distaste. I didn't know what to do. I hung there in the doorway, feeling foolish, then I started to go.

"Stay and talk to me a minute, Leland. Can you? Please stay . . ." Part plea, part command. Yop, there was going to be more: a brisk hard set. What are you doing there, under my wife's bed? Boss, ever'body got to be *somewhere.* Hyuk hyuk. And here is where I am, smack in the bosom of the little-used homestead (*little-used* now we'd entered the flood tide of history, that is). Kee-rist: will kids some day actually *study* the incredible muddles the Prof-O has got himself glued up in? Never thought of it that way before.

"And what have you been doing with yourself evenings?" Ah, that was more like it. Bishop to knight five and buckle your safety belts. I ensconced myself in the Prof's chair, ankle over knee. Loose in the saddle. It is my duty to warn you that anything you have can be taken away from you. Including your jewelry. However: if she thought for one off-bop second she was going to pry any devastating admissions out of me she was stark and raving. We are moving on two different planets, Nelly Bly.

"Nothing much," I said. "Four muggings, one political assassination —messy business, that—three Peeping—" *"Can't* you be serious!—" Leaning toward me all at once, her face astonishing. Really fierce. Shocked me. Good Nell, forthright, principled Nell, the Judge's dutiful daughter. Jesus. Why is it I can never shake off that cold spasm of guilt, inadequacy, whatcvei the hell? Of course the Prof can't, either—and he's holding the big marbles. Felt scared suddenly, watching her. As though she weren't my mother at all but some celestial spook, getting ready to lay bare my quivering soul under the lights at Fenway Park. And at the same time I wanted to hurt her with all my might, make her weep and beg for mercy on her knobbly knees. So much for the psychic life.

"Oh yes," I said slowly, "I can be serious." "Then do me that courtesy . . . I mean, have you been here in Cambridge often?" Hey now, watch out for that one. Low bridge. "Fairly often. Haven't had all the time in the world, I mean this job is a killer . . ." "You must be careful, Leland. You look very thin and tired." Yep: standard tactics. Open with fear, switch to solicitude. Hearties, give us some ti-i-i-ime to break the man down. "Oh, that," I said, "—that's just Revolutionary's Nerves. All the tension of plotting and skullduggery, nocturnal raids—if you don't do it at night, when *can* you? Like some other things. Marat, Robespierre, Bakunin—those yo-yos were dead from lack of sleep half the time. Didn't you know that?"

But instead of lashing out at me she looked up at the portrait of Gramp. Searching for divine intercession. Rotten likeness—all softened, none of the flint ferocity. Or the other part either, the goofy sardonic humor. Like the time we made the Hallowe'en dummy and tied it to the breakwater so it would bob around in the swells. Standing there, his legs blue from the October water, studying his handiwork with pride. "Your mother always thinks there's a corpse out here, ax murder victim or some such. We'll give her a real turn." Which it did, of course. Old Grampus laughing that crazy wheezing laugh, turtle eyes streaming . . . Society portraits. Christ, the capacity for human vanity is limitless. Though to do the old crocodile credit he always hated it: wouldn't have it down at the Paling.

"Have you seen Miss Hoyt?"

Just like that. Simple, direct question, without preamble. God, she is something. Why in Torquemada is it that knowing the haymaker is coming, setting up for it, half *praying* for it almost, I'm never ready when it comes? Do I *want* to be eviscerated, spread-eagled? And yet her expression was not so much contemptuous as diffident, pleading for something. Why was that? I said: "It's funny, but I'm stuck with the impression that's *my* business. Of course that's just an educated guess." Her lips came together neatly then. "I wish that were true. I'm afraid it's not." "What the hell do you mean by that?" I demanded. She looked afraid again, her eyes brushing me quickly. Yes, afraid. "Have you seen her, been in touch with her recently?"

"*Well* . . ." I said. "Why all the maternal interest, out of the blue? In my degenerate ways?" "I have to know. That's all." She kept falling over her words, gazing at me tensely. There was a fair-sized silence. "Leland . . . have you—been with her, during—during the past few weeks?" I socked the arm of the chair and said, "For Christ sake, Mother! I don't think I feel like answering that. I'm damned if I see if it's—" "Well, I think you'd better." "And just why is that?" I shouted.

"Because I've just had—some extraordinary news. I think you ought to know about it." She looked away at that phony portrait, back to me again. "Your father is having an affair with her."

I didn't know what my face looked like. I just stared at her. Yes, that was what she'd said, all right all right. I burst out laughing. "It's true," she said. That quiet, dogged manner that could wear away obsidian. "For Christ sake!" I yelled at her. "What the hell are you talking about? That's the craziest piece of bullshit I've ever heard . . ." "It's true," she said again. "All right—how do you know?" "Because I do, that's all."

I jumped up and went to the front windows and yanked the draperies aside. Two bouncy girls, not Cliffies, not townies. A smiling young man with his head shaved, wearing a Buddhist robe of brilliant orange. Last week when I called she'd said she was feeling lousy. She hadn't been home all weekend. At the meeting she was all business, the way she always was. All plans. Thursday her phone didn't answer. But that was just the quarrel. My fault. Wasn't it? The old Yorktown elm out front was dead now, its bark peeling away in long hidelike strips: a disease they couldn't check. Like the stupid system. They were going to cut it down soon.

I turned around. "That's ridiculous—you realize how ridiculous, how completely preposterous this is?" She nodded somberly, her piercing blue eyes steady. "Don't you think I'd know about something like this?" I demanded. "Only you can answer that, Leland."

Sheer rage, I felt then. I could have killed then, easily, anyone can at one time or another, it just takes the right combinations. Jumbo is wrong: anyone can. Her face was still set, almost composed in its stern certitude. That sureness! I could fling myself against that wall until my flesh was torn to rags, all my bones ground to powder. Like Peggy. Standing in the upstairs hall with the scissors in her hand. "I'm going to make her hurt. *Hurt!* You'll see. I'll make her cry out so we'll *all* hear it!" "Peg, look, she didn't mean—" "Don't tell me what she didn't mean, she means *everything* she means! She's cut all of *us* up—let *go* of me!" God bless our happy home. Why did I stop her?

And then I began to get it. Little by little. A touch too slowly to be a good pro quarterback. But I get there. In time. The Prof-O is dead right, Nell should have been running one of those Zenda countries featuring military balls and lace at the throat. Of course. Of course! Accusation, sugared with solicitude—and then the duster . . .

"How nice," I said. "How bloody convenient. What better way to get me to break off with her: right? Sorry to have been so obtuse, Maman." She closed her eyes. "That's a cruel thing to say, Leland." "Is it, now?" "Yes. At a moment like this. A cruel, bitter thing." "That's the way it works, though. Isn't it? I mean, that's the essential strategy: I throw her over, maybe even slap her around a bit for good measure—wouldn't that please your freaky Victorian soul?—and declare war on Dad at the same time . . ."

"I don't know what it was that made you so cruel. I truly don't know." She began to shake her head slowly, her hands squeezed tight in her lap. I waited for the passing shot: she always had one. But she just kept staring at me, and then her face froze in the strangest way. ". . . Dorothy Meigs," she said in a low voice. "I had to hear this from that vicious, tale-bearing creature, I had to sit and listen to her tell *me*—" Her cheeks and chin underwent a funny little tremor, and her eyes filled. "After all the years together, the struggles and disappointments, all the years . . . and then finally we reached—"

She was crying, a hoarse stormy weeping, her back perfectly straight. My mother. Crying. I'd seen her weep only once before, a thousand years ago, when Mrs. Timmons died of amoebic dysentery in Damascus. And even then she hadn't cried like this. I went over to her and stood there, I put my hand on her shoulder and then took it away. I didn't know what to think, everything had gone all funny. "Look, it's impossible," I told her. "How could it happen, *how*—? He has to be down in *Washington,* for Christ sake, handing out the good word. Look, he's old enough to be her *father*—"

"Then go over there yourself, go on and see for yourself!" Her face quivering, a mass of lines. A desperate, frightened old woman's. "Oh, it's so *wrong* of him," she groaned. "After all these hard years. So wrong, so selfish—"

Across the street now everything looked just the same. Why shouldn't it? The Giomartis' cat, a tough overgrown orange tom, walked across the porch like a Gay Nineties café bouncer and sat on the railing, washing a hind leg.

It was still impossible. Clearly and sheerly impossible. My father, United States Secretary of State, Llanfear Professor of History at Harvard University, *my own father* could actually have been behind that door, there behind that tilted shade—

Why should he? He never had time for people anyway, his *work* was too important. The night Charlie Willis died in the infirmary all I kept getting were Miss Pyttka and Miss Ross and a man named Simpson. Nobody could locate him, *busy* you see. And the snow kept melting on my hair and dripping on the nickels and quarters on the shelf and I kept dropping them all over the floor of the God damn phone booth, I couldn't reach him and it was the only time I really prayed for him to be there, drop whatever fucking stupid paper-passing he was engaged in and talk to me quietly. The only time, and he wasn't there. Shit, nobody's there when you need them most. Nobody.

The Buddhist type in the apricot silk robe was going by. No, another one, thinner, with a bell in his hand. Some Lost Horizon splinter sect, floating through a holy dream world. Like Malicoat out at that kooky Berkshire commune. "It's a complete experience, man. I mean, it's a case of *realizing* your possible self, you know?" Rat's nest of a beard speckled with bread crumbs, overalls stiff with cow dung. "See, we've put all that mechanistic crap behind us—we're creating the energy field for a new culture, really. It's written in *I Ching* that spontaneous affection is the basis of all human union. Isn't that a groove?" And then the beatific smile, his teeth brown and tiny inside all that beard. "I mean can you *comprehend* that?"

"How about the spontaneous affection of the CIA?" I said. "What about the military-industrial-defense triangle? How do they fit into the energy field?" Shaking his head like Moses disappointed in all twelve tribes. "Don't you see, Land baby, you're still *competing*. Putting your own ego in opposition to the Establishment, dig? Forget it, withdraw your hostility. The whole thing's going to self-destruct anyway in five, ten years . . ." Looking off at the grayed magenta hills, a mad and patriarchal gaze. Storm door for a dining table, soggy piles of watercress and dandelion greens on the peeling brown surface, a beat-up loom in the corner like a crashed flying machine. Two crows in Mother Hubbards stirring a big black pot full of something gelatinous and putrid—soy paste, eucalyptus leaves? —half a dozen brats, God alone knew whose, squalling and crawling and crapping all over the floor. New converts to the energy field. Praise the lord and pass the dandelion greens.

I pulled a copy of the *Globe* out of my hip pocket. The French ambassador had again offered his good offices in the mounting Burma crisis. A high government source favored stern measures to insure the immediate return of the American mission. Vosz that meant, as who over the age of seven didn't know. Yes, there he was on page two, walking with the President in the woods at Camp Goliath, glaring away, clutching at the air. All that *power*. I closed my eyes but he was still there, with those God damned wrap-around mauve shades. And I pleaded with him to let Smitty off, I mean I *begged* the no-good son of a bitch. Even smashed. *Why did I do it!*

My hands were trembling. Blown my cool. Shit, yes, and why not. And all the time of course he was planning to bury Smitty for life. *For life*. Only gave him another chance to put somebody down. What got into me? All that far-out bullshit about the centuries going by like freight trains and the microscopic *insignificance* of man, world without end, mountains of bat turd, amen. Donlund and that ice freak Félice. *That's what you want, isn't it?* he said. *You have to act, then. Not pose game theories.* That shadow glare, like an old mountain king.

Is he right? "You're always thinking in terms of absolutes, Blackburn." Bushy gawping at me, a starved heron, keening on about Regis Debray and the Revolution Within the Revolution, the historical need to force the

populace to choose sides. And Jillie saying wearily, "It failed, it *failed*—
in Bolivia and Chicago and Paris and everywhere else. It's only effective
when the people are ready to move—when they're either hopelessly oppressed or they've been educated to take concerted action. The Marighella
line is the true one. Look, Lenin's prediction has come true—urban man is
being forced out of the process of production. And the only way he'll wake up
to the true state of affairs is if he sees the essential vulnerability of the
Establishment. *That's* our line, not comic sideshows. We're a minority, we
always will be—face it! The only way we can make our weight count is to
find the precise pressure point, and jab right there." "Mao," Jumbo said.
"Exactly. At that single point even a small force can wield superiority. I
mean there he'll be—in New York City where we can get *at* him. Standing
right there in front of the Council on Foreign Relations. The act will be
the symbol. When would we get another chance like this?"

Horns, voices down on Mount Auburn Street, the radio in the next
room pushing pollution-free (!) gasoline. Jumbo sweating in the faded
khaki shirt, squinting against a spiral of cigarette smoke, head tilted.
"Going to be pretty hard to make it go the way we want it to," he said.
"I mean with all the flunkies they'll have milling around there." "I don't
think so," Jillie answered. "The thing is to make sure we entirely surround
the car so they can't drive off, the way Semmes did in San Francisco. And
there's got to be plenty of wire running back to the panel truck. Also there
ought to be two of us with mikes, in case something goes wrong with mine
or I get blocked off or something."

Looking at each of us, her eyes flashing pure emeralds. "No shouting,
no violence. Perfect silence. The way the Wobblies greeted Wilson in Seattle
—the most effective thing they could have done, they say he came all apart
after that scene. That's going to be the hard part. You'll have to stress this
with your people: the whole show hinges on that discipline. But once he's
engaged we've got him. Either he refuses to answer us and breaks away—
in which case it's a clear confession of guilt, broadcast live for all to hear.
Or he comes back at me, which is what I think he'll do. And we'll force
those admissions out of him, with America listening in, and a tape of the
whole exchange for further—"

There she was. Just like that. On cue. Closing the door behind her
smartly, skipping down the steps in white slacks and that sleeveless green
shirt with the mandarin collar, she always looks good without sleeves, with
those shoulders. She knows it, too. Moving briskly along the far sidewalk,
head held high. She walks so *proudly*. Light on her face, the trace of a
smile. Been laughing? Or remembering something? If she were moving in
my sights now, just below the left breast, squeezing off, now, *now*. Pa-
chooonggg. Why did I think that? Zonksville. I had to fight to keep from
glancing down the counter toward lovable, huggable Tony P. Sliding out of

sight now above the frantic helmets of the car roofs. So proud, so free and proud.

Impossible. Absolutely, totally impossible.

Wasn't it? Jesus, wasn't it? The shade, the window were the same. Joys of a timid voyeur. The eye's the window of the soul. And fear has a thousand eyes. Yes indeedy. That's what's so rare in Jillie: that hard white gimlet-point that can pierce an issue, strip back the blubber, involve others. It's not brains especially, or simple enthusiasm or organizing power or even eloquence. It's something more elusive: the faculty for getting people to see something the way you see it, make them feel it's their own. The Prof's got it, Donlund's got it to burn. Proud, certain, persuasive. I only fabricate it, and the fraud shows. I know it shows. But even so.

"Hey, I missed you, Jill," I'd told her last Tuesday. "I know. I'm wasted, Land. I need to split for a while. Change the script. I really do." Frowning at the torn print, the jumble of books and magazines. She did look all strung-out, those pale blue shadow-smudges under her eyes and her lower lip slack: lost little girl. But more, oh so much more. She always looked particularly beautiful when she was tired. "You wouldn't like to give me a lovely island in the Seychelles, would you? Where are the Seychelles?" "Indian Ocean." "Well, I want to go there. I want to go right on out of this century, where they've never heard of embarrassing the center of power or any of the rest of it." Leaning back against the bookcase with her eyes closed, eyelids upslanted, exotic, her expression faintly troubled as though she were trying to remember something deep back. I thought of her dead, then. Cold and still, beyond anyone's reach. I wanted her as I never had before, I wanted to take her, pick her up and enter her right there, standing, her legs wrapped around my waist, move with her gasping from room to room, my face buried in her breasts—

And then I said it, I don't really know why, it just came out. "Marry me." Her eyes popped open. *"What?—?"* "I mean it, Jill." I did: like you know if I married her, if we made love all that afternoon and evening she would never die. Her face so weird then—as if she were really looking *at* me for the first time in two years. "What's that for?" I said. Her expression didn't change, it scared me a little. I said it again: "Marry me, Jill." It was, I don't know, so *important* at that instant; everything she'd meant to me from that night, driving back late after the New London thing, with Bushy and Jumbo arguing about Regis Debray and Jillie said, "Oh, screw all that —look at the *sky!*" and there up ahead were stars in powder-soft clusters drifting toward us like magic flares. And the next evening back at her place after the flick she said, "You're a lovely boy, but I better tell you—I'm not a great one for sleeping around," and I said, "Oh, shut up, I want you," and I swung her back on to the couch, light as a feather. And my God it was good, richer and deeper than I'd ever had it, catching all the rings of love.

And at the end—the very end—she was smiling at me, her eyes full with tears. And I said, "My God, you're sensational. Do you know that?" I said: "Don't tell me that's routine—I won't believe it," and she laughed: "Oh, no! No, it's not routine . . ."

But this other afternoon last week she frowned at the poster, biting savagely at her hangnails. She's always biting at her hangnails since she quit smoking. "What did you quit smoking for?" I said. "Made a pact," she answered. "A pact with who?" She gave me a quick, covert glance. "Myself." After a minute I said, "I'm serious, you know." "No, you're not." "Damn it, I *am* . . ." But she walked over to that battleship of a table. "Don't be ridiculous," she said. "You know it's out of the question." "You're not going to start in on ages again, are you?" "Of course not," she snapped, "age hasn't anything to do with it." "Well, what, then?" "Land, you know I don't believe in all that bourgeois rot, and neither do you. Want another?" She tilted her empty glass toward me. I followed her into the kitchen and watched her cutting up a lime neatly, cool green gondolas. She was always drinking Tom Collins with lime these days. I came up behind her and put my face to her hair. "I love your hair," I said. "It's so springy and fine, so full of life." "It's a stupid mess," she answered, "it's all the salt." "Salt?" I said. "What do you mean?"

That quick flashing look, eyes curiously bright, very green and wide. "—Oh, salt water, I mean. I went to the beach last weekend." "Really? I thought you went to Connecticut." "Changed my mind." "I see. Where'd you go?" "Cape Ann. Near Cape Ann." "Where? Annisquam, you mean?" "Christ, *I* don't know, Land. Some beach up there . . ." Handing me my drink, irritated with me. She was lying, I could tell. And I couldn't leave it there, I had to push it all the way to the wall. "How was it?" "Lovely." "I thought you hated cold water," I said. "And besides, it rained like a bastard all day Sunday. Or didn't it where you were swimming?" Staring at me hotly now. "I wasn't aware that we had any particular obligations to each other." "You weren't." "No, I wasn't. I think we ought to drop this." "And suppose I don't want to?" I demanded. I wanted to hurt her now; and wanting to, of course I did. But it wasn't like the other quarrels, there wasn't that sense of an underlying presence, the beat of desire beneath it. I could tell. Round and round, and all of a sudden I was talking like Nell, boring in like Nell, I could hear myself, and I broke off.

She said, "I'm *tired,* Land, can't you see that?—I'm half dead on my feet, I can't think clearly about anything. We've never laid any chains on. Why now?" I said: "You give freedom so it won't be used. That's what *real* love, real marriage is!" She shook her head in a kind of weary wonder. "You take too much for granted." And I shouted, "Don't worry, I won't assume a single frigging thing from here on out!" and I ripped on out of there and walked halfway to Lynn, talking to myself. Yet even then, slamming my hand against the lamp posts and chain-link fences and cursing, I had the sense that in spite of my goading *she* was the one who wanted the row . . .

But even so it was impossible. Wasn't it? Jesus, wasn't it?

I chewed on the salty ice in the coke. What the fuck was I still sitting here for? Really? Some sign from on high, a star hanging over the house, streaming red-white-and-blue sparklers? What was I, scared to go over there?

I got up, squeegeeing around in my jeans for change. Now. I'd go over now, before she finished shopping, I'd be sitting there in the elephant chair when she got back, it would be more natural that way. More casual. Wouldn't it? We could pick up where we left off.

The street was hotter than before. I could feel the heat curl up against my eyelids. The leaves on the spindly trees hung wearily, gray on their undersides, waiting for a wind change, for rain. Everything was waiting for something. A foul odor of asphalt and burning rubber, the way empires smell when they're beginning to come apart at the seams. The kids were still playing with the wiffle ball. As I crossed over the batter connected, a straight-away fly, and one of the fielders came backpedaling awkwardly, his arms raised like a muezzin calling the faithful, stumbled into me. I shoved him away and the plastic shell fell free with a fragile clattering sound, danced away across the asphalt. Unreal. The kid, my height but younger, whirled around and said, "Watch it . . ." *"You* watch it," I told him. Glaring at me, panting, red hair, and cool blue eyes, like Nell's. "What's the matter with *you—?"*

I ignored him and walked on across the street, feeling their hatred between my shoulder blades and not giving a damn. Along the crooked walk, the shattered cement like cut-rate ruins, up on the porch, the sad boards squeaking. The big tom watched me with sour suspicion, a long raw gash over the rag of an ear.

The key wouldn't turn. I withdrew it, glanced down the street, thrust it home again—at the same instant saw the new brass disc inside the worn collar. Had it changed. Of course. Of course! Cute as a bug. Well, that was all right too, I'd just wait right here on the porch railing with old Battling Nelson, we'd tell each other—

The door was flung open. My father. In a blue sport shirt hanging open, his hair all messed up, saying, "I thought you always—" And then staring at me.

My father.

I walked past him into the room and over to the mausoleum table. I picked up one of the magazines lying on it and began furling it into a smooth cylinder, very tight ——————————————————————

FIFTEEN

WATCHING HIS SON'S STRAIGHT, tense back, Blackburn closed the door. He started to button his sport shirt, dismissed the impulse irritably. His heart was drumming, and it shook him. For once in his life he could think of nothing to say.

Land had turned, holding a furled magazine in his fist. *"Well,* now . . ." he said. His face gave an odd little quiver, as though he were on the verge of laughter, but his eyes were black and very shiny. "Well, if it isn't old Pomp-and-Circ himself . . . Kind of a little surprise party, isn't it?"

Blackburn nodded once, he didn't know why. Lying on the bed trying to read, thinking a slow, wild tumult of thoughts, he'd heard the key in the lock and imagined that Jillie, her arms full of groceries, was having trouble letting herself in. He felt off-balance, beleaguered and angry, confronted this way; and yet at the same time there was a curious sense of relief. It must have shown on his face—*something* must have shown on his face, because Land all at once smashed the magazine against the table's edge.

"—perfect!" he cried. "Oh Jesus, it's too good, it's really just too God damned perfect for words." His face, which had gone dead white at the door, was now flushed and dark. "And I didn't believe it—I thought it was some kind of freaky con game."

"Land," Blackburn said. His voice was curiously unsteady and it vexed him. "I'd like to explain a few things to you."

"No! Not this time." Leland jabbed at his belly with the magazine. *"I'll* do the explaining this time. Okay?"

"Land . . ."

"Just a sweet piece of paternal goodwill. To see that sonny-boy doesn't get *too* involved with someone of *dubious background* . . . what the fuck do you think I am!"

"Land, if you'd—"

"No, I said no! I don't want to hear anything from you. Anything! Trust," he muttered savagely, twisting and twisting the magazine. "Sure. All that high talk. Trust and the obligations of the man of moral purpose in today's troubled world—you know what I think of all that? I think it's a running river of shit, that's what I think! Just for starters . . . Can't leave anybody alone, can you? Hell, no—somebody might have a slice of his own life, a free moment or two you can't control, and riveted Jesus, we can't have something like that, can we? And you call *us* cynical!" The boy laughed harshly, shaking his head. "The rootless younger generation, spurning all the grand old values . . . Who's the cynic now? the cold-blooded operator? I mean, under all the silver words and sunny hours—"

"All right, Land!" Blackburn broke in with heat, checked himself. "This isn't what you think."

"No? No? What do I think? Hey? How d'you *want* me to read it?"

"Things happen sometimes—things you can't foresee . . ."

"Just don't care what you do, do you? Oh God, how I hate your very guts. You shameless son of a bitch—!"

He flung the magazine from him with all his might and ran at his father then, his arms flailing. Blackburn blocked one blow on his forearm, grunted with the force of another on his ribs, his neck—reached out instinctively and clutched Land to him, pinioning one arm, bore him back against the table which shuddered with their weight. The boy was so strong! Much stronger than he would have believed. A short, violent struggle while Blackburn held him hard—then flung him gently on to the couch and stood above him, panting.

"All right, Land," he said softly. "All right, now."

Leland braced himself with his hands, his eyes black with fury, and for an instant Blackburn was afraid of what he might do, how he might cope with him. Then it passed; the boy rubbed his nose and cheek with his knuckles, breathing thickly and coughing. Blackburn hooked his thumbs in his trouser pockets, thinking of Lee glaring up at him, raging, long ago. *Go fatten on someone else for a change—you've used us long enough!* . . . Good Christ, did *everything* have to repeat itself throughout time? No. Only certain things.

Land was muttering something. Blackburn extended an arm and the boy fell silent, watching him. He said: "Things happen to people . . . Can't you—look, can't you conceive of a man, a middle-aged man, finding himself in love for the first time in his life?"

"In love!" Land gave a gasping, raging bark of laughter. "Love . . . *you—?*"

"Yes. Is that so impossible to imagine?"

"Impossible? No, it's not impossible. It's just grotesque, that's all."

"Why—because it's happened to me?"

The boy struck his hands against his thighs. "Do you actually expect me to believe that?"

"Yes. I ask you to. Yes."

". . . And it just happened. Just like that. After twenty-five years, the whole world over—and it just *happened* to be the girl I'm planning to marry."

"—Marry," Blackburn echoed him.

"What a lovely coincidence, wouldn't you say? Who the hell do you think you're kidding?"

"Land, listen to me. Please listen."

"You're incapable of falling in love. No way. You wouldn't know how."

Blackburn chafed his neck with the heel of his hand, watching his son. It was incredible that Land could be saying these things to him; here in this room. Out in the street there was a hoot of laughter, and an answering voice called: "No—that's three! *Three* away . . ."

"Land," he began again, in a different voice. "I want to tell you something. About me. I tried to live a certain way—a way I thought was right. I know, I know—" he interrupted himself hurriedly to still his son's retort "—but that was how I saw it then. A kind of code, and I tried to live by it . . . Your grandfather—I owed him so much. So very much, you can't know how terribly deeply I was indebted to him. And then, there was your Uncle Lee . . ."

Land cried: "What do you want—a medal or a goof ball? What does any of that matter to me! What's it got to do with us here, right now?"

"A lot. Believe me, a whole lot. Look, I wanted nothing more on this earth than to do the right thing—"

"But there was always the old career too, wasn't there? All those steppingstones to the groovy Hall of Mirrors—so what did it matter what you did to people along the way? I always thought you were a little bit better than the rest of them. I believed that. But you're not, you're just what they say you are—a cold-blooded power-broker without a drop—not a drop!—of humanity—"

"Can't you—"

"You never loved me, or Peg or Mother either. Not one time! And now you want me to believe *this?*"

"Land, that's not true . . . Your mother and I—you can know very little of our problems. I'm not sure we've ever understood them ourselves."

"Enough—I know enough." He threw one long arm toward the door. "She's over at the house right now, crying her heart out. I know that much. Do you? Hell no, of course you don't. Or care less. Sure, she's a sad, fucked-up career wife—but at least she's crying, and that's more than you can say . . ."

Blackburn looked down at his hands. Land had learned about this from Nell, then. And that meant that Nell had heard it from—someone else. He felt a sharp twinge of anguish that the boy had had to find out in this way, but that was no more than the surface emotion: the veins ran deeper. He had betrayed his son now, had he? as he'd betrayed all the others—the Judge, Lee, Nell, Peg . . . Yes, apparently he had. And yet he had not meant to do that, any of it. It wasn't malice, nor even selfishness or carelessness, but something much stealthier—

"—apologies and good nights," Land was saying with cold savagery. "Don't bother. The train's pulled out. You think I give a sick cat's drop over how you fouled up your life? You want to lie to yourself, that's all right, that's your affair. But what's rotten is you lied to *us*. You prated away year in, year out about how virtue will be recognized and good will prevail. When all that counts is power and who wields it. You knew how it was. So you moved in on my girl—my girl, yes!—the same way. Don't stand there and try to tell me anything different because I know better! I've found out what the real score is. What do I care about the shit you've piled up around yourself? I only care what's happened right here, right now . . ."

"Then what can I say that you will listen to?" Blackburn demanded. "What is it you want?"

"Just one thing: clear the hell out! Split! That's all," the boy answered tightly, and his eyes filled. "Why did you have to do this—this one thing, to me? of all the big, brave, earth-shattering things you could do? *Why—?*"

Because of all the years I didn't. Blackburn almost said it aloud—he bit it off at the last instant. It was the truth—a kind of terrible final truth, he knew—but there was no sense in giving it voice, it wouldn't mean anything to this desperate, raging young man. He could run on ad nauseam about his dreams of service and accomplishment, what had and had not happened to him over the gray wash of years—that subtle deflection of purpose, the slow defeat of dreams, and what this swift green love had come to mean to him, what he still wanted to stand for, really stand for— but all Land would see was that he had made the choice long ago, when he had snatched at that first chance for power . . .

He ran his hand through his hair, staring at the photograph of the terrified Vietnamese woman trying to ford the river; staring at nothing. No, it was not the world he had told his children about, not exactly . . . but wasn't it better, kinder to expect a world of generosity, a space for hope—yes, a nobler way people *could* act at their best? Had that been wrong of him? Had he failed to prepare his children for the jungle of avarice and brutality and thus incurred their final contempt? Maybe he had . . .

"Ego." His son's voice was lower now, implacable, a bit heavy. "Boy, you've got enough of it to fill the Grand Canyon . . . What *you* want, what gives *you* thrills and chills—everyone else can go to hell in a leaky bucket. Can't bear for anyone else to have anything, can you? No, because that might pluck a dowel from your plume—Christ, you're hopeless!" He raised his hands suddenly, and Blackburn braced himself; but Land dropped his arms again and shook his head in slow, raging wonder from side to side. "But there's more to it, too, of course. Isn't there? You think I'm some kind of submoron that I haven't got *this* figured out? I've done my classical homework. Oh, sure. Else what's a Hahhhvahd education for? Maybe it even put some frosting on the cake . . ."

The boy's face was held in that steady, malignant smile. His son, his flesh and blood, his body's spawning. There he sat: slender, uncommonly handsome, savage in his defiance—and Jillie hanging like some rare and delicate pendant between them, between their estranged generations . . . But this other thing. Yes, it was there, he could not deny it—the stealthiest, side-slipping shadow, the thick, slow beat of his heart; deeper than dream, farther-flung than fantasy. He was conscious of a sudden sharp pressure in his viscera, his loins, which scattered his thoughts like a burst bag of steel pellets. *Roots,* the image pressed him, what works deep in the earth controls the forms we see and glorify; and then, *the broken wall, the burning roof and tower, and Agamemnon dead.*

"Love," Jillie had said one lazy afternoon, her lips caught in a slow, languid smile, "love isn't your deep blue sea—love's an underground river nobody's ever charted . . ." For an instant, staring wildly at his son, he wanted to flee the house—then was swept with wrath, headlong and prideful, as focused as his anger at Tremayne two days before. Clasping his hands he interlocked his fingers, twisting them remorselessly, burdened now with an almost insupportable need to strike the boy, to silence him. But to say he actually wanted to—no, he would not think of that, he would not. Why couldn't he get himself in hand? He was like an unhelmed ship careening on bare poles through the blackest wilderness of gales—he no longer knew what he thought, or where it might lead, or why.

"—I can't help myself!" he burst out all at once. "Can't you see that? I can't *do* anything else . . ."

Leland's face contorted in the most furious disdain. "Bullshit. Everybody can help *everything* he does—you told me that yourself once. Or doesn't it apply now?—like anything else that proves inconvenient . . . But Jesus, what a boot for you, eh? I mean talk about *elementals*—the sheer satisfaction of getting right down to hardpan, matching cocks with sonny-boy—"

Blackburn snapped: "There's no need to say things like that!"

"No?" The boy laughed harshly again: the vein in his throat stood out like a rich blue cord. "Why not? It's *there*—are you going to deny it? You're not my father, she's not my girl? What a glorious way to cut sonny-boy down to size!"

"Land, I've never—"

"What do you care about a little university secretary half your age? You've got the whole motherfucking *world* to play with, as it stands! Isn't that enough for you? Even you?"

They had been father and son for nineteen years. They had watched divers rise glistening and golden from the sea off Nyaga Shima, they had ridden on camels through the narrow rose walls of Petra, they had lain snug in their sleeping bags on Gay Head and talked about tidal waves and plankton and why the stars winked, why they looked brighter when you didn't stare at them directly . . .

"Look, Dad . . ." Leland was bent forward over his knees, his face oddly strained. "Look—I want you to pull out. I'm asking you. This is very important to me. Really very important. You understand?"

Blackburn shook his shoulders loose and bowed his head. He wished with all his heart he could simply nod once and walk through that scratched and overpainted door—and he could not. He would rather cut off his right hand at the wrist. How curious for him—for good, steady Paul Blackburn, public servant—to have come to this! The essential tragedy of life, he thought with confused urgency, is that the hardest choices come upon us at the wrong times.

Slowly, with infinite reluctance he shook his head. "I'm sorry, Land," he said. "I can't give her up."

There was another strained silence. Then Land said flatly: "I misjudged you."

"I'm sorry for that."

"All right. If that's how you want it. I've got this to· say: just don't be sur—"

The door swung open. Jillie, her hip thrust against a bulging paper bag, poised against the thick afternoon light. Her eyes moved to Blackburn, to Land, back to Blackburn again. There was nothing but silence. Watching Jillie and the boy, their vulnerable—but oh, their radiant— youth, Blackburn felt his heart pounding; despite the past weeks, despite everything, he had not realized what pure anguish he could feel at such a moment. Then Jillie, looking full at him, said: "I told you so," in a dull, troubled voice; and his heart leaped in immense exultation and relief.

Leland had sprung to his feet. "Isn't that touching!" he cried. "Isn't that just too touching . . . *What* did you tell him?"

"Land, there's no—"

"No—let's do it right—just like a real zazzy sophisticated Noel Coward production: 'Harry, darling, the magic was never really there, we were caught up in an insupportable dream' . . . Hey, you're really moving up now, aren't you, baby? Eager-beaver college boys won't do. Too *ineffectual,* right? And the act is the symbol. Hey, isn't it, though!"

"That's enough, Land," Blackburn said.

"This doesn't concern you," Leland retorted, "—just stay out of this one." But his voice lacked purpose now. With Jillie there in the room, Blackburn saw, the naked force of their personal struggle had vanished— all their antagonism was refracted through her presence as through a huge and uncertain lens. Jillie herself was silent; she had set the groceries down in a chair and now, dogged and wan, watched the boy as he lashed out at her.

"I'm sorry, Land," she said lamely. "I tried to . . . Well: I *am* sorry."

"And what can you say, dear, after you've said you're sorry?" He moved with alacrity toward the door, turned and looked at her again. "Well, that kind of affects the old operational planning, wouldn't you say? I'll pass the word along." His eyes swung with quick malice to his father. "You're always running off at the mouth about consequences. Awareness of consequences marks the responsible man, remember?—Oh my, but you've been eloquent about that! All right, now there are going to be plenty of consequences. Plenty!" He nodded rapidly, his mouth hard. "Just look out for yourself, that's all. Look out . . ."

He drew the door smartly closed behind him, his feet thumped on the steps. Then there was silence.

Jillie let herself down on the couch and said: "Want a drink?" Blackburn shook his head. "Well, I do. How'd he get in, for God's sake?"

"I let him in. By mistake. I thought it was you coming back."

"Lovely. Well, that sort of flips it right in the fan, doesn't it?" For a moment she watched him very levelly, her jade eyes wide. "There's something else," she declared. "Isn't there? Please tell me. I have the right to know."

He sighed, and rubbed his neck. "He found out from Eleanor," he said with reluctance. "That's why he came by. I guess. I don't know how she found out."

"Oh, my." Her hands were jammed into a curiously prayerful pose between her thighs. "Oh my oh my . . . What are you going to do?"

"I don't know. I'm not sure there's anything to do.—What did he mean—now there are going to be plenty of consequences?"

She shrugged impatiently. "How should I know? He says a lot of wild things."

"He's so violent! That headlong fury. I worry sometimes he'll—" He broke off, remembering Judge Seaver in his study that long-ago summer afternoon, thinking then of Land the night of the Diplomacy game— the friction-taped baseball rumbling toward him along the floor, the taut leap of panic, and Land's gaze in the lamplight furious, importunate, rapt . . . Buttoning his shirt absently Blackburn eyed his girl. "He told me he's going to marry you."

Her eyes flashed up at him. *"Marry—!"*

"That's what he said."

"Oh, that's from the last time I saw him. When I broke it off, the way you wanted. We had a good row over it. He gets obsessed with the idea every once in a while. He thinks it'll solve something."

—Ah, but it would, Blackburn thought with a small fierce pang. Actions solve dilemmas; sometimes. Actions are irreparable. He found himself glancing tensely around the room. He was always astonished at its lack of personal mementoes. His own home was littered with souvenirs of travel, tokens of discovery, gifts exchanged—jade animals, exotic daggers, coral blooms; here in this welter of disheveled periodicals and old letters and stained coffee cups there was nothing he could see except a pebble from the beach at Tashawena, black as jet, girdled with one slender band . . .

"I've hurt the boy," he said suddenly. "Hurt him badly."

She made a sharp, impatient gesture. "Somebody always gets hurt. What did you expect?"

It's not *your* son, he started to say—bit it off; it was hardly an answer. Knowing the world knew about them now had swept him with a loose, prideful elation. Why didn't she feel any of this? *Diplomats, women and crabs.* Charming, cultivated, aristocratic John Hay, Teddy Roosevelt's "fine figurehead," who had married money and position and insured his career—

"It's funny," he went on, musing, aloud; he felt constrained to talk, examine this new rush of contradictory emotions. "I ought to be torn in two with guilt. And yet I don't feel anything like that. I'm sorry I've hurt him, God knows I am; but this is *mine.* Even Land can't change that . . ." He picked up the pebble, set it down again. "He said it was all Greek: the classic antagonism. He put it a touch more graphically."

"Well, isn't it?"

"I suppose so. Somehow I think it's simpler than that . . . Jill, it's the first time in my life I've done something *I* wanted to do. Yes, wanted. Weird, isn't it? Mother and School and the Army and Foreign Service and the University and the Department. That slow parade. I wanted respect, and I earned it. But it wasn't *me*—what *I* wanted, with all my heart and soul and guts. Do you see what I mean? I'd given up hope of love. I can see that now. I didn't think I rated it, somehow."

"Everybody rates it." But her voice was toneless and heavy. The balance of things had shifted again: what had brought him relief and a kind of wanton pride had turned her resentful and sullen. Something had shifted under his feet. She was moving away from him, slipping off into herself somewhere, and momentarily it shook him—he wanted to strike down all barriers between them, surge around her like a full-course tide, enfold her utterly.

". . . I want to tell you how I feel," he said with lame insistence. Abruptly he remembered a shuffleboard game on the old *Excalibur,* going out to Damascus. A boisterous easterly gale: everyone, even Eleanor, had been sick, and by the fourth day only he and two other men were still on their feet—an Australian rancher named Connell and a diamond merchant from Brussels. They'd drunk beer and shouted at each other; spray had soaked them, the scarred wooden discs had curved eerily with the mountainous roll of the ship. You never had the slightest idea where your shots would wind up . . .

"Poor Paul," she was saying softly, watching him. "Descending from the marble halls to these dreary digs. Peeling paint and a leaky john."

"You're here," he answered.

"And it's booby-trapped, every inch of it. For the first unwary step. Danger, high tension . . . Life is so messy, isn't it? This kind of life."

"Life is immense—it's glorious. Don't say that."

"Did you really want this? If you'd known what you were letting yourself in for that night down in—"

"Jillie, stop it!"

He went toward her automatically. Every now and then she would fall into this bleak, deprecatory pattern, a mood he saw as morbid and unprofitable; but this afternoon her expression was so comfortless he felt obscurely alarmed. Was it so fragile, so hopeless a love as all that? It couldn't be, he *knew* it couldn't be . . .

"What we have is everything," he murmured. And now, putting his two hands on each side of her lovely face, he heard it clearly, several blocks away—the shivering, reedy call of a barrel organ.

> *Together we*
> *Could have found a love*
> > *true as Xanadu, or Cathay . . .*
> *Did you need to be free?*
> *Why did you turn away?*

"A hurdy-gurdy!" he exclaimed. "I didn't know there were any still around."

"He's a fat little old guy with a leather vest and a bandanna handkerchief tied around his neck. Another anachronism."

"You're no anachronism—you're my girl for all seasons. My emerald love . . . Jillie." He felt nothing for her but an overwhelming tenderness; he wanted to lay at her feet all the glories of East and West, sapphires and silks and floating gardens. But her body when he embraced her was tense for the first time.

"You do love me, don't you?" he heard himself say. The need to hear her say the words was a clamor deep in his veins.

"Yes, I love you—oh my God, yes." With her head back and her eyes closed she looked fragile, childlike, utterly defenseless. Holding her lightly, protectively Blackburn thought of her here in this room, weeping, that first afternoon, with the rain drumming in the downspouts.

"There's too much to fight off, Paul. There's just too much standing in the way. Don't you see that?"

"No. No, I don't see any such thing . . ."

It was true. She had brought him life, like apples gathered in her skirt, as she'd once said; as simply and purely as that. They'd stripped the scales from each other's hearts. Most people didn't live: they did time, like drugged prisoners with the illusion but not the reality of freedom. What could stand in the way of their swaying golden net, their five-pointed star? He was speaking rapidly now, summoning all his eloquence, the softest blandishments and still she hung in his arms inert, despondent, waiting. Waiting for what? For him to set her free? But that wasn't possible—they'd gone too far for that, they'd found too wild a glory, too green . . .

> Still I can't find the key—
> Where did we go astray?

"What does it matter what they think?" he concluded. "Whether they know or not? any of them? Look, all my happiness—all my effectiveness in this world comes from us, right here, together. What we are."

"All the more reason, then," she murmured.

"All the more reason *what?* What are you saying?"

"Look, Paul—I bring people trouble. Cause trouble."

"You've brought me every soaring thing a woman can bring a man . . ."

"It's always been this way. I can't seem to help it. Even with Smitty I should have kept—"

"Jillie, this is superstitious and absurd. You're taking some coincidences, some bad luck—"

"No. It's true. Trouble follows me like an ugly old dog."

"And so you'd just—let us go?" he cried, exasperated. "Is that what you want? Just let it all slide away?"

"It isn't what I want. You know that. It's what'll happen."

Her voice—resigned, implacable—filled him with panic. This was unthinkable, it could not be. It simply could not be. "Jillie, I need you, I need you beyond anything else in this world—you *know* that, why are you talking this way? It's just morbid, and—and childish . . ."

"Maybe so. Maybe you're right. Only see, it's coming all apart anyhow."

"It's *not coming apart—!*"

"If your wife knows, it's just a matter of time. All the knives will be out soon. Do you think she's going to keep it to herself? Or whoever it was told *her?*"

He locked his fingers together, staring at them. "They know anyway."

"They? Who? Who knows?"

"Jim Torgerson's people. FBI. The Internal Security crowd. Shelly hit me with it the other night. I told him to go take a flying leap."

"The FBI . . . Look, Paul," her voice was shaking, "—it can't keep going along like this! It'll destroy you . . ."

"No," he said stubbornly. "It won't. Only your not loving me would destroy me now."

She whirled away from him with that swift, flowing Brancusi movement he loved. "You don't know what you're saying! Jesus Christ, you're Secretary of *State* . . ."

"All right then, they can take me as I am. With you, your lover—yes! That's how it'll be."

"Oh, don't be such an idiot! We're not FDR and Lucy Mercer. Do you think Brickley will keep it to himself if he finds out? You're caught in webs within webs. You've got to go back down there tonight and start shifting the gears again—"

He cried softly: "Yes, and for years I did *everything* they wanted. Sat up till all hours reading, drafting reports—always there, on call, ready to drop everything for some God damned overinflated crisis in Pongo-Bongo. Steady, dutiful old Blackburn. The same, my lord, and thy poor servant ever. All right! Now *I'm* going to walk toward the summer, for a change. Seek out my own enviable isles . . ."

"Dear Paul." She came up to him then, her body curved to his like a spanned bow; her fingers traced a corner of his mouth. "My sleek brown seal. Dear Paul. My A & P delivery boy from San Francisco who loves to mend things, put them back together again. If they'll let him. If they haven't got it splashed all over the front page by tomorrow morning . . ." She shivered, a quick involuntary spasm. "I'm afraid," she said with a kind of derisive wonder. "Funny. Me, afraid. Before, I didn't care—what I did, what happened. Now I'm in a great blue panic, all the time. You pay, don't you? For everything. Loving you brought me all alive again—but it turned me afraid again, too." As if reciting a lesson she pronounced: "For every pleasure there is a counterbalancing pain. How funny you never see that."

"—It doesn't matter," he broke in on her urgently. "It's what we hold here between us that matters. Life is what you take hold of and make your own—the clay you fashion . . ."

She shook her head, with the saddest smile he'd ever seen. "I know you think that, darling. But you're wrong. Life is the cards you're dealt: the shapes people make of *your* clay."

"I'll never believe that—never, never believe that," he answered. But holding her desperately, his face buried deep in her hair, hearing the wind-roar of the early evening traffic, the barely audible thread of melody from the hurdy-gurdy, he was afraid that she was right.

SIXTEEN

"BODAWYIN'S primary concern was, as you would imagine, the temper of the American response," Adrian Pommeroy went on. He held a small sheaf of notes firmly in one hand but he hadn't once looked at them—he hadn't been known to consult his notes in forty-five years—and his eyes darted around the long table before fastening on the President, who sat hunched forward on his elbows, frowning, his eyes snapping behind their steel-rimmed glasses. "His feeling—and he was most emphatic about this—was that events have proceeded too far for any reasonable accommodation, especially in view of Naungapaya's unqualified support of these shocking Chinese charges. I was present at the cabinet meeting where it was decided—unanimously—to place Burma on a war footing."

"You mean they're actually contemplating going it alone, Adrian?" the President asked.

"Faute de mieux, Mr. President. Of course they will let their ultimate actions be guided by whatever course we pursue. But Bodawyin quite naturally sees his present dilemma as clearly intolerable—the direct result of our endorsement of Naungapaya." His gaze came to rest on Blackburn. "In a very palpable sense, the chickens have already come home to roost."

"The Greater Asian Treaty Organization endorsed Prince Naungapaya as head of the new state of Dhotal," Blackburn said quietly.

"Of course, I was forgetting." Inclining his head one notch Pommeroy smiled. "Forgive me, Paul. They *did* decide to go along with us at that, didn't they?" The smile vanished. "What this means to Bodawyin—and therefore to the Burmese people—is another divided nation. Still another Korea, Germany, Vietnam. And the inauguration of a policy of subversion they are ill-equipped to counter in the long run. They are under no illusions about Naungapaya's intentions, particularly the fact that he is Peking's fair-haired boy. And now, with this preposterous move by the Chinese to try to expel us from the Security Council, they are fearful that any submissive posture on our part will usher in a new period of Chinese aggression."

Blackburn made no reply. Pommeroy, after one last significant glance, looked away and went on urbanely with his report. Erect, slender in his elegant gray-and-white cord jacket, with his clipped cavalry mustache and full silver hair, he looked the perfect prep school master: indulgent, mettlesome, tradition-obsessed—until one noticed the firm, perfectly chiseled lips, the flash of steel in his fine blue eyes. He was seventy-seven and he looked barely sixty-five—the salubrious favors of an illustrious career had kept him young, as he himself liked to say. It *had* been illustrious. He had been credited with holding Turkey neutral singlehanded in the dark days of '42, and later with helping to choke off the flow of tungsten to a desperate Third Reich; but his finest hour had been at Potsdam as the brilliant Under Secretary who had held everything together for a nervous new President and a choleric, inept Secretary of State—outlasting the French, out-patronizing the British, outinsulting the Russians: a trim, forceful personi-fication of those years of thunder, when there truly seemed to be nothing the Arsenal of Democracy could not do.

His versatility was immense, and it was matched by his confidence. He had served in a bewildering variety of roles for successive presidents— special consultant, unofficial adviser, minister without portfolio, emissary extraordinaire. He was famous for his pipe-stem tweeds, his cufflinks, his Rob Roy cocktails, his inveterate Anglophilia. Because of a certain gaunt arrogance, a fastidiousness and insistence on protocol they called him the Sacred Ibis—but with affection. He was a legend, from his Locke's Homburg to his Peel boots: urbane, witty, aggressive, the only American diplomat invested with real glamour. "They simply can't do without me," he would say with his quick, mischievous smile. "I know where all the bodies are buried!"

Now here he was again, just back from a flying trip to Burma and the Triangle (the President, with one of his impetuous hunches, had dis-patched him as Ambassador-at-Large over the combined opposition of Vosz and Blackburn), looking—maddeningly—even more fit than when he had departed, formulating his phrases with the old precision, staring the room into absorbed attention.

"—not simply the governing classes but the populace as a whole is deeply aroused. U Lapsut told me in confidence he has received solemn guarantees from both Thailand and Khotiane in the event of any aggressive action from Peking. Not to mention Taipei, who as I've said has made the handsome offer of sixteen divisions . . ."

Blackburn bowed his head and suppressed a long sigh. It was easy enough to imagine what the mission had been like: the helicopter flights and jeep rides, the reviews and briefings, inevitably accompanied by Bodaw-yin and Simmons and their military advisers; leading him surely and gra-ciously to what they wanted him to see—no, worse, what he himself wanted to see: a vigorous, model East Asian democracy, valiantly main-taining its integrity in the shadow of the Yellow Hordes . . .

Foxy old fossil. Jillie, fist on her lip, an eerily bent spatula in her hand, something behind her sizzling and popping. *Hanging onto the big clock— both hands. Why doesn't he read the papers? At least take a stroll down to the corner espresso once in a while, tune in on us peons?*

"I'm really indebted to you, Adrian," the President was saying. "We all are, I know." Taking off his glasses he shook out a large white handkerchief and began to rub the lenses vigorously between thumb and forefinger. "On the basis of your trip, what conclusions did you draw?"

Pommeroy placed one hand over his wrist and traced a line of his notes with the seal ring on his little finger. "The situation is distinctly analogous to Berlin in the summer of Sixty-One. The Communists are obviously probing, seeking to test our will to resist. Even the Thais are convinced these nerve gas charges by Peking are no more than a pretext for deeper designs. It's quite evident that our position—both as guarantor of GATO and guiding force in Southeast Asia itself—is hanging seriously in the balance. Especially after the lamentable concessions made to Peking at New Delhi. If it should appear that we are unwilling to secure the proper safeguards for our own citizens—"

"I think it ought to be remembered that Peking also made extensive concessions at New Delhi, Mr. Ambassador," Blackburn broke in. Somehow he had never been able to call his old superior by his first name; and Pommeroy's manner had never encouraged it.

"Oh yes—they can be free enough with *promises* when nothing definitive is at stake."

"There's a great deal at stake here, I'd say."

"Indeed there is." The Ibis' steely gaze riveted on him again. "And the question at issue is whether or not we are going to take a firm stand, serve as a rallying point for the little people out there . . ."

Blackburn smiled. "I thought they were all little people out there. Or does alignment magically alter a man's stature?"

Someone down the table snorted—it sounded like Ernie Hazbrouck. Pommeroy said: "You know perfectly well what I mean," and looked away irritably. "I hardly feel this is an occasion for levity, Paul."

"I was genuinely interested in your distinction. I think it has a definite bearing on our decision."

The Ambassador-at-Large sat still more erectly and said, "I doubt if anyone, whatever his motives, can impugn the nature of my service to this country or my attitude toward any other—least of all a relative newcomer to the field of diplomacy."

"That's telling him, Adrian," Donlund said, and laughed.

Blackburn suppressed a smile this time. Not a thing had changed between them since the afternoon Pommeroy, once again Under Secretary, had come in to him at Far East desk and told him about the Administration's decision to send the 1st Marine Division to Danang.

"Isn't it a bit impetuous?" he'd said. "I mean, in the light of this new peace feeler from Hanoi . . . Do we really have all the information, for a step like this?"

"The decison has been made, Paul. That is the line of policy."

"It seems—awfully irrevocable. Has everyone really thought where this could take us?"

The Ibis' eyes had widened, the drawn cheeks had flexed above the pointed cavalryman's mustache. "You don't seem to understand, Blackburn. You're not here to think. Your duty is to *implement what has been decided.*"

"Yes, Mr. Secretary." And he had implemented—until, sickened at the willful stupidities and the lies and the losses, he had resigned and gone back to Cambridge.

Now time had reversed their roles, if not their attitudes. Under the cold rebuke, Blackburn knew, lay the long resentment, the patterns of politics and faction and machination that had led straight to this present moment: here sat this 47-year-old renegrade schoolman in the one post above all others Adrian Pommeroy had wanted with all his heart—and never got. He had been "in line" for it on several occasions, of course. He might have had it if Stevenson had won in '52; it was said Lovett had blocked his chances in '60; Kennedy had been thinking of him seriously as Rusk's replacement in '64—but then had come Dallas; his Establishment hauteur had not been congenial to Johnson, who in any event appreciated Rusk's feline deference; and the current President (Vosz had told Blackburn once) felt Pommeroy was too testy and authoritarian for the job. That provided the final deferment; even the Ibis must have known. Only a miracle—or an unparalleled catastrophe—would ever give it to him now.

Blackburn let his breath out slowly, listening to the Ambassador-at-Large's answer to a query of Fred Semmes. Maybe he should have had it, maybe he deserved it more than any of the rest of them; but now, at this third meeting of the Executive Committee in two days—though it was the first one the President had attended—irritable with lack of sleep, worn down by the visceral scene with Land and the abortive quarrel with Jillie, harassed by the mounting avalanche of Department problems and an ominous sense of how the Executive winds were blowing, he thought sharply, The hell with him, he's had his day, and his day is as dead as the Pax Romana; this is not Berlin, or Cuba, or—most emphatically—South Vietnam. Which was at the root of it, too. Pommeroy had, Blackburn knew, thoroughly disapproved of that letter to State from Khotiane: the young consul had been soft on communism—and worst of all, he had survived the charge that had crushed so many others . . .

The whole thing's racial, anyway. You can't help it, you're all pumped full of that old Kipling formaldehyde. Do you think for one swift minute we'd ever have dropped the bomb on Germany? Oh sure, Hitler was a a bastard, check, but he was our kind of bastard, you know? Nice and white-like-me—a member of the club . . .

"Reiny," the President was saying now with a trace of impatience, "lay out the options for us, will you?"

Vosz gave a short, violent bark of a cough, tilted his cropped head at an alarming angle and said without preamble:

"Option One: We negotiate with the Chinese through the intercession of a third power for release of the Mission. India and Thailand have both approached our embassies. Advantages: We avoid direct confrontation with Peking, gain time for mobilization of public opinion. Disadvantages: One: The action will strike GATO nations as suppliant in view of Chinese intransigence. Two: We lack an adequate bargaining lever in such negotiations . . ."

It was a typical Vosz performance, delivered with dry precision. Blackburn idly watched Joe Carter and Reiny's man Wentzel down at the far end of the table, hurriedly writing it all down, taking the minutes. We could submit to United Nations arbitration. This would afford the opportunity for the introduction of UN inspection teams, thus peeling open the Chinese lockout; but there was the possibility that world opinion might favor the Chinese—and there was the grave danger that Peking would act before the UN could air the problem and make any dispositions. We could submit a further protest to Peking, we could issue a flat ultimatum for return of the Mission under threat of (a) quarantine of the China coast, (b) surgical strikes on the interior, (c) overt declaration of war. We could launch a surprise attack on China, either air strikes or full-scale amphibious assault and invasion—

All the things we could do: which were not so many, really, and there were getting to be fewer every day. Time and pressure closed off the options, one by one. A typical Vosz presentation. And yet there was something different about it—the aggressive edge of personal zest was missing. Which was strange . . .

"This would invite a probable Russian entry, with the virtual certainty of global nuclear war."

Yes, that certainly ought to be listed under the disadvantages. The Presidential Adviser stopped as abruptly as he had begun and threw himself back in his chair; his hands were out of sight beneath the wood.

"There's still another possibility, Reiny," Ernie Hazbrouck said gravely from down the table. "A variant on your surgical strikes. That would be a special operation to bring out the Mission." The heads swung toward him. "I'm not recommending it," he said with a wintry smile. "I only want to point out that it does exist as an option."

"An air drop, you mean?" the President said. "Is that feasible, Ernie?"

"It might be brought off."

"How?"

"An air brigade, helicoptered in. Two fighter wings. It would depend on requisite speed and deception."

"Where are they being held, do we know?"

"Kunming, sir," Tremayne answered. "We're quite certain of that."

The President bent forward still farther, hitching up his trousers. "Sounds awfully risky to me," he said. "If we did pull it off it could look as though we were guilty as charged. Springing the desperado before the wheels of justice can turn. You know? And if we didn't pull it off . . ."

The thought hung in the air a moment. No one said anything. The President's gaze, intent, irritated, roved from Blackburn to Vosz to Donlund and back again. "Jesus!" he muttered. "How'd we ever get into this thing so deep, anyway? How did things drift this *far*—*?*" Again he jerked harshly at his trousers—that invariable barometer of his impatience—and stared hard at the map of China tacked to a display frame across the room. But there was no solace in that vast, bulging land with its whites and ochres shading off from the western mountains and desert into the lush green lowlands; it was like trying to embrace a redwood, or measure the sea in bucketsful . . .

"Well, I want a straw vote first, with supporting argument. What are your inclinations, Fred?"

Semmes pushed the neat stack of papers slowly back and forth in front of him, trimming and retrimming them with his soft, square hands. "I'd say Bodawyin is the key issue. I think Adrian put the case very well. If we aren't willing to afford protection to our own citizens—sent out there on an errand of mercy, for God's sake—what trust can the GATO powers put in our word? I'd have to say I'd favor an ultimatum of some sort. We've got too much at stake there to back down now. Without our taking a firm line, the régime will certainly collapse. Five of the rubber plantations have stopped production, the teak industry is faltering, the Competrin people tell me they can't sustain operations for two more weeks." He looked at the President mildly. "I'm happy to say the projected loan wouldn't entail going over to the Hill—it would be mainly a matter of surplus arms, which would only have the effect of reducing costs in my section."

The President nodded. Blackburn could see his mind ticking it off: Good for the budget, it would go over well with Congress, it would even tidy up some of that leftover hardware lying around. Well, that was to be expected.

"Shelly?" the President said. "Your views?"

Tremayne ran a pencil up and down over his handsome, pointed chin. "In terms of a firm line, nearly all our reports are encouraging. Unrest in both Yunnan and the Chuang Autonomous Region are high, the anticipated plebiscite was almost certain to favor independence. The

Chinese army is in the midst of an arduous reorganization. Our sources out of Nam Lieu and Hong Kong tell us that Peking has already set a target date for the trial and execution of our Mission. I think we ought to hit hard and hit fast and get them out of there."

"You're in favor of Ernie's air drop and rescue, then?"

"Yes, sir. I am."

No, I take it all back—it isn't racial, it's just plain sexual. Look— every war ends with a bunch of dry-balled old men sitting round a table and coming to terms, right? That's what they call it, isn't it?—coming to terms. Usually the same old bastards that were sitting around the table at the BEGINNING, flexing their wasted biceps and uttering patriotic grunts. And the only thing that's happened in BETWEEN is that a lot of kids have got their heads blown off. Which of course was just what the old sons of bitches wanted anyway, right?

The President said: "How about you, Reiny?"

Vosz pulled his hand out of his pocket, peered up at the ceiling. "I'm of two minds," he admitted. "In view of the current Indian offer, I would favor mediation—that is, provided Delhi can secure an immediate response from Peking." There were some expressions of mild surprise, and his head swung quickly right and left, although there was no telling where his eyes had journeyed behind the shades. He said carefully: "The problem of world opinion is not to be lightly regarded here."

"World opinion—!" Donlund, facing him, gave vent to his rich, easy chuckle. "I thought world opinion was the Shangri-La of timid souls, Reiny."

Vosz did not smile. "There are occasions on which it exerts a certain force. In the Third Middle East Crisis, you will recall, Hassan Dagh's decision to withdraw from—"

"Okay, okay—spare us the doctoral essay. We've got the message."

"I was only making an analogy. Nothing more."

The President went on with his private poll-taking. Ernie Hazbrouck was of course for an ultimatum; Walt Maitland, the soft-spoken Attorney General, favored direct negotiations through France's good offices; young Jim Roper, the President's Special Counsel, had fallen for the air drop scheme; Miles Stout, without once looking at Blackburn, launched on a series of hyperqualified negatives which seemed to advocate a quarantine of the China coast. Down by a six-to-two score, now. Yet Blackburn found himself staring at Vosz. The Squeezer's manner, even at such crises, was invariably a garrulous pitch bordering on raillery—now it had vanished. He sounded uncertain, off-balance. He knew Vosz often took a position opposed to the President's view for what he called dialectical purposes, to be sure his chief had considered all the options or until he saw his views had crystallized. But this was different. What was the matter? Well: support—

of a sort—and from a most unexpected quarter. He'd take it anywhere he could get it. Six to two. Jesus. The President's face was impassive, but he had hitched at his trouser legs again.

You know what you're all like, Paul? The typical regional committee-woman. You know what I mean. She's run her husband right into the ground, she's lost control of all five kids, the house is a wreck even with a live-in maid, she drinks like a fish half the day, her sex life is an Arctic horror—and she's just dogged and determined to do good *all over the place. No matter how many more lives she ruins.*

The President said: "Bill?"

Donlund sat perfectly immobile, massive, staring at the great flat brass ashtray in front of him, while the room grew quieter. Deep in the knuckles of his big hand a cigarette smoldered. "It seems to me we've fallen into a curiously rigid posture over the past several years," he said after a moment. "It was well meant, its origins were understandable enough. But it has left us without any real freedom of range."

He looked up then, and his steady, wise, faintly bemused gaze moved around the room. "I don't know whether any of you have noticed, but there's a significant reaction to these options of Reiny's. Everybody's look-ing at them like some kid watching the family doctor taking all those shiny instruments out of his little black bag. It seems to me we ought to think more in terms of what we might gain than what we stand to lose. We're blessed with remarkable assets here, when you add them up: Bodawyin's determination to resist Chinese pressure, the current Sino-Soviet hassle near Ulan Bator, Taipei's offer of sixteen divisions reinforced, the Japanese disaffection over Peking's trade restrictions, India's apprehensions about Kashmir . . . If Peking is determined to make of this relatively trifling incident a massive, all-out showdown, why should we go around with our hearts in our mouths? Let's hand them a twenty-four-hour ultimatum, throw it right back in their laps. And if push comes to shove, when would another occasion as favorable as this one arise? Their nuclear capability is still rudi—"

"Bill, you're not serious!—" He hadn't meant to say it out loud—he was scarcely aware that he had. Donlund's great brick-red face, the staring sapphire eyes swung toward him.

"You bet your nervous life I am."

"But—you were *for* the Mission, you suggested it . . ."

"Exactly. And for just that reason, if for nothing else." The Vice President's face all at once took on an indefinable, forbidding aspect, rock-hard. "How much do we swallow?" he asked the Council. "All you shrewd historians—what would have happened if JFK hadn't drawn the chalk in Cuba? Where would we be now?" He raised the cigarette to his lips and its end flared fiercely, subsided. "Is it the risks that are troubling you? All right, let's consider the risks a couple weeks from now, when our own Mission has been executed to a man, and all those millions of faces from Karachi to Manila begin looking the other way . . ."

Blackburn started to say something else, and stopped. It was impossible. Not Bill Donlund, the Great Conciliator, his resourceful mainstay all these months; not Bill who, when the debate with al-Zobeir was getting out of hand, had actually feigned an attack of acute indigestion to interrupt the meeting before too many harsh words had—

"Paul?"

The President—that bright, inquiring glance, touched with impatience. Last, but—let us hope—not least. He took a deep, even breath and said: "I am solidly opposed to any and all of the 'firm' lines proposed—in fact I'm astonished beyond measure that so many of you favor them, given the circumstances."

Smiles, embarrassment, disgust. Ernie Hazbrouck gave a mirthless grunt, Fred Semmes frowned at his notes, Shelly indifferently inspected his nails. Adrian Pommeroy offered the Council his quick, mischievous smile and said, "Well, gentlemen, it looks like another long afternoon."

"No, it doesn't," the President answered sharply. "We've already given this damned situation time enough—we're going to settle it and we're going to settle it quickly."

"Forgive me if I seem unduly obtuse," Blackburn spoke into the pause, "but in terms of long-range policy I fail to see the value of all this martial fervor."

"This isn't a long-range situation," Tremayne retorted. "We're confronted with a crisis which requires immediate action."

"And therefore it's to be divorced from all patterns of foreign policy in the Far East?" He looked slowly and stubbornly around the long table. "Are we serious about this—really serious? Haven't we learned *anything?* Are Vietnam and the Yalu and Cambodia some kind of dream world— unfortunate adventures that never happened at all? How the Christ many times do we have to play this lousy record—!" His voice was unsteady, it was pitched too high, his instinct told him that; but he couldn't help it. Consternation gripped his belly, warring with disgust. Donlund's sudden defection, the realization that an overwhelming majority of the Council were for various aspects of a hard line, that not a single one of them had advocated UN mediation, enraged him. "What are we doing—are we actually sitting here in this room and planning an invasion of the Asian land mass . . . ?"

"They're not going to go to war over this," Pommeroy told him. "This is just another one of their little trials of strength-and-virtue. If you'd had some field experience in China you'd know that. When they see we mean business they'll back down, never fear."

"Really?" he retorted, stung by the note of condescension. "Really, now? Where did you get that fine, celestial assurance—from the head-master of Groton?"

Pommeroy's head came up, he half rose from his seat. "Now you look here, Blackburn! I'm not going to take that kind of talk from you or anybody else. I'll tell you how I got that assurance—I got it from forty-seven years' service in the field of American diplomacy, when US policy had some muscle behind it . . ."

"Yes, it was so muscular it cost us eighty-five thousand dead—*dead* —in two Asian wars, and just about all the respect and confidence of the rest of the world—"

"Gentlemen, gentlemen!" the President broke in tartly. "Let's drop this—it's getting us exactly nowhere at all . . ." His eyes behind the square, rimmed lenses were snapping, and two small white crescents had appeared just outside the corners of his mouth. If there was anything he hated, Blackburn knew, it was dissension. Opposed views, yes, forceful, even heated argument—but not downright conflict, not within the team itself, and never of a personal nature. That was not the Detroit way: in Detroit one schooled oneself to a dispassionate appraisal of trends, figures, probabilities, yes, one even now and then entertained a few long-shot possibilities—and then arrived by enthusiastic consensus at the true and proper course. Only here they weren't bringing out a new line of cars . . .

"—I'm sorry," Pommeroy was saying in tones that clearly denied he was sorry about anything at all, "genuinely sorry, Mr. President, but I cannot function in an atmosphere of personal vilification and calumny. Most definitely I did not take on an impromptu, exhausting trip to Burma only to be greeted with derision by an academic theoretician half my age . . ."

"Of course, Adrian, of course," Donlund interrupted soothingly. "A time of tensions and tempers, when the passions rise. You've been through more of those than any of us. Paul didn't mean that silly little remark about Groton. Did you, Paul?"

The Vice President was smiling, but there was that edge in his voice, in his eyes—not malice, not threat, but a kind of nameless, implacable force. Blackburn watched him for a moment, then looked at Pommeroy, who was craning his neck about in his neat, stylish collar, his mustache quivering. The Sacred Ibis: there he sat, still living in the bold, aggressive days of the 50s and 60s when the tide of American power had rolled across the seven seas to Kuwait and Pnompenh, when force had been accepted— nay, welcomed—as an essential part of diplomacy; not a last, desperate measure when everything else had failed. The poor, misguided, dangerous old man: and to think that there had been a day when he, Blackburn, had actually envied him . . .

With immense effort he produced a smile. "Of course," he answered.

"That was a perfectly unwarranted remark on my part—I had no right to make it. I'm sure the headmaster of Groton doesn't even recognize the *existence* of the People's Republic of China."

There were smiles here and there. Pommeroy was still glaring at him. He said quickly, sharply to the room: "But if they don't back down. If they don't. What then? No, I haven't seen service in China, either the Chiang or the Mao versions, but I have come to know the Foreign Minister quite well. I know he was a member of an infantry company that crossed the Yangtze under fire against two divisions of Nationalist troops and held a bridgehead for nearly two days—at the age of sixteen. I know him well enough to know he is not going to be intimidated by muscle-flexing . . . Do you know how many divisions the Japanese had stationed in North China for seven years? I do—so does Ernie. And so does Fred. And that was a worn, weary North China low on weapons and fearful of another one of Chiang's lovely little extermination campaigns . . ."

"There's no need for it to come to that," Tremayne interposed evenly. "No one's said anything about our committing ground forces."

He stared at the CIA chief. "Do you think the GATO countries will support us if we start firing off ultimatums? You're dead wrong if you do. And as for that picture-postcard Taiwan army, it wouldn't last very long— ask Ernie. And what will we do then? What will be left but to go in with both feet? *Are* we contemplating nuclear strikes? You all sound awfully gung ho to me. Has anybody really thought this through, or is it all some kind of John Wayne script?"

"—You know something, Paul?" Donlund said with a curious, slow smile. "You're always against it. Iraq, Uruguay, the Negev, this fisheries hassle . . ." He ticked them off on his blunt, powerful fingers. "You always oppose the use of force. Always. Don't the implications bother you?"

He was invaded with an instant's thick, white fury—struck it down. He would not be provoked; not this way. Not now. There was too much at stake here. "Meaning that I'm a yellow-livered cur?" he answered, smiling. "A pigeon-hearted poltroon?"

"Now, Paul," Donlund murmured, "you know I never used those words."

"Of course you didn't. I did. It's true—when it comes to nuclear nine-pins I'm as chicken as they come . . . Yes: I oppose it. There are very, very few occasions in this world when force can be used to good purpose. Shall we call the roll of the Ambassador's muscular quarter-century? What do we want to prove—that we're more hard-nosed than the heathen Chinee?"

"Paul, it isn't just that, it's a question of *time,*" Semmes broke in tersely. "It's all very well to take a fine moral stand. But *Peking* has forced the issue here, it's not our doing. Even setting aside the safety of the American Mission, if we don't seize the initiative, Bodawyin is almost certain to cave in. He's the only man strong enough to hold it all together."

"The way Diem was, you mean. Or Ky. Or Thieu."

"Stop raking up *history*—if he goes down we'll have a vacuum out there, a flat invitation to the Reds to move in. We've got to move quickly."

There it was. If we don't act now it'll all crash; if we don't move today, now, this minute, it'll all be too late. Cassandra Time Along the Potomac. There was always this sense of crisis, of desperation at these gatherings, it was the atmosphere Washington secretly reveled in: We've got to do this, refuse that, press for the other, we haven't any choice, time is running out, the clock is racing, twenty-seven seconds of playing time remaining . . . They called him dilatory and tender-hearted, the way they had Stevenson, they castigated State for a ponderous, procrastinating, vacillating slug buried in its nineteenth-century cocoon—but were there no virtues in moderation, reflection, purposeful delay until at least one *comprehended* the issues? Didn't they ever stop to wonder what lay out there *beyond* the frenzied act? to ask themselves, if there *was* such desperation, such a need for last-ditch hysteria, whether maybe the policy itself wasn't all wrong, whether maybe we were swimming against another one of those looming, irresistible tides of history? Perhaps if we thought a little more and snatched at eleventh-hour exigencies a bit less we might avoid some of the terrible face-offs, the iron hours like this one .. . .

"Just a minute, Fred," the President was saying. Shoving a stack of memoranda away with his elbow he leaned forward. "On what do you base your objections, Paul?"

"A number of things. Our relations with China over the past three years, my recent interview with Ch'en Pu-tsao." He paused. "I don't think he would make a charge as grave as this without some foundation."

"Are you trying to tell us you've accepted these preposterous accusations against our own Mission?" Pommeroy demanded hotly.

"I didn't say that. I said I think he has some foundation for his charges."

"That's why they've neatly sealed it off from the rest of the civilized world, of course."

"They may have their own reasons for doing what they've done. I still remember Tonkin Gulf—I think we all do. We've shut off United States territory from international scrutiny when it has suited our purposes—surely I don't have to remind you of that."

The President said: "You're convinced they've actually been attacked with this gas or poison or biological weapon or whatever it is?"

"Yes, sir, I am. Or that they *believe* it's an attack."

"On what evidence?"

"It's just—an instinct, a feeling. But I know I can trust it."

A mistake—he knew it the moment he'd said it. The President's face assumed that flat, remote expression Blackburn dreaded. "Well: I'm afraid

we've got to have something a little harder than that. Instinct, feeling—
where are your facts and figures, Paul? Give me something to feed the old
computer. Don't just hand me your dream life in a situation like this . . ."

Blackburn bit his lip. Dream life. But he'd let himself in for this. The
President's thinking ran in the nicely defined channels of those well-
illustrated production charts, flow-sheets, accountability columns from the
city of the golden wheel. They were what he understood, what he'd mastered so early and so well, as the celebrated Boy Wonder of 1942. With
tank production in a hopeless maze of snarls and cross-purposes Washington had sent out a frantic call for him, and he'd gone straight to the airport
from the plant without even bothering to pack a bag. It was characteristic
of him. He'd brought order out of chaos in a matter of weeks, had quad-
rupled production in four months more, and it was said of him in those
days that he could tell you the exact number of armored vehicles we had
on hand at any given moment the world over, right down to the last gyro-
scopic mount and bogie wheel. Everything! He'd flooded France with Sher-
mans and Pershings, and Stimson had personally pinned on him the nation's highest civilian decoration after the Battle of the Bulge.

After that he had gone back to Detroit and breathed new life into two
mighty—and faltering—corporations, had led the fight on bad design, restored the functional compact to favor, and broken the grip of the European car on the American market when all the other manufacturers had
panicked and run. No Harvard Business School had prepared him, no
economics chairs in London or New Haven; he had come up from night
school and the assembly line and he had *proved* himself right, not once but
again and again. The charts and figures had never let him down—and so
of course they wouldn't now.

The only trouble was this wasn't a cost-efficiency problem or a new
plastic model he and his staff were going over piece by piece after hours,
picking it apart. At the root of this problem were human beings, as touchy
and devious and misguided as their minds and hearts could make them. It
was a world of intuition, feeler, conjecture, the single murky choice among
a hundred conflicting intangibles—and what could he tell the Boy Wonder
of Bloomfield Hills in the face of that? The President had to *know*—and
now he didn't, he couldn't because all the game counters had been changed.
There were things on this earth, thank God—yes, thank God!—that
weren't soluble by computer; and the hazardous, grazing course between
nation-states was most certainly one of them . . .

"Unless I'm very much mistaken," the President was saying to him,
"none of the Chinese or Burmese are going to the polls here in November.
It may sound crass to voice the thought, but I've got to reckon with public
opinion. The Naungapaya deal was not entirely popular, as you know.
Brickley and Posla and the conservative press are out for blood. And I
doubt very much if the public will suffer what they interpret as another

piece of passive acquiescence very gladly—especially with American lives at stake. The Mission has got to be extricated or I am going to be in very serious trouble. And because I will be, so will all of you." He paused a moment. "We can't escape the weight of public opinion. Why should we? We have to reckon with it whether we like it or not. All of us."

Blackburn was conscious of a sudden thin visceral tensing, the pressure on a new and different nerve. He knows then, he thought, watching the President's face. Of course. Someone had seen fit to tell him; for the good of the nation, of course. Tremayne's expression was perfectly impassive, but in Pommeroy's eyes there hung an unmistakable malignant gleam. Reiny, he told himself, Reiny's told the Chief—but there was Vosz hunched low in his seat looking diminutive and unhappy. What the hell was going on? There was the pressure, of course—it was always there in one form or another, and now it was congealing steadily, gaining momentum from its own irrefutable logic, thrusting them toward a haste they feared even as they yielded to it.

Yet that wasn't it—there was something else here, something he couldn't define. Something was all wrong . . .

"Look, Paul," the President said suddenly. "Let's try to take hold of this thing once and for all. Now, you're in sharp disagreement with just about everybody around this table—all right, that's your privilege. But all you've done is raise negative reasons: you're against this and that and the other. What are you prepared to do constructively? What are you pushing?"

They were all watching him now: Semmes with two fat fingers hooked inside his wrinkled collar; Tremayne bored, the Ibis exasperated and vengeful, Reiny troubled and sullen, squeezing that damned black rubber grip in a frenzy. The Vice President's face he could not read.

"Yes, I have a plan," he said. "Not precisely one of Reiny's options. A full and formal defense of our position at the Security Council."

"Oh-my-God," Pommeroy burst out, "—Archie Grace will start telling the world about his palmy days in Brussels . . ."

"Archie won't be handling it," Blackburn answered him shortly. "I will go there myself and personally answer Peking's charges, one by one. I'll ask for inspection teams to police and inspect the areas affected, and an international tribunal to examine the evidence and assign responsibility —and culpability—where it exists. I flatter myself I can plead our cause a touch more effectively than Archie Grace."

"What good will all that do?" Donlund demanded. "There simply isn't *time*. You're playing into their hands—by the time you've put all that creaky old machinery in motion Drachenfels and our people in the Mission will be dead and buried. The Chinese want to burn them and that's what they'll do."

"I think not. Ch'en has given me solemn assurances that his govern-

ment would not move against the Mission while the Security Council proceedings were in session."

"The word of a Chinese Communist," the Ibis scoffed.

"That's right. Look, you're all saying they want to push us to the wall
—slaughter the Mission, crush Bodawyin, set up a trial by combat. I say
they don't want any of these things. Look at the evidence. On the eleventh
Ch'en reacted quickly to my invitation; on the fifteenth Peking asked for
an emergency meeting of the SC—the day before the date of the trials was
announced: August thirtieth, five weeks away. Two days ago Chou En-lai
had that very conciliatory interview with Harrison Salisbury; and yesterday
Peking informed me that disciplinary action is being taken against the
officers involved in the seizure of the Pao Shan consulate. Do you think
these actions represent the behavior of a government that wants war? No
—they're the exact opposite, they're the deliberately patterned moves of a
government that wants at all cost to avoid it. If they wanted a face-off, our
humiliation, even war, they would have executed the Mission three weeks
ago and been done with it. And they would *never* have apologized for the
Pao Shan incident, as they in fact did."

He faced the President directly. "What have we to lose by this
course? It keeps most of the options open. If the charges prove to be false,
or ill-taken—as I hope to God they are—we have Reiny's international
support enlisted fully in our favor. If the Chinese block the inspection
teams or persist in their trial-and-execution gambit we can always revert
to sterner measures." He glanced at Tremayne. "And if by some chance
they should be able to substantiate their charges in any way, I think we
ought to know that, too."

"You're not trying to tell us you actually think our Mission could
have been guilty of something like this, do you, Blackburn?" Pommeroy
cried again in astonishment.

"I'd like to keep an open mind, Mr. Ambassador. Stranger things than
that have happened in this decade—some of them even involved Americans. Yes, I'd like to get at the truth," he heard himself say with a vehemence that surprised him. "Your hole card, Bill: I'd like to see it. There's
been entirely too much smog surrounding this whole affair—Naungapaya's
strange intransigence, and Ch'en Pu-tsao's charge. And we've had this
nasty surprise about our engineering wizard Drachenfels. Let's clear the atmosphere, small we? The fact is, our position—our dilemma—is a moral
one: until we can establish before an international tribunal that we had no
part in this vicious operation—if it is that—our position is tainted and the
Chinese attitude must remain hostile. And in my opinion justifiably so . . .
Don't worry," he turned again to Pommeroy, "if the SC airing fails there
will still be the chance to deal out death and destruction in abundance.
War, like the poor, is always with us, gentlemen."

"Not true, of course," the Ibis retorted, "since we will already have yielded leverage with your course of appeasement."

Blackburn forced himself to smile for the last time. "Not quite the word I'd have chosen, Mr. Ambassador."

"I dare say it's not."

"In any event I'll try not to feel maligned by a veteran Cold Warrior twice my age."

To Blackburn's surprise the President gave his abrupt, rather nasal chuckle and said: "You two shake hands and make up, will you? We can't have our two top diplomats at daggers drawn. Who knows?—in another few days you both may have something to *really* fight about."

For a long moment he stared at the great map of China, his hands clasped behind his head, his mouth working. The room was quite still except for Roper, who was also taking down the minutes, writing furiously with an incredibly scratchy pencil. There was nothing more for anyone to say, and everyone suddenly sensed this—all the points had been made, the gages thrown: it all rested in the hands of the man with the square, steel-rimmed glasses and neatly combed straight hair. Blackburn thought, *Thank God and all the stars in heaven I'm not sitting in that chair*—and was astonished at the intensity of his emotion: he had never felt precisely that before.

"All right," the President said all at once, and rocked forward. "We'll try it your way first, Paul. I hope you're in top forensic form—it better be the defense of the century." He smiled, but his glance had turned steely and flat—Blackburn remembered that for all his celebrated affability there were those back in Detroit who still called him "the Ice Man" with dread in their voices. "When do they convene?"

"Thursday afternoon, Mr. President."

"All right. I think this is as far as we can go. Reiny, when's that New York speech of yours set for the Council?"

"Thursday evening, sir."

"Everything at once. As usual. Come on back with me, will you?—there are a few things we've got to hammer out. Good afternoon, gentlemen."

There was a low murmured chorus, and the meeting broke up quickly. Rising, Blackburn encountered the others. Vosz, hurrying out behind the President, threw him a covert look that seemed to embrace both gratification and alarm. Hazbrouck nodded genially, Semmes cocked his head in wry reservation and shrugged. At the door Adrian Pommeroy whirled around, white-faced and irate.

"Don't think for one minute this absurd scheme of yours will solve anything, because it won't!"

"Come on, Adrian," Donlund rumbled, "go to your corner and

breathe deep. You've lost the round." Easing the Ibis through the door he grinned at Blackburn, who nodded unsmiling. He didn't for the life of him know which he felt more keenly, elation or apprehension. What he did feel was tired to death.

Joe Carter was waiting for him in the hall, solemn with worry.

"Hello, Joe," he said. "Waiting to bear the body away?"

"Mr. Secretary . . . I'm afraid I have some news for you. News that's not too good."

Jillie, he thought with a pierce of pure anguish. Something terrible, out of nothing. Jillie. While I've been wrangling with these baboons. "What is it?" he asked quietly.

"It's your mother, sir. She's had a stroke—a severe one. She's seriously ill. Your wife just called."

SEVENTEEN

"ALL RIGHT, ALL RIGHT," Jillie Hoyt said hotly, "—but *murder* . . . !"

The word hung in the air a moment, thick as gas; died away. In this bare, white, underfurnished room of Smitty's with its low black leather hikieis and raffia mats the word had no meaning: it sounded like a dozen others. But the edge of outrage in her voice had reached them. Jumbo Erikson shook his massive shoulders once and sighed through his nose. Bushy Slatin, peering out from his shag rug of hair like a mad fox in a thicket, kept blinking at nothing and grinning nervously. Maury Adelman started to say something and changed it into a dry, thin cough behind his hand. Were they really going to buy it, then—a disastrous, crack-brained scheme like this? Only Land was gazing full at her, his face frozen in that glittering, malignant stare.

"Murder," he retorted, "for Christ sake—murder. It's simple insecticide."

"—I wouldn't joke about this!" she almost shouted.

"Don't con yourself for one cheap second I'm joking!"

"Our group's never been into violence, not from the beginning—let alone shooting people . . ."

"Yes, and look where it's got us. A nice, polite, debating team. You want to write an editorial for the fucking *Crimson?* You think that would cut some kind of ice with Smitty right now?"

"Look, you accepted certain conditions when you joined Sirius. We all did. And the primary one was rejection of armed struggle."

"Then maybe it's time to change the script!" He forced his voice lower, and his eyes narrowed. It was only the second time she'd seen him since the afternoon at her place, with Paul. "Our chief gets busted for ninety-nine years, and so we roll over and play dead. You want to be the laughingstock of every group from here to San Francisco?"

"How do you know what the rest of us want?" she demanded. "The last time we got together about this we had the broadcast confrontation all worked out in detail. And everybody was satisfied with it . . ."

"Well, maybe that just doesn't *apply* any longer, Hoyt. Maybe it's *obsolete*. You know?"

He turned away, bent over the unfolded paper with its careful drawing, and the photos. He had decided to ignore her. He started talking to the others like a salesman pushing some article of dubious value. "All right now, here's the way it plays. The Council is right here, the corner building. These black doors with the lions' heads. Here's Park, running south, where these trees are. Now here, diagonally across Park, is Hunter. And right here—" he drew a quick, angry circle around a window near the south end of the building "—is the room. Third floor. Bushy and I checked it all out. The rec room is on the southwest corner, here. As you go down the corridor there's a kitchen, then a utility room nobody uses after ten in the morning. It's even got a lock on the inside. Here's the angle from the window—what you'll see when they pull up."

"Yeah, but afterward," Maury murmured. "You're up there on the third floor. What happens then?"

Land looked at him. "Then you put the rifle back in the florist's box and slide it behind the set-tubs. Remove your gloves, walk, do not run, to the stairs opposite the elevators. Kids are going up and down the stairs all the time. Descend to the main floor and walk out. The car will be on Sixty-ninth, live-parked at the hydrant here, booted and spurred and ready to ride. What could be simpler?"

"Wouldn't leave much time," Jumbo said, studying the snapshots. "Just that little distance from the curb to the door."

"It's not a track meet, Erikson. They'll be milling around, saying hello and telling each other how wonderful they all are. With those crazy purple glasses and that penguin-head crew cut you can't miss him . . ."

There was another silence. Jumbo sat chewing on the edge of his thumb, Maury kept scowling at the plans and pulling at the neck of his shiny Mao tunic.

"All beautifully figured out," Jillie said with flat scorn. "*Cased* is the word, I think. Just like a neat Italian moom pitcher." The other three looked at her then, startled, a bit resentful, as though she'd just shaken them awake. "Everything all worked out beautifully—except for *why* you've dreamed up such a stupid, crazy-ass deal. Oh, what's the matter with you!" She glared at Land; she had recovered from her initial shock now, she was simply angry. "You want to wind up like the Panthers? You *want* them to hunt down every last one of you and wipe you out—is that it? Destroy yourselves as a revolutionary force in one adventurist, suicidal—"

"That's where you're wrong, Hoyt," Land said, and his face was all at once hard and homely, transformed. "Dead wrong. Your *real* suicide is the sad-sack yo-yo who *doesn't* fight back and gets racked up anyway. You're always screaming about symbolic actions—all right. Here it is. With bells."

"But it isn't symbolic, it's *killing a man!* And to what purpose? You'll only make him a martyr . . ."

"Fine. Martyrs don't wield any power. They made the Kennedys martyrs, King too. And what harm did it do the bastards who starched them? All it meant was that people who might have done certain things couldn't do them. Because they were dead. Don't yak to me about the power of martyrdom. *Men* are what count—living, breathing men with defined aims and the power to realize them. Not some sick, sad memory feeding an eternal flame. That's all a crock of shit."

"But—it'll be the end! Of Sirius. Of all of us!"

"Well . . ." His gaze held hers, black with contempt. "What about Smitty—anything about Smitty crossed your mind?"

"It's Smitty I *am* thinking about. He taught us to act, not to react."

"It's the end for *him,* isn't it? *Isn't it?* Or have you had a change of heart? Especially now the price has gone up?"

She made no reply. He turned to the others again, struck the map, the photos with the flat of his hand. "It's perfect, can't you see? The President's own Special Adviser gets splashed; right on the doorsteps of the Foreign Policy Establishment. Nothing we could ever do would have such impact! Talk about heavy action . . ."

"You're serious," Jillie said. "You're really serious about this."

Land looked at her a long moment. "You're a crummy broad. You know that?"

"Hey now, cool it, Land," Jumbo told him.

"You could give me that much," Land went on to Jillie, his voice shaking. *"Yes,* I'm serious! I'm as serious as you can get and still—" He stopped himself with an effort. "We're going to do it. We're going to do it because we've got to. Can't you see that? *We can't let him get away with it.* If we let Vosz bury Smitty like this we can never hold our heads up again. Never!"

Jillie said quietly: "So let's shoot him, in the back. In cold blood."

"What's all this stupid moral bullshit about? Listen to the lady— do you think *they've* ever shown any moral scruples?" He held up his two index fingers, a liturgical gesture, half comical. "A life for a life. Yeah! They've done the escalating, not us. If that's the way he wants it, that's the way it'll be, you hear? That's the way it'll fucking well be!"

There was a silence, heightened by the dry susurrus of traffic down on Mount Auburn Street. Jillie sat silently, picking at her nails. It was happening again. All over again, only instead of Terry and Karen and Tom it was Land and Jumbo and Bushy. Kids sitting around in stripped rooms planning something deadly. Something certain to fail. She hated it— all at once and fully she wanted to be free of it, put it behind her forever, ideologies and plans and that light-sick clutch high in the belly that some loved, and others even lived by, but which never failed to fill her with nausea and dread.

Logic, we're not into logic, we're into action and action alone!

Unhappily she watched the others. Smitty. They were all thinking of

Smitty, thinking about holding up their heads again. She saw the pale face with its snub nose, the overlarge brown eyes that never seemed to blink even when he was reading. Flights of wry levity, snatches of song, snips and scraps of abstruse information, all of it held in a scholarly graven image that had never fooled her from the first. He'd drawn his armor on, as everyone does. But with Smitty it was different: he never peeled it off, not even when he was doing imitations of Dustin Hoffman or Big Bill Donlund or Werner von Braun. Not even when he'd kissed her. She had only gone to bed with him once, a brief surrender to what she wasn't exactly sure, a quiet maternal thing—or no, simply a gentle enfolding, a comforting; and yes, the furtive hope that something might come of it. There had always been that, then. It hadn't been very successful. He had apologized to her with a kind of formal stiffness, almost as though he'd taken advantage of her. She'd told him it didn't matter; which it didn't basically. They'd sat in the middle of the bed and smoked. After a while he'd muttered, "It's always been like this with me. Always." And then suddenly he'd plunged his head between her breasts. He'd slept in her arms for hours without moving a muscle. The only time . . . All because of Smitty. They were sitting here in this black-and-white Chinese room debating savage things, all because of Smitty. He'd had a plan to shiver the center of power, he'd put years into its execution and brought it off consummately . . . and he'd been erased as a social creature in one—

"Who do you have in mind?"

It was Jumbo. He was looking stolidly at Land.

"I figured we'd draw lots for it, cut cards or something. That's the fairest way. Maury's the best shot—Maury and you. But hell, marksmanship is no problem at that range."

"—Jumbo ought to do it," Bushy exclaimed suddenly. "Jumbo Blasts Squeezer: what a fucking headline!"

Land leaped to his feet and seized Bushy by the shirt collar with both hands. "One more stupid remark like that and I'm going to punch you one in the mouth. Are you on something, Slatin? *Are you?*"

Bushy shook his crazy headful of hair. "No, Land—you know I kicked it, you know that . . ."

"Dizzy bastard." With a nervous thrust of his body Land moved to one of the windows. His face, in profile, looked scornful and a little demented. "What do you think this is, Slatin, some frigging game?"

"You ever shoot anybody?" Jumbo said. He was still hunched over like an uncompleted Rodin, work boots and a denim shirt with the sleeves cut off at the shoulder seam.

"Hell no, I've never shot anybody! Have you?" The big man nodded. "When was that?"

"Vietnam."

Another word that rang in the room. Jillie thought of Dave—the homely, lined face; faded now, faded nearly out of sight, effaced by Paul. Everything had been effaced by Paul.

"Two kids, in a rice paddy," Jumbo was saying with heavy reluctance. "I didn't know they were kids. I thought one of them had a weapon. Turned out to be some funny kind of grub hoe." He sighed thickly through his nose again. "They told us even the kids were planting mines. Maybe they were. They didn't look to me like they'd been planting any mines. Of course they were dead, then."

Land swung away from the window. "What do you want to do, Erikson—back out? Is that it?"

"I never said I was in."

"Just forget about it, right? That all you owe Smitty? That sandlot plan of Hoyt's? Stand there with our silly microphones pleading, actually *debating* with that vicious little swine—*no!* You God—damn—fools, he'll never change, I *know* the son of a bitch! I've watched him for years . . ."

"That's not my point, Blackburn."

"What are you trying to say, Erikson—you think I can't do it? Just try me!"

He couldn't do it. Jumbo was right. It was all fantasies, deadly phantoms. Smitty could kill, she'd always known it, there was that cold white diamond-point at the pit of his soul, he could kill someone and raise a forkful of roast beef to his lips the next moment, chew and swallow it. Land could not. He would blow it, hit an assistant or some Council flunky. He would be caught and they would put him away too, wipe him out.

She couldn't go on sitting here like this much longer. She couldn't do it again, she had lived all this before, this *shit,* she was sick to death of it, she wanted to see Paul, she wanted to go rowing on the Inlet with him and eat cold broiled chicken and potato chips and listen to him talk about the white towers of Damascus. She didn't want to watch Land's mouth quivering, that straight dark line struck diagonally across his cheek as the rage worked in him. Nerving himself to it, the way Terry had. Marco Retzlaff once said we were all instinctive killers, with only the veneer of civilization to prevent us from hacking each other to bits. But it was a lot more complicated than that. There were the destructive and the affectionate—and then there were the limbo people, the swayed . . .

"There *is* an alternative," she heard herself say in her steadiest voice. "Of course I realize it might lack that romantic, suicidal glow."

"Oh, wow—I can imagine what *you've* got in mind! A televised—"

But it was her turn to ignore him now. Jumbo had given her the opening she'd wanted. "You're leaving yourselves with no levarage. Can't you see that? All right, you kill him if you're lucky. Or unlucky. And that's the end of the line. End of him, end of us. But with Vosz in your hands, alive, you can force concessions. Just like the V.P.R. in Brazil. Kidnap him and you've got your symbolic action, plus a trading card. You can start negotiations, seize headlines and hold them."

"Same penalty, kidnapping as murder," Maury Adelman said tersely. "Isn't it?"

"But you have bargaining power," she insisted. "A life for a life, all right—only with purpose. That's the way to force Smitty's release. *If* that's what you really want, I mean."

"Got it all worked out, have you, Hoyt?" Land was still standing by the window. He never hooked his fingers in his trouser pockets the way Paul did, he hardly ever put his hands in his pockets at all.

"I know a hopeless, dead-end scheme when I see one."

"What makes you think it would work? How do you know the high brass won't sacrifice him?"

"Because the President values him."

"Makes sense," Jumbo murmured.

"—Why don't you keep your smart ass out of this!" Land shouted at her. "You had nothing to do with this project—you weren't even around when I tried to reach you after they threw the book at Smitty." His upper lip curled. "Plans and policy. All full of piss and vinegar as long as it's *theory,* as long as you don't have to lay your ass on the line, as long as somebody *else* is around to kick ass in your behalf—"

"Fuck off, Land. I was into political action when you were reading *Winnie the Pooh.*"

"Then how come you're all wimpy on this project? Wouldn't be having a conflict of interest, would you?"

"What's that for?"

"I mean maybe you've had a change of heart, of late. You know?"

The others were watching them uneasily now. She would have to force it. She would have to find out how far he was willing to go to block her.

"Why is that?" she asked steadily. "Why should I have changed?"

He clasped his long fingers, interlocked them; fingers that had caressed her nipples and belly and thighs, and later fretted her hair, lying silent in the early evening watching together the light sink into dusk. So very strange . . .

"I couldn't say," he offered with sullen care. "I thought you might have found a new cause or something."

He wouldn't, then. The others didn't know about her and Paul. And he wasn't going to open it up. He was beside himself that he couldn't attack her directly, confute and humiliate her, and this sudden knowledge excited her curiously even as it saddened. It was as though some ancient

tyrant had condemned them, hating each other, to remain lovers—an
enforced cohabitation in which wounds were to replace caresses, savage
innuendo the full gaze of desire.

"Either way you win," he pursued. "Know what I mean?"

"No, I don't."

"Sure you do." He would not let go. He would give anything to
wound her, she saw—anything except the admission that his own father
had supplanted him in her bed. He was ridiculous, he was spiteful, he was
capable of almost anything. *Assassination,* for God's sweet sake! And
under it ran that unquenchable need to force the issue, alter the substance
of things forever. "It can't be for nothing!" he'd cried one night at her
place, right after the FBI had caught Smitty. "That's the one thing I can't
stand—that it could wind up as nothing at all . . ." Like most passionate
natures he was sure of himself only in the grip of sensation. Abstract
thought had no real meaning for him; what he sought was the scald of
emotion, the dense, tactile comfort of the act.

Which could be said of her, too, truth to tell . . .

"Risky game, playing both ends against the middle. You can *really*
get burned that way, you know?" He was pressing hard, daring himself to
say it in spite of himself. *"They* won't protect you when the hammer comes
down—don't think they will! I know them."

"Look, Blackburn," Jumbo said heavily, "I don't know what you've
got going between you and it's none of my business. But I've known Jillie
a while longer than you and nobody's ever called—"

"Yeah, well, there's a few things you don't happen to know, old
buddy." His eyes had never left her face. "You see, there's a story going
around that she's become an Establishment playmate, a—"

"Look, love, there are stories going around about everybody in Cambridge," she broke in on him, "—even you." Exasperated, furious, she
decided there was only one way to stop him. "Speaking of heavy projects:
what are you hanging back for? After all, why accept substitutes? Why
not do what you *really* want—why don't you kill your old man?"

Slatin burst into his high-pitched laughter, Maury made a murmur of
protest. Land's eyes dilated, he gave a violent wrench of his whole body.
Then he too laughed wildly. "Oh no—that's too easy! Way too easy!" He
couldn't stop laughing. "No no no—*that* requires other techniques! Very
different plans . . ." But as he subsided she could see the points of fear in
his eyes. He *had* thought of it—and its harsh, cold expression here in this
room, where the others heard it and wondered, momentarily sterilized his
ferocity.

Before he could recover she turned to the other three, treating the
kidnapping plan as though agreed-upon, stressing its advantages, thinking
of Paul in the window seat, his hair a sticky, ruffled cock's comb from
swimming, reading aloud from *The Green Helmet;* and beyond him the

plumed heron solitary in the reeds. When Land came back at her again she said flatly: "I say we put it to a vote. I'm in favor of kidnapping. Who else is for it?"

"I am," Maury said. Jumbo lifted one big hand and let it fall again.

"You God damned fools," Land muttered. "Can't you see she's just working you?"

"She's right, Blackburn. It makes more sense, any way you look at it."

"There isn't time anyway—it isn't thirty hours . . ."

"Sure there is," she said. "We've got the people. We use the same set-up as the broadcast-confrontation, only we grab him instead of talking to him." She picked up the map and snapshots. "How big is this reserved space in front of the building?"

"Two car lengths," Bushy said. "Maybe more. But you can't park there, it's—"

"I know that. What's this across from it—a hydrant?"

"Yes."

"Perfect. We live-park there with the best car we've got—Maury's Olds maybe, something with room for six or seven. Then we live-park the panel truck back here—what are these, town houses?"

"Yeah, and a private school."

"All right, we double-park back here as if we're making a delivery. We let them pull in, then straddle the street with the panel truck to block off anything coming behind them. How many people does he usually have with him? There's the fat little sweaty one—"

"Wentzel."

"Yes, Wentzel. And the one who always wears gray flannel suits no matter how hot it is, some kind of secretary–yes man."

"A bodyguard?" Maury said.

"I doubt it. He's always carrying a briefcase. And the driver. That shouldn't be hard."

"What if he's got a motorcycle escort, something like that?" Jumbo asked.

"He didn't have one when he was up here last spring. The President has discouraged the practice. He feels they're ostentatious."

"Should be easy, then," Bushy said. "We jump him, hustle him into the sedan and run down Park."

"No," she said. "Better to cross Park, stay on Sixty-eighth."

"But if the lights are wrong—those cabs come down there at fifty, fifty-five. We'll get killed . . ."

"Then we'll have people out. Stop them. It's only for a few seconds." She peered at a photo Bushy had just set down. It seemed to be a refrigerator capped by a beach umbrella. "What on earth's that?"

"A street vendor. He sells popsicles, hot dogs, goop like that. Nice little guy. I talked with him while Land was doing the Dash Hammett."

"Will he still be there at six-thirty?"

"Sure. He stays late, summer evenings. Catches the kids coming from the Park."

"Good. Some of us can be buying stuff from him, hanging around eating it. And the phone booth."

"There's a police phone, too. On the street lamp stanchion." Bushy giggled, scratching his beard. "They can call the cops from it after the caper."

"And if anything *should* go wrong it'll be just a demonstration."

"Is something going to go wrong?" Land asked her softly.

"I said, *In the event something did.*"

He nodded. "You're not going to be in on this, you know."

"Why not?"

"No women. It'll be too rough." His eyes glittered. "We want beef for this—broads will be a liability. Anyway, you're in policy *planning*. Right? Isn't that right, Erikson?"

Jumbo nodded. "You sit this one out, Jill. All the women."

"Oh now, come on—"

"Okay," Land retorted, "we'll vote on it."

They did: it was a unanimous decision to exclude her. Land was watching her again, grinning tightly. She accepted the verdict with good grace and they went on planning the abduction. She arranged the disposition of their twenty-six people: four in the getaway car, eight in the panel truck, eight around the vendor, six to stop traffic north and south on Park. There was a long discussion over where to take Vosz—in the end it was decided to run him downtown to Maury's apartment in the Village, to avoid the risk of getting stopped on major arteries.

Jillie found herself watching Land covertly as they talked. The brief elation she'd felt at diverting all the crazy assassination talk had given way to that sense of deep confusion and dismay that surrounded her days now. What was she doing here, in this hot, antiseptic room? What was she doing anywhere? She longed for a cigarette and watched Jumbo talking, his lips moving slowly, his great calves straining against the faded levis, and Bushy crouched over a legal pad scribbling, looking goatlike now in profile, a Renaissance scribe in mauve velour shirt and bellbottoms. Bushy was the only one of them who ought to be in Cambridge: he at least looked the part. Jumbo had no business being in graduate school, he ought to be working a bridle over the head of some crazy-eyed yearling or, gauntleted, easing a spruce log against the furry arc of the blade in a saffron rain of sawdust. Everybody was doing the wrong thing. Paul should be a philosopher-recluse measuring the state versus the individual, the individual versus the state, Land should be a reform candidate for Congress, standing on the hood of a station wagon at Kendall Square haranguing a crowd, she herself should be . . . she should be—well . . .

Jesus, wasn't anybody right for his role, had we all walked on to the wrong sets without time to learn the appropriate lines? No—Smitty was. Smitty had done what he was meant to do, somehow or other. She did not question it. Vosz too. The two of them were walking toward disaster, they would destroy each other.

"No phony diffidence, no hanging back," Maury was saying in his over-enunciated lawyer's voice. "They've got to get out there and stop that traffic coming down . . ."

"I'll talk to them," Jumbo answered.

Preserve us all from certainty, she thought—only after a second realized it was something Paul had said one afternoon at Tashawena. Yes. Nothing was simple any more, there were other people walking other roads, and they weren't all beasts and bigots and fools. Paul was the bleeding Establishment all right; and yet he'd tried to turn things around where he could . . .

The meeting had broken up. Land was out of the door before she'd even got to her feet. Pursued by a nameless urgency she hurried down the narrow, shabby stairs and burst out into heat and sunlight. Grimy Cambridge summer afternoon. There he was, a good block away now, moving toward the river with his loose, ambling stride, so unlike Paul's neat purposeful step. They were so unlike, so *foreign* to each other . . .

She ran a little, slowed to a walk and called his name. He turned, scowling, not really stopping, and she ran again.

"I want to talk to you," she said, coming up to him.

"Do you, now." But still he hung there, uncertain, his eyes pained and forbidding, and when she moved past him he fell into step beside her.

"Where are you going?" she asked lightly.

"You want a full dossier on my movements? For State Department clearance?"

"Oh, shut up." She stared ahead, frowning, trying to think. "Don't you have to go to work?"

"Got myself canned." He grinned without mirth at her surprised glance. "Sick of it anyway. Besides, I wanted my hands free. For other things."

They came out on the Drive, crossed to the river bank. Couples sprawled on the worn grass sunbathing, making love in a welter of books, soft drink cans, newspapers. Bound in their somnambulistic movements, half naked, bathed in sunlight, bordered by the still water and the towers they were like participants in some vast slow rite of love, a new race of anthropoids just stirred into being. She glanced at Land, who was peering about him morosely: he looked hunted, vengeful, groping toward some new and cruel solution.

"You *are* going along with it, aren't you, Land?" she said suddenly. "What's been decided."

He stopped and faced her a moment. "You think I'm going to double-cross the group? The lone assassin?" The corners of his mouth drew down. "*I'm* not the one who's copping out. Or is it selling out."

"There's no need to be abusive."

"Isn't there?"

"I just mean—you'll be careful: won't you?"

"What the hell do you care?"

"Well. I do." His high nearness, the midsummer heat, the tension of the meeting were working in her like some fearsome yeast—she felt all at once unstable, prey to a thousand outlandish sensations. It was impossible, surrounded by this lazy, crazy modern-day Seurat, that in twenty-four hours they were going to do what they had planned to do. Impossible—like everything else. She tried to fix her attention on a couple who were blowing through grass blades, making thin, bleating sounds.

Aloud she said: "I didn't want it this way, you know."

"Is that right. How *did* you want it?"

"I don't know—"

"Hell, I'd think this would serve your purposes beautifully."

"Look, I'm sorry—I want to say I'm sorry, Land . . ."

"Where's your frigging violin." His eyes moved over the recumbent figures as though they were a species of agricultural parasite. "Something in a real gone minor key. Maybe we could get up an act. If you're not too busy evenings, I mean."

"—Don't go down there," she said suddenly. "To New York."

He gazed at her in quick angry amazement. "Now just what the fuck is that for?"

"I mean just this one time. Just this once." What *had* she said that for? Why in God's sweet name did she always say something before she'd thought it through? But it was true, she knew it . . .

"Woman's intuition," he was saying coldly. "Is that it? Baby Calpurnia in her nightgown. A lioness hath whelped in the streets, and graves have yawned dee-blah dee-blah dee-blah. Or do you want me offstage for some rusier ruse? Got guilt pangs?"

"You haven't any right to say something like that . . ."

"—*I've got a right to say anything I want to say.*" His voice was low and threatening. "Anything! You got that?"

But it was different: what she felt for Smitty, what she owed him for making her think, drive her mind away from the blue bottle of Seconal, the knife blades in Hoffritz windows. Land didn't know anything about that, he couldn't. Smitty had pulled together the ragged, demoralized scraps of the old New Left, or some of them anyway, he'd given them back dignity and cohesion and a sense of purpose, and she had helped him. They'd accomplished something, for a while at least. But that wasn't all of it. What they'd done was what they'd wanted to do, their own harsh answers. *Their* answers, though: *their* needs and not anyone else's. And even then maybe they were wrong. Were they? Did it always move toward death, was there a built-in, inevitable escalation? Revolution becomes protest becomes violence becomes murder. Maybe they couldn't have gone any other way, she and Smitty, because of what they were and what they'd seen and done. Maybe Smitty was already destroyed—maybe she herself was. But Land was different: Land had life in him, the hot green responses of life, and possibilities. Anyone could see that. He could go beyond Paul. He must. To walk the dark, crooked corridors of Smitty's world would destroy him.

"Please, Land," she murmured. They were down near the base of the footbridge. No one was near them except one couple with long blond hair and matelot shirts, look-alikes. "I'm all mixed up . . ."

"Aren't you ever! Boy, aren't you ever." He was looking away from her across the river. "You don't care about anybody on earth but yourself. Never have. For the simple reason that you can't put yourself on the line with anybody. You're *suspicious.*" He uttered the word as if it were a new, incurable and not very presentable disease. "You're suspicious of everybody, all the time."

"Look, Land, I didn't—"

"I was wrong about you," he went on in that same curiously distant, speculative tone. "I mean I never fell for all that Joan-of-Arc-on-the-barricades bullshit. But I thought you were committed, a battler. But you're not. All the time you're really standing there outside it all. Just like the big brass, the lord high muckety-mucks themselves . . ."

She bit her lip. "If I am like that—maybe it's because I've had the rug pulled out from under me once too often."

"—Oh, don't shove me that!" he snarled, and the couple near them turned curious pale eyes like sea flowers in their direction. "Everybody's had the bloody rug pulled out once too often. You think you're unique? But *you* got suspicious. You decided to look for it everywhere you went: perfidy, in hearts and spades. All the underhanded bastards who were going to let you down, sooner or later. And *that* left you off the hook—that gave you the old green light to step outside the circle . . ." His face all at once contorted. "Is that why it was so easy?" he demanded, his voice shaking. "Because you knew *he* wouldn't care, either? Is that it?"

"No." She shook her head vehemently. "It's not that way at all . . ."

"Of course not. It's the love of the fucking century."

She stared down at her shoes moving. She felt a pure regret—she didn't know why; a bitter, spreading sadness. Things always went this way—whatever you did you were bound to mess up one way or another. In his fury he could see only one thing, and she could not tell him how irreparably wrong he was. He was going to get hurt in this thing tomorrow, something really bad was going to happen . . . Watching his face working, she was suddenly swept by sexual desire, she wanted him as she never had before. She thought, half-aghast, half-curious, I'm going crazy, really crazy, what in God's name is the *matter* with me—!

"Land," she heard herself say. "Land, I'll marry you. If you want."

He gave her a sharp, wild look—then laughed harshly. "Hey now, there's a gasper!"

"There isn't anything between me and—Paul. It was a flash thing, a lark. I did it to get at Vosz," she went on, shocked beyond amazement at so monstrous a lie. But she had to, somehow: anything, anything to allay this savage, boundless grief. "I was drawn to you the moment I saw you. At the Arsenal rally. Remember?"

"Why don't you *drop* it—!" He'd raised his hand, he was clearly going to hit her. Then he lowered it, as though it were an alien mechanism that interested him deeply. "You'll do anything, won't you?" he said. "Say anything if it'll work somebody for something or other. You're rotten all the way down. I may be a simple-minded type but I can decode *you*. You—"

He stood there cursing her in a stony monotone. Well, they were only words, dirty worn-out words, she'd heard them all before. It was this other thing, it was all going wrong, and terrible—

"Please, Land. There's something I want to say . . ."

"I'll see you around, Hoyt. You recline here on the sylvan fucking banks of the Charles and ponder the human condition. Okay? Me, I've got things to do. People to see. You know how it is."

He moved quickly away now, as though genuinely glad to be rid of her and her lies. She sat down on the matted, weary grass, her hands locked around her knees. The moonflower couple were paying no attention to her. On the river a man in a singles shell slid along, the slick dun plate of water moving rather than boat and oarsman. A lean, bony face, a face like Judge Seaver's: the arrogant and certain, the enemy . . . She smiled faintly. Paul was neither arrogant nor certain, he was rocked and riddled with doubts, misgivings; was that apparent to her now only because she knew and loved him, feared for him? Was that what the heart did? Were the others—all those bold, summary men she'd hated all these years, inveighed against—were some of them like him? troubled and unsure at heart?

The shell was gone; had slipped away under the footbridge. There was no trace of it on the still water. *History is nothing but the actions of men in pursuit of their ends.* True. Probably. Maybe. Was no subtler distinction to be made between Bismarck's pursuit, say, and Saint Augustine's? She had believed in certain things so sternly, so devoutly, scant weeks ago—now none of it mattered, nothing on this earth mattered except Paul.

She was like everyone else, then, all the women she'd detested: she wanted nothing so much as to live with and love one man, restore him, guard him—

She was hooked. At long last. The realization pleased her deeply. What Land had said *had* been true of her—the irony of it was his accusation came too late: she was no longer guilty as charged. Life was so cram-jam full of ironies, sly surprises! She'd hated Paul so that first afternoon, she'd have given quite literally everything she owned if she could have wounded him mortally. Now the most glancing thought of hurt to him washed her with dread . . .

Three students at the edge of the water were tossing a Frisbee, a plastic yellow disc that hovered above them in the still, heavy air, some menacing Martian craft—then human hands snatched it to the status of a toy. Actions of men in pursuit of their ends. Yes—if you qualified it to read *ends they themselves would never recognize.* There lay the single, unalterable law, if there was one. If there was anything you could call a law. Lenin in the sealed railroad car returning to a shattered Russia could have had no idea where his actions would lead. And even the best-laid plans—

Her gaze focused sharply on the Frisbee which, overthrown, was floating on the water like a weird yellow mushroom. Something was wrong, really wrong. It was too neat, too easy. Land had said Jean Tyler had contacted him from Washington over the time change in Vosz's arrival. But Jean wasn't that close to the White House Basement, she didn't know anybody in Vosz's office, she'd told her that not three months ago. And something like this, a security measure, would be guarded. Very closely guarded. How did Jean know about it, then?

She was frowning hard now. The Frisbee players were clustered at the water's edge; a gangling red-haired boy had rolled up his trousers and was wading out toward the platter. Someone had told Jean, then. Someone high up who wanted Vosz intercepted, wanted the confrontation to take place. For his own purposes.

A trap, then. Was it? Why hadn't Land or Jumbo seen it? Yet why bother to crush Sirius? Vosz wouldn't care—Sirius was no threat, not really, now he had Smitty. Vosz was scheduled to arrive at 6:30. Paul would be downtown at the UN arguing the Drachenfels case, probably at the same time. Strange. Maybe whoever had done this *wanted* it to succeed—or partially succeed: it could bring down both Paul and Vosz in one stroke. Someone who knew all about Land's work in Sirius, who knew—

She was on her feet. *Tremayne,* she thought without a second's doubt, recalling the overpretty face, the easy urbanity. He would know all these things and more. That long, aristocratic nose which had been out of joint ever since Paul had secured full State Department authority over all CIA activities overseas. Tremayne would know all these things and more. She had to warn Paul. She had to get down to New York and warn him as quickly as she could.

She was hurrying now, half-running through the close heat; her mouth was dry. Around her the sprawled figures on the river bank looked like nothing so much as the wounded and dying over whom the tide of battle had just rolled.

EIGHTEEN

THE ROOM—HIGH-CEILINGED, with the massive chaste molding and ten-foot-high bow windows of the Bullfinch era, the golden age—sloped off in darkness from the solitary lamp beside the bed. A blued, ashen light high over the river seemed to promise dawn, but dawn was still far away. Two forty-three. Blackburn, in his shirt sleeves and with his collar opened, sat perfectly still in the uncomfortable Hepplewhite armchair and watched the woman who had given birth to him. She lay propped on a small hill of pillows, her head sunk in their white mass, her arms extended slackly above the neatly folded sheet. The sudden swelling had smoothed out the wrinkles in her face; now, near death, Adelaide Blackburn looked younger and prettier than she had in years. Her lips, strangely slack now—she had held them with such resolution in health—fell away in an expression of almost grateful resignation. At rare intervals her eyes would open, doll-like and unsure, and rest on her son.

"It's Paul, Mother," he would say then, "—I'm here, Mother. I'm right here with you," and she would nod like a dutiful little girl, or frown in stunned consternation. Now and then she would take his hand with a faint, convulsive pressure—once she thrust it away in swift petulance, rocking her head dreamlike, muttering things he couldn't catch. He couldn't tell if she knew he was here with her or not.

"She recognizes your voice," the nurse, the more talkative one, had told him when he'd first come in. "There. See her head turn? She knows your voice."

Now, six hours and a weary tumult of thoughts later, he wasn't at all sure. What was certain was the slow, unbearably dilatory clucking gasp for breath, another, another—then silence, in which the world seemed to hang in dreadful suspension; then the hoarse gasping laboriously began all over again, and Paul, bent forward tensely, would see her expression brighten or grow stern as memories skipped across the poorly lighted wall of her mind.

Two forty-seven. He scowled at his watch, unfastened the band and slipped it in his pocket. The night crept on, more slowly than any night in his life. He tried to think, to rivet his mind on the tempestuous session of ExComm that afternoon, Peking's latest note, the rebuttal he must make at the Security Council tomorrow—today—Donlund's sudden, stunning opposition, Vosz's sullen evasiveness, the welter of options . . . but his mother would stir and speak, and it would all fall to a jumble at the pit of his mind. Everything was rushing toward a crisis, hurtling unhelmed and unforeseen, and he wasn't up to it. His need to call Jillie, to hear her voice, was a stark physical ache deep in his belly—once he was horrified to find he had actually put his hand on the bedside phone, though he knew it had been removed from its jack the day before.

The wind sighed in the trees outside, a sound like rain. The night nurse entered and gave his mother an injection, changed the drainage apparatus. She was a short dark girl given to quick, impatient movements that made Blackburn angry.

"Be careful, can't you?" he said sharply. "She's in pain . . ."

The nurse threw him a savage, sidelong glance and moved away. All the nurses were cross, Eleanor had told him, because Adelaide had refused to let herself be taken out to Peter Bent Brigham or anywhere else. This had occasioned some tense colloquies at the end of the upstairs hall. Blackburn had argued for moving her. Who knew how long she might hang on? She might need special care, special facilities—could they cope with anything that might arise? Eleanor, tense, bleak, said No, they ought to respect her wishes, especially at a time like this; and Doctor Stainforth had concurred with a wistful grimace as if to say: "What does it matter, really, where she is, in the few hours left to her?" He had been gently emphatic that she would not outlast the night.

There were voices in the street below: young, heedless voices. A boy laughed and said, "I don't mean anything I say. When are you going to latch on to that?" and a girl answered: "Oh, *nobody* means anything they say . . ." Their steps clattered on the worn brick, heading toward the Square, and Blackburn imagined them swaying hand-in-hand, the shaggy, outlandish clothes, the slumped, sliding gait; so unlike the quiet circumspection of his own youth. The Korean generation, they had called him and his immediate successors, the Silent Generation: contained, uncertain, clutching at tangibles. Yet were they really so inadequate, so worthy of contempt? They had done the best they could with what they'd been dealt; hadn't they?

His mother stirred, her head turned with dreamy deliberation. Her forearm came up, the first two fingers raised, peremptory and still; then dropped. Gently, stirred by memory he took her hand again but she plucked it away and muttered, "I don't want *you* . . ."

Abashed he stared at her, telling himself she was under sedation, that she had him confused with someone else, her mind was wandering; but he wasn't sure. She had always known who and what she wanted; she'd kept all his report cards, his diplomas and theses, had studded them with marginal comments in her own small, firm hand; even the speeches he'd given as Secretary she'd evaluated—quite deftly, he'd had to admit, even if a trifle presumptuously; after all, even Adelaide Whitcombe Blackburn couldn't have known *everything* that had been in her son's mind at such moments.

". . . Mumma," she murmured now. And then: "Such a *pretty* hat! . . ." Skipping back and forth in time—her spirit, after a lifetime of ordered purpose, roving free. Chained here to this uncomfortable chair, hearing the nurse moving in the adjoining room, thinking of Jillie, the hard pain high in his belly and the climbing menace of the Drachenfels Crisis, for a moment he almost envied his mother: she had smashed all the locks of obligation, shattered the cage of time. Perhaps you could achieve that only twice in life—at the edge of death, and in the swallow-dance of early childhood . . .

Once when he'd been four or five he'd got lost in Gump's Department Store. It was during the Christmas season. His mother must have stepped to another counter, or perhaps she'd spoken to him and he hadn't been paying attention. Or maybe he'd wandered off by himself, he didn't remember. But there'd been nothing in his life up to that time to equal it. One moment he was walking serenely along holding his mother's sleeve, conscious of a festive world, benign with colored lights and jingling music—the very next he was utterly alone in a cavern choked with great figures that bumped and banged him wherever he turned. He gave one last, terrified look in all directions, and then he opened his mouth and roared.

And then there was a voice, soothing and deep. He opened his eyes again. A man with a hat whose brim turned up all the way around and a small thin neat mustache was crouched in front of him. A man he'd never seen before, who was wiping his face with a big white handkerchief that smelled of pipe tobacco and asking him his name. "Paul," he answered, soothed. "Paul? That's a good name, that's a fine name . . ." The man had straightened now and taken his hand, they were going along somewhere together when like a curious echo he heard his name spoken again— a sharp, tense voice he knew well enough. His mother was standing there. Familiarity swept over him, pleasure, he cried her name in glee. But something was wrong. His mother's face was stern with distrust, with fear. There was danger here, then. But why? She said something. The man's face changed too, went long with surprise; his smile froze in an unnatural way, his hands were moving in nervous little gestures—then he had slipped off through the crowds.

"*Paul.*" His mother's face was close, her eyes were boring into his. Crouching she had both hands on his shoulders. That was a bad thing he had done, very bad. He was never to do a thing like that again. If they should ever be separated in any way, he was to stand right where he was, stand right there and *wait for Mother*. Did he understand that? He was not to speak to strangers—if a man came up to him and said he was his father he was *not* to take his hand.

"—But he didn't say he was my father," he'd protested, frightened now and close to tears.

"That doesn't matter," his mother said, and she was looking at him in such deadly earnest that he forgot to cry. No matter who came up to him he was to say he was waiting for his mother. He was not to listen to strangers, ever . . . Did he understand?

Did he? He didn't know, he really didn't know. Somehow it seemed to him it had been at the center of everything—that fierce, frightened dictum: in some way at the heart of his life. And he'd obeyed her, he'd always obeyed her—and yet there had been the instinctive impulse to reach out, take the proffered alien hand in his . . .

God, he was tired: as sheerly weary as he'd ever been. He'd always had the public servant's scorn for weariness, shouldering it aside as indulgence, an affliction of the weak or oversensitive; but now he felt it not as a momentary infirmity but some kind of baleful emanation clouding his judgment and clogging his responses. There was so much to be done, so cruelly little time to do it. Brickley and the superhawks had attacked him savagely in the Senate earlier that evening as the apostle of the New Appeasement—it wasn't hard to guess where that phrase had originated; de Mortier was incensed at what he'd chosen to call a blatant rebuff to his good offices; Shiraga was urging dissolution of GATO, Bodawyin remained hysterical over the possibilities of a Chinese invasion, Van Kleeck in an astonishing flash had advocated breaking off diplomatic relations with Peking; and now, worst of all, here was Donlund clearly pressing for an ultimatum, while Drachenfels and the Mission—

From the bed there came the agonizingly slow, rattling gasp for air. Adelaide Blackburn strained to raise herself from the pillows, her fine slim head swinging slowly from side to side.

". . . Mother?" he murmured, leaning forward. "Mother? Do you want to be higher on the pillows? Higher up?"

She raised her hand again in that deliberate admonitory gesture, and he fell silent; but her arm dropped, she sank back troubled, muttering inaudibly. Then there was a small gathering of her forces and all at once an urgent plea, fearful, eager: "*Rick*—!" and then—unmistakably—a cry of pure joy: "Oh Rick, dearest . . ." Then it too passed, and her lips curved in a sad, slow smile.

He found he was gripping the chair arms hard, scarcely breathing himself. So there it was. After all the years of estrangement, vilification, embittered disdain the unfettered heart sought out some long-ago golden moment and reveled in its sunlight . . . she had not despised his father, then: only what she thought he stood for—what she herself had feared. Yes. How astonishing, how beautifully wayward life was! All the proud towers of will could crumble like so much sand before a single blow of the traduced, exuberant heart . . .

"That's it, *now* you've got it!" His father in a sparkling white shirt, cuffs turned up, his curly dark hair glinting against the bottle green of live oaks. "You step forward with your left foot as you throw. Like this, see? It's all one rhythm, an easy rhythm. *That's* the stuff! You bet." Curious—he always thought of Rick Blackburn moving in sunlight, the windy, gold-dust sunlight of October. *You bet.* His father would take a bet on anything—a Stanford game, the make of an oncoming car, the weather: money moved through his hands like a live green thing. Once Paul had seen him slip a man several bills in a coatroom. "Why'd you do that, Dad?" he'd asked later.

"Because he's down on his luck, son." The swift wink, the nod. "Every man's bound to be down on his luck, some time or other."

Luck had been Rollicking Rick's talisman—a glittering, fast-flowing stream one was either in or out of, an Aladdin's lamp that called up the omnipotent djinn or stubbornly reverted to the status of an old pot. Luck was everything; without it no amount of effort was availing. Adelaide had abominated the very idea. "What your father is fond of calling *luck* is nothing more or less than an utter lack of self-discipline and perseverance, a sorry surrender to chance. We make our own ways in this world, Paul. Don't you forget that."

True—but only in part. His father had been right, too: you did what you could, carried your own misshapen load as valiantly as possible; but even then you needed those skirts of happy chance to grab hold of. The man who didn't see that was blinded—either by vanity or lack of imagination. And his mother had never seen that . . . What a Janus-marriage it had been: his father had rushed emotionally into the future ("Why hell, there's no place this country can't go, Paul—you'll live to see the day when everyone's got his own autogyro, radiophones, solar heat—my God, you won't even recognize this country in twenty years! Or the world either, for that matter"), his mother had gazed steadfastly into the past ("They lived lives of *purpose* in your grandfather's time, Paul, a true gentility, not this shabby worship of notoriety and spurious wealth. Why, your grandfather wouldn't even have *spoken* to some of these people in Washington now, giving themselves airs") . . .

And he, their sole and troubled offspring—where did he look? what banner had he clung to? His father had taught him how to throw a baseball and he'd chosen to be a swimmer; his mother had taught him deference to the conventions and unflinching adherence to principle—and so he had fallen irretrievably in love with a girl exactly two-thirds his age, a girl unalterably opposed to everything he stood for. And just what did all that prove? Nothing, everything. In the end, at the sticking place, all firmest dedication and resolve to the contrary, we yielded to the still, green prompting of the heart. Wasn't that the deepest, the only truth? Take his father now—laughing, head back, the sun a fine roseate gold on his face, the varnished rod bowed like a whiplash frozen, and across the still water the pickerel's wake danced and glittered, scattering diamonds. "You see, Paul? There's nothing to it when your luck's running . . ." But no, it was something larger than that, something more sinister, it circled them in stealthy menace, relentless and vast; he started to cry out in alarm, glanced up at his father who was still smiling through his exertions, absorbed; he didn't see the danger. Something grazed the boat's bottom, jarring them subtly, voices rose around them in the mist—

"—I'll call him."

He opened his eyes to a subdued flurry of movement around him, around the bed. The nurse, Eleanor, their maid Signe, her hair loose over her shoulders. Asleep, he'd fallen asleep despite his best intentions. Daylight mocked the bedside lamp, restored the dimensions of the room. But something in the movements of the three women alerted him.

"What is it?" he asked. "What's the matter?"

Eleanor threw him a swift, preoccupied glance. "She's gone."

". . . But she's better, she was *better*—!" He stood up, his hand to his face. None of them made any reply, went on at their task. Beyond them his mother looked suddenly smaller, defeated and rather petulant.

"When . . . ?" he heard himself say. He was conscious of a straining great pressure in him, a still void of time which precedes the largest catastrophes: the bulging stillness before a tower's falling. He found he was standing in the blued light of the hall, his mouth open, trying to breathe, it was quite hard to breathe—

She had always been there. That was the thing: whether he saw her three evenings a week or held down some jungle consulate ten thousand miles away, it made no difference—there had always been the reassurance of that firm, uncompromising zeal, like a moss-covered wall at one's back, an intaglio of standards against which he could measure all intentions, all achievements, the obligations of the man of purpose . . . Now it was gone, there was nothing there behind him, nothing precisely like that. It was going to take—he was going to need some time.

He took a deep breath, then another. He was suddenly immensely hungry, half starved. He went downstairs, his hand on the polished rosewood railing—watched himself in slow surprise. He had never taken hold of the railing before.

"Paul."

Eleanor was standing at the door to the study. Her face was even more gaunt from strain and exhaustion; the line of the jaw, the faintly bulging temples were oddly accentuated.

She said: "I'd like to talk with you a moment." There was just the faintest hitch in his stride and she caught it; her face hardened a bit more. Then she turned and went into the study.

He stepped inside, said, "Will you make the arrangements? I've got to call Sid right away. And Joe."

She shook her head like a girl. "I want to talk about us. Now."

"Can't it wait? Look, I've—"

"No. It can't. It's waited far too long as it is."

He drew the study door gently closed. "Nell, I'm incredibly tired, relations with Peking are in a desperately bad way, I've got to give a very important speech before the Security Council in a matter of hours . . ."

"The fact is that we're actually here in the same room, under the same roof—God knows when I'll see you again. We seem to have—"

She broke off. He cried softly: "Nell, my mother has just died!"

"Yes. Your mother has died. I've eased her last hours as best I could. And here we are. That's just what I mean." She paused, arched her back wearily, and he thought how perfectly typical it was of her to force a discussion at a moment like this: that awful, graceless candor riding on the old arrogance—he could have smiled; at any other time he might have smiled.

"I'd like to know what you intend to do, Paul."

"Do?" he echoed. "I intend to finish this speech, and huddle with Sid and Archie Grace at the—"

"—You know perfectly well what I meant!" She put her hand to her neck, trembling, and he saw that she was struggling as hard as he to control herself. "I'm sorry," she added lamely, "I can't seem to talk about this dispassionately." She threw him a swift, sharp glance. "I've learned about you and—Miss Hoyt," she said. "As you can see. As you must have known I would."

Still fighting the raw sense of loss, of instability, he too felt robbed of grace itself. "I'm sorry you had to learn it through—someone else."

"It wasn't terribly pleasant."

". . . It was a very sudden thing. I didn't know what to do."

"I'd have hoped you would have come to me about it first."

He opened his mouth to speak, closed it again. Moved by her tone, that old gauche vulnerability, he had been tempted to go on, but the implication in her last remark—that he come suppliant to her authority, for permission to live—my God, to *live!*—checked him. Remembering she had told Land, his heart hardened again. "I'm afraid it was a bit more complicated than that." After a moment he murmured: "I'm sorry if it caused you grief."

"*If*—?" She looked at him incredulously, her lips moving. "*If* . . . do you mean to say you were in any doubt about it?"

He made a distressed, impatient gesture. "I'm sorry, Nell—but look now, God knows our marriage isn't all it might have been." The cliché nettled him. "To put it mildly. You know that as well as I do."

". . . No," she admitted after a little pause. "It hasn't been, of late." A strange, musing tone that made him glance at her. It never was, he thought irascibly but told himself, No, no, let it pass—imagining Jillie in the room here, whirling around, her hands and hair flying; the violent, probably obscene rejoinders. *Jillie* . . .

"It hasn't been—right," his wife was saying. "That's true. You haven't given it a chance."

"*I*—haven't given it . . . ?" He gaped at her as if she had just stepped out of a column of fire.

She said abruptly: "Paul, let's go away. Can't we go away?"

"Away? Away where?"

"I don't know—Taormina. The Greek Islands. Somewhere by ourselves, Paul."

The fearful entreaty in her eyes, her movements, the sheer absurdity of the idea pushed him off-balance, exasperated him all over again. "Nell, I can no more leave this—"

But she wouldn't let him finish. "A second honeymoon, that's what it would be—they even call it that." Her voice throbbed in the room, low, propitiatory—not Eleanor Seaver Blackburn's voice at all. "Just be by ourselves, Paul—a chance for things to be the way they used to . . . you've got to give us that chance. You have to."

She was serious; he could see that she believed this. He saw the rose-ruddy rock walls of Petra, the lifting salt-cube terraces of Mykonos under a flat white sky. *Things were* never *the way they used to be!* he wanted to shout at her with arm-waving theatricality, *can't you admit that? They never were, we never had a love, the plunging, sense-darkened inebriation of love—you never felt it either, don't try to tell me you did!* . . . But he couldn't say it—that or any of the other teeming accusations. He could not say them. Pity, a nameless contrition held him silent. She believed it had been there once, she had told herself that until her lonely, timorous heart believed it; and beyond that—ah God! far beyond that—she had no way of knowing how fearfully barren their life together had been. Nothing he could say would ever convince her. Wife and mother of two grown children she was yet his virgin, and the world's. And was she to blame for that? Was she, when all was said and done? The thought softened him, blunted the impulse toward recrimination. Anything but complete honesty was unthinkable in the face of that terrible, poignant little girl's gaze.

"It isn't what you think," he said as gently as he knew how. "I'm in love with her, Nell. Utterly and finally. In love with her."

Her head went back, she turned with a frightened, feral gesture. "No —I don't believe it . . ."

"It's true, though."

She looked down at her hands for some seconds, still as stone. Torn between exasperation and affection he watched her, thinking for no reason at all of an amethyst ring he had given her on their fifth wedding anniversary. Soon afterward he'd noticed she hadn't been wearing it, and one night he asked her, hadn't she liked it, really? Oh yes!—she loved it, it was the dearest ring she'd ever owned. Then why wasn't she wearing it? But that was just it, it was so very precious to her, she didn't want to risk losing the stone . . .

". . . I always knew it would happen," she said finally in a low voice, so low he could hardly hear her. "You would leave me. Some day. I always knew it. You never loved me the way I love you."

And then she gave way, her face breaking up in little waves: first the small firm mouth, then the cheeks and chin, then her ice-blue eyes, the full, gently domed brows—a mounting flood of grief; but silent. He stirred, pressed his arms against his sides. Standing there before her he wanted to feel only the deepest sorrow, the heaviest contrition—and he could not: her very anguish—and God knew it was real enough—was still edged with accusation. *You never loved me the way—*

There was a soft, low persistent knocking at the study door. They both started, and Eleanor said: "Not now, please. Just a minute . . ." and looked down at her hands again. Her face, inclined, looked impossibly dry and haggard, a maze of wrinkles. It was true: he'd never loved her as he should have. He'd tried to, and failed, and then had recognized the failure and striven consciously, arduously to make up for that lack in other ways. But it hadn't been enough: how could it? If he had loved her— really loved her—she would not have aged like that. Love withheld aged us, crippled us, just as praise withheld turned our entrails to stone. Maybe if he'd loved her as he loved Jillie—with that fierce, sight-clouding need, so that his veins could run fire and his very guts turn on themselves at the mere thought that he might not see her again—maybe if he'd loved Nell like that she would have come alive under his hands and lips, burst into passion like some ripe green pod . . . But something small and obstinate beneath his heart knew this wasn't so. It just wasn't so.

There was, painfully, cruelly, nothing he could say.

She stiffened then, her eyes flashed up at him like a Greenland sea. "Well, you didn't," she answered for him. "I know. But that's not all there is to it. Not after twenty-five years of life together and a family and everything else, it's not that easy, do you understand? No, you don't, I can see that . . . Even if you *were* pretending—no! It's not, Paul . . ."

"I was not pretending," he answered.

—I tried to will my love, he wanted to say, I thought I could force it to suffice—but can't you see the difference? And love can't be willed, I can see that now, I know that now, it's as clear as any October sky: love is like the southerly, it lifts out of the world's sweet edges and breathes against your eyelids, it falls like spring rain and rises like honeydew, drenching the farthest reaches of the heart—but it wasn't *pretending* . . . In my ignorance I didn't know that, and I failed you. But you failed me too, dear, for fear was in your heart from the beginning, a chilling Arctic fear that mocked the south wind another way, too; your way . . .

Aloud he said: "All I ask you to believe is that I struggled against it as best I could. That I simply could not help myself."

Her lips curved in a small, bitter smile. "They all say that, don't they? Something like that."

"I don't know what they say."

"You never loved me—did you? *Did you?*"

It was terrible to him that he could not deny that anguished cry. But he would do her the honor of honesty, if nothing else. He made no answer.

"Then that's it, you see." She nodded stoically, though her lips were trembling. "Then you should have gone on, gone on as you have."

"I tell you," he burst out, "I couldn't help myself!"

"You should have, anyway—! All you had to do was say no. Why didn't you? Yes, I knew about Michele Franquinet, I was aware of that, any woman would be, any wife—that attraction or whatever you want to call it . . ."

"Nell, no purpose will be—"

"—a matter of attraction, and propinquity, she was so good at turning men to her own purposes, all those suggestions and innuendoes, I watched them do it at school, I despised them for it . . . I set my teeth and endured it, said nothing—but this! This radical, this *slut*—!"

"Eleanor! Control yourself!"

"If it were just sex, if that's all it is . . . but the indignity!" She shut her eyes tightly, as if willing it all away. "That after all these years, all the—the allegiances we owe each other, you would have done this thing, to satisfy whatever needs—"

"Eleanor," he broke in again, "this is fruitless."

"Yes, it's fruitless," she cried softly, her voice hoarse from weeping, "oh yes, it's at least that—at least that!" Her eyes came to rest on his again, great blue discs, and the muscle in her jaw clenched like a cord. "Well, you made a choice with me, long ago. Yes. A decision. You decided to use me for your own devices . . ."

"—Nell, that's not true!" he stammered.

"No? No? What is it, then—since you admit you had no love for me? What would you like to call it? *No!*—We made a life, decided on a life together, a bargain, I hewed to my line in fair weather and foul—and now you've got to hew to yours. You'll destroy your career, you know," she said, almost as an afterthought.

"Maybe."

"No—it's certain. Probably you already have." She looked out toward the bright, hot morning wearily, almost casually. "Perhaps it's just as well. Part of you always wanted it, anyway . . . It will complete your revenge."

He looked at her. "Revenge?"

"What do you think it was—*devotion?* You never looked very hard, did you? Never looked very closely into the real reason you walked away from Lee that afternoon at Stonewall Beach . . ."

It was too much. Here, now, at seven-thirty of the morning on which his mother had died, his nerves rasped raw with sleeplessness and worry, and now this oldest, cruelest charge of all. Bitterly he said: "Look, I've suffered over that for thirty years—worried and pondered and sweated it until I was sick to my very guts. Are you saying—are you trying to say I *wanted* him to die? That's beneath you, Nell. Really beneath you."

"Is it? Think about it. Oh yes, I know, he was headstrong and—and defiant and wild, he was in real agony that spring.—He hated it. But he stood for it, all the same, you see."

"Stood for *what?*"

"For this." She swept one of her long, slender hands around her once, again, to include not only this house but in widening concentric spheres Harvard, Boston, Cape Cod and the Islands—the proud, rude citadel of the Eastern littoral. "All this. Everything you wanted to destroy."

"Destroy—!" he cried. *"Destroy*—you're stark, raving mad! I've loved it more than anything else in my whole life . . ."

"Yes," she said with her father's voice. "More than anything else in this world. That's true. You loved it too much. You wanted to be a part of it so badly you turned it all inside out. You twisted it into its opposite."

"You don't even know what you're—"

"Oh, yes. You wanted it, all right. Is it so difficult to see? Because you thought you were more worthy of it than Lee. Well, you weren't, you never were—as witness this sordid business."

"That's simply not true, that's ridiculous!"

"I know you'll never see it, Paul. Or admit it if you should. It's too painful, and you never could bear pain very well. But it's true, just the same. In his shoes. My father's son. And what was the only way you could do it? Tell me."

"Nell, that's monstrous . . . and cruel—"

"Yes. Truth is cruel. I know."

Her eyes, narrowed now with pain and fatigue, were perfectly steady. For the first time he turned away and gripped the shoulder of the sleepy Cambodian idol on the mantel. He felt provoked, embittered, half-stunned, his thoughts whirling like a flock of crazed birds. What was she saying? Excessive admiration, she was saying. Excessive admiration, obsessive worship of an object, a person, a way of life slipped imperceptibly into envy, hatred's threshold—not true, not true!—it couldn't be true, no one could say he hadn't loved the Seavers and all they stood for with simple, wholehearted sacrifice, with that particular emulation that is the very *proof* of affection . . . and if he *had*—now and then and rarely—idly dreamed of being Silas Seaver's son, why should that—for Christ's sake, why should that mean he actually *sought*—no! it was not true, none of it!

But if it *were* true . . .

The room, the house now rested in complete stillness, made more massive by a confused mutter of voices and heavy equipment outside. He found he was holding his breath furtively, gripping the cool gray stone. He tried to say something, could not; his mouth was dry as meal. Eleanor was watching him, but sadly now—a kind of fearful sadness he'd never seen before, never quite that . . . He shut his eyes. With that slow, quaking visceral shock that never fails to herald the most fearsome revelations, he knew it was true. He had envied Leland Seaver, deeply and terribly—even when guarding him most resolutely from ruin. He had loved Lee, but he had hated him, too, for scorning the patrimony he himself worshipped . . . But it was so eminently *laudable,* this world, with its peculiar grace and assurance, its fine austerity. The exemplary land, its very pre-eminence a silent rebuke to the brash, open-handed, rootless extravagance of the West Coast . . .

His father's world. *Rick!* his mother had called, just before dying. *Oh Rick, dearest* . . . In his fearful need he had spurned it, wished it out of sight—all that breezy, generous, Western egalitarian Irish heritage. But the price had been a consumptive envy: a short step from thinking, "I love this new Eastern world, I want to be accepted by it, to *be* it, I wish this man were my real father," to thinking, "In the strength of my love, my loyalty, my desire I am more worthy than the son, I want to supplant him, destroy him, marry his sister—become in fact and deed the true son and heir—"

What a short, stealthy step it was . . .

Was it true? Was it? But that was only half the price. The other part was self-denial. For there was the part of him that knew he never could be Lee, no matter what. He was Rollicking Rick Blackburn's boy, loving wit, travel, new faces and fresh lands, the spendthrift virtues; conscious of differences, troubled by anomalies and crosswinds. He was not Leland Seaver and could never be, by definition—and in the pit of his awareness he knew that, too, he'd always known it. Hadn't he?

He passed his hand over his face, which was slick with sweat, half-conscious of a shout in the street, and what sounded like the powdery rattle of a chain hoist. Nell's eyes still held on his, unwavering; and he saw, with a heavy, boundless dismay, that for all her puerile severity she was nevertheless tougher than he, and braver, because she had foregone the comfort of received illusions. Her truths, such as they were, at least had the supreme virtue of being her own. He had sought the favor of alien ways, alien gods . . .

But what, then? Was admiration only envy's other face? Did the two inevitably merge, so that love—admiration, emulation, desire—could only turn through some obscene alchemy into hatred? Were we all so many helpless pawns in the face of such a cosmic cheat? *Envy, to which th'ignoble mind's a slave, Is emulation in the learn'd or brave* . . . He'd always believed that in his bright credulity—and he'd been wrong. He had hated his father's legacy because he'd feared it, then; for years convinced himself he'd been living by reason. And this was where it had led. For every repudiation there was a corresponding cost—rather than divest oneself of a burden one merely assumed another, more expensive one. And this was what it had cost him: a suppressed desire for Leland Seaver's destruction, and after that—

There was a sudden, snarling bellow out in the street, shocking in the morning stillness. He exclaimed, "Jesus!" stepped to the window and flung back the curtain—saw the pick-up trucks, the upward looking, helmeted men, the looping suspended lines and a figure high in the branches. The Yorktown elm. Of all days—! In a paroxysm of wrathful release he flung open the door and half ran from the room.

"Paul," Eleanor called after him. *"Paul—"*

He hurried down the front steps into the still heat, pushed open the iron gate and called up into the snarling clamor: "Hey! You turn that thing off!" The woodcutter, well-braced in one of the higher crotches, went on rocking the chain saw with deft care. Silver chips drifted down like untimely snow. The racket was impregnable, maddening. Blackburn seized one of the helpers by the shoulder and roared: "Tell him! Tell him to turn that damned thing off—!"

The assistant, a slender boy with a ridged brow and large, hooked Adam's apple, was staring at him in pop-eyed astonishment. Quickly he yanked on a nearby line, and made desisting motions with his gloved hands. The flatulent bellow stopped. The sawyer peered down, a broad red face under the canary yellow hard hat, and called: "What's the matter?"

"Come down out of there!" Blackburn shouted up. "Right away. Come on! Who told you to cut down this tree today?"

The woodcutter scowled. "Listen, Mac, they said take it down this morning—"

"And I said come down out of there!" If the man had been standing in front of him at that moment he would have hit him with his fists, a piece of plank—anything available. He was sweating and trembling; the shaggy, heavy-booted figure above him wobbled and wavered as if underwater. "A woman—" His voice broke. He fought to hold it steady and hard, but he couldn't say the words. "—a woman is very sick in there, this is no time for any such racket as this! You come down out of that tree . . ."

The woodcutter stared down at him for a moment: then with quick, disgusted movements attached the saw to a lanyard and began to lower it through the dead, silvered branches. Blackburn, watching, clenched his hands, clenched them again.

"I'm sorry, sir," the helper said. "We didn't know anything about no sick woman. All they told us was, they've had this request in, four, five weeks . . ."

"That's all right. All right. Just so long as you don't bring it down today." Blackburn turned and went back up the walk, stumbled on the second step and nearly fell. Inside the foyer he stopped, swaying—all at once put his hand to his mouth. Chewing on his knuckles he began to cry slowly, harshly, staring at the brass nameplate on the door.

NINETEEN

"—WONDERFUL PRESENCE OF MIND, KITTY," Archibald Grace declared. "It's something that's never failed her, never once. Of how many women of your acquaintance could that be said, Jacobi? Answer me honestly, now."

"None," Jacobi answered. "Not one."

"Ah, that's why Kitty is so formidable." Grace gave a short exhalation of breath—Jacobi couldn't tell whether it signified gratification or despair—and waved briskly to Sven Bjornson of the Swedish delegation, who was talking with Piers-Monckton. "There was the final toast—to Franco-American understanding, may it never lose its vaunted luster—and then we all rose, and De Gaulle offered Kitty his arm. She was wearing her royal blue silk that evening, do you remember it?"

"Not that I can recall."

"Lovely thing. Anyway, it was stiffened by a crinoline petticoat, and it was at precisely that moment she felt *something let go*. Yes!" Grace chuckled genially, his eyes darting birdlike around the Council chamber. "Ah, the unforeseen hazards of the diplomatic life, Jacobi! There were the assembled grandees, there stood France in all his gloomy, martial grandeur. What do you think she did?"

"I—I can't imagine," Jacobi answered. He'd been up all night working on the speech, and since Blackburn had flown in from Boston had been rewriting feverishly, arguing over various points; and his natural irascibility was mounting minute by minute, listening to the United Nations Ambassador's tales of pomp and glory and waiting for the session to get under way.

"Of course she realized instantly there was no time for repairs. So she did a quick little shimmy and let the blasted crinoline fall, gave it a good swift judicious kick under the table. And turning to the savior of modern France threw him her most disarming smile." Grace drew two fingers down the side of his pink, perfectly shaved cheek, and nodded with frosty courtesy to Dohturov of the Soviet Union, who nodded genially back. "The General, who had more of an eye for the female form divine than you might have suspected, bestowed on her one of his most significant glances, and *voilà!* they led the exodus into the main salon. But lord, you should have seen the women's eyes!"

Jacobi, seated beside Grace in one of the advisers' chairs placed behind the Chief of Mission's seat at the Security Council table, thought crossly, Why in God's name have I deserved *this*. The Chamber always depressed him anyway. With its green and tan décor and eerily slanted walls, the enormous silken tapestry resolutely shutting out the afternoon light, it looked like a stage-set erected by some empty-headed Maecenas for a dreadful, amateurish drama. The Norwegian mural with its tortuously inept naked bodies writhing like foetuses in antiseptic sepia wombs, particularly offended him. It was like everything else at the United Nations— staid and pompous and passé, a doddering actress insisting on patterns of adulation that had no basis in reality. Misconceived and traduced at its very birth, shattered on the obdurate rock of the veto, the thirty-odd years since San Francisco had only revealed the ponderous façade that failed to shield its ineffectuality. What a *chance* missed . . .

Glumly he watched Blackburn talking with quick intensity to Parracini, the Italian Ambassador. Paul however believed in it, defended it as idea and institution. "World opinion *does* mean something," he'd said to Jacobi and Hudela, flying up from the Capital the night before. "Do you think the action on Korea, the resolutions on Yugoslavia in Fifty-One and Algeria in Sixty would have been possible without the moral force the General Assembly exerts? Don't be too quick to write it all off. At the very worst it keeps us talking . . . Or do you think that's just bushwah, too?"

". . . I think you're sticking your neck way out, sir," he'd answered. "And to no good purpose. If Peking abandons its position on the Drachenfels trials it won't be because of any Security Council debate, it'll be because of pressure exerted from Moscow or Paris. Or because Comrade Ch'en figures another line of attack will prove more effective."

"Maybe. But the resolution, Sid. Suppose we can turn the action . . ."

"It's just a front, Mr. Secretary," Mike had broken in with some urgency. "They're using it for propaganda purposes. It's a loudspeaker. They want to make a big thing out of this, score a lot of points. Why else would Ch'en be coming over to run it?"

"Sure, I know. Well, maybe we'll do the scoring. He won't be up against Archie this time." There was the sudden, infectious grin; then it fled, and the fatigue lines flowed back around the Secretary's eyes. "We've got to work with it. Don't you see? We've got to. There's this pressure building up all over—couldn't you feel it yesterday, at ExComm?"

"Yes," Jacobi had said, "I could feel it."

"This thing seems to have taken on a life of its own—feeding on itself, building its own momentum. It scares me." He'd massaged his eyes and nose tiredly, gazing out at the depthless void beyond the window. "Hell, I know it's eighty per cent window dressing—the UN. Yes, and twenty per cent PA system. But it's all we've got, to hold off the thunder and lightning . . ."

"There's our villain," Archie Grace was saying now. The thin four-teen-karat gold pen in his fingers traversed like a pigmy gun barrel the tan wood horseshoe and stopped at the massive squat figure of Kuranda of Umbara, who was sitting perfectly still in the President's chair in the midst of the genial general commotion, the arrivals and greetings, his head propped on his massive forearms, brooding like Ashurbanipal. "How'd you like to meet *him* in an underpass on a dark and stormy night, eh? Black Messiah Number Five-A. Going to lead all dem oppressed tarbabies out ob de layand ob bondage, yassuh." Grace had a great reputation as a parlor mime. Jacobi, unsmiling, thought of the note-passing with Carter at the Co-Ax meeting when Vosz had called Joe an aboriginal blackamoor; he glanced back to the observers' section but Joe was still checking with the Department's Operations Center from the US Mission offices across the street.

Aloud he said: "Oh, they're uppity. Uppity's the word."

Grace's smile vanished, replaced by that expression of injured, bilious discomfiture that had earned him the nickname of Puffles among the Department's younger, less reverent souls. "Oh, it's easy for you to talk," he retorted. "You haven't done a tour out there. You haven't had to put up with the insults and chaos and comic opera." Watching Kuranda his eyes narrowed. "Two-faced, conniving little beggar . . . Give them a little authority and right away they begin to feel they're some ebony reincarnation of Ivan the Terrible. And of course this is his big chance, the blessed moment he's been waiting for—to play off the Inscrutable East against the Decadent West. All of it nicely calculated to display his talents as potential leader of the Pan-African Federation. And they'll swallow it," he ended cholerically. "They'll gobble it down plug, rod and reel."

"You don't feel the Secretary's tactics are sound, then?"

"Sound?" The Ambassador's eyes rolled up to meet Jacobi's; his foxy bon vivant's face became all at once older and much harder. "Sound? I suppose so. Who knows? In this bear garden anything's possible. Of course it hasn't a damned thing to do with *statecraft,* with getting on with the real business of the world's work, I can tell you that."

"Oh well, if it doesn't pan out we can always blame the niggers, can't we?" Jacobi said. Grace gave him a furious, outraged look and sank into sullen silence. He seemed neither distressed nor elated that Paul had decided to take over the delegation for the purpose of rebutting the Chinese charges. In UN service only two types seemed to survive: the extroverts and demagogues who used it as a proscenium arch for their performances—a publicity power base for their ambitions back home; and the manipulators, who held no illusions whatever about this Forum of the Peoples and who forever moved behind the scenes with a resolute delicacy, pressing for confidential "understandings." Poor old Puffles, with his last-century habits of protocol, his starchy ambassadorships in Paris and Athens and

Istanbul, fell into neither category. The underlying cynicism in the place had bitten into his soul like acid, until nothing was left but patrician snobbery and bile.

The room was filling rapidly now; the galleries were already crowded. Above their heads in the press booths there were feverish preparations—the major networks had apparently decided this one was worth shooting into the hearthsides of America. Well they might. Jacobi looked around again for Carter, failed to find him, encountered directly behind him the placid face of Mike Hudela, who murmured: "Greatest show on earth."

"Beats Christians-and-Lions."

"Now you're just being superior," Senator Frank Church, Grace's Deputy Chief of Delegation, chided him.

"Don't forget the flucking tigers," Hudela added. "Paper and sabertooth."

Jacobi started to reply, suddenly broke off; he had felt the quickened tension in the hall, the gathering anticipatory murmur, even before he turned. Ch'en Pu-tsao was entering at the head of his group. He moved quickly, though without any appearance of haste, hands loose at his sides. His eyes, as black as his short, wiry hair, shone warmly under the lights and gave evidence of a boundless energy, balancing the resolute cast to the lips. Everything about him bespoke force, resilience, a fine tensile strength; a man in full command of his powers.

Just as he reached his seat Paul broke away from Parracini and headed for his own chair, and their eyes met across the horseshoe. Jacobi, watching, thought again how much alike they were, for all the differences. Each had the same broad, strong face with its short nose and square jaw, the deep-set, level eyes. Both were plain, unprepossessing men, even a touch homely, but graced with an uncommon animation—that uniquely purposeful magic that reaches into men's minds and effects changes there, impels the tide of great events. Ch'en nodded, the American nodded back. It was a brief enough glance, not at all hostile, even with a suggestion of warmth; but there was the unmistakable electric shock of two champions in open, accepted confrontation, mighty issues joined. The whole room saw it, and the murmur grew.

At that moment Kuranda, with his exquisite African sense of timing, began to tap his gavel: slow, rhythmic strokes of wood on wood. And caught by the swift, unnatural quiet in the chamber Jacobi started as if wakened. It's Ch'en—he met the idea, astonished he hadn't seen it as clearly before—Paul knew he was coming and couldn't resist it. Main event, fifteen rounds . . . and may the best man win.

But that was an American tradition—

"This emergency session of the Security Council is now declared in session," Kuranda was saying in his deep, nicely modulated French, "and the delegates will please be in order. The meeting is held at the request of the People's Republic of China, protesting the alleged dissemination of poisonous gases on her sovereign territory on the part of the United States, and presenting a resolution for the expulsion of the latter nation from this body in violation of Article Thirty-three of the Charter." There was a mutter in the galleries, contentious and harsh. Kuranda raised his head in slow, ponderous rebuke and the sound subsided. "These constitute grave charges indeed, and they will receive a full—and respectful—hearing." Again he paused, then said crisply: "The chair now recognizes the distinguished delegate from the People's Republic of China, Foreign Minister Ch'en Pu-tsao."

"And now the gospel according to Saint Mao," Grace muttered sourly.

Ch'en leaned forward a little toward the microphone, his hands clasped, and Jacobi watched delegates and observers switch to the English or French translations.

"Mr. President, fellow delegates. The charges my government brings are indeed grave, as our distinguished President has said. It is a matter of profound regret that my nation, so recently instated as a permanent member of this august body, should find it necessary to burden the Council with them. Let me assure the Council they are not advanced lightly, nor were they arrived at in a casual manner."

He paused and his eyes moved around the crescent of table with interest. He was speaking without notes, and Jacobi was struck all over again by the balance of subtlety and force in the man.

"Mr. President, in one sense my people should not have been unduly surprised, for China has pursued a singular destiny in modern times. For well over a century she has been the victim of incursions and assaults which no western power has ever had to endure. There were the impositions of the so-called China Trade, the 'concessions,' and the establishment of foreign enclaves in our own cities. *Concessions,*" he repeated, and his eyes glittered. "The Treaty Ports, the legalizing of opium, the foreign legations. We were raw material for the twin zeal of missionaries and Standard Oil—none of which was assuaged or averted by the mendacious façade of the Open Door. Our door *was* always open, it seemed: forced open by those who came empty-handed and left with pockets well-lined. These conditions were blandly accepted by the civilized powers of the West as the inevitable result of Chinese weakness, Manchu venality. There was even advanced the interesting theory that these things were necessary and proper because the Chinese were inferior people—indeed that the entire yellow race, like the black race, being inherently inferior, was receiving its just deserts." There was a low murmur from the African delegations and another muttering echo from the gallery, resentful and ominous; and glancing upward Ch'en smiled softly. "The only difficulty, Mr. President, was that we did not *feel* inferior.

"I will not dwell on the anguished years of Japanese invasion, when our land was cruelly ravaged; when, although my government took the unprecedented action of offering to fight under the direct command of the brilliant American general Joseph Stilwell, all Lend Lease and military aid nevertheless continued to go to Chiang Kai-shek, that guileful pretender to democracy, who hoarded these same supplies—not to repel the Japanese invaders but to use them against his own countrymen, to maintain his warlord regime of tyranny and corruption . . ."

"Don't you love history made easy?" Archie Grace murmured—and across the oval Ch'en seemed to be smiling directly at the Ambassador, though he could not possibly have heard him.

"Xenophobic, we were called. Victims of á Yenan Complex, psychotic recluses peering out at the civilized world from caves of suspicion and hate. But Mr. President, attitudes do not spring from the earth: they are responses to circumstance. The abandoned child draws into himself, the despised laborer seeks to assert his dignity.

"It is not my purpose to weary this august Council with a historical dissertation on the long parade of invasion and indignity which brought my people to the very edge of despair. With the acceptance of the true China in the world community, with the advent of the new Administration in the United States, we were assured that those barbaric attitudes were a thing of the past, which we were to put behind us in a new era of open negotiation and good feeling. It was in that spirit, Mr. President, that we accepted these assurances and agreed at New Delhi to the creation of the new state of Dhotal—even though it involved a cession of sovereign Chinese territory, and the presence of international inspection teams. It was in that spirit that we welcomed the GATO Technical Assistance Mission to Yunnan as an earnest of good faith. If the western powers could, at long last, relinquish their predilection for annexing choice morsels of our land and resources, surely *we* could put our suspicions behind us and accept this errand of mercy."

He nodded firmly. "Yes. This errand of international mercy to a stricken area of the earth. That is what it professed tó be, and that is how we accepted it." His eyes rested on Blackburn's a brief moment, then passed on. "Imagine our uneasiness therefore, Mr. President, when reports spread of a mysterious malady in remote places—a sickness that evaded medical analysis, that spread with curious stealth until whole villages and towns lay stunned in terrible apathy. Yes, picture to yourself our alarm when investigation by our authorities resulted in the apprehension of several men—shall I call them men, Mr. President? Shall I honor them with the proud title of humanity?"

So intent was Jacobi in watching the Foreign Minister, following the sharp, melodic lift and drop of Mandarin, searching for nuance, that he only then became aware of Joe Carter bent over Blackburn's chair. The Secretary was holding a piece of paper in his hand. His face was impassive but the very set of his head bespoke that controlled tension Jacobi had learned to recognize instantly. Turning back now, the Secretary passed the paper to Jacobi, thrust it into his hands.

"Read that, Sid. Read it."

> TOP SECRET, PERSONAL TO ASSISTANT SECRETARY FAR EAST FROM AMERICAN CONSUL, PAO SHAN. EVADED CAPTURE BY PROVISIONAL DHOTALESE FORCES DURING SEIZURE AND LOOTING PAO SHAN CONSULATE. POSSESS INCONTROVERTIBLE PROOF DRACHENFELS AND ASSISTANTS HERTZ AND MCKINLOCH SOWING NERVE GAS K-432 ALONG UPPER SALWEEN, VICINITY LUSHUI AND MENG-PO-LO WITH CIA KNOWLEDGE AND SUPPORT. REPORT FOLLOWS. URGENTLY REQUEST CABLE SOONEST. COCKSWAIN UMPHLETT.

One afternoon when he was twelve Jacobi had come home from school to find his mother hysterical with grief and his sisters frightened into silence. His Aunt Thelma, tremulous but holding on to herself, had taken him aside and told him: his father had committed suicide. He remembered staring at her puffy old maid's face, watching the cords in her throat, the mole below her left ear, while the awful awareness burned its way into the center of his heart and lodged there forever. His father, who had been undaunted by any crisis large or small—who had in a sense been the mainstay of De Kalb Avenue—was gone. Had run out on them. They were alone now, and defenseless. Now again there was the same yawning, distended dread, the same flutter of malignant wings. *Umphlett,* he thought, *Umphlett!* My God—

He looked up, his face burning. Ch'en Pu-tsao was proceeding smoothly, pointing to the map now, to the area just northwest of Yao-kuan, but he hadn't heard one word. Paul's eyes were fastened on his with unnatural intensity.

"Chief," he murmured, "let me check—"

"No. I've got to run this one down myself." With a single deft movement the Secretary removed his earphones and said, "Archie, take over for me, will you? I've got to go across the street for a moment."

Grace blinked at him, his lips puffed. "All right. You mean—you want me to go ahead and answer the charges?"

"If need be, yes. I expect to be back in time, though. Just hold the fort."

"If you say so."

"Yes, I say so . . ." Blackburn's voice was edged with exasperation, but his face was expressionless. Rising he turned to Jacobi and Carter. "Come on. Let's get over there." They moved quickly toward the great teak doors. Paul was saying to Joe Carter: "Where'd he send it from? Bhamo? Myitkyina?"

"No, sir. It's from Pao Shan."

"Pao Shan—the *consulate*? But that's impossible—"

"He must have got in there somehow."

"Well, has he contacted Van? Has he—"

But Ch'en's voice pursued them now, calling—Jacobi could hear him with perfect clarity.

"He withdraws, Mr. President! The Secretary of State of this great, this civilized nation! Why does he hurry away at this particular moment? Is it because he is afraid to learn the truth—to face what lay behind this widely publicized errand of mercy?" The Foreign Minister was on his feet, his homely bronze face dark with anger; he held in one hand a small glass phial that winked in the saffron light. Blackburn, who had caught the denunciatory tone and probably his title, had turned and was gazing impassively at his antagonist.

"What's he saying? He's accusing me—"

"Yes," Jacobi answered, "of skipping out."

"Is he unwilling, Mr. President, to discover exactly what were the contents of this ampoule? Does he shrink from the admission that all past professions of friendship lie exposed as the most grotesque mockery in the face of this evidence? Does he fear, Mr. President, the full and terrible disclosure of a conspiracy he knows in his heart was engineered and executed by the high agencies of his own *government!* . . ."

There was a sudden, clamorous uproar in the gallery above them, shocking in its abruptness. Jacobi saw a large group on its feet, gesticulating, waving small placards, chanting in unison: *"Chi-com lies! Save our Mission! Chi-com lies!"* Guards were hurrying down the aisles, pushing against the densely swaying mass which began to fight back now, still chanting its slogans, a deafening reverberation in the high chamber. Blackburn's face, upturned, looked all at once tense and shaken.

"What's the matter with them? Have they gone crazy?"

"YAF bunch," Carter answered.

"I know—but how'd they get in like that? in force?"

Kuranda's gavel sounded again, flat and resonant against the uproar. "Disruption of the proceedings of this Council will not be tolerated!" he cried in a voice like thunder. "The chair orders that these demonstrators be removed from the chamber! *The chair orders it!*"

A pitched battle was going on now: the chant had subsided, broken into sharp, isolate cries—the energy of the group was now directed toward resisting expulsion as long as possible. More guards were coming down the aisles but the faction skillfully, doggedly held its place, surging, recoiling in a flurry of starkly lettered cardboard and flailing arms.

". . . Diversionary tactic," Blackburn was saying with a small, wry smile. "I never thought I'd be beholden to the Young Americans for Freedom, for anything . . . Let's go, boys."

But still he hung back, gazing across the great blond curve of the table where beyond the heads of the press representatives Ch'en still stood, watching him with that alert, penetrating glance—and what seemed to be the bitterest disappointment Jacobi had ever beheld in another man's eyes.

It seemed doubtful enough. It seemed downright impossible, approached from any angle at all. A man who as protocol officer in Lahore had confused the name of the Nawab Tandahur with that of his most detested rival, who had managed to fall out of a ceremonial barge on the Uyu during Muharram; a man who couldn't control the extracurricular antics of his own wife—

"What real confidence can you put in anything he says, anyway?"

Blackburn, sitting at Grace's desk at the United States Mission on First Avenue, found himself staring at an enlarged framed photograph of Archie and Kate being greeted by Franco at some formal function in Madrid, and looked away irritably. The others were quiet but he didn't expect any answer to the question. Who in his right mind would? Yet it had seemed to betray his past support of the Cockswain—glumly he wished he hadn't said it.

His search for confirmation had been disastrous. He'd got exactly nowhere at all. He'd been unable to contact the President—Frank Greggson, his secretary, reached in Detroit, informed him the President had just started to give the first of three speeches there. Vosz was in flight to New York, on the way to giving *his* address to the Council on Foreign Relations. Why, for Christ sake, had everyone in Washington decided to go around making speeches? Himself included, of course. Fred Semmes was inspecting a new missile base in Texas. Nobody would tell him where Tremayne was; like a city cop, the CIA was as always unavailable just when you needed them most. After a good deal of ranting and roaring Blackburn had got through to Shelly's deputy, Tom Barrow, who'd assured him they had nothing more on Drachenfels than he already knew, but that he expected to be in touch with the Director in an hour or so; which was a great help. There were times when the obduracy of government, its sheer multitudinous diffusion of activities, could make you want to smash every pane of glass within—

Bent forward he gripped his head, which was splitting. Things kept skidding away from the corners of his eyes—an unmistakable sign of exhaustion he'd learned to recognize and guard against over the years; but there was no time now for Rest and Rehabilitation. Time was in the saddle now, whirling along with the fearsome dance of an immense sweepsecond hand around a dial as cold as the moon; minute after minute while he sat here and the choices narrowed, the possibilities for conciliation gave way to harsher, less tractable measures. He remembered a feeling like this during his college days when he'd had to swim three events, the sense that the clock was moving too fast, some nefarious kind of sorcery had speeded it up and there was no time, bound in the glaucous seethe of water and the hollow, muted roar of the crowd, to finish the race, no time to complete this very lap, reach the black-lined wall. He hated the sensation. Diplomacy was a leisured art—and it couldn't be. Blackburn's Lament.

Sid and Joe were regarding him with a kind of fearful deference he would have found amusing at any other time. He gazed at them a moment, said aloud: "Poor Umphlett. Confusion still stalks him like the plague. Of course it could be a plant by the Chinese."

"That's why he used his nickname, Chief. To preclude that interpretation."

"But they could know about it . . ."

"With that spelling? Highly doubtful."

"True enough. —There's no way you can contact him, Joe?"

"Not without ESP, sir. De Leo says there's been nothing more out of there. Dead silence."

"Then why in God's name did he say: *Send cable soonest?*"

Carter shrugged. "That's the Cockswain. I suppose he means for us to cable the embassy. Or maybe Kunming. Van says he hopes to be in touch with him in six, seven hours, maybe . . ."

"Lovely." For want of anything else to do Blackburn kept running his eyes along the lines of the cable. "Proof. Of course it's possible that proof to Umphlett could be something we would not accept at all."

". . . Chief, you can't give that speech." Sid was looking at him with blunt, importunate force, his hands on his knees.

"You think he's right? It's true?" Sid said nothing. "But why? Why should poor star-crossed Umphlett be right this time, and everyone else be wrong?"

There was a short silence. Jacobi rubbed his bony hands back and forth on his trousers, his face screwed up like an old sage's. "But— the pieces still don't fit," he cried. "There's too many parts missing . . . Doesn't it seem funny to you that you can't reach anybody right now?"

"Now hold on, Sid. The President—"

"The President, okay. But what about Tremayne, Semmes, what about Vosz? Why, at this key moment, should they all be so unavailable?"

"Look, Sid, Reiny had this speech scheduled weeks ago—months, for all I know . . ." He paused, full of consternation; in his turmoil and exhaustion there was an almost overpowering impulse to agree, to behold conspiracies in every rustle of the curtains. "You mean you actually think I'm being left out on the end of a great big dirty limb, with everybody in Washington, D.C. trying to saw it off—?"

"It happened to Stevenson over the Cuba flap—if they were prepared to fake those photos of the aircraft markings to snow him, there isn't much they won't do, is there? They lied to Sebald about all that CIA stuff in Burma in Fifty-Three. They wouldn't even cut our own Intelligence Director in on the Bay of Pigs invasion force, they left Rogers in the dark at first over the Peking overtures. Chief, you've got *enemies* down there . . ."

"And you, Joe? You go along with Sid, here?"

Carter shifted his gaze. "I'm not sure I go quite as far as Sid on this. But yes, I think something's very fishy out there—I agree that you ought not to make that defense."

"But all we've got is this God damn crazy cable of Umphlett's—Jesus Christ, *Umphlett's!* There's so damned much at stake . . ."

Neither of them made any reply. Enemies. Hell yes, he had enemies enough. Who didn't? He ran his hand through his hair; he felt actively frightened at the thought. That men could—that there could actually be underfoot a coherent plan . . . The sense he'd had since the long bedside vigil and the quarrel with Nell early that morning, of massive forces moving darkly against him, driving toward some grim and unpredictable solution increased, swung his thoughts in looping, eerie patterns.

"All right," he heard himself say with heat. "We'll settle it for good." He picked up the phone. "Vice President Donlund's office, please. This is Secretary Blackburn." There was Bill, then. Bill wouldn't let him down. Christ, there had to be *somebody* who could give him something definitive in the face of all these maddening wraiths of—

"Vice President Donlund's office." Hélène Ransome, cool and competent and impervious.

"Hello, Hélène? This is Paul Blackburn. Is the Veep in? I need to speak to him—it's a matter of extreme urgency."

"Would you hold on, Mr. Secretary."

There was an interminable pause, then Donlund's deep, easy voice answered. In spite of the Tuesday hassle in ExComm Blackburn felt a slow, dense wave of relief.

"Bill, I'm calling you from Archie's office. We're on scrambler. Can you talk at your end?"

"Yes, sure. How's it going up there? We ahead or behind?"

"I can't say yet. Bill, I've just had a rather disquieting report from one of my people in the area—to the effect that Drachenfels definitely does have a CIA connection."

"For God's sake—I thought you said Van was convinced—"

"This is from one of my consuls, on the ground."

"Can you trust it?"

"Of course I can!" he retorted sharply, stung all at once by the reply. "What kind of a question is that?"

"Have you checked with Shelly?"

"I can't reach Shelly. *Or* Fred. I can't get hold of anybody who can clear this up . . . Look, Bill," he said tensely, and the sense of congealing pressure rode down on his shoulders, "I know we don't see eye to eye on this thing; but we've always been square with each other. Open and above board. In a few minutes I'm going across the street and try to make as strong and eloquent a defense as I can against some very serious charges. Now I think under the circumstances I have the right to know if anyone does. Bill, what's the story? What's really going on?"

There was the slightest of pauses, barely discernible, and then: "Nothing, Paul. You've got what there is to tell."

"All right, that does it!" he answered hotly, "I've had enough. I never thought you'd hold out on me, and I'm God damned if I can see why. Do you *want* to blow the whole game? I can tell you right now— and you can tell Shelly and Reiny and the President for me—I'm not going to make that speech unless I have the full story."

"Now hold on, Paul—"

"I'm sick of holding on, when I don't have anything to hold on to! Don't play around with me, Bill!"

"No, now hold on, hold on—I don't want you mad at me along with everyone else . . ." Again the briefest of pauses. "I don't even know that I ought to tell you this, without clearance—"

"Clearance from whom? from *God?*"

"It was a sensitive issue, extremely sensitive. The thing is, Drachenfels did have an Agency connection."

"Jesus Christ. When was this?"

"Some years back. After the Aswan Dam project. He turned over some information to the Agency, some very vital information on projected Egyptian missile sites; and the Soviet agents were after him. There was a certain amount of cloak-and-dagger grab-ass—you know how these things can get—and he was accused of murdering a Soviet agent."

"Yes, I've got that far," Blackburn answered coldly. "More or less. Even though we had to dig *that* out on our own.—All right: what *more* is there?"

"That's it, Paul. Drachenfels was acquitted and that was that. It was considered necessary to give him an alias—that's what all that Diefenbach background stuff was all about."

"The CIA set that up."

"Yes, that's right. To protect him from further Soviet reprisal. Trust me on this."

"Why in hell should I?"

There was another short pause, and Donlund said somberly: "Because we've known each other and worked together for years. Because we both come from the poor old maligned West Coast. Because we both lost our fathers early in life. *I* don't know. Make up your own reasons.

Look, I'm telling you all I can—none of us knew much about it, even then. It was very tightly held . . ."

Blackburn found himself smiling bitterly. "Ours but to do and die, eh?" he murmured. "Well, it won't wash, Bill. It won't carry the old load. If all this is ancient history, why is Shelly holding out on me this way? or you, for that matter? How can I put credence in *anything* this Drachenfels is mixed up in—how do I know he hasn't stuffed bubonic plague pellets into every frigging well in Yunnan?"

"Now don't take that attitude."

"What attitude do you *expect* me to take! Who's playing on which side of the line? I don't rate this, Bill. I really don't. No; I think I'll sit this one out. I'll let Archie deliver one of his silvery travelogues on the Prater in spring . . ."

"All right, Paul." The Vice President's voice had altered again—it was both harder and more concessionary. "I didn't want to tell you this—I figured you'd see it as trying to influence you unduly. Do you know who found Drachenfels innocent in that murder indictment? Who presided over the case? Silas Darcey Seaver."

Blackburn put his hand flat on the desk top. "Deuermann," he said gently, like a sigh.

"Yeah, sure, that was his real name. You knew about it, then."

"A little."

"Well, then. Do you mean to tell me the Judge would have cleared him of a murder charge if he wasn't all right? What more do you want?"

Well: that did change everything, no doubt about it. That put a very different construction on it all. If Federal Magistrate Seaver had come to the conclusion that he was innocent—

"Paul?" Donlund's voice pursued him. "You there?"

"Yes. I'm here."

"I know this is a thorny one. But the stakes are awfully big, you know."

"I know."

"All I can say is, if Judge Seaver's word isn't good enough for you nothing ever will be. Now go on over there. The President is counting on you to take 'em apart, plank by plank. All right?"

"I'll see."

He put the phone carefully back in its cradle and told the others. Carter nodded with a troubled air, but Sid shook his head stubbornly.

"I still don't buy it, Chief. It feels all wrong. You said so, yourself . . ."

He gripped his hands. "But think it through. I can't fly in the face of *policy* until I know what I'm about. Not without better evidence than this . . . No, for the time being I'm obligated to go along with what's been formulated."

"But if the Chinese *should* be right?" Jacobi said softly. "What then? You're leaving yourself with no room for maneuver, you'll have no credibility with anybody, anywhere in the whole mucked-up world . . ."

Which was true, too. Everything was true. And false. And shading off into a thousand confusions. It did still *feel* wrong, the instincts and intimations of two decades counseled caution, equivocation, further inquiry. But there wasn't time, there wasn't time for anything but action now—and pushing aside his suspicions were Bill's reluctant candor, and that unswerving probity of the Judge. And beyond that Ch'en Pu-tsao's eyes in the Council chamber facing him over the heads of the press table, animate with accusation, with contempt—

"I've got to do it, boys," he said with level finality. "I haven't any other choice, really."

"You have, Mr. Secretary," Sid said in the same soft tone. "But it's your decision."

TWENTY

"Sir! Mr. Carter—aren't you? *Sir—*"

Carter turned abruptly. The girl, slender in a turquoise jersey, was pulling at his sleeve—a gesture fearful and imperious. He frowned at her.

"Aren't you Assistant Secretary Carter?"

"Yes," he answered. "What is it?"

"Oh, thank God! I hoped it was you—I wasn't sure . . ." She gave a sudden nervous smile, shook her hair back from her throat and said, "I've got to see Secretary Blackburn immediately—I have a very important message for him."

He nodded automatically, moving toward the elevators. They were always around at such moments—worried-looking Hartsdale housewives and aspirant PhDs from Barnard, convinced they had the grand solution to the current crisis. "You'll have to contact the conference officer—check with one of the girls at the phones, over there. Now if you'll excuse me—"

"I've tried that—they won't let me call him. They won't even take a note to him . . ." She looked suddenly worn and tremulous, her green eyes wide; on the edge of tears. An attractive girl, with fine shoulders and a rich sensuality just beneath the surface. "They make it impossible, I've been here for two hours! I had to sneak in through that door, there . . ." She gestured toward one of the glass doors connecting the delegates' entrance with the visitors' section. "I've *got* to see him—can't you take me in with you?"

She had been walking with him toward the elevators, her hand still touching his sleeve now and then. Something in her manner was different from the run-of-the-mill samaritans; but, irritated at the fruitless conversation with the Operations Center down at State, the maddening absence of any further word out of Dhotal or the Triangle or all of far Cathay, worried over the new, grim turn of events, that dizzy neurotic bastard Umphlett, he said in his most brusque, official voice:

"I'm afraid that's impossible. The Secretary is in the Council now. You'll have to excuse me—"

"Oh . . ." She glanced around her wildly, increased her grip on his arm. The professional diffidence of secretaries and advisers and press people around them seemed only to increase her concern. "Look, you don't know me—who I am. I'm Jillian Hoyt. I'm—a friend of the Secretary. A good friend. I know he'll see me, I'm not trying to crash my way in or anything . . ."

He stopped in mid-stride and faced her. So this was the girl. Stout had told him about her one evening—a circuitous solicitude which failed to disguise the gloating malice underlying it. Danger, his mind had registered automatically, watching the Under Secretary's face, the smooth, slack jowls, the pigeon's lips. Big trouble. He had listened, made no comment, gone his way. It was no business of his if Blackburn was shacked up with fifty girls. Yet he had found himself curious, for all that—and oddly, subtly disconcerted. The Secretary had always seemed so balanced, self-contained: his course charted, his life set. You could imagine Andy Stinchfield involved with a chick, or Mike Hudela or that bastard Vosz—hell, you could picture the Squeezer groping and grappling with a dozen big-boned rapacious groupies all at once; but somehow not Paul Blackburn. And little by little the fine cynicism that had been his own mainstay had given way to more passionate sentiments: as he'd noticed the Secretary's increasing exasperation, the lapses of concentration, the sudden brief unfocused flares of temper, he'd begun to resent her, whoever she might be. Didn't she see what she was doing? She was fouling up the life of a very important man, a superior man . . .

Now here she was, distraught, peremptory, clinging to his arm for dear life. He felt a touch off-balance—he'd imagined an older woman, someone more elegant and assured, not a headlong girl: she seemed on the point of flying off somewhere, like some vivid tropical bird.

"Please," she said. She had sensed his changed attitude—she knew he knew about her, he could tell—because she seemed to sway nearer him, become more entreating. She attracted him sharply, and this irritated him more than anything else. "Please let me see him, talk to him—just five minutes. Just two . . ."

"I would if I could but it really is impossible," he repeated. "He's addressing the Council, right now. You must know that."

She bit her lip, gave that flashing glance around the lobby, the small planes of her face catching the light prettily. Then she made up her mind and said: "There's a plan. To intercept Reinhold Vosz. This afternoon, right outside the Council on Foreign Relations. Uptown."

Oh Jesus Q. Christ, he thought, staring at her. Wouldn't you just know it. The Chinese charges and Umphlett's crazy cable out of the boondocks, and the Chief's phone conversation with Donlund—and now this. That son of a bitch Vosz would be the death of them yet. *If* what she said was accurate, of course.

"Whose plan?" he demanded, more harshly than he'd intended.

"What? It doesn't matter *who*—"

"Of course it does. How do you know this?"

"Because I know—look, can't I talk with him? I won't impose, I know how busy he is—I *know* he'll want to hear about this."

"You simply don't understand. He really is speaking right now, they're in session. If there's some kind of demonstration up there—"

"It's more than that—it's a plan to kidnap him," she said with sudden vehemence. "I've just found out. Someone in the government, high up in the government, has told them about Vosz's route—as a trap, so they'll fall into the trap. So as to hurt both Vosz and Paul, don't you see?"

Somberly, impassively he nodded, thinking of Nancy Shattuck. Nancy had even looked like this girl—long loose hair, the whiplike body, the volatile responses . . . He'd been excited at first: elated and prideful to have this beautiful white girl going to the games with him, sharing his bed. "People ought to live according to their best impulses," she'd told him once. "Society can't dictate anything to anybody." Ah, but it could, though; oh my yes indeedy, it could. In spite of all his cool, hard caution she'd almost got him kicked out of college; she'd caused him to quarrel disastrously with his best friend. She'd almost finished him before he'd got started. She'd been just like this Hoyt girl, chock-full of high ideals and emotional largesse—and it always led to big trouble. He'd thought then, embittered and savage, that it was purely his comeuppance, the consequences of reaching for forbidden fruit; but he'd been wrong—there was simply this kind of woman, who confused everything, who always tried to have it both ways.

"Even if your information *is* reliable," he said coldly, "the Secretary has more important things to worry about right now."

"But this is terribly important!"

"Everything is relative, Miss Hoyt."

"Don't you understand?" she cried. "They've set this up, a lot of people are going to get hurt and it doesn't have to happen at all . . . Look, I don't give a damn what you think of me—but don't you care what this will do to Paul?"

He saw that she actively disliked him; and this, coupled with all the other pressures, infuriated him. All his easy providence fled.

"I care a lot about what happens to the Secretary," he said with sudden soft anger. "How about you, baby?"

Her head went back, her eyes flared. "—You bastard," she said in low, threatful intensity, "you're just along for the ride. Aren't you?"

"That's it."

"You're all alike—you wouldn't join the truly militant movements, oh no! All walled up in black—black power, black muslimism, black panthers, black black black—go ahead! Ruin him, then! You—"

She leaped at him in a little frenzy but he was quicker, caught first one wrist and then the other and held them against his chest.

"Reg'lar li'l ol' wahhhldcat, ain't you?" he said in a slow, even drawl, insultingly. "You really know how to do it, don't you, baby?" She looked frightened and unsure now, struggling, and it pleased him—too much, he knew, but he couldn't help it. Christ! That the Chief should have got himself messed up with one of these!

"For your information it so happens he's right now trying to keep some fat old H-bombs from falling on your pretty little ass. Or haven't you got the picture?"

"I've got the picture all right—"

"Why don't you just throw it over and go home to Daddy?"

She stopped struggling then and drew back, her face stiff, her eyes dead green with hate. ". . . If you don't tell him about this I'll kill you," she whispered. "And that's a promise."

"You do that." He released her, grinning broadly through more turmoil than he would have believed, and turned toward the opened elevator. "You do that thing, Miss Hoyt."

Trembling she glared at the closed elevator doors through which Carter had passed: doors which, when closed, looked more final than any others. The grip of his fingers around her wrists was still active, a quaking pressure; her heart was beating soddenly. Pompous, cold-blooded creep—! Probably hoped to wreck it all, bring down everybody and everything, survive all alone in a bomb crater at 138th and Lenox, come out later gloating at the corpses and the rubble. What did he care? More whites than blacks would perish. And Paul had put him into that job—

One of the guards, round-shouldered and paunchy, was eyeing her suspiciously. Turning away she drifted back toward the information desks near the front entrance. Despondency dulled her rage now. What did it matter? The essential thing had been to get him to give the message to Paul, at the very least: now he would cheerfully die first.

"You idiot," she muttered through clenched teeth. You won't get another chance like that, don't think you will. You're your own worst enemy. Yes. Just like everybody else.

People kept crowding up to the information desks, asking for names, asking for numbers. There was a fat, buttery little man—he looked like a Malay—who glanced speculatively at her, and a gaunt Norseman with hands like the hands on Romanesque statuary, who stared at her forbiddingly, his eyes pale as ice in deep shadow. There is no barrier so insurmountable as the one between those who have entrée and those who do not, she told herself; the whole pitiful bloody history of mankind could be wrapped up in that sentence. Paul's very nearness, his total inaccessibility, made her wild. All day she'd tried to get through to him, encountering a succession of supercilious, faintly amused voices: he was not in his office in Washington, or in his suite at the Carlyle, nor in the Delegates' Lounge; at least that was what they'd told her. Now he was here, a few walls and corridors away—and he might as well be in Burma. They should have worked out some signal between them, some goofy provocative countersign so he'd have known it was she. But how were they to know she'd need to contact him officially?

You lordly bastards! she wanted to shout at the diplomats and clerks and flunkeys. You think you're so humping important and today I just may be more important than any of you—the most disgustingly valuable person in this loony fish bowl . . .

The hell with that nonsense: what was she going to do? She stood on one foot, biting on a hangnail, thinking of Maury live-parked beside the hydrant in the Oldsmobile, his soft almond eyes sliding toward the Council entrance, Land and Jumbo and the others in the panel truck down the block, sweating in the heat, waiting. She could prevent all this from happening. How? Call the cops? No: the old aversion checked that impulse. Were they there now, hidden behind the sedate east-side foyers? She could contact the Council—but that would only mean cops, anyway: and she couldn't do that. Not to Land . . .

Three men moved past her—swarthy, heavy-set men with brown moons of faces and that peculiar self-satisfied walk that snaps the leg out from the knee. They were talking loudly and laughing—a language she couldn't identify. Power made men top-lofty and vain and smug: it did. Look at them—they felt nothing could touch them, ever. One of the men dropped a cigarette from a leather case; it rolled along the shining black-and-white squares and she followed its diminutive course thinking, Do they have to make the UN foyer look *exactly* like a stupid chessboard?

She couldn't wait any longer—it was after six now. A few seconds more she hung there, swinging her shoulder bag aimlessly—abruptly whirled around and hurried out through the whistling, ponderous glass doors into the open plaza. Light and hope reigned here, freed of the gloomy harsh corridors inside. She squinted up at the towering green glass façade. Hopeless, hopeless! Nothing good would ever come of it. The Congress was still dancing while they all burned. She should have forced her way in somehow. *I'm Secretary Blackburn's lover, consort, paramour, inamorata and I* will *be treated with the respect befitting my station*—*!* Watch their goggling faces. What a lot of words for it there were. Like sex. Like—

The cabs were all taken, they always were. Summertime, and the thieving is jazzy. Her eyes poured over some embassy car, all dove gray and black, its engine idling richly, momentarily abandoned by its chauffeur—resisted the almost ungovernable impulse. You *are* an outlaw, she told herself with a catch of wonder, of fear, hurrying away toward the gates, you think like one, you want to act like one. Why not? Tear up the avenue through the lights, siren going, scattering frightened pedestrians left and right. A merry chase. Why merry? The Hoyts were unstable, Grandma Kendrick always said. Yet it was her mother who had gone to pieces . . .

God *damn* it!—why wasn't there ever a free taxi? She hadn't done anything right. Children filed past her in noisy, disheveled columns to see the UN, the adults in charge shouting at them. Chiseled high on the gray stone the prophet's vision caught her eye, angered her all over again. Consummate idiots—no swords were ever going to be beaten into anything but more and better swords, no nation would ever pass up the use of force if force would serve its ends. Whoever *was* running this sorry carnival should never have put the faculty for reason in the brain of an animal.

A cab. Empty, on the far side of the street. Frantically she waved, raced across just as the lights turned, saw at the same moment a woman hurrying down the avenue, her face red under a yellow ice-cream-cup hat: a tired, heavy-bodied wobble, one arm waving. Too slow. Had the money but not the agility. Jillie tumbled in and banged the door shut, watching the woman's glaring, outraged eyes.

"Park and Sixty-eighth," she said to the glass. "And if you drive faster than you should I'll double your fare."

"How fast is that, bootsie?"

The driver's eyes, locked in the tight rectangle of mirror, were crinkled and small, glinting. Bronx wise guy. Indolently he picked up speed, peering at a passing carryall, and she saw his face: slack mouth, amused calculating glance, slick leathery skin. She knew him: he was always the one who obscured other people's view at the movies, propositioned waitresses and turned up the TV too loudly in bars. Rules were never for these slobs, they knew all the angles and never got caught, they could brazen anything out with cool insolence. They would have made the most incomparable political activists—but no, they were always the reactionaries, the superpatriots. They were always on the side of law-and-order, except where it cramped *them*. She had long since given up on their breed.

"I mean drive it just as fast as you possibly can, will you?" she said tersely, angered at the suppliant edge in her voice.

He yawned, a foggy growl; his arm, hairy and thick, lay across the top of the wheel. "No, I mean no kidding, is it important?"

"Do you think I'd ask you if it wasn't?"

"Sweetheart, I've had them ask me anything you can trouble your pretty little head about." His lips curled in greasy, grand disdain. "You wouldn't believe the things some of these dizzy chicks have asked me . . . Now if somebody's sick or dying—"

"That's it," she said tightly, "somebody's dying."

His eyes narrowed with suspicion. He muttered something inaudible, then: "What are you, a sweet little kidder?"

She burst out, "Will you just *drive—!*"

"Look, you just asked me to break the law, risk my hack license, now what's the story? You leveling or putting me on?"

She made no answer; sat hating the back of his head, the blackened creases in his neck above the orange sport shirt, hating all arrogant, argumentative, self-righteous souls everywhere on earth. He missed a light through sheer malicious sloth and began playing with the radio—settled on a Harlem rock band, tenor voices in demented howling chorus. Groaning she looked for another empty cab: they were all taken. No, there was one behind them, slowing. She lurched over, pressed the door handle—saw a man step out to the vacant cab from the curb.

"Hey, what's that all about?" the driver demanded.

"Nothing, *nothing* . . ."

"You riding with me, or what?"

She banged the door shut again and gripped her elbows. God damn this filthy city! Everything dreary had happened to her here in New York. The last time she'd seen Smitty had been here, at the zoo in Central Park, because they were already after him. His face looked tight with strain, but his eyes still held that steely, devilish levity. "This will do it," he'd said. "This'll make it all worthwhile. All our effort. You'll see." The neatly lettered sign behind him said *Ursus horribilis;* one of the grizzlies had stared at her relentlessly out of vacant, translucent eyes. Smitty had insisted on buying a large sausage-shaped red balloon though she worried it might call attention to them. The string had broken right afterward on Fifth, and they'd watched it sway forlornly off beyond the gray stone.

Years before they'd sat on the sisal mat in the living room in Casey Streeter's pad on Eleventh Street, in front of the fireplace you couldn't light, arguing about Proudhon and Mao and Bakunin or writing pieces for *Grapnel* or planning the removal of sensitive government papers. It was at Casey's she'd held his head between her breasts all that long night, while the car lights swept across the ceiling and the rain lashed the windows like fine rice. And it was here in New York, too, just outside the IBM Building that the FBI had caught him. All those dreamy schemes—so much of it had been lacking in reality. This was reality.

Sunlight splashed in her eyes from the rear window of a car up ahead, kept flashing, dazzling her no matter how she twisted and turned. The last time she'd seen Dave had been here, too—an October day raw with an east wind and low-dipping smoke from the Con Ed stacks, a smell of death and dissolution in the air. They had walked and walked, from the Westbury down to Herald Square and then over to the river, as if by walking they could evade time's consuming rush. And finally, scarcely talking, they had surrendered to time and taken the airport limousine out to Kennedy. New York, where everything began and everything—

The cab stopped with a jolt that threw her against the front seat. She cried, *"Jesus!"*

"Look, bootsie," the driver said, "whyn't you just sit back and relax, ah?"

"Why don't you drive more sensibly?"

"Look, I been pushing a hack in this town for eight years, *nine* years, and I never had no complaint from nobody. Not till you come along . . ."

She shut her eyes, shut him and the rock band out of her thoughts; saw Paul in the still water at Tashawena Inlet, his hair plastered against his head, a happy seal. *You'll be swimming like a mink in six weeks. I can teach anyone to swim—even a lead-sinker type like you!* When she'd leaped at him he'd sunk without a ripple, and turning round and round on herself, knowing he was tricking her, she'd still become more and more fearful as the seconds passed. Love was a cheat—instead of making you brave it turned you fearful: all that tumbling, glorious sea-surge, that gossamer golden net to lose. Fears . . . Once, kidding, she'd called him "Frisco"— she'd been amazed at the vehemence of his objection. "Why, what's the matter? It's just a nickname." "Not to me it isn't. Don't call me that." But he wouldn't tell her why.

Here she was: leaving Paul, running north toward Land. She was caught betwen them, she would always be pulled right, pulled left, yanked limb from limb. What *was* she doing? She could see Paul's face, hurt and disapproving, the way it had been that rainy afternoon at the cabin a few light-years ago. Make up your mind, he was saying: which side are you on? make up your wandering mind . . .

The cab swerved left sharply. She opened her eyes. The traffic was worse—trucks seemed to rise up out of the sweating asphalt around them like tin-metal mushrooms. They were stopped again, behind a blocklike orange van that said MALOOF HI-FI. The cab driver—his name was Herbert Kravitz—was singing along with the Negro rock group. She said violently: "Why didn't you go up Park?"

"What? With all that traffic?"

"It couldn't have been any worse than this!"

"Now she tells me how to *get* there . . ."

She looked away again, raging. A clock in a dress shop said 6:32. Too late. She was already too late, it had started, she'd waited too long, there was nothing she could do. She felt ashamed, frightened—bound in a disaster whose discovery would destroy them all. *If there's one thing I can tell you, Jillian, one thing in this miserable, wretched life I've learned, it is: Don't ever depend on a man. For anything!* Her mother's face, disordered and feverish and shaking. That first day at Bannersley, waiting in the wind, the long aching cold, and he never showed up. Hoyts were unstable. Hoyts were—

Sixty-seventh Street. Finally, my God, finally and everlastingly! Running west past the dulled brownstones, the jazzed-up tan and magenta façades. Her throat was choked with dust, her heart was pounding so violently her hands were shaking. It wasn't going to work. There was going to be a heavy reckoning levied for this, beyond anything any of them knew. She could feel it. "Our lives are one long atonement," Paul had said once in a bleak moment, and she'd laughed and said: "That's medieval theology—

you don't mean to tell me you *swallow* that goop?" and he'd smiled that lovely boyish gentle smile . . .

The traffic lurched ahead again; they moved across Lexington, climbing toward Park—and at that moment she heard the high, metallic scream of a siren and a patrol car shot up the Avenue in front of them. They eased up to the light and looking north she saw it then—a scurrying confusion of cars and people, horns, a whistle in shrill, staccato bursts. Two young men came running hard down the far side of the street, glancing back fearfully, their hair flying. One of them looked like Don—

"Hey," the cab driver said with smug wonder. "There's some kind of demonstration going on up there, some radical deal . . ."

"I know," she said, and lifted the worn green flap of her bag, for money. "This is near enough."

His head craned around to her, inquisitive and harsh. "What do you mean, you know?"

She thrust five dollars toward the change tray. "Nothing. Nothing."

"Hey. I asked you a question."

"—And I'm telling you to mind your own business!"

He hitched himself around in the seat, jabbed a sweating, hairy arm at the windshield where now she could see white helmets moving above the turrets of cars. "That *is* my business, in case you don't know it, bootsie —that happens to be the business of *every* loyal American. In case you—"

"Oh shut up!" she shouted. "Just shut up, you big fat loudmouth fascist fool—!" She snapped open the door and leaped out, almost falling.

"You little bitch—*hey!*" he roared.

She watched him lunging across to open his rider-side front door; cried, "Screw you!" and ran, realized she still held the bill in her fist. She laughed once in high, exultant rage. Good. Good! That was the price he paid for playing vigilante, yard dog for the mucking Establishment: everybody paid for his convictions. "A patriot," she breathed through her teeth, dodging through the knots of people, forcing her way. "Filthy slob patriot—" But overpowering everything now was her fear, her need to get there, be at the source of that clamor and confusion at the far corner. A patrol car squealed to a stop ahead of her, rocking on its springs, and three cops jumped out. A genteel, middle-aged couple turned blank, amazed faces toward her and the woman said, *"Well!* . . ." her voice fading into a prolonged shout from up the street. She ran on, her mouth dry, reached the corner.

There across the intersection was the panel truck, a festive yellow elephant cut off by patrol cars and surrounded by crowds—a dense mass that contracted and swelled like some gross organism, broke apart and again coalesced. All wrong, it had gone all wrong. Where was the Olds— had they got him and got away? She heard what she thought was a chant, drowned suddenly in a bedlam of car horns and shouts. Near her a boy in a buckskin vest was being dragged along by two policemen, his head hanging limply. Slick wet ribbons of blood glistened under his hair. She peered at him wildly, couldn't tell who it was. Tricked. They'd been tricked, she'd known it. More police were coming from Madison, clumps of baby-blue helmets, and the wail of sirens rose like the lament for a doomed city. Fear held her motionless. She had caused this, had she? all this savagery? There was another violent surge around the truck. She caught a glimpse of a white, snarling face above the commotion, a hand flailing—all at once driven out of sight below the thrusting blue backs.

"*Land!*" she screamed. Oh, the dirty, dirty—

Filled with a hatred so pure it pressed on joy she ran toward the panel truck.

There was a shock—she had left her body, was tumbling through slow waves of time. Spin falling. Sky and glass and concrete swept in high, lazy eddies, swirling toward the funnel core of a gleaming baton adorned with vines that slowly, carefully, oh so cleverly revealed itself as a nightstick with its black leather thong. Lying in the gutter. How careless. For some reason it was important to pick it up. But her arm would not move. She stirred nonetheless, sought to reach the nightstick—and out of the numb capricious lightness came pain in wires, on points, in heavy pulsing waves. "Oh," she murmured. The nightstick darkened, receded. A wrathful, frightened face was peering down at her now, another—what did they think they were *doing?*—but too bright, they hurt her eyes. So angry!

Someone was speaking to her, she could hear the words clearly enough but they made no sense, funny melodious sounds. Words are easy, like the wind; fearful friends are here to bind. No. Are hurt in mind.

"Oh," she said, or did not say. Help. Help me. Now. Pain embraced her in coils, in noisome crushing toils that drowned all thought. She was conscious only of light, far too bright light, and then shadow, arched on discordant, distant sounds. The intersection was deserted, none of it had happened. Dream, then? Good. Dreams were—

Vaguely, abruptly she felt she was being moved. Oh no. No. If she could only see! Some awful mistake, irreparable, and now it was dark, quite dark, and the pain drew back, waiting. There was something she wanted, but it was not here, she was never going to find it in this dark, threatful place. The thing was to be clear!

Movement, rocking. She was falling backward, an axis at the small of her back and she was spinning, tumbling backward endlessly, this had to stop! *Paul.* She had to see Paul, it was absolutely essential, oh nothing mattered but to be with him, her hands held deep in his. This bad thing—she needed to see him and he'd put it right. I want to see. Secretary Blackburn. United States Secretary of State. Nothing irregular, we are good friends, close friends, is there anything so disreputable about that? It's only natural for the human animal to fall—or rise? yes, rise—in the close green embrace—

But nobody. Nobody was where she was now. And all at once, like a break in massed clouds, the storm's burning eye, she understood what had happened to her. Oh Paul, she told him, I'm so sorry—see what I've done. Oh forgive me.

Hands were moving on her. Foreign hands, she hated them. *They* were causing this terrible weight on her chest, her belly, had joined forces with the pain. Now please help me, she asked the hands, please leave me alone; but they refused, crushed her terribly, a cold spiraling that set her drifting toward the steep blank edge of something. No! she said, *oh no!*—but it was waiting for that, her cry, it caught her with its whirling painful cone, skidded off all at once to a hollow, ringing dark.

TWENTY-ONE

THE LONG STONE FOYER was swarming. Faces kept turning to meet Blackburn's—they looked oddly dazed, as though confounded, slapped with surprise. Usually he hurried past them, a purposeful principal moving through the waves and screens of extras, unmindful. Now he sought their faces as eagerly as they sought his.

"You say she was here?" he asked Carter. "Right here?"

The Assistant Secretary nodded. He was wearing his best Corromantee chieftain's look, his hair high and bristling, but there was a shade of awkward reticence that puzzled Blackburn. Something had passed between them; but there was no time to go into that now. He had to find her. If she was here it meant Land was probably involved. Yes, Land was involved, he knew it in his bones . . . But first he had to find his girl.

"Did you tell her to wait for me here?"

"No, sir. She knew you were speaking—I said I didn't know how long you'd be tied up. She might have felt more comfortable in the visitors' section."

Blackburn threw him a quick, searching glance. "That's possible—all right. Let's try in there. If she's—"

Mustafa Rizza of Turkey pressed close to him, smelling of toilet water and paregoric, and offered elaborate, fawning congratulations on his speech. A few steps farther on the delegate from Somaliland nearly ran against him, gave a nervous frightened smile and veered away. The fortunes of diplomacy. Sid swung open the high glass door and they passed through, encountering groups of whooping children in disorderly clumps and files. Above their heads the great gold-plated ball of the Foucault Pendulum swung over its slender grid in ponderous, inexorable majesty, tracing the earth's rotation. It was going to fall, explode on impact and obliterate them all—an instantaneous, irresistible thought. You're tired, he told himself crossly, tired and spooky.

Customarily he was elated after speaking, but this time it hadn't come off at all well. His moment had come, he'd spoken as eloquently as he'd known how. He had denied categorically any CIA involvement in the American Mission to the Burma Triangle. He had spoken of the imperative need for trust between nations as a logical extension of trust between men, he had called for an end to the spirit of retaliation and cited Erasmus and Confucius and St. Augustine—and all the while Ch'en Pu-tsao had heard him out with black contempt and the delegates had bestowed on him that attitude of punctilious politesse he knew all too well. They didn't believe what he was saying: it was that simple. The dutiful applause which had greeted his final words had been worse than silence, worse than obloquy. They didn't believe him. Drained, depressed, he'd listened as the debate wore on. When Carter had passed him the note telling of his meeting with Jillie he had snatched at it like a man drowning.

But she wasn't here, anywhere that he could see. A little boy in a New York Mets baseball cap flung against his legs, crowing something, and a young woman with a face like an Aztec shrilled: "Jaimayyyy! I'm going to *break your arm!"*

"She's probably gone on up there," Jacobi was saying.

"To the—abduction or whatever it is?"

"Well, she didn't know how long you'd be pinned here."

"But what good could *she* do?"

Sid shrugged. "Just a supposition. It's almost six-twenty now, Chief."

"You're right. We're wasting time. Let's go."

At the curb outside the Delegates' Entrance two reporters came running toward them. He waved them away with his hand and ducked into the limousine but they surged up against the window.

"Mr. Secretary, just a word on this latest—"

"Sorry, boys, I really can't spare a moment."

"But sir, in the light of this new dev—"

"I'm sorry, I really am. Council on Foreign Relations," he told Stollens. "And make it as fast as you decently can." They swung away around the circle and out through the gate into First Avenue. The reporters were still standing at the curb staring after them, puzzled. Jacobi's face was wearing the old dour, disapproving expression. "Don't worry, Sid. We'll get right back down here. Rabindi will take hours—he's never had an audience like this in his whole life."

Sid looked even gloomier and muttered: "If they're really going to kidnap the little son of a bitch . . ."

"Perfect solution to an insoluble dilemma, Sid. Coop Reiny up with the militants for a week or so, let him harangue them at leisure: break the back of the anarchist movement. Who knows? They might even water down some of Reiny's views." But their smiles were listless: worry and despondency had them all. Gazing at the chaotic rush of store fronts and stoops Blackburn saw Land's face, slick with sweat, importunate, lost. *All right, now there are going to be plenty of consequences!* I did it, then. Shoved him into this just as clearly as if I'd ordered him to do it. Worse—he wouldn't have obeyed me if I'd ordered him. Did I? Yes, probably . . . What a maddening manner of creature we were, when you thought about it: if you had time to stop and think—

At a corner he saw the dull green news hutch, the black calligraphy of headlines—leaned forward impulsively and flicked on the radio. The voice, urbane and touched with urgency, leaped at him:

"—*engaged in various espionage operations in South America and Asia for several years. It is not known if he is connected with the nerve gas charges brought by the Chinese at the United Nations Security Council this afternoon, although this most recent development has raised speculation in many quarters, despite Secretary Blackburn's emphatic denial of any such connection in his rebuttal at the Council, just concluded. I repeat—this bulletin has just been handed me: A high government spokesman has admitted that Dr. Kurt Drachenfels, head of the International Rescue and Reclamation Mission to Dhotal, now in the custody of the Chinese government awaiting trial on charges of crimes against humanity, has been an employee of the Central Intelligence Agency and has been engaged in various espionage operations—*"

A broken, seamed face was squinting at him out of the opening in the news vendor's hutch, eyeing him askance. Behind him dimly he heard a horn bleat, then several in a ragged chorus.

"Chief . . ." Sid, staring at him with bitter, mournful eyes. "Oh, my God no—*Chief* . . ."

He could neither nod nor shake his head; sat there gazing at Sid, the sliding crazy-quilt panels of the shop windows, while the shock rode up through his belly and loins.

Not possible

Sid was saying something, talking to Joe but he didn't hear him; he was looking stolidly at the carpeted floor of the limousine between his feet, tracing the scuffs and scars his shoes had made; dread and disbelief kept washing against his temples. Not possible. They couldn't have done this. Not this. Certain covert actions, surreptitious maneuvers, yes, even power plays undertaken in anger . . . but not this: not the calculated seeding—

"Timed it perfectly, didn't they?" Joe was saying with cold savage scorn. "Washington release, all right. Had to come right from the top."

"Chief," Sid was leaning toward him, his mouth slack. "Chief—you've got no place to go . . ."

Not possible. It was simply—not—possible. *Shelly.* After all those years . . . They wanted it, then. War with China. They had deliberately provoked it.

"Chief, don't you see? That's why Vosz shut up, he was going to say something. After you hauled him out of the water, remember? And then he clammed up again." Numbly Blackburn shook his head. "Because the Judge used the name. He was upset about it, remember?"

Remember. There was everything and nothing to remember. Where were they *going*? Where in the name of all that was decent and honorable—

". . . Well," he said, and licked his lips, fighting for calm, for a semblance of control. "There's been a sea change, all right. We'll have to shorten sail. And then some."

The other two were silent. Sid looked fearful and sullen, Joe's eyes glittered with rage. *A Negro and a Jew and an Irish-mun,* the refrain danced in his head, *the more you whip 'em, the faster they run* . . .

"Well," he went on, "let's see how the Squeezer is making out first, shall we?"

"Oh, *he'll* land on his feet," Sid burst out with sudden vehemence. "He'll be lecturing the kids on the joys of protective reaction strikes in Rarotonga . . . I'm damned if I know why you want to bail him out. He's engineered this whole rotten business."

"No. It's Tremayne," Joe answered. "They never change, the fucking CIA. Jesus, you should have seen them in Bangkok. They monkey around and monkey around, a sneaky little insurrection here, a secret airfield there, a few nicely placed assassinations and it gets in their bloodstream, like malaria—they can't *think* any other way . . ."

Jacobi snorted. "Don't be ridiculous—Tremayne couldn't have pulled any of it off without Administration help. It's Vosz: I knew it! Power-drunk little son of a bitch. He's schemed for something like this for—"

He broke off. The siren rose hard behind them, a sudden outrageous soprano shriek. Stollens eased over and the ambulance went by them swiftly. Blackburn caught a glimpse of a white-coated attendant bent forward, arranging something. Hard on its heels came a patrol car, its dome light flashing a dull garnet in the dusty sunlight. Blackburn slid back the glass panel and said to Stollens: "Follow them, George."

"Sir?"

"Get right behind them if you can. Push her."

Jebb, the security guard sitting up front with Stollens, said, "Mr. Secretary, I don't think you ought to get mixed up in this . . ."

"We are. We are, anyway. Get on up there." A nameless urgency had hold of him, dread and anticipation fused. There was trouble up here, too— he wanted to meet it, come to grips with it, solve it or be struck down by it. Yet he had no clear sense of purpose. The two people most dear to him in life were probably up ahead there, in that great commotion and crush of traffic. At 67th Street a motorcycle trooper waved them violently west; the ambulance, the cruiser shot on through. Stollens slowed.

"Go on!" Blackburn said. Stollens swung wide around the man, ran on for most of the next block until two more helmeted police blocked their progress.

"Mr. Secretary," Jebb began, "this is too—"

"You'll have to go back—you can't go on here," one cop called.

"Secretary of State, official business," Stollens answered haughtily.

The officer peered in. "I'm sorry, I have no authority—it's police vehicles only."

Stollens began loudly: "This is the *Secretary*—"

"Forget it, George," Blackburn said. "I'll walk it."

He flung open the door on the driver's side and leaped out, began to push his way quickly through the crowd. Little knots of people bunched and scattered around him curiously, like sparrows. At the flower-patterned mall in the center of the avenue Blackburn saw a boy running, tripped sprawling—rolling over and over against a screen of putteed legs.

Jebb's voice behind him cried: "Mr. Secretary! You can't—"

He made no answer. At the entrance to the Council he could see a yellow panel truck blocked on all sides by patrol cars; in and among the vehicles what looked like a dozen or so people were dodging and fighting, hemmed in by police, who were swinging their sticks and shouting to each other. In the street a vendor's cart lay on its side, a spidery bicycle wheel crushed against the tin, its gay little orange-and-black parasol smashed flat; a sea bird's skeleton. One of the motorcycle cops was sitting on the curb and an ambulance orderly was bent over him, dabbing at his eye. A knot of people was crowded in the entrance to the Council, and across the street a thin boy in glasses and a denim jacket was moving in a skittering, crablike retreat behind a sports car, pursued by several police.

"Chief!" Sid was shouting against the din, which was terrific. "You be careful, now!"

He made no reply—all at once slipped and nearly fell to one knee. Looking down he saw long red smears beneath his feet, bright and pure against the dirty asphalt. So bright and clean.

"Jesus," he muttered weakly. Someone drove against him: a boy with long blond hair who kept twisting and writhing away from an assailant. A trooper had hold of his collar and was slashing at him with his stick. In contrast to the enveloping uproar these two made no sound beyond a dry, hoarse panting.

"—*No,* now," Blackburn said. To keep himself from falling he had caught the boy, who flung at him a wild, terrified glance. At that moment the policeman swung again. Blackburn heard the crack of the club, flat as a ruler slap, and the boy went limp, his weight full against Blackburn's arms. And still the cop kept slashing, panting with his exertions, while Blackburn twisted and turned, trying to shield the boy, feeling shaken and unready, thinking fearfully, This has got to stop, this is—

"All right, cool it!" Joe Carter had thrust his way through, had pulled the policeman around by the shoulder. "Now knock it off!"

The officer whirled, his eyes wide, the palest blue; raised the club again and swung it. Carter stopped it on his uplifted arm. The cop cursed, snatched at Carter's seersucker jacket, swung again: there was the same flat slapping sound, and Joe staggered back with a grunt, gave way.

Blackburn felt himself move then. The blow had released him—all his sense of self-possession, of eased certainty, had come back. Nothing was moving too quickly for him now, nothing was beyond him. In one sure movement he lowered the boy to the ground, straightened and stepped inside the officer's upraised arm, caught it and wrenched it back and down with all his strength. The cop cried out, the club fell clattering on the asphalt.

"Now cut that out!" he roared. He thrust the officer away and stepped in front of Joe. The man backed off holding his shoulder, calling something. Two more police rushed at them menacingly.

Blackburn shouted: "Touch this man again you'll spend the rest of your life in a cage! I promise you!"

They all paused now, uncertain. The first officer was still holding his shoulder. And then Jebb had moved between them, his powerful arms outstretched, speaking in low, forceful tones. A police captain with a torn blouse confronted Blackburn and said hotly: "Who are you?"

"I am Paul Blackburn. Secretary of State of the United States," he answered calmly, "and I am looking for my son."

The captain blinked. "Your son?"

"That's what I said. My son is here somewhere. Find him. And a girl named Jillian Hoyt. H-O-Y-T. Now get on it!"

"Yes, sir."

"And I want to see Reinhold Vosz. Assistant to the President. Is he all right?"

"Yes, he's—he's here somewhere. I don't—"

"He's over there, Chief." Sid was pointing to a police cruiser double-parked on the avenue. "Sitting in the car."

"Right. Wait for me." At the sight of Vosz's cropped bullet head in the back of the patrol car, Blackburn was conscious of a raging disappointment—then a perfectly cold, matter-of-fact assurance. Someone—a reporter, a plainclothesman—ran against him and he pushed him aside. He was all right again. He was the only still point in a terrible, careening world. He walked over to the patrol car. Vosz looked up, his eyes as usual vacant and timorous without the glasses.

"Paul," he croaked. He was holding a handkerchief to the side of his face. One sleeve of his jacket was torn completely off, his pink-striped shirt was smeared with dirt and sweat. Cyrus Hammond, President of the Council, was sitting beside him. Hammond was saying rapidly:

"It's a terrible thing, a terrible thing. That this could happen here, right here before our eyes—"

"Would you mind, Cy?" Blackburn said. "I'd like to speak to Doctor Vosz alone."

Hammond's mouth opened, his pink, genial face looked blank with surprise. "Why certainly, certainly," he responded. "Of course—I had no idea . . ." He opened the door and got out with fussy alacrity.

"Paul," Vosz was saying, "they surrounded me before I knew what had happened, they pulled me into a car, that car up there—"

Blackburn swung into the place vacated by Hammond and studied the Presidential Adviser for a few seconds. "Looks as though you'll have to get yourself still another pair of goggles."

"What? Yes—they pulled them off and smashed them. One of them stamped on them—my glasses! I *saw* him . . ." He was trembling, drenched in sweat. "Butcher, they called me," he cried hoarsely. "Yes! Death's-head! They wanted to kill me—one of them spat in my face. Mine! If the police hadn't come up just then—"

"All right, Reiny," Blackburn said quietly. "Let's have it."

Vosz gazed at him blankly. "Have what? What do you mean?"

"It's all over, Reiny. It's out. Somebody's blown the old whistle. Now I want the full story."

The little man's eyes wavered and blinked. "What—has happened? I know nothing, I've been—"

"No. It won't do." Blackburn reached out and gripped Vosz's shoulder, dug his thumb into the hollow of the clavicle with slow, sure pressure. "It won't do, Reiny. Umphlett caught them with the goods."

"I don't understand . . ."

"No! I want it now. Plain and unvarnished. All of it."

The Presidential Assistant hesitated, his jaw working oddly; then he looked away, mopping at his face. "I see," he said in a very different tone. "Yes. Well, it wasn't my idea, you understand—they came to me with the plan. Shelly himself said it was feasible in view of the Soviet connection, the superlative cover Drachenfels had. And in country like that, inaccessible, those mountains . . ." He licked his lips, gazing palely out at the confused milling of police and bystanders. "It was the only way to redress the balance, you see . . ."

"Nerve gas?" Blackburn whispered. *"Nerve gas—?"*

"What difference does it make—gas or napalm or bombs? That in itself is immaterial, the objective was a total Sino-Soviet rupture—even war if possible. It was a valid enough option, especially once Drachenfels contacted the Soviet team at Meng-p'eng. Like that plan of Max Taylor's for infiltrating combat troops under the cover of flood relief in Vietnam— you remember . . . " He faltered, his face quivered at something he saw in the Secretary's eyes. "There was no point in telling you, Paul—you'd have opposed it, you know you would, you always oppose every circuitous procedure—"

"Circuitous."

"Well yes, you know what I mean. The unorthodox action. He said it was the chance of a lifetime to set the Chinese back once and for all, a Soviet confrontation like that. And Shelly agreed, Shelly himself said it was precisely the kind of penetration the Agency had been—"

"Who?" Blackburn demanded suddenly. "Who said?"

"Donlund. It was his idea from the first. He pushed it. He said we'd never be suspected after the biological warfare treaty, the destruction of weapons at Pine Bluff. I could supply the cylinders from Hughbryce, no one would ever question it at my level. It was just the sort of thing Drachenfels could execute flawlessly, with a cholera epidemic as cover. There was every chance the Chinese would crack under the strain and blow it all."

"*Bill Donlund . . .*"

"Yes. He put it all together, he and Shelly, and they—"

"And you bought it."

"It seemed essentially sound. Don't you see, it was merely a sort of controlled experiment." He paused again, licked his lips. "It made sense as a tactic, viewed in that light. I didn't realize it would grow into—into something like this. I mean—"

"What you mean, Reiny, is that you're a moral dwarf."

Blackburn looked away. He felt mortally sick with shock and disgust. *Bill Donlund.* Donlund, who had supported his policies with such unflappable skill, who had defended the Sudan mediation, the Middle East détente, GATO, the formal China recognition . . . And it had all been a ruse, an elaborate plan to gain his confidence, lower his guard.

But to put nerve gas in the water children would drink . . .

"I began to have doubts, I did," Vosz was running on in gray panic, "after they caught them with the—the evidence, I don't know how that happened, and you requested that interview with Ch'en Pu-tsao. I didn't see where they were headed, I swear I didn't—I was going to tell you . . ."

"Were you, now."

"I swear it, Paul. The day you—the day the boat capsized. I didn't realize what Donlund wanted—under everything else, I mean. That's why I backed you Tuesday at ExComm, I thought we could still ease away from it."

"Yet you let me go down there and argue our innocence before the whole world, when you *knew* it was a lie. When you knew it would come out."

"No, I thought—I honestly thought it could remain inconclusive at the very least, undemonstrable at the very—"

"Oh, shut up!"

There was a short silence. Jacobi approached the car and Blackburn waved him away with a shake of his head. The fighting outside was over now; only police and police vehicles were visible.

"Don't you understand?" Vosz cried, a hoarse entreaty. "I made a mistake, a mistake in judgment, that's all—it's not my fault if they've run away with it . . ."

"No," Blackburn said with quiet heat. "Not good enough. You only backed off when you felt it wasn't panning out. Like McNamara and Bundy and the others. Not because it was a dirty, rotten piece of business from the very start." He turned and faced the Presidential Adviser. "Now you listen

to me, Reiny. You chose it: you *chose* the world of power and action—
and so you're going to be judged on those terms. The world won't give a
rat's ass about all your clever options. And the world is right. They're
going to judge you on what you've accomplished and on nothing else—just
like the rest of us. And don't you forget it."

He opened the door then, felt Vosz clutch at his arm. "—But how did
they know?" he cried. "Only my assistants knew, a few others. The flight,
the route, time of arrival here—how did they know?"

Blackburn paused—said in a low, derisive voice: "Perfectly elemen-
tary, Reiny. You'd lost faith in the operation, hadn't you? You were dragging your feet. With all those PhDs and LLDs you ought to be able to
figure that one out."

"Oh `. . . I see."

"You're catching on."

"Paul—what are you going to do now?"

He turned and looked back at Vosz. "I'm going to try to mop up after
you. And I very much doubt if there's a mop absorbent enough for the job."

"No, Paul—" Vosz reached out of the car window, his blunt fingers
clutched again at the Secretary's sleeve. "Help me, Paul. You've got to help
me . . ."

Somberly Blackburn shook his head. "No dice, Reiny. The hell with
you. You wanted the fun of playing God and Mammon and avenging angel
and all the rest of it and so the hell with you. You help yourself. I've got
better things to do."

He left the patrol car and walked over to where Sid and Joe were
talking with Wentzel and Hammond and the police captain. They looked
up as he approached—the quick, unhappy glance of people caught in a
misfortune not of their making, but which they expect to be blamed for.

"Well?" he asked the captain.

"We don't have anything on him, sir. Your son. Nothing specific, that
is. The entire group has been taken into custody downtown."

"I see." Grimly he watched the final three or four militants being
herded into a police wagon. The last of them, a thin, gangling boy with
long blond hair and a beard, was weeping, his head back, holding his left
arm close to his body. One of the police shoved him forward and he gave
a quick, low cry, ducked out of sight. All around them the crowd had
thickened again until it became a dense, menacing presence. Police swarmed
about the panel truck and another car, an Oldsmobile sedan, writing down
information and calling to each other with that peculiar excitement that follows violence successfully terminated. The street was littered with newspaper and broken glass.

"—terrible, a terrible shock to all of us," Hammond was saying in his
overenunciated, breathless manner. His little round squirrel's eyes fastened
on Blackburn. "There are bound to be repercussions, the most unpleasant

repercussions, aren't there?"

"No question about it," the Secretary answered.

"Did you know Leland was involved, Mr. Secretary?"

"Of course," Blackburn said easily, "—that's why I waited so long before coming up here—I wanted to give him every chance to bring it off,
don't you know." Joe Carter gave a mirthless snort of laughter, and Blackburn said, "How do you feel, Joe? Morning-after head?"

"Just fine, sir. Us darkies got harder skulls than the Sassenachs, you
know. Skull come in two pieces rather than three, make it harder to punc-
ture."

"Sagittal sutures thickened by the African sun," Sid added gravely.
"It's what makes them unbeatable in the prize ring."

"Tha's whah we developed the *Afffro* hairdo." Joe's accent was getting heavier by the minute. "Cushion all those blows from the Man . . ."

Hammond was looking at them all with fastidious alarm; Wentzel was
scowling suspiciously. Blackburn wanted to laugh.

"Yes," Hammond said, "well, I ought to be seeing to Doctor Vosz—
I must confess I feel guilty about the whole episode." Trailed by Wentzel
he hurried away through the blue uniforms.

"What did he have to say for himself, Chief?" Jacobi asked.

"A lot of things," he answered heavily. "A whole lot."

"He admit it was his baby?"

"No, it runs deeper than that. Even *you* cool cynics may be surprised."

"Not me." Carter shook his head. "Not one time."

"We'll see.—Oh, you'll hear it all. Fear not. I'll unfold the happy details on the way down . . . Well, I think we've seen all we need to," he
said, running his eyes over the shifting crowd, the rude practical celerity of
the police: the gray wooden horses disposed to shut off traffic on 68th, the
cars and cabs briskly waved south on the Avenue. A quick town, familiar
with violence and tragedy, quick to dispose of it and move on to fresh crises.
In a few hours everything would be "taken care of," the vehicles im-
pounded, the débris in the street cleaned up, charges lodged against the
offenders. Nothing of this savage moment would remain . . . He must
see Land, find out how he was, where Jillie was, what had happened; nobody here would have any coherent idea.

"Let's move on to other terrors," he said flatly. "Where's Stollens?
They haven't locked *him* up, have they?"

They were at the edge of the crowd when he saw the battered green
suede shoulder bag. A helmeted cop, engaged in conversation with some
others, was swinging it idly by its strap. At the sight of it Blackburn felt
his throat tighten, as though with intense cold.

"—Officer!" he called. The cop turned in casual inquiry. "That bag.
Where'd you get it?"

"Accident case—she was involved in an accident here. Somebody found it after the—"

"What happened?"

"She was running in the street. Trouble is there was no identification in it—" He broke off, watching Blackburn's face. "You recognize it? You know her?"

"Yes," he heard himself say thickly. "Her name is Jillian Hoyt."

"Chief . . ." Jacobi murmured behind him in warning. "Let me—"

"Jillian Hoyt," he repeated. "What happened—where is she?"

"I don't know, sir. They took her in one of the ambulances, is all I know.—Hey, Harry," he called to a massive black patrolman, "where'd they take that girl, you know?"

"Special Surgery, I think."

"She was hurt?—hurt badly?" Blackburn demanded. He felt very light of bone, removed from earth, removed forever from all well-being; the cop's swarthy, handsome face had become curiously bright, invested with lights that glowed and faded subtly.

"Look at that."

He followed the gauntleted fingers to the dented fender and smashed headlight of the patrol car. Her body had made that. The impact of her body. Glass lay in glittering little jewels and pendants on the rim of the bumper. He put his hand to his mouth, staring. Something had swollen vastly inside his chest and throat. His skin was burning.

Oh God. Oh have mercy. Please, God. Oh have mercy—

He swung away blindly and bumped into Cy Hammond, who had come hurrying up to him and was saying something about Ambassador Grace and a message from Washington, a message of the most extreme urgency. He shook his head and walked away across the avenue, motioning vaguely to Joe and Sid. He could not trust himself to speak.

TWENTY-TWO

——————————————— IT FEELS ALL—TWISTED. And grating." Bushy's voice. "I can't stand it, ah Go-o-o-od . . ." And as if his words had turned up some nerve in my head the pain shot in again—a thin, piercing rush that made me groan out loud, I couldn't help it. Pain. Behind my eye, over and behind my brain somewhere. Now I knew what pain was, oh Jesus yes, first time in my life. Broke my arm falling off that wall in Kobe, and there was that time I had whatever it was I had in Cau Luong, but nothing like this. Oh impaled Jesus, nothing remotely close to this.

"Anyway," Maury's voice said, "we did it. We kept discipline." "Oh shit," I said, "ain't that peachy." It felt better to rant and rage along, it shoved the pain off. A little. "You looking forward to a citation? quiet little ceremony in the Rose Garden?" "Even so, it's important," Maury answered. "Look what they'd have on us now if we'd done it the way you wanted, Blackburn." "Oh my yes," I said, "murder at least. At the very least. Think of that." Sweat kept running into my eyes, stinging, and I closed them again. Down the block a cell door clanked shut and there was a chorus of greetings, threats and laughter. Welcome to Club Bastinado: no cover, no minimum.

"Jumbo," I said, "you're full of shit. You hear me?" He muttered something, I couldn't tell what. He was lying on the floor holding his shirt against his mouth. The blood was still creeping back down through his ears and hair and gathering in a sticky pool behind his head. "Well, I know now," I told him. "I can kill. You're as full of green shit as a holiday goose. I could have killed every last one of the bastards. Blasted their fat greasy faces, their beer guts, ripped their nuts off—oh yes! Don't tell me I couldn't." "Good for you," Jumbo said—or something like it, his voice was so muffled I could hardly hear him. "Yes—good for me," I answered. "And feel nothing but pure joy. Pure lovely fucking joy."

The bars were cool and smooth against my back, a kind of comfort. My head felt as if it was going to break apart, big hair-covered eggshell, and spill everything all over the floor—picture postcards of Kobe and Petra, sailing races on the Sound, fights with the Prof-O and Queen Nell, other prime mementoes. What shit! The pain kept swelling like yeast, filling up my skull, getting ready to burst, I was so close to crying, I could tell; and I was not going to. I was not. No matter what. "Suckered right in," I told them. "You poor, misguided sons of bitches," I told them. "What led you to think you could ever get away with it?" "Your source loused us up," Maury answered, "your wonderful infallible inside source." "Don't be ridiculous." "Do you think it was an accident—that cruiser?" "Don't hit *me* with that," I said, "I was never for it, remember? If we'd shot the son of a bitch the way I wanted to, none of this would have happened. You let her talk you into it." "Who?" he said. "Joan of Lorraine. Who the stupid fuck do you think? Sat there and let her lead you around by your whangs. You poor witless slobs." "Ah, you're crazy, Blackburn." "That's right," I said, "good and crazy. And so are you."

Silence then. No answer to that, all right all right. The air against my face was slow and foul. That universal stink of prisons: sweaty clothing and coal-tar oil and urine, and something else with no name. Debasement. Yes. Abandon hope all ye who guess wrong. Bushy cried out again, and I held my hand gently cupped over the side of my head and let the moment come flooding back, the leaping golden moment with the Carey limousine gliding up at the entrance like a long black boat and the doors opening, all of us piling out of the panel truck and moving dreamlike through the warm, still air, Vosz turning as I grabbed his arm, all teeth. "What is the *matter* with you? Unhand me." Oh my sweet, perforated Christ. Unhand me. Wanted to howl with laughter, shouted at him instead, I don't remember what. Passer-by backing away from us, his face lopsided with surprise. Joys of rubbernecking in Fun City.

Across the street I reached out to open the car door and he started to struggle then, slammed me against the door, my God he was strong, Jumbo barely able to hold his other arm. Suddenly dawned on me we should have manacled him first, *then* got him in the car. Or slugged him and thrown him in. Mistake. He flung me off, I couldn't believe it, hit Jumbo once before I caught him again, got a headlock on him, all my strength now, full of rage, dragged him with me bodily into the back seat, held him while his hand clawed at my face and neck, till Jumbo got the cuffs on him. Then I did what I've wanted to do for years—tore those purple fucking cheaters off his face and threw them on the floor and stomped on them, heard them crunch and splinter. And now I could see the fear in his eyes. He was full of fear, sick with it, he was afraid to die. "Filthy little butcher," I told him, "you're going to get it now. Oh yes! What you've been dishing out. Your turn now." Someone—a girl—shouting at us from down the street, a high, plaintive wail.

It's true: all life does run toward one moment, emerald clear—one moment your whole aching life builds to, and everything afterward is numb going-through-the-motions. But that moment is pure raining glory, the true communion, forever and ever, world-without-end amen: those weak amber eyes with flecks of red in them, drawn wide with terror, and the shiny little bubble of saliva at the corner of his mouth. "He's a coward," Grampus said once, "he has a coward's mouth," and the Prof-O said, "We all have

cowards' mouths sometimes, don't you think?" and Gramp shook his head
crossly and answered, "No, I think what I *said*. There is a true coward's
mouth, and he has it. He draws his strength from the reactions of others,
he has no moral keel of his own . . ." And then sitting there panting, watching the points of fear spread in his silly trout's eyes—all at once I saw he
didn't recognize me. I could tell. It was impossible! I looked away, thinking of the cruelest thing I could say, the guys had the avenue blocked and
Maury started forward—and there was the cruiser sliding in front of us,
right there, sliding nearer and nearer, like the king of all bad dreams—

"I know it's broken," Bushy was saying. "I *know* it is . . ." Crying,
holding his arm across his hollow chest. "Dislocated," Jumbo muttered
through his shirt. "No, it's broken, it's broken all to pieces, oh I can't
hack it, I can't—" "Shut your mealy mouth," I told him, "nobody in this
world gives a swift shit whether your ass is broken or not. Can't you see
that?" Was coming all apart myself now, God how I wanted to let go.
Only hate could hold it off, hate thick as soup, hard as diorite. That one
I got, his nose broke and spread under my fist, I made him cry out, just
before they—

"What'll we get?" a kid named Lewis was asking nobody in particular. "Capital offense," someone answered anyway. "Yeah, but we didn't
all of us try to kidnap him—I was only stopping traffic . . ." Jesus please
us. And now the prizes and awards. "Well, but it was only *attempted*
kidnapping, we didn't carry it off—" "Yeah," I said, 'it's like rape and
partial rape. If you only penetrate *four* inches instead of eight—I assume
you *do* have eight inches, Lewis—you only get forty years instead of
eighty." "You're one mean son of a bitch, Blackburn," Maury said, "you
really took after your old man." "That's right," I said, "blood will tell,
every time out."

All the things I could be doing at this moment. If I weren't here.
Could have gone on that student exchange deal to São Paulo, could have
done that sailing thing to the Marquesas with Doc Avellar. Could be
studying in Widener, writing editorials at the Crime, drinking at Cronin's,
could even be dug in at Tony P's watching the Giomartis' tiger tom slouched
on that broken-down porch washing his hind leg to the right of the door,
that tilted shade—

"Oh," Bushy cried softly. "Oh Christ." Bubbles of sweat on his face,
his eyes hooked on mine. "Oh somebody, help me. Help me, Land . . ."

I grabbed the cell door and shook it: a high, clashing roar that rang
in my head beyond the pain and scared me. I shook and shook it, the
whole block erupted in hoots and hollers. "Hey now, *listen* to that man—!"
"Tear it down, Daddy . . ." "Dig that *ac*-tivist!" I liked hearing them
yell, it pumped strength into me somehow. When I opened my eyes a cop
was standing there in front of me. Soft round face, snub nose, pale gray
eyes flat along the upper lids: a baby's eyes inverted. He was smiling—

a genial smile, yet sad. "What's the trouble, Slim?" I said, "Get us a doctor, will you? This man's in real trouble." "Is that right?" "Now look, God damn it, you send for a doc—"

Fire. Pure fire flowing over my right hand. My hands weren't there, they were at my sides, I'd whipped them away from the iron, and now pain came soaking up through the fire. Smiling sweetly the cop raised his hand again: a flat leather strap. Or was it rubber? or wood? I still couldn't see it. That grin. The grin should have told me. "You want more, Slim? That it?" My eyes had filled with tears, I hated myself for that, and across the alley the drunks and hotshots and hoods were roaring with delight. "Oooh, didn't he stop one!" *"Look* out, Slim—that's the baby bull pizzle!" "That's the blue blivot, man . . ." Jumbo's unawakened proletarian heroes. They were on his side. His. I couldn't open my hand or close it. The guard was still smiling amiably, watching me. "You got any further requests, Slim? Through channels?"

Breath came back then, the old wild rage. "—You cheap, yellow son-of-a-bitching slob," I gasped. His face turned beaming, a delighted surprise. The block was in pandemonium. Someone had hold of me, Jumbo, one big arm around my chest. "No, Land, no—sir, he's been hit in the head, he's out of his skull—" "Shut up!" I cried, "—you fat-ass motherfucker, you love it, don't you? You get your kicks . . ." "All right, Slim," the cop said. He swung up a wad of keys on a snap-ring and started going through them. I watched him in a hard cone of fear, still cursing him. I couldn't stop myself, Jumbo and somebody else holding me, everyone else backing away from the bars. He started to open the door and then a voice shouted to him from down the row, a different voice, and he stopped and looked at me. "I'll be back, Slim. Don't go away, now. I'll be back."

He walked away, a funny swaying walk. The punks in the other tank were working up a storm of joyful anticipation. Watch the *ac*-tivist scream for mercy. "Take it easy, Land," Jumbo was muttering, "—you're only digging yourself in deeper . . ." I was shaking all over, shaking like a fever type. The back of my hand was swollen like a football. "Fuck him," I said. "Fuck them all the way down to hell." Hate was all there was in the world, hate was the glue that held you together—I saw it now, like a stab: the French Resistance leader strapped down in the terrible bathtub of Dijon, the anarchist captured by the Czar's Cossacks, the Arab messenger on the rack at Damascus—all that endless march of the desperate and weary, the cornered. Hate alone could carry you where nothing else could. It alone could change the world.

Two black studs coming down the alley, trailed by a guard, a different one. Easy lifting stride and lots of sleepy disdain. Green jackets, purple bellbottoms. One of them waved to me as he passed, a contemptuous flap of a foot-long pink hand. "How they hanging, man." "Up yours,"

I said. Then the crash and clang of the door, followed by echoing catcalls. Bushy still sobbing thickly, his head pressed now against the concrete as if it were nailed there.

It's the lights in a jailhouse that get you down. That endless, mean yellow light: too bright to let you hide, too dim to let you see. I held my hand perfectly still and gazed up at the solitary bulb, a dying planet. A light to destroy time by. One moment—and you spend the rest of your life paying for it. Existentialism, 100 proof. How many people live that way: soldiers, actors, athletes. Thieves and lovers.

But to have failed: that was what was unendurable—to pay this price after failing. "You'll make a martyr of him," she said, and I laughed in her face, hating her, reading her game. Well, now we've made a bloody hero of him: Veerless Voszdick, the watch-charm Defender of the Faith. "You equate everything with success," she told me once, "you don't see a particular demonstration as one small step in the long march of revolutionary activity from the beginning of time." And I said: "Tell that to all the poor bastards who've rotted away in prisons and labor gangs from the beginning of time. You tell them."

I'd stopped shaking almost, but my hand hurt so I couldn't think about anything at all if I moved it. The skin looked funny to me: shiny and blue, not my skin at all. Unreal. What I was now had nothing to do with what I'd been or thought or done before. My whole goofy chemistry was altered, like some marsh bird sprouting a horned head and scales. I would never be what I had been. There are no truths but private truths.

Everyone is alone, all the time. No discharge. "Real loneliness," she murmured to me one night late. "You don't know what it is, Land, you've never felt that." "I know what loneliness is," I said, and she smiled and rubbed her head slowly on the pillow, back and forth, and said, "No, you don't, darling, and I hope you never do." There are no truths but—

The guard was back, that tippy-toe swaying gait, strangely feminine. Jumbo was watching me over the scarlet sponge of his shirt, shaking his head slowly. My body was a bass drum, thumping. He stopped at the door, fingering the ring of keys. I could not keep from looking at him. He was smiling at me, that sad and genial smile. "Hello, Slim. I'm back." I didn't say anything. The tank, the whole cell block was strangely quiet. I thought, He'll have to come and get me, I'll sit here until he drags me out —then in the next instant I thought, No, you toad-faced monster, I won't give you the cheap satisfaction. But my legs, my hands wouldn't move.

He opened the cell door and stood with his hands on his hips and said: "Blackburn." I did it, then, I made my legs move and started to get to my feet. When he saw me get up his face went vacant with surprise. "You Blackburn?" I nodded. He stepped back, frowning, and said, "All right, let's go." Now there was fresh whooping and rebel-yelling up and down the block, the animals thirsting for the blood of one of their own.

Jumbo had hold of my arm. "Hang on to yourself now, Land. Don't blow up." "Easy does it," I told him. But my voice wasn't steady at all.

I walked out to where the guard stood waiting, holding my eyes on his, telling myself I would not flinch. But it was no good, when he reached out I jerked badly. But he only snapped a handcuff on my wrist, the good hand, and said, "Come on, move it." Somewhere else, then. Private suite, I was shaking again, my head slamming as hard as my heart, dread going in greasy waves over my body, scalp to knees, scalp to knees. Jesus. This would not do. It simply would not do. Still, he'd been surprised at the name. Why was that? He hadn't put the other end of the manacle over his own wrist, he was holding it loosely in two fingers. I went on down the row, my scalp and neck crawling, trying to think, turned right into another corridor, silent this time, into a room.

My father. Coat open, no tie, hair all messed up. Of course. Of course! Felt a slow, sick, awful rush of relief, legs pure jelly and sand. "Hello, Land," he said. "You all right?" I made no answer. I thought for a moment I was going to collapse right there on the floor, cry and puke and fill my pants. I took a lot of air into my lungs and held it. The Prof said to the guard: "Leave us alone together for a moment, will you?" A fractional pause and then the cop's voice: "It's not customary, sir. In a case where—" "I said *you may leave us.* I think I can answer for my son's good conduct. Is that clear?" The tone that brooks no rejoinder, the voice of power. All my anger came back, I felt loose. The guard, discomfited, no longer smiling, left the room. Then all smiles stopped together. Except mine. "Well—Prof-O," I said. "Come down to gloat?" He shook his head dully; he was twisting a newspaper in his hands, furling it tighter and tighter. "No, I didn't come down to gloat." "Thought you'd have too much on your mind, over at the UN. Rattling the old saber and all." His face was drawn, his eyes puffy and narrowed from lack of sleep: could barely see the points of the pupils.

"Are you all right, Land?" he asked again. "Sure," I said. "Never better. You look kind of strung out yourself. Burdens of command, I suppose. Or aren't things rolling as planned?" He didn't say anything, though he looked as if he wanted to, as if he were trying to decide what to say, and it goaded me a little. "Well, you got a bit of a scare," I said. "For a while, anyway. A little while. Didn't you?" He gave me a curious, distraught look as though I'd just shaken him out of a sound sleep. "Yes," he said. "Oh, yes." A funny tone, not the customary zing. "Well," I went on, "that's how it goes—you win one, you lose one . . ."

"Oh no," he answered; a casual, dull tone. "No, I've lost it all." "What do you mean?" "Just that. I'm through." He snapped the newspaper open and threw it on the desk, and I stared at the headlines. DRACHENFELS CIA AGENT: US IN 24-HOUR ULTIMATUM TO PEKING. "But—you were *at* the UN . . . ." "How true." I kept looking from him to the paper, I didn't get it: then I did. The old crosseroo. The shaft. How bloody neat. "So they sold you out, too," I said softly. "Looks like it." I laughed, a narrow imitation of a laugh, but he was staring at a girlie calendar on the wall, a round-faced chick with breasts like those swinging Italian milk cheeses. Paraffin injection or whatever. But he didn't say anything else, just kept gazing at the photo stupidly while I watched him out of the corner of my eye. So he was a victim, too. Someone still higher up had been planning *his* execution. Any rumbler can slay.

"Well, that's a jolt," I said. "A—jolly—jolt. Of course that's how the game is played, isn't it?" "No, that's not how the game is played." But he wasn't arguing, he didn't seem to give a damn, he threw the words away like trash in a basket. "But that's my affair—things have gone way beyond me now. Or Reiny, either . . ." "No, but I mean that's Realpolitik, isn't it? Man bites dog, and above all, CYDA—which translates: Cover Your Delicate Ass. When you're into power, I mean." He looked at me. "Weren't you?" he said. "Wasn't I what?" "Into power. Or is it only altruism when a revolutionary wants it?" I laughed again. "That's how much you know— we're trying to *rid* the world of power." "No!" he said with sudden quick heat. "Don't delude yourself about that. Power is with you every minute of the day. With every last mother's son of us. It shadows us like Faust's sneaky black dog. Oh yes. To hate is power, to spurn love is power—" "And to *take* love," I cried, "what's that?—ah?" "—Oh yes," he said, and all of a sudden his eyes filled, "oh yes, that's power, too. I know . . . Land," he said, "try not to hold me off. Just this once. I'm asking—for your help, now." "Well, you'll never get it!" I shouted. "Never. Forget it!" "Land," he said in a queer, frightened voice, "try not to hate me . . ." Oh transpierced Jesus! "You can't order anybody's love, or obedience either," I shouted at him, "you'd better get that through your diplomatic skull. You have to earn it, like everything else—you remember you said that? It was one of your favorite themes. You remember that?" He nodded, swallowing, nodded rapidly. But he didn't say anything more.

I'd have given the Golconda mine to be able to sit down. But he looked even worse, which was a comfort. He looked old and beaten, I'd beaten him just by standing here. Had I? "Land . . ." he started again, but it was something he was afraid to say, I could tell. I'd never seen him so afraid: it filled me with a black, unholy joy. He would stand there as long as he couldn't say it and I could whip him, standing here. For all the crimes he'd committed in our name. And one above all the others. Oh yes.

"You look pretty rugged, Prof-O," I told him, "—you look as if *you'd* been uptown, battling the fuzz." "I was." I stared at him. "*You* were up there? Up at the Council?" He nodded again. "I got there late. Too late." "Hey, I'm sorry you missed the main event. When the good old Seventh Cavalry came up and saved the languishing maiden from the scrimey redskins—" All at once that made me think of something queer, and I stopped. I was shaking again, the pain and dizziness came back in flat, seeping fans, like night tide. I put my hand to my head, furious with myself for the gesture. "Sorry," I said. "I'm a little zonky right now. Like maybe we better break off this parley, okay?" "No, Land—" he began again, that begging tone, and then I said it, I don't know why, I swore I'd never mention her name in front of him again. I said: "I had the funniest feeling, up there. Right in the middle of the ruckus . . . I thought Jillie was up there, yelling at me. Weird, isn't it?" "She was." I looked at him hard. "Jillie? Up there? That's crazy—we said no women . . . You mean—they stuck her in here, she's in here with us?" "No. I've just seen her." He glanced at me fearfully and put his hands together, lacing the fingers that way I hated, cracking his knuckles. "Land, she was hurt. She was hit by a car." His face was working oddly, he kept looking down. "She—was hurt very badly . . . Land, she's dead."

Everything lurched, stiffened. "Dead?" I said. *"Killed*—?" He nodded at me quickly. His face was perfectly firm and tears were running down his cheeks. "Oh no," I cried, I couldn't help it. "No, no, *no* . . . !" He said nothing at all, just watched me with that frightened, beaten look. I couldn't stand on my feet any longer. That was all. Everything let go all at once, there wasn't anything more I could do. I said, "Oh, Dad . . ." I started to fall, started to go toward him and sagged down into his arms. "Oh, Dad," I said. I was crying now, I'd come all apart, after all my resolves and fury, there wasn't anything I could do about it, I felt his arms holding me hard against him and that was all that mattered, oh Jesus all. I could feel his body shaking—slow, choked sobs like gasping for air. "Oh Dad," I cried, "I did it all wrong, everything—they tricked me, too, they tricked us . . ." "I know," he said. "Dad, they broke my head and my hand—oh Dad I *hurt* so!" "It's all right, lad," he said, the way he used to when I was little and had hurt myself, "it's all right. It's all right, now." They'd beaten me, I knew it now, they'd won, and I wanted to tell him, I wanted him to hold me. "It's all right, Land, never you mind now . . ." Tears were still streaking his face, glistening in the high, mean light. He looked old and sick and beaten, as if he'd never recover, never smile that glorious smile of his again. Like us, like me. We were alike now, they'd beaten us and all we had now was each other.

"Oh Dad, I'm sorry," I said. "Forgive me." "Never you mind, now, Land," he said. And looking up at him, holding him hard, I knew hate wouldn't do it, ever, hate wasn't enough at all ————————————————

TWENTY-THREE

"—TOLD ME POINTEDLY that in his opinion the only solution would be a formal apology, and full restitution and indemnities."

"From a *major power?*—he must be out of his mind . . ."

"He said the admission of CIA complicity leaves no other viable alternatives, all that jazz."

That laugh she had, two notes half an octave apart, her head thrown back to the light, so jubilant. Once she said love makes you timid as well as reckless, when was that? They all run together. The way she'd lift her skirt above her knees, funny little curtsey parody, looking up from under her brows, and say, "It's a gasper!"—the way she would reach out and her fingers would move along one corner of my mouth—

Don't think of that. You can't. *You can't.*

"You mean he flatly rejected any intercessory role whatever?"

"He went farther than that—said he very much doubted if the doctrine of indefeasible allegiance applied when the subject in question had broken every law of human decency. Got quite nasty before he was through."

"Jesus, that's what I love about these African potentates—they're so grateful for all you've done for them. Where the hell do you think Kuranda would be today without United States backing?"

It was as though he'd been beating his way along some undersea cavern: a burdensome black journey under mountains of rock, with no hope of emerging in the light of day. Everything at once, was all he could think, hollowly; everything crashing at once, too much to hold off. I can't stand this. Can't stand sitting here like this much longer. The big, ugly plane, stripped of all comforts, swayed and creaked through the night, its engines roaring mountainously; the voices of his staff went on behind him, pitched above the engines' clamor—irate, speculative, wry— and Blackburn heard them, but distantly, feeling in their stead his son's broken, anguished weeping, that beloved face utterly bloodless and drawn under the suspended tubes and bottles, her cheeks catching the shifting planes of light—

"It's the second note that's the crusher," Sid was saying in his flat, nasal, sourball-comedian's voice, "it leaves no room for maneuver. Dismantling of all our Asian bases—my God, *Mahatma Gandhi* wouldn't go along with that . . ."

"Unless maybe Peking could be induced to withdraw support for Naungapaya as a quid pro quo," Mike Hudela answered. "What about that?" And Blackburn stirred listlessly, knowing before he said it what Jacobi would say: that the Chinese regarded the Dhotal question as already settled, that it clearly had no relevance to the Drachenfels Crisis and must therefore be kept separate . . . Which was true enough. Probably. Maybe. "The duty of the radical intellectual is implacable hostility to power," she'd said once. "That's the trouble with you political phallus types—you want to move all the grand levers . . ." Throwing her arms wide—a happy, heedless child. "When all you need is a palm-fringed isle and me!"

No. He shut his eyes, fighting for control, coherence, fighting to hold his thoughts on China, the crisis—but with his eyes closed the sensation was worse: he was conscious of nothing but distending voids of loss and betrayal, betrayal and loss, the ceaseless rush of black water. Did it matter who ceded what, who pressed for what? The game of nations. Donlund and his clique—or dupes—had sought war, had laid the groundwork in great stealth and on the most inhuman level; the Chinese in their perfectly understandable rage were reacting savagely. The world was sliding toward the edge again—and this time he did not for the life of him see what could stop it. The very shape of things was altered. The world *was* square, as the pre-Copernicans had claimed, it was a great big spinning cube and they were all gliding toward that rim somewhere out in the far Pacific, to fall eternally through space, through fire . . .

"What's Ragozhin's position? Any chance of Russian mediation?"

"They're dealing themselves out. Strict neutrality."

"How about Jack De Leo—isn't he close to that fat man in the Chinese embassy? Lin Kwei-liang?"

"Jim Roper told me emphatically no action of any sort is to be undertaken without full White House clearance."

Words. But they had no meaning: he'd been dropped among another race of beings who chirped about time warps or plantations on the ocean floor. Betrayal and loss, and a hollow dark stunned emptiness that fanned outward from the pit of his belly, turned him sick and trembling, filled his eyes relentlessly with tears. He had to think, *keep his mind on things!*— he had to, events were running swiftly away from him. Hanging somewhere now above Philadelphia in one of Fred Semmes' notorious Economy Specials (they'd told him at Kennedy they didn't have anything else serviceable at the moment), an Air Force 707 with no inner skin; huddled on olive-drab jump seats with the steam, or vapor—or poison gas, for all he knew—seeping through the ancient air conditioning and the engines' bellow beyond all tolerance; swallowing and blowing his nose incessantly to clear the pressure in his head, he was inundated by the absolute and utter meaninglessness of all human activity over sixty centuries. What in Christ's sweet name did any of them think they were doing? Who for that matter could ever have deluded himself that he had solved anything at all?

So many words. Charles Francis Adams, cold and punctilious, still smarting under the pressures and indignities of two long years, told Russell: "It would be superfluous to point out to your lordship that this is war." The Earl of Shrewsbury wrote an old friend, "Had I a son I would sooner breed him a hangman than a statesman." Palmerston, reckless and debonaire, cried: "It cannot be made, it shall not be made, it will not be made; but if it *were* made there would be war between France and England for possession of Egypt." "I have discovered the art of deceiving diplomats," Cavour observed; "I speak the truth, and they never believe me." And Wooton in bitter reflection, "An ambassador is an honest man sent to lie abroad for the commonwealth."

What a pompous, dismal parade. "In the struggle between nationalities, one nation is the hammer and the other the anvil," von Bülow stubbornly instructed. "Speech was given to man to disguise his thoughts," noted lame, corrupt old Talleyrand. And Napoleon, after the Treaty of Amiens: "What a beautiful fix we are in now; peace has been declared!" Lord Grey wrote pompously, "Diplomacy consists in taking the next obvious step," and Richard Harding Davis told young Griscom at the height of the Smyrna crisis: "Few boys of twenty-eight are given a battleship to play with. Be very careful it doesn't go off." The Russian Minister Izvolsky, at the end of the terrible summer weeks of 1914, danced on the balcony of the foreign ministry and shouted exultantly: *"C'est ma guerre!"* And Bacon, so sardonic and so sage: "Nothing doth more harm in a state than that cunning men pass for wise—"

"Mr. Secretary . . ."

He opened his eyes again. Joe Carter was standing above him, swaying with the lurching motion of the plane.

"Hello, Joe," he said.

"May I speak to you for a moment, sir? I know you were probably asleep. But I've got to."

"Of course." He forced himself to grin. "Had enough of government service? Want to get into something nice and clean, like white slavery or cutting heroine?"

Unsmiling Carter lowered himself to a kneeling position beside the Secretary. "I've got to tell you this. It's—on my mind."

"Go ahead."

"I had a kind of a thing with—with Miss Hoyt. When we met in the lobby, there." He held one hand loosely in the other, was shaking it rhythmically up and down. "She insisted on seeing you, I told her you were speaking. And then we got into a kind of a hassle. She thought I was trying to block her seeing you, and she grabbed hold of me, she was pretty upset—and then *I* got sore, and told her off. Sort of." He looked up, his face mournful and hard. "I'm afraid she went up there because of me. I've got to say it."

Blackburn watched him for the briefest moment, thinking many things. "No," he said, "she'd have gone up there anyway."

"I'm not entirely sure of that, sir. If I'd said—"

"No. It was what she had to do, don't you see? She'd have gone anyway."

Carter licked his lips and shook his head slowly. "I wouldn't have had it happen for the world. Not for the whole world . . ."

"I know, Joe."

"I've never regretted anything so much in all my life."

"Don't worry about it, now." The tears had started up in his eyes again; he clenched his fist in a spasm. If only Joe hadn't had to tell him that now! The need to weep, to break down and empty his heart was overpowering. A grief so green, so sharp as this! He kept coming all apart, no matter how hard he tried not to; and he couldn't afford it. Not now, not these rushing, merciless hours—

"We do for ourselves, Joe," he murmured; he put his hand blindly on the Assistant Secretary's hard young shoulder. "We do. It's taken me a rather long time to find that out, but it's the lean-and-mean truth of the matter. We betray ourselves, in deepest consequence."

"I wish I could believe that."

"You will. One day."

Carter hesitated again, shaking his held hand in a slow rhythm. "I want you to know that no matter what happens from here on in, working with you has been the single great experience of my life. I mean that."

". . . Thanks, Joe. That's a comforting thing to hear tonight. I won't forget it."

Smiling, shaky, he clapped him on the shoulder again, let him go sadly. Something in Joe would always believe he'd caused her death, no matter what anyone else said. And it was possible. Distinctly possible. Guilt. We had so much of it to carry in this life—and who save God Himself could say which were just, which inadvertent? "You feel guilt, of course, but it is not related to me," she'd said once, "—and you shouldn't even feel that, really. Guilt and regret—they're not the same thing. Even I know that. You worked so hard trying to be a ring-tailed Calvinist-Yankee-Puritan-moralist you half killed yourself at it. But that dear, wild Celtic heart wouldn't let you . . ." "Daytime love is best," she said once, her green eyes large and full of sunlight, "then I can watch you in all your glory. You *are* glorious, you know. I love your chest muscles— do you know that?—that rich deep curve, from swimming I suppose. And your smooth flat belly and hard thighs and oh, your golden arrow that turns me into showers of emeralds and seafronds and all green flowing things. Why should voyeur be a dirty word? Ridiculous. Every lover is a voyeur—or damned well ought to be. Darling, when you're gone it's as if I'd been cleft in two. Yes actually, cleft in—"

No. Ah God. God help me now. You've got to put it *down*—!

He leaned forward and put his head in his hands. He was too soft, too vulnerable for this post. He wanted the fine, professional toughness of his predecessors—something of that killer instinct Acheson had singled out as the primary virtue of the First Secretary; he lacked the remote, feline evasions of Rusk—God, maybe even the fierce self-righteousness of Dulles was better than this . . . It was falsity that brought on disaster, and nothing else: deceit, self-delusion, guile—its hydra heads. But he had failed to search out falsity, unmask it—hadn't he? That was his job and he had failed.

He cared too much about people, that was the root of the trouble. He worried about them until their fleshed presence dulled that all-essential capacity for dispassionate, ruthless appraisal on which the successful pursuit of his office rested. He had asked too much of a reflective, credulous nature, and behold the melancholy result: the country hurtling toward war, his career in ruins, his son in desperate trouble, his wife estranged; and his girl, his lovely green-gold girl who'd swung him toward life, the white birds soaring, who'd gazed out at the festive, prideful spinnakers on the Sound, her eyes shining like stars, and cried, "They make me think of jewels and spices, and gold moidores!"—

He gave a low moan and pressed his face against the dense cold glass of the window. He had to crush it behind him now, he *had* to. Did he think he was the only public servant whose heart had ever been ripped open with loss? Great Christ, who ever *had* been equipped for this post, or any other? His predecessors . . . Stupid with grief, helpless now before the murderous rush of events he wished with all his heart he could reach out and speak to them, grasp their hands, call upon that long and august company beset with grim possibilities, maddening choices: Madison, scared half out of his wits on learning that Livingston and Monroe had blithely committed him to the purchase of half a continent—for which there were no funds at all; Seward snatching at land in all directions, predicting that Mexico City would become the capital of the American people—even urging war with all of Europe as a means of uniting the country; Jefferson in the jaws of the Anglo-Spanish nutcracker—rescued from a maze of desperate choices when the whole crazy Nootka Sound Incident suddenly blew over; Rusk coldly execrating Heren over the British refusal to send troops to Vietnam: ("All we needed was one regiment. The Black Watch would have done. But you wouldn't. Well don't expect us to save you again. They can invade Sussex, and we wouldn't do a damn thing about it."); his boyhood idol Webster drafting and redrafting the ameliorative reply to Fox in the McLeod Case, and then insuring that insufferable braggart's acquittal by bringing a Washington judge all the way up to Niagara County to preside over the trial; the irrepressible John Hay pleading—unsuccessfully, always unsuccessfully—with TR over the incredible warning to Germany and France that if they supported Russia, he personally would back Japan; crusty old Cord Hull raging at the perfidy of the Japanese envoys ("Scoundrels and piss-ants, every one of them!") . . .

Those had been the names, not the captains or the pathfinders, that had snatched at his boyish fancies: these men who had intimated, improvised, conciliated, turned away wrath; who had sought, at the mercy of their talents, to hold the pitching, careening Republic on course. In his stark ambition he had wanted more than anything else on earth to be part of that company—of men too subtle, too proud (even perhaps too able?) to be President; and then to his vast amazement he had got the post he'd sought . . .

All his predecessors. Had they once thought, all of them, that they could ride the whirlwind, guide Arcturus and his sons—even (with luck) end their tours with a comparatively clean slate? Yes, probably. But what had each of them thought when finally he had stepped down?

"—it simply won't work, Joe! It won't *work*, things have gone too far for that now . . ."

Sid's voice, exasperated and affectionate. They were still talking there behind him, brain-storming, snatching at straws. Rousing himself he leaned forward and peered down through the undersize port—saw, even at this late hour, the clusters of lights like spilled trays of jewels. They were down there, in their millions and tens of millions. They had ridden brontosaurus combines in the choking midsummer heat or slid on roller-creepers beneath the foul undersides of cars, they'd ferried the kids to school or sat under those crazy beehive helmets of hair dryers—complaining about taxes, looking forward to the Saturday ballgame, the weekend up at the lake . . . They had turned off the eleven o'clock news with tired exasperation (another God damned international crisis! couldn't those idiots in Washington keep things running along smoothly for even a *couple* of months?) and gone to bed, sprawled under one badly wrinkled sheet, lulled by the low, thrumming pulse of the air conditioner, dreaming what dreams?

Sleeping now, most of them. They had put their trust in him, they'd expected him to solve it all. It had been his job, and he had failed them. He was powerless now, or nearly so. Other lips had the President's ear, not his. So he'd been duped, he was shorn of credulity—so what? Let's move on, let's get someone who isn't such a pigeon; someone tougher, more practical. They had robbed him of power by withdrawing their trust, their confidence: he'd had only the power they'd given him, and now it was gone.

Mike Hudela was talking—a low, insistent recitative while the others listened dejectedly. The noise of the plane's engines in the unencased fuselage was stunningly oppressive. Far below the highway lights were muted and blue, the neon signs danced like carnival delights. The people. The multitude, the rabble, the great unwashed, the man in the street, the many-headed monster, Mr. John Q. Public, *profanum vulgus,* the venal herd. Who were they? As individuals generous, selfish, impetuous, unsure. As a mob . . . The way of the revolution—Land's way, and Jillie's—was to use heads and hearts to secure its ends, and he'd long ago seen the folly inherent in that course: what good lay in reaching some mythical El Dorado when the beneficiary had already been turned into a robot wound up by dogma, powered by coercion? No, the road he'd chosen was better, he would always believe that—an abiding faith in the individual's capacity for excellence, in the ultimate soundness of the common man. It lay at the heart of the great liberal tradition, and he would not disavow it— not even at this anguished hour.

But what of *him?* up here, hanging in space, pressing his sweaty forehead against the glass? He had used charm, a certain aggressiveness to reach those ends, he'd gone a certain distance with them; yet the very use of that charm, that opportunism had softened him along the way—had it?—deflected his purpose, corrupted his vision of what must be done. And what, then, lay behind that? "Part of you always wanted it anyway. It will complete your revenge." Nell's eyes, very level and blue, resting on his: measuring him finally. He'd sought power, yes: power was the gateway to all realization—wasn't it? But it didn't stop there. The exercise of power demanded a ruthless self-righteousness, a kind of blind certitude his scrupulous introspection and sense of responsibility had always mistrusted. Yes, it was true, he'd felt it . . .

And so—he had feared power, even as he sought it, even after he'd held it. He had feared it, and the price had been disaster. Naturally. He was not an Adrian Pommeroy, knowing in the marrow of his bones that he was born to lead, to direct, secure in his conviction of what was best for the country; nor was he a Fred Semmes, who wanted to wield power for its own sake, for the personal gratification it afforded. No; he had repudiated both roles, he had fallen between the two stools. Fearing power, he had hated it—and hence misused it. Was that too harsh? No. This was hardly an hour for palliatives.

He sneezed, sneezed again, blew his nose compulsively. He was coming down with a cold. On top of everything else . . . All that frantic effort, all those monumental struggles in the stately corridors. Well, he was powerless now, or very nearly: prey to Donlund's cunning, his own misplaced scrupulosity: a Secretary of State without presidential support or public confidence, a man only lately reborn—whose new life had been severed. He'd had it. What in God's sweet name could he do in the face of such an avalanche of hate and betrayal? A twenty-four-hour ultimatum, of which more than eight hours were already gone . . . Slumped here in this roaring warehouse with wings, his head splitting with fatigue, he could see it all unfolding with the gathering rush of classic tragedy: the code clerks running into the offices of their chiefs of mission, the submarine and bomber crews eyeing each other narrowly as they armed their terrible cargo—all of it set in motion from that ghostly, cramped room deep in the White House basement with its chattering Telex machines and its huge Mercator map whose deadly multicolored lights illuminated eerily the strained, tense faces—and the intoxicant adrenalin surge this moment never failed to bring. To some, that was. To some . . .

"All that is necessary for the triumph of evil is that good people do nothing."

He sighed, a long, shuddering expulsion of breath, passed his hand through his hair. Was that true? That simple adage of Burke's—it had always been a favorite of his, credo and clarion alike, the wellspring of an alert citizenry who would not accede to tyranny in any form, who would not be driven or deceived . . .

He peered out of the dense glass window again, peered down hungrily. Fewer lights now: even as he watched some of them winked out, the night gathered force. But he *was* still Secretary of State; and they were still down there, crammed with distressful bread, trusting to him—or God damn it, to somebody—to push away the final terror. They did not deserve what was being risked in their name; in their innermost hearts they did not approve of this course—he knew it without question. Because he knew them better than the Pommeroys or the Semmeses ever would. They deserved better than this deadly preparation: even misguided, indifferent, biased they deserved better.

He heaved himself out of the cramped seat, cursing Fred Semmes and his lunatic economies, went aft and stood with his arms on the bulkhead, bracing himself, and said:

"I'm going to go see the President. As soon as we land."

They looked up at him startled, as though he'd just suggested some outlandish prank. Jacobi said: "Gee, I don't know, Chief—"

"Well, I do. He'll see me, don't worry about that. He's got to see me."

Sid was watching him warily. "I don't know what you've got in mind, but I'm not sure it's the most judicious moment to see him. The word's gone out, he's going to the nation tomorrow noon—*this* noon . . ."

"He'll have to see me first." He shook himself loose in his jacket, rolling his shoulders, staring at each of them in turn. "We're not through yet. Not quite. There's a way out of this, a solution. Now what have you high-salaried specialists thought of that I can use?"

"I'm afraid we haven't got anything, sir," Hudela said simply. "A personal appeal . . . Even if by some miracle you *were* able to talk him into calling off the dogs, it's impossible to get around this last China cable.

No government on earth could agree to even *part* of its conditions and survive for twelve hours."

"What about something really dramatic, then? Burma for Korea?"

"The trouble is it's an unconditional demand. Any suggestion of bargaining now, any backing off . . ."

"It's not like them," Sid mused. He was chewing on his ball-point pacifier. "To leave no fall-back position at all. Not their style."

Crouching close they forced their voices over the racket of the motors, throwing out suggestions and batting them away, while the old ship tipped and creaked and lumbered its way down toward the Capital. The Potomac made a slender black ribbon through the soft maze of lights. Blackburn kept sneezing, Sid kept starting to say *Gesundheit* out of life-long habit and checking himself. It *was* impassable, the last Peking note. My God: to consent to withdrawal from all Thai and Japanese bases, to say nothing of the JUSMAG teams in Bangladesh—this in addition to formal apology, and full restitution. Sid was right, it wasn't at all like the Chinese. But the Drachenfels Affair wasn't at all like anything else, either. The Peking note was a signal, a grim sort of signal; he saw that clearly enough. They felt *we* were unconditionally committed to hostilities, hence the counter—they had taken the hardest conceivable line, just to make the knot more binding. Your ten and raise you twenty.

But why *now?* Why, after an essentially conciliatory position, should the Chinese have come on so savagely? It didn't make sense . . . Yet it did, of course. There was a reason—there was always a reason. There was something he couldn't quite put his finger on, something that rasped at the far edges of his mind. He hadn't thought it out; he hadn't gone deep enough. He kept seeing Ch'en Pu-tsao's face across the table livid with rage, right after Joe had handed him Umphlett's cable. He wasn't sure he'd ever seen such contempt in a man's face. It didn't fit, didn't go with anything else that had happened. *Track down the incongruous element, isolate it, analyze it correctly and it will often hold the solution.* Wily, mettlesome old Acheson had told them that once, long ago.

Right after he'd got Umphlett's cable . . .

Yes. There it was.

"We can solve it," he said aloud. "It may not all be as hopeless as it looks. I'll tell you one thing: Peking did not want to send that last note." He nodded at them briskly; they were all gazing up at him as though he'd just cracked up for good.

"We're not reading them correctly," he went on. "The key to the whole business is Umphlett's cable."

"Oh-my-God," Sid groaned. "Chief, we don't—"

"No, now you listen, all of you. Joe, you say you can't reach him. There's been no further word out of Pao Shan. He gets off that one flash to Washington—but no word to Van, not even a copy."

"That's our boy."

"No. Even the Cockswain wouldn't have done that. Don't you see? He sent that one cable because they let him, they wanted him to send it. They even let him stick in his own little personal verification code."

"But if they didn't know what it was—"

"Sid, it stuck out like a sore thumb. They could have cut it. Anyway, that doesn't matter: the point is, they let it go through . . . It's Ch'en, it's the way he moves, I know it is. He probably talked them into it, Fa-Hsieng and the others. It kept it confidential, within the Department, it handed us the option to back off in the light of new evidence, etcetera, etcetera. Don't you see, he was giving us a last, clean chance. That cable was Peking's signal every bit as much as Umphlett's."

Joe said: "Then why in hell hasn't the dumb bastard stayed on the phone?"

"Ah, that's asking too much. Look at what had happened: they *knew* it was true, they knew our government was involved on some level. Maybe that was all Ch'en could extract from the hard-line faction. They've got their superhawks too, don't forget. Anyway, the ultimatum took care of that. They couldn't believe we wouldn't back off once we got the flash, you see. Then when the Administration turned on the live steam they figured it was all over, we were bent on battle; and they clamped down on Pao Shan. And *that* is why Ch'en was so angry down at the Security Council. He decided he must have been wrong about me, that I'd known about it all along. Nothing makes you madder than the sense that someone you've trusted has just let you down. This last note of theirs is utterly inconsistent with their whole pattern of response."

"Yes, but they *did* send it, sir," Hudela said tersely. "There it is. They've *taken* the step, they're not going to back off from it now."

"I suppose so." Blackburn stared dejectedly at his feet, the eerie wisps of vapor that kept seeping up through the floor plates. *War is the usual condition of Europe. A thirty years' supply of causes of war is always on hand.* Who had said that? Somebody who knew what the score was, all right. If Peking was utterly convinced we sought war—

"Why not ignore it?"

He raised his head. Joe Carter's face was perfectly impassive, vintage Corromantee warrior chieftain; but his eyes were gleaming.

"Ignore it—!" Sid cried. "Ignore what, for God's sake?"

"The second note. Pretend we haven't received it yet—reply to the earlier one. Yesterday's cable."

Blackburn laughed once and nodded. The Trollope Ploy. Of course. Of course! The Khrushchev notes over Cuba. At heart intuitive, he saw the possibilities at once. It felt right, it was moving right.

"That's it, Joe. That's the answer. Good going."

"Bush league," Jacobi said in derision. "Just because it worked for

Bobby Kennedy that time, and then by luck. One of them was written in the Russian Foreign Office anyway, wasn't it? It's not the same situation."

"It never is, Sid."

"What makes you think it's going to work twice? Besides, even if you get away with that you're still stuck with the formal apology."

"That's all right—I'll take my chances with that part of it. It's like they say: take the cash and let the credit go." He grinned at his assistant; he felt suddenly full of energy, invested with some purpose. Sometimes all you needed was the thin edge of a wedge. "Come on, Sid. You're just miffed because you didn't think of it first. Why do the Jews *always* distrust the Blacks?"

Sid gazed at him a moment. "Solomon," he answered gravely. "It was our big moment. Top banana on the Levantine circuit. And then he had to get mixed up with the Queen of Sheba—she was black as the ace of spades, you know."

"Is that right," Carter said. "I always thought she was sepia."

"No—black. Jet black. Everything went downhill after that. She tricked him—took over the palace, shoved women in all the top administrative posts, legalized the numbers game, decreed elephants as official transportation. Jerusalem was never the same again."

"She had those hot, crazy African corpuscles," Joe retorted. "Man, she had too much pezazz for a smart young circuit judge who scribbled poetry and played the oboe, an egghead twice her age—"

He broke off, all at once aware of painful analogies, with a quick distressed sidewise glance at Blackburn. The Secretary smiled softly at him and said: "You've both of you got it wrong. She never went to bed with him at all. They were just good friends who liked to play together in chamber-music groups. The whole alliance was engineered by Hiram of Tyre. It was a CIA operation from start to finish." He clutched the back of Sid's chair as the old ship canted over wildly now, creaking like a windjammer rounding the Horn. "Now let's get out of this flying trash bucket and do battle one more time."

The West Wing entrance to the White House was deserted except for the security detail. The air felt damp and mephitic, faintly ominous; the streets had that hollow stillness only two o'clock in the morning can evoke. The President had been preoccupied and abrupt on the phone—no one could miss the overtone of irascibility and censure. He had told Blackburn to come on ahead, but the Secretary had no illusions: he was out of it, now. He had forfeited the right to the imperial quip, the easy mild profanity. He had got out of the cab and started along the path when a figure emerged from the shadows, moving solidly yet lightly away from him. There was no mistaking the broad back, the slight roll to the massive shoulders, the curious short stride. Blackburn uttered the one word:

"Donlund."

The Vice President stopped and turned, a feigned surprise. "Well, Paul! The prodigal returns."

He offered his hand. Blackburn ignored it, watching him. Donlund's face was flushed, his gray eyes quick and exultant. He looked huge and supremely self-assured; he looked invincible.

"No," Blackburn answered. "The bad penny."

A moment longer Donlund held there, with that hooded, inquiring glance, the sardonic smile. He lowered his hand. "You romantics . . ." Again he started to move on.

Blackburn said: "No—you don't walk away from me like that. Not tonight. I've got something to say."

"Very well. Let's have it. I've been with the President since eleven and I'm pressed for time."

"Time." Blackburn started to add something more, and stopped. He was standing here, at the West Wing entrance to the White House, face to face with the man who had become renowned over two decades for his balance, his mastery of the measured approach, the style unflappable; who had sat with him time and again through the night's late watches, when all the other voices had been raised in rancor—

"—Why?" he half whispered, staring. "I want to know *why!*"

The Vice President's expression was perfectly bland, remote. "Reasons of my own. They don't concern you."

The night wind stirred the branches of the plane tree above their heads. Across the lawn, near the entrance, a guard was eyeing them with tactful circumspection, out of earshot: two VIPs conferring in a time of crisis. A time of—

"It isn't going to work, you know," Blackburn said finally. "I'm going to block it. This time, anyway."

Donlund smiled. "You cling to your illusions, Paul. The Council is with me to a man. So's the President, which is more to the point." He glanced at his watch. "Now if you'll excuse me, I've a number of rather urgent—"

"Umphlett," he murmured bitterly. All the grief and humiliation of the past day and night swept over him. "Poor, ineffectual little Cockswain. Who'd have believed it . . . The only person who dug out the simple truth."

The Vice President moved restively. "It's immaterial. The fat is in the fire."

"Hybris. That's in character . . . Figured you could risk the CIA disclosure—that would knock me out of there—and *still* bring it all off. Sure. The momentum would be too great by then, they'd all go along, nobody would throw himself in front of the chariot. Well, it won't work."

"Don't tell me what will or won't work," Donlund said sharply. "I know *exactly* how things work—which is something you never will."

"By lying—all the way down the line?"

"I falsified nothing."

"I'm talking about the truth, Donlund."

"Truth—there is no such animal as truth. There are only components of fact and how you field them."

"What about that cock-and-bull story over the phone? About the Judge acquitting Drachenfels on that murder charge?"

"What about it?"

"I happen to know he *did* murder the man—Mike checked it out for me. That one of the components?"

Donlund's eyes were wide and baleful. "Yes. The naked facts."

"Are you trying to tell me my father-in-law would acquit a defendant he knew to be guilty—?"

"Precisely that, Blackburn. Precisely that. Pressure was applied. Drachenfels had already given us a lot of sensitive information, even then; but he had ways of learning still more. The Man got into it personally. I was there. And so the Judge agreed to acquit him. You go look it up. As they say." His eyes glinted with amused contempt. "Why all the consternation? Yes—there's the rock-ribbed, incorruptible Yankee you've been worshipping all these years. A phiz of uncompromising rectitude—and feet of good old Gay Head clay."

"And how that must have pleased you. To see a man everybody—"

"It neither pleased me nor displeased me. It was just another in a series of facts. He was a judge, he was in politics, the inner circles. He knew how things worked. It's *you* who put him on that pedestal—he never was there. You're just paying for your obsessions. Like everybody else."

Blackburn ran his hand through his hair. The guard in his white belt and hat was still watching them. Again he had that sense of things going past him too rapidly, of objects sliding off the ends of his fingers. The need to shout at the top of his lungs was almost unsuppressible. His heart was pounding thickly. He said: "You . . . you Judas."

It was as though the name had released a spring. Donlund made a sudden lurching movement toward the Secretary, checked himself. "Oh no," he said tightly, "not I! *I'm* not the Judas. It's you gutless liberals with your egghead Harvard scruples and your dreams of gentility—too good to get down in the muck with the rest of us, too *fine-grained* . . ." His mouth went slack with disdain. "You were never your own master—you sold out to the bastards from the moment you went east to school. A flock of gilded roosters, that's what you thought. And how have they paid you off? You think one of them, even one, will support you now? Pommeroy, Stout, Harriman, Bundy—go ahead, talk to them, see what they say . . ."

He struck his hands together once, fist in palm. "Well, you're through. And so are they. We're going to have a new deal now—and the West Coast will be holding all the cards."

"Consummate," Blackburn said quietly. He felt calm again. There was a curious relief in this torrent of revelation. He felt stripped of all illusion, somber, even proud. "And the way to this new golden age is to scorch mainland China with H-bombs."

"If need be, if need be." Donlund's eyes flashed once. "It won't come to that."

"But of course it might. That's the exciting part, isn't it?"

"They'll back off from their hard-nosed game. They have their options."

"And how about us? Do we think about backing off? Can't you ever dare a little forbearance, a little compassion?"

"—*Compassion!*"

Again it was as if he had touched a spring. The Vice President took a short, deliberate step toward Blackburn and raised one of his big hands: a heavy, admonitory gesture, infinitely more threatening than if he had swung. His eyes held a soft, bright intensity the Secretary had never seen before.

"Do you know something, Blackburn? You remind me of my father. A man of peace, a man of God . . . Do you know how he died? He was a credulous type. Like you, Blackburn. He thought people were *good*— his mission was to help souls, not causes. I stood there and watched him trying to appeal to their nobler natures. The victorious Red Army. A touching scene, Jesus to the legionaries. He thought he *owed* them something, you see. I was fifteen years old." He raised two fingers to the side of his face, a strange, dreamy gesture. "They ran him through the belly. And then they held the point of a bayonet that far from my right eye and they told me to repeat after them. *Yeh Su Chi Tu shih mo kuei, wo pu chieh shou t'a.* Sure, you have enough Mandarin for that. 'My Jesus Christ is the devil and I deny him.' Another kind of credo, you see. Don't talk to me about compassion, Blackburn. There's no need to be any more of a fool than you already are."

There was complete silence between them. From off to the south there came a low, slow mutter of thunder, and the wind stirred in the high branches of the trees. Blackburn locked his fingers together. A sense of mission. The zealots. Preserve us from the missionaries, if nothing else. If nothing else on earth. He heard himself say: "And for that terrible moment you would risk war. Destroy seven hundred million human beings."

Donlund expelled his breath as though he had been carrying an intolerable weight through some dark, unfamiliar place. "I told you it didn't concern you. It's no skin off your ass."

"Strange. I was so wrong about you."

"Let's say you haven't understood me."

"No—I don't mean in that way. That's beyond question.—No, it's you who are the romantic, not I. I didn't see that. But I do now." Blackburn hooked his fingers in his trouser pockets. "After all these years, all the things you've done . . . I wonder that you haven't been able to forgive yourself."

Donlund gazed back at him with inexpressible hatred. "Do you," he said. "Well you see, I lack your lofty Brahmin sentiments. As I told you." He turned away, then swung back as though he had suddenly remembered the occasion for their quarrel. "A piece of advice, Blackburn. Don't oppose this. The skids are greased, the chocks are pulled. If you want to survive, if you want to keep any part of your ass above water, don't oppose it."

He moved off into the dark with that curiously short, brisk stride. Blackburn stood looking after him, listening to the far-off mumble of thunder, the leading edges of wind through the trees.

TWENTY-FOUR

THE PRESIDENT was standing bent over his desk in his shirt sleeves, writing on a yellow pad. He was angry—that much was apparent at a glance: his eyes held that certain hard shine, the lower lip was thrust forward—most important of all were those pale, white crescents at the corners of his mouth. He nodded once, went on writing furiously. Jim Roper was sitting in a nearby chair, reading something and frowning; he smiled in greeting but said nothing. Blackburn nodded in return and walked slowly up to the President's desk.

"Paul," the President said in a tone that withheld rather than welcomed. "What kept you?" He studied the Secretary's face. "Are you ill?"

"No, sir. I'm not ill."

"You certainly look terrible."

"I'm sorry to keep you waiting. I met Vice President Donlund on his way out. We—had an exchange of views."

The President grunted, dropped the pencil, and with a tight, impatient gesture pulled his coat from the back of his chair and swung it over his shoulder. "Come on, you can tell me whatever you need to on the way—I've got to get downstairs."

Blackburn said: "Could I see you for just five minutes, Mr. President? Here. Before you go."

"You can talk down there, can't you?"

"No. I'm afraid I can't." He glanced at Roper whose expression was frank with warning. Had he gone too far? Possibly. In any event he'd have to chance it. "I'd be grateful for just a few minutes, Mr. President. I think you may want to hear what I have to say."

The Chief Executive grimaced, rubbed a knuckle harshly back and forth under his nose. "All right. Go on down, Jim—I'll be with you in a minute or so." As the door closed behind Roper he dropped his coat in his chair and half sat on a corner of his desk, swinging one foot rapidly. "I must tell you I'm very disappointed, Paul. Disappointed and dismayed. I had no idea you'd lost control of things so badly."

Blackburn opened his mouth to speak, closed it again. The President eyed him irately, hitching hard at his trousers. "You asked for full authority over all other agencies abroad. And I consented—it was precisely to avoid the possibility of any such mess as this that I made certain you had that authority. Do I make myself clear?"

Blackburn said quietly: "I accept the responsibility, sir."

"You'd better—I'll tell you that. You'd damned well better."

"I accept the responsibility for what has happened. But you and I both know that two important branches of this government deliberately withheld crucial information from my—"

"Where was your own intelligence section? What were they doing? It was your responsibility to find out. Most particularly in an operation of this nature. But no, you had some success at New Delhi, or what you thought was some success—"

"Mr. President—"

"Let me finish! You got these assurances of conciliation out of Peking, it all sounded marvelous, and you deluded yourself into thinking Utopia was on the way. Open covenants openly arrived at. Well, it *isn't* all that simple and you ought to know that by now. It's dog-eat-dog, tunnel in the dark, get the drop on him before he hits you—and God help the credulous fool in rose-colored glasses who decides, for whatever high-minded reasons, to let his guard down."

Blackburn cried: "Yes, I was such a credulous fool that I believed in the honorable assurances of a Vice President of the United States!"

". . . And that was precisely your mistake." The President's eyes were narrowed, glistening and quite hard; his face was white and drawn. He too, it was obvious enough, had spent the past few nights without sleep. "Who the hell gave you the right to trust him? any more than anyone else? It's your job not to trust *anybody*. You ought to know that by now. What do you think power is all about, anyway? Do you think *they're* running on trust and mutual affection, over there?"

He swung his head away, eastward, across the room; his bifocals flashed once in the light from the lamp as he nodded grimly. "You know, we learn things in the rough-and-tumble school of politics, Paul, that you academic types don't. I was never fooled about Bill Donlund. I knew he was emotionally involved over China—the missionary thing. It's you who swallowed that Great Compromiser line. I knew he was only holding back until he found the opening he wanted. You Ivy Leaguers come into government and buy the face the politician shows you—because basically you have contempt for it. Yes. But we're not always as dumb as you think."

There was a little pause. Forcing himself to speak calmly Blackburn said, "Am I to understand there is no basic difference between controlled intelligence operations and a scheme to poison—to paralyze—the men, women and children of an entire province?"

"Of course there's a difference, but that's not the point! The point is the situation you've stuck us all with right now. This minute." He pointed two joined fingers at the Secretary's wishbone. "I felt I could leave the day-to-day conduct of this Republic's foreign affairs in your hands and I did just that—and here we are, faced with the worst crisis in years. Look at us: discredited at the UN, the whole Drachenfels Mission about to be executed, this last Chinese note demanding we get our tails out of Southeast Asia in toto . . . and now this crazy kidnapping attempt on Reiny." He shook his head angrily. "I talked with him only an hour ago. He's all broken up, he tells me they beat him to a pulp, if it hadn't been for—"

"Not quite," the Secretary broke in. "I saw him myself, up at the Council. That isn't what's eating him."

"Yes, what were you doing up there? Your son was there too, I'm told. Is that true?"

"He was one of the participants, yes."

"Christ Almighty, Paul! Just whose side are you on, anyway? Have you been playing some kind of double game with me?"

Blackburn said tightly: "You have no right to say that, Mr. President."

"I hope not—by God, I hope not! And this girl, the Hoyt girl—a terrible thing, terrible . . . How did all this get started—how did it go so far? Haven't you had things in hand at *all?*"

Jillie. The thought of her now, at this instant, was a great cold blade entering his vitals. Resolutely he thrust it away, drove her out of his mind as though she had never been; put down his rage.

"Mr. President," he said quietly, "let's not rake up recriminations. We're beyond them now. Far beyond them. I was wrong—I assume the responsibility, as you must know I would. I accepted evidence I never should have. But here we are, on the brink, and I swear to you I made the most solemn vow I know that we'd never be there during my term as your First Secretary . . .

"Mr. President, please believe me that the Chinese will not give way on this issue. They are riding on the same defensive patterns that characterized our own conduct at the turn of the century. We outgrew it—a lot of it, anyway—and maybe they will, too. But they won't acquiesce here, now. The triumphs of the past five years have been too heady after the long freeze. They're in *their* Teddy Roosevelt phase, charging around, flexing muscles and telling off a forest of potential enemies . . . And yet even then they've held back. I'd hope to convince you of that, sir. They've held their hand. They sought the Security Council forum, they delayed on the Drachenfels trials, Ch'en made what was tantamount to a personal appeal to me . . . But our ultimatum has driven them off course. Ch'en's group —the moderation group—is losing influence. If we push them it'll go over to Fa-Hsieng and the hardliners. And if they decide to fight—"

The President's cheek flexed once. "If they decide to fight, we will win."

Blackburn nodded. "Yes. This time. But the river keeps on flowing. There are such long consequences in every move. Even the easiest, even the slightest. Yes. We would win. Probably. But the cost of such a victory! We will not have the support of a single power on this earth—not the Soviet Union, not Britain, not even El Salvador. We will have forfeited every last vestige of what respect remains to us. Everything your Administration has come to mean—the great power moving prudently, reflectively—will be gone. And what will be served? The Drachenfels Mission will un- doubtedly either be put to death or die under our own bombs, the Secu- rity Council position cannot possibly be retrieved by violence—we will in- sure beyond hope of salvage our expulsion from the United Nations . . . Do we seriously want to emulate Imperial Germany, despised and feared by everyone, reveling in our very ostracism?"

"That's a strained analogy, Paul. We're not a bunch of saber-rattling Junkers and everyone knows it. Look, this is no time for history lessons—"

"All right—then we should shun this course for the simple reason that it's wrong. Nothing else. The moral damage to this country in the Vietnam adventure was terrible, but it was not irreparable—not quite. We will never recover from the wanton destruction of China. Never . . . You're right, this is no time for history. But it still is true: there has never been a case throughout the long, perilous course of human affairs where *in the long run* it has not paid to act morally in international relations . . . Mr. President, I beg you to rescind this ultimatum."

It was one sentence too many: he'd had to utter it, given the circum- stances; but it was still one too many. The President came to his feet in that quick, irascible way, thrusting himself away from the desk with both arms as if he were crippled.

"I can't," he said tersely. "Things have gone too far for that, Paul— I couldn't if I wanted to. You must realize that . . ." Outside the open window the approaching thunder growled like subterranean explosions; he stared off into the dark for a moment, his head cocked, listening— turned abruptly back. "Look, I'm not interested in might-have-beens, dreams of some God damned mythical concert of nations in the sky. I'm responsible to two hundred and fifty million people for the security and prestige of this country. Now, here, today. No ifs, ands or buts. In keep- ing one step ahead of the rest of the pack—I'm *answerable* to them, Paul, can't you see that? You've never run for office, you don't realize what that means. They elected me. My job is to lead them, sure, but to lead where they will follow. They'd never put up with a stand-down—if I withdrew that ultimatum now the Capitol dome would blow right off and sail away like a flying saucer. And you know it. I know the mood of the country, and it's not blindly acquiescent, I can tell you . . ."

"But it's not jingo, either," Blackburn answered, "—they'd follow you if you drew back. Sometimes to draw back is to lead. To display the courage, the forbearance of a truly great power, to admit publicly to a misdeed and make it right—what could be more commendable? Or more practical? Why should we fear it so? Look at them: Johnson got escalation all mixed up with dominoes and being tough, and it destroyed him in one week; Nixon tried to play it cute, dragging out the war for years in spite of all his promises, raids into Laos and Cambodia and blockades and bombing Hanoi to rubble, and it eventually brought him to grief in ways he never foresaw . . . Who can be generous if not the most awesome power on earth—?"

The President shook his head doggedly. "That's not the way I see it. Even without the ultimatum, Peking was coming out of this looking pretty hot. And now this last ridiculous demand. Withdrawal from all Asian bases! Maybe Donlund's right—maybe if they *are* seeking a military showdown it's better to have it now than six months from now."

"You can't mean that . . ."

"Don't tell me what I can't mean!" the President snapped. "No. It's out of the question." He snatched up his jacket again. "We're wasting time, I've got to get down there."

All right. Blackburn took his hands out of his pockets. All right, then: something he *could* put in the computer.

He said aloud: "Then I guess I'd better tender my resignation, sir."

The President stopped short. "You wouldn't. Not now—not right now . . ."

"I don't see any other course for me. And I will have to go to the press as well."

The Chief Executive's face underwent a curious little quivering change —that indefinable hardness crept into it, like rock under great heat. "I thought you were loyal, Paul," he said with ominous restraint. "I thought I could always count on your loyalty. No matter what."

"You can, sir. Within certain limits."

"There are no limits. One is loyal or one is not. You know that."

Revolt against authority which is not aimed at the common good ceases to be seditious. Jillie, sitting on the old couch under the—

He bent to an agony that nearly made him groan, and answered: "If authority is wrong, acting ruinously or even unwisely, if government seeks to hold its position through duplicity or ill-considered violence, what then? No, sir. I've been cozened and hoodwinked, my honesty has been publicly impugned. I think you must agree I have the right to give my side of this affair."

The President struck the desk with the flat of his hand. Blackburn had never seen him as angry as this. "By God, you *are* a recalcitrant! They told me you were one at heart and I didn't believe them. Have you stopped to think, in your righteous liberal wrath, what this could do to the Party? Not just me, but the Party—has that occurred to you?"

"Mr. President, I find it hard to equate the health of the Party with the lives of several million human beings."

"It won't come to that, I tell you—Fred is certain their ICBM range is incapable of strikes anywhere but on our northwest coast. So is Ernie. They have no secret bases in this hemisphere, we know that. Do you think I would risk a second-strike capability if it were a tangible threat? You have things all out of proportion . . ."

"Do I?" he said softly. "If one boy is killed in an ill-conceived act of aggression—one single boy!—his death is more terrible than all the men who have died defending their homes since the beginning of time. Make no mistake about that, Mr. President. We say we are the leaders of the free peoples because we believe that the individual matters. That his rights are as valid as all the needs of the Golden Horde. All right. So be it. How much more terrible, then, the loss of one boy sacrificed to a twisted cause?"

It was curious: here at the ragged edge of things, beleaguered, his nerves stripped raw from the relentless pressures of the past two days, so utterly whipped he could hardly stay on his feet, Blackburn saw that it was the President, not he, who was losing control of the argument; overborne, traduced, exhausted he could nonetheless outsteady the cold-eyed Boy Wonder of Bloomfield Hills. And this was—he realized with a pang of contrition—because the Chief Executive knew, for all his prating of team loyalty and the practical needs of the situation, that his First Secretary was right. He was in the right. It was his one slender sheet to windward.

He said aloud: " 'Justice, sir, is the great interest of man on earth.' A great American said that. A Secretary of State, too. Yes, you would risk the loss of public approval today—in return for its most certain gratitude for all time. Not a bad exchange."

"—It might have been possible twenty-four hours ago. Even twelve." The President hitched up his trousers savagely. "But now I have no choice—in the face of that note anything that even *smells* of conciliation will have the reactionary press on me like the hounds of heaven. Even if I wanted to, I couldn't untie the knot. You've left me no way out. Can't you see that?"

Necessity: the tyrant's plea. Stern old John Milton. The image-breaker. "Yes, I see that. But there is a way out."

"And what might that be?"

Blackburn took a deep breath and said: "Ignore the latest note, sir. Answer the earlier one—rescind the ultimatum in the light of new evidence and offer formal apologies to Peking."

There was a quick, flat clap of thunder right over the garden that broke off in a rough series of mutterings; a gust of wind lifted several papers off the surface of the desk and sent them whirling across the floor. The President started, threw back his head.

"What? And admit before the whole world that I'm not master in my own house? See here, I'm not a five-ply intellectual like you but I know my history, too. The Hartford Convention nonsense smashed the Federalists, and the slavery issue broke the Whigs—I'm not going to preside over the destruction of the Democratic Party as the 'party of appeasement' or some such drivel. These issues are a good deal larger than you or I."

"Indeed they are, Mr. President."

"Don't use that tone to me, Paul," the President muttered. The rising wind whistled high against the screening and more papers riffled and rose. The President caught up the olive-drab model of the Sherman tank and banged it down on them. "Things are not always as simple as they might seem to certain romantic liberals. Heady stuff, I know. But I can't afford the luxury."

Someone is going to call me a romantic liberal once too often, Blackburn thought. Really and truly. Aloud he said: "I'm sorry, sir. I know you're under tremendous pressure—no one knows that better than I. It's just that I've never wanted to convince someone of something so badly in all my life. It's made me—overanxious, I suppose. The immense stakes here . . ."

"How do you know they'd accept that tactic, anyway?"

Blackburn thought: Because of past designs, historical parallels, diplomatic signals, psychological motivations—all that swarm of intangibles that cause people to take the actions they do. Because I've done my homework for all these backbreaking years. That's why. Aloud he said, "Because of the cumulative weight of evidence since last Tuesday. And because I know my man. Ch'en. It isn't anything that will fit in the computer, but I'm sure of it just the same. He wants to pull back every bit as much as I do."

The President glared at a violent blued shutter-flash of lightning beyond the windows; absently he kept pushing the shiny little tank back and forth over the rumpled papers. A clock struck somewhere, drowned in the high seethe of wind. After a long moment his eyes, snapping, bloodshot, rose to Blackburn's and held there.

"All right. You say there's nothing you've ever wanted more than this—a détente here. Is that correct?"

"Yes, it is, Mr. President."

"All right. I will give the order to revoke the ultimatum and offer full apology to Peking and all commensurate indemnities and restitution." He stood up again and jammed his fingers deep inside his belt. "On one condition. That you assume full responsibility for the entire affair and tender our apologies in your name; and that you resign from office immediately thereafter. That's my price."

There was a tear—his thumbnail was torn badly, he'd done it some time during the day. Probably in that scuffle with the cop up at the Council. Funny he hadn't noticed it before this. Blackburn pressed on the white fissure with his fingers, smoothing it absently. Well, there it was. Right on the line. It was raining now—a hard, steady downpour that hissed on the leaves. Where was his raincoat? He'd lost it, left it somewhere, God knew where.

Right on the line. He saw with a certain soft shock that part of him had been hoping he could retain the post, survive the chain of disasters. Somehow, some way. The final self-delusion. Save ceremony, save general ceremony . . . It was hard, hard to let go. But it was more than that, it was something else: that he should be charged with that same deadly perfidy he abhorred, that history should hold *him* guilty—

"Well?" the President said—and in his eyes Blackburn could see the faintest glint of cynical amusement. "How about it?"

The Ice Man. The Secretary smiled a slow, sad smile. "Very good, Mr. President. I will draft a reply to the earlier note at once, for your approval." He paused, raised his voice against the mounting wash of rain. "You will rescind the ultimatum right away, then?" The President nodded once. "Very good. My resignation will be effective as soon as the negotiations are satisfactorily completed."

"Paul, it's understood that you won't go to the press on this?"

The President's gaze was perfectly impassive, almost solemn. It was true: the President was harder than he could ever be. He could never ask of a man what the Chief of State had just demanded of him.

"Yes, sir. I'll bow out with all decorum and restraint. You have my word on it."

"Good." The Chief Executive moved toward the door. "We'll put all this behind us, then. Damn Drachenfels mess . . . God Almighty, it'll be good to have it over and done with."

"Yes, Mr. President." Watching his chief he gave a very different smile and said quietly: "A footnote to history."

The storm had passed over the city, bowling on seaward. The streets were cool now and almost pure, swept free of the scour of humanity. Above the roofs there hung a faint, dove flush of dawn.

He was unemployed—or about to be, which amounted to the same thing. It was a curious sensation. Dirt lay deep in his nails, his face felt stiff with sleeplessness and dried sweat; fatigue had seeped into every corner of his body, had taken complete possession of him. He was walking up New Hampshire Avenue, why he didn't really know, only that he wanted to walk by himself. He'd sent Stollens home hours before, and he'd refused a ride with Sid. He wanted to walk through this sleeping city, going nowhere in particular, too tired to make any plans, too tired to think—merely to roll gently in sensations, like some abandoned hulk in the easterly swells. Ahead of him the dawn wind—the residue of the storm —lifted something in the gutter, a piece of placard or perhaps a sodden sheet of newspaper, and a cat slipped in a dun shadow around a corner and flowed through a wrought-iron fence.

He sighed and blew his nose; he'd caught a cold, all right: a daisy. Emotional disturbances caused colds, his mother had been fond of saying. Emotional disturbances . . .

After the interview with the President he'd hurried back to State where the others were waiting for him, routed Ch'en Pu-tsao out of bed (was he really asleep? could *anybody* connected with this grinding agony have fallen asleep this night?) and through Sid's linguistic good offices informed him of the sudden *démarche* and the forthcoming formal apology from Washington. There was a silence at the other end of the line; a silence so long Blackburn began to entertain the idea that Ch'en had mandatory instructions to reject anything short of Peking's final demands—either that or he'd fainted dead away from shock. Then the Foreign Minister said:

"My government will be relieved at this turn of events. Profoundly relieved."

"There is the understanding, then, that Peking considers its conditions to have been met?"

"You have my full assurances, Mr. Secretary . . . I would like to congratulate you on a most statesmanlike decision."

"Thank you," Blackburn replied. "I have one request: that your government issue the firmest instructions that there be no public rejoicing, no claims of victory. This crisis has been too grave, the circumstances too terrible for such indulgences."

"That is true." Again the prolonged silence.

"Do I have your assurances on this point also, Mr. Minister?"

"Without qualification, Mr. Secretary." Still Ch'en hung fire. Blackburn could almost see him hunched over the phone, grappling with the problem, threading it laboriously, speculating, analyzing—finally getting it; or most of it, anyway. "I understand. Again I must congratulate you." And then the exclamation: "I would not have thought it possible . . ."

"Neither, to tell the truth, would I."

"An ancient philosopher of ours—a philosopher not especially in favor these days—once said: 'The commander of the forces of a large State may be carried off, but the will of even a common man cannot be taken from him.' You have courage, Mr. Secretary." Ch'en seemed to be making an effort to keep his voice even. "What a tremendous sacrifice to the cause of peace . . ."

"Thank you, Mr. Minister," Blackburn said gently. "Sleep well."

That done, he had turned to the succeeding steps. He had issued orders, arranged for a dozen logical or outlandish contingencies, and then drafted the apology with that slow, prideful care in the eloquence and precision of each word that had been the trademark of his office; it had received presidential approval and gone off. He had prodded Hudela and rebuked Stout and comforted Carter and commiserated with Jacobi. He had felt all at once tireless and masterful, supremely competent. The irony pleased him: here, on the edge of complete powerlessness, he was more effective than he had ever been.

And now he was through. There was nothing to do now but keep on top of it, watch it unfold: the disarming of missiles, the stand-down of troop concentrations, the assignment of UN inspection teams to move through the affected area to bring such help as they could, assess compensations; the slow, blessed relaxation of tensions—the eclipse of that image he still held in his mind's eye, of two enormous ships rushing soundlessly toward collision in a dense fog . . .

Ahead of him, in a crack in the cement, he saw a coin, bent down—realized even as he picked it up it was one of those tear-away beer can tabs. Without thought he slipped the ring segment over his forefinger and moved on, gripping the sharp metal. What would he do now? He would never be trusted again: he would never be considered for high office or low. He would not even be approached for one of the foundation sinecures. What had Bryan said after his resignation in the teeth of another war? "I go out into the dark . . ." Yes. The dark.

Adrian Pommeroy would succeed him, probably. The President had been surprised and delighted by his Burma report—his urbanity, his mettlesome aggressiveness. That was what would be wanted now. The Ibis had enemies over on the Hill, but he would please the hard-liners; he would put "muscle" back into American foreign policy. The scepter he'd despaired of all these years would finally fall into his shapely, well-manicured hands, and he would wield it with ingenuity and force. Adrian Pommeroy would not be harried by doubts.

Well: he himself had tenure back at Cambridge; and that would be it. Lifting his gaze he seemed to see them all, like the measured concrete intervals of L'Enfant's proud avenue—the years stretching on ahead, gray and interminable. A dull pavane. He would turn dour and "difficult," like all the others, riddled with pettiness and punctilio; walking through his lectures, his private thoughts wandering away, unfocused and bitter. And then he would put on his overshoes and burberry and plod through the dirty snow with a dogged, abstracted air, mindful always of the sudden glances bright with recognition, the furtive queries and still more furtive explanations. He would serve as a caveat, an object lesson for ambitious young graduate students, a subject for cautious late-evening speculations on governmental responsibility and the limits of power; as likely as not mocked by the Kissingers and Rusks and Bundys, who had convinced themselves that the wrong course was right in order to hold power, to stay in power . . . Life was so marvelously rife with ironies: the bravest things one ever did were misconstrued.

He sneezed again, abruptly, whipped out his handkerchief—glanced up as the police car slid almost soundlessly by; the eyes of the rider-side cop passed over him with quick professional interest, passed on indifferently. Staring back, Blackburn thought of the state trooper leaning in the car window on the ride up to Somerville that afternoon. "You want to be careful, sir," the trooper had said. "We don't want to lose *you* . . ."

Well: he would turn his back on them now, the power-seekers, the captains and the kings. He would walk through the tired March snow, holding deep in his heart's eye that gorgeous, sun-voluptuous blazonry of sail, and Jillie's face animate and rapt; those fugitive hours in the wind-filled cabin at Tashawena when he had been all alive, really *in life*—when he had been, pridefully and tenderly, all a man could be. She had brought him his manhood, a surging new awareness of life, the sap springing at the heart of all things. His green-gold girl. He would remember when he sat alone over coffee at the Faculty Club or walked the great shaded loop of the Charles toward Watertown, when he encountered Eleanor's hollow, wary face over the Lowestoft at dinner; it would never leave him—the very memory of it was more than most people had ever glimpsed in all their straitened, prudent, love-empty lives—

His eyes had filled again; he closed his fists in a spasm of anguish. So short! So cruelly short a time together. That was what was—that was what would take some time getting used to. Well. A link, all the same—a green-gold link in a chain that reached all the way from that shy offering of Lee's below the osprey's nest on the Inlet to his own son's cry of anguish this past evening. It was all one indissoluble chain—he could see that now —an unreckoning pursuit of life, the rainbow shell. To feel, to walk always toward the summer, follow one's own spendthrift dreams. "We are our own legend," she'd said once. It would be a quiet legend. But it was his.

Sour, dour old Gerontion was wrong—it was not true that neither fear nor courage saved us. He would never believe that, his pierced heart knew better. Defeat—oh yes. Defeat was probably inevitable, but a man might still shape the *quality* of that defeat. Wasn't that true enough? Come what may, we all of us had more freedom than we ever availed ourselves of—though that, sadly, seemed to be the lesson we learned last of all. Life was so immensely hard to fathom! Most of us wanted, however misguided or troubled we might be, to do the right thing—and to our dismay our briefest acts engendered consequences that echoed down the very end of time: we found ourselves extending both delight and anguish with the same hand. Yet for all that, was a man never to act, to dare? For beyond that melancholy truth lay the most awesome injunction of all: we persist in denying the heart's deepest cry at our mortal peril . . .

At the corner he heard a harsh metallic clatter—saw down the block the coveralled figure swing a ridged, shiny garbage can up to the armored maw of the truck. Reiny's thrasonic baboon, doing his job. The world might teeter on the knife-edge of Armageddon, but the garbage had to be collected nevertheless. Someone shouted once, the truck crept on.

He had to get back to New York right away and see Land. Maybe they'd mitigate things a bit, maybe he could even talk paranoid old Reiny into dropping the charges. After all, the boy was a minor, that ought to count for something; and they *hadn't* kidnapped him, worse luck. His fancy was still piqued by the image of Vosz, tied to a chair in some ratty Greenwich Village walk-up, incessantly haranguing his sullen captors with the punitive customs of the Choctaws, the Ibwawe—

But the grip of Land's arms on his body had been such a bond at that moment. Such *solace*.

And Nell? What of Nell? Would she accept his "ruin"? Understand it? Oddly, he felt she would, somehow—if she chose to understand anything. But what a pity that a part of her would enjoy it: the sea captain's wife, confronting her man who had lost his ship, who returned home on a strange deck, a passenger. What a pity . . .

The Judge was different. The Judge would be incensed, then disgusted—then he would withdraw completely into his hobbies, his increasingly confused tangle of memories. Still, he'd remembered one face, one name, all right . . . Walking more slowly Blackburn frowned, passed a hand through his hair. He could never speak of that. Even to mention it to Nell would serve no purpose—it would be a gratuitous piece of cruelty and there had been enough of that, all around. Silas Seaver would remain the intransigent, incorruptible hawk. And yet—irony of all crowning ironies!—that a Seaver should, after all, have betrayed a Blackburn—

In any event it wasn't the Judge's problem any longer: it was his. Yes, his. Men gave way, finally, inevitably, somewhere. At some point a tiny bit of caulking gave way, then the strake—and the sea rushed in: expediency, ambition, cynicism, vengeance, naiveté—everyone had his own peculiar mortal wound, the bullet with his name on it. Yes, and misplaced veneration, too. Of course the President was right in one sense: he should not have trusted Donlund blindly, as he had—even when Donlund had brought up the Judge as evidence. It was unwise to make a habit of believing men would be better than they had it in them to be, especially when you were riding in the eye of the hurricane. The President had been right, according to his lights—he could see that: the Administration must be cleared, the Party preserved intact, a scapegoat found to take the heat; his First Secretary's unwarranted gullibility had led to the crisis—ergo, that First Secretary should extricate them all, and then tactfully remove his corpse from the premises. QED. It was good, cost-effective logic proceeding from a well-defined data base, it was managerially sound . . .

And yet was it the long truth of the matter? Was the sad, wayward human race advanced any farther along the road? Wasn't what we did out of largeness of heart or just plain affectionate *need*—wasn't that more important ultimately than all the cool, hard-headed practicality of *dux* and *rex?* Didn't those spendthrift—

He started, his thoughts broke and scattered. Two cars swooped in from 23rd Street and tore around Washington Circle: sports cars open to the cool damp air, filled with girls perched triumphantly on the seatbacks, calling to each other, waving, howling like maenads. A night on the town in little old Foggy Bottom. They roared on past him around the circle, the first ivory, the second fire-truck red—a flatulent clamor that was almost frightening in the dawn stillness. Wearily, bemused he watched them —saw the red Ferrari swerve to a stop in a squeal of brakes, roar back toward him and stop again with a jerk, nearly spilling the girls into the street.

"—*crazy* man!" one of them sang. "Arnie, you're *ape*-O . . ."

The door was flung open and Arnold Shamlur—it was unmistakably he—swung out of it, pitched forward, righted himself ponderously and fell back against the car's side. He was wearing a loose-knit canary-and-emerald turtleneck and bellbottoms and his face was thunderous from a two-day growth of beard.

"Old Talley-randy-ro!" he crowed. "I thought so. Never forget a face. *Or* an ass." He approached Blackburn, swaying; his eyes were dancing with excitement. "Trudging home after a hard night over the old cauldron, sport? Fixing to get us all properly fricasseed—right? Right?"

"I wouldn't say that."

"—Who *is* he?" one of the girls was saying in a harsh stage whisper. The other answered, *"I* don't know—some fucking pal of Arnie's." She was shakily aiming a Bell & Howell at Blackburn, her thin white face contracted behind the lens, the gnat whirring of the machine.

"Hey, I hear the word is out," the Secretary for Cultural Affairs pursued. "I hear the Man is mighty pissed off—I hear they're going to nail your ass to the Smithsonian door and charge admission. Of course it won't be a very *lengthy* exhibit . . . Hey, are you getting this?" Lurching, he wheeled back to the girls. "Are you shooting, muffie?"

"Yo, Daddy," the girl with the camera said. She seemed to Blackburn to be aiming it somewhere in the vicinity of their bellies. The meeting of Goethe and Napoleon at Frankfurt am Main. Recorded for posterity. Forty centuries look down on you. In spite of himself he went into a sneezing fit. The girl cursed, and all at once the face of the other one, a plump blonde, filled with boundless awe. She cried, "It's Mr. *Black*burn!"

"You're my curtain," Shamlur went on, oblivious. "Third act curtain. Been gathering material for Shamlur's Last Shit. Know something? The only true art is accident. I just figured it out." He ran the back of his hand across his forehead, which was slick with sweat. "Going to be called *Almanach de Golgotha*—got it? Or: 'Songs My Sainted Mother Never Had the Balls to Teach Me' . . ."

"Good title," Blackburn said.

"Bet your doogie-dunking ass." He whipped a pint flask out of his hip pocket with the alacrity of a draw-fighter and offered it. "Want a slug?" Blackburn shook his head. "Well, I do. A final snort. A last, all-consuming gurgle. Know?" Shamlur tilted his head and drank, his thoat pumping, lowered it with reluctance. "It's about a simple tool who worships God all his life, soaks up the Ten Commandments, Beatitudes, all that shit. And then he finds out—quite by accident—that God and the devil have switched roles. As a kind of teleological gag. Everything good brings about evil, and viva voce." He grinned his cunning, malevolent grin. "What you think, Talley? Think I've got time to finish it? for the archives?"

"Sure, I do."

"Sheeee-it, you've got to say that—*I* know. But before the big crunch, I mean. The grand squasheroo . . ."

"Do you *want* all this, Arnie?" the girl with the Bell & Howell said irritably.

"Of *course* I want it—it's the last scene! . . . dizzy gash," he muttered. He bent forward again, gleefully vengeful. *"Où sont les neiges,* Blackie? Ah? The mushroom ones, I mean."

"No mushroom clouds."

"Going to ride it out, are you? down in the old cellar? Ah, you bishop-belting diplomats! Always a way out, nifty-shifty . . ."

"Let's go, Arnie," the plump blonde called. "You're making so much *noise* . . ."

He turned, visited on her a magisterial, forbidding glance. "Just jam it up your Houbigant snatch, baby-ducks: this is important—*I've* got the genius to see it even if you don't." He swung back to the Secretary again, his face still marked with that feverish, exultant air. "So you've finally done it: the Big Doom, with bells. Are you ready, Talley? ready to look down that lonesome road, before you travel on?" The idea of singing the last phrase appealed to him. He had a surprisingly good baritone; it soared above the austere façades and hovered there, echoing plaintively.

"Arnie," the thin-faced brunette hissed, lowering the camera.

"Just get it. That's all I ask—just get it on film. Then we're going up on the roof and wait for it. The grand fin-alley. Want to come, Frisco? wait up with us? Seems only fitting, watch the curtain rise on your own *oeuvre*—"

"No Doomsday, Arnie," Blackburn said. "No war. Sorry. It's all been averted."

Shamlur paused uncertainly, blinking. "What you giving me?" All the tense excitement went out of him. He looked baffled, his eyes darted around the circle. "Called it off?" he stammered. *"Called it off . . . ?"*

"That's right. Just another international incident. You know how it is."

"For creep's sake . . ." He turned back to the Ferrari numbly, stumbled against the hood, fending it off with his hands. "But then . . . then—"

Blackburn opened the car door. "That's right, Arnie. Nothing to do now but go on living."

Shamlur reared back all at once. ". . . You don't deserve it!" he roared at the circle, his fists raised high, glaring, his eyes rolling in his head. "You don't *deserve* to live, you bastards—you hear me?"

Hear me? Hear me? the circle echoed.

Then he collapsed into the bucket seat, banging his forehead on the wheel. "The hell with it," he muttered. "The bloody hell with it."

Blackburn closed the door. "It's okay, Arnie," he said. "Go home. Go to bed, pal."

"It's true, Mr. Blackburn?" the girl with the camera asked. "We're not going to go to war with China?"

"No. We're not."

"Are you sure?"

He smiled. "Yes. I'm sure."

"—a miracle," Shamlur said sullenly, wrestling with the gear shift, an elaborate chrome T-handle set deep into a streamlined box. "That's all I can say. A snatch-gobbling miracle . . ."

Blackburn put his hands on the door frame. "Arnie, there are no such things as miracles. There are only the commitments or defections of men." He nodded to the girls and walked away westward.

"Hey, Frisco-baby!" He turned. Shamlur was pointing a massive arm at him. "Hey you know, that's good. Can I have that line?"

The Secretary nodded, turned and went on walking slowly up the avenue in the mounting green light.